THE MYSTERY OF EDWIN DROOD
and Other Stories

THE MYSTERY OF
EDWIN DROOD
and Other Stories

◆

Charles Dickens

With illustrations to
The Mystery of Edwin Drood by
S. L. FILDES
and illustrations to
Master Humphrey's Clock by
HABLOT K. BROWNE (PHIZ)

Introduction and Notes by
PETER PRESTON
University of Nottingham

WORDSWORTH CLASSICS

In loving memory of
MICHAEL TRAYLER
the founder of Wordsworth Editions

3

Readers who are interested in other titles from
Wordsworth Editions are invited to visit our website at
www.wordsworth-editions.com

For our latest list and a full mail-order service, contact
Bibliophile Books, 5 Thomas Road, London E14 7BN
TEL: +44 (0)20 7515 9222 FAX: +44 (0)20 7538 4115
E-MAIL: orders@bibliophilebooks.com

This edition first published 1998 by Wordsworth Editions Limited
8B East Street, Ware, Hertfordshire SG12 9HJ
Introduction and Notes added 2005

ISBN 978-1-85326-729-1

Typeset in Great Britain by Antony Gray
Printed and bound by Clays Ltd, St Ives plc

GENERAL INTRODUCTION

Wordsworth Classics are inexpensive editions designed to appeal to the general reader and students. We commissioned teachers and specialists to write wide ranging, jargon-free introductions and to provide notes that would assist the understanding of our readers rather than interpret the stories for them. In the same spirit, because the pleasures of reading are inseparable from the surprises, secrets and revelations that all narratives contain, we strongly advise you to enjoy this book before turning to the Introduction.

General Adviser
KEITH CARABINE
Rutherford College
University of Kent at Canterbury

INTRODUCTION

The Mystery of Edwin Drood

What should you think of the idea of a story beginning in this way? – Two people, boy and girl, or very young, going apart from one another, pledged to be married after many years – at the end of the book. The interest to arise out of the tracing of their separate ways, and the impossibility of telling what will be done with that impending fate. [*Letters*, XII, 377][1]

Dickens's letter to John Forster, written in mid-July 1869, gives the first written hint of his search for a subject for his new novel. *Our Mutual Friend* had finished publication in the autumn of 1865 and for Dickens an unusually long interval had elapsed between novels,

---

1 Full details of all books and articles quoted or cited in this Introduction may be found in the Bibliography.

during which he had been fully occupied with reading tours in Britain and the United States and the editing and management of his weekly periodical *All the Year Round*. Nonetheless, by the spring of 1869 he had begun to feel that it was time for him to begin a new full-length novel. By 6 August 1869, however, he had moved on from his original idea of a betrothed couple (although this motif was retained in *Edwin Drood*) and was describing to Forster another idea: 'I laid aside the fancy I told you of, and have a very curious and new idea for my new story. Not a communicable idea (or the interest of the book would be gone), but a very strong one, though difficult to work' (*Letters*, XII, pp. 389–90).

It was not until the autumn of 1869 that Dickens began any serious work on *Edwin Drood*. Exhausted by a demanding programme of work, he experienced a serious breakdown in health in the spring of 1869 and spent the summer and early autumn recuperating at Gad's Hill, his home in Kent. Early in October, accompanied by his American publisher J. T. Fields, his tour manager George Dolby and two police officers, he visited an opium den in Shadwell, by the Thames in London. At about the same time, Dolby and Fields went with him on a visit to the cathedral city of Canterbury, where Dickens was horrified to discover the apathetic attitude of many of the clergy towards their vocation. Material gained on these visits found its way into *Edwin Drood*, but some dimensions of the plot were planted in Dickens's mind as early as January 1867.

In that month Dickens was in Cambridge, Massachusetts where he visited the Harvard Medical School accompanied by the American writer Oliver Wendell Holmes.[2] Dickens had remembered that in 1849 John White Webster, Professor of Chemistry and Mineralogy at Harvard, had murdered a local physician, Dr George Parkman, and disposed of his body in his anatomy laboratory. The Medical School made a deep impression on Dickens, and he told his fellow novelist Edward Bulwer-Lytton that he found the localities of the murder ' . . . horribly grim, private. Cold and quiet; the identical furnace smelling fearfully (some anatomical broth in it I suppose) as if the body were still there; jars of pieces of mortality standing about . . . and bodies near us ready to be carried into the next morning's lecture. (13? January 1867; *Letters*, XII, p. 12). It was characteristic of Dickens to be fascinated by the macabre associations of rooms where bodies were

---

2 Holmes (1809–94) was a Harvard medical graduate and eventually became Professor of Anatomy and Physiology at the university (1847–82). He was one of America's best-known men of letters, celebrated as a poet and essayist.

dissected, preserved or cremated. Mr Krook in *Bleak House* (1854–56) is a victim of spontaneous combustion and is reduced to a kind of 'anatomical broth'; while Silas Wegg in *Our Mutual Friend* asks about the welfare of his amputated leg every time he visits Mr Venus's taxidermist's shop, which is full of 'pieces of mortality', human and otherwise.

Dickens was also curious about the personality of Webster, a respectable academic transformed into a convicted murderer. From what he was told of Webster Dickens concluded that he 'was always a secretly cruel man' and that the murder revealed his true personality. This view was confirmed by an anecdote Dickens heard from Longfellow.[3] At a dinner party at Webster's house about a year before the murder the host ordered the lights to be extinguished and a bowl of burning minerals placed on the table so that his guests could see how frightening they looked by this light:

> . . . every man was looking, horror-stricken, at his neighbour, when Webster was seen bending over the bowl with a rope round his neck, holding up the end of the rope, with his head on one side and tongue lolled out, to represent a hanged man!
>
> [*Letters*, XII, p. 13][4]

Webster's staging of this seemingly proleptic drama suggests a macabre sense of humour and the *mise en scène* with its distinctive stage lighting was bound to appeal to Dickens's imagination. It revealed another, disturbing dimension of Webster's character, usually concealed behind a mask of conventionality and professionalism. The Parkman-Webster story thus offered Dickens a model for a tale of divided personality, murder, body-disposal, detection and conviction.[5]

On 18 October 1869 he told William Macready that he was 'in the preliminary agonies of a new book' (*Letters*, XII, 423) and throughout

3 Henry Wadsworth Longfellow (1807–82) was perhaps the most revered poet in America in the mid-nineteenth century and was also extremely popular in England. From 1836–54 he was Professor of French and Spanish at Harvard and so, like Holmes, was a colleague of Webster.

4 There is an excellent account of the Parkman case in Simon Schama's *Dead Certainties* and Robert Tracy has written a helpful article on the connections between the case and the novel.

5 Margaret Cardwell, in her 1972 edition of the novel, points out that in the months before he began work on *Edwin Drood*, two of the stories he accepted for *All the Year Round*, 'Fatal Zero' (1868–9) and *The Disappearance of John Acland* by Robert Lytton (1869), suggest Dickens's interest in curious psychological states and mysterious disappearances (p. xx).

the winter of 1868–69 he worked steadily on *Edwin Drood*. Although there were reports that he was in difficulties with the novel, it is equally possible that Dickens was unwilling to reveal too much about the progress of a book that depended so much on the gradual revelation of character and motive. However, Dickens's work on the novel overlapped with his final series of public readings and the continuing obligations of *All the Year Round*, so that he was, as he told G. H. Lewes 'really hard put to it occasionally' (26 February 1870; *Letters*, XII, p. 472).

Dickens had contracted with Chapman for a comparatively short novel to be published in twelve monthly instalments, and the first part (dated April) appeared at the end of March 1870 and was an immediate success: 'We have been doing wonders with No.1 of Edwin Drood', Dickens wrote enthusiastically to Fields. 'It has very, very far outstripped every one of its predecessors' (*Letters*, XII, p. 510). This was no exaggeration: 50, 000 copies of the monthly numbers were printed, compared with 40, 000 for *Our Mutual Friend*, its immediate predecessor, and 38, 000 for *Little Dorrit* (1855–57). Meanwhile, Dickens was well ahead with the writing and on 14 January had told Fields that

> Forster . . . thinks No. 2 [Chaps. 6–9] of the new book a clincher . . . There is a curious interest steadily working up to No. 5 [Chaps. 17–20] which requires a good deal of art and self-denial. I think also, apart from characters and picturesqueness, that the young people are placed in a very novel situation. – So I hope. – At Nos. 5 and 6 [Chaps. 21–3] the story will turn upon an interest suspended until the end. [*Letters*, XII, p. 465]

In the event, Numbers 2 and 3, issued in April and May, were the last that Dickens saw in print. He died at Gad's Hill on 9 June 1870,[6] and Numbers 4, 5 and 6, published at the end of June, July and August, were seen through the press by a grieving Forster.

*   *   *

In a novel where much of the action takes place in and around a cathedral, it is not surprising that the language should be rich in religious associations. These are derived from three sources. The first

---

6 In the appendix to the Penguin reissue of *The Invisible Woman* Claire Tomalin raises the intriguing possibility that Dickens was actually taken ill while visiting his mistress Ellen Ternan at her house in Peckham, south London and was conveyed, unconscious, to Gad's Hill, where he died soon afterwards.

is the language of cathedral life, of dean and sacristan, canon and verger, aisle, nave, tomb and chancel. Then there are direct quotations from or allusions to biblical stories and texts, from both Old and New Testaments. Finally, there is Dickens's extensive use of the Book of Common Prayer, familiar to anybody who regularly attended Church of England Services. Indeed, in some instances what appear to be references to the Bible are actually to the Book of Common Prayer, identifiable by slight differences in the translation of biblical quotations used for liturgical purposes. This language adds appropriate colour to the narrative, giving a sense of the atmosphere and rhythm of cathedral life. But the choice of allusions is by no mean random and the stories and texts used by Dickens gather into some highly significant clusters that convey or emphasise the themes of the novel.

One such cluster concerns sin, guilt, repentance and punishment. An early evocation of sin occurs in the first scene in the opium den, with a reference to the 'unclean spirit' and Jesus's casting out of devils (p. 6). This central motif of the novel is also suggested by one of Dickens's notes for the first number: 'Touch the key note/ "When the Wicked Man" '. This quotation occurs at the end of Chapter 1 (see p. 6) and alludes to a text from Ezekiel – 'when the wicked man turneth away from his wickedness that he hath committed, and doeth that which is lawful and right, he shall save his soul alive' – a text which occurs in both morning and evening prayers in *The Book of Common Prayer*, and is immediately followed by a quotation from Psalm 51: 'I acknowledge my transgressions: and my sin is ever before me.' Readers have already witnessed Jasper's transgressive behaviour in the opium den, and as the narrative proceeds it becomes clear that he is planning further transgressions, for which some day he will have to answer. The use of these allusions raises the question of whether Jasper will acknowledge the reality of his wickedness, repent and accept his punishment.

The fact that the crime to be committed in the novel will be the murder of a close relative is suggested by a sequence of references to the story of Cain and Abel which begins after it becomes clear that Edwin Drood has disappeared. When Neville Landless is set upon by one of the parties searching for Edwin, he tells them ' "If eight men, or four men, or two men, or two men, set upon one . . . the one has no chance but to set his mark upon some of them" " (p. 145), which alludes to Genesis 4:15: 'And the Lord set a mark upon Cain, lest any finding him should kill him'. A few minutes later Neville encounters Jasper with another search party: ' "Where is my nephew?' asked Mr

Jasper, wildly. 'Where is your nephew?' repeated Neville. 'Why do you ask me?" ' (p. 146). This echoes Genesis 4: 9: 'And the Lord said unto Cain, Where is Abel thy brother? And he said, I know not: Am I my brother's keeper?'. When Neville, regarded as the chief suspect in Drood's disappearance, flees from Cloisterham he does so 'with a blight upon his name and fame' (p. 160), which refers to God's punishment of Cain: 'And Cain said unto the Lord, My punishment is greater that I can bear. Thou has driven me out this day from the face of the earth; and from thy face I shall be hid; and I shall be fugitive and a vagabond in the earth; and it shall come to pass; that every one that findeth me shall slay me' (Genesis 4: 13–14).' He later tells Mr Crisparkle, who remains convinced of his innocence, that he feels ' "marked and tainted" '. And the egregious Mr Honeythunder, equally convinced that Neville is the murderer, cries 'Abel! Cain! I hold no terms with Cain!' (p.163).

In the course of the same exchange, Mr Honeythunder reminds Crisparkle of the commandment, 'Thou shalt do no murder'; and Crisparkle, less willing to rush to judgement, reminds him of another: 'Thou shalt not bear false witness against thy neighbour' (p. 163). Indeed, the energetic, practical and right-minded Crisparkle carries the message of a Christianity that is more understanding and for-giving than Jasper's despair or Honeythunder's punitive aggression. When he tells Honeythunder that he believes his first duty as a priest 'is towards those who are in necessity and tribulation, who are desolate and oppressed' (p. 164) his words derive from the Litany in *The Book of Common Prayer*: 'We beseech thee to hear us, good Lord. That it may please thee to succour, help, and comfort, all that are in danger, necessity, and tribulation.' Crisparkle's words also reflect Dickens's own preference for the New Testament message of love and redemption.

Edwin Drood also contains a large number of references to Shake-speare's *Macbeth*, a tragedy in which the sense of guilt weighs heavily upon the protagonists . The first allusion to the play occurs in what might appear to be a neutral, even slightly comic passage about 'that sedate and clerical bird, the rook' and his behaviour 'when he wings homeward towards nightfall' (p.7). The analogous lines in *Macbeth* are: 'Light thickens, and the crow/ Makes wing to th' rooky wood' (3, 2, 50–1). The verbal echo is distant, but there is a striking similarity in atmosphere and time of day, and when we recall that Shakespeare's lines occur in the scene before Banquo's murder, Dickens's oblique allusion becomes more sinister. A similar sense of foreboding is evoked by means of an allusion to *Macbeth* on the night of Edwin's disappearance. A strong wind rises and '[c]himneys topple in the streets' (p. 143), just as on the night of Duncan's murder 'The night has been unruly. Where we lay,/ Our chimneys were blown down, (and, as they say)/ Lamentings heard i' th' air; strange screams of death' (2, 3, 54–56).

Macbeth also helps Dickens to create the novel's sense of guilt. In Chapter X, Crisparkle is described as going for a swim 'as confident in the sweetening powers of Cloisterham Weir and a wholesome mind, as Lady Macbeth was hopeless of all the seas that roll' (pp. 86–7). There is no obvious likeness between Crisparkle and Lady Macbeth, but these words clearly direct readers to well-known locations in *Macbeth*: 'Will all great Neptune's oceans wash this blood/ Clean from my hand? No: this hand will rather/ The multitudinous seas incarnadine,/ Making the green one red' and 'All the perfumes of Arabia will not sweeten this little hand' (2, 2, 57–60; 5, 1, 50–2). The apparently unlikely coupling of Crisparkle with Lady Macbeth draws attention to an allusion that is anticipatory in terms of the plot, since it is in Cloisterham Weir that some of Edwin's belongings are found, apparently providing proof that he has been murdered. At the same time, it powerfully evokes the idea of an ineradicable blood-stain and thus intensifies the effect of the allusions to the mark of guilt carried by Cain. Similarly, when Crisparkle visits Jasper to tell him about Neville's promise to apologise to Edwin and keep silent about his feelings for Rosa, he comes upon Jasper asleep. Suddenly woken, Jasper cries out ' "What is the matter? Who did it?" ' (p. 92), echoing Macbeth's words when he first sees Banquo's ghost: 'Which of you have done this?' (3, 4, 47). Again Dickens appears to place in his text a hint that points towards murder, even before Edwin's disappearance; and just as Banquo's ghost is a projection of Macbeth's guilt, invisible to everyone except the murderer, so the reader might assume that Jasper is similarly haunted by his own actions.

In the last chapter he completed, Dickens returns Jasper to the opium den in Shadwell where, in his delirium, he tells Princess Puffer, ' "I did it so often, and through such vast expanses of time, that when it was really done, it seemed not worth the doing, it was done so soon" ' (p. 226). This apparent confession echoes and recasts Macbeth's words: 'If it were done when 'tis done, then 'twere well/ It were done quickly' (1, 7, 1–2). When he goes on to say that ' "time and place are both at hand" ' (p. 227), he echoes Lady Macbeth's lines from the same scene in the play: 'Nor time, nor place,/ Did then adhere, and yet you would make both:/ They have made themselves, and that their fitness now/ Does unmake you' (1, 7, 51–54). In this manner, by drawing on another and very familiar text, Dickens suggests, rather than narrates, what may have happened to Edwin.

*   *   *

The narrative of *Edwin Drood* exhibits a persistent pull to the east, more so than in any other of Dickens's novels. The opening scene, with its references to Lascars and Chinamen and Jasper's drug-induced Arabian Nights visions of scimitars, dancing girls and white elephants, introduces the motif and establishes some of the terms by which it will be developed. Jasper's visions relate to a European view of the east that is both imaginary and political, composed of orientalist fantasies and the hard facts of colonialism.[7] Britain's active role in the opium trade in India and China ensured a continuing supply of the drugs for British addicts, and this truth lies beneath Jasper's regular escapes from his increasingly irksome and meaningless duties in Cloisterham.

Egypt is the most significant eastern country in *Edwin Drood*. Edwin tells Jasper that he plans to go 'engineering into the East' (p. 16), to participate in the technological colonialism that during the nineteenth century saw British engineers undertake numerous major projects in the Middle East and Asia. Edwin later specifies that he plans to go to Egypt, and in the course of a playful conversation with Rosa he strikes a serious note when he speaks of Rosa's need to take ' "a sensible interest in triumphs of engineering skill: especially when they are to change the whole condition of an undeveloped country" ' (p. 24). Rosa's response – ' "Lor!" ' – is a deflating reaction to Edwin's solemnity, but her fiancé has an earnest belief in his civilising mission. For Rosa, Egypt is a less enticing prospect: she is wary of ' "Arabs, and Turks, and fellahs, and people" '; and at Miss Twinkleton's she has been fed with the new knowledge of Egyptology that has become available as a result of recent excavations and is bored by ' "Tiresome old burying-grounds! Isises, and Ibises, and Cheopses, and Pharaohses" ' (p. 25). By the end of the conversation, however, the Egyptian motif takes on a more sinister note:

> 'Why, I thought you Egyptian boys could look into a hand and see all sorts of phantoms. Can't you see a happy Future?'
>   For certain, neither of them sees a happy Present, and the gate opens and closes, and one goes in, and the other goes away.
>   [p. 28]

7 Edward Said's *Orientalism* is the pioneering work on this subject. See also Eve Sedgwick Kosofsky's extremely interesting chapter on the novel.

At the beginning of Chapter VIII, just before he quarrels with Neville, Edwin says that he plans ' "to wake up Egypt a little" ' by ' "[d]oing, working, engineering" ' (p. 101). This further expression of Edwin's sense of colonial mission, like his remarks to Rosa, is founded on a sense that Egypt is in a somnolent, underdeveloped state in need of European knowledge and energy. But the chapter also takes up Rosa's remark about the alleged Egyptian power of reading the future, and contains other references to Edwin's destiny, spoken by Jasper, which appear to articulate both his pride in Edwin's abilities and his observation of the offhand ease with which his nephew approaches life, but which might also be a revelation of the uncle's true feelings about their respective positions. Further, Jasper appears to cloak any application of these remarks solely to himself by enlisting Neville as sharing his situation rather than Edwin's:

> 'See where he lounges so easily, Mr Neville! The world is all before him where to choose. A life of stirring work and interest, a life of change and excitement, a life of domestic ease and love! Look at him! . . . See how little he heeds it all!' Jasper proceeds in a bantering vein. 'It is hardly worth his while to pluck the golden fruit that hangs ripe on the tree for him. And yet consider the contrast, Mr Neville . . . You and I have no prospect . . . but the tedious unchanging round of this dull place.'   [p. 64]

Jasper's comments, supposedly intended to ease the atmosphere, actually incite the two young men to further conflict, and their quarrel reaches its climax when Edwin throws at Neville a pointedly racist insult in response to the other's remark that he is ' "a common fellow and a common boaster" ': " 'You may know a black common fellow, or a black common boaster, when you see him (and no doubt you have a large acquaintance that way); but you are no judge of white men" ' (p. 66). This grossly insensitive remark is what we might expect of Edwin, who is emerging as an unsympathetic character, but his comments highlight what Neville and Helena Landless contribute to the novel's eastern motif. They have been brought up in Ceylon and their lengthy residence overseas makes them outsiders in England. They represent a threatening otherness and a puzzling uncertainty of both racial and social assignment. Colonialism is acceptable when practised in distant lands, but reminders of its existence in an English cathedral city are more troubling and unsettling. Furthermore, Helena and Neville seem to carry with them what Cloisterham perceives as an alien fluidity of temperament and behaviour, a dangerous doubleness – intensified by their twinship – and a wavering sense of identity: they might not only disguise themselves as strangers, but also, potentially, as each other.[8]

*   *   *

In his biography of Dickens, after quoting the writer's new plan for his next novel (see p. vi above), John Forster goes on to outline the development of the plot:

> . . . The story . . . was to be that of the murder of a nephew by his uncle; the originality of which was to consist in the review of the murderer's career by himself at the close, when its temptations were to be dwelt upon as if, not he the culprit, but some other man were the tempted.   [Forster, Book XI, Chap II]

Forster gives further details of how the body of the victim will be discovered and identified and the murderer hunted down and unmasked, as well as of who will marry whom and who will die heroically in the pursuit of the villain. By using phrases like 'I learnt immediately afterwards' and 'So much was told to me before any of the book was written', Forster claims privileged access to information about how the plot would develop. He and Dickens were close friends who saw each other almost daily, and it is highly probable that Dickens shared with his principal literary confidant his ideas about the novel. At the same time, however, Forster admits that there is no written evidence that this is exactly how the plot of the novel would have worked out, since Dickens wrote nothing of *Edwin Drood* beyond what was published, and nor did he leave any notes of his intentions. Forster's outline of the plot may have as much to do with his own perception of desirable and appropriate outcomes in terms of punishment, marriage and the necessary sacrifice of sympathetic characters, as with anything that might have developed in the writing of the novel.

Yet readerly desire and curiosity are always at play as we make our way through a narrative and construct ever-changing possible futures for the characters. In this sense reading is an intensely active experience, engaging readers' judgement and imagination as well as their stock of expectations derived from the reading of other stories. This collaboration between reader and writer, or reader and text becomes problematic, however, when the text is unfinished. Writerly co-operation is withdrawn, the collaborative endeavour is abruptly

8 For a brilliant general discussion of the ideas of twinning and doubling in literature, see Karl Miller's *Doubles* (Oxford; Oxford University Press, 1987).

halted and further information is withheld, so that readers are no longer able to check their guesses, hopes and fears against 'real' outcomes. Therefore, as Stephen Connor writes, '[t]he fragmentary condition of *The Mystery of Edwin Drood* can never be self-sufficient, will always call for the reconstructive participation of its future readers . . . the dead hand of narrative finality lies more clammily upon an unfinished novel than on a finished one. An unfinished novel seems everywhere, and insistently, to broach the question of its closure, seems at every point held in the detention of its absent, withheld ending' (Connor, p. 86). G. K. Chesterton touches on another consequence of the permanent suspension of closure when he remarks that 'a finished tale may give a man immortality in the light and literary sense; but an unfinished tale suggests another immortality more essential and more strange' (Chesterton, p. 223). Inevitably, therefore, much writing about the novel has concentrated on its absent ending and speculated about the likely outcome of the plot. By 1912 J. Cuming Walters was able to publish *The Complete Mystery of Edwin Drood*, which contain the text of the novel together with an extensive survey (complete with fold-out table summarising the various 'solutions' proposed) of speculations, continuations and sequels. Walters's bibliography lists almost 100 items, most of them from the years 1905–12: even a symposium in the *Dickensian* for April 1908, hopefully (or perhaps despairingly) entitled 'Last Words on the Drood Mystery', failed to stem the flow. [9] Writers were fairly evenly divided between Edwin being dead or alive – the most popular murderer in the former case being Jasper, the most popular explanation in the latter being that he has gone to Egypt, whence he eventually returns to confront Jasper. Bazzard, Drood, Grewgious, Helena and Neville Landless, Tartar and 'a detective' are all suggested as the real identity of Mr Datchery. Most commentators expect Neville Landless to die, Rosa to marry Tartar and Helena, Crisparkle. Jasper is variously redeemed, hanged, commits suicide and dies of shock when Edwin reappears. Chesterton, perhaps wisely, is of the view that with Dickens's death, the mysteries of the novel are forever insoluble.

Even if we think we have 'solved' the mystery, more mysteries will remain. A plausible and not particularly ingenious version of events might be that Jasper, driven by jealousy of Edwin's position and his

9 In 1912 Walters himself published *Clues to the Mystery of Edwin Drood* which occasioned a considerable press controversy and animated a whole new generation of literary detectives.

love for Rosa, plots to kill his nephew and conceal his remains in the cathedral. Somehow this plot misfires and he throws an unconscious Edwin into Cloisterham Weir. Edwin escapes but leaves his watch and shirtpin so that people will assume that he is dead. He then returns in disguise as Mr Datchery, to expose Jasper and clear Neville's name. However, this version of events immediately gives rise to a number of questions. Why doesn't Edwin struggle out of the water, go to the authorities in Cloisterham, have Jasper arrested before he can do any more damage and save everybody a great deal of trouble and heartbreak? Perhaps Edwin, like John Harmon with Bella in *Our Mutual Friend*, is *testing* Rosa, to see how she will react to his death. But this would presuppose that Edwin *cared* how Rosa felt about him; that he is really in love with her all along, and seizes on his disappearance as an opportunity for Rosa to discover her real feelings for him. A more cynical reader would no doubt suggest that for Edwin to have exposed Jasper so early in the plot would not have given Dickens the full-length story he required. But by 1870 Dickens was a highly experienced novelist who would not have embarked on a full-length novel if he did not believe that he had enough material to complete it. If Datchery is Edwin in disguise (and that he is *someone* in disguise seems to be one of the few things agreed on by most readers) then there is a good reason for his decision to adopt a false identity and watch and wait by his open door. And there is a more intriguing possibility to consider: that the greatest mysteries, unrevealed even to the author at the midway point in his narrative, lie forever locked in the tortured mind of John Jasper.

Master Humphrey's Clock

It would be easy to dismiss *Master Humphrey's Clock* as a frame lacking its canvas, and the history of this short-lived periodical appears to support such a view. But Dickens never undertook literary projects lightly, especially when they offered full control over his medium, and a fresh challenge always roused his energies and stimulated his imagination. After the enormous success of his first three novels, *The Pickwick Papers* (1836–37), *Oliver Twist* (1837–39) and *Nicholas Nickleby* (1838–39), all published in monthly numbers, Dickens was concerned that his public had tired of this mode of publication and wanted something new. Drawing on his experience as editor (1837–1839) of the monthly *Bentley's Miscellany*, in which *Oliver Twist* was serialised, Dickens suggested to his publishers Chapman and Hall a weekly miscellany whose contents would be framed in the setting of a club. Dickens would at first be editor and sole author, and would receive £50 from each issue, as well as a half-share of profits. He calculated that, assuming weekly sales of 50,000 copies, a two-year run would bring Chapman and Hall a profit of £5000, while Dickens himself would earn £11000.[10]

Sales of the first number, in April 1840, exceeded even Dickens's optimistic projections: 60,000 copies were printed and sold and another 10,000 were ordered. After this brilliant start, however, sales for the second and third numbers dropped sharply. Dickens kept his head, but prudently revised the proofs of the 'little child-story' (*Letters*, II, p. 50) in Number 4 in such a way that it could be extended if necessary. In the event, the second instalment of *The Old Curiosity Shop* did not appear until Number 7, and while the novel entirely occupied Numbers 8 and 10, the miscellany format returned for Numbers 9 and 11. The convention of Master Humphrey as narrator of Little Nell's story was abandoned by the end of Chapter 3 (Number 8), however, and numbers 12 to 45 were wholly devoted to *The Old Curiosity Shop*. The rise in sales, which at one time reached 100,000 a week, suggests that readers did not regret the absence of Master Humphrey and his friends. They returned briefly to introduce *Barnaby Rudge*, and once again when that novel was completed. In the final number of the periodical Master Humphrey dies: his clock 'has stopped for ever' (p. 350).

What, then, do these remainders of a long-defunct literary periodical offer the modern reader? The overall device of a club of elderly gentlemen telling one another stories, mostly set in the past, now seems at best quaint and at worst artificial. The resurrection, presumably in response to uncertain sales figures, of Pickwick, Sam Weller and his father, even smacks of desperation. But the nature of Dickens's imagination is such that even in the slightest stories, which we might think were created simply to fill a required space each week, the author's characteristic preoccupations are likely to emerge. Childhood, London, the dangers of idealising the past – these are motifs that run through the tales narrated by the club members. And in the revelation of Master Humphrey's identity as the single gentleman of *The Old Curiosity Shop*, or in the further revelation, in the penultimate paragraph, that Jack Redburn's past may have made its way into *Barnaby Rudge*, there is a fascinating rupture of the fictional frame, as material from the novels leaks into a setting that claims reality but is itself fictive.

10 The cover price was 3d, with collected monthly parts at 1/-.

'Hunted Down', 'Holiday Romance' and 'George Silverman's Explanation'

All three of these stories were written to commission for American periodicals, and they demonstrate Dickens's fame and literary standing as well as the payments he could command for even a comparatively short piece of writing. Indeed, so considerable were the financial rewards that in the case of 'Hunted Down' Dickens was persuaded to interrupt work on *A Tale of Two Cities*. 'I thought that I could not have been tempted at this time', Dickens wrote to Robert Bonner, proprietor of the magazine the *New York Ledger*, 'to engage in any undertaking, however short, but the literary project which will come into existence next month'. This letter is dated 29 March 1859 and *A Tale of Two Cities* began to appear in *All the Year Round* in April. 'But', Dickens continued, 'your proposal is so handsome that it changes my resolution, and I cannot refuse it' (*Letters*, IX, pp. 44–45). Bonner had offered the substantial sum of £1000, and was delighted to have pulled off a coup, proudly announcing in a newspaper advertisement that 'this is the first time that a tale has been written expressly and solely for an American periodical by such an eminent author' (*Letters*, IX, p. 44n). The story appeared in the *New York Ledger* in three weekly parts in August–September 1859, and in two parts, in *All the Year Round* in August 1860.

For the plot and main character of 'Hunted Down', Dickens went back over twenty years, to June 1837, when he and the actor William Macready, visited in Newgate prison the forger and poisoner Thomas Wainewright. Born in 1794, Wainewright had been an art critic and a painter who exhibited at the Royal Academy in the 1820s, but began a criminal career in 1826 when he forged a Bank of England money order, and went on to poison a number of relatives for monetary gain. He was convicted of forgery, transported to Tasmania and died there in 1847. Dickens was always fascinated by what drives apparently respectable individuals to commit criminal acts, so it is not surprising that he should have been interested in seeing Wainewright. He left no contemporary account of this visit, but Macready's diary contains an interesting glimpse of what took place, describing Wainewright as a 'wretched man overlaid with crime', apparently cheerful 'but in the pride of our nature . . . eradicated or trodden down—it was a most depressing sight' (27 June 1837; Macready, pp. 401–2)

Much of the interest of 'Hunted Down' lies in the uncovering of Slinkton's true character by the narrator, Mr Sampson. At first sight,

Sampson, after thirty years in a Life Assurance office, cut off from the world and wholly devoted to business, seems an unlikely detective. But he is a shrewd observer, with a keen sense of the gap between appearance and reality: the plate glass partition that replaces the solid wall between his room and the office in which he works enables him to observe visitors and to draw conclusions about their behaviour. Sampson immediately perceives that Slinkton is insincere, a manipulative character who uses the force of his personality to persuade others to accept his view of events. His strongly marked centre parting, like a path along his head, is an effective image for the power he has in leading people's thoughts in his chosen direction, and an important moment occurs when the narrator thinks to himself ' "I *won't* go up the track, and I *will* go on the grass" ' (p. 357). This ability to think along routes other than those signposted, which Slinkton either fails to perceive or gravely underestimates, enables Sampson to outwit his opponent.

The early sections of the story, in which Dickens constructs the personality of his narrator and suggests the falsity in Slinkton's nature, are subtle and effective. The fourth section, set on the beach at Scarborough as darkness falls, also has some power as Dickens increases the tension, not least by the way in which he suggests that crime can threaten even in the most ordinary of settings. By contrast, the final section is disappointing, as the narrative gallops towards a resolution that requires too much exposition from Sampson and Beckwith/ Meltham. There is material here for a much longer story which might have explored more fully Slinkton's motivation and the complexity of his deceptions as well as Meltham's association with Slinkton's nieces. The ending also strains credulity when it is revealed that the supposedly sickly Meltham has been able to sustain a convincing disguise as Beckwith and find time to double as the old East India Company director on Scarborough beach. On the other hand, Meltham's determination bears out Dickens's belief in the power of a few right-minded people, armed with strong principles and acute powers of perception (perhaps like Tartar, Crisparkle and Grewgious in *Edwin Drood*) to confront and overcome evil.

Dickens remembered the commission from Bonner when, in March 1867, he received a request from J. R. Osgood, agent in England for the American publishers Ticknor and Field, asking for a story for their children's magazine *Our Young Folks* for a payment of £1000. 'The length of the whole,' he told Osgood on 29 March 1867, 'shall certainly not be less than that of the story "Hunted Down" which I wrote . . . for a New York paper some years ago'. But he would not be bound by this limit, and told Osgood that 'nothing could compensate me for slighting my art' (*Letters*, XI, p. 343). The story was ready by the end of July and appeared in four instalments between January and May 1868 under the title 'Holiday Romance'; it was published almost simultaneously in *All the Year Round*. Dickens's personal investment in this charming tale of innocent childhood fantasy is suggested by his remarks to Percy Fitzgerald: 'I am glad you like the children, and particularly glad you like the pirate. I remember very well when I had a general idea of occupying that place in history at the same age. But I loved more desperately than Boldheart' (28 April 1867; *Letters*, XII, p. 707).

The origins of 'George Silverman's Explanation' are more complicated, just as the story itself is more complex and enigmatic. It was written on commission for Ticknor and Fields, for their periodical *Atlantic Monthly*. When the commission came, in the spring of 1867, Dickens was seeking a subject for his next novel and among his ideas was a story that would end with a villain writing a death-cell confession and explanation Then, in April 1867, while walking between reading engagements in Preston and Blackburn, Dickens and George Dolby came across Hoghton Towers, a partially ruined sixteenth and seventeenth century manor house. Dickens recorded the decisive effect of this discovery in a letter to W. H. Wills: 'The main idea of the narrator's position towards the other people, was the idea I *had* for my next novel in A. Y. R. But it is very curious that I did not in the least see how to begin his state of mind, until I walked into Hoghton Towers' (28 June 1867; *Letters*, XII, p. 385). Dickens then worked quickly, so that Dolby was able to deliver the manuscript when he visited the United States in August 1867.

The story takes up Dickens's half-formed idea of a man writing an account and justification of his life, and was as much of a surprise to its author as it obviously was to Wills:

> I am glad you see a certain unlikeness to any thing, in the American story; and I hope that when you see it complete, you will think still better of it. Upon myself, it has made the strangest impression of reality and originality!! And I feel as if I had read something (by somebody else) which I should never get out of my mind!!! [28 June 1867; *Letters*, XII, p. 385]

Dickens's striking sense of detachment from his own work and the impression he gives of being somehow haunted by the story, perhaps relates to the shifting tone of Silverman's narrative, its blend of humility and arrogance, self-blame and self-exculpation. It represents one of the few examples of Dickens taking full advantage of the strengths offered by compression: what makes a deep impression over twenty or so pages would be intolerable at greater length.

The circumstances of Silverman's life are extraordinary in themselves, and the narrative is powerfully driven by Dickens's always acute awareness of the child's vulnerability in a rapidly developing mass society; his sense that children could easily become 'lost' or displaced in both moral and class terms, in the chaos and indifference of the modern industrial system. The early parts of the story are set in Preston and Birmingham, both centres of industrialisation. Preston was the town that Dickens chose to visit when seeking material for his 'industrial' novel *Hard Times* (1854), where it is recreated as Coketown, and his memories had been refreshed when he read there on 25 April 1867. The unexpected discovery of Hoghton Towers, completed the settings that Dickens needed in which to create Silverman's solipsistic vision: the subterranean claustrophobia of a foetid Preston cellar; the stifling moral environment of a Birmingham conventicle; and the reminder of past splendours in a ruined manor.

Is Silverman to be pitied or despised? It is the great achievement of this story that both views are possible, because the shifting tone of the narrative constantly plays on the reader's responses. On the one hand, it is possible to understand how Silverman internalises the view, instilled in him first by his mother and then by Brother Hawkyard, that he is a reprehensibly worldly creature. His worldliness, observed from beyond the enclosed and almost hallucinatory worlds of the cellar and the chapel, consists of an understandable desire to enjoy some basic human comforts. Yet when he acquires these comforts his pride in his own accomplishments is soured by a self-flagellating guilt. The tensions of his situation set up in Silverman a series of deeply ambivalent feelings, his indulgence of which perhaps take him beyond the reader's sympathy. Memories of the hardships he has endured make him resentful and self-pitying; self-pity leads to a perverted self-regard combined with a specious humility, which in turn leads to a kind of self-justification that can no longer distinguish reality from fantasy. Silverman may have been rescued from poverty, but there is a sense in which he remains forever trapped in that dark Preston cellar.

PETER PRESTON
Senior Lecturer in Literary Studies
Centre for Continuing Education, University of Nottingham

CLOISTERHAM AND ROCHESTER: A NOTE

For his creation of Cloisterham Dickens drew upon the topography of the cathedral city of Rochester on the River Medway in north-east Kent. It was a city and a countryside that Dickens knew well: from 1817 (when he was five years old) until 1823 he lived in the nearby town of Chatham, also on the Medway, where his father was a clerk in the naval dockyard. In 1856 he was able to purchase Gad's Hill Place at Higham, a few miles north of Rochester, a house he had admired in childhood and which he used as his country home until his death. The marshy landscape so memorably evoked in the opening paragraphs of *Great Expectations* lies to the east, and the row of child graves that gave Dickens the idea for Pip's dead brothers, as well as Crisparkle's (see p. 42), is to be found close by in Cooling churchyard. Many of the places mentioned in *Edwin Drood* can be identified as being re-creations of locations in Rochester; others combine features from more than one building or area; and others again are entirely imaginary. Equally significant for an understanding of the novel, however, is the way in which Dickens employs places, especially the cathedral, in a symbolic manner as part of the 'mystery' with which the book is concerned.

Among the identifiable locations is 'the old stone gatehouse' (p.8) where John Jasper lives. It has features in common with all three of the gates near Rochester cathedral – College Gate, Deanery Gate and Priory Gate – but is closest to College Gate, now known as Chertsey's Gate. Miss Twinkleton keeps her school in The Nun's House, the 'venerable brick edifice' (p.17) with its 'sly faces carved on spout and gable', which is based on Eastgate House in the High Street. It was never used as a convent but it housed a girls' school at the time Dickens was writing the novel. Mr Sapsea's house stands opposite Eastgate House, and had previously been used by Dickens as the basis for Uncle Pumblechook's shop in *Great Expectations*. Mr Tope, the head verger of the cathedral, also lives in the High Street, in a house adjoining Jasper's, and it is here that the mysterious Mr Datchery takes lodgings when he arrives in Cloisterham (see pp.176–7). The 'drooping and despondent little theatre' (p.18) refers to

Rochester's Theatre Royal, also know as the Lyceum, built in 1791 and standing at the bottom of Star Hill. When Rosa and Edwin talk seriously about their future 'among the quiet walks in the neighbourhood of the cathedral and the river' (p.130), they are on the Esplanade, on the east bank of the Medway.

The 'crazy wooden house of two low storeys . . . a house all warped and distorted, like the morals of the travellers' (p. 41) is the Traveller's Twopenny, which appears to be based on Kitt's Lodging House, also called the Fourpenny Lodging House, near the High Street. Dickens no doubt halved the lodging charge to emphasise the low point it occupied in the housing chain. In order to reach the 'narrow back lane' where the Twopenny stands, Jasper and Durdle cross 'what was once the vineyard belonging to what was once the monastery' (p. 41). The 'Vines' is a walk to the south of the cathedral, beyond Minor Canon Row on the site of a former vineyard. Although there was a Benedictine monastery near the cathedral in Rochester, the city has no monastic ruins and the 'beetling fragment of monastery ruin' (p.85) that Crisparkle is fond of climbing actually occupies some of the site of Rochester Castle, which apart from a passing reference to 'the pile close at hand' (p. 8) does not appear in the novel.

Many scenes take place in and around the cathedral and its 'echoing Close' (p.7). Such details as 'the iron railing of the burial-ground' or 'the old cloister-arches' (p. 36) draw on Dickens's detailed knowledge of Rochester's cathedral precinct. The 'paved Quaker settlement . . . up in a shady corner' (p.18) does not refer to any area associated with Quakerism and is occasioned by the plainness and quietness of the location. For Minor Canon Corner, where Rev. Crisparkle lives with his mother, Dickens made only a small change to the name of Minor Canon Row, a terrace of houses built for the clergy in the 1720s and 1730s, which stands in St Margaret's Street on the south side of the cathedral close. Crisparkle lives in the house at west end of the terrace, which is close to Prior's Gate. The Deanery, a 'snug old redbrick house' (p. 9), stands near the old chapter house ruins at the east end of Rochester cathedral. .

Details of the cathedral itself are also drawn from what Dickens knew of Rochester. The 'massive grey square tower' (p. 3) is immediately recognisable (although the fourteenth century tower familiar to Dickens was rebuilt in the twentieth century), while the 'low arched cathedral door' (p.7) from which the Dean and Mr Tope emerge adjoins the great west door on the north. That 'great western-folding door' at Rochester, through which Mr Grewgious peers, as if

' "down the throat of Old Time" ' (p. 80), is a magnificent example of Norman work from the second half of the twelfth century. Jasper's moonlight tour of the cathedral with Durdles, supposedly undertaken because he is, as he tells Sapsea, ' "a lover of the picturesque" ' (p. 110), clearly has a more sinister purpose, and Dickens modifies some details of the layout of Rochester to increase the dramatic effect. Their descent into the crypt 'by a small side door' (p.115) refers to the door in the south choir aisle by which gives access to one of the largest crypts in England. But the 'winding staircase of the great tower', also visible in the illustration on the cover of the monthly parts of the novel, differs from that in Rochester, while the view 'into the moonlit nave' is not possible from the 'level low-arched galleries' of the triforium (p. 117). Cloisterham/ Rochester 'fair to see in the moon-light', is certainly visible from the top of the tower, which also overlooks 'that stillest part' (p. 118), the graveyard. As Wendy Jacobson points out, it is here that anyone falling or thrown from the tower would land; and Durdles's mild attack of calenture emphasises how easy such a fall might be (Jacobson, p. 119).

The dramatic advantage of this topography is that the main characters live very close to one another, combining convenience with claustrophobia. They can move quickly and easily between houses; but at the same time, as Mr Datchery finds, their movements can also be readily observed. Eavesdropping and spying occur throughout the novel: the tight-knit community of the cathedral close makes it difficult to live a private life – which is one of the things that Jasper finds intolerable and why he travels to London for a kind of escape. And if Jasper *is* planning to murder Edwin and conceal his remains in the cathedral, his plan is the more desperate and daring because of the proximity of many keen-eyed and inquisitive people.

It is from Jasper's point of view that some of the more negative and disturbing visions of Cloisterham are seen. The city first appears, out of place as it were, in his opium-induced dream with which the novel opens, thus establishing Cloisterham as somewhere that exists partly in the real world and partly in Jasper's fevered imagination. But the novel's narrative voice, without underwriting Jasper's view, creates its own forbidding vision of the 'monotonous silent city' with its 'oppressive respectability', and where '[a]ll things . . . are of the past' (pp.17–18) Troubling images constantly appear and the prose, with its frequently decelerating rhythms, adds to the effect of a city that depresses and confines more than it uplifts and liberates. As the Dean, Tope and Crisparkle look towards Jasper's gatehouse home 'the deep cathedral bell strikes the hour [and] a ripple of wind goes through these at a distance, like a ripple of the solemn sound that hums through tomb and tower, broken niche and defaced statue, in the pile close at hand' (p.8). When Jasper and Tope look down on the city from the top of the cathedral tower, Cloisterham is at first 'fair to see in the moonlight', but the passage soon strikes a note of melancholy with the 'ruined habitations and sanctuaries of the dead', and then of disturbance with the river 'winding from the mist on the horizon, as though that were its source, already heaving with a restless knowledge of its approach to the sea' (p. 118). The reader is always conscious of how many dead lie around the characters, whether it be in the city's many graveyards or in the cathedral's tombs, with which Durdles is so familiar and about which Jasper shows so much curiosity (see pp. 115–6).

The cathedral is in fact both deeply compromised and threatened with desecration, presided over by the amiable but ineffectual Dean and its music directed by the bored and disaffected Jasper. Only Crisparkle, as his name suggests, offers any prospect of enlightenment, but he is in a relatively junior and powerless position in the cathedral's hierarchy. One of the most remarkable passages in the novel occurs when Grewgious looks in at the cathedral through its west door and sees darkness where light might be expected:

> . . . gloomy shadows began to deepen in corners; and damps began to rise from deep patches of stone; and jewels, cast upon the pavement of the nave from stained glass by the declining sun, began to perish. Within the grill-gate of the chancel, up the steps surmounted loomingly by the fast-darkening organ, white robes could be dimly see, and one feeble voice, rising and falling in a cracked monotonous mutter, could at intervals be faintly heard.
>
> [p. 80]

The passage then turns to a brief evocation of the freer, brighter world outside the cathedral, before returning to the 'grey, murky, and sepulchral' interior, 'the cracked monotonous mutter', which is then drowned by 'a sea of music' which eventually 'beat[s] its life out' (p. 76). Somewhere between the feeble 'dying voice' of the church establishment, and Jasper's passionate, desperate but quickly subsiding outburst of music, the spiritual life of the cathedral, with its intended message of salvation and forgiveness, disappears. And it is in this sense, much more than in the identification of 'real' places that Cloisterham and its cathedral are central to an understanding of *The Mystery of Edwin Drood*.

BIBLIOGRAPHY

Works by Charles Dickens and his contemporaries

The Letters of Charles Dickens, vol. II, ed. Madeline House and Graham Storey, Clarendon Press, Oxford 1969

The Letters of Charles Dickens, vol. IX, ed. Graham Storey, Clarendon Press, Oxford 1997

The Letters of Charles Dickens, vol. XI, ed. Graham Storey, Clarendon Press, Oxford 1999

The Letters of Charles Dickens, vol. XII, ed. Graham Storey, Clarendon Press, Oxford 2002

Master Humphrey's Clock and *A Child's History of England*, Oxford: Oxford University Press, 1958

The Mystery of Edwin Drood ed. Margaret Cardwell, Clarendon Press, Oxford 1972

The Mystery of Edwin Drood ed. Arthur J. Cox, with an introduction by Angus Wilson, Penguin, Harmondsworth 1974

The Mystery of Edwin Drood ed. Margaret Cardwell, Oxford World's Classics, Oxford 1982

The Mystery of Edwin Drood ed. Steven Connor, J. M. Dent, Everyman Classics, London, 1996

The Mystery of Edwin Drood ed. David Paroissien, Penguin, London 2002

The Diaries of William Macready, ed. William Toynbee, 2 vols, Chapman & Hall, London, 1912

Biography

Peter Ackroyd, *Dickens*, Sinclair-Stevenson, London 1990; revised 1994

John Forster, *Life of Charles Dickens* (1872–4), ed. A. J. Hoppé, 2 vols, Dent, London 1969

Edgar Johnson, *Charles Dickens: his Tragedy and Triumph*, Gollancz, London 1953

Fred Kaplan, *Dickens: a Biography*, Hodder and Stoughton, London 1988

Grahame Smith, *Charles Dickens: a Literary Life*, Macmillan Press, Basingstoke 1993

Angus Wilson, *The World of Charles Dickens*, Secker and Warburg, London 1970

Social, political and cultural Context

Asa Briggs, *The Age of Improvement*, Longman, London 1959

Asa Briggs, *Victorian People*, Penguin Books, Harmondsworth 1965

Jerome H. Buckley, *The Victorian Temper: a Study in Literary Culture*, Cass, London 1966

William F. Houghton, *The Victorian Frame of Mind 1830–1870*, Yale University Press, London 1957

John Sutherland, *Victorian Novelists and Publishers*, Athlone Press, London 1976

Alison Winter, *Mesmerized: Powers of Mind in Victorian Britain*, University of Chicago Press, London and Chicago, 1998

General critical works on Dickens

John Butt and Kathleen Tillotson, *Dickens at Work*, Methuen, London, 1957

John Carey, *The Violent Effigy: A Study of Dickens's Imagination*, Faber, London, 1973, 1991

G. K. Chesterton, *Charles Dickens*, Methuen, London 1906

G. K. Chesterton, *Criticisms and Appreciations of the Work of Charles Dickens*, London: J. M. Dent, 1933

Philip Collins (ed), *Charles Dickens: The Critical Heritage*, Routledge, London 1971

George Gissing, *Charles Dickens: a Critical Study* (1898), Blackie, London 1926

J. R. Harvey, *Victorian Novelists and their Illustrators*, Sidgwick and Jackson, London 1970

Humphry House, *The Dickens World*, Oxford University Press, Oxford 1940

F. R. and Q. D. Leavis, *Dickens the Novelist*, Chatto and Windus, London 1970

John Lucas, *The Melancholy Man: A Study of Dickens's Novels*, Methuen, London 1970, 1980

J. Hillis Miller, *Charles Dickens: the World of His Novels*, Harvard University Press, Cambridge, MA 1958

George Orwell, 'Charles Dickens' (1940) in *The Collected Essays, Journalism and Letters of George Orwell*, ed. Sonia Orwell and Ian Angus, vol. 1, pp. 454–504

Robert L. Patten, *Charles Dickens and his Publishers*, Clarendon Press, Oxford 1978

Michael Slater, *Dickens on Women*, Dent, London 1983

Stephen Wall (ed), *Charles Dickens: a Critical Anthology*, Penguin Books, Harmondsworth 1970

On The Mystery of Edwin Drood

Felix Aylmer, *Dickens Incognito*, Rupert Hart-Davis, London 1959

Felix Aylmer, *The Drood Case*, Rupert Hart-Davis, London 1964

Philip Collins, 'The Mysteries in *Edwin Drood*' in *Dickens and Crime*, Routledge, London, 1962, 1964, pp. 290–319

Steven Connor, 'Dead? Or Alive? *Edwin Drood* and the Work of Mourning', *Dickensian*, 89 (1993), 85–102

Arthur J. Cox, 'Magnetic Sympathy in *The Mystery of Edwin Drood*' Part I: 'Mr Crisparkle Takes a Memorable Nightwalk' Part II: 'Neville Landless Sets Out on a Pilgrimage', *Dickensian*, 96 (2000), 127–50, 209–42

Ray Dubberke, 'Dating *Edwin Drood*', *Dickensian*, 88 (1992), 19–24

Charles Faulkner, 'Drood and the Bean-Stalk', *Dickensian*, 80 (1984), 74–88

Wendy S. Jacobson, *The Companion to The Mystery of Edwin Drood*, Allen & Unwin, London 1986

Fred Kaplan, *Dickens and Mesmerism: the Hidden Springs of Fiction*, Princeton University Press, Princeton NJ 1975)

Elsie Karbacz and Robert Raven, 'The Many Mysteries of *Edwin Drood*', *Dickensian*, 90 (1990), 5–17

Simon Schama, 'Death of a Harvard Man' in *Dead Certainties: Unwarranted Speculations*, Granta Books, London 1991, pp. 73–318

Eve Kosofsky Sedgwick, 'Up the Postern Stair: *Edwin Drood* and the Homophobia of Empire' in *Between Men: English Literature and Male Homosocial Desire*, Columbia University Press, New York 1985, pp. 180–200

Edward Said, *Orientalism*, Routledge & Kegan Paul, London 1978

John Thacker, *Edwin Drood: Antichrist in the Cathedral*, Vision Press, London 1990

Claire Tomalin, *The Invisible Woman: the Story of Nelly Ternan and Charles Dickens*, Viking, London 1990; with additional material, Penguin, London, 1991

Robert Tracy, 'Disappearances: George Parkman and Edwin Drood', *Dickensian*, 96 (2000), 101–17

J. Cuming Walters, *The Complete Mystery of Edwin Drood by Charles Dickens: the History, Continuations and Solutions (1870–1912)*, Chapman & Hall, London 1912

CONTENTS

MASTER HUMPHREY'S CLOCK

HUNTED DOWN
page 351

HOLIDAY ROMANCE

GEORGE SILVERMAN'S EXPLANATION
page 409

NOTES

THE MYSTERY OF EDWIN DROOD

The Dawn[1]

AN ANCIENT English cathedral town? How can the ancient English cathedral town be here? The well-known massive grey square tower of its old cathedral? How can that be here? There is no spike of rusty iron in the air, between the eye and it, from any point of the real prospect. What is the spike that intervenes, and who has set it up? Maybe it is set up by the sultan's orders for the impaling of a horde of Turkish robbers, one by one. It is so, for cymbals clash, and the sultan goes by to his palace in long procession. Ten thousand scimitars flash in the sunlight, and thrice ten thousand dancing girls strew flowers. Then follow white elephants caparisoned in countless gorgeous colours and infinite in number and attendants.[2] Still the cathedral tower rises in the background, where it cannot be, and still no writhing figure is on the grim spike. Stay! Is the spike so low a thing as the rusty spike on the top of a post of an old bedstead that has tumbled all awry? Some vague period of drowsy laughter must be devoted to the consideration of this possibility.

Shaking from head to foot, the man whose scattered consciousness has thus fantastically pieced itself together, at length rises, supports his trembling frame upon his arms, and looks around. He is in the meanest and closest of small rooms. Through the ragged window curtain, the light of early day steals in from a miserable court. He lies, dressed, across a large unseemly bed, upon a bedstead that has indeed given way under the weight upon it. Lying, also dressed and also across the bed, not longwise, are a Chinaman, a Lascar,[3] and a haggard woman. The two first are in a sleep or stupor; the last is blowing at a kind of pipe, to kindle it. And as she blows, and shading it with her lean hand, concentrates its red spark of light, it serves in the dim morning as a lamp to show him what he sees of her.

'Another?' says this woman,[4] in a querulous, rattling whisper. 'Have another?'

He looks about him, with his hand to his forehead.

'Ye've smoked as many as five since ye come in at midnight,' the woman goes on, as she chronically complains. 'Poor me, poor me, my head is so bad. Them two come in after ye. Ah, poor me, the business is slack, is slack! Few Chinamen[5] about the docks, and fewer Lascars, and no ships coming[6] in, these say! Here's another ready for ye, deary. Ye'll remember like a good soul, won't ye, that the market price is dreffle[7] high just now? More than three shillings and sixpence for a thimbleful! And ye'll remember that nobody but me (and Jack Chinaman t'other side the court; but he can't do it as well as me) has the true secret of mixing it? Ye'll pay up accordingly, deary, won't ye?'

She blows at the pipe as she speaks, and, occasionally bubbling at it, inhales much of its contents.

'Oh me, oh me, my lungs is weak, my lungs is bad! It's nearly ready for ye, deary. Ah, poor me, poor me, my poor hand shakes like to drop off! I see ye coming to, and I ses to my poor self, "I'll have another ready for him, and he'll bear in mind the market price of opium, and pay according." Oh my poor head! I makes my pipes of old penny ink-bottles, ye see, deary – this is one – and I fits in a mouthpiece, this way, and I takes my mixter out of this thimble with this little horn spoon;[8] and so I fills, deary. Ah, my poor nerves! I got Heavens-hard drunk for sixteen year afore I took to this; but this don't hurt me, not to speak of. And it takes away the hunger as well as wittles, deary.'

She hands him the nearly-emptied pipe, and sinks back, turning over on her face.

He rises unsteadily from the bed, lays the pipe upon the hearth-stone, draws back the ragged curtain, and looks with repugnance at his three companions. He notices that the woman has opium-smoked herself into a strange likeness of the Chinaman. His form of cheek, eye and temple, and his colour, are repeated in her. Said Chinaman convulsively wrestles with one of his many gods or devils, perhaps, and snarls horribly. The Lascar laughs and dribbles at the mouth. The hostess is still.

'What visions can *she* have?' the waking man muses, as he turns her face towards him, and stands looking down at it. 'Visions of many butchers' shops, and public-houses, and much credit? Of an increase of hideous customers, and this horrible bedstead set upright again, and this horrible court swept clean? What can she rise to, under any quantity of opium, higher than that! – Eh?'

He bends down his ear, to listen to her mutterings.

In the court

'Unintelligible!'

As he watches the spasmodic shoots and darts that break out of her face and limbs, like fitful lightning out of a dark sky, some contagion in them seizes upon him: insomuch that he has to withdraw himself to a lean armchair by the hearth – placed there, perhaps, for such emergencies – and to sit in it, holding tight, until he has got the better of this unclean spirit of imitation.[9]

Then he comes back, pounces on the Chinaman, and seizing him with both hands by the throat, turns him violently on the bed. The Chinaman clutches the aggressive hands, resists, gasps and protests.

'What do you say?' A watchful pause. 'Unintelligible!'

Slowly loosening his grasp as he listens to the incoherent jargon with an attentive frown, he turns to the Lascar and fairly drags him forth upon the floor. As he falls, the Lascar starts into a half-risen attitude, glares with his eyes, lashes about him fiercely with his arms, and draws a phantom knife. It then becomes apparent that the woman has taken possession of this knife, for safety's sake; for, she too starting up, and restraining and expostulating with him, the knife is visible in her dress, not in his, when they drowsily drop back, side by side.

There has been wild chattering and clattering enough between them, but to no purpose. When any distinct word has been flung into the air, it has had no sense or sequence. Wherefore 'unintelligible!' is again the comment of the watcher, made with some reassured nodding of his head, and a gloomy smile. He then lays certain silver money on the table, finds his hat, gropes his way down the broken stairs, gives a good morning to some rat-ridden door-keeper, in bed in a black hutch beneath the stairs, and passes out.

That same afternoon, the massive grey square tower of an old cathedral[10] rises before the sight of a jaded traveller. The bells are going for daily vesper service,[11] and he must needs attend it, one would say, from his haste to reach the open cathedral door. The choir are getting on their sullied white robes, in a hurry, when he arrives among them, gets on his own robe, and falls into the procession filing in to service. Then the sacristan locks the iron-barred gates that divide the sanctuary from the chancel,[12] and all of the procession, having scuttled into their places, hide their faces; and then the intoned words, '*When the wicked man* – '[13] rise among groins of arches and beams of roof, awakening muttered thunder.

CHAPTER 2

A Dean and a Chapter Also[14]

WHOSOEVER has observed that sedate and clerical bird,[15] the rook, may perhaps have noticed that when he wings his way homeward[16] towards nightfall, in a sedate and clerical company, two rooks will suddenly detach themselves from the rest, will retrace their flight for some distance, and will there poise and linger; conveying to mere men the fancy that it is of some occult importance to the body politic that this artful couple should pretend to have renounced connection with it.

Similarly, service being over in the old cathedral with the square tower, and the choir scuffling out again, and divers venerable persons of rook-like aspect dispersing, two of these latter retrace their steps, and walk together in the echoing Close.[17]

Not only is the day waning, but the year.[18] The low sun is fiery and yet cold behind the monastery ruin, and the Virginia creeper[19] on the cathedral wall has showered half its deep-red leaves down on the pavement. There has been rain this afternoon, and a wintry shudder goes among the little pools on the cracked, uneven flag-stones, and through the giant elm trees as they shed a gust of tears. Their fallen leaves lie strewn thickly about.[20] Some of these leaves, in a timid rush, seek sanctuary within the low-arched cathedral door; but two men coming out resist them, and cast them forth[21] again with their feet; this done, one of the two locks the door with a goodly key, and the other flits away with a folio music-book.

'Mr Jasper was that, Tope?'

'Yes, Mr Dean.'

'He has stayed late.'

'Yes, Mr Dean. I have stayed for him, your reverence. He has been took a little poorly.'

'Say "taken", Tope – to the dean,' the younger rook interposes in a low tone with this touch of correction, as who should say: 'You may offer bad grammar to the laity, or the humbler clergy, not to the dean.'

Mr Tope, Chief Verger[22] and Showman, and accustomed to be

high with excursion parties, declines with a silent loftiness to perceive that any suggestion has been tendered to him.

'And when and how has Mr Jasper been taken – for, as Mr Crisparkle has remarked, it is better to say taken – taken – ' repeats the dean; 'when and how has Mr Jasper been taken – '

'Taken, sir,' Tope deferentially murmurs.

' – poorly, Tope?'

'Why, sir, Mr Jasper was that breathed – '

'I wouldn't say "that breathed", Tope,' Mr Crisparkle interposes with the same touch as before. 'Not English – to the dean.'

'Breathed to that extent,' the dean (not unflattered by this indirect homage) condescendingly remarks, 'would be preferable.'

'Mr Jasper's breathing was so remarkably short' – thus discreetly does Mr Tope work his way round the sunken rock – 'when he came in, that it distressed him mightily to get his notes out: which was perhaps the cause of his having a kind of fit on him after a little. His memory grew *dazed*' – Mr Tope, with his eyes on the Reverend Mr Crisparkle, shoots this word out, as defying him to improve upon it – 'and a dimness and giddiness crept over him as strange as ever I saw: though he didn't seem to mind it particularly, himself. However, a little time and a little water brought him out of his *daze*.' Mr Tope repeats the word and its emphasis, with the air of saying: 'As I *have* made a success, I'll make it again.'

'And Mr Jasper has gone home quite himself, has he?' asks the dean.

'Your reverence, he has gone home quite himself. And I'm glad to see he's having his fire kindled up, for it's chilly after the wet, and the cathedral had both a damp feel and a damp touch this afternoon, and he was very shivery.'

They all three look towards an old stone gatehouse crossing the Close, with an arched thoroughfare passing beneath it. Through its latticed window, a fire shines out upon the fast-darkening scene, involving in shadow the pendent masses of ivy and creeper covering the building's front. As the deep cathedral bell strikes the hour, a ripple of wind goes through these at their distance, like a ripple of the solemn sound that hums through tomb and tower, broken niche and defaced statue, in the pile close at hand.

'Is Mr Jasper's nephew with him?' the dean asks.

'No, sir,' replied the Verger, 'but expected. There's his own solitary shadow betwixt his two windows – the one looking this way, and the one looking down into the High Street – drawing his own curtains now.'

'Well, well,' says the dean, with a sprightly air of breaking up the little conference, 'I hope Mr Jasper's heart may not be too much set upon his nephew.[23] Our affections, however laudable, in this transitory world,[24] should never master us; we should guide them, guide them. I find I am not disagreeably reminded of my dinner by hearing my dinner-bell. Perhaps, Mr Crisparkle, you will, before going home, look in on Jasper?'

'Certainly, Mr Dean. And tell him that you had the kindness to desire to know how he was?'

'Ay; do so, do so. Certainly. Wished to know how he was. By all means. Wished to know how he was.'

With a pleasant air of patronage, the dean as nearly cocks his quaint hat as a dean in good spirits may, and directs his comely gaiters towards the ruddy dining-room of the snug old redbrick house where he is at present 'in residence'[25] with Mrs Dean and Miss Dean.

Mr Crisparkle, minor canon,[26] fair and rosy, and perpetually pitching himself head-foremost into all the deep running water in the surrounding country; Mr Crisparkle, minor canon, early riser, musical, classical, cheerful, kind, good-natured, social, contented, and boy-like; Mr Crisparkle, minor canon and good man, lately 'coach' upon the chief pagan high roads, but since promoted by a patron (grateful for a well-taught son) to his present Christian beat; betakes himself to the gatehouse, on his way home to his early tea.

'Sorry to hear from Tope that you have not been well, Jasper.'

'Oh, it was nothing, nothing!'

'You look a little worn.'

'Do I? Oh, I don't think so. What is better, I don't feel so. Tope has made too much of it, I suspect. It's his trade to make the most of everything appertaining to the Cathedral, you know.'

'I may tell the dean – I call expressly from the dean – that you are all right again?'

The reply, with a slight smile, is: 'Certainly; with my respects and thanks to the dean.'

'I'm glad to hear that you expect young Drood.'

'I expect the dear fellow every moment.'

'Ah! He will do you more good than a doctor, Jasper.'

'More good than a dozen doctors. For I love him dearly, and I don't love doctors, or doctors' stuff.'

Mr Jasper is a dark man of some six-and-twenty, with thick, lustrous, well-arranged black hair and whiskers. He looks older than he is, as dark men often do. His voice is deep and good, his face and figure are good, his manner is a little sombre. His room is a little sombre, and may have had its influence in forming his manner. It is mostly in shadow. Even when the sun shines brilliantly, it seldom touches the grand piano in the recess, or the folio music-books on the stand, or the bookshelves on the wall, or the unfinished picture of a blooming schoolgirl hanging over the chimneypiece; her flowing brown hair tied with a blue riband, and her beauty remarkable for a quite childish, almost babyish, touch of saucy discontent, comically conscious of itself. (There is not the least artistic merit in this picture, which is a mere daub; but it is clear that the painter has made it humorously – one might almost say, revengefully – like the original.)

'We shall miss you, Jasper, at the "Alternate Musical Wednesdays"[27] tonight; but no doubt you are best at home. Good-night. God bless you! "Tell me, shep–herds,[28] te–e–ell me; tell me–e–e, have you seen (have you seen, have you seen, have you seen) my–y–y Flo–o–ora–a pass this way!" ' Melodiously good minor canon the Reverend Septimus[29] Crisparkle thus delivers himself, in musical rhythm, as he withdraws his amiable face from the doorway and conveys it downstairs.

Sounds of recognition and greeting pass between the Reverend Septimus and somebody else, at the stair-foot. Mr Jasper listens, starts from his chair, and catches a young fellow in his arms, exclaiming: 'My dear Edwin!'

'My dear Jack! So glad to see you!'

'Get off your greatcoat, bright boy, and sit down here in your own corner. Your feet are not wet? Pull your boots off. Do pull your boots off.'

'My dear Jack, I am as dry as a bone. Don't moddley-coddley,[30] there's a good fellow. I like anything better than being moddley-coddleyed.'

With the check upon him of being unsympathetically restrained in a genial outburst of enthusiasm, Mr Jasper stands still, and looks on intently at the young fellow, divesting himself of his outward coat, hat, gloves, and so forth. Once for all, a look of intentness and intensity – a look of hungry, exacting, watchful, and yet devoted affection – is always, now and ever afterwards, on the Jasper face whenever the Jasper face is addressed in this direction. And whenever it is so addressed, it is never, on this occasion or on any other, dividedly addressed; it is always concentrated.

'Now I am right, and now I'll take my corner, Jack. Any dinner, Jack?'

Mr Jasper opens a door at the upper end of the room, and discloses a small inner room pleasantly lighted and prepared, wherein a comely dame is in the act of setting dishes on table.

'What a jolly old Jack it is!' cries the young fellow, with a clap of his hands. 'Look here, Jack; tell me; whose birthday is it?'

'Not yours, I know,' Mr Jasper answers, pausing to consider.

'Not mine, you know? No; not mine, I know! Pussy's!'

Fixed as the look the young fellow meets is, there is yet in it some strange power of suddenly including the sketch over the chimneypiece.

'Pussy's, Jack! We must drink many happy returns to her. Come, uncle; take your dutiful and sharp-set nephew in to dinner.'

As the boy (for he is little more) lays a hand on Jasper's shoulder, Jasper cordially and gaily lays a hand on *his* shoulder, and so Marseillaise-wise[31] they go in to dinner.

'And, Lord! here's Mrs Tope!' cries the boy. 'Lovelier than ever!'

'Never you mind me, Master Edwin,' retorts the verger's wife; 'I can take care of myself.'

'You can't. You're much too handsome. Give me a kiss because it's Pussy's birthday.'

'I'd Pussy you, young man, if I was Pussy, as you call her,' Mrs Tope blushingly retorts, after being saluted. 'Your uncle's too much wrapped up in you, that's where it is. He makes so much of you, that it's my opinion you think you've only to call your Pussys by the dozen, to make 'em come.'

'You forget, Mrs Tope,' Mr Jasper interposes, taking his place at the table with a genial smile, 'and so do you, Ned, that uncle and nephew are words prohibited here by common consent and express agreement. For what we are going to receive His holy name be praised!'

'Done like the dean! Witness, Edwin Drood! Please to carve, Jack, for I can't.'

This sally ushers in the dinner. Little to the present purpose, or to any purpose, is said while it is in course of being disposed of. At length the cloth is drawn, and a dish of walnuts and a decanter of rich-coloured sherry are placed upon the table.

'I say! Tell me, Jack,' the young fellow then flows on: 'do you really and truly feel as if the mention of our relationship divided us at all? *I* don't.'

'Uncles as a rule, Ned, are so much older than their nephews,' is the reply, 'that I have that feeling instinctively.'

'As a rule! Ah, maybe! But what is a difference in age of half a dozen years or so? And some uncles, in large families, are even younger than their nephews. By George, I wish it was the case with us!'

'Why?'

'Because if it was, I'd take the lead with you, Jack, and be as wise as Begone, dull Care! that turned a young man grey, and Begone, dull Care! that turned an old man to clay.[32] – Halloa, Jack! Don't drink.'

'Why not?'

'Asks why not, on Pussy's birthday, and no happy returns proposed! Pussy, Jack, and many of 'em! Happy returns, I mean.'

Laying an affectionate and laughing touch on the boy's extended hand, as if it were at once his giddy head and his light heart, Mr Jasper drinks the toast in silence.

'Hip, hip, hip, and nine times nine, and one to finish with, and all that, understood. Hooray, hooray, hooray! – And now, Jack, let's have a little talk about Pussy. Two pairs of nutcrackers? Pass me one, and take the other.' Crack! 'How's Pussy getting on Jack?'

'With her music? Fairly.'

'What a dreadfully conscientious fellow you are, Jack! But *I* know, Lord bless you! Inattentive, isn't she?'

'She can learn anything, if she will.'

'*If* she will! Egad, that's it. But if she won't?'

Crack! – on Mr Jasper's part.

'How's she looking, Jack?'

Mr Jasper's concentrated face again includes the portrait as he returns: 'Very like your sketch indeed.'

'I *am* a little proud of it,' says the young fellow, glancing up at the sketch with complacency, and then shutting one eye, and taking a corrected prospect of it over a level bridge of nutcrackers in the air: 'Not badly hit off from memory. But I ought to have caught that expression pretty well, for I have seen it often enough.'

Crack! – on Edwin Drood's part.

Crack! – on Mr Jasper's part.

'In point of fact,' the former resumes, after some silent dipping among his fragments of walnut with an air of pique, 'I see it whenever I go to see Pussy. If I don't find it on her face, I leave it there. – You know I do, Miss Scornful Pert. Booh!' With a twirl of the nutcrackers at the portrait.

Crack! crack! crack! Slowly, on Mr Jasper's part.

Crack! Sharply on the part of Edwin Drood.

Silence on both sides.

'Have you lost your tongue, Jack?'

'Have you found yours, Ned?'

'No, but really; – isn't it, you know, after all – '

Mr Jasper lifts his dark eyebrows enquiringly.

'Isn't it unsatisfactory to be cut off from choice in such a matter? There, Jack! I tell you! If I could choose, I would choose Pussy from all the pretty girls in the world.'

'But you have not got to choose.'

'That's what I complain of. My dead and gone father and Pussy's dead and gone father must needs marry us together by anticipation. Why the – Devil, I was going to say, if it had been respectful to their memory – couldn't they leave us alone?'

'Tut, tut, dear boy,' Mr Jasper remonstrates, in a tone of gentle deprecation.

'Tut, tut? Yes, Jack, it's all very well for *you*. *You* can take it easily. *Your* life is not laid down to scale, and lined and dotted out for you, like a surveyor's plan. *You* have no uncomfortable suspicion that you are forced upon anybody, nor has anybody an uncomfortable suspicion that she is forced upon you, or that you are forced upon her. *You* can choose for yourself. Life, for *you*, is a plum with the natural bloom on; it hasn't been over-carefully wiped off for *you* – '

'Don't stop, dear fellow. Go on.'

'Can I anyhow have hurt your feelings, Jack?'

'How can you have hurt my feelings?'

'Good Heaven, Jack, you look frightfully ill! There's a strange film come over your eyes.'

Mr Jasper, with a forced smile, stretches out his right hand, as if at once to disarm apprehension and gain time to get better. After a while he says faintly: 'I have been taking opium for a pain[33] – an agony – that sometimes overcomes me. The effects of the medicine steal over me like a blight or a cloud, and pass. You see them in the act of passing; they will be gone directly. Look away from me. They will go all the sooner.'

With a scared face the younger man complies by casting his eyes downward at the ashes on the hearth. Not relaxing his own gaze on the fire, but rather strengthening it with a fierce, firm grip upon his elbow-chair, the elder sits for a few moments rigid, and then, with thick drops standing on his forehead, and a sharp catch of his breath, becomes as he was before. On his so subsiding in his chair, his nephew gently and assiduously tends him while he quite recovers. When Jasper is restored, he lays a tender hand upon his nephew's shoulder, and, in a tone of voice less troubled than the purport of his words – indeed with something of raillery or banter in it – thus addresses him: 'There is said to be a hidden skeleton in every house; but you thought there was none in mine, dear Ned.'

'Upon my life, Jack, I did think so. However, when I come to consider that even in Pussy's house – if she had one – and in mine – if I had one – '

'You were going to say (but that I interrupted you in spite of myself) what a quiet life mine is. No whirl and uproar around me, no distracting commerce or calculation, no risk, no change of place, myself devoted to the art I pursue, my business my pleasure.'

'I really was going to say something of the kind, Jack; but you see, you, speaking of yourself, almost necessarily leave out much that I should have put in. For instance: I should have put in the foreground your being so much respected as lay precentor, or lay clerk,[34] or whatever you call it, of this cathedral; your enjoying the reputation of having done such wonders with the choir; your choosing your society, and holding such an independent position in this queer old place; your gift of teaching (why, even Pussy, who don't like being taught, says there never was such a master as you are!), and your connection.'

'Yes; I saw what you were tending to. I hate it.'

'Hate it, Jack?' (Much bewildered.)

'I hate it. The cramped monotony of my existence grinds me away by the grain. How does our service sound to you?'

'Beautiful! Quite celestial!'

'It often sounds to me quite devilish. I am so weary of it. The echoes of my own voice among the arches seem to mock me with my daily drudging round. No wretched monk who droned his life away in that gloomy place, before me, can have been more tired of it than I am. He could take for relief (and did take) to carving demons out of the stalls and seats and desks.[35] What shall I do? Must I take to carving them out of my heart?'

'I thought you had so exactly found your niche in life, Jack,' Edwin Drood returns, astonished, bending forward in his chair to lay a sympathetic hand on Jasper's knee, and looking at him with an anxious face.

'I know you thought so. They all think so.'

'Well, I suppose they do,' says Edwin, meditating aloud. 'Pussy thinks so.'

'When did she tell you that?'

'The last time I was here. You remember when. Three months ago.'

'How did she phrase it?'

'Oh, she only said that she had become your pupil, and that you were made for your vocation.'

The younger man glances at the portrait. The elder sees it in him.

'Anyhow, my dear Ned,' Jasper resumes, as he shakes his head with a grave cheerfulness, 'I must subdue myself to my vocation: which is much the same thing outwardly. It's too late to find another now. This is a confidence between us.'

'It shall be sacredly preserved, Jack.'

'I have reposed it in you, because – '

'I feel it, I assure you. Because we are fast friends, and because you love and trust me, as I love and trust you. Both hands, Jack.'

As each stands looking into the other's eyes, and as the uncle holds the nephew's hands, the uncle thus proceeds: 'You know now, don't you, that even a poor monotonous chorister and grinder of music – in his niche – may be troubled with some stray sort of ambition, aspiration, restlessness, dissatisfaction, what shall we call it?'

'Yes, dear Jack.'

'And you will remember?'

'My dear Jack, I only ask you, am I likely to forget what you have said with so much feeling?'

'Take it as a warning, then.'

In the act of having his hands released, and of moving a step back, Edwin pauses for an instant to consider the application of these last words. The instant over, he says, sensibly touched: 'I am afraid I am but a shallow, surface kind of fellow, Jack, and that my headpiece is none of the best. But I needn't say I am young; and perhaps I shall not grow worse as I grow older. At all events, I hope I have something impressible within me, which feels – deeply feels – the disinterestedness of your painfully laying your inner self bare, as a warning to me.'

Mr Jasper's steadiness of face and figure becomes so marvellous that his breathing seems to have stopped.

'I couldn't fail to notice, Jack, that it cost you a great effort, and that you were very much moved, and very unlike your usual self. Of course I knew that you were extremely fond of me, but I really was not prepared for your, as I may say, sacrificing yourself to me in that way.'

Mr Jasper, becoming a breathing man again without the smallest stage of transition between the two extreme states, lifts his shoulders, laughs, and waves his right arm.

'No; don't put the sentiment away, Jack; please don't; for I am very much in earnest. I have no doubt that that unhealthy state of mind which you have so powerfully described is attended with some real suffering, and is hard to bear. But let me reassure you, Jack, as to the chances of its overcoming me. I don't think I am in the way of it. In some few months less than another year, you know, I shall carry Pussy off from school as Mrs Edwin Drood. I shall then go engineering into the East,[36] and Pussy with me. And although we have our little tiffs now, arising out of a certain unavoidable flatness that attends our lovemaking, owing to its end being all settled beforehand, still I have no doubt of our getting on capitally then, when it's done and can't be helped. In short, Jack, to go back to the old song I was freely quoting at dinner (and who knows old songs better than you?), my wife shall dance, and I will sing, so merrily pass the day.[37] Of Pussy's being beautiful there cannot be a doubt – and when you are good besides, Little Miss Impudence,' once more apostrophising the portrait, 'I'll burn your comic likeness, and paint your music-master another.'

Mr Jasper, with his hand to his chin, and with an expression of musing benevolence on his face, has attentively watched every animated look and gesture attending the delivery of these words. He remains in that attitude after they are spoken, as if in a kind of fascination attendant on his strong interest in the youthful spirit that he loves so well. Then he says with a quiet smile: 'You won't be warned, then?'

'No, Jack.'

'You can't be warned, then?'

'No, Jack, not by you. Besides that I don't really consider myself in danger, I don't like your putting yourself in that position.'

'Shall we go and walk in the churchyard?'

'By all means. You won't mind my slipping out of it for half a moment to the Nuns' House, and leaving a parcel there? Only gloves for Pussy; as many pairs of gloves as she is years old today. Rather poetical, Jack?'

Mr Jasper, still in the same attitude, murmurs: ' "Nothing half so sweet in life",[38] Ned!'

'Here's the parcel in my greatcoat pocket. They must be presented tonight, or the poetry is gone. It's against regulations for me to call at night, but not to leave a packet. I am ready, Jack!'

Mr Jasper dissolves his attitude, and they go out together.

CHAPTER 3

The Nuns' House

FOR SUFFICIENT REASONS, which this narrative will itself unfold as it advances, a fictitious name must be bestowed upon the old cathedral town. Let it stand in these pages as Cloisterham. It was once possibly known to the Druids by another name, and certainly to the Romans by another, and to the Saxons by another, and to the Normans by another; and a name more or less in the course of many centuries can be of little moment to its dusty chronicles.

An ancient city, Cloisterham, and no meet dwelling-place for any one with hankerings after the noisy world. A monotonous, silent city, deriving an earthy flavour throughout from its Cathedral crypt, and so abounding in vestiges of monastic graves, that the Cloisterham children grow small salad[39] in the dust of abbots and abbesses, and make dirt-pies of nuns and friars; while every plough-man in its outlying fields renders to once puissant lord treasurers, archbishops, bishops, and suchlike, the attention which the ogre in the story-book desired to render to his unbidden visitor, and grinds their bones to make his bread.[40]

A drowsy city, Cloisterham, whose inhabitants seem to suppose, with an inconsistency more strange than rare, that all its changes lie behind it, and that there are no more to come. A queer moral to derive from antiquity, yet older than any traceable antiquity. So silent are the streets of Cloisterham (though prone to echo on the smallest provocation), that of a summer day the sun-blinds of its shops scarce dare to flap in the south wind; while the sun-browned tramps, who pass along and stare, quicken their limp a little, that they may the sooner get beyond the confines of its oppressive respectability. This is a feat not difficult of achievement, seeing that the streets of Cloisterham city are little more than one narrow street by which you get into it and get out of it: the rest being mostly disappointing yards with pumps in them and no thorough-fare – exception made of the Cathedral Close, and a paved Quaker settlement, in colour and general confirmation very like a Quakeress's bonnet, up in a shady corner.

In a word, a city of another and a bygone time is Cloisterham, with its hoarse cathedral bell, its hoarse rooks hovering about the cathedral tower, its hoarser and less distinct rooks in the stalls far beneath. Fragments of old wall, saint's chapel, chapter-house, convent and monastery, have got incongruously or obstructively built into many of its houses and gardens, much as kindred jumbled notions have become incorporated into many of its citizens' minds. All things in it are of the past. Even its single pawnbroker takes in no pledges, nor has he for a long time, but offers vainly an unredeemed stock for sale, of which the costlier articles are dim and pale old watches apparently in a cold perspiration, tarnished sugar-tongs with ineffectual legs, and odd volumes of dismal books. The most abundant and the most agreeable evidences of progressing life in Cloisterham are the evidences of vegetable life in many gardens; even its drooping and despondent little theatre has its poor strip of garden, receiving the foul fiend,[41] when he ducks from its stage into the infernal regions, among scarlet-beans[42] or oyster shells, according to the season of the year.

In the midst of Cloisterham stands the Nuns' House: a venerable brick edifice, whose present appellation is doubtless derived from the legend of its conventual uses. On the trim gate enclosing its old courtyard is a resplendent brass plate flashing forth the legend: 'Seminary for Young Ladies. Miss Twinkleton'. The house-front is so old and worn, and the brass plate is so shining and staring, that the general result has reminded imaginative strangers of a battered old beau with a large modern eye-glass stuck in his blind eye.

Whether the nuns of yore, being of a submissive rather than a stiff-necked generation,[43] habitually bent their contemplative heads to avoid collision with the beams in the low ceilings of the many chambers of their house; whether they sat in its long low windows telling their beads for their mortification, instead of making neck-laces of them for their adornment; whether they were ever walled up alive in odd angles and jutting gables of the building for having some ineradicable leaven of busy mother Nature in them which has kept the fermenting world alive ever since;[44] these may be matters of interest to its haunting ghosts (if any), but constitute no item in Miss Twinkleton's half-yearly accounts. They are neither of Miss Twinkleton's inclusive regulars, nor of her extras. The lady who undertakes the poetical department of the establishment at so much (or so little) a quarter has no pieces in her list of recitals bearing on such unprofitable questions.

As, in some cases of drunkenness, and in others of animal

magnetism,[45] there are two states of consciousness which never clash, but each of which pursues its separate course as though it were continuous instead of broken (thus, if I hide my watch when I am drunk, I must be drunk again before I can remember where), so Miss Twinkleton has two distinct and separate phases of being. Every night, the moment the young ladies have retired to rest, does Miss Twinkleton smarten up her curls a little, brighten up her eyes a little, and become a sprightly Miss Twinkleton whom the young ladies have ever seen. Every night, at the same hour, does Miss Twinkleton resume the topics of the previous night, comprehending the tenderer scandal of Cloisterham, of which she has no knowledge whatever by day, and references to a certain season at Tunbridge Wells[46] (airily called by Miss Twinkleton in this state of her existence 'The Wells'), notably the season wherein a certain finished gentleman (compassionately called by Miss Twinkleton, in this stage of her existence, 'foolish Mr Porters') revealed a homage of the heart, whereof Miss Twinkleton, in her scholastic state of existence, is as ignorant as a granite pillar. Miss Twinkleton's companion in both states of existence, and equally adaptable to either, is one Mrs Tisher: a deferential widow with a weak back, a chronic sigh, and a suppressed voice, who looks after the young ladies' wardrobes, and leads them to infer that she has seen better days. Perhaps this is the reason why it is an article of faith with the servants, handed down from race to race, that the departed Tisher was a hairdresser.

The pet pupil of the Nuns' House is Miss Rosa Bud, of course called Rosebud; wonderfully pretty, wonderfully childish, wonderfully whimsical. An awkward interest (awkward because romantic) attaches to Miss Bud in the minds of the young ladies, on account of its being known to them that a husband has been chosen for her by will and bequest, and that her guardian is bound down to bestow her on that husband when he comes of age. Miss Twinkleton, in her seminarial state of existence, has combated the romantic aspect of this destiny by affecting to shake her head over it behind Miss Bud's dimpled shoulders, and to brood on the unhappy lot of that doomed little victim. But with no better effect – possibly some unfelt touch of foolish Mr Porters has undermined the endeavour – than to evoke from the young ladies a unanimous bedchamber cry of 'Oh, what a pretending old thing Miss Twinkleton is, my dear!'

The Nuns' House is never in such a state of flutter as when this allotted husband calls to see little Rosebud. (It is unanimously understood by the young ladies that he is lawfully entitled to this privilege, and that if Miss Twinkleton disputed it, she would be instantly taken up and transported.)[47] When his ring at the gate-bell is expected, or takes place, every young lady who can, under any pretence, look out of the window, looks out of the window; while every young lady who is 'practising', practises out of time; and the French class becomes so demoralised that the mark goes round[48] as briskly as the bottle at a convivial party in the last century.

On the afternoon of the day next after the dinner of two at the gatehouse, the bell is rung with the usual fluttering results.

'Mr Edwin Drood to see Miss Rosa.'

This is the announcement of the parlour-maid in chief. Miss Twinkleton, with an exemplary air of melancholy on her, turns to the sacrifice, and says, 'You may go down, my dear.' Miss Bud goes down, followed by all eyes.

Mr Edwin Drood is waiting in Miss Twinkleton's own parlour: a dainty room, with nothing more directly scholastic in it than a terrestrial and a celestial globe. These expressive machines imply (to parents and guardians) that even when Miss Twinkleton retires into the bosom of privacy, duty may at any moment compel her to become a sort of Wandering Jewess,[49] scouring the earth and soaring through the skies in search of knowledge for her pupils.

The last new maid, who has never seen the young gentleman Miss Rosa is engaged to, and who is making his acquaintance between the hinges of the open door, left open for the purpose, stumbles guiltily down the kitchen stairs, as a charming little apparition, with its face concealed by a little silk apron thrown over its head, glides into the parlour.

'Oh! it *is* so ridiculous!' says the apparition, stopping and shrinking. 'Don't, Eddy!'

'Don't what, Rosa?'

'Don't come any nearer, please. It *is* so absurd.'

'What is absurd, Rosa?'

'The whole thing is. It *is* so absurd to be an engaged orphan; and it *is* so absurd to have the girls and the servants scuttling about after one, like mice in the wainscot; and it *is* so absurd to be called upon!'

The apparition appears to have a thumb in the corner of its mouth while making this complaint.

'You give me an affectionate reception, Pussy, I must say.'

'Well, I will in a minute, Eddy, but I can't just yet. How are you?' (very shortly).

'I am unable to reply that I am much the better for seeing you, Pussy, inasmuch as I see nothing of you.'

This second remonstrance brings a dark, bright, pouting eye out from a corner of the apron; but it swiftly becomes invisible again, as the apparition exclaims: 'Oh good gracious! you have had half your hair cut off!'

'I should have done better to have had my head cut off, I think,' says Edwin, rumpling the hair in question, with a fierce glance at the looking-glass, and giving an impatient stamp. 'Shall I go?'

'No; you needn't go just yet, Eddy. The girls would all be asking questions why you went.'

'Once for all, Rosa, will you uncover that ridiculous little head of yours and give me a welcome?'

The apron is pulled off the childish head, as its wearer replies: – 'You're very welcome, Eddy. There! I'm sure that's nice. Shake hands. No, I can't kiss you, because I've got an acidulated drop[50] in my mouth.'

'Are you at all glad to see me, Pussy?'

'Oh, yes, I'm dreadfully glad! Go and sit down. – Miss Twinkleton.'

It is the custom of that excellent lady when these visits occur, to appear every three minutes, either in her own person or in that of Mrs Tisher, and lay an offering on the shrine of Propriety by affecting to look for some desiderated article. On the present occasion Miss Twinkleton, gracefully gliding in and out, says in passing: 'How do you do, Mr Drood? Very glad indeed to have the pleasure. Pray excuse me. Tweezers. Thank you!'

'I got the gloves last evening, Eddy, and I like them very much. They are beauties.'

'Well, that's something,' the affianced replies, half grumbling. 'The smallest encouragement thankfully received. And how did you pass your birthday, Pussy?'

'Delightfully! Everybody gave me a present. And we had a feast. And we had a ball at night.'

'A feast and a ball, eh? These occasions seem to go off tolerably well without me, Pussy.'

'De–lightfully!' cries Rosa, in a quite spontaneous manner, and without the least pretence of reserve.

'Hah! And what was the feast?'

'Tarts, oranges, jellies and shrimps.'

'Any partners at the ball?'

'We danced with one another, of course, sir. But some of the girls made game to be their brothers. It *was* so droll!'

'Did anybody make game to be – '

'To be you? Oh dear yes!' cries Rosa, laughing with great

enjoyment. 'That was the first thing done.'

'I hope she did it pretty well,' says Edwin rather doubtfully.

'Oh, it was excellent! – I wouldn't dance with you, you know.'

Edwin scarcely seems to see the force of this; begs to know if he may take the liberty to ask why?

'Because I was so tired of you,' returns Rosa. But she quickly adds, and pleadingly too, seeing displeasure in his face: 'Dear Eddy, you were just as tired of me, you know.'

'Did I say so, Rosa?'

'Say so! Do you ever say so? No, you only showed it. Oh, she did it so well!' cries Rosa, in a sudden ecstasy with her counterfeit betrothed.

'It strikes me that she must be a devilish impudent girl,' says Edwin Drood. 'And so, Pussy, you have passed your last birthday in this old house.'

'Ah, yes!' Rosa clasps her hands, looks down with a sigh, and shakes her head.

'You seem to be sorry, Rosa.'

'I am sorry for the poor old place. Somehow, I feel as if it would miss me, when I am gone so far away, so young.'

'Perhaps we had better stop short, Rosa?'

She looks up at him with a swift bright look; next moment shakes her head, sighs, and looks down again.

'That is to say, is it, Pussy, that we are both resigned?'

She nods her head again, and after a short silence, quaintly bursts out with: 'You know we must be married, and married from here, Eddy, or the poor girls will be so dreadfully disappointed!'

For the moment there is more of compassion, both for her and for himself, in her affianced husband's face, than there is of love. He checks the look, and asks: 'Shall I take you out for a walk, Rosa dear?'

Rosa dear does not seem at all clear on this point, until her face, which has been comically reflective, brightens. 'Oh, yes, Eddy; let us go for a walk! And I tell you what we'll do. You shall pretend that you are engaged to somebody else, and I'll pretend that I am not engaged to anybody, and then we shan't quarrel.'

'Do you think that will prevent our falling out, Rosa?'

'I know it will. Hush! Pretend to look out of the window – Mrs Tisher!'

Through a fortuitous concourse of accidents, the matronly Tisher heaves in sight, says, in rustling through the room like the legendary ghost of a dowager in silken skirts: 'I hope I see Mr Drood well; though I needn't ask, if I may judge from his complexion. I trust I disturb no one; but there *was* a paper-knife – Oh, thank you, I am sure!' and disappears with her prize.

'One other thing you must do, Eddy, to oblige me,' says Rosebud. 'The moment we get into the street, you must put me outside, and keep close to the house yourself – squeeze and graze yourself against it.'

'By all means, Rosa, if you wish it. Might I ask why?'

'Oh! because I don't want the girls to see you.'

'It's a fine day; but would you like me to carry an umbrella up?'

'Don't be foolish, sir. You haven't got polished leather boots on,' pouting, with one shoulder raised.

'Perhaps that might escape the notice of the girls, even if they did see me,' remarks Edwin, looking down at his boots with a sudden distaste for them.

'Nothing escapes their notice, sir. And then I know what would happen. Some of them would begin reflecting on me by saying (for *they* are free) that they never will on any account engage themselves to lovers without polished leather boots. Hark! Miss Twinkleton. I'll ask for leave.'

That discreet lady being indeed heard without, enquiring of nobody in a blandly conversational tone as she advances: 'Eh? Indeed! Are you quite sure you saw my mother-of-pearl button-holder on the work-table in my room?' is at once solicited for walking leave, and graciously accords it. And soon the young couple go out of the Nuns' House, taking all precautions against the discovery of the so vitally defective boots of Mr Edwin Drood: precautions, let us hope, effective for the peace of Mrs Edwin Drood that is to be.

'Which way shall we take, Rosa?'

Rosa replies: 'I want to go to the Lumps-of-Delight shop.'

'To the – ?'

'A Turkish sweetmeat, sir. My gracious me, don't you understand anything? Call yourself an Engineer, and not know *that*?'

'Why, how should I know it, Rosa?'

'Because I am very fond of them. But Oh! I forgot what we are to pretend. No, you needn't know anything about them; never mind.'

So he is gloomily borne off to the Lumps-of-Delight shop, where Rosa makes her purchase, and, after offering some to him (which he rather indignantly declines), begins to partake of it with great zest: previously taking off and rolling up a pair of little pink gloves, like rose-leaves, and occasionally putting her little pink fingers to her rosy lips, to cleanse them from the Dust of Delight that comes off the Lumps.

'Now, be a good-tempered Eddy, and pretend. And so you are engaged?'

'And so I am engaged.'

'Is she nice?'

'Charming.'

'Tall?'

'Immensely tall!' Rosa being short.

'Must be gawky, I should think,' is Rosa's quiet commentary.

'I beg your pardon; not at all,' contradiction rising in him. 'What is termed a fine woman; a splendid woman.'

'Big nose, no doubt,' is the quiet commentary again.

'Not a little one, certainly,' is the quick reply (Rosa's being a little one).

'Long pale nose, with a red knob in the middle. I know the sort of nose,' says Rosa, with a satisfied nod, and tranquilly enjoying the Lumps.

'You *don't* know the sort of nose, Rosa,' with some warmth; 'because it's nothing of the kind.'

'Not a pale nose, Eddy?'

'No.' Determined not to assent.

'A red nose? Oh! I don't like red noses. However; to be sure she can always powder it.'

'She would scorn to powder it,' says Edwin, becoming heated.

'Would she? What a stupid thing she must be! Is she stupid in everything?'

'No; in nothing.'

After a pause, in which the whimsically wicked face has not been unobservant of him, Rosa says: 'And this most sensible of creatures likes the idea of being carried off to Egypt; does she, Eddy?'

'Yes. She takes a sensible interest in triumphs of engineering skill: especially when they are to change the whole condition of an undeveloped country.'[51]

'Lor!' says Rosa, shrugging her shoulders, with a little laugh of wonder.

'Do you object,' Edwin enquires, with a majestic turn of his eyes downward upon the fairy figure: 'do you object, Rosa, to her feeling that interest?'

'Object? my dear Eddy! But really, doesn't she hate boilers and things?'

'I can answer for her not being so idiotic as to hate Boilers,' he returns with angry emphasis; 'though I cannot answer for her views about Things; really not understanding what Things are meant.'

'But don't she hate Arabs, and Turks, and Fellahs, and people?'

'Certainly not.' Very firmly.

'At least she *must* hate the Pyramids? Come, Eddy?'

'Why should she be such a little – tall, I mean – goose, as to hate the Pyramids, Rosa?'

'Ah! you should hear Miss Twinkleton,' often nodding her head, and much enjoying the Lumps, 'bore about them, and then you wouldn't ask. Tiresome old burying-grounds! Isises, and Ibises, and Cheopses, and Pharaohses;[52] who cares about them? And then there was Belzoni,[53] or somebody, dragged out by the legs, half-choked with bats and dust. All the girls say: Serve him right, and hope it hurt him, and wish he had been quite choked.'

The two youthful figures, side by side, but not now arm-in-arm, wander discontentedly about the old Close; and each sometimes stops and slowly imprints a deeper footstep in the fallen leaves.

'Well!' says Edwin, after a lengthy silence. 'According to custom. We can't get on, Rosa.'

Rosa tosses her head, and says she don't want to get on.

'That's a pretty sentiment, Rosa, considering.'

'Considering what?'

'If I say what, you'll go wrong again.'

'*You'll* go wrong, you mean, Eddy. Don't be ungenerous.'

'Ungenerous! I like that!'

'Then I *don't* like that, and so I tell you plainly,' Rosa pouts.

'Now, Rosa, I put it to you. Who disparaged my profession, my destination – '

'You are not going to be buried in the Pyramids, I hope?' she interrupts, arching her delicate eyebrows. 'You never said you were. If you are, why haven't you mentioned it to me? I can't find out your plans by instinct.'

'Now, Rosa, you know very well what I mean, my dear.'

'Well then, why did you begin with your detestable red-nosed giantesses? And she would, she would, she would, she would, she *would* powder it!' cries Rosa, in a little burst of comical contradictory spleen.

'Somehow or other, I never can come right in these discussions,' says Edwin, sighing and becoming resigned.

'How is it possible, sir, that you ever can come right when you're always wrong? And as to Belzoni, I suppose he's dead – I'm sure I hope he is – and how can his legs or his chokes concern you?'

'It is nearly time for your return, Rosa. We have not had a very happy walk, have we?'

'A happy walk? A detestably unhappy walk, sir. If I go upstairs the moment I get in and cry till I can't take my dancing lesson, you are responsible, mind!'

'Let us be friends, Rosa.'

'Ah!' cries Rosa, shaking her head and bursting into real tears, 'I wish we *could* be friends! It's because we can't be friends, that we try one another so. I am a young little thing, Eddy, to have an old heartache; but I really, really have, sometimes. Don't be angry. I know you have one yourself too often. We should both of us have done better, if What is to be had been left What might have been. I am quite a little serious thing now, and not teasing you. Let each of us forbear, this one time, on our own account, and on the other's!'

Disarmed by this glimpse of a woman's nature in the spoilt child, though for an instant disposed to resent it as seeming to involve the enforced infliction of himself upon her, Edwin Drood stands watching her as she childishly cries and sobs, with both hands to the handkerchief at her eyes, and then – she becoming more composed, and indeed beginning in her young inconstancy to laugh at herself for having been so moved – leads her to a seat hard by, under the elm trees.

'One clear word of understanding, Pussy dear. I am not clever out of my own line – now I come to think of it, I don't know that I am particularly clever in it – but I want to do right. There is not – there may be – I really don't see my way to what I want to say, but I must say it before we part – there is not any other young – '

'Oh no, Eddy! It's generous of you to ask me; but no, no, no!'

They have come very near to the cathedral windows, and at this moment the organ and the choir sound out sublimely. As they sit listening to the solemn swell, the confidence of last night rises in young Edwin Drood's mind, and he thinks how unlike this music is to that discordance.

'I fancy I can distinguish Jack's voice,' is his remark in a low tone in connection with the train of thought.

'Take me back at once, please,' urges his affianced, quickly laying her light hand upon his wrist. 'They will all be coming out directly; let us get away. Oh, what a resounding chord! But don't let us stop to listen to it; let us get away!'

Her hurry is over as soon as they have passed out of the Close. They go arm-in-arm now, gravely and deliberately enough, along the old High Street, to the Nuns' House. At the gate, the street

Under the tress

being within sight empty, Edwin bends down his face to Rosebud's.

She remonstrates, laughing, and is a childish schoolgirl again.

'Eddy, no! I'm too sticky to be kissed. But give me your hand, and I'll blow a kiss into that.'

He does so. She breathes a light breath into it and asks, retaining it and looking into it: 'Now say, what do you see?'

'See, Rosa?'

'Why, I thought you Egyptian boys could look into a hand and see all sorts of phantoms. Can't you see a happy Future?'

For certain, neither of them sees a happy Present, as the gate opens and closes, and one goes in, and the other goes away.[54]

CHAPTER 4

Mr Sapsea

ACCEPTING THE JACKASS as the type of self-sufficient stupidity and conceit – a custom, perhaps, like some few other customs, more conventional than fair – then the purest jackass in Cloisterham is Mr Thomas Sapsea, auctioneer.

Mr Sapsea 'dresses at'[55] the dean; has been bowed to for the dean, in mistake; has even been spoken to in the street as My Lord,[56] under the impression that he was the bishop come down unexpectedly, without his chaplain. Mr Sapsea is very proud of this, and of his voice, and of his style. He has even (in selling landed property) tried the experiment of slightly intoning in his pulpit, to make himself more like what he takes to be the genuine ecclesiastical article. So, in ending a sale by public auction, Mr Sapsea finishes off with an air of bestowing a benediction on the assembled brokers, which leaves the real dean – a modest and worthy gentleman – far behind.

Mr Sapsea has many admirers; indeed, the proposition is carried by a large local majority, even including non-believers in his wisdom, that he is a credit to Cloisterham. He possesses the great qualities of being portentous and dull, and of having a roll in his speech, and another roll in his gait; not to mention a certain gravely flowing action with his hands, as if he were presently going to confirm the individual with whom he holds discourse. Much nearer sixty years of age than fifty, with a flowing outline of stomach, and horizontal creases in his waistcoat; reputed to be rich; voting at elections in the strictly respectable interest; morally satisfied that nothing but he himself has grown since he was a baby; how can dunder-headed Mr Sapsea be otherwise than a credit to Cloisterham, and society?

Mr Sapsea's premises are in the High Street, over against the Nuns' House. They are of about the period of the Nuns' House, irregularly modernised here and there, as steadily deteriorating generations found, more and more, that they preferred air and light to fever and the plague. Over the doorway is a wooden effigy, about half life-size, representing Mr Sapsea's father, in a curly wig and toga, in the act of selling. The chastity of the idea, and the natural appearance of the little finger, hammer, and pulpit, have been much admired.

Mr Sapsea sits in his dull ground-floor sitting-room, giving first on his paved backyard; and then on his railed-off garden. Mr Sapsea has a bottle of port wine on a table before the fire – the fire is an early luxury, but pleasant on the cool, chill autumn evening – and is characteristically attended by his portrait, his eight-day clock,[57] and his weather-glass. Characteristically, because he would uphold himself against mankind, his weather-glass against weather, and his clock against time.

By Mr Sapsea's side on the table are a writing-desk and writing materials. Glancing at a scrap of manuscript, Mr Sapsea reads it to himself with a lofty air, and then, slowly pacing the room with his thumbs in the arm-holes of his waistcoat, repeats it from memory: so internally, though with much dignity, that the word 'Ethelinda' is alone audible.

There are three clean wine glasses in a tray on the table. His serving-maid entering, and announcing, 'Mr Jasper is come, sir,' Mr Sapsea waves, 'Admit him,' and draws two wine glasses from the rank, as being claimed.

'Glad to see you, sir. I congratulate myself on having the honour of receiving you here for the first time.' Mr Sapsea does the honours of his house in this wise.

'You are very good. The honour is mine and the self-congratulation is mine.'

'You are pleased to say so, sir. But I do assure you that it is a satisfaction to me to receive you in my humble home. And that is what I would not say to everybody.' Ineffable loftiness on Mr Sapsea's part accompanies these words, as leaving the sentence to be understood: 'You will not easily believe that your society can be a satisfaction to a man like myself; nevertheless, it is.'

'I have for some time desired to know you, Mr Sapsea.'

'And I, sir, have long known you by reputation as a man of taste. Let me fill your glass. I will give you, sir,' says Mr Sapsea, filling his own:

> 'When the French come over,
> May we meet them at Dover!'[58]

This was a patriotic toast in Mr Sapsea's infancy, and he is therefore fully convinced of its being appropriate to any subsequent era.

'You can scarcely be ignorant, Mr Sapsea,' observes Jasper, watching the auctioneer with a smile as the latter stretches out his legs before the fire, 'that you know the world.'

'Well, sir,' is the chuckling reply, 'I think I know something of it; something of it.'

'Your reputation for that knowledge has always interested and surprised me, and made me wish to know you. For Cloisterham is a little place. Cooped up in it myself, I know nothing beyond it, and feel it to be a very little place.'

'If I have not gone to foreign countries, young man – ' Mr Sapsea begins, and then stops. 'You will excuse me calling you young man, Mr Jasper? You are much my junior.'

'By all means.'

'If I have not gone to foreign countries, young man, foreign countries have come to me. They have come to me in the way of business, and I have improved upon my opportunities. Put it that I take an inventory, or make a catalogue. I see a French clock. I never saw him before, in my life, but I instantly lay my finger on him and say "Paris!" I see some cups and saucers of Chinese make, equally strangers to me personally: I put my finger on them, then and there, and I say "Pekin, Nankin and Canton". It is the same with Japan, with Egypt, and with bamboo and sandalwood from the East Indies; I put my finger on them all. I have put my finger on the North Pole before now, and said "Spear of Eskimo make, for half a pint of pale sherry!"'

'Really? A very remarkable way, Mr Sapsea, of acquiring a knowledge of men and things.'

'I mention it, sir,' Mr Sapsea rejoins, with unspeakable complacency, 'because, as I say, it don't do to boast of what you are; but show how you came to be it, and then you prove it.'

'Most interesting. We were to speak of the late Mrs Sapsea.'

'We were, sir.' Mr Sapsea fills both glasses, and takes the decanter into safe keeping again. 'Before I consult your opinion as a man of taste on this little trifle' – holding it up – 'which is *but* a trifle, and still has required some thought, sir, some little fever of the brow, I ought perhaps to describe the character of the late Mrs Sapsea, now dead three quarters of a year.'

Mr Jasper, in the act of yawning behind his wine glass, puts down that screen and calls up a look of interest. It is a little impaired in its expressiveness by his having a shut-up gape still to dispose of, with watering eyes.

'Half a dozen years ago, or so,' Mr Sapsea proceeds, 'when I had enlarged my mind up to – I will not say to what it now is, for that might seem to aim at too much, but up to the pitch of wanting another mind to be absorbed in it – I cast my eye about me for a nuptial partner. Because, as I say, it is not good for man to be alone.'[59]

Mr Jasper appears to commit this original idea to memory.

'Miss Brobity at that time kept, I will not call it the rival establishment to the establishment at the Nuns' House opposite, but I will call it the other parallel establishment down town. The world did have it that she showed a passion for attending my sales, when they took place on half-holidays, or in vacation time. The world did put it about that she admired my style. The world did notice that as time flowed by, my style became traceable in the dictation-exercises of Miss Brobity's pupils. Young man, a whisper even sprang up in obscure malignity, that one ignorant and besotted churl (a parent) so committed himself as to object to it by name. But I do not believe this. For is it likely that any human creature in his right senses would so lay himself open to be pointed at, by what I call the finger of scorn?'[60]

Mr Jasper shakes his head. Not in the least likely. Mr Sapsea, in a grandiloquent state of absence of mind, seems to refill his visitor's glass, which is full already; and does really refill his own, which is empty.

'Miss Brobity's Being, young man, was deeply imbued with homage to Mind. She revered Mind, when launched, or, as I say, precipitated, on an extensive knowledge of the world. When I made my proposal, she did me the honour to be so overshadowed with a species of Awe, as to be able to articulate only the two words, "Oh Thou!" meaning myself. Her limpid blue eyes were fixed upon me, her semi-transparent hands were clasped together, pallor overspread her aquiline features, and, though encouraged to proceed, she never did proceed a word further. I disposed of the parallel establishment by private contract, and we became as nearly one as could be expected under the circumstances. But she never could, and she never did, find a phrase satisfactory to her perhaps-too-favourable estimate of my intellect. To the very last (feeble action of liver), she addressed me in the same unfinished terms.'

Mr Jasper has closed his eyes as the auctioneer has deepened his voice. He now abruptly opens them, and says, in unison with the deepened voice, 'Ah!' – rather as if stopping himself on the extreme verge of adding – 'men!'

'I have been since,' says Mr Sapsea, with his legs stretched out, and solemnly enjoying himself with the wine and the fire, 'what you behold me; I have been since a solitary mourner; I have been since, as I say, wasting my evening conversation on the desert air.[61] I will not say that I have reproached myself; but there have been times when I have asked myself the question: What if her husband had been nearer on a level with her? If she had not had to look up quite so high, what might the stimulating action have been upon the liver?'

Mr Jasper says, with an appearance of having fallen into dreadfully low spirits, that he 'supposes it was to be'.

'We can only suppose so, sir,' Mr Sapsea coincides. 'As I say, Man proposes, Heaven disposes.[62] It may or may not be putting the same thought in another form; but that is the way I put it.'

Mr Jasper murmurs assent.

'And now, Mr Jasper,' resumes the auctioneer, producing his scrap of manuscript, 'Mrs Sapsea's monument having had full time to settle and dry, let me take your opinion, as a man of taste, on the inscription I have (as I before remarked, not without some little fever of the brow) drawn out for it. Take it in your own hand. The setting out of the lines requires to be followed with the eye, as well as the contents with the mind.'

Mr Jasper complying, sees and reads as follows:

ETHELINDA,
Reverential Wife of
MR THOMAS SAPSEA,
AUCTIONEER, VALUER, ESTATE AGENT, &C.,
OF THIS CITY,
Whose Knowledge of the World,
Though somewhat extensive,
Never brought him acquainted with
A SPIRIT
More capable of
LOOKING UP TO HIM.
STRANGER, PAUSE
And ask thyself the Question,
CANST THOU DO LIKEWISE?
If Not,
WITH A BLUSH RETIRE.

Mr Sapsea having risen and stationed himself with his back to the fire, for the purpose of observing the effect of these lines on the countenance of a man of taste, consequently has his face towards the door, when his serving-maid, again appearing, announces, 'Durdles is come, sir!' He promptly draws forth and fills the third wine glass, as being now claimed, and replies, 'Show Durdles in.'

'Admirable!' quoth Mr Jasper, handing back the paper.

'You approve, sir?'

'Impossible not to approve. Striking, characteristic and complete.'

The auctioneer inclines his head, as one accepting his due and giving a receipt; and invites the entering Durdles to take off that glass of wine (handing the same), for it will warm him.

Durdles is a stonemason; chiefly in the gravestone, tomb, and monument way, and wholly of their colour from head to foot. No man is better known in Cloisterham. He is the chartered libertine[63] of the place. Fame trumpets him a wonderful workman – which, for aught that anybody knows, he may be (as he never works); and a wonderful sot – which everybody knows he is. With the Cathedral crypt he is better acquainted than any living authority; it may even be than any dead one. It is said that the intimacy of this acquaintance began in his habitually resorting to that secret place, to lock-out the Cloisterham boy-populace, and sleep off fumes of liquor: he having ready access to the cathedral, as contractor for rough repairs. Be this as it may, he does know much about it, and, in the demolition of impedimental fragments of wall, buttress and pavement, has seen strange sights. He often speaks of himself in the third person; perhaps being a little misty as to his own identity, when he narrates; perhaps impartially adopting the Cloisterham nomenclature in reference to a character of acknowledged distinction. Thus he will say, touching his strange sights: 'Durdles come upon the old chap,' in reference to a buried magnate of ancient time and high degree, 'by striking right into the coffin with his pick. The old chap gave Durdles a look with his open eyes, as much as to say, "Is your name Durdles? Why, my man, I've been waiting for you a devil of a time!" And then he turned to powder.' With a two-foot rule always in his pocket, and a mason's hammer all but always in his hand, Durdles goes continually sounding and tapping all about and about the cathedral; and whenever he says to Tope: 'Tope, here's another old 'un in here!' Tope announces it to the dean as an established discovery.

In a suit of coarse flannel with horn buttons, a yellow neckerchief with draggled ends, an old hat more russet-coloured than black, and laced boots of the hue of his stony calling, Durdles leads a hazy, gypsy sort of life, carrying his dinner about with him in a small bundle, and sitting on all manner of tombstones to dine. This dinner of Durdles's has become quite a Cloisterham institution: not only because of his never appearing in public without it, but because of its having been, on certain renowned occasions, taken into custody along with Durdles (as drunk and incapable), and exhibited before the bench of justices[64] at the town hall. These occasions, however, have been few and far apart: Durdles being as seldom drunk as sober. For the rest, he is an old bachelor, and he lives in a little antiquated hole of a house that was never finished: supposed to be built, so far, of stones stolen from the city wall. To this abode there is an approach, ankle-deep in stone chips, resembling a petrified grove of tombstones, urns, draperies, and broken columns, in all stages of sculpture. Herein two journeymen incessantly chip, while two other journeymen, who face each other, incessantly saw stone, dipping as regularly in and out of their sheltering sentry-boxes as if they were mechanical figures emblematical of Time and Death.[65]

To Durdles, when he has consumed his glass of port, Mr Sapsea entrusts that precious effort of his Muse. Durdles unfeelingly takes out his two-foot rule, and measures the lines calmly, alloying them with stone-grit.

'This is for the monument, is it, Mr Sapsea?'

'The Inscription. Yes.' Mr Sapsea waits for its effect on a common mind.

'It'll come in to a eighth of an inch,' says Durdles. 'Your servant, Mr Jasper. Hope I see you well.'

'How are you Durdles?'

'I've got a touch of the Tombatism on me, Mr Jasper, but that I must expect.'

'You mean the Rheumatism,' says Sapsea, in a sharp tone. (He is nettled by having his composition so mechanically received.)

'No, I don't. I mean, Mr Sapsea, the Tombatism. It's another sort from Rheumatism. Mr Jasper knows what Durdles means. You get among them tombs afore it's well light on a winter morning, and keep on, as the Catechism says, a-walking in the same all the days of your life,[66] and *you'll* know what Durdles means.'

'It is a bitter cold place,' Mr Jasper assents, with an antipathetic shiver.

'And if it's bitter cold for you, up in the chancel, with a lot of live breath smoking out about you, what the bitterness is to Durdles, down in the crypt among the earthy damps there, and the dead breath of the old 'uns,' returns that individual, 'Durdles leaves you to judge – Is this to be put in hand at once, Mr Sapsea?'

Mr Sapsea, with an author's anxiety to rush into publication, replies that it cannot be out of hand too soon.

'You had better let me have the key then,' says Durdles.

'Why, man, it is not to be put inside the monument!'

'Durdles knows where it's to be put, Mr Sapsea; no man better. Ask 'ere a man in Cloisterham whether Durdles knows his work.'

Mr Sapsea rises, takes a key from a drawer, unlocks an iron safe let into the wall, and takes from it another key.

'When Durdles puts a touch or a finish upon his work, no matter where, inside or outside, Durdles likes to look at his work all round, and see that his work is a-doing him credit,' Durdles explains, doggedly.

The key proffered him by the bereaved widower being a large one, he slips his two-foot rule into a side-pocket of his flannel trousers made for it, and deliberately opens his flannel coat, and opens the mouth of a large breast-pocket within it, before taking the key to place it in that repository.

'Why, Durdles!' exclaims Jasper, looking on amused, 'you are undermined with pockets!'

'And I carries weight in 'em too, Mr Jasper. Feel those!' producing two other large keys.

'Hand me Mr Sapsea's likewise. Surely this is the heaviest of the three.'

'You'll find 'em much of a muchness, I expect,' says Durdles. 'They all belong to monuments. They all open Durdles's work. Durdles keeps the keys of his work mostly. Not that they're much used.'

'By the by,' it comes into Jasper's mind to say, as he idly examines the keys, 'I have been going to ask you, many a day, and have always forgotten. You know they sometimes call you Stony Durdles, don't you?'

'Cloisterham knows me as Durdles, Mr Jasper.'

'I am aware of that, of course. But the boys sometimes – '

'Oh! if you mind them young imps of boys – ' Durdles gruffly interrupts.

'I don't mind them any more than you do. But there was a discussion the other day among the choir, whether Stony stood for Tony;' clinking one key against another.

('Take care of the wards,[67] Mr Jasper.')

'Or whether Stony stood for Stephen;' clinking with a change of keys.

('You can't make a pitch pipe of 'em, Mr Jasper.')

'Or whether the name comes from your trade. How stands the fact?'

Mr Jasper weighs the three keys in his hand, lifts his head from his idly stooping attitude over the fire, and delivers the keys to Durdles with an ingenuous and friendly face.

But the stony one is a gruff one likewise, and that hazy state of his is always an uncertain state, highly conscious of its dignity, and prone to take offence. He drops his two keys back into his pocket one by one, and buttons them up; he takes his dinner-bundle from the chair-back on which he hung it when he came in; he distributes the weight he carries, by tying the third key up in it, as though he were an ostrich, and liked to dine off cold iron;[68] and he gets out of the room, deigning no word of answer.

Mr Sapsea then proposes a hit at backgammon, which, seasoned with his own improving conversation, and terminating in a supper of cold roast beef and salad, beguiles the golden evening until pretty late. Mr Sapsea's wisdom, being, in its delivery to mortals, rather of the diffuse than the epigrammatic order, is by no means expended even then; but his visitor intimates that he will come back for more of the precious commodity on future occasions, and Mr Sapsea lets him off for the present, to ponder on the instalment he carries away.

CHAPTER 5

Mr Durdles and Friend

JOHN JASPER, on his way home through the Close, is brought to a standstill by the spectacle of Stony Durdles, dinner-bundle and all, leaning his back against the iron railing of the burial-ground enclosing it from the old cloister-arches; and a hideous small boy in rags flinging stones at him as a well-defined mark in the moonlight. Sometimes the stones hit him, and sometimes they miss him, but Durdles seems indifferent to either fortune. The hideous small boy, on the contrary, whenever he hits Durdles, blows a whistle of triumph through a jagged gap, convenient for the purpose, in the front of his mouth, where half his teeth are wanting; and whenever he misses him, yelps out 'Mulled[69] agin!' and tries to atone for the failure by taking a more correct and vicious aim.

'What are you doing to the man?' demands Jasper, stepping out into the moonlight from the shade.

'Making a cock-shy[70] of him,' replies the hideous small boy.

'Give me those stones in your hand.'

'Yes, I'll give 'em you down your throat, if you come a-ketching hold of me,' says the small boy, shaking himself loose, and backing. 'I'll smash your eye, if you don't look out!'

'Baby-devil that you are, what has the man done to you?'

'He won't go home.'

'What is that to you?'

'He gives me a 'apenny to pelt him home if I ketches him out too late,' says the boy. And then chants, like a little savage, half stumbling and half dancing among the rags and laces of his dilapidated boots:

> 'Widdy widdy wen!
> I–ket–ches–'im–out–ar–ter–ten,
> Widdy widdy wy!
> Then–'e–don't–go–then–I shy –
> Widdy widdy wake-cock warning!'[71]

– with a comprehensive sweep on the last word, and one more delivery at Durdles.

This would seem to be a poetical note of preparation,[72] agreed upon, as a caution to Durdles to stand clear if he can, or to betake himself homeward.

John Jasper invites the boy with a beck of his head to follow him (feeling it hopeless to drag him, or coax him), and crosses to the iron railing where the Stony (and stoned) One is profoundly meditating.

'Do you know this thing – this child?' asks Jasper, at a loss for a word that will define this thing.

'Deputy,' says Durdles, with a nod.

'Is that its – his – name?'

'Deputy,' assents Durdles.

'I'm manservant up at the Travellers' Twopenny[73] in Gasworks Garding,' this thing explains. 'All us manservants at Travellers' Lodgings is named Deputy. When we're chock full and the Travellers is all abed I come out for my 'elth.' Then withdrawing into the road, and taking aim, he resumes:

'Widdy widdy wen!
I–ket–ches–'im–out–ar–ter–'

'Hold your hand,' cries Jasper, 'and don't throw while I stand so
near him, or I'll kill you! Come, Durdles; let me walk home with
you tonight. Shall I carry your bundle?'

'Not on any account,' replies Durdles, adjusting it. 'Durdles was
making his reflections here when you come up, sir, surrounded by
his works, like a poplar author. Your own brother-in-law – '
introducing a sarcophagus within the railing, white and cold in the
moonlight. 'Mrs Sapsea – ' introducing the monument of that
devoted wife. 'Late Incumbent – ' introducing the Reverend Gentleman's broken column. 'Departed Assessed Taxes – ' introducing a
vase and towel, standing on what might represent the cake of soap.
'Former Pastrycook and Muffin-maker, much respected – ' introducing a gravestone. 'All safe and sound here, sir, and all Durdles's
work. Of the common folk, that is merely bundled up in turf and
brambles,[74] the less said the better. A poor lot, soon forgot.'

'This creature, Deputy, is behind us,' says Jasper, looking back. 'Is
he to follow us?'

The relations between Durdles and Deputy are of a capricious
kind; for, on Durdles's turning himself about with the slow gravity
of beery suddenness, Deputy makes a pretty wide circuit into the
road and stands on the defensive.

'You never cried Widdy Warning before you begun tonight,' says
Durdles, unexpectedly reminded of, or imagining, an injury.

'Yer lie, I did,' says Deputy, in his only form of polite contradiction.

'Own brother, sir,' observes Durdles, turning himself about again,
and as unexpectedly forgetting his offence as he had recalled or
conceived it; 'own brother to Peter the Wild Boy![75] But I gave him
an object in life.'

'At which he takes aim?' Mr Jasper suggests.

'That's it, sir,' returns Durdles, quite satisfied; 'at which he takes
aim. I took him in hand and gave him an object. What was he
before? A destroyer. What work did he do? Nothing but destruction. What did he earn by it? Short terms in Cloisterham jail. Not a
person, not a piece of property, not a winder, not a horse, nor a dog,
nor a cat, nor a bird, nor a fowl, nor a pig, but what he stoned, for
want of an enlightened object. I put that enlightened object before
him, and now he can turn his honest halfpenny by the three
penn'orth a week.'

'I wonder he has no competitors.'

'He has plenty, Mr Jasper, but he stones 'em all away. Now, I don't know what this scheme of mine comes to,' pursues Durdles, considering about it with the same sodden gravity; 'I don't know what you may precisely call it. It ain't a sort of a – scheme of a National Education?'[76]

'I should say not,' replies Jasper.

'*I* should say not,' assents Durdles; 'then we won't try to give it a name.'

'He still keeps behind us,' repeats Jasper, looking over his shoulder; 'is he to follow us?'

'We can't help going round by the Travellers' Twopenny, if we go the short way, which is the back way,' Durdles answers, 'and we'll drop him there.'

So they go on; Deputy, as a rear rank of one, taking open order, and invading the silence of the hour and place by stoning every wall, post, pillar, and other inanimate object, by the deserted way.

'Is there anything new down in the crypt, Durdles?' asks John Jasper.

'Anything old, I think you mean,' growls Durdles. 'It ain't a spot for novelty.'

'Any new discovery on your part, I meant.'

'There's a old 'un under the seventh pillar on the left as you go down the broken steps of the little underground chapel as formerly was; I make him out (so fur as I've made him out yet) to be one of them old 'uns with a crook. To judge from the size of the passages in the walls, and of the steps and doors, by which they come and went, them crooks must have been a good deal in the way of the old 'uns! Two on 'em meeting promiscuous must have hitched one another by the mitre pretty often, I should say.'

Without any endeavour to correct the literality of this opinion, Jasper surveys his companion – covered from head to foot with old mortar, lime, and stone grit – as though he, Jasper, were getting imbued with a romantic interest in his weird life.

'Yours is a curious existence.'

Without furnishing the least clue to the question, whether he receives this as a compliment or as quite the reverse, Durdles gruffly answers: 'Yours is another.'

'Well! inasmuch as my lot is cast in the same old earthy, chilly, never-changing place, Yes. But there is much more mystery and interest in your connection with the cathedral than in mine. Indeed, I am beginning to have some idea of asking you to take me on as a sort of student, or free 'prentice, under you, and to let me go about with you sometimes, and see some of these odd nooks in which you pass your days.'

The Stony One replies, in a general way, 'All right. Everybody knows where to find Durdles, when he's wanted.' Which, if not strictly true, is approximately so, if taken to express that Durdles may always be found in a state of vagabondage somewhere.

'What I dwell upon most,' says Jasper, pursuing his subject of romantic interest, 'is the remarkable accuracy with which you would seem to find out where people are buried. – What is the matter? That bundle is in your way; let me hold it.'

Durdles has stopped and backed a little (Deputy, attentive to all his movements, immediately skirmishing into the road), and was looking about for some ledge or corner to place his bundle on, when thus relieved of it.

'Just you give me my hammer out of that,' says Durdles, 'and I'll show you.'

Clink, clink. And his hammer is handed him.

'Now, lookee here. You pitch your note, don't you, Mr Jasper?'

'Yes.'

'So I sound for mine. I take my hammer, and I tap.' (Here he strikes the pavement, and the attentive Deputy skirmishes at a rather wider range, as supposing that his head may be in requisition.) 'I tap, tap, tap. Solid! I go on tapping. Solid still! Tap again. Hallo! Hollow! Tap again, persevering. Solid in hollow! Tap, tap, tap, to try it better. Solid in hollow; and inside solid, hollow again! There you are! Old 'un crumbled away in stone coffin, in vault!'

'Astonishing!'

'I have even done this,' says Durdles, drawing out his two-foot rule (Deputy meanwhile skirmishing nearer, as suspecting that Treasure may be about to be discovered, which may somehow lead to his own enrichment, and the delicious treat of the discoverers being hanged by the neck, on his evidence, until they are dead).[77] 'Say that hammer of mine's a wall – my work. Two; four; and two is six,' measuring on the pavement. 'Six foot inside that wall is Mrs Sapsea.'

'Not really Mrs Sapsea?'

'Say Mrs Sapsea. Her wall's thicker, but say Mrs Sapsea. Durdles taps that wall represented by that hammer, and says, after good sounding: "Something betwixt us!" Sure enough, some rubbish has been left in that same six-foot space by Durdles's men!'

Jasper opines that such accuracy 'is a gift'.

'I wouldn't have it at a gift,' returns Durdles, by no means receiving the observation in good part. 'I worked it out for myself. Durdles comes by *his* knowledge through grubbing deep for it, and having it up by the roots when it don't want to come. – Hallo, you Deputy!'

'Widdy!' is Deputy's shrill response, standing off again.

'Catch that ha'penny. And don't let me see any more of you tonight, after we come to the Travellers' Twopenny.'

'Warning!' returns Deputy, having caught the halfpenny, and appearing by this mystic word to express his assent to the arrangement.

They have but to cross what was once the vineyard, belonging to what was once the monastery, to come into the narrow back lane wherein stands the crazy wooden house of two low storeys currently known as the Travellers' Twopenny: a house all warped and distorted, like the morals of the travellers, with scant remains of a lattice-work porch over the door, and also of a rustic fence before its stamped-out garden; by reason of the travellers being so bound to the premises by a tender sentiment (or so fond of having a fire by the roadside in the course of the day), that they can never be persuaded or threatened into departure, without violently possessing themselves of some wooden forget-me-not, and bearing it off.

The semblance of an inn is attempted to be given to this wretched place by fragments of conventional red curtaining in the windows, which rags are made muddily transparent in the night-season by feeble lights of rush or cotton dip[78] burning dully in the close air of the inside. As Durdles and Jasper come near, they are addressed by an inscribed paper lantern over the door, setting forth the purport of the house. They are also addressed by some half-dozen other hideous small boys – whether twopenny lodgers or followers or hangers-on of such, who knows! – who, as if attracted by some carrion-scent of Deputy in the air, start into the moonlight, as vultures might gather in the desert, and instantly fall to stoning him and one another.

'Stop, you young brutes,' cries Jasper angrily, 'and let us go by!'

This remonstrance being received with yells and flying stones, according to a custom of late years comfortably established among the police regulations of our English communities, where Christians are stoned on all sides, as if the days of Saint Stephen[79] were revived, Durdles remarks of the young savages, with some point, that 'they haven't got an object', and leads the way down the lane.

At the corner of the lane, Jasper, hotly enraged, checks his companion and looks back. All is silent. Next moment, a stone coming rattling at his hat, and a distant yell of 'Wake-Cock! Warning!' followed by a crow, as from some infernally-hatched Chanticleer,[80] apprising him under whose victorious fire he stands, he turns the corner into safety, and takes Durdles home: Durdles stumbling among the litter of his stony yard as if he were going to turn head foremost into one of the unfinished tombs.

John Jasper returns by another way to his gatehouse, and entering softly with his key, finds his fire still burning. He takes from a locked press a peculiar-looking pipe, which he fills – but not with tobacco – and, having adjusted the contents of the bowl, very carefully, with a little instrument, ascends an inner staircase of only a few steps, leading to two rooms. One of these is his own sleeping chamber: the other is his nephew's. There is a light in each.

His nephew lies asleep, calm and untroubled. John Jasper stands looking down upon him, his unlighted pipe in his hand, for some time, with a fixed and deep attention. Then, hushing his footsteps, he passes to his own room, lights his pipe, and delivers himself to the spectres it invokes at midnight.

CHAPTER 6

Philanthropy in Minor Canon Corner

THE REVEREND SEPTIMUS CRISPARKLE (Septimus, because six little brother Crisparkles before him went out, one by one, as they were born, like six weak little rushlights, as they were lighted),[81] having broken the thin morning ice near Cloisterham Weir with his amiable head, much to the invigoration of his frame, was now assisting his circulation by boxing at a looking-glass with great science and prowess. A fresh and healthy portrait the looking-glass presented of the Reverend Septimus, feinting and dodging with the utmost artfulness, and hitting out from the shoulder with the utmost straightness, while his radiant features teemed with innocence, and soft-hearted benevolence beamed from his boxing-gloves.

It was scarcely breakfast-time yet, for Mrs Crisparkle – mother, not wife of the Reverend Septimus – was only just down, and waiting for the urn. Indeed, the Reverend Septimus left off at this very moment to take the pretty old lady's entering face between his boxing-gloves and kiss it. Having done so with tenderness, the Reverend Septimus turned to again, countering with his left, and putting in his right, in a tremendous manner.

'I say, every morning of my life, that you'll do it at last, Sept,' remarked the old lady, looking on; 'and so you will.'

'Do what, ma dear?'

'Break the pier-glass,[82] or burst a blood-vessel.'

'Neither, please God, ma dear. Here's wind, ma. Look at this!' In a concluding round of great severity, the Reverend Septimus administered and escaped all sorts of punishment, and wound up by getting the old lady's cap into Chancery – such is the technical term used in scientific circles by the learned in the Noble Art[83] – with a lightness of touch that hardly stirred the lightest lavender or cherry riband on it. Magnanimously releasing the defeated, just in time to get his gloves into a drawer and feign to be looking out of the window in a contemplative state of mind when a servant entered, the Reverend Septimus then gave place to the urn and other preparations for breakfast. These completed, and the two alone again, it was pleasant to see (or would have been, if there had been anyone to see it, which there never was), the old lady standing to say the Lord's Prayer aloud, and her son, minor canon nevertheless, standing with bent head to hear it, he being within five years of forty: much as he had stood to hear the same words from the same lips when he was within five months of four.

What is prettier than an old lady – except a young lady – when her eyes are bright, when her figure is trim and compact, when her face is cheerful and calm, when her dress is as the dress of a china shepherdess: so dainty in its colours,[84] so individually assorted to herself, so neatly moulded on her? Nothing is prettier, thought the good minor canon frequently, when taking his seat at table opposite his long-widowed mother. Her thought at such times may be condensed into the two words that oftenest did duty together in all her conversations: 'My Sept!'

They were a good pair to sit breakfasting together in Minor Canon Corner, Cloisterham. For Minor Canon Corner was a quiet place in the shadow of the cathedral, which the cawing of the rooks, the echoing footsteps of rare passers, the sound of the cathedral bell, or the roll of the cathedral organ, seemed to render more quiet than absolute silence. Swaggering fighting men had had their centuries of ramping and raving about Minor Canon Corner, and beaten serfs had had their centuries of drudging and dying there, and powerful monks had had their centuries of being sometimes useful and sometimes harmful there, and behold they were all gone out of Minor Canon Corner, and so much the better. Perhaps one of the highest uses of their ever having been there was that there might be left behind that blessed air of tranquillity which pervaded Minor Canon Corner, and that serenely romantic state of the mind – productive for the most part of pity and forbearance – which is engendered by a sorrowful story that is all told, or a pathetic play that is played out.

Red-brick walls harmoniously toned down in colour by time, strong-rooted ivy, latticed windows, panelled rooms, big oaken beams in little places, and stone-walled gardens where annual fruit yet ripened upon monkish trees, were the principal surroundings of pretty old Mrs Crisparkle and the Reverend Septimus as they sat at breakfast.

'And what, ma dear,' enquired the minor canon, giving proof of a wholesome and vigorous appetite, 'does the letter say?'

The pretty old lady, after reading it, had just laid it down upon the breakfast-cloth. She handed it over to her son.

Now, the old lady was exceedingly proud of her bright eyes being so clear that she could read writing without spectacles. Her son was also so proud of the circumstance, and so dutifully bent on her deriving the utmost possible gratification from it, that he had invented the pretence that he himself could *not* read writing without spectacles. Therefore he now assumed a pair, of grave and prodigious proportions, which not only seriously inconvenienced his nose and his breakfast, but seriously impeded his perusal of the letter. For, he had the eyes of a microscope and a telescope combined, when they were unassisted.

'It's from Mr Honeythunder, of course,' said the old lady, folding her arms.

'Of course,' assented her son. He then lamely read on: ' "Haven of Philanthropy,[85] Chief Offices, London, Wednesday.– Dear Madam – I write in the – ;" In the what's this? What does he write in?'

'In the chair,' said the old lady.

The Reverend Septimus took off his spectacles, that he might see her face, as he exclaimed: 'Why, what should he write in?'

'Bless me, bless me, Sept,' returned the old lady, 'you don't see the context! Give it back to me, my dear.'

Glad to get his spectacles off (for they always made his eyes water), her son obeyed: murmuring that his sight for reading manuscript got worse and worse daily.

' "I write," ' his mother went on, reading very perspicuously and precisely, ' "from the chair, to which I shall probably be confined for some hours." '

Septimus looked at the row of chairs against the wall, with a half-protesting and half-appealing countenance.

' "We have," ' the old lady read on with a little extra emphasis, ' "a meeting of our Convened Chief Composite Committee of Central and District Philanthropists, at our Head Haven as above; and it is their unanimous pleasure that I take the chair." '

Septimus breathed more freely, and muttered: 'Oh! if he comes to *that*, let him,'

' "Not to lose a day's post, I take the opportunity of a long report being read, denouncing a public miscreant – " '

'It is a most extraordinary thing,' interposed the gentle minor canon, laying down his knife and fork to rub his ear in a vexed manner, 'that these philanthropists are always denouncing somebody. And it is another most extraordinary thing that they are always so violently flush of miscreants!'

' "Denouncing a public miscreant – " ' – the old lady resumed, ' "to get our little affair of business off my mind. I have spoken with my two wards, Neville and Helena Landless, on the subject of their defective education, and they give in to the plan proposed; as I should have taken good care they did, whether they liked it or not." '

'And it is another most extraordinary thing,' remarked the minor canon in the same tone as before, 'that these philanthropists are so given to seizing their fellow-creatures by the scruff of the neck, and (as one may say) bumping them into the paths of peace.[86] I beg your pardon, ma dear, for interrupting.'

' "Therefore, dear Madam, you will please prepare your son, the Reverend Mr Septimus, to expect Neville as an inmate to be read with,[87] on Monday next. On the same day Helena will accompany him to Cloisterham, to take up her quarters at the Nuns' House, the establishment recommended by yourself and son jointly. Please likewise to prepare for her reception and tuition there. The terms in both cases are understood to be exactly as stated to me in writing by yourself when I opened a correspondence with you on this subject, after the honour of being introduced to you at your sister's house in town here. With compliments to the Reverend Mr Septimus, I am, dear Madam, Your affectionate brother (in philanthropy), Luke Honeythunder." '[88]

'Well, ma,' said Septimus, after a little more rubbing of his ear, 'we must try it. There can be no doubt that we have room for an inmate, and that I have time to bestow upon him, and inclination too. I must confess to feeling rather glad that he is not to be Mr Honeythunder himself. Though that seems wretchedly prejudiced – does it not? – for I never saw him. Is he a large man, ma?'

'I should call him a large man, my dear,' the old lady replied after some hesitation, 'but that his voice is so much larger.'

'Than himself?'

'Than anybody.'

'Hah!' said Septimus. And finished his breakfast as if the flavour of the Superior Family Souchong,[89] and also of the ham and toast and eggs, were a little on the wane.

Mrs Crisparkle's sister, another piece of Dresden china, and matching her so neatly that they would have made a delightful pair of ornaments for the two ends of any capacious old-fashioned chimneypiece, and by right should never have been seen apart, was the childless wife of a clergyman holding corporation preferment in London City.[90] Mr Honeythunder in his public character of professor of philanthropy had come to know Mrs Crisparkle during the last re-matching of the china ornaments (in other words during her last annual visit to her sister), after a public occasion of a philanthropic nature, when certain devoted orphans of tender years had been glutted with plum buns, and plump bumptiousness. These were all the antecedents known in Minor Canon Corner of the coming pupils.

'I am sure you will agree with me, ma,' said Mr Crisparkle, after thinking the matter over, 'that the first thing to be done is to put these young people as much at their ease as possible. There is nothing disinterested in the notion, because we cannot be at our ease with them unless they are at their ease with us. Now, Jasper's nephew is down here at present; and like takes to like, and youth takes to youth. He is a cordial young fellow, and we will have him to meet the brother and sister at dinner. That's three. We can't think of asking him, without asking Jasper. That's four. Add Miss Twinkleton and the fairy bride that is to be,[91] and that's six. Add our two selves, and that's eight. Would eight at a friendly dinner at all put you out, ma?'

'Nine would, Sept,' returned the old lady, visibly nervous.

'My dear ma, I particularise eight.'

'The exact size of the table and the room, my dear.'

So it was settled that way: and when Mr Crisparkle called with his mother upon Miss Twinkleton, to arrange for the reception of Miss Helena Landless at the Nuns' House, the two other invitations having reference to that establishment were proffered and accepted.

Miss Twinkleton did, indeed, glance at the globes, as regretting that they were not formed to be taken out into society; but became reconciled to leaving them behind. Plain instructions were then despatched to the philanthropist for the departure and arrival, in good time for dinner, of Mr Neville and Miss Helena; and stock for soup became fragrant in the air of Minor Canon Corner.

In those days there was no railway[92] to Cloisterham, and Mr Sapsea said there never would be. Mr Sapsea said more; he said there never should be. And yet, marvellous to consider, it has come to pass, in these days, that express trains don't think Cloisterham worth stopping at, but yell and whirl through it on their larger errands, casting the dust off their wheels as a testimony against its insignificance. Some remote fragment of main line to somewhere else there was, which was going to ruin the money market[93] if it failed, and church and state if it succeeded, and (of course), the constitution, whether or no; but even that had already so unsettled Cloisterham traffic, that the traffic, deserting the high road, came sneaking in from an unprecedented part of the country by a back stable-way, for many years labelled at the corner: 'Beware of the Dog'.

To this ignominious avenue of approach, Mr Crisparkle repaired, awaiting the arrival of a short, squat omnibus, with a disproportionate heap of luggage on the roof – like a little Elephant with infinitely too much Castle[94] – which was then the daily service between Cloisterham and external mankind. As this vehicle lumbered up, Mr Crisparkle could hardly see anything else of it for a large outside passenger seated on the box, with his elbows squared, and his hands on his knees, compressing the driver into a most uncomfortably small compass, and glowering about him with a strongly marked face.

'Is this Cloisterham?' demanded the passenger, in a tremendous voice.

'It is,' replied the driver, rubbing himself as if he ached, after throwing the reins to the ostler. 'And I never was so glad to see it.'

'Tell your master to make his box-seat wider, then,' returned the passenger. 'Your master is morally bound – and ought to be legally, under ruinous penalties – to provide for the comfort of his fellow-man.'

The driver instituted, with the palms of his hands, a superficial perquisition into the state of his skeleton; which seemed to make him anxious.

'Have I sat upon you?' asked the passenger.

'You have,' said the driver, as if he didn't like it at all.

'Take that card, my friend.'

'I think I won't deprive you on it,' returned the driver, casting his eyes over it with no great favour, without taking it. 'What's the good of it to me?'

'Be a member of that society,' said the passenger.

'What shall I get by it?' asked the driver.

'Brotherhood,' returned the passenger, in a ferocious voice.

'Thankee,' said the driver, very deliberately, as he got down; 'my mother was contented with myself, and so am I. I don't want no brothers.'

'But you must have them,' replied the passenger, also descending, 'whether you like it or not. I am your brother.'

'I say!' expostulated the driver, becoming more chafed in temper, 'not too fur! The worm *will*, when – '[95]

But here Mr Crisparkle interposed, remonstrating aside, in a friendly voice: 'Joe, Joe, Joe! don't forget yourself, Joe, my good fellow!' and then, when Joe peaceably touched his hat, accosting the passenger with: 'Mr Honeythunder?'

'That is my name, sir.'

'My name is Crisparkle.'

'Reverend Mr Septimus? Glad to see you, sir. Neville and Helena are inside. Having a little succumbed of late, under the pressure of my public labours, I thought I would take a mouthful of fresh air, and come down with them, and return at night. So you are the Reverend Mr Septimus, are you?' surveying him on the whole with disappointment, and twisting a double eyeglass by its ribbon, as if he were roasting it, but not otherwise using it. 'Hah! I expected to see you older, sir.'

'I hope you will,' was the good-humoured reply.

'Eh?' demanded Mr Honeythunder.

'Only a poor little joke. Not worth repeating.'

'Joke? Ay; I never see a joke,' Mr Honeythunder frowningly retorted. 'A joke is wasted upon me, sir. Where are they? Helena and Neville, come here! Mr Crisparkle has come down to meet you.'

An unusually handsome lithe young fellow, and an unusually handsome lithe girl; much alike; both very dark, and very rich in colour; she of almost the gypsy type; something untamed about them both; a certain air upon them of hunter and huntress; yet withal a certain air of being the objects of the chase, rather than the followers. Slender, supple, quick of eye and limb; half shy, half defiant; fierce of look; an indefinable kind of pause coming and going on their whole expression, both of face and form, which might be equally likened to the pause before a crouch or a bound. The rough mental notes made in the first five minutes by Mr Crisparkle would have read thus, *verbatim*.

He invited Mr Honeythunder to dinner, with a troubled mind (for the discomfiture of the dear old china shepherdess lay heavy on it), and gave his arm to Helena Landless. Both she and her brother, as they walked all together through the ancient streets, took great delight in what he pointed out of the cathedral and the monastery ruin, and wondered – so his notes ran on – much as if they were beautiful barbaric captives brought from some wild tropical dominion. Mr Honeythunder walked in the middle of the road, shouldering the natives out of his way, and loudly developing a scheme he had for making a raid on all the unemployed persons in the United Kingdom, laying them every one by the heels in jail, and forcing them, on pain of prompt extermination, to become philanthropists.

Mrs Crisparkle had need of her own share of philanthropy when she beheld this very large and very loud excrescence on the little party. Always something in the nature of a boil upon the face of society, Mr Honeythunder expanded into an inflammatory wen in Minor Canon Corner. Though it was not literally true, as was facetiously charged against him by public unbelievers, that he called aloud to his fellow-creatures: 'Curse your souls and bodies, come here and be blessed!' still his philanthropy was of that gunpowderous sort that the difference between it and animosity was hard to determine. You were to abolish military force, but you were first to bring all commanding officers who had done their duty, to trial by court-martial for that offence, and shoot them.[96] You were to abolish war, but were to make converts by making war upon them, and charging them with loving war as the apple of their eye. You were to have no capital punishment, but were first to sweep off the face of the earth all legislators, jurists and judges, who were of the contrary opinion. You were to have universal concord, and were to get it by eliminating all the people who wouldn't, or conscientiously couldn't, be concordant. You were to love your brother as yourself,[97] but after an indefinite interval of maligning him (very much as if you hated him), and calling him all manner of names. Above all things, you were to do nothing in private, or on your own account. You were to go to the offices of the Haven of Philanthropy, and put your name down as a member and a professing philanthropist. Then, you were to pay up your subscription, get your card of membership and your riband and medal, and were evermore to live upon a platform, and evermore to say what Mr Honeythunder said, and what the treasurer said, and what the sub-treasurer said, and what the committee said, and what the sub-committee said, and what the secretary said, and what the vice-secretary said. And this was usually said in the unanimously-carried resolution under hand and seal, to the effect: 'That this assembled body of professing philanthropists views, with indignant scorn and contempt, not unmixed with utter detestation and loathing abhorrence – ' in short, the baseness of all those who do not belong to it, and pledges itself to make as many obnoxious statements as possible about them, without being at all particular as to facts.

The dinner was a most doleful breakdown. The philanthropist deranged the symmetry of the table, sat himself in the way of the waiting, blocked up the thoroughfare, and drove Mr Tope (who assisted the parlour-maid) to the verge of distraction by passing plates and dishes on, over his own head. Nobody could talk to anybody, because he held forth to everybody at once, as if the company had no individual existence, but were a meeting. He impounded the Reverend Mr Septimus as an official personage to be addressed or kind of human peg to hang his oratorical hat on, and fell into the exasperating habit, common among such orators, of impersonating him as a wicked and weak opponent. Thus, he would ask: 'And will you, sir, now stultify yourself by telling me – ?' and so forth, when the innocent man had not opened his lips, nor meant to open them. Or he would say: 'Now see, sir, to what a position you are reduced. I will leave you no escape. After exhausting all the resources of fraud and falsehood, during years upon years; after exhibiting a combination of dastardly meanness with ensanguined daring, such as the world has not often witnessed; you have now the hypocrisy to bend the knee before the most degraded of mankind, and to sue and whine and howl for mercy!' Whereat the unfortunate minor canon would look in part indignant and in part perplexed; while his worthy mother sat bridling, with tears in her eyes, and the remainder of the party lapsed into a sort of gelatinous state, in which there was no flavour or solidity, and very little resistance.

But the gush of philanthropy that burst forth when the departure of Mr Honeythunder began to impend, must have been highly gratifying to the feelings of that distinguished man. His coffee was produced, by the special activity of Mr Tope, a full hour before he wanted it. Mr Crisparkle sat with his watch in his hand for about the same period, lest he should overstay his time. The four young people were unanimous in believing that the cathedral clock struck three-quarters, when it actually struck but one. Miss Twinkleton estimated the distance to the omnibus at five-and-twenty minutes' walk, when it was really five. The affectionate kindness of the whole circle hustled him into his greatcoat, and shoved him out into the moonlight, as if he were a fugitive traitor with whom they sympathised, and a troop of horse were at the back door. Mr Crisparkle and his new charge, who took him to the omnibus, were so fervent in their apprehensions of his catching cold, that they shut him up in it instantly and left him, with still half an hour to spare.

CHAPTER 7

More Confidences than One

'I KNOW VERY LITTLE of that gentleman, sir,' said Neville to the minor canon as they turned back.

'You know very little of your guardian?' the minor canon repeated.

'Almost nothing!'

'How came he – '

'To *be* my guardian? I'll tell you, sir. I suppose you know that we come (my sister and I) from Ceylon?'[98]

'Indeed, no.'

'I wonder at that. We lived with a stepfather there. Our mother died there, when we were little children. We have had a wretched existence. She made him our guardian, and he was a miserly wretch who grudged us food to eat, and clothes to wear. At his death, he passed us over to this man; for no better reason, that I know of, than his being a friend or connection of his, whose name was always in print and catching his attention.'

'That was lately, I suppose?'

'Quite lately, sir. This stepfather of ours was a cruel brute as well as a grinding one. It is well he died when he did, or I might have killed him.'

Mr Crisparkle stopped short in the moonlight and looked at his hopeful pupil in consternation.

'I surprise you, sir?' he said, with a quick change to a submissive manner.

'You shock me; unspeakably shock me.'

The pupil hung his head for a little while, as they walked on, and then said: 'You never saw him beat your sister. I have seen him beat mine, more than once or twice, and I never forgot it.'

'Nothing,' said Mr Crisparkle, 'not even a beloved and beautiful sister's tears under dastardly ill-usage;' he became less severe, in spite of himself, as his indignation rose; 'could justify those horrible expressions that you used.'

'I am sorry I used them, and especially to you, sir. I beg to recall them. But permit me to set you right on one point. You spoke of my sister's tears. My sister would have let him tear her to pieces, before she would have let him believe that he could make her shed a tear.'

Mr Crisparkle reviewed those mental notes of his, and was neither at all surprised to hear it, nor at all disposed to question it.

'Perhaps you will think it strange, sir,' – this was said in a hesitating voice – 'that I should so soon ask you to allow me to confide in you, and to have the kindness to hear a word or two from me in my defence?'

'Defence?' Mr Crisparkle repeated. 'You are not on your defence, Mr Neville.'

'I think I am, sir. At least I know I should be, if you were better acquainted with my character.'

'Well, Mr Neville,' was the rejoinder. 'What if you leave me to find it out?'

'Since it is your pleasure, sir,' answered the young man, with a quick change in his manner to sullen disappointment: 'since it is your pleasure to check me in my impulse, I must submit.'

There was that in the tone of this short speech which made the conscientious man to whom it was addressed uneasy. It hinted to him that he might, without meaning it, turn aside a trustfulness beneficial to a misshapen young mind and perhaps to his own power of directing and improving it. They were within sight of the lights in his windows, and he stopped.

'Let us turn back and take a turn or two up and down, Mr Neville, or you may not have time to finish what you wish to say to me. You are hasty in thinking that I mean to check you. Quite the contrary. I invite your confidence.'

'You have invited it, sir, without knowing it, ever since I came here. I say "ever since", as if I had been here a week. The truth is, we came here (my sister and I) to quarrel with you, and affront you, and break away again.'

'Really?' said Mr Crisparkle, at a dead loss for anything else to say.

'You see, we could not know what you were beforehand, sir; could we?'

'Clearly not,' said Mr Crisparkle.

'And having liked no one else with whom we have ever been brought into contact, we had made up our minds not to like you.'

'Really?' said Mr Crisparkle again.

'But we do like you, sir, and we see an immeasurable difference between your house and your reception of us, and anything else we have ever known. This – and my happening to be alone with you – and everything around us seeming so quiet and peaceful after Mr Honeythunder's departure – and Cloisterham being so old and grave and beautiful, with the moon shining on it – these things inclined me to open my heart.'

'I quite understand, Mr Neville. And it is salutary to listen to such influences.'

'In describing my own imperfections, sir, I must ask you not to suppose that I am describing my sister's. She has come out of the disadvantages of our miserable life as much better than I am as that cathedral tower is higher than those chimneys.'

Mr Crisparkle in his own breast was not so sure of this.

'I have had, sir, from my earliest remembrance, to suppress a deadly and bitter hatred. This has made me secret and revengeful. I have been always tyrannically held down by the strong hand. This has driven me, in my weakness, to the resource of being false and mean. I have been stinted of education, liberty, money, dress, the very necessaries of life, the commonest pleasures of childhood, the commonest possessions of youth. This has caused me to be utterly wanting in I don't know what emotions, or remembrances, or good instincts – I have not even a name for the thing, you see! – that you have had to work upon in other young men to whom you have been accustomed.'

'This is evidently true. But this is not encouraging,' thought Mr Crisparkle as they turned again.

'And to finish with, sir: I have been brought up among abject and servile dependents, of an inferior race, and I may easily have contracted some affinity with them. Sometimes, I don't know but that it may be a drop of what is tigerish in their blood.'

'As in the case of that remark just now,' thought Mr Crisparkle.

'In a last word of reference to my sister, sir (we are twin children), you ought to know, to her honour, that nothing in our misery ever subdued her, though it often cowed me. When we ran away from it (we ran away four times in six years, to be soon brought back and cruelly punished), the flight was always of her planning and leading. Each time she dressed as a boy,[99] and showed the daring of a man. I take it we were seven years old when we first decamped; but I remember, when I lost the pocketknife with which she was to have cut her hair short, how desperately she tried to tear it out, or bite it off. I have nothing further to say, sir, except that I hope you will bear with me and make allowance for me.'

'Of that, Mr Neville, you may be sure,' returned the minor canon. 'I don't preach more than I can help, and I will not repay your confidence with a sermon. But I entreat you to bear in mind, very seriously and steadily, that if I am to do you any good, it can only be with your own assistance; and that you can only render that, efficiently, by seeking aid from heaven.'

'I will try to do my part, sir.'

'And, Mr Neville, I will try to do mine. Here is my hand on it. May God bless our endeavours!'

They were now standing at his house-door, and a cheerful sound of voices and laughter was heard within.

'We will take one more turn before going in,' said Mr Crisparkle, 'for I want to ask you a question. When you said you were in a changed mind concerning me, you spoke, not only for yourself, but for your sister too?'

'Undoubtedly I did, sir.'

'Excuse me, Mr Neville, but I think you have had no opportunity of communicating with your sister, since I met you. Mr Honeythunder was very eloquent; but perhaps I may venture to say, without ill-nature, that he rather monopolised the occasion. May you not have answered for your sister without sufficient warrant?'

Neville shook his head with a proud smile.

'You don't know, sir, yet, what a complete understanding can exist between my sister and me, though no spoken word – perhaps hardly as much as a look – may have passed between us. She not only feels as I have described, but she very well knows that I am taking this opportunity of speaking to you, both for her and for myself.'

Mr Crisparkle looked in his face, with some incredulity; but his face expressed such absolute and firm conviction of the truth of what he said, that Mr Crisparkle looked at the pavement, and mused, until they came to his door again.

'I will ask for one more turn, sir, this time,' said the young man, with a rather heightened colour rising in his face. 'But for Mr Honeythunder's – I think you called it eloquence, sir?' (somewhat slyly.)

'I – yes, I called it eloquence,' said Mr Crisparkle.

'But for Mr Honeythunder's eloquence, I might have had no need to ask you what I am going to ask you. This Mr Edwin Drood, sir: I think that's the name?'

'Quite correct,' said Mr Crisparkle. 'D–r–double o–d.'

'Does he – or did he – read with you, sir?'

'Never, Mr Neville. He comes here visiting his relation, Mr Jasper.'

'Is Miss Bud his relation too, sir?'

('Now, why should he ask that, with sudden superciliousness?' thought Mr Crisparkle.) Then he explained, aloud, what he knew of the little story of their betrothal.

'Oh! *that's* it, is it?' said the young man. 'I understand his air of proprietorship now!'

This was said so evidently to himself, or to anybody rather than Mr Crisparkle, that the latter instinctively felt as if to notice it would be almost tantamount to noticing a passage in a letter which he had read by chance over the writer's shoulder. A moment afterwards they re-entered the house.

Mr Jasper was seated at the piano as they came into his drawing-room, and was accompanying Miss Rosebud while she sang. It was a consequence of his playing the accompaniment without notes, and of her being a heedless little creature, very apt to go wrong, that he followed her lips most attentively, with his eyes as well as hands; carefully and softly hinting the keynote from time to time. Standing with an arm drawn round her, but with a face far more intent on Mr Jasper than on her singing, stood Helena, between whom and her brother an instantaneous recognition passed, in which Mr Crisparkle saw, or thought he saw, the understanding that had been spoken of, flash out. Mr Neville then took his admiring station, leaning against the piano, opposite the singer; Mr Crisparkle sat down by the china shepherdess; Edwin Drood gallantly furled and unfurled Miss Twinkleton's fan; and that lady passively claimed that sort of exhibitor's proprietorship in the accomplishment on view, which Mr Tope, the verger, daily claimed in the cathedral service.

The song went on. It was a sorrowful strain of parting, and the fresh young voice was very plaintive and tender. As Jasper watched the pretty lips, and ever and again hinted the one note, as though it were a low whisper from himself, the voice became less steady, until all at once the singer broke into a burst of tears, and shrieked out, with her hands over her eyes: 'I can't bear this! I am frightened! Take me away!'

With one swift turn of her lithe figure Helena laid the little beauty on a sofa, as if she had never caught her up. Then, on one knee beside her, and with one hand upon her rosy mouth, while with the other she appealed to all the rest, Helena said to them: 'It's nothing; it's all over; don't speak to her for one minute, and she is well!'

Jasper's hands had, in the same instant, lifted themselves from the keys, and were now poised above them, as though he waited to resume. In that attitude he yet sat quiet: not even looking round, when all the rest had changed their places and were reassuring one another.

'Pussy's not used to an audience; that's the fact,' said Edwin Drood. 'She got nervous, and couldn't hold out. Besides, Jack, you are such a conscientious master, and require so much, that I believe you make her afraid of you. No wonder.'

'No wonder,' repeated Helena.

'There, Jack, you hear! You would be afraid of him, under similar circumstances, wouldn't you, Miss Landless?'

'Not under any circumstances,' returned Helena.

Jasper brought down his hands, looked over his shoulder, and begged to thank Miss Landless for her vindication of his character. Then he fell to dumbly playing, without striking the notes, while his little pupil was taken to an open window for air, and was otherwise petted and restored. When she was brought back, his place was empty. 'Jack's gone, Pussy,' Edwin told her. 'I am more than half afraid he didn't like to be charged with being the monster who had frightened you.' But she answered never a word, and shivered, as if they had made her a little too cold.

Miss Twinkleton now opining that indeed these were late hours, Mrs Crisparkle, for finding ourselves outside the walls of the Nuns' House, and that we who undertook the formation of the future wives and mothers of England[100] (the last words in a lower voice, as requiring to be communicated in confidence) were really bound (voice coming up again) to set a better example than one of rakish habits, wrappers were put in requisition, and the two young cavaliers volunteered to see the ladies home. It was soon done, and the gate of the Nuns' House closed upon them.

The boarders had retired, and only Mrs Tisher in solitary vigil awaited the new pupil. Her bedroom being within Rosa's, very little

At the piano

introduction or explanation was necessary, before she was placed in charge of her new friend, and left for the night.

'This is a blessed relief, my dear,' said Helena. 'I have been dreading all day that I should be brought to bay at this time.'

'There are not many of us,' returned Rosa, 'and we are good-natured girls; at least the others are; I can answer for them.'

'I can answer for you,' laughed Helena, searching the lovely little face with her dark, fiery eyes, and tenderly caressing the small figure. 'You will be a friend to me, won't you?'

'I hope so. But the idea of my being a friend to you seems too absurd, though.'

'Why?'

'Oh, I am such a mite of a thing, and you are so womanly and handsome. You seem to have resolution and power enough to crush me. I shrink into nothing by the side of your presence even.'

'I am a neglected creature, my dear, unacquainted with all accomplishments, sensitively conscious that I have everything to learn, and deeply ashamed to own my ignorance.'

'And yet you acknowledge everything to me!' said Rosa.

'My pretty one, can I help it? There is a fascination in you.'

'Oh! is there though?' pouted Rosa, half in jest and half in earnest. 'What a pity Master Eddy doesn't feel it more!'

Of course her relations towards that young gentleman had been already imparted in Minor Canon Corner.

'Why, surely he must love you with all his heart!' cried Helena, with an earnestness that threatened to blaze into ferocity if he didn't.

'Eh? Oh, well, I suppose he does,' said Rosa, pouting again; 'I am sure I have no right to say he doesn't. Perhaps it's my fault. Perhaps I am not as nice to him as I ought to be. I don't think I am. But it *is* so ridiculous!'

Helena's eyes demanded what was.

'*We* are,' said Rosa, answering as if she had spoken. 'We are such a ridiculous couple. And we are always quarrelling.'

'Why?'

'Because we both know we are ridiculous, my dear!' Rosa gave that answer as if it were the most conclusive answer in the world.

Helena's masterful look was intent upon her face for a few moments, and then she impulsively put out both her hands and said: 'You will be my friend and help me?'

'Indeed, my dear, I will,' replied Rosa, in a tone of affectionate childishness that went straight and true to her heart; 'I will be as good a friend as such a mite of a thing can be to such a noble creature as you. And be a friend to me, please; I don't understand myself: and I want a friend who can understand me, very much indeed.'

Helena Landless kissed her, and retaining both her hands said: 'Who is Mr Jasper?'

Rosa turned aside her head in answering: 'Eddy's uncle, and my music-master.'

'You do not love him?'

'Ugh!' She put her hands up to her face, and shook with fear or horror.

'You know that he loves you?'

'Oh, don't, don't, don't!' cried Rosa, dropping on her knees, and clinging to her new resource. 'Don't tell me of it! He terrifies me. He haunts my thoughts, like a dreadful ghost. I feel that I am never safe from him. I feel as if he could pass in through the wall when he is spoken of.' She actually did look round, as if she dreaded to see him standing in the shadow behind her.

'Try to tell me more about it, darling.'

'Yes, I will, I will. Because you are so strong. But hold me the while, and stay with me afterwards.'

'My child! You speak as if he had threatened you in some dark way.'

'He has never spoken to me about – that. Never.'

'What has he done?'

'He has made a slave of me with his looks. He has forced me to understand him, without his saying a word; and he has forced me to keep silence, without his uttering a threat. When I play, he never moves his eyes from my hands. When I sing, he never moves his eyes from my lips. When he corrects me, and strikes a note, or a chord, or plays a passage, he himself is in the sounds, whispering that he pursues me as a lover, and commanding me to keep his secret. I avoid his eyes, but he forces me to see them without looking at them. Even when a glaze comes over them (which is sometimes the case), and he seems to wander away into a frightful sort of dream in which he threatens most, he obliges me to know it, and to know that he is sitting close at my side, more terrible to me than ever.'

'What is this imagined threatening, pretty one? What is threatened?'

'I don't know. I have never even dared to think or wonder what it is.'

'And was this all, tonight?'

'This was all; except that tonight when he watched my lips so closely as I was singing, besides feeling terrified I felt ashamed and passionately hurt. It was as if he kissed me, and I couldn't bear it, but cried out. You must never breathe this to anyone. Eddy is devoted to him. But you said tonight that you would not be afraid of him, under any circumstances, and that gives me – who am so much afraid of him – courage to tell only you. Hold me! Stay with me! I am too frightened to be left by myself.'

The lustrous gypsy-face drooped over the clinging arms and bosom, and the wild black hair fell down protectingly over the childish form. There was a slumbering gleam of fire in the intense dark eyes, though they were then softened with compassion and admiration. Let whomsoever it most concerned look well to it!

CHAPTER 8

Daggers Drawn

THE TWO YOUNG MEN, having seen the damsels, their charges, enter the courtyard of the Nuns' House, and finding themselves coldly stared at by the brazen door-plate, as if the battered old beau with the glass in his eye were insolent, look at one another, look along the perspective of the moonlit street, and slowly walk away together.

'Do you stay here long, Mr Drood?' says Neville.

'Not this time,' is the careless answer. 'I leave for London again, tomorrow. But I shall be here, off and on, until next Midsummer; then I shall take my leave of Cloisterham, and England too; for many a long day, I expect.'

'Are you going abroad?'

'Going to wake up Egypt a little,' is the condescending answer.

'Are you reading?'

'Reading?' repeats Edwin Drood, with a touch of contempt. 'No. Doing, working, engineering.[101] My small patrimony was left a part of the capital of the firm I am with, by my father, a former partner; and I am a charge upon the firm until I come of age; and then I step into my modest share in the concern. Jack – you met him at dinner – is, until then, my guardian and trustee.'

'I heard from Mr Crisparkle of your other good fortune.'

'What do you mean by my other good fortune?'

Neville has made his remark in a watchfully advancing, and yet furtive and shy manner, very expressive of that peculiar air already noticed, of being at once hunter and hunted. Edwin has made his retort with an abruptness not at all polite. They stop and interchange a rather heated look.

'I hope,' says Neville, 'there is no offence, Mr Drood, in my innocently referring to your betrothal?'

'By George!' cries Edwin, leading on again at a somewhat quicker pace; 'everybody in this chattering old Cloisterham refers to it I wonder no public-house has been set up, with my portrait for the sign of the Betrothed's Head. Or Pussy's portrait. One or the other.'

'I am not accountable for Mr Crisparkle's mentioning the matter to me, quite openly,' Neville begins.

'No; that's true; you are not,' Edwin Drood assents.

'But,' resumes Neville, 'I am accountable for mentioning it to you. And I did so, on the supposition that you could not fail to be highly proud of it.'

Now, there are these two curious touches of human nature working the secret springs of this dialogue. Neville Landless is already enough impressed by Little Rosebud to feel indignant that Edwin Drood (far below her) should hold his prize so lightly. Edwin Drood is already enough impressed by Helena, to feel indignant that Helena's brother (far below her) should dispose of him so coolly, and put him out of the way so entirely.

However, the last remark had better be answered. So, says Edwin: 'I don't know, Mr Neville' (adopting that mode of address from Mr Crisparkle), 'that what people are proudest of, they usually talk most about; I don't know either, that what they are proudest of, they most like other people to talk about. But I live a busy life, and I speak under correction by you readers, who ought to know everything, and I dare say do.'

By this time they had both become savage; Mr Neville out in the open; Edwin Drood under the transparent cover of a popular tune, and a stop now and then to pretend to admire picturesque effects in the moonlight before him.

'It does not seem to me very civil in you,' remarks Neville, at length, 'to reflect upon a stranger who comes here, not having had your advantages, to try to make up for lost time. But, to be sure, I was not brought up in "busy life", and my ideas of civility were formed among heathens.'

'Perhaps, the best civility, whatever kind of people we are brought up among,' retorts Edwin Drood, 'is to mind our own business. If you will set me that example, I promise to follow it.'

'Do you know that you take a great deal too much upon yourself?' is the angry rejoinder, 'and that in the part of the world I come from, you would be called to account for it?'

'By whom, for instance?' asks Edwin Drood, coming to a halt, and surveying the other with a look of disdain.

But, here a startling right hand is laid on Edwin's shoulder, and Jasper stands between them. For, it would seem that he, too, has strolled round by the Nuns' House, and has come up behind them on the shadowy side of the road.

'Ned, Ned, Ned!' he says; 'we must have no more of this. I don't like this. I have overheard high words between you two. Remember, my dear boy, you are almost in the position of host tonight. You belong, as it were, to the place, and in a manner represent it towards a stranger. Mr Neville is a stranger, and you should respect the obligations of hospitality. And, Mr Neville,' laying his left hand on the inner shoulder of that young gentleman, and thus walking on between them, hand to shoulder on either side: 'you will pardon me; but I appeal to you to govern your temper too. Now, what is amiss? But why ask! Let there be nothing amiss, and the question is superfluous. We are all three on a good understanding, are we not?'

After a silent struggle between the two young men who shall speak last, Edwin Drood strikes in with: 'So far as I am concerned, Jack, there is no anger in me.'

'Nor in me,' says Neville Landless, though not so freely; or perhaps so carelessly. 'But if Mr Drood knew all that lies behind me, far away from here, he might know better how it is that sharp-edged words have sharp edges to wound me.'

'Perhaps,' says Jasper, in a soothing manner, 'we had better not qualify our good understanding. We had better not say anything having the appearance of a remonstrance or condition; it might not seem generous. Frankly and freely, you see there is no anger in Ned. Frankly and freely, there is no anger in you, Mr Neville?'

'None at all, Mr Jasper.' Still, not quite so frankly or so freely; or, be it said once again, not quite so carelessly perhaps.

'All over then! Now, my bachelor gatehouse is but a few yards from here, and the heater is on the fire, and the wine and glasses are on the table, and it is not a stone's throw from Minor Canon Corner. Ned, you are up and away tomorrow. We will carry Mr Neville in with us, to take a stirrup-cup.'[102]

'With all my heart, Jack.'

'And with all mine, Mr Jasper.' Neville feels it impossible to say less, but would rather not go. He has an impression upon him that he has lost hold of his temper; feels that Edwin Drood's coolness, so far from being infectious, makes him red-hot.

Mr Jasper, still walking in the centre, hand to shoulder on either side, beautifully turns the refrain of a drinking song, and they all go up to his rooms. There, the first object visible, when he adds the light of a lamp to that of the fire, is the portrait over the chimneypiece. It is not an object calculated to improve the under-standing between the two young men, as rather awkwardly reviving the subject of their difference. Accordingly, they both glance at it consciously, but say nothing. Jasper, however (who would appear from his conduct to have gained but an imperfect clue to the cause of their late high words), directly calls attention to it.

'You recognise that picture, Mr Neville?' shading the lamp to throw the light upon it.

'I recognise it, but it is far from flattering the original.'

'Oh, you are hard upon it! It was done by Ned, who made me a present of it.'

'I am sorry for that, Mr Drood.' Neville apologises, with a real intention to apologise; 'if I had known I was in the artist's presence – '

'Oh, a joke, sir, a mere joke,' Edwin cuts in, with a provoking yawn. 'A little humouring of Pussy's points! I'm going to paint her gravely, one of these days, if she's good.'

The air of leisurely patronage and indifference with which this is said, as the speaker throws himself back in a chair and clasps his hands at the back of his head, as a rest for it, is very exasperating to the excitable and excited Neville. Jasper looks observantly from the one to the other, slightly smiles, and turns his back to mix a jug of mulled wine at the fire. It seems to require much mixing and compounding.

'I suppose, Mr Neville,' says Edwin, quick to resent the indignant protest against himself in the face of young Landless, which is fully as visible as the portrait, or the fire, or the lamp: 'I suppose that if you painted the picture of your lady love – '

'I can't paint,' is the hasty interruption.

'That's your misfortune, and not your fault. You would if you could. But if you could, I suppose you would make her (no matter what she was in reality) Juno, Minerva, Diana and Venus,[103] all in one. Eh?'

'I have no lady love, and I can't say.'

'If I were to try my hand,' says Edwin, with a boyish boastfulness getting up in him, 'on a portrait of Miss Landless – in earnest, mind you; in earnest – you should see what I could do!'

'My sister's consent to sit for it being first got, I suppose? As it never will be got, I am afraid I shall never see what you can do. I must bear the loss.'

Jasper turns round from the fire, fills a large goblet glass for Neville, fills a large goblet glass for Edwin, and hands each his own; then fills for himself, saying: 'Come, Mr Neville, we are to drink to my nephew, Ned. As it is his foot that is in the stirrup – metaphori-cally – our stirrup-cup is to be devoted to him. Ned, my dearest fellow, my love!'

Jasper sets the example of nearly emptying his glass, and Neville follows it. Edwin Drood says, 'Thank you both very much,' and follows the double example.

'Look at him,' cries Jasper, stretching out his hand admiringly and tenderly, though rallyingly too. 'See where he lounges so easily, Mr Neville! The world is all before him where to choose.[104] A life of stirring work and interest, a life of change and excitement, a life of domestic ease and love! Look at him!'

Edwin Drood's face has become quickly and remarkably flushed with the wine; so has the face of Neville Landless. Edwin still sits thrown back in his chair, making that rest of clasped hands for his head.

'See how little he heeds it all!' Jasper proceeds in a bantering vein. 'It is hardly worth his while to pluck the golden fruit that hangs ripe on the tree for him.[105] And yet consider the contrast, Mr Neville. You and I have no prospect of stirring work and interest, or of change and excitement, or of domestic ease and love. You and I have no prospect (unless you are more fortunate than I am, which may easily be), but the tedious unchanging round of this dull place.'

'Upon my soul, Jack,' says Edwin, complacently, 'I feel quite apologetic for having my way smoothed as you describe. But you know what I know, Jack, and it may not be so very easy as it seems, after all. May it, Pussy?' To the portrait, with a snap of his thumb and finger. 'We have got to hit it off yet; haven't we, Pussy? You know what I mean, Jack.'

His speech has become thick and indistinct. Jasper, quiet and self-possessed, looks to Neville, as expecting his answer or comment. When Neville speaks, *his* speech is also thick and indistinct.

'It might have been better for Mr Drood to have known some

On dangerous ground

hardships,' he says, defiantly.

'Pray,' retorts Edwin, turning merely his eyes in that direction, 'pray why might it have been better for Mr Drood to have known some hardships?'

'Ay,' Jasper assents, with an air of interest; 'let us know why?'

'Because they might have made him more sensible,' says Neville, 'of good fortune that is not by any means necessarily the result of his own merits.'

Mr Jasper quickly looks to his nephew for his rejoinder.

'Have *you* known hardships, may I ask?' says Edwin Drood, sitting upright.

Mr Jasper quickly looks to the other for his retort.

'I have.'

'And what have they made you sensible of?'

Mr Jasper's play of eyes between the two holds good throughout the dialogue, to the end.

'I have told you once before tonight.'

'You have done nothing of the sort.'

'I tell you I have. That you take a great deal too much upon yourself.'

'You added something else to that, if I remember?'

'Yes, I did say something else.'

'Say it again.'

'I said that in the part of the world I come from, you would be called to account for it.'

'Only there?' cries Edwin Drood, with a contemptuous laugh. 'A long way off, I believe? Yes; I see! That part of the world is at a safe distance.'

'Say here, then,' rejoins the other, rising in a fury. 'Say anywhere! Your vanity is intolerable, your conceit is beyond endurance; you talk as if you were some rare and precious prize, instead of a common boaster. You are a common fellow, and a common boaster.'

'Pooh, pooh,' says Edwin Drood, equally furious, but more collected; 'how should you know? You may know a black common fellow, or a black common boaster, when you see him (and no doubt you have a large acquaintance that way); but you are no judge of white men.'

This insulting allusion to his dark skin infuriates Neville to that violent degree that he flings the dregs of his wine at Edwin Drood, and is in the act of flinging the goblet after it, when his arm is caught in the nick of time by Jasper.

'Ned, my dear fellow!' he cries in a loud voice; 'I entreat you, I command you, to be still!' There has been a rush of all the three, and a clattering of glasses and overturning of chairs. 'Mr Neville, for shame! Give this glass to me. Open your hand, sir. I *will* have it!'

But Neville throws him off, and pauses for an instant, in a raging passion, with the goblet yet in his uplifted hand. Then he dashes it down under the grate, with such force that the broken splinters fly out again in a shower; and he leaves the house.

When he first emerges into the night air, nothing around him is still or steady; nothing around him shows like what it is; he only knows that he stands with a bare head in the midst of a blood-red whirl, waiting to be struggled with, and to struggle to the death.

But, nothing happening, and the moon looking down upon him as if he were dead after a fit of wrath, he holds his steam-hammer beating head and heart, and staggers away. Then, he becomes half-conscious of having heard himself bolted and barred out, like a dangerous animal; and thinks what shall he do?

Some wildly passionate ideas of the river dissolve under the spell of the moonlight on the cathedral and the graves, and the remembrance of his sister, and the thought of what he owes to the good man who has but that very day won his confidence and given him his pledge. He repairs to Minor Canon Corner, and knocks softly at the door.

It is Mr Crisparkle's custom to sit up last of the early household, very softly touching his piano and practising his favourite parts in concerted vocal music. The south wind that goes where it lists,[106] by way of Minor Canon Corner on a still night, is not more subdued than Mr Crisparkle at such times, regardful of the slumbers of the china shepherdess.

His knock is immediately answered by Mr Crisparkle himself. When he opens the door, candle in hand, his cheerful face falls, and disappointed amazement is in it.

'Mr Neville! In this disorder! Where have you been?'

'I have been to Mr Jasper's, sir. With his nephew.'

'Come in.'

The minor canon props him by the elbow with a strong hand (in a strictly scientific manner, worthy of his morning trainings), and turns him into his own little book-room, and shuts the door.'

'I have begun ill, sir. I have begun dreadfully ill.'

'Too true. You are not sober, Mr Neville.'

'I am afraid I am not, sir, though I can satisfy you at another time that I have had a very little indeed to drink, and that it overcame me in the strangest and most sudden manner.'

'Mr Neville, Mr Neville,' says the minor canon, shaking his head with a sorrowful smile; 'I have heard that said before.'

'I think – my mind is much confused, but I think – it is equally true of Mr Jasper's nephew, sir.'

'Very likely,' is the dry rejoinder.

'We quarrelled, sir. He insulted me most grossly. He had heated that tigerish blood I told you of today, before then.'

'Mr Neville,' rejoins the minor canon, mildly, but firmly: 'I request you not to speak to me with that clenched right hand. Unclench it, if you please.'

'He goaded me, sir,' pursues the young man, instantly obeying, 'beyond my power of endurance. I cannot say whether or no he meant it at first, but he did it. He certainly meant it at last. In short, sir,' with an irrepressible outburst, 'in the passion into which he lashed me, I would have cut him down if I could, and I tried to do it.'

'You have clenched that hand again,' is Mr Crisparkle's quiet commentary.

'I beg your pardon, sir.'

'You know your room, for I showed you to it before dinner; but I will accompany you to it once more. Your arm, if you please. Softly, for the house is all abed.'

Scooping his hand into the same scientific elbow-rest as before, and backing it up with the inert strength of his arm, as skilfully as a police expert, and with an apparent repose quite unattainable by novices, Mr Crisparkle conducts his pupil to the pleasant and orderly old room prepared for him. Arrived there, the young man throws himself into a chair, and, flinging his arms upon his reading-table, rests his head upon them with an air of wretched self-reproach.

The gentle minor canon has had it in his thoughts to leave the room, without a word. But looking round at the door, and seeing this dejected figure, he turns back to it, touches it with a mild hand, says 'Good-night!' A sob is his only acknowledgment. He might have had many a worse; perhaps, could have had few better.

Another soft knock at the outer door attracts his attention as he goes downstairs. He opens it to Mr Jasper, holding in his hand the pupil's hat.

'We have had an awful scene with him,' says Jasper, in a low voice.

'Has it been so bad as that?'

'Murderous!'

Mr Crisparkle remonstrates: 'No, no, no. Do not use such strong words.'

'He might have laid my dear boy dead at my feet. It is no fault of his, that he did not. But that I was, through the mercy of God, swift and strong with him, he would have cut him down on my hearth.'

The phrase smites home. 'Ah!' thinks Mr Crisparkle, 'his own words!'

'Seeing what I have seen tonight, and hearing what I have heard,' adds Jasper, with great earnestness, 'I shall never know peace of mind when there is danger of those two coming together, with no one else to interfere. It was horrible. There is something of the tiger in his dark blood.'

'Ah!' thinks Mr Crisparkle, 'so he said!'

'You, my dear sir,' pursues Jasper, taking his hand, 'even you, have accepted a dangerous charge.'

'You need have no fear for me, Jasper,' returns Mr Crisparkle, with a quiet smile. 'I have none for myself.'

'I have none for myself,' returns Jasper, with an emphasis on the last pronoun, 'because I am not, nor am I in the way of being, the object of his hostility. But you may be, and my dear boy has been. Good night!'

Mr Crisparkle goes in, with the hat that has so easily, so almost imperceptibly, acquired the right to be hung up in his hall; hangs it up; and goes thoughtfully to bed.

CHAPTER 9

Birds in the Bush

ROSA, HAVING NO RELATION that she knew of in the world, had, from the seventh year of her age, known no home but the Nuns'. House, and no mother but Miss Twinkleton. Her remembrance of her own mother was of a pretty little creature like herself (not much older than herself it seemed to her), who had been brought home in her father's arms, drowned. The fatal accident had happened at a party of pleasure. Every fold and colour in the pretty summer dress, and even the long wet hair, with scattered petals of ruined flowers still clinging to it, as the beloved young figure, in its sad, sad beauty lay upon the bed, were fixed indelibly in Rosa's recollection. So were the wild despair and the subsequent bowed-down grief of her poor young father, who died broken-hearted on the first anniversary of that hard day.

The betrothal of Rosa grew out of the soothing of his year of mental distress by his fast friend and old college companion, Drood: who likewise had been left a widower in his youth. But he, too, went the silent road into which all earthly pilgrimages merge, some sooner, and some later; and thus the young couple had come to be as they were.

The atmosphere of pity surrounding the little orphan girl when she first came to Cloisterham, had never cleared away. It had taken brighter hues as she grew older, happier, prettier; now it had been golden, now roseate, and now azure; but it had always adorned her with some soft light of its own. The general desire to console and caress her, had caused her to be treated in the beginning as a child much younger than her years; the same desire had caused her to be still petted when she was a child no longer. Who should be her favourite, who should anticipate this or that small present, or do her this or that small service; who should take her home for the holidays; who should write to her the oftenest when they were separated, and whom she would most rejoice to see again when they were reunited; even these gentle rivalries were not without their slight dashes of bitterness in the Nuns' House. Well for the poor nuns, in their day, if they hid no harder strife under their veils and rosaries!

Thus Rosa had grown to be an amiable, giddy, wilful, winning little creature; spoilt, in the sense of counting upon kindness from all around her; but not in the sense of repaying it with indifference. Possessing an exhaustless well of affection in her nature, its sparkling waters had freshened and brightened the Nuns' House for years, and yet its depths had never yet been moved: what might betide when that came to pass; what developing changes might fall upon the heedless head, and light heart, then; remained to be seen.

By what means the news that there had been a quarrel between the two young men overnight, involving even some kind of onslaught by Mr Neville upon Edwin Drood, got into Miss Twinkleton's establishment before breakfast, it is impossible to say. Whether it was brought in by the birds of the air,[107] or came blowing in with the very air itself, when the casement windows were set open; whether the baker brought it kneaded into the bread, or the milkman delivered it as part of the adulteration of his milk; or the housemaids, beating the dust out of their mats against the gateposts, received it in exchange deposited on the mats by the town atmosphere; certain it is that the news permeated every gable of the old building before Miss Twinkleton was down, and that Miss Twinkleton herself received it through Mrs Tisher, while yet in the act of dressing; or (as she might have expressed the phrase to a parent or guardian of a mythological turn) of sacrificing to the Graces.[108]

Miss Landless's brother had thrown a bottle at Mr Edwin Drood.

Miss Landless's brother had thrown a knife at Mr Edwin Drood.

A knife became suggestive of a fork; and Miss Landless's brother had thrown a fork at Mr Edwin Drood.

As in the governing precedence of Peter Piper, alleged to have picked the peck of pickled pepper, it was held physically desirable to have evidence of the existence of the peck of pickled pepper which Peter Piper was alleged to have picked;[109] so, in this case, it was held psychologically important to know why Miss Landless's brother threw a bottle, knife or fork – or bottle, knife *and* fork – for the cook had been given to understand it was all three – at Mr Edwin Drood?

Well, then! Miss Landless's brother had said he admired Miss Bud. Mr Edwin Drood had said to Miss Landless's brother that he had no business to admire Miss Bud. Miss Landless's brother had then 'up'd' (this was the cook's exact information) with the bottle, knife, fork and decanter (the decanter now coolly flying at everybody's head, without the least introduction), and thrown them all at Mr Edwin Drood.

Poor little Rosa put a forefinger into each of her ears when these rumours began to circulate, and retired into a corner, beseeching not to be told any more; but Miss Landless, begging permission of Miss Twinkleton to go and speak with her brother, and pretty plainly showing that she would take it if it were not given, struck out the more definite course of going to Mr Crisparkle's for accurate intelligence.

When she came back (being first closeted with Miss Twinkleton, in order that anything objectionable in her tidings might be retained by that discreet filter), she imparted to Rosa only what had really taken place; dwelling with a flushed cheek on the provocation her brother had received, but almost limiting it to that last gross affront as crowning 'some other words between them', and, out of consideration for her new friend, passing lightly over the fact that the other words had originated in her lover's taking things in general so very easily. To Rosa direct, she brought a petition from her brother that she would forgive him; and, having delivered it with sisterly earnestness, made an end of the subject.

It was reserved for Miss Twinkleton to tone down the public mind of the Nuns' House. That lady, therefore, entering in a stately manner what plebeians might have called the schoolroom, but what, in the patrician language of the head of the Nuns' House, was euphuistically, not to say round-aboutedly, denominated 'the apartment allotted to study', and saying with a forensic air, 'Ladies!' all rose. Mrs Tisher at the same time grouped herself behind her chief, as representing Queen Elizabeth's first historical female friend at Tilbury fort.[110] Miss Twinkleton then proceeded to remark that Rumour, ladies, had been represented by the bard of Avon – needless were it to mention the immortal Shakespeare, also called the Swan of his native river,[111] not improbably with some reference to the ancient superstition that that bird of graceful plumage (Miss Jennings will please stand upright) sang sweetly on the approach of death, for which we have no ornithological authority – Rumour,[112] ladies, had been represented by that bard – hem! –

who drew
The celebrated Jew,[113]

as painted full of tongues. Rumour in Cloisterham (Miss Ferdinand will honour me with her attention) was no exception to the great limner's portrait of Rumour elsewhere. A slight *fracas* between two young gentlemen occurring last night within a hundred miles of these peaceful walls (Miss Ferdinand, being apparently incorrigible, will have the kindness to write out this evening, in the original language, the first four fables of our vivacious neighbour, Monsieur La Fontaine)[114] had been very grossly exaggerated by Rumour's voice. In the first alarm and anxiety arising from our sympathy with a sweet young friend, not wholly to be dissociated from one of the gladiators in the bloodless arena in question (the impropriety of Miss Reynolds's appearing to stab herself in the hand with a pin, is far too obvious, and too glaringly unladylike, to be pointed out), we descended from our maiden elevation to discuss this uncongenial and this unfit theme. Responsible enquiries having assured us that it was but one of those 'airy nothings'[115] pointed at by the poet (whose name and date of birth Miss Giggles will supply within half an hour), we would now discard the subject, and concentrate our minds upon the grateful labours of the day.

But the subject so survived all day, nevertheless, that Miss Ferdinand got into new trouble by surreptitiously clapping on a paper moustache at dinner-time, and going through the motions of aiming a water-bottle at Miss Giggles, who drew a tablespoon in defence.

Now, Rosa thought of this unlucky quarrel a great deal, and thought of it with an uncomfortable feeling that she was involved in it, as cause, or consequence, or what not, through being in a false position altogether as to her marriage engagement. Never free from such uneasiness when she was with her affianced husband, it was not likely that she would be free from it when they were apart. Today, too, she was cast in upon herself, and deprived of the relief of talking freely with her new friend, because the quarrel had been with Helena's brother, and Helena undisguisedly avoided the subject as a delicate and difficult one to herself. At this critical time, of all times, Rosa's guardian was announced as having come to see her.

Mr Grewgious had been well selected for his trust, as a man of incorruptible integrity, but certainly for no other appropriate quality discernible on the surface. He was an arid, sandy man, who, if he had been put into a grinding-mill, looked as if he would have ground immediately into high-dried snuff. He had a scanty flat crop of hair, in colour and consistency like some very mangy yellow fur tippet; it was so unlike hair, that it must have been a wig, but for the stupendous improbability of anybody's voluntarily sporting such a head. The little play of feature that his face presented, was cut deep into it, in a few hard curves that made it more like work; and he had certain notches in his forehead, which looked as though Nature had been about to touch them into sensibility or refinement, when she had impatiently thrown away the chisel, and said: 'I really cannot be worried to finish off this man; let him go as he is.'

With too great length of throat at his upper end, and too much anklebone and heel at his lower; with an awkward and hesitating manner; with a shambling walk; and with what is called a near sight – which perhaps prevented his observing how much white cotton stocking he displayed to the public eye, in contrast with his black suit – Mr Grewgious still had some strange capacity in him of making on the whole an agreeable impression.

Mr Grewgious was discovered by his ward, much discomfited by being in Miss Twinkleton's company in Miss Twinkleton's own sacred room. Dim forebodings of being examined in something, and not coming well out of it, seemed to oppress the poor gentleman when found in these circumstances.

'My dear, how do you do? I am glad to see you. My dear, how much improved you are. Permit me to hand you a chair, my dear.'

Miss Twinkleton rose at her little writing-table, saying, with general sweetness, as to the polite universe: 'Will you permit me to retire?'

'By no means, madam, on my account. I beg that you will not move.'

'I must entreat permission to *move*,' returned Miss Twinkleton, repeating the word with a charming grace; 'but I will not withdraw, since you are so obliging. If I wheel my desk to this corner window, shall I be in the way?'

'Madam! In the way!'

'You are very kind. Rosa, my dear, you will be under no restraint, I am sure.'

Here Mr Grewgious, left by the fire with Rosa, said again: 'My dear, how do you do? I am glad to see you, my dear.' And having waited for her to sit down, sat down himself.

'My visits,' said Mr Grewgious, 'are, like those of the angels – not that I compare myself to an angel.'

'No, sir,' said Rosa.

'Not by any means,' assented Mr Grewgious. 'I merely refer to my visits, which are few and far between.[116] The angels are, we know very well, upstairs.'

Miss Twinkleton looked round with a kind of stiff stare.

'I refer, my dear,' said Mr Grewgious, laying his hand on Rosa's, as the possibility thrilled through his frame of his otherwise seeming to take the awful liberty of calling Miss Twinkleton my dear; 'I refer to the other young ladies.'

Miss Twinkleton resumed her writing.

Mr Grewgious, with a sense of not having managed his opening point quite as neatly as he might have desired, smoothed his head from back to front as if he had just dived, and were pressing the water out – this smoothing action, however superfluous, was habitual with him – and took a pocket-book from his coat-pocket, and a stump of black-lead pencil from his waistcoat-pocket.

'I made,' he said, turning the leaves: 'I made a guiding memorandum or so – as I usually do, for I have no conversational powers whatever – to which I will, with your permission, my dear, refer. "Well and happy." Truly. You are well and happy, my dear? You look so.'

'Yes, indeed, sir,' answered Rosa.

'For which,' said Mr Grewgious, with a bend of his head towards the corner window, 'our warmest acknowledgments are due, and I am sure are rendered, to the maternal kindness and the constant care and consideration of the lady whom I have now the honour to see before me.'

This point, again, made but a lame departure from Mr Grewgious, and never got to its destination; for, Miss Twinkleton, feeling that the courtesies required her to be by this time quite outside the conversation, was biting the end of her pen, and looking upward, as waiting for the descent of an idea from any member of the Celestial Nine[117] who might have one to spare.

Mr Grewgious smoothed his smooth head again, and then made another reference to his pocket-book; lining out 'well and happy', as disposed of.

' "Pounds, shillings and pence", is my next note. A dry subject for a young lady, but an important subject too. Life is pounds, shillings, and pence. Death is – ' A sudden recollection of the death of her two parents seemed to stop him, and he said in a softer tone, and evidently inserting the negative as an afterthought: 'Death is *not* pounds, shillings and pence.'

His voice was as hard and dry as himself, and Fancy might have ground it straight, like himself, into high-dried snuff. And yet, through the very limited means of expression that he possessed, he seemed to express kindness. If Nature had but finished him off, kindness might have been recognisable in his face at this moment. But if the notches in his forehead wouldn't fuse together, and if his face would work and couldn't play, what could he do, poor man!

' "Pounds, shillings and pence". You find your allowance always sufficient for your wants, my dear?'

Rosa wanted for nothing, and therefore it was ample.

'And you are not in debt?'

Rosa laughed at the idea of being in debt. It seemed, to her inexperience, a comical vagary of the imagination. Mr Grewgious stretched his near sight to be sure that this was her view of the case. 'Ah!' he said, as comment, with a furtive glance towards Miss Twinkleton, and lining out pounds, shillings and pence: 'I spoke of having got among the angels! So I did!'

Rosa felt what his next memorandum would prove to be, and was blushing and folding a crease in her dress with one embarrassed hand, long before he found it.

' "Marriage". Hem!' Mr Grewgious carried his smoothing hand down over his eyes and nose, and even chin, before drawing his chair a little nearer, and speaking a little more confidentially: 'I now touch, my dear, upon the point that is the direct cause of my troubling you with the present visit. Otherwise, being a particularly angular man, I should not have intruded here. I am the last man to intrude into a sphere for which I am so entirely unfitted. I feel, on these premises, as if I was a bear – with the cramp – in a youthful cotillion.'[118]

His ungainliness gave him enough of the air of his simile to set Rosa off laughing heartily.

'It strikes you in the same light,' said Mr Grewgious, with perfect calmness. 'Just so. To return to my memorandum. Mr Edwin has been to and fro here, as was arranged. You have mentioned that, in your quarterly letters to me. And you like him, and he likes you.'

'I *like* him very much, sir,' rejoined Rosa.

'So I said, my dear,' returned her guardian, for whose ear the timid emphasis was much too fine. 'Good. And you correspond.'

'We write to one another,' said Rosa, pouting, as she recalled their epistolary differences.

'Such is the meaning that I attach to the word "correspond" in this application, my dear,' said Mr Grewgious. 'Good. All goes well, time moves on, and at this next Christmastime it will become necessary, as a matter of form, to give the exemplary lady in the corner window, to whom we are so much indebted, business notice of your departure in the ensuing half-year. Your relations with her are far more than business relations, no doubt; but a residue of business remains in them, and business is business ever. I am a particularly angular man,' proceeded Mr Grewgious, as if it suddenly occurred to him to mention it, 'and I am not used to give anything away. If, for these two reasons, some competent proxy would give *you* away, I should take it very kindly.'

Rosa intimated, with her eyes on the ground, that she thought a substitute might be found, if required.

'Surely, surely,' said Mr Grewgious. 'For instance, the gentleman who teaches dancing here – he would know how to do it with graceful propriety. He would advance and retire in a manner satisfactory to the feelings of the officiating clergyman, and of yourself, and the bridegroom, and all parties concerned. I am – I am a particularly angular man,' said Mr Grewgious, as if he had made up his mind to screw it out at last: 'and should only blunder.'

Rosa sat still and silent. Perhaps her mind had not got quite so far as the ceremony yet, but was lagging on the way there.

'Memorandum, "Will". Now, my dear,' said Mr Grewgious, referring to his notes, disposing of 'Marriage' with his pencil, and taking a paper from his pocket; 'although I have before possessed you with the contents of your father's will, I think it right at this time to leave a certified copy of it in your hands. And although Mr

Edwin is also aware of its contents, I think it right at this time likewise to place a certified copy of it in Mr Jasper's hand – '

'Not in his own!' asked Rosa, looking up quickly. 'Cannot the copy go to Eddy himself?'

'Why, yes, my dear, if you particularly wish it; but I spoke of Mr Jasper as being his trustee.'

'I do particularly wish it, if you please,' said Rosa, hurriedly and earnestly; 'I don't like Mr Jasper to come between us, in any way.'

'It is natural, I suppose,' said Mr Grewgious, 'that your young husband should be all in all. Yes. You observe that I say, I suppose. The fact is, I am a particularly unnatural man, and I don't know from my own knowledge.'

Rosa looked at him with some wonder.

'I mean,' he explained, 'that young ways were never my ways. I was the only offspring of parents far advanced in life, and I half believe I was born advanced in life myself. No personality[119] is intended towards the name you will so soon change when I remark that while the general growth of people seem to have come into existence buds, I seem to have come into existence a chip. I was a chip – and a very dry one – when I first became aware of myself. Respecting the other certified copy, your wish shall be complied with. Respecting your inheritance, I think you know all. It is an annuity of two hundred and fifty pounds. The savings upon that annuity, and some other items to your credit, all duly carried to account, with vouchers, will place you in possession of a lump-sum of money, rather exceeding seventeen hundred pounds. I am empowered to advance the cost of your preparations for your marriage out of that fund. All is told.'

'Will you please tell me,' said Rosa, taking the paper with a prettily knitted brow, but not opening it: 'whether I am right in what I am going to say? I can understand what you tell me, so very much better than what I read in law-writings. My poor papa and Eddy's father made their agreement together, as very dear and firm and fast friends, in order that we, too, might be very dear and firm and fast friends after them?'

'Just so.'

'For the lasting good of both of us, and the lasting happiness of both of us?'

'Just so.'

'That we might be to one another even much more than they had been to one another?'

'Just so.'

'It was not bound upon Eddy, and it was not bound upon me, by any forfeit, in case – '

'Don't be agitated, my dear. In the case that it brings tears into your affectionate eyes even to picture to yourself – in the case of your not marrying one another – no, no forfeiture on either side. You would then have been my ward until you were of age. No worse would have befallen you. Bad enough perhaps!'

'And Eddy?'

'He would have come into his partnership derived from his father, and into its arrears to his credit (if any), on attaining his majority, just as now.'

Rosa, with her perplexed face and knitted brow, bit the corner of her attested copy, as she sat with her head on one side, looking abstractedly on the floor, and smoothing it with her foot.

'In short,' said Mr Grewgious, 'this betrothal is a wish, a senti-ment, a friendly project, tenderly expressed on both sides. That it was strongly felt, and that there was a lively hope that it would prosper, there can be no doubt. When you were both children, you began to be accustomed to it, and it *has* prospered. But circum-stances alter cases; and I made this visit today, partly, indeed principally, to discharge myself of the duty of telling you, my dear, that two young people can only be betrothed in marriage (except as a matter of convenience, and therefore mockery and misery) of their own free will, their own attachment, and their own assurance (it may or it may not prove a mistaken one, but we must take our chance of that) that they are suited to each other, and will make each other happy. Is it to be supposed, for example, that if either of your fathers were living now, and had any mistrust on that subject, his mind would not be changed by the change of circumstances involved in the change of your years? Untenable, unreasonable, inconclusive, and preposterous!'

Mr Grewgious said all this, as if he were reading it aloud; or, still more, as if he were repeating a lesson. So expressionless of any approach to spontaneity were his face and manner.

'I have now, my dear,' he added, blurring out 'Will' with his pencil, 'discharged myself of what is doubtless a formal duty in this case, but still a duty in such a case. Memorandum, "Wishes". My dear, is there any wish of yours that I can further?'

Rosa shook her head, with an almost plaintive air of hesitation in want of help.

'Is there any instruction that I can take from you with reference to your affairs?'

'I – I should like to settle them with Eddy first, if you please,' said Rosa, plaiting the crease in her dress.

'Surely, surely,' returned Mr Grewgious. 'You two should be of one mind in all things. Is the young gentleman expected shortly?'

'He has gone away only this morning. He will be back at Christmas.'

'Nothing could happen better. You will, on his return at Christmas, arrange all matters of detail with him; you will then communicate with me; and I will discharge myself (as a mere business acquaintance) of my business responsibilities towards the accomplished lady in the corner window. They will accrue at that season.' Blurring pencil once again. 'Memorandum, "Leave". Yes. I will now, my dear, take my leave.'

'Could I,' said Rosa, rising, as he jerked out of his chair in his ungainly way: 'could I ask you, most kindly to come to me at Christmas, if I had anything particular to say to you?'

'Why, certainly, certainly,' he rejoined; apparently – if such a word can be used of one who had no apparent lights or shadows about him – complimented by the question. 'As a particularly angular man, I do not fit smoothly into the social circle, and consequently I have no other engagement at Christmastime than to partake, on the twenty-fifth, of a boiled turkey and celery sauce with a – with a particularly angular clerk I have the good fortune to possess, whose father, being a Norfolk farmer, sends him up (the turkey up), as a present to me, from the neighbourhood of Norwich. I should be quite proud of your wishing to see me, my dear. As a professional receiver of rents, so very few people *do* wish to see me that the novelty would be bracing.'

For his ready acquiescence, the grateful Rosa put her hands upon his shoulders, stood on tiptoe, and instantly kissed him.

'Lord bless me!' cried Mr Grewgious. 'Thank you, my dear! The honour is almost equal to the pleasure. Miss Twinkleton, madam, I have had a most satisfactory conversation with my ward, and I will now release you from the encumbrance of my presence.'

'Nay, sir,' rejoined Miss Twinkleton, rising with a gracious condescension: 'say not encumbrance. Not so, by any means. I cannot permit you to say so.'

'Thank you, madam. I have read in the newspapers,' said Mr Grewgious, stammering a little, 'that when a distinguished visitor (not that I am one: far from it) goes to a school (not that this is one: far from it), he asks for a holiday, or some sort of grace. It being now the afternoon in the – college – of which you are the eminent head, the young ladies might gain nothing, except in name, by having the rest of the day allowed them. But if there is any young lady at all under a cloud, might I solicit – '

'Ah, Mr Grewgious, Mr Grewgious!' cried Miss Twinkleton, with a chastely-rallying forefinger. 'Oh, you gentlemen, you gentlemen! Fie for shame, that you are so hard upon us poor maligned disciplinarians of our sex, for your sakes! But as Miss Ferdinand is at present weighed down by an incubus' – Miss Twinkleton might have said a pen-and-ink-ubus[120] of writing out Monsieur La Fontaine – 'go to her, Rosa my dear, and tell her the penalty is remitted, in deference to the intercession of your guardian, Mr Grewgious.'

Miss Twinkleton here achieved a curtsy, suggestive of marvels happening to her respected legs, and which she came out of nobly, three yards behind her starting-point.

As he held it incumbent upon him to call on Mr Jasper before leaving Cloisterham, Mr Grewgious went to the gatehouse, and climbed its postern stair. But Mr Jasper's door being closed, and presenting on a slip of paper the word 'Cathedral', the fact of its being service-time was borne into the mind of Mr Grewgious. So he descended the stair again, and, crossing the Close, paused at the great western folding-door of the cathedral, which stood open on the fine and bright, though short-lived, afternoon, for the airing of the place.

'Dear me,' said Mr Grewgious, peering in, 'it's like looking down the throat of Old Time.'[121]

Old Time heaved a mouldy sigh from tomb and arch and vault; and gloomy shadows began to deepen in corners; and damps began to rise from green patches of stone; and jewels, cast upon the pavement of the nave from stained glass by the declining sun, began to perish. Within the grill-gate of the chancel,[122] up the steps surmounted loomingly by the fast-darkening organ, white robes could be dimly seen, and one feeble voice, rising and falling in a cracked, monotonous mutter, could at intervals be faintly heard. In the free outer air, the river, the green pastures, and the brown arable lands, the teeming hills and dales, were reddened by the sunset; while the distant little windows in windmills and farm homesteads, shone, patches of bright beaten gold. In the cathedral, all became grey, murky and sepulchral, and the cracked monotonous mutter went on like a dying voice, until the organ and the choir burst forth, and drowned it in a sea of music. Then the sea fell, and the dying voice made another feeble effort, and then the sea rose high, and beat its life out, and lashed the roof, and surged among the arches, and pierced the heights of the great tower; and then the sea was dry, and all was still.

Mr Grewgious had by that time walked to the chancel-steps, where he met the living waters coming out.

'Nothing is the matter?' Thus Jasper accosted him, rather quickly. 'You have not been sent for?'

'Not at all, not at all. I came down of my own accord. I have been to my pretty ward's, and am now homeward bound again.'

'You found her thriving?'

'Blooming indeed. Most blooming. I merely came to tell her, seriously, what a betrothal by deceased parents is.'

'And what is it – according to your judgement?'

Mr Grewgious noticed the whiteness of the lips that asked the question, and put it down to the chilling account of the cathedral.

'I merely came to tell her that it could not be considered binding, against any such reason for its dissolution as a want of affection, or want of disposition to carry it into effect, on the side of either party.'

'May I ask, had you any especial reason for telling her that?'

Mr Grewgious answered somewhat sharply: 'The especial reason of doing my duty, sir. Simply that.' Then he added: 'Come, Mr Jasper; I know your affection for your nephew, and that you are quick to feel on his behalf. I assure you that this implies not the least doubt of, or disrespect to, your nephew.'

'You could not,' returned Jasper, with a friendly pressure of his arm, as they walked on side by side, 'speak more handsomely.'

Mr Grewgious pulled off his hat to smooth his head, and, having smoothed it, nodded it contentedly, and put his hat on again.

'I will wager,' said Jasper, smiling – his lips were still so white that he was conscious of it, and bit and moistened them while speaking: 'I will wager that she hinted no wish to be released from Ned.'

'And you will win your wager, if you do,' retorted Mr Grewgious. 'We should allow some margin for little maidenly delicacies in a young motherless creature, under such circumstances, I suppose; it is not in my line; what do you think?'

'There can be no doubt of it.'

'I am glad you say so. Because,' proceeded Mr Grewgious, who had all this time very knowingly felt his way round to action on his remembrance of what she had said of Jasper himself: 'because she seems to have some little delicate instinct that all preliminary arrangements had best be made between Mr Edwin Drood and herself, don't you see? She don't want us, don't you know?'

Jasper touched himself on the breast, and said, somewhat indistinctly: 'You mean me.'

Mr Grewgious touched himself on the breast, and said: 'I mean us. Therefore, let them have their little discussions and councils together, when Mr Edwin Drood comes back here at Christmas; and then you and I will step in, and put the final touches to the business.'

'So, you settled with her that you would come back at Christmas?' observed Jasper. 'I see! Mr Grewgious, as you quite fairly said just now, there is such an exceptional attachment between my nephew and me, that I am more sensitive for the dear, fortunate, happy, happy fellow than for myself. But it is only right that the young lady should be considered, as you have pointed out, and that I should accept my cue from you. I accept it. I understand that at Christmas they will complete their preparations for May, and that their marriage will be put in final train by themselves, and that nothing will remain for us but to put ourselves in train also, and have everything ready for our formal release from our trusts, on Edwin's birthday.'

'That is my understanding,' assented Mr Grewgious, as they shook hands to part. 'God bless them both!'

'God save them both!' cried Jasper.

'I said, bless them,' remarked the former, looking back over his shoulder.

'I said, save them,' returned the latter. 'Is there any difference?'

CHAPTER 10

Smoothing the Way

IT HAS BEEN OFTEN ENOUGH REMARKED that women have a curious power of divining the characters of men, which would seem to be innate and instinctive; seeing that it is arrived at through no patient process of reasoning, that it can give no satisfactory or sufficient account of itself, and that it pronounces in the most confident manner even against accumulated observation on the part of the other sex. But it has not been quite so often remarked that this power (fallible, like every other human attribute) is for the most part absolutely incapable of self-revision; and that when it has delivered an adverse opinion which by all human lights is subsequently proved to have failed, it is undistinguishable from prejudice, in respect of its determination not to be corrected. Nay, the very possibility of contradiction or disproof, however remote, communicates to this feminine judgement from the first, in nine cases out of ten, the weakness attendant on the testimony of an interested witness; so personally and strongly does the fair diviner connect herself with her divination.

'Now, don't you think, ma dear,' said the minor canon to his mother one day as she sat at her knitting in his little book-room, 'that you are rather hard on Mr Neville?'

'No, I do *not*, Sept,' returned the old lady.

'Let us discuss it, ma.'

'I have no objection to discuss it, Sept. I trust, my dear, I am always open to discussion.' There was a vibration in the old lady's cap, as though she internally added: 'and I should like to see the discussion that would change *my* mind!'

'Very good, ma,' said her conciliatory son. 'There is nothing like being open to discussion.'

'I hope not, my dear,' returned the old lady, evidently shut to it.

'Well! Mr Neville, on that unfortunate occasion, commits himself under provocation.'

'And under mulled wine,' added the old lady.

'I must admit the wine. Though I believe the two young men were much alike in that regard.'

'I don't,' said the old lady.

'Why not, ma?'

'Because I *don't*,' said the old lady. 'Still, I am quite open to discussion.'

'But, my dear ma, I cannot see how we are to discuss, if you take that line.'

'Blame Mr Neville for it, Sept, and not me,' said the old lady, with stately severity.

'My dear ma! why Mr Neville?'

'Because,' said Mrs Crisparkle, retiring on first principles, 'he came home intoxicated, and did great discredit to this house, and showed great disrespect to this family.'

'That is not to be denied, ma. He was then, and he is now, very sorry for it.'

'But for Mr Jasper's well-bred consideration in coming up to me, next day, after service, in the nave itself, with his gown still on, and expressing his hope that I had not been greatly alarmed or had my rest violently broken, I believe I might never have heard of that disgraceful transaction,' said the old lady.

'To be candid, ma, I think I should have kept it from you if I could: though I had not decidedly made up my mind. I was following Jasper out, to confer with him on the subject, and to consider the expediency of his and my jointly hushing the thing up on all accounts, when I found him speaking to you. Then it was too late.'

'Too late, indeed, Sept. He was still as pale as gentlemanly ashes at what had taken place in his rooms overnight.'

'If I *had* kept it from you, ma, you may be sure it would have been for your peace and quiet, and for the good of the young men, and in my best discharge of my duty according to my lights.'

The old lady immediately walked across the room and kissed him: saying, 'Of course, my dear Sept, I am sure of that.'

'However, it became the town-talk,' said Mr Crisparkle, rubbing his ear, as his mother resumed her seat, and her knitting, 'and passed out of my power.'

'And I said then, Sept,' returned the old lady, 'that I thought ill of Mr Neville. And I say now, that I think ill of Mr Neville. And I said then, and I say now, that I hope Mr Neville may come to good, but I don't believe he will.' Here the cap vibrated again considerably.

'I am sorry to hear you say so, ma – '

'I am sorry to say so, my dear,' interposed the old lady, knitting on firmly, 'but I can't help it.'

' – for,' pursued the minor canon, 'it is undeniable that Mr Neville is exceedingly industrious and attentive, and that he improves apace, and that he has – I hope I may say – an attachment to me.'

'There is no merit in the last article, my dear,' said the old lady, quickly; 'and if he says there is, I think the worse of him for the boast.'

'But, my dear ma, he never said there was.'

'Perhaps not,' returned the old lady; 'still, I don't see that it greatly signifies.'

There was no impatience in the pleasant look with which Mr Crisparkle contemplated the pretty old piece of china as it knitted; but there was, certainly, a humorous sense of its not being a piece of china to argue with very closely.

'Besides, Sept, ask yourself what he would be without his sister. You know what an influence she has over him; you know what a capacity she has; you know that whatever he reads with you, he reads with her. Give her her fair share of your praise, and how much do you leave for him?'

At these words Mr Crisparkle fell into a little reverie, in which he thought of several things. He thought of the times he had seen the brother and sister together in deep converse over one of his own old college books; now, in the rimy mornings, when he made those sharpening pilgrimages to Cloisterham Weir; now, in the sombre evenings, when he faced the wind at sunset, having climbed his favourite outlook, a beetling fragment of monastery ruin; and the two studious figures passed below him along the margin of the river, in which the town fires and lights already shone, making the landscape bleaker. He thought how the consciousness had stolen upon him that in teaching one, he was teaching two; and how he had almost insensibly adapted his explanations to both minds – that with which his own was daily in contact, and that which he only approached through it. He thought of the gossip that had reached him from the Nuns' House, to the effect that Helena, whom he had mistrusted as so proud and fierce, submitted herself to the fairy-bride (as he called her), and learnt from her what she knew. He thought of the picturesque alliance between those two, externally so very different. He thought – perhaps most of all – could it be that these things were yet but so many weeks old, and had become an integral part of his life?

As, whenever the Reverend Septimus fell a-musing, his good mother took it to be an infallible sign that he 'wanted support', the blooming old lady made all haste to the dining-room closet, to produce from it the support embodied in a glass of Constantia[123] and a home-made biscuit. It was a most wonderful closet, worthy of Cloisterham and of Minor Canon Corner. Above it, a portrait of Handel in a flowing wig[124] beamed down at the spectator, with a knowing air of being up to the contents of the closet, and a musical air of intending to combine all its harmonies in one delicious fugue. No common closet with a vulgar door on hinges, openable all at once, and leaving nothing to be disclosed by degrees, this rare closet had a lock in midair, where two perpendicular slides met; the one falling down, and the other pushing up. The upper slide, on being pulled down (leaving the lower a double mystery), revealed deep shelves of pickle-jars, jam-pots, tin canisters, spice-boxes, and agreeably outlandish vessels of blue and white, the luscious lodgings of preserved tamarinds and ginger. Every benevolent inhabitant of this retreat had his name inscribed upon his stomach. The pickles, in a uniform of rich brown double-breasted buttoned coat, and yellow or sombre drab continuations, announced their portly forms, in printed capitals, as WALNUT, GHERKIN, ONION, CABBAGE, CAULI-FLOWER, MIXED and other members of that noble family. The jams, as being of a less masculine temperament, and as wearing curlpapers, announced themselves in feminine calligraphy, like a soft whisper, to be RASPBERRY, GOOSEBERRY, APRICOT, PLUM, DAMSON, APPLE and PEACH. The scene closing on these charmers, and the lower slide ascending, oranges were revealed, attended by a mighty japanned[125] sugar-box, to temper their acerbity if unripe. Home-made biscuits waited at the Court of these Powers, accompanied by a goodly fragment of plum-cake, and various slender ladies' fingers,[126] to be dipped into sweet wine and kissed. Lowest of all, a compact leaden-vault enshrined the sweet wine and a stock of cordials, whence issued whispers of Seville Orange, Lemon, Almond and Caraway-seed. There was a crowning air upon this closet of closets, of having been for ages hummed through by the cathedral bell and organ, until those venerable bees had made sublimated honey of every-thing in store; and it was always observed that every dipper among the shelves (deep, as has been noticed, and swallowing up head, shoulders and elbows) came forth again mellow-faced, and seeming to have undergone a saccharine transfiguration.

The Reverend Septimus yielded himself up quite as willing a victim to a nauseous medicinal herb-closet, also presided over by the china shepherdess, as to this glorious cupboard. To what amazing infusions of gentian, peppermint, gillie flower, sage, parsley, thyme, rue, rosemary and dandelion did his courageous stomach submit itself! In what wonderful wrappers, enclosing layers of dried leaves, would he swathe his rosy and contented face, if his mother suspected him of a toothache! What botanical blotches would he cheerfully stick upon his cheek, or forehead, if the dear old lady convicted him of an imperceptible pimple there! Into this herbaceous penitentiary, situated on an upper staircase-landing: a low and narrow whitewashed cell, where bunches of dried leaves hung from rusty hooks in the ceiling, and were spread out upon shelves, in company with portentous bottles: would the Reverend Septimus submissively be led, like the highly popular lamb who has so long and unresistingly been led to the slaughter,[127] and there would he, unlike that lamb, bore nobody but himself. Not even doing that much, so that the old lady were busy and pleased, he would quietly swallow what was given him, merely taking a corrective dip of hands and face into one great bowl of dried rose-leaves, and into the other great bowl of dried lavender, and then would go out, as confident in the sweetening powers of

Cloisterham Weir and a wholesome mind, as Lady Macbeth was hopeless of those of all the seas that roll.[128]

In the present instance the good minor canon took his glass of Constantia with an excellent grace, and, so supported to his mother's satisfaction, applied himself to the remaining duties of the day. In their orderly and punctual progress they brought round vesper service and twilight. The cathedral being very cold, he set off for a brisk trot after service; the trot to end in a charge at his favourite fragment of ruin, which was to be carried by storm, without a pause for breath.

He carried it in a masterly manner, and, not breathed even then, stood looking down upon the river. The river at Cloisterham is sufficiently near the sea to throw up oftentimes a quantity of seaweed. An unusual quantity had come in with the last tide, and this, and the confusion of the water, and the restless dipping and flapping of the noisy gulls, and an angry light out seaward beyond the brown-sailed barges that were turning black, foreshadowed a stormy night. In his mind he was contrasting the wild and noisy sea with the quiet harbour of Minor Canon Corner, when Helena and Neville Landless passed below him. He had had the two together in his thoughts all day, and at once climbed down to speak to them together. The footing was rough in an uncertain light for any tread save that of a good climber; but the minor canon was as good a climber as most men, and stood beside them before many good climbers would have been half-way down.

'A wild evening, Miss Landless! Do you not find your usual walk with your brother too exposed and cold for the time of year? Or at all events, when the sun is down, and the weather is driving in from the sea?'

Helena thought not. It was their favourite walk. It was very retired.

'It is very retired,' assented Mr Crisparkle, laying hold of his opportunity straightway, and walking on with them. 'It is a place of all others where one can speak without interruption, as I wish to do. Mr Neville, I believe you tell your sister everything that passes between us?'

'Everything, sir.'

'Consequently,' said Mr Crisparkle, 'your sister is aware that I have repeatedly urged you to make some kind of apology for that unfortunate occurrence which befell on the night of your arrival here.' In saying it he looked to her, and not to him; therefore it was she, and not he, who replied: 'Yes.'

'I call it unfortunate, Miss Helena,' resumed Mr Crisparkle, 'forasmuch as it certainly has engendered a prejudice against Neville. There is a notion about that he is a dangerously passionate fellow, of an uncontrollable and furious temper: he is really avoided as such.'

'I have no doubt he is, poor fellow,' said Helena, with a look of proud compassion at her brother, expressing a deep sense of his being ungenerously treated. 'I should be quite sure of it from your saying so; but what you tell me is confirmed by suppressed hints and references that I meet with every day.'

'Now,' Mr Crisparkle again resumed, in a tone of mild though firm persuasion, 'is not this to be regretted, and ought it not to be amended? These are early days of Neville's in Cloisterham, and I have no fear of his outliving such a prejudice, and proving himself to have been misunderstood. But how much wiser to take action at once, than to trust to uncertain time! Besides, apart from its being politic, it is right. For there can be no question that Neville was wrong.'

'He was provoked,' Helena submitted.

'He was the assailant,' Mr Crisparkle submitted.

They walked on in silence, until Helena raised her eyes to the minor canon's face, and said, almost reproachfully: 'Oh, Mr Crisparkle, would you have Neville throw himself at young Drood's feet, or at Mr Jasper's, who maligns him every day? In your heart you cannot mean it. From your heart you could not do it, if his case were yours.'

'I have represented to Mr Crisparkle, Helena,' said Neville, with a glance of deference towards his tutor, 'that if I could do it from my heart, I would. But I cannot, and I revolt from the pretence. You forget, however, that to put the case to Mr Crisparkle as his own, is to suppose Mr Crisparkle to have done what I did.'

'I ask his pardon,' said Helena.

'You see,' remarked Mr Crisparkle, again laying hold of his opportunity, though with a moderate and delicate touch, 'you both instinctively acknowledge that Neville did wrong. Then why stop short, and not otherwise acknowledge it?'

'Is there no difference,' asked Helena, with a little faltering in her manner; 'between submission to a generous spirit, and submission to a base or trivial one?'

Before the worthy minor canon was quite ready with his argument in reference to this nice distinction, Neville struck in: 'Help me to clear myself with Mr Crisparkle, Helena. Help me to convince him that I cannot be the first to make concessions without mockery and falsehood. My nature must be changed before I can do so, and it is not changed. I am sensible of inexpressible affront, and deliberate aggravation of inexpressible affront, and I am angry. The plain truth is, I am still as angry when I recall that night as I was that night.'

'Neville,' hinted the minor canon, with a steady countenance, 'you have repeated that former action of your hands, which I so much dislike.'

'I am sorry for it, sir, but it was involuntary. I confessed that I was still as angry.'

'And I confess,' said Mr Crisparkle, 'that I hoped for better things.'

'I am sorry to disappoint you, sir, but it would be far worse to deceive you, and I should deceive you grossly if I pretended that you had softened me in this respect. The time may come when your powerful influence will do even that with the difficult pupil whose antecedents you know; but it has not come yet. Is this so, and in spite of my struggles against myself, Helena?'

She, whose dark eyes were watching the effect of what he said on Mr Crisparkle's face, replied – to Mr Crisparkle, not to him: 'It is so.' After a short pause, she answered the slightest look of enquiry conceivable, in her brother's eyes, with as slight an affirmative bend of her own head; and he went on: 'I have never yet had the courage to say to you, sir, what in full openness I ought to have said when you first talked with me on this subject. It is not easy to say, and I have been withheld by a fear of its seeming ridiculous, which is very strong upon me down to this last moment, and might, but for my sister, prevent my being quite open with you even now. I admire Miss Bud, sir, so very much, that I cannot bear her being treated with conceit or indifference; and even if I did not feel that I had an injury against young Drood on my own account, I should feel that I had an injury against him on hers.'

Mr Crisparkle, in utter amazement, looked at Helena for corroboration, and met in her expressive face full corroboration, and a plea for advice.

'The young lady of whom you speak is, as you know, Mr Neville, shortly to be married,' said Mr Crisparkle, gravely; 'therefore your admiration, if it be of that special nature which you seem to indicate, is outrageously misplaced. Moreover, it is monstrous that you should take upon yourself to be the young lady's champion against her chosen husband. Besides, you have seen them only once. The young lady has become your sister's friend; and I wonder that your sister, even on her behalf, has not checked you in this irrational and culpable fancy.'

'She has tried, sir, but uselessly. Husband or no husband, that fellow is incapable of the feeling with which I am inspired towards the beautiful young creature whom he treats like a doll. I say he is as incapable of it, as he is unworthy of her. I say she is sacrificed in being bestowed upon him. I say that I love her, and despise and hate him!' This with a face so flushed, and a gesture so violent, that his sister crossed to his side, and caught his arm, remonstrating, 'Neville, Neville!'

Thus recalled to himself, he quickly became sensible of having lost the guard he had set upon his passionate tendency, and covered his face with his hand, as one repentant and wretched.

Mr Crisparkle, watching him attentively, and at the same time meditating how to proceed, walked on for some paces in silence. Then he spoke: 'Mr Neville, Mr Neville, I am sorely grieved to see in you more traces of a character as sullen, angry and wild as the night now closing in. They are of too serious an aspect to leave me the resource of treating the infatuation you have disclosed as undeserving serious consideration. I give it very serious consideration, and I speak to you accordingly. This feud between you and young Drood must not go on. I cannot permit it to go on any longer, knowing what I now know from you, and you living under my roof. Whatever prejudiced and unauthorised constructions your blind and envious wrath may put upon his character, it is a frank, good-natured character. I know I can trust to it for that. Now, pray observe what I am about to say. On reflection, and on your sister's representation, I am willing to admit that, in making peace with young Drood, you have a right to be met half-way. I will engage that you shall be, and even that young Drood shall make the first advance. This condition fulfilled, you will pledge me the honour of a Christian gentleman that the quarrel is for ever at an end on your side. What may be in your heart when you give him your hand, can only be known to the Searcher of all hearts;[129] but it will never go well with you, if there be any treachery there. So far, as to that; next as to what I must again speak of as your infatuation. I understand it to have been confided to me, and to be known to no other person save your sister and yourself. Do I understand aright?'

Helena answered in a low voice: 'It is only known to us three who are here together.'

'It is not at all known to the young lady, your friend?'

'On my soul, no!'

'I require you, then, to give me your similar and solemn pledge, Mr Neville, that it shall remain the secret it is, and that you will take no other action whatsoever upon it than endeavouring (and that most earnestly) to erase it from your mind. I will not tell you that it will soon pass; I will not tell you that it is the fancy of the moment; I will not tell you that such caprices have their rise and fall among the young and ardent every hour; I will leave you undisturbed in the belief that it has few parallels or none, that it will abide with you a long time, and that it will be very difficult to conquer. So much the more weight shall I attach to the pledge I require from you, when it is unreservedly given.'

The young man twice or thrice essayed to speak, but failed.

'Let me leave you with your sister, whom it is time you took home,' said Mr Crisparkle. 'You will find me alone in my room by and by.'

'Pray do not leave us yet,' Helena implored him. 'Another minute.'

'I should not,' said Neville, pressing his hand upon his face, 'have needed so much as another minute, if you had been less patient with me, Mr Crisparkle, less considerate of me, and less unpretendingly good and true. Oh, if in my childhood I had known such a guide!'

'Follow your guide now, Neville,' murmured Helena, 'and follow him to heaven!'

There was that in her tone which broke the good minor canon's voice, or it would have repudiated her exaltation of him. As it was, he laid a finger on his lips, and looked towards her brother.

'To say that I give both pledges, Mr Crisparkle, out of my innermost heart, and to say that there is no treachery in it, is to say nothing!' Thus Neville, greatly moved. 'I beg your forgiveness for my miserable lapse into a burst of passion.'

'Not mine, Neville, not mine. You know with whom forgiveness lies, as the highest attribute conceivable. Miss Helena, you and your brother are twin children. You came into this world with the same dispositions, and you passed your younger days together surrounded by the same adverse circumstances. What you have overcome in yourself, can you not overcome in him? You see the rock that lies in his course. Who but you can keep him clear of it?'

'Who but you, sir?' replied Helena. 'What is my influence, or my weak wisdom, compared with yours!'

'You have the wisdom of love,' returned the minor canon, 'and it was the highest wisdom ever known upon this earth, remember. As to mine – but the less said of that commonplace commodity the better. Good night!'

She took the hand he offered her, and gratefully and almost

reverently raised it to her lips.

'Tut!' said the minor canon softly, 'I am much overpaid!' and turned away.

Retracing his steps towards the Cathedral Close, he tried, as he went along in the dark, to think out the best means of bringing to pass what he had promised to effect, and what must somehow be done. 'I shall probably be asked to marry them,' he reflected, 'and I would they were married and gone! But this presses first.'

He debated principally whether he should write to young Drood, or whether he should speak to Jasper. The consciousness of being popular with the whole cathedral establishment inclined him to the latter course, and the well-timed sight of the lighted gatehouse decided him to take it. 'I will strike while the iron is hot,' he said, 'and see him now.'

Jasper was lying asleep on a couch before the fire, when, having ascended the postern-stair and received no answer to his knock at the door, Mr Crisparkle gently turned the handle and looked in. Long afterwards he had cause to remember how Jasper sprang from the couch in a delirious state between sleeping and waking, and crying out: 'What is the matter? Who did it?'[130]

'It is only I, Jasper. I am sorry to have disturbed you.'

The glare of his eyes settled down into a look of recognition, and he moved a chair or two, to make a way to the fireside.

'I was dreaming at a great rate, and am glad to be disturbed from an indigestive after-dinner sleep. Not to mention that *you* are always welcome.'

'Thank you. I am not confident,' returned Mr Crisparkle, as he sat himself down in the easy-chair placed for him, 'that my subject will at first sight be quite as welcome as myself; but I am a minister of peace, and I pursue my subject in the interests of peace. In a word, Jasper, I want to establish peace between these two young fellows.'

A very perplexed expression took hold of Mr Jasper's face; a very perplexing expression too, for Mr Crisparkle could make nothing of it.

'How?' was Jasper's enquiry, in a low and slow voice, after a silence.

'For the "how" I come to you. I want to ask you to do me the great favour and service of interposing with your nephew (I have already interposed with Mr Neville), and getting him to write you a short note, in his lively way, saying that he is willing to shake hands. I know what a good-natured fellow he is, and what influence you

Mr Crisparkle is overpaid

have with him. And without in the least defending Mr Neville, we must all admit that he was bitterly stung.'

Jasper turned that perplexed face towards the fire. Mr Crisparkle continuing to observe it, found it even more perplexing than before, inasmuch as it seemed to denote (which could hardly be) some close internal calculation.

'I know that you are not prepossessed in Mr Neville's favour,' the minor canon was going on, when Jasper stopped him: 'You have cause to say so. I am not, indeed.'

'Undoubtedly; and I admit his lamentable violence of temper, though I hope he and I will get the better of it between us. But I have exacted a very solemn promise from him as to his future demeanour towards your nephew, if you do kindly interpose; and I am sure he will keep it.'

'You are always responsible and trustworthy, Mr Crisparkle. Do you really feel sure that you can answer for him so confidently?'

'I do.'

The perplexed and perplexing look vanished.

'Then you relieve my mind of a great dread, and a heavy weight,' said Jasper; 'I will do it.'

Mr Crisparkle, delighted by the swiftness and completeness of his success, acknowledged it in the handsomest terms.

'I will do it,' repeated Jasper, 'for the comfort of having your guarantee against my vague and unformed fears. You will laugh – but do you keep a diary?'

'A line for a day; not more.'

'A line for a day would be quite as much as my uneventful life would need, heaven knows,' said Jasper, taking a book from a desk, 'but that my diary is, in fact, a diary of Ned's life too. You will laugh at this entry; you will guess when it was made:

Past midnight – After what I have just now seen, I have a morbid dread upon me of some horrible consequences resulting to my dear boy, that I cannot reason with or in any way contend against. All my efforts are vain. The demoniacal passion of this Neville Landless, his strength in his fury, and his savage rage for the destruction of its object, appal me. So profound is the impression, that twice since I have gone into my dear boy's room, to assure myself of his sleeping safely, and not lying dead in his blood.

'Here is another entry next morning:

Ned up and away. Light-hearted and unsuspicious as ever. He

laughed when I cautioned him, and said he was as good a man as Neville Landless any day. I told him that might be, but he was not as bad a man. He continued to make light of it, but I travelled with him as far as I could, and left him most unwillingly. I am unable to shake off these dark intangible presentiments of evil – if feelings founded upon staring facts are to be so called.

'Again and again,' said Jasper, in conclusion, twirling the leaves of the book before putting it by, 'I have relapsed into these moods, as other entries show. But I have now your assurance at my back, and shall put it in my book, and make it an antidote to my black humours.'

'Such an antidote, I hope,' returned Mr Crisparkle, 'as will induce you before long to consign the black humours to the flames. I ought to be the last to find any fault with you this evening, when you have met my wishes so freely; but I must say, Jasper, that your devotion to your nephew has made you exaggerative here.'

'You are my witness,' said Jasper, shrugging his shoulders, 'what my state of mind honestly was, that night, before I sat down to write, and in what words I expressed it. You remember objecting to a word I used, as being too strong? It was a stronger word than any in my diary.'

'Well, well. Try the antidote,' rejoined Mr Crisparkle; 'and may it give you a brighter and better view of the case! We will discuss it no more now. I have to thank you for myself, thank you sincerely.'

'You shall find,' said Jasper, as they shook hands, 'that I will not do the thing you wish me to do, by halves. I will take care that Ned, giving way at all, shall give way thoroughly.'

On the third day after this conversation, he called on Mr Crisparkle with the following letter:

My DEAR JACK – I am touched by your account of your interview with Mr Crisparkle, whom I much respect and esteem. At once I openly say that I forgot myself on that occasion quite as much as Mr Landless did, and that I wish that bygone to be a bygone, and all to be right again.

Look here, dear old boy. Ask Mr Landless to dinner on Christmas Eve (the better the day the better the deed), and let there be only we three, and let us shake hands all round there and then, and say no more about it.

My dear Jack, ever your most affectionate,

EDWIN DROOD

PS – Love to Miss Pussy at the next music-lesson.

'You expect Mr Neville, then?' said Mr Crisparkle.

'I count upon his coming,' said Mr Jasper.

CHAPTER 11

A Picture and a Ring

BEHIND THE MOST ANCIENT PART of Holborn, London, where certain gabled houses some centuries of age still stand looking on the public way, as if disconsolately looking for the Old Bourne[131] that has long run dry, is a little nook composed of two irregular quadrangles called Staple Inn.[132] It is one of those nooks the turning into which out of the clashing street imparts to the relieved pedestrian the sensation of having put cotton in his ears, and velvet soles on his boots. It is one of those nooks where a few smoky sparrows twitter in smoky trees, as though they called to one another, 'Let us play at country,' and where a few feet of garden-mould and a few yards of gravel enable them to do that refreshing violence to their tiny understandings. Moreover, it is one of those nooks which are legal nooks, and it contains a little hall, with a little lantern in its roof,[133] to what obstructive purposes devoted, and at whose expense, this history knoweth not.

In the days when Cloisterham took offence at the existence of a railroad afar off, as menacing that sensitive constitution, the property of us Britons, the odd fortune of which sacred institution it is to be in exactly equal degrees croaked about, trembled for, and boasted of, whatever happens to anything, anywhere in the world: in those days no neighbouring architecture of lofty proportions had arisen to overshadow Staple Inn. The westering sun bestowed bright glances on it, and the southwest wind blew into it unimpeded.

Neither wind nor sun, however, favoured Staple Inn one December afternoon towards six o'clock, when it was filled with fog, and candles shed murky and blurred rays through the windows of all its then-occupied sets of chambers; notably from a set of chambers in a corner house in the little inner quadrangle, presenting in black and white over its ugly portal the mysterious inscription:

P
J T
1747 [134]

In which set of chambers, never having troubled his head about the inscription, unless to bethink himself at odd times, on glancing up at it, that haply it might mean Perhaps John Thomas or Perhaps Joe Tyler, sat Mr Grewgious writing by his fire.

Who could have told, by looking at Mr Grewgious, whether he had ever known ambition or disappointment? He had been bred to the bar, and had laid himself out for chamber practice; to draw deeds; 'convey the wise it call,' as Pistol says.[135] But conveyancing and he had made such a very indifferent marriage of it that they had separated by consent – if there can be said to be separation where there has never been coming together.

No. Coy conveyancing would not come to Mr Grewgious. She was wooed, not won, and they went their several ways. But an arbitration being blown towards him by some unaccountable wind, and he gaining great credit in it as one indefatigable in seeking out right and doing right, a pretty fat receivership[136] was next blown into his pocket by a wind more traceable to its source. So, by chance, he had found his niche. Receiver and agent now to two rich estates, and deputing their legal business, in an amount worth having, to a firm of solicitors on the floor below, he had snuffed out his ambition (supposing him to have ever lighted it), and had settled down with his snuffers for the rest of his life under the dry vine and fig tree[137] of PJT, who planted in 1747.

Many accounts and account-books, many files of correspondence, and several strong boxes, garnished Mr Grewgious's room. They can scarcely be represented as having lumbered it, so conscientious and precise was their orderly arrangement. The apprehension of dying suddenly, and leaving one fact or one figure with any incompleteness or obscurity attaching to it, would have stretched Mr Grewgious stone-dead any day. The largest fidelity to a trust was the lifeblood of the man. There are sorts of lifeblood that course more quickly, more gaily, more attractively; but there is no better sort in circulation.

There was no luxury in his room. Even its comforts were limited to its being dry and warm, and having a snug though faded fireside. What may be called its private life was confined to the hearth, and an easy-chair, and an old-fashioned occasional round table that was brought out upon the rug after business hours, from a corner where it elsewise remained turned up like a shining mahogany shield.

Behind it, when standing thus on the defensive, was a closet, usually containing something good to drink. An outer room was the clerk's room; Mr Grewgious's sleeping-room was across the common stair; and he held some not empty cellarage at the bottom of the common stair. Three hundred days in the year, at least, he crossed over to the hotel in Furnival's Inn[138] for his dinner, and after dinner crossed back again, to make the most of these simplicities until it should become broad business day once more, with PJT, date 1747.

As Mr Grewgious sat and wrote by his fire that afternoon, so did the clerk of Mr Grewgious sit and write by *his* fire. A pale, puffy-faced, dark-haired person of thirty, with big dark eyes that wholly wanted lustre, and a dissatisfied doughy complexion, that seemed to ask to be sent to the baker's, this attendant was a mysterious being, possessed of some strange power over Mr Grewgious. As though he had been called into existence, like a fabulous familiar,[139] by a magic spell which had failed when required to dismiss him, he stuck tight to Mr Grewgious's stool, although Mr Grewgious's comfort and convenience would manifestly have been advanced by dispossessing him. A gloomy person, with tangled locks, and a general air of having been reared under the shadow of that baleful tree of Java[140] which has given shelter to more lies than the whole botanical kingdom, Mr Grewgious, nevertheless, treated him with unaccountable consideration.

'Now, Bazzard,' said Mr Grewgious, on the entrance of his clerk: looking up from his papers as he arranged them for the night: 'what is in the wind besides fog?'

'Mr Drood,' said Bazzard.

'What of him?'

'Has called,' said Bazzard.

'You might have shown him in.'

'I am doing it,' said Bazzard.

The visitor came in accordingly.

'Dear me!' said Mr Grewgious, looking round his pair of office candles. 'I thought you had called and merely left your name and gone. How do you do, Mr Edwin? Dear me, you're choking!'

'It's this fog,' returned Edwin; 'and it makes my eyes smart, like cayenne pepper.'

'Is it really so bad as that? Pray undo your wrappers. It is fortunate I have so good a fire; but Mr Bazzard has taken care of me.'

'No I haven't,' said Mr Bazzard at the door.

'Ah! then it follows that I must have taken care of myself without observing it,' said Mr Grewgious. 'Pray be seated in my chair. No. I beg! Coming out of such an atmosphere, in *my* chair.'

THE MYSTERY OF EDWIN DROOD

Edwin took the easy-chair in the corner; and the fog he had brought in with him, and the fog he took off with his greatcoat and neck-shawl, was speedily licked up by the eager fire.

'I look,' said Edwin, smiling, 'as if I had come to stop.'

' – By the by,' cried Mr Grewgious; 'excuse my interrupting you; do stop. The fog may clear in an hour or two. We can have dinner in from just across Holborn. You had better take your Cayenne pepper here than outside; pray stop and dine.'

'You are very kind,' said Edwin, glancing about him as though attracted by the notion of a new and relishing sort of gypsy party.

'Not at all,' said Mr Grewgious; '*you* are very kind to join issue with a bachelor in chambers, and take pot luck. And I'll ask,' said Mr Grewgious, dropping his voice, and speaking with a twinkling eye, as if inspired with a bright thought: 'I'll ask Bazzard. He mightn't like it else. Bazzard!'

Bazzard reappeared.

'Dine presently with Mr Drood and me.'

'If I am ordered to dine, of course I will, sir,' was the gloomy answer.

'Save the man!' cried Mr Grewgious. 'You're not ordered; you're invited.'

'Thank you, sir,' said Bazzard; 'in that case I don't care if I do.'

'That's arranged. And perhaps you wouldn't mind,' said Mr Grewgious, 'stepping over to the hotel in Furnival's, and asking them to send in materials for laying the cloth. For dinner we'll have a tureen of the hottest and strongest soup available, and we'll have the best made-dish[141] that can be recommended, and we'll have a joint (such as a haunch of mutton), and we'll have a goose, or a turkey, or any little stuffed thing of that sort that may happen to be in the bill of fare – in short, we'll have whatever there is on hand.'

These liberal directions Mr Grewgious issued with his usual air of reading an inventory, or repeating a lesson, or doing anything else by rote. Bazzard, after drawing out the round table, withdrew to execute them.

'I was a little delicate, you see,' said Mr Grewgious, in a lower tone, after his clerk's departure, 'about employing him in the foraging or commissariat department. Because he mightn't like it.'

'He seems to have his own way, sir,' remarked Edwin.

'His own way?' returned Mr Grewgious. 'Oh dear no! Poor fellow, you quite mistake him. If he had his own way, he wouldn't be here.'

'I wonder where he would be!' Edwin thought. But he only thought it, because Mr Grewgious came and stood himself with his back to the other corner of the fire, and his shoulder-blades against the chimneypiece, and collected his skirts for easy conversation.

'I take it, without having the gift of prophecy, that you have done me the favour of looking in to mention that you are going down yonder – where I can tell you, you are expected – and to offer to execute any little commission from me to my charming ward, and perhaps to sharpen me up a bit in my proceedings? Eh, Mr Edwin?'

'I called, sir, before going down, as an act of attention.'

'Of attention!' said Mr Grewgious. 'Ah! of course, not of impatience?'

'Impatience, sir?'

Mr Grewgious had meant to be arch – not that he in the remotest degree expressed that meaning – and had brought himself into scarcely supportable proximity with the fire, as if to burn the fullest effect of his archness into himself, as other subtle impressions are burnt into hard metals. But his archness suddenly flying before the composed face and manner of his visitor, and only the fire remaining, he started and rubbed himself.

'I have lately been down yonder,' said Mr Grewgious, rearranging his skirts; 'and that was what I referred to when I said I could tell you you are expected.'

'Indeed, sir! Yes; I knew that Pussy was looking out for me.'

'Do you keep a cat down there?' asked Mr Grewgious.

Edwin coloured a little as he explained: 'I call Rosa Pussy.'

'Oh, really,' said Mr Grewgious, smoothing down his head; 'that's very affable.'

Edwin glanced at his face, uncertain whether or no he seriously objected to the appellation. But Edwin might as well have glanced at the face of a clock.

'A pet name, sir,' he explained again.

'Umps,' said Mr Grewgious, with a nod. But with such an extraordinary compromise between an unqualified assent and a qualified dissent, that his visitor was much disconcerted.

'Did PRosa – ' Edwin began by way of recovering himself.

'PRosa?' repeated Mr Grewgious.

'I was going to say Pussy, and changed my mind; – did she tell you anything about the Landlesses?'

'No,' said Mr Grewgious. 'What is the Landlesses? An estate? A villa? A farm?'

'A brother and sister. The sister is at the Nuns' House, and has become a great friend of P – '

'PRosa's,' Mr Grewgious struck in, with a fixed face.

'She is a strikingly handsome girl, sir, and I thought she might have been described to you, or presented to you perhaps?'

'Neither,' said Mr Grewgious. 'But here is Bazzard.'

Bazzard returned, accompanied by two waiters – an immovable waiter, and a flying waiter; and the three brought in with them as much fog as gave a new roar to the fire. The flying waiter, who had brought everything on his shoulders, laid the cloth with amazing rapidity and dexterity; while the immovable waiter, who had brought nothing, found fault with him. The flying waiter then highly polished all the glasses he had brought, and the immovable waiter looked through them. The flying waiter then flew across Holborn for the soup, and flew back again, and then took another flight for the made-dish, and flew back again, and then took another flight for the joint and poultry, and flew back again, and between whiles took supplementary flights for a great variety of articles, as it was discovered from time to time that the immovable waiter had forgotten them all. But let the flying waiter cleave the air as he might, he was always reproached on his return by the immovable waiter for bringing fog with him, and being out of breath. At the conclusion of the repast, by which time the flying waiter was severely blown, the immovable waiter gathered up the tablecloth under his arm with a grand air, and having sternly (not to say with indignation) looked on at the flying waiter while he set the clean glasses round, directed a valedictory glance towards Mr Grewgious, conveying: 'Let it be clearly understood between us that the reward is mine, and that nil is the claim of this slave,' and pushed the flying waiter before him out of the room.

It was like a highly-finished miniature painting representing My Lords of the Circumlocution Department,[142] Commandership-in-Chief of any sort, Government. It was quite an edifying little picture to be hung on the line in the National Gallery.[143]

As the fog had been the proximate cause of this sumptuous repast, so the fog served for its general sauce. To hear the outdoor clerks sneezing, wheezing, and beating their feet on the gravel was a zest far surpassing Doctor Kitchener's. To bid, with a shiver, the unfortunate flying waiter shut the door before he had opened it, was a condiment of a profounder flavour than Harvey.[144] And here let it be noticed, parenthetically, that the leg of this young man, in its application to the door, evinced the finest sense of touch: always preceding himself and tray (with something of an angling air about it), by some seconds: and always lingering after he and the tray had disappeared, like Macbeth's leg when accompanying him off the stage with reluctance to the assassination of Duncan.[145]

The host had gone below to the cellar, and had brought up bottles of ruby, straw-coloured and golden drinks, which had ripened long ago in lands where no fogs are, and had since lain slumbering in the shade. Sparkling and tingling after so long a nap, they pushed at their corks to help the corkscrew (like prisoners helping rioters to force their gates), and danced out gaily. If PJT in 1747, or in any other year of his period, drank such wines – then, for a certainty, PJT was Pretty Jolly Too.

Externally, Mr Grewgious showed no signs of being mellowed by these glowing vintages. Instead of his drinking them, they might have been poured over him in his high-dried snuff form, and run to waste, for any lights and shades they caused to flicker over his stolid face. Neither was his manner influenced. But, in his wooden way, he had observant eyes for Edwin; and when at the end of dinner, he motioned Edwin back to his own easy-chair in the fireside corner, and Edwin sank luxuriously into it after very brief remonstrance, Mr Grewgious, as he turned his seat round towards the fire too, and smoothed his head and face, might have been seen looking at his visitor between his smoothing fingers.

'Bazzard!' said Mr Grewgious, suddenly turning to him.

'I follow you, sir,' returned Bazzard; who had done his work of consuming meat and drink in a workmanlike manner, though mostly in speechlessness.

'I drink to you, Bazzard; Mr Edwin, success to Mr Bazzard!'

'Success to Mr Bazzard!' echoed Edwin, with a totally unfounded appearance of enthusiasm, and with the unspoken addition: 'What in, I wonder!'

'And may! – ' pursued Mr Grewgious, 'I am not at liberty to be definite – may! – my conversational powers are so very limited that I know I shall not come well out of this – may! – it ought to be put imaginatively, but I have no imagination – may! – the thorn of anxiety is as near the mark as I am likely to get – may it come out at last!'

Mr Bazzard, with a frowning smile at the fire, put a hand into his tangled locks, as if the thorn of anxiety were there; then into his waistcoat, as if it were there; then into his pockets, as if it were there. In all these movements he was closely followed by the eyes of Edwin, as if that young gentleman expected to see the thorn in action. It was not produced, however, and Mr Bazzard merely said: 'I follow you, sir, and I thank you.'

'I am going,' said Mr Grewgious, jingling his glass on the table with one hand, and bending aside under cover of the other, to whisper to Edwin, 'to drink to my ward. But I put Bazzard first. He mightn't like it else.'

This was said with a mysterious wink; or what would have been a wink, if, in Mr Grewgious's hands, it could have been quick enough. So Edwin winked responsively, without the least idea what he meant by doing so.

'And now,' said Mr Grewgious, 'I devote a bumper to the fair and fascinating Miss Rosa. Bazzard, the fair and fascinating Miss Rosa!'

'I follow you, sir,' said Bazzard, 'and I pledge you!'

'And so do I!' said Edwin.

'Lord bless me,' cried Mr Grewgious, breaking the blank silence which of course ensued: though why these pauses *should* come upon us when we have performed any small social rite, not directly inducive of self-examination or mental despondency, who can tell? 'I am a particularly angular man, and yet I fancy (if I may use the word, not having a morsel of fancy) that I could draw a picture of a true lover's state of mind, tonight.'

'Let us follow you, sir,' said Bazzard, 'and have the picture.'

'Mr Edwin will correct it where it's wrong,' resumed Mr Grewgious, 'and will throw in a few touches from the life. I dare say it is wrong in many particulars, and wants many touches from the life, for I was born a chip, and have neither soft sympathies nor soft experiences. Well! I hazard the guess that the true lover's mind is completely permeated by the beloved object of his affections. I hazard the guess that her dear name is precious to him, cannot be heard or repeated without emotion, and is preserved sacred. If he has any distinguishing appellation of fondness for her, it is reserved for her, and is not for common ears. A name that it would be a privilege to call her by, being alone with her own bright self, it would be a liberty, a coldness, an insensibility, almost a breach of good faith, to flaunt elsewhere.'

It was wonderful to see Mr Grewgious sitting bolt upright, with his hands on his knees, continuously chopping this discourse out of himself: much as a charity boy with a very good memory might get his catechism[146] said: and evincing no correspondent emotion whatever, unless in a certain occasional little tingling perceptible at the end of his nose.

'My picture,' Mr Grewgious proceeded, 'goes on to represent (under correction from you, Mr Edwin), the true lover as ever impatient to be in the presence or vicinity of the beloved object of his affections; as caring very little for his case in any other society; and as constantly seeking that. If I was to say seeking that, as a bird seeks its nest, I should make an ass of myself, because that would trench upon[147] what I understand to be poetry; and I am so far from trenching upon poetry at any time, that I never, to my knowledge, got within ten thousand miles of it. And I am besides totally unacquainted with the habits of birds, except the birds of Staple Inn, who seek their nests on ledges, and in gutter-pipes and chimney-pots, not constructed for them by the beneficent hand of nature. I beg, therefore, to be understood as foregoing the bird's-nest. But my picture does represent the true lover as having no existence separable from that of the beloved object of his affections, and as living at once a doubled life and a halved life. And if I do not clearly express what I mean by that, it is either for the reason that, having no conversational powers, I cannot express what I mean, or that, having no meaning, I do not mean what I fail to express. Which, to the best of my belief, is not the case.'

Edwin had turned red and turned white as certain points of this picture came into the light. He now sat looking at the fire, and bit his lip.

'The speculations of an angular man,' resumed Mr Grewgious, still sitting and speaking exactly as before, 'are probably erroneous on so globular a topic. But I figure to myself (subject, as before, to Mr Edwin's correction) that there can be no coolness, no lassitude, no doubt, no indifference, no half-fire and half-smoke state of mind, in a real lover. Pray am I at all near the mark in my picture?'

As abrupt in his conclusion as in his commencement and progress, he jerked this enquiry at Edwin, and stopped when one might have supposed him in the middle of his oration.

'I should say, sir,' stammered Edwin, 'as you refer the question to me – '

'Yes,' said Mr Grewgious, 'I refer it to you, as an authority.'

'I should say, then, sir,' Edwin went on, embarrassed, 'that the picture you have drawn is generally correct; but I submit that perhaps you may be rather hard upon the unlucky lover.'

'Likely so,' assented Mr Grewgious, 'likely so. I am a hard man in the grain.'

'He may not show,' said Edwin, 'all he feels; or he may not – '

There he stopped so long, to find the rest of his sentence, that Mr Grewgious rendered his difficulty a thousand times the greater by unexpectedly striking in with: 'No, to be sure; he *may* not!'

After that, they all sat silent; the silence of Mr Bazzard being occasioned by slumber.

'His responsibility is very great, though,' said Mr Grewgious at length, with his eyes on the fire.

Edwin nodded assent, with *his* eyes on the fire.

'And let him be sure that he trifles with no one,' said Mr Grewgious; 'neither with himself, nor with any other.'

Edwin bit his lip again, and still sat looking at the fire.

'He must not make a plaything of a treasure. Woe betide him if he does! Let him take that well to heart,' said Mr Grewgious.

Though he said these things in short dry sentences, much as the supposititious charity boy just now referred to might have repeated a verse or two from the Book of Proverbs, there was something dreamy (for so literal a man) in the way in which he now shook his right forefinger at the live coals in the grate, and again fell silent.

But not for long. As he sat upright and stiff in his chair, he suddenly rapped his knees, like the carved image of some queer Joss[148] or other coming out of its reverie, and said: 'We must finish this bottle, Mr Edwin. Let me help you. I'll help Bazzard too, though he *is* asleep. He mightn't like it else.'

He helped them both, and helped himself, and drained his glass, and stood it bottom upward on the table, as though he had just caught a bluebottle in it.

'And now, Mr Edwin,' he proceeded, wiping his mouth and hands upon his handkerchief: 'to a little piece of business. You received from me, the other day, a certified copy of Miss Rosa's father's will. You knew its contents before, but you received it from me as a matter of business. I should have sent it to Mr Jasper, but for Miss Rosa's wishing it to come straight to you, in preference. You received it?'

'Quite safely, sir.'

'You should have acknowledged its receipt,' said Mr Grewgious; 'business being business all the world over. However, you did not.'

'I meant to have acknowledged it when I first came in this evening, sir.'

'Not a businesslike acknowledgment,' returned Mr Grewgious; 'however, let that pass. Now, in that document you have observed a few words of kindly allusion to its being left to me to discharge a little trust, confided to me in conversation, at such time as I in my discretion may think best.'

'Yes, sir.'

'Mr Edwin, it came into my mind just now, when I was looking at the fire, that I could, in my discretion, acquit myself of that trust at no better time than the present. Favour me with your attention half a minute.'

He took a bunch of keys from his pocket, singled out by the

candlelight the key he wanted, and then, with a candle in his hand, went to a bureau or escritoire, unlocked it, touched the spring of a little secret drawer, and took from it an ordinary ring-case made for a single ring. With this in his hand, he returned to his chair. As he held it up for the young man to see, his hand trembled.

'Mr Edwin, this rose of diamonds and rubies, delicately set in gold, was a ring belonging to Miss Rosa's mother. It was removed from her dead hand, in my presence, with such distracted grief as I hope it may never be my lot to contemplate again. Hard man as I am, I am not hard enough for that. See how bright these stones shine!' opening the case. 'And yet the eyes that were so much brighter, and that so often looked upon them with a light and a proud heart, have been ashes among ashes, and dust among dust,[149] some years! If I had any imagination (which it is needless to say I have not), I might imagine that the lasting beauty of these stones was almost cruel.'

He closed the case again as he spoke.

'This ring was given to the young lady who was drowned so early in her beautiful and happy career, by her husband, when they first plighted their faith to one another. It was he who removed it from her unconscious hand, and it was he who, when his death drew very near, placed it in mine. The trust in which I received it was that, you and Miss Rosa growing to manhood and womanhood, and your betrothal prospering and coming to maturity, I should give it to you to place upon her finger. Failing those desired results, it was to remain in my possession.'

Some trouble was in the young man's face, and some indecision was in the action of his hand, as Mr Grewgious, looking steadfastly at him, gave him the ring.

'Your placing it on her finger,' said Mr Grewgious, 'will be the solemn seal upon your strict fidelity to the living and the dead. You are going to her, to make the last irrevocable preparations for your marriage. Take it with you.'

The young man took the little case, and placed it in his breast.

'If anything should be amiss, if anything should be even slightly wrong, between you; if you should have any secret consciousness that you are committing yourself to this step for no higher reason than because you have long been accustomed to look forward to it; then,' said Mr Grewgious, 'I charge you once more, by the living and by the dead, to bring that ring back to me!'

Here Bazzard awoke himself by his own snoring; and, as is usual in such cases, sat apoplectically staring at vacancy, as defying vacancy to accuse him of having been asleep.

'Bazzard!' said Mr Grewgious, harder than ever.

'I follow you, sir,' said Bazzard, 'and I have been following you.'

'In discharge of a trust, I have handed Mr Edwin Drood a ring of diamonds and rubies. You see?'

Edwin reproduced the little case, and opened it; and Bazzard looked into it.

'I follow you both, sir,' returned Bazzard, 'and I witness the transaction.'

Evidently anxious to get away and be alone, Edwin Drood now resumed his outer clothing, muttering something about time and appointments. The fog was reported no clearer (by the flying waiter, who alighted from a speculative flight in the coffee interest), but he went out into it; and Bazzard, after his manner, 'followed' him.

Mr Grewgious, left alone, walked softly and slowly to and fro, for an hour and more. He was restless tonight, and seemed dispirited.

'I hope I have done right,' he said. 'The appeal to him seemed necessary. It was hard to lose the ring, and yet it must have gone from me very soon.'

He closed the empty little drawer with a sigh, and shut and locked the escritoire, and came back to the solitary fireside.

'Her ring,' he went on. 'Will it come back to me? My mind hangs about her ring very uneasily tonight. But that is explainable. I have had it so long, and I have prized it so much! I wonder – '

He was in a wondering mood as well as a restless; for, though he checked himself at that point, and took another walk, he resumed his wondering when he sat down again.

'I wonder (for the ten-thousandth time, and what a weak fool I, for what can it signify now!) whether he confided the charge of their orphan child to me because he knew – Good God, how like her mother she has become!

'I wonder whether he ever so much as suspected that someone doted on her, at a hopeless, speechless distance, when he struck in and won her. I wonder whether it ever crept into his mind who that unfortunate someone was!

'I wonder whether I shall sleep tonight! At all events, I will shut out the world with the bedclothes, and try.'

Mr Grewgious crossed the staircase to his raw and foggy bed-room, and was soon ready for bed. Dimly catching sight of his face in the misty looking-glass, he held his candle to it for a moment.

'A likely someone, *you*, to come into anybody's thoughts in such an aspect!' he exclaimed. 'There! there! there! Get to bed, poor man, and cease to jabber!'

With that, he extinguished his light, pulled up the bedclothes around him, and with another sigh shut out the world. And yet there are such unexplored romantic nooks in the unlikeliest men that even old tinderous and touchwoody PJT Possibly Jabbered Thus, at some odd times, in or about 1747.

CHAPTER 12

A Night with Durdles

WHEN MR SAPSEA has nothing better to do, towards evening, and finds the contemplation of his own profundity becoming a little monotonous in spite of the vastness of the subject, he often takes an airing in the Cathedral Close and thereabout. He likes to pass the churchyard with a swelling air of proprietorship, and to encourage in his breast a sort of benignant-landlord feeling, in that he has been bountiful towards that meritorious tenant, Mrs Sapsea, and has publicly given her a prize. He likes to see a stray face or two looking in through the railings, and perhaps reading his inscription. Should he meet a stranger coming from the churchyard with a quick step, he is morally convinced that the stranger is 'with a blush retiring', as monumentally directed.

Mr Sapsea's importance has received enhancement, for he has become Mayor of Cloisterham.[150] Without mayors, and many of them, it cannot be disputed that the whole framework of society – Mr Sapsea is confident that he invented that forcible figure – would fall to pieces. Mayors have been knighted for 'going up' with addresses:[151] explosive machines intrepidly discharging shot and shell into the English Grammar. Mr Sapsea may 'go up' with an address. Rise, Sir Thomas Sapsea! Of such is the salt of the earth.[152]

Mr Sapsea has improved the acquaintance of Mr Jasper, since their first meeting to partake of port, epitaph, backgammon, beef and salad. Mr Sapsea has been received at the gatehouse with kindred hospitality; and on that occasion Mr Jasper seated himself at the piano, and sang to him, tickling his ears – figuratively – long enough to present a considerable area for tickling. What Mr Sapsea likes in that young man is that he is always ready to profit by the wisdom of his elders, and that he is sound, sir, at the core. In proof of which, he sang to Mr Sapsea, that evening, no kickshaw ditties,[153] favourites with national enemies, but gave him the genuine George III home-brewed; exhorting him (as 'my brave boys') to reduce to a smashed condition all other islands but this island, and all continents, peninsulas, isthmuses, promontories, and other geographical forms of land soever, besides sweeping the seas in all directions. In short, he rendered it pretty clear that Providence made a distinct mistake in originating so small a nation of hearts of oak,[154] and so many other verminous peoples.

Mr Sapsea, walking slowly this moist evening near the churchyard with his hands behind him, on the lookout for a blushing and retiring stranger, turns a corner, and comes instead into the goodly presence of the dean, conversing with the verger and Mr Jasper. Mr Sapsea makes his obeisance, and is instantly stricken far more ecclesiastical than any Archbishop of York or Canterbury.[155]

'You are evidently going to write a book about us, Mr Jasper,' quoth the dean; 'to write a book about us. Well! We are very ancient, and we ought to make a good book. We are not so richly endowed in possessions as in age; but perhaps you will put *that* in your book, among other things, and call attention to our wrongs.'

Mr Tope, as in duty bound, is greatly entertained by this.

'I really have no intention at all, sir,' replies Jasper, 'of turning author or archaeologist. It is but a whim of mine. And even for my whim, Mr Sapsea here is more accountable than I am.'

'How so, Mr Mayor?' says the dean, with a nod of good-natured recognition of his fetch.[156] 'How is that, Mr Mayor?'

'I am not aware,' Mr Sapsea remarks, looking about him for information, 'to what the Very Reverend the Dean does me the honour of referring.' And then falls to studying his original in minute points of detail.

'Durdles,' Mr Tope hints.

'Ay!' the dean echoes; 'Durdles, Durdles!'

'The truth is, sir,' explains Jasper, 'that my curiosity in the man was first really stimulated by Mr Sapsea. Mr Sapsea's knowledge of mankind and power of drawing out whatever is recluse or odd around him, first led to my bestowing a second thought upon the man: though of course I had met him constantly about. You would not be surprised by this, Mr Dean, if you had seen Mr Sapsea deal with him in his own parlour, as I did.'

'Oh!' cries Sapsea, picking up the ball thrown to him with

ineffable complacency and pomposity; 'yes, yes. The Very Reverend the Dean refers to that? Yes. I happened to bring Durdles and Mr Jasper together. I regard Durdles as a character.'

'A character, Mr Sapsea, that with a few skilful touches you turn inside out,' says Jasper.

'Nay, not quite that,' returns the lumbering auctioneer. 'I may have a little influence over him, perhaps; and a little insight into his character, perhaps. The Very Reverend the Dean will please to bear in mind that I have seen the world.' Here Mr Sapsea gets a little behind the dean, to inspect his coat-buttons.

'Well!' says the dean, looking about him to see what has become of his copyist: 'I hope, Mr Mayor, you will use your study and knowledge of Durdles to the good purpose of exhorting him not to break our worthy and respected choirmaster's neck; we cannot afford it; his head and voice are much too valuable to us.'

Mr Tope is again highly entertained, and, having fallen into respectful convulsions of laughter, subsides into a deferential murmur, importing that surely any gentleman would deem it a pleasure and an honour to have his neck broken, in return for such a compliment from such a source.

'I will take it upon myself, sir,' observes Sapsea loftily, 'to answer for Mr Jasper's neck. I will tell Durdles to be careful of it. He will mind what *I* say. How is it at present endangered?' he enquires, looking about him with magnificent patronage.

'Only by my making a moonlight expedition with Durdles among the tombs, vaults, towers and ruins,' returns Jasper. 'You remember suggesting, when you brought us together, that as a lover of the picturesque,[157] it might be worth my while?'

'*I* remember!' replies the auctioneer. And the solemn idiot really believes that he does remember.

'Profiting by your hint,' pursues Jasper, 'I have had some day-rambles with the extraordinary old fellow, and we are to make a moonlight hole-and-corner exploration tonight.'

'And here he is,' says the dean.

Durdles with his dinner-bundle in his hand, is indeed beheld slouching towards them. Slouching nearer, and perceiving the dean, he pulls off his hat, and is slouching away with it under his arm, when Mr Sapsea stops him.

'Mind you take care of my friend,' is the injunction Mr Sapsea lays upon him.

'What friend o' yourn is dead?' asks Durdles. 'No orders has come in for any friend o' yourn.'

Durdles cautions Mr Sapsea against boasting

'I mean my live friend there.'

'Oh! him?' says Durdles. 'He can take care of himself, can Mister Jarsper.'

'But do you take care of him too,' says Sapsea.

Whom Durdles (there being command in his tone) surlily surveys from head to foot.

'With submission to his reverence the dean, if you'll mind what concerns you, Mr Sapsea, Durdles he'll mind what concerns him.'

'You're out of temper,' says Mr Sapsea, winking to the company to observe how smoothly he will manage him. 'My friend concerns me, and Mr Jasper is my friend. And you are my friend.'

'Don't you get into a bad habit of boasting,' retorts Durdles, with a grave cautionary nod. 'It'll grow upon you.'

'You are out of temper,' says Sapsea again; reddening, but again winking to the company.

'I own to it,' returns Durdles; 'I don't like liberties.'

Mr Sapsea winks a third wink to the company, as who should say: 'I think you will agree with me that I have settled *his* business;' and stalks out of the controversy.

Durdles then gives the dean a good evening, and adding, as he puts his hat on, 'You'll find me at home, Mister Jarsper, as agreed, when you want me; I'm a-going home to clean myself,' soon slouches out of sight. This going home to clean himself is one of the man's incomprehensible compromises with inexorable facts; he, and his hat, and his boots, and his clothes, never showing any trace of cleaning, but being uniformly in one condition of dust and grit.

The lamplighter now dotting the quiet Close with specks of light, and running at a great rate up and down his little ladder with that object – his little ladder under the sacred shadow of whose inconvenience generations had grown up, and which all Cloisterham would have stood aghast at the idea of abolishing[158] – the dean withdraws to his dinner, Mr Tope to his tea and Mr Jasper to his piano. There, with no light but that of the fire, he sits chanting choir-music in a low and beautiful voice, for two or three hours; in short, until it has been for some time dark, and the moon is about to rise.

Then he closes his piano softly, softly changes his coat for a pea-jacket,[159] with a goodly wicker-cased bottle in its largest pocket, and putting on a low-crowned, flap-brimmed hat, goes softly out. Why does he move so softly tonight? No outward reason is apparent for it. Can there be any sympathetic reason crouching darkly within him?

Repairing to Durdles's unfinished house, or hole in the city wall, and seeing a light within it, he softly picks his course among the gravestones, monuments, and stony lumber of the yard, already touched here and there, sidewise, by the rising moon. The two journeymen have left their two great saws sticking in their blocks of stone; and two skeleton journeymen out of the Dance of Death[160] might be grinning in the shadow of their sheltering sentry-boxes, about to slash away at cutting out the gravestones of the next two people destined to die in Cloisterham. Likely enough, the two think little of that now, being alive, and perhaps merry. Curious, to make a guess at the two; – or say one of the two!

'Ho! Durdles!'

The light moves, and he appears with it at the door. He would seem to have been 'cleaning himself' with the aid of a bottle, jug and tumbler; for no other cleansing instruments are visible in the bare brick room with rafters overhead and no plastered ceiling, into which he shows his visitor.

'Are you ready?'

'I am ready, Mister Jarsper. Let the old 'uns come out if they dare, when we go among their tombs. My spirit is ready for 'em.'

'Do you mean animal spirits, or ardent?'[161]

'The one's the t'other,' answers Durdles, 'and I mean 'em both.'

He takes a lantern from a hook, puts a match or two in his pocket wherewith to light it, should there be need; and they go out together, dinner-bundle and all.

Surely an unaccountable sort of expedition! That Durdles himself, who is always prowling among old graves and ruins like a ghoul – that he should be stealing forth to climb, and dive, and wander without an object, is nothing extraordinary; but that the choirmaster or anyone else should hold it worth his while to be with him, and to study moonlight effects in such company is another affair. Surely an unaccountable sort of expedition, therefore!

' 'Ware that there mound by the yard-gate, Mister Jarsper.'

'I see it. What is it?'

'Lime.'

Mr Jasper stops, and waits for him to come up, for he lags behind. 'What you call quicklime?'[162]

'Ay!' says Durdles; 'quick enough to eat your boots. With a little handy stirring, quick enough to eat your bones.'

They go on, presently passing the red windows of the Travellers' Twopenny, and emerging into the clear moonlight of the Monks' Vineyard. This crossed, they come to Minor Canon Corner: of which the greater part lies in shadow until the moon shall rise higher in the sky.

The sound of a closing house-door strikes their ears, and two men come out. These are Mr Crisparkle and Neville. Jasper, with a strange and sudden smile upon his face, lays the palm of his hand upon the breast of Durdles, stopping him where he stands.

At that end of Minor Canon Corner the shadow is profound in the existing state of the light: at that end, too, is a piece of old dwarf wall, breast high, the only remaining boundary of what was once a garden, but is now the thoroughfare. Jasper and Durdles would have turned this wall in another instant; but, stopping so short, stand behind it.

'Those two are only sauntering,' Jasper whispers; 'they will go out into the moonlight soon. Let us keep quiet here, or they will detain us, or want to join us, or what not.'

Durdles nods assent, and falls to munching some fragments from his bundle. Jasper folds his arms upon the top of the wall, and, with his chin resting on them, watches. He takes no note whatever of the minor canon, but watches Neville, as though his eye were at the trigger of a loaded rifle, and he had covered him, and were going to fire. A sense of destructive power is so expressed in his face, that even Durdles pauses in his munching, and looks at him, with an unmunched something in his cheek.

Meanwhile Mr Crisparkle and Neville walk to and fro, quietly talking together. What they say cannot be heard consecutively; but Mr Jasper has already distinguished his own name more than once.

'This is the first day of the week,' Mr Crisparkle can be distinctly heard to observe, as they turn back; 'and the last day of the week is Christmas Eve.'

'You may be certain of me, sir.'

The echoes were favourable at those points, but as the two approach, the sound of their talking becomes confused again. The word 'confidence', shattered by the echoes, but still capable of being pieced together, is uttered by Mr Crisparkle. As they draw still nearer, this fragment of a reply is heard: 'Not deserved yet, but shall be, sir.' As they turn away again, Jasper again hears his own name, in connection with the words from Mr Crisparkle: 'Remember that I said I answered for you confidently.' Then the sound of their talk becomes confused again; they halting for a little while, and some earnest action on the part of Neville succeeding. When they move once more, Mr Crisparkle is seen to look up at the sky, and to point before him. They then slowly disappear; passing out into the moonlight at the opposite end of the Corner.

It is not until they are gone, that Mr Jasper moves. But then he turns to Durdles, and bursts into a fit of laughter. Durdles, who still has that suspended something in his cheek, and who sees nothing to laugh at, stares at him until Mr Jasper lays his face down on his arms to have his laugh out. Then Durdles bolts the something, as if desperately resigning himself to indigestion.

Among those secluded nooks there is very little stir or movement after dark. There is little enough in the high tide of the day, but there is next to none at night. Besides that the cheerfully frequented High Street lies nearly parallel to the spot (the old cathedral rising between the two), and is the natural channel in which the Cloisterham traffic flows, a certain awful hush pervades the ancient pile, the cloisters and the churchyard after dark which not many people care to encounter. Ask the first hundred citizens of Cloisterham, met at random in the streets at noon, if they believed in ghosts, and they would tell you no; but put them to choose at night between these eerie precincts and the thoroughfare of shops, and you would find that ninety-nine declared for the longer round and the more frequented way. The cause of this is not to be found in any local superstition that attaches to the precincts – albeit a mysterious lady, with a child in her arms and a rope dangling from her neck, has been seen flitting about there by sundry witnesses as intangible as herself – but it is to be sought in the innate shrinking of dust with the breath of life in it from dust out of which the breath of life has passed; also, in the widely diffused, and almost as widely unacknowledged, reflection: 'If the dead do, under any circumstances, become visible to the living, these are such likely surroundings for the purpose that I, the living, will get out of them as soon as I can.'

Hence, when Mr Jasper and Durdles pause to glance around them, before descending into the crypt by a small side door, of which the latter has a key, the whole expanse of moonlight in their view is utterly deserted. One might fancy that the tide of life was stemmed by Mr Jasper's own gatehouse. The murmur of the tide is heard beyond; but no wave passes the archway, over which his lamp burns red behind his curtain, as if the building were a lighthouse.

They enter, locking themselves in, descend the rugged steps, and are down in the crypt. The lantern is not wanted, for the moonlight strikes in at the groined windows, bare of glass, the broken frames for which cast patterns on the ground. The heavy pillars which support the roof engender masses of black shade, but between them there are lanes of light. Up and down these lanes they walk, Durdles discoursing of the 'old 'uns' he yet counts on disinterring, and slapping a wall in which he considers 'a whole family on 'em' to be stoned and earthed up, just as if he were a familiar friend of the family. The taciturnity of Durdles is for the time overcome by Mr Jasper's wicker bottle, which circulates freely – in the sense, that is to say, that its contents enter freely into Mr Durdles's circulation, while Mr Jasper only rinses his mouth once, and casts forth the rinsing.

They are to ascend the great tower. On the steps by which they rise to the cathedral, Durdles pauses for new store of breath. The steps are very dark, but out of the darkness they can see the lanes of light they have traversed. Durdles seats himself upon a step. Mr Jasper seats himself upon another. The odour from the wicker bottle (which has somehow passed into Durdles's keeping) soon intimates that the cork has been taken out; but this is not ascertainable through the sense of sight, since neither can descry the other. And yet, in talking, they turn to one another, as though their faces could commune together.

'This is good stuff, Mister Jarsper!'

'It is very good stuff, I hope – I bought it on purpose.'

'They don't show, you see, the old 'uns don't, Mister Jarsper!'

'It would be a more confused world than it is, if they could.'

'Well, it *would* lead towards a mixing of things,' Durdles acquiesces: pausing on the remark, as if the idea of ghosts had not previously presented itself to him in a merely inconvenient light, domestically or chronologically. 'But do you think there may be ghosts of other things, though not of men and women?'

'What things? Flower-beds and watering-pots? Horses and harness?'

'No. Sounds.'

'What sounds?'

'Cries.'

'What cries do you mean? Chairs to mend?'[163]

'No. I mean screeches. Now I'll tell you, Mr Jarsper. Wait a bit till I put the bottle right.' Here the cork is evidently taken out again, and replaced again. 'There! *now* it's right! This time last year, only a few days later, I happened to have been doing what was correct by the season, in the way of giving it the welcome it had a right to expect, when them town-boys set on me at their worst. At length I gave 'em the slip, and turned in here. And here I fell asleep. And what woke me? The ghost of a cry. The ghost of one terrific shriek, which shriek was followed by the ghost of the howl of a dog: a long, dismal, woeful howl, such as a dog gives when a person's dead. That was *my* last Christmas Eve.'

'What do you mean?' is the very abrupt, and, one might say, fierce retort.

'I mean that I made enquiries everywhere about, and that no living ears but mine heard either that cry or that howl. So I say they was both ghosts; though why they came to me, I've never made out.'

'I thought you were another kind of man,' says Jasper, scornfully.

'So I thought myself,' answers Durdles with his usual composure; 'and yet I was picked out for it.'

Jasper had risen suddenly, when he asked him what he meant, and he now says, 'Come; we shall freeze here; lead the way.'

Durdles complies, not over-steadily; opens the door at the top of the steps with the key he has already used; and so emerges on the cathedral level, in a passage at the side of the chancel. Here, the moonlight is so very bright again that the colours of the nearest stained-glass window are thrown upon their faces. The appearance of the unconscious Durdles, holding the door open for his companion to follow, as if from the grave, is ghastly enough, with a purple hand across his face, and a yellow splash upon his brow; but he bears the close scrutiny of his companion in an insensible way, although it is prolonged while the latter fumbles among his pockets for a key confided to him that will open an iron gate, and enable them to pass to the staircase of the great tower.

'That and the bottle are enough for you to carry,' he says, giving it to Durdles; 'hand your bundle to me; I am younger and longer-winded than you.' Durdles hesitates for a moment between bundle and bottle; but gives the preference to the bottle as being by far the better company, and consigns the dry weight to his fellow-explorer.

Then they go up the winding staircase of the great tower, toilsomely, turning and turning, and lowering their heads to avoid the stairs above, or the rough stone pivot around which they twist. Durdles has lighted his lantern, by drawing from the cold, hard wall a spark of that mysterious fire which lurks in everything, and, guided by this speck, they clamber up among the cobwebs and the dust. Their way lies through strange places. Twice or thrice they emerge into level, low-arched galleries, whence they can look down into the moonlit nave; and where Durdles, waving his lantern, waves the dim angels' heads upon the corbels of the roof, seeming to watch their progress. Anon they turn into narrower and steeper staircases, and the night-air begins to blow upon them, and the chirp of some startled jackdaw or frightened rook precedes the heavy beating of wings in a confined space, and the beating down of dust and straws upon their heads. At last, leaving their light behind a stair – for it blows fresh up here – they look down on Cloisterham, fair to see in the moonlight: its ruined habitations and sanctuaries of the dead, at the tower's base; its moss-softened red-tiled roofs and redbrick houses of the living, clustered beyond; its river winding down from the mist on the horizon, as though that were its source, and already heaving with a restless knowledge of its approach towards the sea.

Once again, an unaccountable expedition this! Jasper (always moving softly with no visible reason) contemplates the scene, and especially that stillest part of it which the cathedral overshadows. But he contemplates Durdles quite as curiously, and Durdles is by times conscious of his watchful eyes.

Only by times, because Durdles is growing drowsy. As aeronauts[164] lighten the load they carry, when they wish to rise, similarly Durdles has lightened the wicker bottle in coming up. Snatches of sleep surprise him on his legs, and stop him in his talk. A mild fit of calenture[165] seizes him, in which he deems that the ground so far below, is on a level with the tower, and would as lief walk off the tower into the air as not. Such is his state when they begin to come down. And as aeronauts make themselves heavier when they wish to descend, similarly Durdles charges himself with more liquid from the wicker bottle, that he may come down the better.

The iron gate attained and locked – but not before Durdles has tumbled twice, and cut an eyebrow open once – they descend into the crypt again, with the intent of issuing forth as they entered. But, while returning among those lanes of light, Durdles becomes so very uncertain, both of foot and speech, that he half drops, half throws himself down, by one of the heavy pillars, scarcely less heavy than itself, and indistinctly appeals to his companion for forty winks of a second each.

'If you will have it so, or must have it so,' replies Jasper, 'I'll not leave you here. Take them, while I walk to and fro.'

Durdles is asleep at once; and in his sleep he dreams a dream.

It is not much of a dream, considering the vast extent of the domains of dreamland and their wonderful productions; it is only remarkable for being unusually restless and unusually real. He dreams of lying there, asleep, and yet counting his companion's footsteps as he walks to and fro. He dreams that the footsteps die away into distance of time and of space, and that something touches him, and that something falls from his hand. Then something clinks and gropes about, and he dreams that he is alone for so long a time, that the lanes of light take new directions as the moon advances in her course. From succeeding unconsciousness he passes into a dream of slow uneasiness from cold; and painfully awakes to a perception of the lanes of light – really changed, much as he had dreamed – and Jasper walking among them, beating his hands and feet.

'Holloa!' Durdles cries out, unmeaningly alarmed.

'Awake at last?' says Jasper, coming up to him. 'Do you know that your forties have stretched into thousands?'

'No.'

'They have though.'

'What's the time?'

'Hark! The bells are going in the tower!'

They strike four quarters, and then the great bell strikes.

'Two!' cries Durdles, scrambling up; 'why didn't you try to wake me, Mister Jarsper?'

'I did. I might as well have tried to wake the dead – your own family of dead, up in the corner there.'

'Did you touch me?'

'Touch you! Yes. Shook you.'

As Durdles recalls that touching something in his dream, he looks down on the pavement, and sees the key of the crypt door lying close to where he himself lay.

'I dropped you, did I?' he says, picking it up, and recalling that part of his dream. As he gathers himself up again into an upright position, or into a position as nearly upright as he ever maintains, he is again conscious of being watched by his companion.

'Well?' says Jasper, smiling, 'are you quite ready? Pray don't hurry.'

'Let me get my bundle right, Mister Jarsper, and I'm with you.' As he ties it afresh, he is once more conscious that he is very narrowly observed.

'What do you suspect me of, Mister Jarsper?' he asks, with drunken displeasure. 'Let them as has any suspicions of Durdles name 'em.'

'I've no suspicions of you, my good Mr Durdles; but I have suspicions that my bottle was filled with something stiffer than either of us supposed. And I also have suspicions,' Jasper adds, taking it from the pavement and turning it bottom upwards, 'that it's empty.'

Durdles condescends to laugh at this. Continuing to chuckle

when his laugh is over, as though remonstrant with himself on his drinking powers, he rolls to the door and unlocks it. They both pass out, and Durdles relocks it, and pockets his key.

'A thousand thanks for a curious and interesting night,' says Jasper, giving him his hand; 'you can make your own way home?'

'I should think so!' answers Durdles. 'If you was to offer Durdles the affront to show him his way home, he wouldn't go home.

> Durdles wouldn't go home till morning;[166]
> And *then* Durdles wouldn't go home,

Durdles wouldn't.' This with the utmost defiance.

'Good-night, then.'

'Good-night, Mister Jarsper.'

Each is turning his own way, when a sharp whistle rends the silence, and the jargon is yelped out:

> 'Widdy widdy wen!
> I–ket–ches–'im–out–ar–ter–ten,
> Widdy widdy wy!
> Then–'e–don't–go–then–I shy –
> Widdy widdy wake-cock warning!'

Instantly afterwards, a rapid fire of stones rattles at the cathedral wall, and the hideous small boy is beheld opposite, dancing in the moonlight.

'What! Is that baby-devil on the watch there!' cries Jasper in a fury: so quickly roused, and so violent, that he seems an older devil himself. 'I shall shed the blood of that impish wretch! I know I shall do it!' Regardless of the fire, though it hits him more than once, he rushes at Deputy, collars him, and tries to bring him across. But Deputy is not to be so easily brought across. With a diabolical insight into the strongest part of his position, he is no sooner taken by the throat than he curls up his legs, forces his assailant to hang him, as it were, and gurgles in his throat, and screws his body, and twists, as already undergoing the first agonies of strangulation. There is nothing for it but to drop him. He instantly gets himself together, backs over to Durdles, and cries to his assailant, gnashing the great gap in front of his mouth with rage and malice: 'I'll blind yer, s'elp me! I'll stone yer eyes out, s'elp me! If I don't have yer eyesight, bellows me!'[167] At the same time dodging behind Durdles, and snarling at Jasper, now from this side of him, and now from that: prepared, if pounced upon, to dart away in all manner of curvilinear directions, and, if run down after all, to grovel in the dust with one defensive leg up, and cry: 'Now, hit me when I'm down! Do it!'

'Don't hurt the boy, Mister Jarsper,' urges Durdles, shielding him. 'Recollect yourself.'

'He followed us tonight, when we first came here!'

'Yer lie, I didn't!' replies Deputy, in his one form of polite contradiction.

'He has been prowling near us ever since!'

'Yer lie, I haven't,' returns Deputy. 'I'd only jist come out for my 'elth when I see you two a-coming out of the kin-freederel. If

I–ket–ches–'im–out–ar–ter–ten!'

(with the usual rhythm and dance, though dodging behind Durdles) 'it ain't *my* fault, is it?'

'Take him home, then,' retorts Jasper, ferociously, though with a strong check upon himself, 'and let my eyes be rid of the sight of you!'

Deputy, with another sharp whistle, at once expressing his relief, and his commencement of a milder stoning of Mr Durdles, begins stoning that respectable gentleman home, as if he were a reluctant ox. Mr Jasper goes to his gatehouse, brooding. And thus, as everything comes to an end, the unaccountable expedition comes to an end – for the time.

CHAPTER 13

Both at Their Best

MISS TWINKLETON's establishment was about to undergo a serene hush. The Christmas recess was at hand. What had once, and at no remote period, been called, even by the erudite Miss Twinkleton herself, 'the half'; but what was now called, as being more elegant, and more strictly collegiate, 'the term',[168] would expire tomorrow. A noticeable relaxation of discipline had for some few days pervaded the Nuns' House. Club suppers had occurred in the bedrooms, and a dressed tongue had been carved with a pair of scissors, and handed round with the curling tongs. Portions of marmalade had likewise been distributed on a service of plates constructed of curlpaper; and cowslip wine had been quaffed from the small squat measuring glass in which little Rickitts (a junior of weakly constitution) took her steel drops daily.[169] The housemaids had been bribed with various fragments of riband, and sundry pairs of shoes more or less down at heel, to make no mention of crumbs in the beds; the airiest costumes had been worn on these festive occasions; and the daring Miss Ferdinand had even surprised the company with a sprightly solo on the comb-and-curlpaper, until suffocated in her own pillow by two flowing-haired executioners.

Nor were these the only tokens of dispersal. Boxes appeared in the bedrooms (where they were capital at other times), and a surprising amount of packing took place, out of all proportion to the amount packed. Largess, in the form of odds and ends of cold cream and pomatum,[170] and also of hairpins, was freely distributed among the attendants. On charges of inviolable secrecy, confidences were interchanged respecting golden youth of England expected to call 'at home'[171] on the first opportunity. Miss Giggles (deficient in sentiment) did indeed profess that she, for her part, acknowledged such homage by making faces at the golden youth; but this young lady was outvoted by an immense majority.

On the last night before a recess, it was always expressly made a point of honour that nobody should go to sleep, and that ghosts should be encouraged by all possible means. This compact invariably broke down, and all the young ladies went to sleep very soon, and got up very early.

The concluding ceremony came off at twelve o'clock on the day of departure; when Miss Twinkleton, supported by Mrs Tisher, held a drawing-room[172] in her own apartment (the globes already covered with brown Holland),[173] where glasses of white wine and plates of cut pound-cake[174] were discovered on the table. Miss Twinkleton then said: Ladies, another revolving year had brought us round to that festive period at which the finest feelings of our nature bounded in our – Miss Twinkleton was annually going to add 'bosoms', but annually stopped on the brink of that expression, and substituted 'hearts'. Hearts; our hearts. Hem! Again a revolving year, ladies, had brought us to a pause in our studies – let us hope our greatly advanced studies – and, like the mariner in his bark, the warrior in his tent, the captive in his dungeon, and the traveller in his various conveyances, we yearned for home. Did we say, on such an occasion, in the opening words of Mr Addison's impressive tragedy:

> The dawn is overcast, the morning lowers
> And heavily in clouds brings on the day,
> The great, th' important day – ?[175]

Not so. From horizon to zenith all was *couleur de rose*, for all was redolent of our relations and friends. Might *we* find *them* prospering as *we* expected; might *they* find *us* prospering as *they* expected! Ladies, we would now, with our love to one another, wish one another goodbye, and happiness, until we met again. And when the time should come for our resumption of those pursuits which (here a general depression set in all round), pursuits which, pursuits which. . . then let us ever remember what was said by the Spartan general, in words too trite for repetition, at the battle it were superfluous to specify.[176]

The handmaidens of the establishment, in their best caps, then handed the trays, and the young ladies sipped and crumbled, and the bespoken coaches began to choke the street. Then leave-taking was not long about; and Miss Twinkleton, in saluting each young lady's cheek, confided to her an exceedingly neat letter, addressed to her next friend at law,[177] 'with Miss Twinkleton's best compliments' in the corner. This missive she handed with an air as if it had not the least connection with the bill, but were something in the nature of a delicate and joyful surprise.

So many times had Rosa seen such dispersals, and so very little did she know of any other home, that she was contented to remain where she was, and was even better contented than ever before, having her latest friend with her. And yet her latest friendship had a blank place in it of which she could not fail to be sensible. Helena Landless, having been a party to her brother's revelation about Rosa, and having entered into that compact of silence with Mr Crisparkle, shrank from any allusion to Edwin Drood's name. Why she so avoided it, was mysterious to Rosa, but she perfectly perceived the fact. But for the fact, she might have relieved her own little perplexed heart of some of its doubts and hesitations, by taking Helena into her confidence. As it was, she had no such vent: she could only ponder on her own difficulties, and wonder more and more why this avoidance of Edwin's name should last, now that she knew – for so much Helena had told her – that a good understanding was to be re-established between the two young men, when Edwin came down.

It would have made a pretty picture, so many pretty girls kissing Rosa in the cold porch of the Nuns' House, and that sunny little creature peeping out of it (unconscious of sly faces carved on spout and gable peeping at her) and waving farewells to the departing coaches, as if she represented the spirit of rosy youth abiding in the place to keep it bright and warm in its desertion. The hoarse High Street became musical with the cry, in various silvery voices, 'Goodbye, Rosebud darling!' and the effigy of Mr Sapsea's father over the opposite doorway seemed to say to mankind: 'Gentlemen, favour me with your attention to this charming little last lot left behind, and bid with a spirit worthy of the occasion!' Then the staid street, so unwontedly sparkling, youthful and fresh for a few rippling moments, ran dry, and Cloisterham was itself again.

If Rosebud in her bower[178] now waited Edwin Drood's coming with an uneasy heart, Edwin for his part was uneasy too. With far less force of purpose in his composition than the childish beauty, crowned by acclamation fairy queen of Miss Twinkleton's establishment, he had a conscience, and Mr Grewgious had pricked it. That gentleman's steady convictions of what was right and what was wrong in such a case as his, were neither to be frowned aside nor laughed aside. They would not be moved. But for the dinner in Staple Inn, and but for the ring he carried in the breast pocket of his coat, he would have drifted into their wedding-day without another pause for real thought, loosely trusting that all would go well, left alone. But that serious putting him on his truth to the living and the dead had brought him to a check. He must either give the ring to Rosa, or he must take it back. Once put into this narrowed way of action, it was curious that he began to consider Rosa's claims upon him more unselfishly than he had ever considered them before, and began to be less sure of himself than he had ever been in all his easy-going days.

'I will be guided by what she says, and by how we get on,' was his decision, walking from the gatehouse to the Nuns' House. 'Whatever comes of it, I will bear his words in mind, and try to be true to the living and the dead.'

Rosa was dressed for walking. She expected him. It was a bright, frosty day, and Miss Twinkleton had already graciously sanctioned fresh air. Thus they got out together before it became necessary for either Miss Twinkleton, or the deputy high-priest Mrs Tisher, to lay even so much as one of those usual offerings on the shrine of Propriety.

'My dear Eddy,' said Rosa, when they had turned out of the High Street, and had got among the quiet walks in the neighbourhood of the cathedral and the river: 'I want to say something very serious to you. I have been thinking about it for a long, long time.'

'Goodbye, Rosebud darling!'

'I want to be serious with you too, Rosa dear. I mean to be serious and earnest.'

'Thank you, Eddy. And you will not think me unkind because I begin, will you? You will not think I speak for myself only, because I speak first? That would not be generous, would it? And I know you are generous!'

He said, 'I hope I am not ungenerous to you, Rosa.' He called her Pussy no more. Never again.

'And there is no fear,' pursued Rosa, 'of our quarrelling, is there? Because, Eddy,' clasping her hand on his arm, 'we have so much reason to be very lenient to each other!'

'We will be, Rosa.'

'That's a dear good boy! Eddy, let us be courageous. Let us change to brother and sister from this day forth.'

'Never be husband and wife?'

'Never!'

Neither spoke again for a little while. But after that pause he said, with some effort: 'Of course I know that this has been in both our minds, Rosa, and of course I am in honour bound to confess freely that it does not originate with you.'

'No, nor with you, dear,' she returned, with pathetic earnestness. 'That sprung up between us. You are not truly happy in our engagement; I am not truly happy in it. Oh, I am so sorry, so sorry!' And there she broke into tears.

'I am deeply sorry too, Rosa. Deeply sorry for you.'

'And I for you, poor boy! And I for you!'

This pure young feeling, this gentle and forbearing feeling of each towards the other, brought with it its reward in a softening light that seemed to shine on their position. The relations between them did not look wilful, or capricious, or a failure, in such a light; they became elevated into something more self-denying, honourable, affectionate, and true.

'If we knew yesterday,' said Rosa, as she dried her eyes, 'and we did know yesterday, and on many, many yesterdays, that we were far from right together in those relations which were not of our own choosing, what better could we do today than change them? It is natural that we should be sorry, and you see how sorry we both are; but how much better to be sorry now than then!'

'When, Rosa?'

'When it would be too late. And then we should be angry, besides.'

Another silence fell upon them.

'And you know,' said Rosa innocently, 'you couldn't like me then;

and you can always like me now, for I shall not be a drag upon you, or a worry to you. And I can always like you now, and your sister will not tease or trifle with you. I often did when I was not your sister, and I beg your pardon for it.'

'Don't let us come to that, Rosa; or I shall want more pardoning than I like to think of.'

'No, indeed, Eddy; you are too hard, my generous boy, upon yourself. Let us sit down, brother, on these ruins, and let me tell you how it was with us. I think I know, for I have considered about it very much since you were here last time. You liked me, didn't you? You thought I was a nice little thing?'

'Everybody thinks that, Rosa.'

'Do they?' She knitted her brow musingly for a moment, and then flashed out with the bright little induction: 'Well, but say they do. Surely it was not enough that you should think of me only as other people did; now, was it?'

The point was not to be got over. It was not enough.

'And that is just what I mean; that is just how it was with us,' said Rosa. 'You liked me very well, and you had grown used to me, and had grown used to the idea of our being married. You accepted the situation as an inevitable kind of thing, didn't you? It was to be, you thought, and why discuss or dispute it?'

It was new and strange to him to have himself presented to himself so clearly, in a glass of her holding up. He had always patronised her, in his superiority to her share of woman's wit. Was that but another instance of something radically amiss in the terms on which they had been gliding towards a lifelong bondage?

'All this that I say of you is true of me as well, Eddy. Unless it was, I might not be bold enough to say it. Only, the difference between us was, that by little and little there crept into my mind a habit of thinking about it, instead of dismissing it. My life is not so busy as yours, you see, and I have not so many things to think of. So I thought about it very much, and I cried about it very much too (though that was not your fault, poor boy); when all at once my guardian came down, to prepare for my leaving the Nuns' House. I tried to hint to him that I was not quite settled in my mind, but I hesitated and failed, and he didn't understand me. But he is a good, good man. And he put before me so kindly, and yet so strongly, how seriously we ought to consider, in our circumstances, that I resolved to speak to you the next moment we were alone and grave. And if I seemed to come to it easily just now, because I came to it all at once, don't think it was so really, Eddy, for oh! it was very, very hard, and oh! I am very, very sorry!'

Her full heart broke into tears again. He put his arm about her waist, and they walked by the riverside together.

'Your guardian has spoken to me too, Rosa dear. I saw him before I left London.' His right hand was in his breast, seeking the ring; but he checked it, as he thought: 'If I am to take it back, why should I tell her of it?'

'And that made you more serious about it, didn't it, Eddy? And if I had not spoken to you, as I have, you would have spoken to me? I hope you can tell me so? I don't like it to be *all* my doing, though it *is* so much better for us.'

'Yes, I should have spoken; I should have put everything before you; I came intending to do it. But I never could have spoken to you as you have spoken to me, Rosa.'

'Don't say you mean so coldly or unkindly, Eddy, please, if you can help it.'

'I mean so sensibly and delicately, so wisely and affectionately.'

'That's my dear brother!' She kissed his hand in a little rapture. 'The dear girls will be dreadfully disappointed,' added Rosa, laughing, with the dewdrops glistening in her bright eyes. 'They have looked forward to it so, poor pets!'

'Ah! but I fear it will be a worse disappointment to Jack,' said Edwin Drood, with a start. 'I never thought of Jack!'

Her swift and intent look at him as he said the words could no more be recalled than a flash of lightning can. But it appeared as though she would have instantly recalled it, if she could; for she looked down, confused, and breathed quickly.

'You don't doubt its being a blow to Jack, Rosa?'

She merely replied, and that evasively and hurriedly: Why should she? She had not thought about it. He seemed, to her, to have so little to do with it.

'My dear child! can you suppose that anyone so wrapped up in another – Mrs Tope's expression: not mine – as Jack is in me, could fail to be struck all of a heap by such a sudden and complete change in my life? I say sudden, because it will be sudden to *him*, you know.'

She nodded twice or thrice, and her lips parted as if she would have assented. But she uttered no sound, and her breathing was no slower.

'How shall I tell Jack?' said Edwin, ruminating. If he had been less occupied with the thought, he must have seen her singular emotion. 'I never thought of Jack. It must be broken to him, before the town-crier knows it. I dine with the dear fellow tomorrow and next day – Christmas Eve and Christmas Day – but it would never do to spoil his feast-days. He always worries about me, and moddley-coddleys in the merest trifles. The news is sure to overset him. How on earth shall this be broken to Jack?'

'He must be told, I suppose?' said Rosa.

'My dear Rosa! who ought to be in our confidence, if not Jack?'

'My guardian promised to come down, if I should write and ask him. I am going to do so. Would you like to leave it to him?'

'A bright idea!' cried Edwin. 'The other trustee. Nothing more natural. He comes down, he goes to Jack, he relates what we have agreed upon, and he states our case better than we could. He has already spoken feelingly to you, he has already spoken feelingly to me, and he'll put the whole thing feelingly to Jack. That's it! I am not a coward, Rosa, but to tell you a secret, I am a little afraid of Jack.'

'No, no! you are not afraid of him!' cried Rosa, turning white, and clasping her hands.

'Why, sister Rosa, sister Rosa, what do you see from the turret?'[179] said Edwin, rallying her. 'My dear girl!'

'You frightened me.'

'Most unintentionally, but I am as sorry as if I had meant to do it. Could you possibly suppose for a moment, from any loose way of speaking of mine, that I was literally afraid of the dear fond fellow? What I mean is that he is subject to a kind of paroxysm, or fit – I saw him in it once – and I don't know but that so great a surprise, coming upon him direct from me whom he is so wrapped up in, might bring it on perhaps. Which – and this is the secret I was going to tell you – is another reason for your guardian's making the communication. He is so steady, precise and exact that he will talk Jack's thoughts into shape, in no time; whereas with me Jack is always impulsive and hurried, and, I may say, almost womanish.'

Rosa seemed convinced. Perhaps from her own very different point of view of 'Jack', she felt comforted and protected by the interposition of Mr Grewgious between herself and him.

And now, Edwin Drood's right hand closed again upon the ring in its little case, and again was checked by the consideration: 'It is certain, now, that I am to give it back to him; then why should I tell her of it?' That pretty sympathetic nature which could be so sorry for him in the blight of their childish hopes of happiness together, and could so quietly find itself alone in a new world to weave fresh wreaths of such flowers as it might prove to bear, the old world's flowers being withered, would be grieved by those sorrowful jewels; and to what purpose? Why should it be? They were but a sign of broken joys and baseless projects; in their very beauty they were (as the unlikeliest of men had said) almost a cruel satire on the loves, hopes, plans of humanity, which are able to forecast nothing, and are so much brittle dust. Let them be. He would restore them to her guardian when he came down; he in his turn would restore them to the cabinet from which he had unwillingly taken them; and there, like old letters or old vows, or other records of old aspirations come to nothing, they would be disregarded, until, being valuable, they were sold into circulation again, to repeat their former round.

Let them be. Let them lie unspoken of, in his breast. However distinctly or indistinctly he entertained these thoughts, he arrived at the conclusion, Let them be. Among the mighty store of wonderful chains that are forever forging, day and night, in the vast ironworks of time and circumstance, there was one chain forged in the moment of that small conclusion, riveted to the foundations of heaven and earth, and gifted with invincible force to hold and drag.

They walked on by the river. They began to speak of their separate plans. He would quicken his departure from England, and she would remain where she was, at least as long as Helena remained. The poor dear girls should have their disappointment broken to them gently, and, as the first preliminary, Miss Twinkleton should be confided in by Rosa, even in advance of the reappearance of Mr Grewgious. It should be made clear in all quarters that she and Edwin were the best of friends. There had never been so serene an understanding between them since they were first affianced. And yet there was one reservation on each side; on hers, that she intended through her guardian to withdraw herself immediately from the tuition of her music-master; on his, that he did already entertain some wandering speculations whether it might ever come to pass that he would know more of Miss Landless.

The bright, frosty day declined as they walked and spoke together. The sun dipped in the river far behind them, and the old city lay red before them, as their walk drew to a close. The moaning water cast its seaweed duskily at their feet, when they turned to leave its margin; and the rooks hovered above them with hoarse cries, darker splashes in the darkening air.

'I will prepare Jack for my flitting soon,' said Edwin, in a low voice, 'and I will but see your guardian when he comes, and then go before they speak together. It will be better done without my being by. Don't you think so?'

'Yes.'

'We know we have done right, Rosa?'

'Yes.'

'We know we are better so, even now?'

'And shall be far, far better so by and by.'

Still there was that lingering tenderness in their hearts towards the old positions they were relinquishing, that they prolonged their parting. When they came among the elm trees by the cathedral, where they had last sat together, they stopped as by consent, and Rosa raised her face to his, as she had never raised it in the old days; – for they were old already.

'God bless you, dear! Goodbye!'

'God bless you, dear! Goodbye!'

They kissed each other fervently.

'Now, please take me home, Eddy, and let me be by myself.'

'Don't look round, Rosa,' he cautioned her, as he drew her arm through his, and led her away. 'Didn't you see Jack?'

'No! Where?'

'Under the trees. He saw us, as we took leave of each other. Poor fellow! he little thinks we have parted. This will be a blow to him, I am much afraid!'

She hurried on, without resting, and hurried on until they had passed under the gatehouse into the street; once there, she asked: 'Has he followed us? You can look without seeming to. Is he behind?'

'No. Yes, he is! He has just passed out under the gateway. The dear, sympathetic old fellow likes to keep us in sight. I am afraid he will be bitterly disappointed!'

She pulled hurriedly at the handle of the hoarse old bell, and the gate soon opened. Before going in, she gave him one last, wide, wondering look, as if she would have asked him with imploring emphasis: 'Oh! don't you understand?' And out of that look he vanished from her view.

CHAPTER 14

When Shall These Three Meet Again?[180]

CHRISTMAS EVE in Cloisterham. A few strange faces in the streets; a few other faces, half strange and half familiar, once the faces of Cloisterham children, now the faces of men and women who come back from the outer world at long intervals to find the city wonderfully shrunken in size, as if it had not washed by any means well in the meanwhile. To these, the striking of the cathedral clock, and the cawing of the rooks from the cathedral tower, are like voices of their nursery time. To such as these, it has happened in their dying hours afar off, that they have imagined their chamber-floor to be strewn with the autumnal leaves fallen from the elm trees in the Close: so have the rustling sounds and fresh scents of their earliest impressions revived when the circle of their lives was very nearly traced, and the beginning and the end were drawing close together.

Seasonable tokens are about. Red berries shine here and there in the lattices of Minor Canon Corner; Mr and Mrs Tope are daintily sticking sprigs of holly into the carvings and sconces of the cathedral stalls, as if they were sticking them into the coat-button-holes of the dean and chapter. Lavish profusion is in the shops: particularly in the articles of currants, raisins, spices, candied peel and moist sugar.[181] An unusual air of gallantry and dissipation is abroad; evinced in an immense bunch of mistletoe hanging in the greengrocer's shop doorway, and a poor little Twelfth Cake, culminating in the figure of a Harlequin[182] – such a very poor little Twelfth Cake, that one would rather called it a Twenty-Fourth Cake or a Forty-Eighth Cake – to be raffled for at the pastrycook's, terms one shilling per member. Public amusements are not wanting. The waxwork which made so deep an impression on the reflective mind of the Emperor of China[183] is to be seen by particular desire, during Christmas week only, on the premises of the bankrupt livery-stable-keeper up the lane; and a new grand comic Christmas pantomime is to be produced at the theatre: the latter heralded by the portrait of Signor Jacksonini[184] the clown, saying 'How do you do tomorrow?'

quite as large as life, and almost as miserably. In short, Cloisterham is up and doing: though from this description the High School and Miss Twinkleton's are to be excluded. From the former establishment the scholars have gone home, every one of them in love with one of Miss Twinkleton's young ladies (who knows nothing about it); and only the handmaidens flutter occasionally in the windows of the latter. It is noticed, by the by, that these damsels become, within the limits of decorum, more skittish when thus entrusted with the concrete representation of their sex, than when dividing the representation with Miss Twinkleton's young ladies.

Three are to meet at the gatehouse tonight. How does each one of the three get through the day?

Neville Landless, though absolved from his books for the time by Mr Crisparkle – whose fresh nature is by no means insensible to the charms of a holiday – reads and writes in his quiet room, with a concentrated air, until it is two hours past noon. He then sets himself to clearing his table, to arranging his books, and to tearing up and burning his stray papers. He makes a clean sweep of all untidy accumulations, puts all his drawers in order, and leaves no note or scrap of paper undestroyed, save such memoranda as bear directly on his studies. This done, he turns to his wardrobe, selects a few articles of ordinary wear – among them, change of stout shoes and socks for walking – and packs these in a knapsack. This knapsack is new, and he bought it in the High Street yesterday. He also purchased, at the same time and at the same place, a heavy walking-stick; strong in the handle for the grip of the hand, and iron-shod. He tries this, swings it, poises it, and lays it by, with the knapsack, on a window-seat. By this time his arrangements are complete.

He dresses for going out, and is in the act of going – indeed has left his room, and has met the minor canon on the staircase, coming out of his bedroom upon the same storey – when he turns back again for his walking-stick, thinking he will carry it now. Mr Crisparkle, who has paused on the staircase, sees it in his hand on his immediately reappearing, takes it from him, and asks him with a smile how he chooses a stick?

'Really I don't know that I understand the subject,' he answers. 'I chose it for its weight.'

'Much too heavy, Neville; *much* too heavy.'

'To rest upon in a long walk, sir?'

'Rest upon?' repeats Mr Crisparkle, throwing himself into pedestrian form. 'You don't rest upon it; you merely balance with it.'

'I shall know better, with practice, sir. I have not lived in a walking country, you know.'

'True,' says Mr Crisparkle. 'Get into a little training, and we will have a few score miles together. I should leave you nowhere now. Do you come back before dinner?'

'I think not, as we dine early.'

Mr Crisparkle gives him a bright nod and a cheerful goodbye; expressing (not without intention) absolute confidence and ease.

Neville repairs to the Nuns' House, and requests that Miss Landless may be informed that her brother is there, by appointment. He waits at the gate, not even crossing the threshold; for he is on his parole not to put himself in Rosa's way.

His sister is at least as mindful of the obligation they have taken on themselves as he can be, and loses not a moment in joining him. They meet affectionately, avoid lingering there, and walk towards the upper inland country.

'I am not going to tread upon forbidden ground, Helena,' says Neville, when they have walked some distance and are turning; 'you will understand in another moment that I cannot help referring to – what shall I say? – my infatuation.'

'Had you not better avoid it, Neville? You know that I can hear nothing.'

'You can hear, my dear, what Mr Crisparkle has heard, and heard with approval.'

'Yes; I can hear so much.'

'Well, it is this. I am not only unsettled and unhappy myself, but I am conscious of unsettling and interfering with other people. How do I know that, but for my unfortunate presence, you and – and – the rest of that former party, our engaging guardian excepted, might be dining cheerfully in Minor Canon Corner tomorrow? Indeed it probably would be so. I can see too well that I am not high in the old lady's opinion, and it is easy to understand what an irksome clog I must be upon the hospitalities of her orderly house – especially at this time of year – when I must be kept asunder from this person, and there is such a reason for my not being brought into contact with that person, and an unfavourable reputation has preceded me with such another person; and so on. I have put this very gently to Mr Crisparkle, for you know his self-denying ways; but still I have put it. What I have laid much greater stress upon at the same time is that I am engaged in a miserable struggle with myself, and that a little change and absence may enable me to come through it the better. So, the weather being bright and hard, I am going on a walking expedition, and intend taking myself out of everybody's way (my own included, I hope) tomorrow morning.'

'When to come back?'

'In a fortnight.'

'And going quite alone?'

'I am much better without company, even if there were anyone but you to bear me company, my dear Helena.'

'Mr Crisparkle entirely agrees, you say?'

'Entirely. I am not sure but that at first he was inclined to think it rather a moody scheme, and one that might do a brooding mind harm. But we took a moonlight walk last Monday night, to talk it over at leisure, and I represented the case to him as it really is. I showed him that I do want to conquer myself, and that, this evening well got over, it is surely better that I should be away from here just now, than here. I could hardly help meeting certain people walking together here, and that could do no good, and is certainly not the way to forget. A fortnight hence, that chance will probably be over, for the time; and when it again arises for the last time, why, I can again go away. Farther, I really do feel hopeful of bracing exercise and wholesome fatigue. You know that Mr Crisparkle allows such things their full weight in the preservation of his own sound mind in his own sound body,[185] and that his just spirit is not likely to maintain one set of natural laws for himself and another for me. He yielded to my view of the matter, when convinced that I was honestly in earnest; and so, with his full consent, I start tomorrow morning. Early enough to be not only out of the streets, but out of hearing of the bells, when the good people go to church.'

Helena thinks it over, and thinks well of it. Mr Crisparkle doing so, she would do so; but she does originally, out of her own mind, think well of it, as a healthy project, denoting a sincere endeavour and an active attempt at self-correction. She is inclined to pity him, poor fellow, for going away solitary on the great Christmas festival; but she feels it much more to the purpose to encourage him. And she does encourage him.

He will write to her?

He will write to her every alternate day, and tell her all his adventures.

Does he send clothes on in advance of him?

'My dear Helena, no. Travel like a pilgrim, with wallet and staff. My wallet – or my knapsack – is packed, and ready for strapping on; and here is my staff!'

He hands it to her; she makes the same remark as Mr Crisparkle, that it is very heavy; and gives it back to him, asking what wood it is? Iron-wood.

Up to this point he has been extremely cheerful. Perhaps the having to carry his case with her, and therefore to present it in its brightest aspect, has roused his spirits. Perhaps the having done so with success is followed by a revulsion. As the day closes in, and the city-lights begin to spring up before them, he grows depressed.

'I wish I were not going to this dinner, Helena.'

'Dear Neville, is it worthwhile to care much about it? Think how soon it will be over.'

'How soon it will be over!' he repeats gloomily. 'Yes. But I don't like it.'

There may be a moment's awkwardness, she cheeringly represents to him, but it can only last a moment. He is quite sure of himself?

'I wish I felt as sure of everything else, as I feel of myself,' he answers her.

'How strangely you speak, dear! What do you mean?'

'Helena, I don't know. I only know that I don't like it. What a strange dead weight there is in the air!'

She calls his attention to those copperous clouds beyond the river, and says that the wind is rising. He scarcely speaks again, until he takes leave of her, at the gate of the Nuns' House. She does not immediately enter, when they have parted, but remains looking after him along the street. Twice he passes the gatehouse, reluctant to enter. At length, the cathedral clock chiming one quarter, with a rapid turn he hurries in.

And so *he* goes up the postern stair.

Edwin Drood passes a solitary day. Something of deeper moment than he had thought has gone out of his life; and in the silence of his own chamber he wept for it last night. Though the image of Miss Landless still hovers in the background of his mind, the pretty little affectionate creature, so much firmer and wiser than he had supposed, occupies its stronghold. It is with some misgiving of his own unworthiness that he thinks of her, and of what they might have been to one another, if he had been more in earnest some time ago; if he had set a higher value on her; if, instead of accepting his lot in life as an inheritance of course, he had studied the right way to its appreciation and enhancement. And still, for all this, and though there is a sharp heartache in all this, the vanity and caprice of youth sustain that handsome figure of Miss Landless in the background of his mind.

That was a curious look of Rosa's when they parted at the gate. Did it mean that she saw below the surface of his thoughts, and down into their twilight depths? Scarcely that, for it was a look of astonished and keen enquiry. He decides that he cannot understand it, though it was remarkably expressive.

As he only waits for Mr Grewgious now, and will depart immediately after having seen him, he takes a sauntering leave of the ancient city and its neighbourhood. He recalls the time when Rosa and he walked here or there, mere children, full of the dignity of being engaged. Poor children! he thinks, with a pitying sadness.

Finding that his watch has stopped, he turns into the jeweller's shop, to have it wound and set. The jeweller is knowing on the subject of a bracelet, which he begs leave to submit, in a general and quite aimless way. It would suit (he considers) a young bride, to perfection; especially if of a rather diminutive style of beauty. Finding the bracelet but coldly looked at, the jeweller invites attention to a tray of rings for gentlemen; here is a style of ring, now, he remarks – a very chaste signet – which gentlemen are much given to purchasing, when changing their condition. A ring of a very responsible appearance. With the date of their wedding-day engraved inside, several gentlemen have preferred it to any other kind of memento.

The rings are as coldly viewed as the bracelet. Edwin tells the tempter that he wears no jewellery but his watch and chain, which were his father's; and his shirt-pin.

'That I was aware of,' is the jeweller's reply, 'for Mr Jasper dropped in for a watch-glass the other day, and, in fact, I showed these articles to him, remarking that if he *should* wish to make a present to a gentleman relative, on any particular occasion . . . But he said with a smile that he had an inventory in his mind of all the jewellery his gentleman relative ever wore; namely, his watch and chain, and his shirt-pin.' Still (the jeweller considers) that might not apply to all times, though applying to the present time. 'Twenty minutes past two, Mr Drood, I set your watch at. Let me recommend you not to let it run down, sir.'

Edwin takes his watch, puts it on, and goes out, thinking: 'Dear old Jack! If I were to make an extra crease in my neckcloth, he would think it worth noticing!'

He strolls about and about, to pass the time until the dinner-hour. It somehow happens that Cloisterham seems reproachful to him today; has fault to find with him, as if he had not used it well; but is far more pensive with him than angry. His wonted careless-ness is replaced by a wistful looking at, and dwelling upon, all the old landmarks. He will soon be far away, and may never see them again, he thinks. Poor youth! Poor youth!

As dusk draws on, he paces the Monks' Vineyard. He has walked to and fro full half an hour by the cathedral chimes, and it has closed in dark, before he becomes quite aware of a woman crouch-ing on the ground near a wicket gate in a corner. The gate commands a cross by-path, little used in the gloaming, and the figure must have been there all the time, though he has but gradually and lately made it out.

He strikes into that path, and walks up to the wicket. By the light of a lamp near it, he sees that the woman is of a haggard appearance, and that her weazen chin is resting on her hands, and that her eyes are staring – with an unwinking, blind sort of steadfastness – before her.

Always kindly, but moved to be unusually kind this evening, and having bestowed kind words on most of the children and aged people he has met, he at once bends down, and speaks to this woman.

'Are you ill?'

'No, deary,' she answers, without looking at him, and with no departure from her strange blind stare.

'Are you blind?'

'No, deary.'

'Are you lost, homeless, faint? What is the matter, that you stay here in the cold so long, without moving?'

By slow and stiff efforts, she appears to contract her vision until it can rest upon him; and then a curious film passes over her, and she begins to shake.

He straightens himself, recoils a step, and looks down at her in a dread amazement; for he seems to know her.

'Good heaven!' he thinks, next moment. 'Like Jack that night!'

As he looks down at her, she looks up at him, and whimpers: 'My lungs is weak; my lungs is dreffle bad. Poor me, poor me, my cough is rattling dry!' and coughs in confirmation horribly.

'Where do you come from?'

'Come from London, deary.' (Her cough still rending her.)

'Where are you going to?'

'Back to London, deary. I came here, looking for a needle in a haystack, and I ain't found it. Look'ee, deary; give me three-and-sixpence, and don't you be afeard for me. I'll get back to London then, and trouble no one. I'm in a business. Ah, me! It's slack, it's slack, and times is very bad! – but I can make a shift to live by it.'

'Do you eat opium?'

'Smokes it,' she replies with difficulty, still racked by her cough. 'Give me three-and-sixpence, and I'll lay it out well, and get back. If you don't give me three-and-sixpence, don't give me a brass farden. And if you do give me three-and-sixpence, deary, I'll tell you something.'

He counts the money from his pocket, and puts it in her hand. She instantly clutches it tight, and rises to her feet with a croaking laugh of satisfaction.

'Bless ye! Hark'ee, dear gen'l'm'n. What's your Chris'en name?'

'Edwin.'

'Edwin, Edwin, Edwin,' she repeats, trailing off into a drowsy repetition of the word; and then asks suddenly: 'Is the short of that name Eddy?'

'It is sometimes called so,' he replies, with the colour starting to his face.

'Don't sweethearts call it so?' she asks, pondering.

'How should I know?'

'Haven't you a sweetheart, upon your soul?'

'None.'

She is moving away, with another 'Bless ye, and thank'ee, deary!' when he adds: 'You were to tell me something; you may as well do so.'

'So I was, so I was. Well, then. Whisper. You be thankful that your name ain't Ned.'

He looks at her quite steadily as he asks: 'Why?'

'Because it's a bad name to have just now.'

'How a bad name?'

'A threatened name. A dangerous name.'

'The proverb says that threatened men live long,' he tells her, lightly.

'Then Ned – so threatened is he, wherever he may be while I am a-talking to you, deary – should live to all eternity!' replies the woman.

She has leaned forward to say it in his ear, with her forefinger shaking before his eyes, and now huddles herself together, and with another 'Bless ye, and thank'ee!' goes away in the direction of the Travellers' Lodging House.

This is not an inspiriting close to a dull day. Alone, in a sequestered place, surrounded by vestiges of old time and decay, it rather has a tendency to call a shudder into being. He makes for the better-lighted streets, and resolves as he walks on to say nothing of this tonight, but to mention it to Jack (who alone calls him Ned), as an odd coincidence, tomorrow; of course only as a coincidence, and not as anything better worth remembering.

Still, it holds to him, as many things much better worth remembering never did. He has another mile or so to linger out before the dinner-hour; and, when he walks over the bridge and by the river, the woman's words are in the rising wind, in the angry sky, in the troubled water, in the flickering lights. There is some solemn echo of them even in the cathedral chime, which strikes a sudden surprise to his heart as he turns in under the archway of the gatehouse.

And so *he* goes up the postern stair.

John Jasper passes a more agreeable and cheerful day than either of his guests. Having no music-lessons to give in the holiday season, his time is his own, but for the cathedral services. He is early among the shopkeepers, ordering little table luxuries that his nephew likes. His nephew will not be with him long, he tells his provision-dealers, and so must be petted and made much of. While out on his hospitable preparations, he looks in on Mr Sapsea; and mentions that dear Ned and that inflammable young spark of Mr Crisparkle's are to dine at the gatehouse today and make up their difference. Mr Sapsea is by no means friendly towards the inflammable young spark. He says that his complexion is 'un-English'. And when Mr Sapsea has once declared anything to be un-English, he considers that thing everlastingly sunk in the bottomless pit.[186]

John Jasper is truly sorry to hear Mr Sapsea speak thus, for he knows right well that Mr Sapsea never speaks without a meaning, and that he has a subtle trick of being right. Mr Sapsea (by a very remarkable coincidence) is of exactly that opinion.

Mr Jasper is in beautiful voice this day. In the pathetic supplication to have his heart inclined to keep this law,[187] he quite astonishes his fellows by his melodious power. He has never sung difficult music with such skill and harmony, as in this day's anthem. His nervous temperament is occasionally prone to take difficult music a little too quickly; today, his time is perfect.

These results are probably attained through a grand composure of the spirits. The mere mechanism of his throat is a little tender, for he wears, both with his singing-robe and with his ordinary dress, a large black scarf of strong close-woven silk,[188] slung loosely round his neck. But his composure is so noticeable, that Mr Crisparkle speaks of it as they come out from vespers.

'I must thank you, Jasper, for the pleasure with which I have heard you today. Beautiful! Delightful! You could not have so outdone yourself, I hope, without being wonderfully well.'

'I *am* wonderfully well.'

'Nothing unequal,' says the minor canon, with a smooth motion of his hand: 'nothing unsteady, nothing forced, nothing avoided; all thoroughly done in a masterly manner, with perfect self-command.'

'Thank you. I hope so, if it is not too much to say.'

'One would think, Jasper, you had been trying a new medicine for that occasional indisposition of yours.'

'No, really? That's well observed; for I have.'

'Then stick to it, my good fellow,' says Mr Crisparkle, clapping him on the shoulder with friendly encouragement, 'stick to it.'

'I will.'

'I congratulate you,' Mr Crisparkle pursues, as they come out of the cathedral, 'on all accounts.'

'Thank you again. I will walk round to the Corner with you, if you don't object; I have plenty of time before my company come; and I want to say a word to you, which I think you will not be displeased to hear.'

'What is it?'

'Well. We were speaking, the other evening, of my black humours.' Mr Crisparkle's face falls, and he shakes his head deploringly. 'I said, you know, that I should make you an antidote to those black humours; and you said you hoped I would consign them to the flames.'

'And I still hope so, Jasper.'

'With the best reason in the world! I mean to burn this year's diary at the year's end.'

'Because you – ?' Mr Crisparkle brightens greatly as he thus begins.

'You anticipate me. Because I feel that I have been out of sorts, gloomy, bilious, brain-oppressed, whatever it may be. You said I had been exaggerative. So I have.'

Mr Crisparkle's brightened face brightens still more.

'I couldn't see it then, because I *was* out of sorts; but I am in a healthier state now, and I acknowledge it with genuine pleasure. I made a great deal of a very little; that's the fact.'

'It does me good,' cries Mr Crisparkle, 'to hear you say it!'

'A man leading a monotonous life,' Jasper proceeds, 'and getting his nerves, or his stomach, out of order, dwells upon an idea until it loses its proportions. That was my case with the idea in question. So

I shall burn the evidence of my case, when the book is full, and begin the next volume with a clearer vision.'

'This is better,' says Mr Crisparkle, stopping at the steps of his own door to shake hands, 'than I could have hoped.'

'Why, naturally,' returns Jasper. 'You had but little reason to hope that I should become more like yourself. You are always training yourself to be, mind and body, as clear as crystal, and you always are, and never change; whereas I am a muddy, solitary, moping weed. However, I have got over that mope. Shall I wait while you ask if Mr Neville has left for my place? If not, he and I may walk round together.'

'I think,' says Mr Crisparkle, opening the entrance-door with his key, 'that he left some time ago; at least I know he left, and I think he has not come back. But I'll enquire. You won't come in?'

'My company wait,' said Jasper, with a smile.

The minor canon disappears, and in a few moments returns. As he thought, Mr Neville has not come back; indeed, as he remembers now, Mr Neville said he would probably go straight to the gatehouse.

'Bad manners in a host!' says Jasper. 'My company will be there before me! What will you bet that I don't find my company embracing?'

'I will bet – or I would, if ever I did bet,' returns Mr Crisparkle, 'that your company will have a gay entertainer this evening.'

Jasper nods, and laughs good-night! He retraces his steps to the cathedral door, and turns down past it to the gatehouse. He sings, in a low voice and with delicate expression, as he walks along. It still seems as if a false note were not within his power tonight, and as if nothing could hurry or retard him. Arriving thus under the arched entrance of his dwelling, he pauses for an instant in the shelter to pull off that great black scarf, and bang it in a loop upon his arm. For that brief time, his face is knitted and stern. But it immediately clears, as he resumes his singing, and his way.

And so *he* goes up the postern stair.

The red light burns steadily all the evening in the lighthouse on the margin of the tide of busy life. Softened sounds and hum of traffic pass it and flow on irregularly into the lonely precincts; but very little else goes by, save violent rushes of wind. It comes on to blow a boisterous gale.

The precincts are never particularly well lighted; but the strong blasts of wind blowing out many of the lamps (in some instances shattering the frames too, and bringing the glass rattling to the ground), they are unusually dark tonight. The darkness is augmented and confused by flying dust from the earth, dry twigs from the trees, and great ragged fragments from the rooks' nests up in the tower. The trees themselves so toss and creak, as this tangible part of the darkness madly whirls about, that they seem in peril of being torn out of the earth: while ever and again a crack, and a rushing fall, denote that some large branch has yielded to the storm.

No such power of wind has blown for many a winter night. Chimneys topple[189] in the streets, and people hold to posts and corners, and to one another, to keep themselves upon their feet. The violent rushes abate not, but increase in frequency and fury until at midnight, when the streets are empty, the storm goes thundering along them, rattling at all the latches, and tearing at all the shutters, as if warning the people to get up and fly with it rather than have the roofs brought down upon their brains.

Still, the red light burns steadily. Nothing is steady but the red light.

All through the night the wind blows, and abates not. But early in the morning, when there is barely enough light in the east to dim the stars, it begins to lull. From that time, with occasional wild charges, like a wounded monster dying, it drops and sinks; and at full daylight it is dead.

It is then seen that the hands of the cathedral clock are torn off; that lead from the roof has been stripped away, rolled up and blown into the Close; and that some stones have been displaced upon the summit of the great tower. Christmas morning though it be, it is necessary to send up workmen to ascertain the extent of the damage done. These, led by Durdles, go aloft; while Mr Tope and a crowd of early idlers gather down in Minor Canon Corner, shading their eyes and watching for their appearance up there.

This cluster is suddenly broken and put aside by the hands of Mr Jasper; all the gazing eyes are brought down to the earth by his loudly enquiring of Mr Crisparkle, at an open window: 'Where is my nephew?'

'He has not been here. Is he not with you?'

'No. He went down to the river last night, with Mr Neville, to look at the storm, and has not been back. Call Mr Neville!'

'He left this morning, early.'

'Left this morning early? Let me in! let me in!'

There is no more looking up at the tower, now. All the assembled eyes are turned on Mr Jasper, white, half-dressed, panting, and clinging to the rail before the minor canon's house.

CHAPTER 15

Impeached

NEVILLE LANDLESS had started so early and walked at so good a pace, that when the church bells began to ring in Cloisterham for morning service, he was eight miles away. As he wanted his breakfast by that time, having set forth on a crust of bread, he stopped at the next roadside tavern to refresh.

Visitors in want of breakfast – unless they were horses or cattle, for which class of guests there was preparation enough in the way of water-trough and hay – were so unusual at the sign of the Tilted Wagon,[190] that it took a long time to get the wagon into the track of tea and toast and bacon; Neville in the interval, sitting in a sanded parlour, wondering in how long a time after he had gone the sneezy fire of damp faggots would begin to make somebody else warm.

Indeed, the Tilted Wagon, as a cool establishment on the top of a hill, where the ground before the door was puddled with damp hoofs and trodden straw; where a scolding landlady slapped a moist baby (with one red sock on and one wanting), in the bar; where the cheese was cast aground upon a shelf, in company with a mouldy tablecloth and a green-handled knife, in a sort of cast-iron canoe; where the pale-faced bread shed tears of crumb over its shipwreck in another canoe; where the family linen, half washed and half dried, led a public life of lying about; where everything to drink was drunk out of mugs, and everything else was suggestive of a rhyme to mugs; the Tilted Wagon, all these things considered, hardly kept its painted promise of providing good entertainment for man and beast. However, man, in the present case, was not critical, but took what entertainment he could get, and went on again after a longer rest than he needed.

He stopped at some quarter of a mile from the house, hesitating whether to pursue the road, or to follow a cart track between two high hedgerows, which led across the slope of a breezy heath, and evidently struck into the road again by and by. He decided in favour of this latter track, and pursued it with some toil; the rise being steep, and the way worn into deep ruts.

He was labouring along, when he became aware of some other pedestrians behind him. As they were coming up at a faster pace than his, he stood aside, against one of the high banks, to let them pass. But their manner was very curious. Only four of them passed. Other four slackened speed, and loitered as intending to follow him when he should go on. The remainder of the party (half a dozen, perhaps) turned and went back at a great rate.

He looked at the four behind him, and he looked at the four before him. They all returned his look. He resumed his way. The four in advance went on, constantly looking back; the four in the rear came closing up.

When they all ranged out from the narrow track upon the open slope of the heath, and this order was maintained, let him diverge as he would to either side, there was no longer room to doubt that he was beset by these fellows. He stopped, as a last test; and they all stopped.

'Why do you attend upon me in this way?' he asked the whole body. 'Are you a pack of thieves?'

'Don't answer him,' said one of the number; he did not see which. 'Better be quiet.'

'Better be quiet?' repeated Neville. 'Who said so?'

Nobody replied.

'It's good advice, whichever of you skulkers gave it,' he went on angrily. 'I will not submit to be penned in between four men there, and four men there. I wish to pass, and I mean to pass, those four in front.'

They were all standing still; himself included.

'If eight men, or four men, or two men, set upon one,' he proceeded, growing more enraged, 'the one has no chance but to set his mark upon some of them.[191] And, by the Lord, I'll do that little, if I am interrupted any farther!'

Shouldering his heavy stick, and quickening his pace, he shot on to pass the four ahead. The largest and strongest man of the number changed swiftly to the side on which he came up, and dexterously closed with him and went down with him; but not before the heavy stick had descended smartly.

'Let him be!' said this man in a suppressed voice, as they struggled together on the grass. 'Fair play! His is the build of a girl to mine, and he's got a weight strapped to his back besides. Let him alone. I'll manage him.'

After a little rolling about, in a close scuffle which caused the faces of both to be besmeared with blood, the man took his knee from Neville's chest, and rose, saying: 'There! Now take him arm-in-arm, any two of you!'

It was immediately done.

'As to our being a pack of thieves, Mr Landless,' said the man, as he spat out some blood, and wiped more from his face; 'you know better than that at midday. We wouldn't have touched you if you hadn't forced us. We're going to take you round to the high road, anyhow, and you'll find help enough against thieves there, if you want it. Wipe his face, somebody; see how it's a-trickling down him!'

When his face was cleansed, Neville recognised in the speaker Joe, driver of the Cloisterham omnibus, whom he had seen but once, and that on the day of his arrival.

'And what I recommend you for the present is, don't talk, Mr Landless. You'll find a friend waiting for you, at the high road – gone ahead by the other way when we split into two parties – and you had much better say nothing till you come up with him. Bring that stick along, somebody else, and let's be moving!'

Utterly bewildered, Neville stared around him and said not a word. Walking between his two conductors, who held his arms in theirs, he went on, as in a dream, until they came again into the high road, and into the midst of a little group of people. The men who had turned back were among the group; and its central figures were Mr Jasper and Mr Crisparkle. Neville's conductors took him up to the minor canon, and there released him, as an act of deference to that gentleman.

'What is all this, sir? What is the matter? I feel as if I had lost my senses!' cried Neville, the group closing in around him.

'Where is my nephew?' asked Mr Jasper, wildly.

'Where is your nephew?' repeated Neville. 'Why do you ask me?'[192]

'I ask you,' retorted Jasper, 'because you were the last person in his company, and he is not to be found.'

'Not to be found!' cried Neville, aghast.

'Stay, stay,' said Mr Crisparkle. 'Permit me, Jasper. Mr Neville, you are confounded; collect your thoughts; it is of great importance that you should collect your thoughts; attend to me.'

'I will try, sir, but I seem mad.'

'You left Mr Jasper last night with Edwin Drood?'

'Yes.'

'At what hour?'

'Was it at twelve o'clock?' asked Neville, with his hand to his confused head, and appealing to Jasper.

'Quite right,' said Mr Crisparkle; 'the hour Mr Jasper has already named to me. You went down to the river together?'

'Undoubtedly. To see the action of the wind there.'

'What followed? How long did you stay there?'

'About ten minutes; I should say not more. We then walked together to your house, and he took leave of me at the door.'

'Did he say that he was going down to the river again?'

'No. He said that he was going straight back.'

The bystanders looked at one another, and at Mr Crisparkle. To whom Mr Jasper, who had been intently watching Neville, said in a low, distinct, suspicious voice: 'What are those stains upon his dress?'

All eyes were turned towards the blood upon his clothes.

'And here are the same stains upon this stick!' said Jasper, taking it from the hand of the man who held it. 'I know the stick to be his, and he carried it last night. What does this mean?'

'In the name of God, say what it means, Neville!' urged Mr Crisparkle.

'That man and I,' said Neville, pointing out his late adversary, 'had a struggle for the stick just now, and you may see the same marks on him, sir. What was I to suppose, when I found myself molested by eight people? Could I dream of the true reason when they would give me none at all?'

They admitted that they had thought it discreet to be silent, and that the struggle had taken place. And yet the very men who had seen it looked darkly at the smears which the bright cold air had already dried.

'We must return, Neville,' said Mr Crisparkle; 'of course you will be glad to come back to clear yourself?'

'Of course, sir.'

'Mr Landless will walk at my side,' the minor canon continued, looking around him. 'Come, Neville!'

They set forth on the walk back; and the others, with one exception, straggled after them at various distances. Jasper walked on the other side of Neville, and never quitted that position. He was silent, while Mr Crisparkle more than once repeated his former questions, and while Neville repeated his former answers; also, while they both hazarded some explanatory conjectures. He was obstinately silent, because Mr Crisparkle's manner directly appealed to him to take some part in the discussion, and no appeal would move his fixed face. When they drew near to the city, and it was suggested by the minor canon that they might do well in calling on the mayor at once, he assented with a stern nod; but he spake no word until they stood in Mr Sapsea's parlour.[193]

Mr Sapsea being informed by Mr Crisparkle of the circumstances under which they desired to make a voluntary statement before him, Mr Jasper broke silence by declaring that he placed his whole reliance, humanly speaking, on Mr Sapsea's penetration. There was no conceivable reason why his nephew should have suddenly absconded, unless Mr Sapsea could suggest one, and then he would defer. There was no intelligible likelihood of his having returned to the river, and been accidentally drowned in the dark, unless it should appear likely to Mr Sapsea, and then again he would defer. He washed his hands as clean as he could[194] of all horrible suspicions, unless it should appear to Mr Sapsea that some such were inseparable from his last companion before his disappearance (not on good terms with previously), and then, once more, he would defer. His own state of mind, he being distracted with doubts, and labouring under dismal apprehensions, was not to be safely trusted; but Mr Sapsea's was.

Mr Sapsea expressed his opinion that the case had a dark look; in short (and here his eyes rested full on Neville's countenance), an un-English complexion. Having made this grand point, he wandered into a denser haze and maze of nonsense than even a mayor might have been expected to disport himself in, and came out of it with the brilliant discovery that to take the life of a fellow-creature was to take something that didn't belong to you. He wavered whether or no he should at once issue his warrant for the committal of Neville Landless to jail, under circumstances of grave suspicion; and he might have gone so far as to do it but for the indignant protest of the minor canon, who undertook for the young man's remaining in his own house, and being produced by his own hands, whenever demanded. Mr Jasper then understood Mr Sapsea to suggest that the river should be dragged, that its banks should be rigidly examined, that particulars of the disappearance should be sent to all outlying places and to London, and that placards and advertisements should be widely circulated imploring Edwin Drood, if for any unknown reason he had withdrawn himself from his uncle's home and society, to take pity on that loving kinsman's sore bereavement and distress, and somehow inform him that he was yet alive. Mr Sapsea was perfectly understood, for this was exactly his meaning (though he had said nothing about it); and measures were taken towards all these ends immediately.

It would be difficult to determine which was the more oppressed with horror and amazement: Neville Landless or John Jasper. But that Jasper's position forced him to be active, while Neville's forced him to be passive, there would have been nothing to choose between them. Each was bowed down and broken.

With the earliest light of the next morning, men were at work upon the river, and other men – most of whom volunteered for the service – were examining the banks. All the livelong day the search went on; upon the river, with barge and pole, and drag and net; upon the muddy and rushy shore, with jackboots, hatchet, spade, rope, dogs, and all imaginable appliances. Even at night, the river was specked with lanterns, and lurid with fires; far-off creeks, into which the tide washed as it changed, had their knots of watchers, listening to the lapping of the stream, and looking out for any burden it might bear; remote shingly causeways near the sea, and lonely points off which there was a race of water, had their unwonted flaring cressets and rough-coated figures when the next day dawned; but no trace of Edwin Drood revisited the light of the sun.

All that day, again, the search went on. Now, in barge and boat; and now ashore among the osiers, or tramping amidst mud and stakes and jagged stones in low-lying places, where solitary water-marks and signals of strange shapes showed like spectres, John Jasper worked and toiled. But to no purpose; for still no trace of Edwin Drood revisited the light of the sun.

Setting his watches for that night again, so that vigilant eyes should be kept on every change of tide, he went home exhausted. Unkempt and disordered, bedaubed with mud that had dried upon him, and with much of his clothing torn to rags, he had but just dropped into his easy-chair, when Mr Grewgious stood before him.

'This is strange news,' said Mr Grewgious.

'Strange and fearful news.'

Jasper had merely lifted up his heavy eyes to say it, and now dropped them again as he drooped, worn out, over one side of his easy-chair.

Mr Grewgious smoothed his head and face, and stood looking at the fire.

'How is your ward?' asked Jasper, after a time, in a faint, fatigued voice.

'Poor little thing! You may imagine her condition.'

'Have you seen his sister?' enquired Jasper, as before.

'Whose?'

The curtness of the counter-question, and the cool, slow manner in which, as he put it, Mr Grewgious moved his eyes from the fire to his companion's face, might at any other time have been exasperating. In his depression and exhaustion, Jasper merely opened his eyes to say: 'The suspected young man's.'

'Do you suspect him?' asked Mr Grewgious.

'I don't know what to think. I cannot make up my mind.'

'Nor I,' said Mr Grewgious. 'But as you spoke of him as the suspected young man, I thought you *had* made up your mind. – I have just left Miss Landless.'

'What is her state?'

'Defiance of all suspicion, and unbounded faith in her brother.'

'Poor thing!'

'However,' pursued Mr Grewgious, 'it is not of her that I came to speak. It is of my ward. I have a communication to make that will surprise you. At least, it has surprised me.'

Jasper, with a groaning sigh, turned wearily in his chair.

'Shall I put it off till tomorrow?' said Mr Grewgious. 'Mind, I warn you, that I think it will surprise you!'

More attention and concentration came into John Jasper's eyes as they caught sight of Mr Grewgious smoothing his head again, and again looking at the fire; but now, with a compressed and determined mouth.

'What is it?' demanded Jasper, becoming upright in his chair.

'To be sure,' said Mr Grewgious, provokingly slowly and internally, as he kept his eyes on the fire: 'I might have known it sooner; she gave me the opening; but I am such an exceedingly angular man, that it never occurred to me; I took all for granted.'

'What is it?' demanded Jasper once more.

Mr Grewgious, alternately opening and shutting the palms of his hands as he warmed them at the fire, and looking fixedly at him sideways, and never changing either his action or his look in all that followed, went on to reply.

'This young couple, the lost youth and Miss Rosa, my ward, though so long betrothed, and so long recognising their betrothal, and so near being married – '

Mr Grewgious saw a staring white face, and two quivering white lips, in the easy-chair, and saw two muddy hands gripping its sides. But for the hands, he might have thought he had never seen the face.

' – This young couple came gradually to the discovery (made on both sides pretty equally, I think), that they would be happier and better, both in their present and their future lives, as affectionate friends, or say rather as brother and sister, than as husband and wife.'

Mr Grewgious saw a lead-coloured face in the easy-chair, and on its surface dreadful starting drops or bubbles, as if of steel.

'This young couple formed at length the healthy resolution of interchanging their discoveries, openly, sensibly and tenderly. They met for that purpose. After some innocent and generous talk, they agreed to dissolve their existing, and their intended, relations, for ever and ever.'

Mr Grewgious saw a ghastly figure rise, open-mouthed, from the easy-chair, and lift its outspread hands towards its head.

'One of this young couple, and that one your nephew, fearful, however, that in the tenderness of your affection for him you would be bitterly disappointed by so wide a departure from his projected life, forbore to tell you the secret for a few days, and left it to be disclosed by me, when I should come down to speak to you, and he would be gone. I speak to you, and he is gone.'

Mr Grewgious saw the ghastly figure throw back its head, clutch its hair with its hands, and turn with a writhing action from him.

'I have now said all I have to say: except that this young couple parted, firmly, though not without tears and sorrow, on the evening when you last saw them together.'

Mr Grewgious heard a terrible shriek, and saw no ghastly figure, sitting or standing; saw nothing but a heap of torn and miry clothes upon the floor.

Not changing his action even then, he opened and shut the palms of his hands as he warmed them, and looked down at it.

CHAPTER 16

Devoted

WHEN JOHN JASPER recovered from his fit or swoon, he found himself being tended by Mr and Mrs Tope, whom his visitor had summoned for the purpose. His visitor, wooden of aspect, sat stiffly in a chair, with his hands upon his knees, watching his recovery.

'There! You've come to nicely now, sir,' said the tearful Mrs Tope; 'you were thoroughly worn out, and no wonder!'

'A man,' said Mr Grewgious, with his usual air of repeating a lesson, 'cannot have his rest broken, and his mind cruelly tormented, and his body overtaxed by fatigue, without being thoroughly worn out.'

'I fear I have alarmed you?' Jasper apologised faintly, when he was helped into his easy-chair.

'Not at all, I thank you,' answered Mr Grewgious.

'You are too considerate.'

'Not at all, I thank you,' answered Mr Grewgious again.

'You must take some wine, sir,' said Mrs Tope, 'and the jelly that I had ready for you, and that you wouldn't put your lips to at noon, though I warned you what would come of it, you know, and you not breakfasted; and you must have a wing of the roast fowl that has been put back twenty times if it's been put back once. It shall all be on table in five minutes, and this good gentleman belike will stop and see you take it.'

This good gentleman replied with a snort, which might mean yes, or no, or anything or nothing, and which Mrs Tope would have found highly mystifying but that her attention was divided by the service of the table.

'You will take something with me?' said Jasper, as the cloth was laid.

'I couldn't get a morsel down my throat, I thank you,' answered Mr Grewgious.

Jasper both ate and drank almost voraciously. Combined with the hurry in his mode of doing it was an evident indifference to the taste of what he took, suggesting that he ate and drank to fortify himself against any other failure of the spirits, far more than to gratify his palate. Mr Grewgious in the meantime sat upright, with no expression in his face, and a hard kind of imperturbably polite protest all over him: as though he would have said, in reply to some invitation to discourse: 'I couldn't originate the faintest approach to an observation on any subject whatever, I thank you.'

'Do you know,' said Jasper, when he had pushed away his plate and glass, and had sat meditating for a few minutes: 'do you know that I find some crumbs of comfort in the communication with which you have so much amazed me?'

'*Do* you?' returned Mr Grewgious, pretty plainly adding the unspoken clause: 'I don't, I thank you!'

'After recovering from the shock of a piece of news of my dear boy, so entirely unexpected, and so destructive of all the castles I had built for him;[195] and after having had time to think of it; yes.'

'I shall be glad to pick up your crumbs,' said Mr Grewgious, dryly.

'Is there not, or is there – if I deceive myself, tell me so, and shorten my pain – is there not, or is there, hope that, finding himself in this new position, and becoming sensitively alive to the awkward burden of explanation in this quarter and that and the other, with which it would load him, he avoided the awkwardness, and took to flight?'

'Such a thing might be,' said Mr Grewgious, pondering.

'Such a thing has been. I have read of cases in which people, rather than face a seven days' wonder,[196] and have to account for themselves to the idle and impertinent, have taken themselves away, and been long unheard of.'

'I believe such things have happened,' said Mr Grewgious, pondering still.

'When I had, and could have, no suspicion,' pursued Jasper, eagerly following the new track, 'that the dear lost boy had withheld anything from me – most of all, such a leading matter as this – what gleam of light was there for me in the whole black sky? When I supposed that his intended wife was here, and his marriage close at hand, how could I entertain the possibility of his voluntarily leaving this place, in a manner that would be so unaccountable, capricious, and cruel? But now that I know what you have told me, is there no little chink through which day pierces? Supposing him to have disappeared of his own act, is not his disappearance more account-able and less cruel? The fact of his having just parted from your ward is in itself a sort of reason for his going away. It does not make his mysterious departure the less cruel to me, it is true; but it relieves it of cruelty to her.'

Mr Grewgious could not but assent to this.

'And even as to me,' continued Jasper, still pursuing the new track, with ardour, and, as he did so, brightening with hope: 'he knew that you were coming to me; he knew that you were entrusted to tell me what you have told me; if your doing so has awakened a new train of thought in my perplexed mind, it reasonably follows that, from the same premises, he might have foreseen the inferences that I should draw. Grant that he did foresee them; and even the cruelty to me – and who am I! – John Jasper, music master, vanishes!' –

Once more, Mr Grewgious could not but assent to this.

'I have had my distrusts, and terrible distrusts they have been,' said Jasper; 'but your disclosure, overpowering as it was at first – showing me that my own dear boy had had a great disappointing reservation from me, who so fondly loved him, kindles hope within me. You do not extinguish it when I state it, but admit it to be a reasonable hope. I begin to believe it possible:' here he clasped his hands: 'that he may have disappeared from among us of his own accord, and that he may yet be alive and well.'

Mr Crisparkle came in at the moment. To whom Mr Jasper repeated: 'I begin to believe it possible that he may have disappeared of his own accord, and may yet be alive and well.'

Mr Crisparkle taking a seat, and enquiring: 'Why so?' Mr Jasper repeated the arguments he had just set forth. If they had been less plausible than they were, the good minor canon's mind would have been in a state of preparation to receive them, as exculpatory of his unfortunate pupil. But he, too, did really attach great importance to the lost young man's having been, so immediately before his disappearance, placed in a new and embarrassing relation towards everyone acquainted with his projects and affairs; and the fact seemed to him to present the question in a new light.

'I stated to Mr Sapsea, when we waited on him,' said Jasper: as he really had done: 'that there was no quarrel or difference between the two young men at their last meeting. We all know that their first meeting was unfortunately very far from amicable; but all went smoothly and quietly when they were last together at my house. My dear boy was not in his usual spirits; he was depressed – I noticed that – and I am bound henceforth to dwell upon the circumstance the more, now that I know there was a special reason for his being depressed: a reason, moreover, which may possibly have induced him to absent himself.'

'I pray to heaven it may turn out so!' exclaimed Mr Crisparkle.

'I pray to heaven it may turn out so!' repeated Jasper. 'You know – and Mr Grewgious should now know likewise – that I took a great prepossession against Mr Neville Landless, arising out of his furious conduct on that first occasion. You know that I came to you, extremely apprehensive, on my dear boy's behalf, of his mad violence. You know that I even entered in my diary, and showed the entry to you, that I had dark forebodings against him. Mr Grewgious ought to be possessed of the whole case. He shall not, through any suppression of mine, be informed of a part of it, and kept in ignorance of another part of it. I wish him to be good enough to understand that the communication he has made to me has hopefully influenced my mind, in spite of its having been, before this mysterious occurrence took place, profoundly impressed against young Landless.'

This fairness troubled the minor canon much. He felt that he was not as open in his own dealing. He charged against himself reproachfully that he had suppressed, so far, the two points of a second strong outbreak of temper against Edwin Drood on the part of Neville, and of the passion of jealousy having, to his own certain knowledge, flamed up in Neville's breast against him. He was convinced of Neville's innocence of any part in the ugly disappearance; and yet so many little circumstances combined so woefully against him, that he dreaded to add two more to their cumulative weight. He was among the truest of men; but he had been balancing in his mind, much to its distress, whether his volunteering to tell these two fragments of truth, at this time, would not be tantamount to a piecing together of falsehood in the place of truth.

However, here was a model before him. He hesitated no longer. Addressing Mr Grewgious, as one placed in authority by the revelation he had brought to bear on the mystery (and surpassingly angular Mr Grewgious became when he found himself in that unexpected position), Mr Crisparkle bore his testimony to Mr Jasper's strict sense of justice, and, expressing his absolute confidence in the complete clearance of his pupil from the least taint of suspicion, sooner or later, avowed that his confidence in that young gentleman had been formed, in spite of his confidential knowledge that his temper was of the hottest and fiercest, and that it was directly incensed against Mr Jasper's nephew by the circumstance of his romantically supposing himself to be enamoured of the same young lady. The sanguine reaction manifest in Mr Jasper was proof even against this unlooked-for declaration. It turned him paler; but he repeated that he would cling to the hope he had derived from Mr Grewgious; and that if no trace of his dear boy were found leading to the dreadful inference that he had been made away with, he would cherish unto the last stretch of possibility the idea that he might have absconded of his own wild will.

Now, it fell out that Mr Crisparkle, going away from this conference still very uneasy in his mind, and very much troubled on behalf of the young man whom he held as a kind of prisoner in his own house, took a memorable night walk.

He walked to Cloisterham Weir.

He often did so, and consequently there was nothing remarkable in his footsteps tending that way. But the preoccupation of his mind so hindered him from planning any walk, or taking heed of the objects he passed, that his first consciousness of being near the weir was derived from the sound of the falling water close at hand.

'How did I come here!' was his first thought, as he stopped.

'Why did I come here!' was his second.

Then he stood intently listening to the water. A familiar passage in his reading, about airy tongues that syllable men's names,[197] rose so unbidden to his ear that he put it from him with his hand, as if it were tangible.

It was starlight. The weir was full two miles above the spot to which the young men had repaired to watch the storm. No search had been made up here, for the tide had been running strongly down at that time of the night of Christmas Eve, and the likeliest places for the discovery of a body, if a fatal accident had happened under such circumstances, all lay – both when the tide ebbed and when it flowed again – between that spot and the sea. The water came over the weir with its usual sound on a cold starlight night, and little could be seen of it; yet Mr Crisparkle had a strange idea that something unusual hung about the place.

He reasoned with himself: What was it? Where was it? Put it to the proof. Which sense did it address?

No sense reported anything unusual there. He listened again, and his sense of hearing again checked the water coming over the weir with its usual sound on a cold starlight night.

Knowing very well that the mystery with which his mind was occupied might of itself give the place this haunted air, he strained those hawk's eyes of his for the correction of his fancy. He got closer to the weir, and peered at its well-known posts and timbers. Nothing in the least unusual was remotely shadowed forth to the sense of sight. But he resolved that he would come back early in the morning.

The weir ran through his broken sleep, all night, and he was back again at sunrise. It was a bright frosty morning. The whole composition before him, when he stood where he had stood last night, was clearly discernible in its minutest details. He had surveyed it closely for some minutes, and was about to withdraw his eyes, when they were attracted keenly to one spot.

He turned his back upon the weir, and looked far away at the sky, and at the earth, and then looked again at that one spot. It caught his sight again immediately, and he concentrated his vision upon it. He could not lose it now, though it was but such a speck in the landscape. It fascinated his sight. His hands began plucking off his coat. For it struck him that at that spot – a corner of the weir – something glistened, which did not move and come over with the glistening water-drops, but remained stationary.

He assured himself of this, he threw off his clothes, he plunged into the icy water and swam for the spot. Climbing the timbers, he took from them, caught among their interstices by its chain, a gold watch, bearing engraved upon its back E.D.

He brought the watch to the bank, swam to the weir again, climbed it and dived off. He knew every hole and corner of all the depths; and dived and dived and dived, until he could bear the cold no more. His notion was, that he would find the body; he only found a shirt-pin sticking in some mud and ooze.

With these discoveries he returned to Cloisterham, and, taking Neville Landless with him, went straight to the mayor. Mr Jasper was sent for, the watch and shirt-pin were identified, Neville was detained, and the wildest frenzy and fatuity of evil report rose against him. He was of that vindictive and violent nature that but for his poor sister, who alone had influence over him, and out of whose sight he was never to be trusted, he would be in the daily commission of murder. Before coming to England he had caused to be whipped to death sundry 'natives' – nomadic persons, encamping now in Asia, now in Africa, now in the West Indies, and now at the North Pole – vaguely supposed in Cloisterham to be always black, always of great virtue, always calling themselves Me, and everybody else Massa or Missie (according to sex), and always reading tracts of the obscurest meaning, in broken English, but always accurately understanding them in the purest mother tongue. He had nearly brought Mrs Crisparkle's grey hairs with sorrow to the grave.[198] (Those original expressions were Mr Sapsea's.) He had repeatedly said he would have Mr Crisparkle's life. He had repeatedly said he would have everybody's life, and become in effect the last man.[199] He had been brought down to Cloisterham from London by an eminent philanthropist, and why? Because that philanthropist had expressly declared: 'I owe it to my fellow-creatures that he should be, in the words of Bentham, where he is the cause of the greatest danger to the smallest number.'[200]

These dropping shots from the blunderbusses of blunder-headedness might not have hit him in a vital place. But he had to stand against a trained and well-directed fire of arms of precision too. He had notoriously threatened the lost young man, and had, according to the showing of his own faithful friend and tutor who strove so hard for him, a cause of bitter animosity (created by himself, and stated by himself), against that ill-starred fellow. He had armed himself with an offensive weapon for the fatal night, and he had gone off early in the morning, after making preparations for departure. He had been found with traces of blood on him; truly, they might have been wholly caused as he represented, but they might not, also. On a search-warrant being issued for the examination of his room, clothes, and so forth, it was discovered that he had destroyed all his papers, and rearranged all his possessions, on the very afternoon of the disappearance. The watch found at the weir was challenged by the jeweller as one he had wound and set for Edwin Drood at twenty minutes past two on that same afternoon; and it had run down, before being cast into the water; and it was the jeweller's positive opinion that it had never been rewound. This would justify the hypothesis that the watch was taken from him not long after he left Mr Jasper's house at midnight, in company with the last person seen with him, and that it had been thrown away after being retained some hours. Why thrown away? If he had been murdered, and so artfully disfigured, or concealed, or both, as that the murderer hoped identification to be impossible, except from something that he wore, assuredly the murderer would seek to remove from the body the most lasting, the best known, and the most easily recognisable things upon it. Those things would be the watch and shirt-pin. As to his opportunities of casting them into the river if he were the object of these suspicions, they were easy. For he had been seen by many persons wandering about on that side of the city – indeed on all sides of it – in a miserable and seemingly half-distracted manner. As to the choice of the spot, obviously such criminating evidence had better take its chance of being found anywhere rather than upon himself or in his possession. Concerning the reconciliatory nature of the appointed meeting between the two young men, very little could be made of that in young Landless's favour; for it distinctly appeared that the meeting originated, not with him, but with Mr Crisparkle, and that it had been urged on by Mr Crisparkle; and who could say how unwillingly, or in what ill-conditioned mood, his enforced pupil had gone to it? The more his case was looked into, the weaker it became in every point. Even the broad suggestion that the lost young man had absconded, was rendered additionally improbable on the showing of the young lady from whom he had so lately parted; for what did she say, with great earnestness and sorrow, when interrogated? That he had, expressly and enthusiastically, planned with her, that he would await the arrival of her guardian, Mr Grewgious. And yet, be it observed, he disappeared before that gentleman appeared.

On the suspicions thus urged and supported, Neville was detained, and re-detained, and the search was pressed on every hand, and Jasper laboured night and day.[201] But nothing more was found. No discovery being made which proved the lost man to be dead, it at length became necessary to release the person suspected of having made away with him. Neville was set at large. Then, a consequence ensued which Mr Crisparkle had too well foreseen. Neville must leave the place, for the place shunned him and cast him out. Even had it not been so, the dear old china shepherdess would have worried herself to death with fears for her son, and with general trepidation occasioned by their having such an inmate. Even had that not been so, the authority to which the minor canon deferred officially would have settled the point.

'Mr Crisparkle,' quoth the dean, 'human justice may err, but it must act according to its lights. The days of taking sanctuary are past.[202] This young man must not take sanctuary with us.'

'You mean that he must leave my house, sir?'

'Mr Crisparkle,' returned the prudent dean, 'I claim no authority in your house. I merely confer with you on the painful necessity you find yourself under of depriving this young man of the great advantages of your counsel and instruction.'

'It is very lamentable, sir,' Mr Crisparkle represented.

'Very much so,' the dean assented.

'And if it be a necessity – ' Mr Crisparkle faltered.

'As you unfortunately find it to be,' returned the dean.

Mr Crisparkle bowed submissively: 'It is hard to prejudge his case, sir, but I am sensible that – '

'Just so. Perfectly. As you say, Mr Crisparkle,' interposed the dean, nodding his head smoothly, 'there is nothing else to be done. No doubt, no doubt. There is no alternative, as your good sense has discovered.'

'I am entirely satisfied of his perfect innocence, sir, nevertheless.'

'We–e–ell!' said the dean, in a more confidential tone, and slightly glancing around him, 'I would not say so, generally. Not generally. Enough of suspicion attaches to him to – no, I think I would not say so, generally.'

Mr Crisparkle bowed again.

'It does not become us, perhaps,' pursued the dean, 'to be partisans. Not partisans. We clergy keep our hearts warm and our heads cool, and we hold a judicious middle course.'

'I hope you do not object, sir, to my having stated in public, emphatically, that he will reappear here, whenever any new suspicion may be awakened, or any new circumstance may come to light in this extraordinary matter?'

'Not at all,' returned the dean. 'And yet, do you know, I don't think,' with a very nice and neat emphasis on those two words: 'I *don't think* I would state it emphatically. State it? Ye–e–es! But emphatically? No–o–o. I *think* not. In point of fact, Mr Crisparkle, keeping our hearts warm and our heads cool, we clergy need do nothing emphatically.'[203]

So Minor Canon Row knew Neville Landless no more; and he went whithersoever he would, or could, with a blight upon his name and fame.[204]

It was not until then that John Jasper silently resumed his place in the choir. Haggard and red-eyed, his hopes plainly had deserted him, his sanguine mood was gone, and all his worst misgivings had come back. A day or two afterwards, while unrobing, he took his diary from a pocket of his coat, turned the leaves, and with an expressive look, and without one spoken word, handed this entry to Mr Crisparkle to read:

> My dear boy is murdered. The discovery of the watch and shirt-pin convinces me that he was murdered that night, and that his jewellery was taken from him to prevent identification by its means. All the delusive hopes I had founded on his separation from his betrothed wife, I give to the winds. They perish before this fatal discovery. I now swear, and record the oath on this page, that I nevermore will discuss this mystery with any human creature until I hold the clue to it in my hand. That I never will relax in my secrecy or in my search. That I will fasten the crime of the murder of my dear dead boy upon the murderer. And, that I devote myself to his destruction.

CHAPTER 17

Philanthropy, Professional and Unprofessional

A FULL HALF A YEAR had come and gone, and Mr Crisparkle sat in a waiting-room in the London chief offices of the Haven of Philanthropy, until he could have audience of Mr Honeythunder.

In his college days of athletic exercises, Mr Crisparkle had known professors of the noble art of fisticuffs, and had attended two or three of their gloved gatherings. He had now an opportunity of observing that as to the phrenological formation of the backs of their heads, the professing philanthropists were uncommonly like the pugilists. In the development of all those organs which constitute, or attend, a propensity to 'pitch into' your fellow-creatures, the philanthropists were remarkably favoured.[205] There were several professors passing in and out with exactly the aggressive air upon them of being ready for a turn-up with any novice who might happen to be on hand that Mr Crisparkle well remembered in the circles of the Fancy. Preparations were in progress for a moral little mill[206] somewhere on the rural circuit, and other professors were backing this or that heavyweight, as good for such or such speech-making hits, so very much after the manner of the sporting publicans that the intended resolutions might have been rounds. In an official manager of these displays much celebrated for his platform tactics, Mr Crisparkle recognised (in a suit of black) the counterpart of a deceased benefactor of his species, an eminent public character, once known to fame as Frosty-Faced Fogo,[207] who in days of yore superintended the formation of the magic circle with the ropes and stakes. There were only three conditions of resemblance wanting between these professors and those. Firstly, the philanthropists were in very bad training: much too fleshy, and presenting, both in face and figure, a superabundance of what is known to pugilistic experts as suet pudding. Secondly, the philanthropists had not the good temper of the pugilists, and used worse language. Thirdly, their fighting code stood in great need of revision, as empowering them not only to bore their man to the ropes, but to bore him to the confines of distraction; also to hit him when he was down, hit him anywhere and anyhow, kick him, stamp upon him, gouge him and maul him behind his back without mercy. In these last particulars the professors of the noble art were much nobler than the professors of philanthropy.

Mr Crisparkle was so completely lost in musing on these similarities and dissimilarities, at the same time watching the crowd which came and went, always, as it seemed, on errands of antagonistically snatching something from somebody, and never giving anything to anybody, that his name was twice called before he heard it. On his at length responding, he was shown by a miserably shabby and underpaid stipendiary philanthropist (who could hardly have done worse if he had taken service with a declared enemy of the human race) to Mr Honeythunder's room.

'Sir,' said Mr Honeythunder, in his tremendous voice, like a schoolmaster issuing orders to a boy of whom he had a bad opinion, 'sit down.'

Mr Crisparkle seated himself.

Mr Honeythunder having signed the remaining few score of a few thousand circulars, calling upon a corresponding number of families without means to come forward, stump up instantly, and be philanthropists, or go to the devil, another shabby stipendiary philanthropist (highly disinterested, if in earnest) gathered these into a basket and walked off with them.

'Now, Mr Crisparkle,' said Mr Honeythunder, turning his chair half round towards him when they were alone, and squaring his arms with his hands on his knees, and his brows knitted, as if he added, I am going to make short work of *you*: 'Now, Mr Crisparkle, we entertain different views, you and I, sir, of the sanctity of human life.'

'Do we?' returned the minor canon.

'We do, sir?'

'Might I ask you,' said the minor canon: 'what are your views on that subject?'

'That human life is a thing to be held sacred, sir.'

'Might I ask you,' pursued the minor canon as before: 'what you suppose to be my views on that subject?'

'By George, sir!' returned the philanthropist, squaring his arms still more, as he frowned on Mr Crisparkle: 'they are best known to yourself.'

'Readily admitted. But you began by saying that we took different views, you know. Therefore (or you could not say so) you must have set up some views as mine. Pray, what views *have* you set up as mine?'

'Here is a man – and a young man,' said Mr Honeythunder, as if that made the matter infinitely worse, and he could have easily borne the loss of an old one, 'swept off the face of the earth by a deed of violence.[208] What do you call that?'

'Murder,' said the minor canon.

'What do you call the doer of that deed, sir?'

'A murderer,' said the minor canon.

'I am glad to hear you admit so much, sir,' retorted Mr Honeythunder, in his most offensive manner; 'and I candidly tell you that I didn't expect it.' Here he lowered heavily at Mr Crisparkle again.

'Be so good as to explain what you mean by those very unjustifiable expressions.'

'I don't sit here, sir,' returned the philanthropist, raising his voice to a roar, 'to be browbeaten.'

'As the only other person present, no one can possibly know that better than I do,' returned the minor canon very quietly. 'But I interrupt your explanation.'

'Murder!' proceeded Mr Honeythunder, in a kind of boisterous reverie, with his platform folding of his arms, and his platform nod of abhorrent reflection after each short sentence of a word. 'Bloodshed! Abel! Cain![209] I hold no terms with Cain. I repudiate with a shudder the red hand when it is offered me.'

Instead of instantly leaping into his chair and cheering himself hoarse, as the brotherhood in public meeting assembled would infallibly have done on this cue, Mr Crisparkle merely reversed the quiet crossing of his legs, and said mildly: 'Don't let me interrupt your explanation – when you begin it.'

'The Commandments say, no murder.[210] *No* murder, sir!' proceeded Mr Honeythunder, platformally pausing as if he took Mr Crisparkle to task for having distinctly asserted that they said: You may do a little murder, and then leave off.

'And they also say, you shall bear no false witness,'[211] observed Mr Crisparkle.

'Enough!' bellowed Mr Honeythunder, with a solemnity and severity that would have brought the house down at a meeting, 'E–e–nough! My late wards being now of age, and I being released from a trust which I cannot contemplate without a thrill of horror, there are the accounts which you have undertaken to accept on their behalf, and there is a statement of the balance which you have undertaken to receive, and which you cannot receive too soon. And let me tell you, sir, I wish that, as a man and a minor canon, you were better employed,' with a nod. 'Better employed,' with another nod. 'Bet-ter em–ployed!' with another and the three nods added up.

Mr Crisparkle rose; a little heated in the face, but with perfect command of himself.

'Mr Honeythunder,' he said, taking up the papers referred to: 'my being better or worse employed than I am at present is a matter of taste and opinion. You might think me better employed in enrolling myself a member of your society.'

'Ay, indeed, sir!' retorted Mr Honeythunder, shaking his head in a threatening manner. 'It would have been better for you if you had done that long ago!'

'I think otherwise.'

'Or,' said Mr Honeythunder, shaking his head again, 'I might think one of your profession better employed in devoting himself to the discovery and punishment of guilt than in leaving that duty to be undertaken by a layman.'

'I may regard my profession from a point of view which teaches me that its first duty is towards those who are in necessity and tribulation, who are desolate and oppressed,'[212] said Mr Crisparkle. 'However, as I have quite clearly satisfied myself that it is no part of my profession to make professions, I say no more of that. But I owe it to Mr Neville, and to Mr Neville's sister (and in a much lower degree to myself), to say to you that I *know* I was in the full possession and understanding of Mr Neville's mind and heart at the time of this occurrence; and that, without in the least colouring or concealing what was to be deplored in him and required to be corrected, I feel certain that his tale is true. Feeling that certainty, I befriend him. As long as that certainty shall last, I will befriend him. And if any consideration could shake me in this resolve, I should be so ashamed of myself for my meanness, that no man's good opinion – no, nor no woman's – so gained, could compensate me for the loss of my own.'

Good fellow! manly fellow! And he was so modest, too. There was no more self-assertion in the minor canon than in the school-boy who had stood in the breezy playing-fields keeping a wicket.[213] He was simply and staunchly true to his duty alike in the large case and in the small. So all true souls ever are. So every true soul ever was, ever is and ever will be. There is nothing little to the really great in spirit.

'Then who do you make out did the deed?' asked Mr Honeythunder, turning on him abruptly.

'Heaven forbid,' said Mr Crisparkle, 'that in my desire to clear one man I should lightly criminate another! I accuse no one,'

'Tcha!' ejaculated Mr Honeythunder with great disgust; for this was by no means the principle on which the philanthropic brotherhood usually proceeded. 'And, sir, you are not a disinterested witness, we must bear in mind.'

'How am I an interested one?' enquired Mr Crisparkle, smiling innocently, at a loss to imagine.

'There was a certain stipend, sir, paid to you for your pupil, which may have warped your judgement a bit,' said Mr Honeythunder, coarsely.

'Perhaps I expect to retain it still?' Mr Crisparkle returned, enlightened. 'Do you mean that too?'

'Well, sir,' returned the professional philanthropist, getting up and thrusting his hands down into his trouser-pockets, 'I don't go about measuring people for caps. If people find I have any about me that fit 'em, they can put 'em on and wear 'em, if they like.[214] That's their look out: not mine.'

Mr Crisparkle eyed him with a just indignation, and took him to task thus: 'Mr Honeythunder, I hoped when I came in here that I might be under no necessity of commenting on the introduction of platform manners or platform manoeuvres among the decent forbearances of private life. But you have given me such a specimen of both, that I should be a fit subject for both if I remained silent respecting them. They are detestable.'

'They don't suit *you*, I dare say, sir.'

'They are,' repeated Mr Crisparkle, without noticing the interruption, 'detestable. They violate equally the justice that should belong to Christians, and the restraints that should belong to gentlemen. You assume a great crime to have been committed by one whom I, acquainted with the attendant circumstances, and having numerous reasons on my side, devoutly believe to be innocent of it. Because I differ from you on that vital point, what is your platform resource? Instantly to turn upon me, charging that I have no sense of the enormity of the crime itself, but am its aider and abettor! So, another time – taking me as representing your opponent in other cases – you set up a platform credulity; a moved and seconded and carried-unanimously profession of faith in some ridiculous delusion or mischievous imposition. I decline to believe it, and you fall back upon your platform resource of proclaiming that I believe nothing; that because I will not bow down to a false God of your making,[215] I deny the true God! Another time you make the platform discovery that war is a vast calamity, and you propose to abolish it by a string of twisted resolutions tossed into the air like the tail of a kite. I do not admit the discovery to be yours in the least, and I have not a grain of faith in your remedy. Again, your platform resource of representing me as revelling in the horrors of a battlefield like a fiend incarnate! Another time, in another of your undiscriminating platform rushes, you would punish the sober for the drunken. I claim consideration for the comfort, convenience, and refreshment of the sober; and you presently make platform proclamation that I have a depraved desire to turn heaven's creatures into swine and wild beasts![216] In all such cases your movers, and your seconders, and your supporters – your regular professors of all degrees, run amuck like so many mad Malays;[217] habitually attributing the lowest and basest motives with the utmost recklessness (let me call your attention to a recent instance in yourself for which you should blush), and quoting figures which you know to be as wilfully one-sided as a statement of any complicated account that should be all creditor side and no debtor, or all debtor side and no creditor. Therefore it is, Mr Honeythunder, that I consider the platform a sufficiently bad example and a sufficiently bad school, even in public life; but hold that, carried into private life, it becomes an unendurable nuisance.'

'These are strong words, sir!' exclaimed the philanthropist.

'I hope so,' said Mr Crisparkle. 'Good-morning.'

He walked out of the Haven at a great rate, but soon fell into his regular brisk pace, and soon had a smile upon his face as he went along, wondering what the china shepherdess would have said if she had seen him pounding Mr Honeythunder in the late little lively affair. For Mr Crisparkle had just enough of harmless vanity to hope that he had hit hard, and to glow with the belief that he had trimmed the philanthropic jacket pretty handsomely.

He betook himself to Staple Inn, but not to PJT and Mr Grewgious. Full many a creaking stair he climbed before he reached some attic rooms in a corner, turned the latch of their unbolted door, and stood beside the table of Neville Landless.

An air of retreat and solitude hung about the rooms and about their inhabitant. He was much worn, and so were they. Their sloping ceilings, cumbrous rusty locks and grates, and heavy wooden bins and beams, slowly mouldering withal, had a prisonous look, and he had the haggard face of a prisoner. Yet the sunlight shone in at the ugly garret-window, which had a penthouse to itself thrust out among the tiles; and on the cracked and smoke-blackened parapet beyond, some of the deluded sparrows of the place rheumatically hopped, like little feathered cripples who had left their crutches in their nests; and there was a play of living leaves at hand that changed the air, and made an imperfect sort of music in it that would have been melody in the country.

The rooms were sparely furnished, but with good store of books. Everything expressed the abode of a poor student. That Mr Crisparkle had been either chooser, lender or donor of the books, or that he combined the three characters, might have been easily seen in the friendly beam of his eyes upon them as he entered.

'How goes it, Neville?'

'I am in good heart, Mr Crisparkle, and working away.'

'I wish your eyes were not quite so large and not quite so bright,' said the minor canon, slowly releasing the hand he had taken in his.

'They brighten at the sight of you,' returned Neville. 'If you were to fall away from me, they would soon be dull enough.'

'Rally, rally!' urged the other, in a stimulating tone. 'Fight for it, Neville!'

'If I were dying, I feel as if a word from you would rally me; if my pulse had stopped, I feel as if your touch would make it beat again,' said Neville. 'But I *have* rallied, and am doing famously.'

Mr Crisparkle turned him with his face a little more towards the light.

'I want to see a ruddier touch here, Neville,' he said, indicating his own healthy cheek by way of pattern. 'I want more sun to shine upon you.'

Neville drooped suddenly, as he replied in a lowered voice: 'I am not hardy enough for that, yet. I may become so, but I cannot bear it yet. If you had gone through those Cloisterham streets as I did; and if you had seen, as I did, those averted eyes, and the better sort of people silently giving me too much room to pass, that I might not touch them or come near them, you wouldn't think it quite unreasonable that I cannot go about in the daylight.'

'My poor fellow!' said the minor canon, in a tone so purely sympathetic that the young man caught his hand, 'I never said it was unreasonable; never thought so. But I should like you to do it.'

'And that would give me the strongest motive to do it. But I cannot yet. I cannot persuade myself that the eyes of even the stream of strangers I pass in this vast city look at me without suspicion. I feel marked and tainted,[218] even when I go out – as I only do – at night. But the darkness covers me then, and I take courage from it.'

Mr Crisparkle laid a hand upon his shoulder, and stood looking down at him.

'If I could have changed my name,' said Neville, 'I would have done so. But as you wisely pointed out to me, I can't do that, for it would look like guilt. If I could have gone to some distant place, I might have found relief in that, but the thing is not to be thought of, for the same reason. Hiding and escaping would be the construction in either case. It seems a little hard to be so tied to a stake,[219] and innocent; but I don't complain.'

'And you must expect no miracle to help you, Neville,' said Mr Crisparkle, compassionately.

'No, sir, I know that. The ordinary fullness of time and circumstances is all I have to trust to.'

'It will right you at last, Neville.'

'So I believe, and I hope I may live to know it.'

But perceiving that the despondent mood into which he was falling cast a shadow on the minor canon, and (it may be) feeling that the broad hand upon his shoulder was not then quite as steady as its own natural strength had rendered it when it first touched him just now, he brightened and said: 'Excellent circumstances for study, anyhow! and you know, Mr Crisparkle, what need I have of study in all ways. Not to mention that you have advised me to study for the difficult profession of the law, specially, and that of course I am guiding myself by the advice of such a friend and helper. Such a good friend and helper!'

He took the fortifying hand from his shoulder, and kissed it. Mr Crisparkle beamed at the books, but not so brightly as when he had entered.

'I gather from your silence on the subject that my late guardian is adverse, Mr Crisparkle?'

The minor canon answered: 'Your late guardian is a – a most unreasonable person, and it signifies nothing to any reasonable person whether he is *ad*verse, *per*verse or the *re*verse.'

'Well for me that I have enough with economy to live upon,' sighed Neville, half wearily and half cheerily, 'while I wait to be learned, and wait to be righted! Else I might have proved the proverb, that while the grass grows, the steed starves!'[220]

He opened some books as he said it, and was soon immersed in their interleaved and annotated passages; while Mr Crisparkle sat beside him, expounding, correcting and advising. The minor canon's cathedral duties made these visits of his difficult to accomplish, and only to be compassed at intervals of many weeks. But they were as serviceable as they were precious to Neville Landless.

When they had got through such studies as they had in hand, they stood leaning on the window-sill, and looking down upon the patch of garden. 'Next week,' said Mr Crisparkle, 'you will cease to be alone, and will have a devoted companion.'

'And yet,' returned Neville, 'this seems an uncongenial place to bring my sister to.'

'I don't think so,' said the minor canon. 'There is duty to be done here; and there are womanly feeling, sense and courage wanted here.'

'I meant,' explained Neville, 'that the surroundings are so dull and unwomanly, and that Helena can have no suitable friend or society here.'

'You have only to remember,' said Mr Crisparkle, 'that you are here yourself, and that she has to draw you into the sunlight.'

They were silent for a little while, and then Mr Crisparkle began anew.

'When we first spoke together, Neville, you told me that your sister had risen out of the disadvantages of your past lives as superior to you as the tower of Cloisterham Cathedral is higher than the chimneys of Minor Canon Corner. Do you remember that?'

'Right well!'

'I was inclined to think it at the time an enthusiastic flight. No matter what I think it now. What I would emphasise is, that under the head of Pride your sister is a great and opportune example to you.'

'Under *all* heads that are included in the composition of a fine character, she is.'

'Say so; but take this one. Your sister has learnt how to govern what is proud in her nature. She can dominate it even when it is wounded through her sympathy with you. No doubt she has suffered deeply in those same streets where you suffered deeply. No doubt her life is darkened by the cloud that darkens yours. But bending her pride into a grand composure that is not haughty or aggressive, but is a sustained confidence in you and in the truth, she has won her way through those streets until she passes along them as high in the general respect as anyone who treads them. Every day and hour of her life since Edwin Drood's disappearance, she has faced malignity and folly – for you – as only a brave nature well directed can. So it will be with her to the end. Another and weaker kind of pride might sink broken-hearted, but never such a pride as hers: which knows no shrinking, and can get no mastery of her.'

The pale cheek beside him flushed under the comparison, and the hint implied in it.

'I will do all I can to imitate her,' said Neville.

'Do so, and be a truly brave man, as she is a truly brave woman,' answered Mr Crisparkle stoutly. 'It is growing dark. Will you go my way with me, when it is quite dark? Mind! it is not I who wait for darkness.'

Neville replied, that he would accompany him directly. But Mr Crisparkle said he had a moment's call to make on Mr Grewgious as an act of courtesy, and would run across to that gentleman's chambers, and rejoin Neville on his own doorstep, if he would come down there to meet him.

Mr Grewgious, bolt upright as usual, sat taking his wine in the dusk at his open window; his wine glass and decanter on the round table at his elbow; himself and his legs on the window-seat; only one hinge in his whole body, like a bootjack.

'How do you do, reverend sir?' said Mr Grewgious, with abundant offers of hospitality, which were as cordially declined as made. 'And how is your charge getting on over the way in the set that I had the pleasure of recommending to you as vacant and eligible?'

Mr Crisparkle replied suitably.

'I am glad you approved of them,' said Mr Grewgious, 'because I entertain a sort of fancy for having him under my eye.'

As Mr Grewgious had to turn his eye up considerably before he could see the chambers, the phrase was to be taken figuratively and not literally.

'And how did you leave Mr Jasper, reverend sir?' said Mr Grewgious.

Mr Crisparkle had left him pretty well.

'And where did you leave Mr Jasper, reverend sir?' Mr Crisparkle had left him at Cloisterham.

'And when did you leave Mr Jasper, reverend sir?' That morning.

'Umps!' said Mr Grewgious. 'He didn't say he was coming, perhaps?'

'Coming where?'

'Anywhere, for instance?' said Mr Grewgious.

'No.'

'Because here he is,' said Mr Grewgious, who had asked all these questions, with his preoccupied glance directed out of the window. 'And he don't look agreeable, does he?'

Mr Crisparkle was craning towards the window, when Mr Grewgious added: 'If you will kindly step round here behind me, in the gloom of the room, and will cast your eye at the second-floor landing window in yonder house, I think you will hardly fail to see a slinking individual in whom I recognise our local friend.'

'You are right!' cried Mr Crisparkle.

'Umps!' said Mr Grewgious. Then he added, turning his face so abruptly that his head nearly came into collision with Mr Crisparkle's: 'what should you say that our local friend was up to?'

The last passage he had been shown in the diary returned on Mr Crisparkle's mind with the force of a strong recoil, and he asked Mr Grewgious if he thought it possible that Neville was to be harassed by the keeping of a watch upon him?

'A watch?' repeated Mr Grewgious musingly. 'Ay!'

'Which would not only of itself haunt and torture his life,' said Mr Crisparkle warmly, 'but would expose him to the torment of a perpetually reviving suspicion, whatever he might do, or wherever he might go.'

'Ay!' said Mr Grewgious musingly still. 'Do I see him waiting for you?'

'No doubt you do.'

'Then *would* you have the goodness to excuse my getting up to see you out, and to go out to join him, and to go the way that you were going, and to take no notice of our local friend?' said Mr Grewgious. 'I entertain a sort of fancy for having *him* under my eye tonight, do you know?'

Mr Crisparkle, with a significant nod complied; and rejoining Neville, went away with him. They dined together, and parted at the yet unfinished and undeveloped railway station:[221] Mr Crisparkle to get home; Neville to walk the streets, cross the bridges, make a wide round of the city in the friendly darkness, and tire himself out.

It was midnight when he returned from his solitary expedition and climbed his staircase. The night was hot, and the windows of the staircase were all wide open. Coming to the top, it gave him a passing chill of surprise (there being no rooms but his up there) to find a stranger sitting on the window-sill, more after the manner of a venturesome glazier than an amateur ordinarily careful of his neck; in fact, so much more outside the window than inside, as to suggest the thought that he must have come up by the water-spout instead of the stairs.

The stranger said nothing until Neville put his key in his door; then, seeming to make sure of his identity from the action, he spoke: 'I beg your pardon,' he said, coming from the window with a frank and smiling air, and a prepossessing address; 'the beans.'

Neville was quite at a loss.

'Runners,' said the visitor. 'Scarlet. Next door at the back.'

'Oh,' returned Neville. 'And the mignonette and wallflower?'

'The same,' said the visitor.

'Pray walk in.'

'Thank you.'

Neville lighted his candles, and the visitor sat down. A handsome gentleman, with a young face, but with an older figure in its robustness and its breadth of shoulder; say a man of eight-and-twenty, or at the utmost thirty; so extremely sunburnt that the contrast between his brown visage and the white forehead shaded out of doors by his hat, and the glimpses of white throat below his neckerchief, would have been almost ludicrous but for his broad temples, bright blue eyes, clustering brown hair, and laughing teeth.

'I have noticed – ' said he. 'My name is Tartar.'[222]

Neville inclined his head.

'I have noticed (excuse me) that you shut yourself up a good deal, and that you seem to like my garden aloft here. If you would like a little more of it, I could throw out a few lines and stays between my windows and yours, which the runners would take to directly. And I have some boxes, both of mignonette and wallflower, that I could shove on along the gutter (with a boathook I have by me) to your windows, and draw back again when they wanted watering or gardening, and shove on again when they were shipshape; so that they would cause you no trouble. I couldn't take this liberty without asking permission, so I venture to ask it. Tartar, corresponding set, next door.'

'You are very kind.'

'Not at all. I beg you will not think so. I ought to apologise for looking in so late. But having noticed (excuse me) that you generally walk out at night, I thought I should inconvenience you least by awaiting your return. I am always afraid of inconveniencing busy men, being an idle man.'

'I should not have thought so, from your appearance.'

'No? I take it as a compliment. In fact, I was bred in the Royal Navy, and was first lieutenant when I quitted it. But, an uncle disappointed in the service leaving me his property on condition that I left the navy, I accepted the fortune, and resigned my commission.'

'Lately, I presume?'

'Well, I had had twelve or fifteen years of knocking about first. I came here some nine months before you; I had had one crop before you came. I chose this place because, having served last in a little corvette, I knew I should feel more at home where I had a constant opportunity of knocking my head against the ceiling. Besides, it would never do for a man who had been aboard ship from his boyhood to turn luxurious all at once. Besides, again, having been accustomed to a very short allowance of land all my life, I thought I'd feel my way to the command of a landed estate by beginning in boxes.'

Whimsically as this was said, there was a touch of merry earnestness in it that made it doubly whimsical.

'However,' said the lieutenant, 'I have talked quite enough about myself. It is not my way, I hope; it has merely been to present myself to you naturally. If you will allow me to take the liberty I have described, it will be a charity, for it will give me something more to do. And you are not to suppose that it will entail any interruption or intrusion on you, for that is far from my intention.'

Neville replied that he was greatly obliged, and that he thankfully accepted the kind proposal.

'I am very glad to take your windows in tow,' said the Lieutenant. 'From what I have seen of you when I have been gardening at mine, and you have been looking on, I have thought you (excuse me) rather too studious and delicate. May I ask, is your health at all affected?'

'I have undergone some mental distress,' said Neville, confused, 'which has stood me in the stead of illness.'

'Pardon me,' said Mr Tartar.

With the greatest delicacy he shifted his ground to the windows again, and asked if he could look at one of them. On Neville's opening it, he immediately sprang out, as if he were going aloft with a whole watch in an emergency and were setting a bright example.

'For heaven's sake,' cried Neville, 'don't do that! Where are you going, Mr Tartar? You'll be dashed to pieces!'

'All well!' said the Lieutenant, coolly looking about him on the housetop. 'All taut and trim here. Those lines and stays shall be rigged before you turn out in the morning. May I take the short cut home, and say good-night?'

'Mr Tartar!' urged Neville. 'Pray! It makes me giddy to see you!'

But Mr Tartar, with a wave of his hand and the deftness of a cat, had already dipped through his scuttle of scarlet runners, without breaking a leaf, and 'gone below'.

Mr Grewgious, his bedroom window-blind held aside with his hand, happened at the moment to have Neville's chambers under his eye for the last time that night. Fortunately his eye was on the front of the house and not the back, or this remarkable appearance and disappearance might have broken his rest as a phenomenon. But Mr Grewgious seeing nothing there, not even a light in the windows, his gaze wandered from the windows to the stars, as if he would have read in them something that was hidden from him. Many of us would, if we could; but none of us so much as know our letters in the stars yet – or seem likely to, in this state of existence – and few languages can be read until their alphabets are mastered.

CHAPTER 18

A Settler in Cloisterham

AT ABOUT THIS TIME a stranger appeared in Cloisterham: a white-haired personage, with black eyebrows. Being buttoned up in a tightish blue surtout, with a buff waistcoat and grey trousers, he had something of a military air, but he announced himself at the Crozier (the orthodox hotel, where he put up with a portmanteau) as an idle dog who lived upon his means; and he farther announced that he had a mind to take a lodging in the picturesque old city for a month or two, with the view of settling down there altogether. Both announcements were made in the coffee-room of the Crozier, to all whom it might or might not concern, by the stranger as he stood with his back to the empty fireplace, waiting for his fried sole, veal cutlet, and pint of sherry. And the waiter (business being chronically slack at the Crozier) represented all whom it might or might not concern, and absorbed the whole of the information.

This gentleman's white head was unusually large, and his shock of white hair was unusually thick and ample. 'I suppose, waiter,' he said, shaking his shock of hair, as a Newfoundland dog might shake his before sitting down to dinner, 'that a fair lodging for a single buffer[223] might be found in these parts, eh?'

The waiter had no doubt of it.

'Something old,' said the gentleman. 'Take my hat down for a moment from that peg, will you? No, I don't want it; look into it. What do you see written there?'

The waiter read: 'Datchery.'

'Now you know my name,' said the gentleman; 'Dick Datchery. Hang it up again. I was saying something old is what I should prefer, something odd and out of the way; something venerable, architectural and inconvenient.'

'We have a good choice of inconvenient lodgings in the town, sir, I think,' replied the waiter, with modest confidence in its resources that way; 'indeed, I have no doubts that we could suit you that far, however particular you might be. But a architectural lodging!' That seemed to trouble the waiter's head, and he shook it.

'Anything cathedraly, now,' Mr Datchery suggested.

'Mr Tope,' said the waiter, brightening, as he rubbed his chin with his hand, 'would be the likeliest party to inform in that line.'

'Who is Mr Tope?' enquired Dick Datchery.

The waiter explained that he was the Verger, and that Mrs Tope had indeed once upon a time let lodgings herself or offered to let them; but that as nobody had ever taken them, Mrs Tope's window-bill, long a Cloisterham institution, had disappeared; probably had tumbled down one day, and never been put up again.

'I'll call on Mrs Tope,' said Mr Datchery, 'after dinner.'

So when he had done his dinner, he was duly directed to the spot, and sallied out for it. But the Crozier being an hotel of a most retiring disposition, and the waiter's directions being fatally precise, he soon became bewildered, and went boggling about and about the cathedral tower, whenever he could catch a glimpse of it, with a general impression on his mind that Mrs Tope's was somewhere very near it, and that, like the children in the game of hot boiled beans and very good butter,[224] he was warm in his search when he saw the tower, and cold when he didn't see it.

He was getting very cold indeed when he came upon a fragment of burial-ground in which an unhappy sheep was grazing. Unhappy, because a hideous small boy was stoning it through the railings, and had already lamed it in one leg, and was much excited by the benevolent sportsmanlike purpose of breaking its other three legs, and bringing it down.

' 'It 'im agin!' cried the boy, as the poor creature leaped; 'and made a dint in 'is wool.'

'Let him be!' said Mr Datchery. 'Don't you see you have lamed him?'

'Yer lie,' returned the sportsman. ' 'E went and lamed isself. I see 'im do it, and I giv' 'im a shy as a widdy-warning to 'im not to go a-bruisin' 'is master's mutton any more.'

'Come here.'

'I won't; I'll come when yer can ketch me.'

'Stay there then, and show me which is Mr Tope's.'

''Ow can I stay here and show you which is Topeseses, when Topeseses is t'other side the kinfreederal, and over the crossings, and round ever so many corners? Stoo-pid! Ya–a–ah!'

'Show me where it is, and I'll give you something.'

'Come on, then.'

This brisk dialogue concluded, the boy led the way, and by and by stopped at some distance from an arched passage, pointing.

'Lookie yonder. You see that there winder and door?'

'That's Tope's?'

'Yer lie; it ain't. That's Jarsper's.'

'Indeed?' said Mr Datchery, with a second look of some interest.

'Yes, and I ain't a-goin' no nearer '*im*, I tell yer.'

'Why not?'

"Cos I ain't a-goin' to be lifted off my legs and 'ave my braces bust and be choked; not if I knows it, and not by 'im. Wait till I set a jolly good flint a-flyin' at the back o' 'is jolly old 'ed some day! Now look t'other side the harch; not the side where Jarsper's door is; t'other side.'

'I see.'

'A little way in, o' that side, there's a low door, down two steps. That's Topeseses with 'is name on a hoval plate.'

'Good. See here,' said Mr Datchery, producing a shilling. 'You owe me half of this.'

'Yer lie. I don't owe yer nothing; I never seen yer.'

'I tell you you owe me half of this, because I have no sixpence in my pocket. So the next time you meet me you shall do something else for me, to pay me.'

'All right, give us 'old.'

'What is your name, and where do you live?'

'Deputy. Travellers' Twopenny, 'cross the green.'

The boy instantly darted off with the shilling, lest Mr Datchery should repent, but stopped at a safe distance, on the happy chance of his being uneasy in his mind about it, to goad him with a demon dance expressive of its irrevocability.

Mr Datchery, taking off his hat to give that shock of white hair of his another shake, seemed quite resigned, and betook himself whither he had been directed.

Mr Tope's official dwelling, communicating by an upper stair with Mr Jasper's (hence Mrs Tope's attendance on that gentleman), was of very modest proportions, and partook of the character of a cool dungeon. Its ancient walls were massive, and its rooms rather seemed to have been dug out of them, than to have been designed beforehand with any reference to them. The main door opened at once on a chamber of no describable shape, with a groined roof, which in its turn opened on another chamber of no describable shape, with another groined roof: their windows small, and in the thickness of the walls. These two chambers, close as to their atmosphere and swarthy as to their illumination by natural light, were the apartments which Mrs Tope had so long offered to an unappreciative city. Mr Datchery, however, was more appreciative. He found that if he sat with the main door open he would enjoy the passing society of all comers to and fro by the gateway, and would have light enough. He found that if Mr and Mrs Tope, living overhead, used for their own egress and ingress a little side stair that came plump into the Precincts by a door opening outward, to the surprise and inconvenience of a limited public of pedestrians in a narrow way, he would be alone, as in a separate residence. He found the rent moderate, and everything as quaintly inconvenient as he could desire. He agreed, therefore, to take the lodging then and there, and money down, possession to be had next evening, on condition that reference was permitted him to Mr Jasper as occupying the gatehouse, of which on the other side of the gateway, the verger's hole-in-the-wall was an appanage or subsidiary part.

The poor dear gentleman was very solitary and very sad, Mrs Tope said, but she had no doubt he would 'speak for her'. Perhaps Mr Datchery had heard something of what had occurred there last winter?

Mr Datchery had as confused a knowledge of the event in question, on trying to recall it, as he well could have. He begged Mrs Tope's pardon when she found it incumbent on her to correct him in every detail of his summary of the facts, but pleaded that he was merely a single buffer getting through life upon his means as idly as he could, and that so many people were so constantly making away with so many other people, as to render it difficult for a buffer of an easy temper to preserve the circumstances of the several cases unmixed in his mind.

Mr Jasper proving willing to speak for Mrs Tope, Mr Datchery, who had sent up his card, was invited to ascend the postern staircase. The mayor was there, Mr Tope said; but he was not to be regarded in the light of company, as he and Mr Jasper were great friends.

'I beg pardon,' said Mr Datchery, making a leg[225] with his hat under his arm, as he addressed himself equally to both gentlemen; 'a selfish precaution on my part, and not personally interesting to anybody but myself. But as a buffer living on his means, and having an idea of doing it in this lovely place in peace and quiet, for remaining span of life, I beg to ask if the Tope family are quite respectable?'

Mr Jasper could answer for that without the slightest hesitation.

'That is enough, sir,' said Mr Datchery.

'My friend the mayor,' added Mr Jasper, presenting Mr Datchery with a courtly motion of his hand towards that potentate, 'whose recommendation is naturally much more important to a stranger than that of an obscure person like myself, will testify in their behalf, I am sure.'

'The worshipful the mayor,' said Mr Datchery, with a low bow, 'places me under an infinite obligation.'

'Very good people, sir, Mr and Mrs Tope,' said Mr Sapsea, with condescension. 'Very good opinions. Very well behaved. Very respectful. Much approved by the dean and chapter.'

'The worshipful the mayor gives them a character,' said Mr Datchery, 'of which they may indeed be proud. I would ask his honour (if I might be permitted) whether there are not many objects of great interest in the city which is under his beneficent sway?'

'We are, sir,' returned Mr Sapsea, 'an ancient city, and an ecclesiastical city. We are a constitutional city, as it becomes such a city to be, and we uphold and maintain our glorious privileges.'

'His honour,' said Mr Datchery, bowing, 'inspires me with a desire to know more of the city, and confirms me in my inclination to end my days in the city.'

'Retired from the army, sir?' suggested Mr Sapsea.

'His honour the mayor does me too much credit,' returned Mr Datchery.

'Navy, sir?' suggested Mr Sapsea.

'Again,' repeated Mr Datchery, 'his honour the mayor does me too much credit.'

'Diplomacy is a fine profession,' said Mr Sapsea, as a general remark.

'There, I confess, his honour the mayor is too many for me,' said Mr Datchery, with an ingenious smile and bow; 'even a diplomatic bird must fall to such a gun.'

Now this was very soothing. Here was a gentleman of a great, not to say a grand, address, accustomed to rank and dignity, really setting a fine example how to behave to a mayor. There was something in that third-person style of being spoken to, that Mr Sapsea found particularly recognisant of his merits and position.

'But I crave pardon,' said Mr Datchery. 'His honour the mayor will bear with me, if for a moment I have been deluded into occupying his time, and have forgotten the humble claims upon my own of my hotel, the Crozier.'

'Not at all, sir,' said Mr Sapsea. 'I too am returning home, and if you would like to take the exterior of our cathedral in your way, I shall be glad to point it out.'

'His honour the mayor,' said Mr Datchery, 'is more than kind and gracious.'

As Mr Datchery, when he had made his acknowledgments to Mr Jasper, could not be induced to go out of the room before the worshipful, the worshipful led the way downstairs; Mr Datchery following with his hat under his arm, and his shock of white hair streaming in the evening breeze.

'Might I ask his honour,' said Mr Datchery, 'whether that gentleman we have just left is the gentleman of whom I have heard in the neighbourhood as being much afflicted by the loss of a nephew, and concentrating his life on avenging the loss?'

'That is the gentleman. John Jasper, sir.'

'Would his honour allow me to enquire whether there are strong suspicions of anyone?'

'More than suspicions, sir,' returned Mr Sapsea; 'all but certainties.'

'Only think now!' cried Mr Datchery.

'But proof, sir, proof must be built up stone by stone,' said the mayor. 'As I say, the end crowns the work.[226] It is not enough that justice should be morally certain; she must be *im*morally certain – legally, that is.'

'His honour,' said Mr Datchery, 'reminds me of the nature of the law. Immoral. How true!'

'As I say, sir,' pompously went on the mayor, 'the arm of the law is a strong arm, and a long arm. That is the way I put it. A strong arm and a long arm.'

'How forcible! – And yet, again, how true!' murmured Mr Datchery.

'And without betraying what I call the secrets of the prison-house[227] – ' said Mr Sapsea; 'the secrets of the prison-house is the term I used on the bench.'

'And what other term than his honour's would express it?' said Mr Datchery.

'Without, I say, betraying them, I predict to you, knowing the iron will of the gentleman we have just left (I take the bold step of calling it iron, on account of its strength), that in this case the long arm will reach, and the strong arm will strike. This is our cathedral, sir. The best judges are pleased to admire it, and the best among our townsmen own to being a little vain of it.'

All this time Mr Datchery had walked with his hat under his arm, and his white hair streaming. He had an odd momentary appearance upon him of having forgotten his hat, when Mr Sapsea now touched it; and he clapped his hand up to his head as if with some vague expectation of finding another hat upon it.

'Pray be covered, sir,' entreated Mr Sapsea; magnificently

implying: 'I shall not mind it, I assure you.'

'His honour is very good, but I do it for coolness,' said Mr Datchery.

Then Mr Datchery admired the cathedral, and Mr Sapsea pointed it out as if he himself had invented and built it: there were a few details indeed of which he did not approve, but those he glossed over, as if the workmen had made mistakes in his absence. The cathedral disposed of, he led the way by the churchyard, and stopped to extol the beauty of the evening – by chance – in the immediate vicinity of Mrs Sapsea's epitaph.

'And by the by,' said Mr Sapsea, appearing to descend from an elevation to remember it all of a sudden; like Apollo shooting down from Olympus to pick up his forgotten lyre;[228] '*That* is one of our small lions. The partiality of our people has made it so, and strangers have been seen taking a copy of it now and then. I am not a judge of it myself, for it is a little work of my own. But it was troublesome to turn, sir; I may say, difficult to turn with elegance.'

Mr Datchery became so ecstatic over Mr Sapsea's composition that, in spite of his intention to end his days in Cloisterham, and therefore his probably having in reserve many opportunities of copying it, he would have transcribed it into his pocket-book on the spot, but for the slouching towards them of its material producer and perpetuator, Durdles, whom Mr Sapsea hailed, not sorry to show him a bright example of behaviour to superiors.

'Ah, Durdles! This is the mason, sir; one of our Cloisterham worthies; everybody here knows Durdles. Mr Datchery, Durdles a gentleman who is going to settle here.'

'I wouldn't do it if I was him,' growled Durdles. 'We're a heavy lot.'

'You surely don't speak for yourself, Mr Durdles,' returned Mr Datchery, 'any more than for his honour.'

'Who's his honour?' demanded Durdles.

'His honour the mayor.'

'I never was brought afore him,' said Durdles, with anything but the look of a loyal subject of the mayoralty, 'and it'll be time enough for me to honour him when I am. Until which, and when, and where,

> Mister Sapsea is his name,
> England is his nation,
> Cloisterham's his dwelling-place,
> Aukshneer's his occupation.'[229]

Here, Deputy (preceded by a flying oyster-shell) appeared upon the scene, and requested to have the sum of threepence instantly 'chucked' to him by Mr Durdles, whom he had been vainly seeking up and down, as lawful wages overdue. While that gentleman, with his bundle under his arm, slowly found and counted out the money, Mr Sapsea informed the new settler of Durdles's habits, pursuits, abode and reputation. 'I suppose a curious stranger might come to see you, and your works, Mr Durdles, at any odd time?' said Mr Datchery upon that.

'Any gentleman is welcome to come and see me any evening if he brings liquor for two with him,' returned Durdles, with a penny between his teeth and certain halfpence in his hands; 'or if he likes to make it twice two, he'll be double welcome.'

'I shall come. Master Deputy, what do you owe me?'

'A job.'

'Mind you pay me honestly with the job of showing me Mr Durdles's house when I want to go there.'

Deputy, with a piercing broadside of whistle through the whole gap in his mouth, as a receipt in full for all arrears, vanished.

The Worshipful and the Worshipper then passed on together until they parted, with many ceremonies, at the Worshipful's door; even then the Worshipper carried his hat under his arm, and gave his streaming white hair to the breeze.

Said Mr Datchery to himself that night, as he looked at his white hair in the gas-lighted looking-glass over the coffee-room chimneypiece at the Crozier, and shook it out: 'For a single buffer, of an easy temper, living idly on his means, I have had a rather busy afternoon!'

CHAPTER 19

Shadow on the Sundial

AGAIN MISS TWINKLETON has delivered her valedictory address, with the accompaniments of white wine and pound-cake, and again the young ladies have departed to their several homes. Helena Landless has left the Nuns' House to attend her brother's fortunes, and pretty Rosa is alone.

Cloisterham is so bright and sunny in these summer days that the cathedral and the monastery ruin show as if their strong walls were transparent. A soft glow seems to shine from within them, rather than upon them from without, such is their mellowness as they look forth on the hot cornfields and the smoking roads that distantly wind among them. The Cloisterham gardens blush with ripening fruit. Time was when travel-stained pilgrims rode in clattering parties through the city's welcome shades; time is when wayfarers, leading a gypsy life between haymaking time and harvest, and looking as if they were just made of the dust of the earth,[230] so very dusty are they, lounge about on cool door-steps, trying to mend their unmendable shoes, or giving them to the city kennels[231] as a hopeless job, and seeking others in the bundles that they carry, along with their yet unused sickles swathed in bands of straw. At all the more public pumps there is much cooling of bare feet, together with much bubbling and gurgling of drinking with hand to spout on the part of these Bedouins;[232] the Cloisterham police meanwhile looking askant[233] from their beats with suspicion, and manifest impatience that the intruders should depart from within the civic bounds, and once more fry themselves on the simmering high-roads.

On the afternoon of such a day, when the last cathedral service is done, and when that side of the High Street on which the Nuns' House stands is in grateful shade, save where its quaint old garden opens to the west between the boughs of trees, a servant informs Rosa, to her terror, that Mr Jasper desires to see her.

If he had chosen his time for finding her at a disadvantage, he could have done no better. Perhaps he has chosen it. Helena Landless is gone, Mrs Tisher is absent on leave, Miss Twinkleton (in her amateur state of existence) has contributed herself and a veal pie to a picnic.

'Oh why, why, why, did you say I was at home!' cried Rosa, helplessly.

The maid replies that Mr Jasper never asked the question.

That he said he knew she was at home, and begged she might be told that he asked to see her.

'What shall I do! what shall I do!' thinks Rosa, clasping her hands.

Possessed by a kind of desperation, she adds, in the next breath, that she will come to Mr Jasper in the garden. She shudders at the thought of being shut up with him in the house; but many of its windows command the garden, and she can be seen as well as heard there, and can shriek in the free air and run away. Such is the wild idea that flutters through her mind.

She has never seen him since the fatal night, except when she was questioned before the mayor, and then he was present in gloomy watchfulness, as representing his lost nephew and burning to avenge him. She hangs her garden-hat on her arm, and goes out. The moment she sees him from the porch, leaning on the sundial, the old horrible feeling of being compelled by him, asserts its hold upon her. She feels that she would even then go back, but that he draws her feet towards him. She cannot resist, and sits down, with her head bent, on the garden-seat beside the sundial. She cannot look up at him for abhorrence, but she has perceived that he is dressed in deep mourning. So is she. It was not so at first; but the lost has long been given up, and mourned for, as the dead.

He would begin by touching her hand. She feels the intention, and draws her hand back. His eyes are then fixed upon her, she knows, though her own see nothing but the grass.

'I have been waiting,' he begins, 'for some time, to be summoned back to my duty near you.'

After several times forming her lips, which she knows he is closely watching, into the shape of some other hesitating reply, and then into none, by turns she answers: 'Duty, sir?'

'The duty of teaching you, serving you as your faithful music-master.'

'I have left off that study.'

'Not left off, I think. Discontinued. I was told by your guardian that you discontinued it under the shock that we have all felt so acutely. When will you resume?'

'Never, sir.'

'Never? You could have done no more if you had loved my dear boy.'

'I did love him!' cries Rosa, with a flash of anger.

'Yes; but not quite – not quite in the right way, shall I say? Not in the intended and expected way. Much as my dear boy was, unhappily, too self-conscious and self-satisfied (but I draw no parallel between him and you in that respect) to love as he should have loved, or as anyone in his place would have loved – must have loved!'

She sits in the same still attitude, but shrinking a little more.

'Then to be told that you discontinued your study with me was to be politely told that you abandoned it altogether?' he suggests.

'Yes,' says Rosa, with sudden spirit, 'The politeness was my guardian's, not mine. I told him that I was resolved to leave off, and that I was determined to stand by my resolution.'

'And you still are?'

'I still am, sir. And I beg not to be questioned any more about it. At all events, I will not answer any more; I have that in my power.'

She is so conscious of his looking at her with a gloating admiration of the touch of anger on her, and the fire and animation it brings with it, that even as her spirit rises, it falls again, and she struggles with a sense of shame, affront and fear, much as she did that night at the piano.

'I will not question you any more, since you object to it so much; I will confess – '

'I do not wish to hear you, sir,' cries Rosa, rising.

This time he does touch her with his outstretched hand. In shrinking from it, she shrinks into her seat again.

'We must sometimes act in opposition to our wishes,' he tells her in a low voice. 'You must do so now, or do more harm to others than you can ever set right.'

'What harm?'

'Presently, presently. You question *me*, you see, and surely that is not fair when you forbid me to question you. Nevertheless, I will answer the question presently. Dearest Rosa! Charming Rosa!'

She starts up again.

This time he does not touch her. But his face looks so wicked and menacing as he stands leaning against the sundial – setting, as it were, his black mark upon the very face of day – that her flight is arrested by horror as she looks at him.

'I do not forget how many windows command a view of us,' he says, glancing towards them. 'I will not touch you again; I will come no nearer to you than I am. Sit down, and there will be no mighty wonder in your music-master's leaning idly against a pedestal and speaking with you, remembering all that has happened, and our shares in it. Sit down, my beloved.'

She would have gone once more – was all but gone – and once more his face, darkly threatening what would follow if she went, has stopped her. Looking at him with the expression of the instant frozen on her face, she sits down on the seat again.

'Rosa, even when my dear boy was affianced to you, I loved you madly; even when I thought his happiness in having you for his wife was certain, I loved you madly; even when I strove to make him more ardently devoted to you, I loved you madly; even when he gave me the picture of your lovely face so carelessly traduced by him, which I feigned to hang always in my sight for his sake, but worshipped in torment for yours, I loved you madly; in the distasteful work of the day, in the wakeful misery of the night, girded by sordid realities, or wandering through paradises and hells of visions into which I rushed, carrying your image in my arms, I loved you madly.'

If anything could make his words more hideous to her than they are in themselves, it would be the contrast between the violence of his look and delivery and the composure of his assumed attitude.

'I endured all in silence. So long as you were his, or so long as I supposed you to be his, I hid my secret loyally. Did I not?'

This lie, so gross, while the mere words in which it is told are so true, is more than Rosa can endure. She answers with kindling indignation: 'You were as false throughout, sir, as you are now. You were false to him, daily and hourly. You know that you made my life unhappy by your pursuit of me. You know that you made me afraid to open his generous eyes, and that you forced me, for his own trusting, good, good sake, to keep the truth from him, that you were a bad, bad man!'

His preservation of his easy attitude rendering his working features and his convulsive hands absolutely diabolical, he returns, with a fierce extreme of admiration: 'How beautiful you are! You are more beautiful in anger than in repose. I don't ask you for your love; give me yourself and your hatred; give me yourself and that pretty rage; give me yourself and that enchanting scorn; it will be enough for me.'

Impatient tears rise to the eyes of the trembling little beauty, and her face flames; but as she again rises to leave him in indignation, and seek protection within the house, he stretches out his hand towards the porch, as though he invited her to enter it.

'I told you, you rare charmer, you sweet witch, that you must stay and hear me, or do more harm than can ever be undone. You asked me what harm. Stay, and I will tell you. Go, and I will do it!'

Again Rosa quails before his threatening face, though innocent of its meaning, and she remains. Her panting breathing comes and goes as if it would choke her; but with a repressive hand upon her bosom, she remains.

'I have made my confession that my love is mad. It is so mad that had the ties between me and my dear lost boy been one silken thread less strong, I might have swept even him from your side, when you favoured him.'

A film come over the eyes she raises for an instant, as though he had turned her faint.

'Even him,' he repeats. 'Yes, even him! Rosa, you see me and you hear me. Judge for yourself whether any other admirer shall love you and live, whose life is in my hand.'

'What do you mean, sir?'

'I mean to show you how mad my love is. It was hawked through the late enquiries by Mr Crisparkle, that young Landless had confessed to him that he was a rival of my lost boy. That is an inexpiable offence in my eyes. The same Mr Crisparkle knows under my hand that I devoted myself to the murderer's discovery and destruction, be he who he might, and that I determined to discuss the mystery with no one until I should hold the clue in which to entangle the murderer as in a net. I have since worked patiently to wind and wind it round him; and it is slowly winding as I speak.'

'Your belief, if you believe in the criminality of Mr Landless, is not Mr Crisparkle's belief, and he is a good man,' Rosa retorts.

'My belief is my own; and I reserve it, worshipped of my soul! Circumstances may accumulate so strongly *even against an innocent man*, that directed, sharpened and pointed, they may slay him. One wanting link discovered by perseverance against a guilty man, proves his guilt, however slight its evidence before, and he dies. Young Landless stands in deadly peril either way.'

'If you really suppose,' Rosa pleads with him, turning paler, 'that I favour Mr Landless, or that Mr Landless has ever in any way addressed himself to me, you are wrong.'

He puts that from him with a slighting action of his hand and a curled lip.

'I was going to show you how madly I love you. More madly now than ever, for I am willing to renounce the second object that has arisen in my life to divide it with you; and henceforth to have no object in existence but you only. Miss Landless has become your bosom friend. You care for her peace of mind?'

'I love her dearly.'

'You care for her good name?'

'I have said, sir, I love her dearly.'

'I am unconsciously,' he observes with a smile, as he folds his hands upon the sundial and leans his chin upon them, so that his talk would seem from the windows (faces occasionally come and go there) to be of the airiest and playfullest – 'I am unconsciously giving offence by questioning again. I will simply make statements, therefore, and not put questions. You do care for your bosom friend's good name, and you do care for her peace of mind. Then remove the shadow of the gallows from her, dear one!'

Jasper's sacrfices

'You dare propose to me to – '

'Darling, I dare propose to you. Stop there. If it be bad to idolise you, I am the worst of men; if it be good, I am the best. My love for you is above all other love, and my truth to you is above all other truth. Let me have hope and favour, and I am a forsworn man for your sake.'

Rosa puts her hands to her temples, and, pushing back her hair, looks wildly and abhorrently at him, as though she were trying to piece together what it is his deep purpose to present to her only in fragments.

'Reckon up nothing at this moment, angel, but the sacrifices that I lay at those dear feet, which I could fall down among the vilest ashes and kiss and put upon my head as a poor savage might. There is my fidelity to my dear boy after death. Tread upon it!'

With an action of his hands, as though he cast down something precious.

'There is the inexpiable offence against my adoration of you. Spurn it!'

With a similar action.

'There are my labours in the cause of a just vengeance for six toiling months. Crush them!'

With another repetition of the action.

'There is my past and my present wasted life. There is the desolation of my heart and my soul. There is my peace; there is my despair. Stamp them into the dust; so that you take me, were it even mortally hating me!'

The frightful vehemence of the man, now reaching its full height, so additionally terrifies her as to break the spell that has held her to the spot. She swiftly moves towards the porch; but in an instant he is at her side, and speaking in her ear.

'Rosa, I am self-repressed again. I am walking calmly beside you to the house. I shall wait for some encouragement and hope. I shall not strike too soon. Give me a sign that you attend to me.'

She slightly and constrainedly moves her hand.

'Not a word of this to anyone, or it will bring down the blow, as certainly as night follows day.[234] Another sign that you attend to me.'

She moves her hand once more.

'I love you, love you, love you! If you were to cast me off now – but you will not – you would never be rid of me. No one should come between us. I would pursue you to the death.'

The handmaid coming out to open the gate for him, he quietly pulls off his hat as a parting salute, and goes away with no greater show of agitation than is visible in the effigy of Mr Sapsea's father opposite. Rosa faints in going upstairs, and is carefully carried to her room and laid down on her bed. A thunderstorm is coming on, the maids say, and the hot and stifling air has overset the pretty dear; no wonder: they have felt their own knees all of a tremble all day long.

CHAPTER 20

A Flight

ROSA NO SOONER CAME to herself than the whole of the late interview was before her. It even seemed as if it had pursued her into her insensibility, and she had not had a moment's unconsciousness of it. What to do, she was at a frightened loss to know: the only one clear thought in her mind was that she must fly from this terrible man.

But where could she take refuge, and how could she go? She had never breathed her dread of him to anyone but Helena. If she went to Helena, and told her what had passed, that very act might bring down the irreparable mischief that he threatened he had the power, and that she knew he had the will, to do. The more fearful he appeared to her excited memory and imagination, the more alarming her responsibility appeared, seeing that a slight mistake on her part, either in action or delay, might let his malevolence loose on Helena's brother.

Rosa's mind throughout the last six months had been stormily confused. A half-formed, wholly unexpressed suspicion tossed in it, now heaving itself up, and now sinking into the deep; now gaining palpability, and now losing it. His self-absorption in his nephew when he was alive, and his unceasing pursuit of the inquiry how he came by his death, if he were dead, were themes so rife in the place, that no one appeared able to suspect the possibility of foul play at his hands. She had asked herself the question, 'Am I so wicked in my thoughts as to conceive a wickedness that others cannot imagine?' Then she had considered, did the suspicion come of her previous recoiling from him before the fact? And if so, was not that a proof of its baselessness? Then she had reflected, 'What motive could he have, according to my accusation?' She was ashamed to answer in her mind, 'The motive of gaining *me*!' And covered her face, as if the lightest shadow of the idea of founding murder on such an idle vanity were a crime almost as great.

She ran over in her mind again all that he had said by the sundial in the garden. He had persisted in treating the disappearance as murder, consistently with his whole public course since the finding of the watch and shirt-pin. If he were afraid of the crime being traced out, would he not rather encourage the idea of a voluntary disappearance? He had unnecessarily declared that if the ties between him and his nephew had been less strong, he might have swept 'even him' away from her side. Was that like his having really done so? He had spoken of laying his six months' labours in the cause of a just vengeance at her feet. Would he have done that, with that violence of passion, if they were a pretence? Would he have ranged them with his desolate heart and soul, his wasted life, his peace and his despair? The very first sacrifice that he represented himself as making for her, was his fidelity to his dear boy after death. Surely these facts were strong against a fancy that scarcely dared to hint itself. And yet he was so terrible a man! In short, the poor girl (for what could she know of the criminal intellect, which its own professed students perpetually misread, because they persist in trying to reconcile it with the average intellect of average men, instead of identifying it as a horrible wonder apart) could get by no road to any other conclusion than that he *was* a terrible man, and must be fled from.

She had been Helena's stay and comfort during the whole time. She had constantly assured her of her full belief in her brother's innocence, and of her sympathy with him in his misery. But she had never seen him since the disappearance, nor had Helena ever spoken one word of his avowal to Mr Crisparkle in regard of Rosa, though as a part of the interest of the case it was well known far and wide. He was Helena's unfortunate brother, to her, and nothing more. The assurance she had given her odious suitor was strictly true, though it would have been better (she considered now) if she could have restrained herself from giving it. Afraid of him as the bright and delicate little creature was, her spirit swelled at the thought of his knowing it from her own lips.

But where was she to go? Anywhere beyond his reach, was no reply to the question. Somewhere must be thought of. She determined to go to her guardian, and to go immediately. The feeling she had imparted to Helena on the night of their first confidence, was so strong upon her – the feeling of not being safe from him, and of the solid walls of the old convent being powerless to keep out his ghostly following of her – that no reasoning of her own could calm her terrors. The fascination of repulsion had been upon her so long, and now culminated so darkly, that she felt as if he had power to bind her by a spell. Glancing out of the window, even now, as she rose to dress, the sight of the sundial on which he had leaned when he declared himself, turned her cold, and made her shrink from it, as though he had invested it with some awful quality from his own nature.

She wrote a hurried note to Miss Twinkleton, saying that she had sudden reason for wishing to see her guardian promptly, and had gone to him; also, entreating the good lady not to be uneasy, for all was well with her. She hurried a few quite useless articles into a very little bag, left the note in a conspicuous place, and went out, softly closing the gate after her.

It was the first time she had ever been even in Cloisterham High Street alone. But knowing all its ways and windings very well, she hurried straight to the corner from which the omnibus departed. It was, at that very moment, going off.

'Stop and take me, if you please, Joe. I am obliged to go to London.'

In less than another minute she was on her road to the railway, under Joe's protection. Joe waited on her when she got there, put her safely into the railway carriage, and handed in the very little bag after her, as though it were some enormous trunk, hundredweights heavy, which she must on no account endeavour to lift.

'Can you go round when you get back, and tell Miss Twinkleton that you saw me safely off, Joe?'

'It shall be done, Miss.'

'With my love, please, Joe.'

'Yes, miss – and I wouldn't mind having it myself!' But Joe did not articulate the last clause; only thought it.

Now that she was whirling away for London in real earnest, Rosa was at leisure to resume the thoughts which her personal hurry had checked. The indignant thought that his declaration of love soiled her; that she could only be cleansed from the stain of its impurity by appealing against it to the honest and true; supported her for a time against her fears, and confirmed her in her hasty resolution. But as the evening grew darker and darker, and the great city impended nearer and nearer, the doubts usual in such cases began to arise. Whether this was not a wild proceeding, after all; how Mr Grewgious might regard it; whether she would find him at the journey's end; how she would act if he were absent; what might become of her, alone, in a place so strange and crowded; how if she had but waited and taken counsel first; whether, if she could now go back, she would not do it thankfully; a multitude of such uneasy speculations disturbed her, more and more as they accumulated. At length the train came into London over the housetops;[235] and down below lay the gritty streets with their yet unneeded lamps aglow, on a hot, light, summer night.

'Hiram Grewgious, Esquire, Staple Inn, London.' This was all Rosa knew of her destination; but it was enough to send her rattling away again in a cab, through deserts of gritty streets, where many people crowded at the corner of courts and byways to get some air, and where many other people walked with a miserably monotonous noise of shuffling of feet on hot paving-stones, and where all the people and all their surroundings were so gritty and so shabby!

There was music playing here and there, but it did not enliven the case. No barrel-organ mended the matter, and no big drum beat dull care away. Like the chapel bells that were also going here and there, they only seemed to evoke echoes from brick surfaces, and dust from everything. As to the flat wind-instruments, they seemed to have cracked their hearts and souls in pining for the country.

Her jingling conveyance stopped at last at a fast-closed gateway, which appeared to belong to somebody who had gone to bed very early, and was much afraid of housebreakers; Rosa, discharging her conveyance, timidly knocked at this gateway, and was let in, very little bag and all, by a watchman.

'Does Mr Grewgious live here?'

'Mr Grewgious lives there, miss,' said the watchman, pointing further in.

So Rosa went further in, and, when the clocks were striking ten, stood on PJT's doorsteps, wondering what PJT had done with his street-door.

Guided by the painted name of Mr Grewgious, she went upstairs and softly tapped and tapped several times. But no one answering, and Mr Grewgious's door-handle yielding to her touch, she went in, and saw her guardian sitting on a window-seat at an open window, with a shaded lamp placed far from him on a table in a corner.

Rosa drew nearer to him in the twilight of the room. He saw her, and he said, in an undertone: 'Good heaven!'

Rosa fell upon his neck, with tears, and then he said, returning her embrace: 'My child, my child! I thought you were your mother! – But what, what, what,' he added, soothingly, 'has happened? My dear, what has brought you here? Who has brought you here?'

'No one. I came alone.'

'Lord bless me!' ejaculated Mr Grewgious. 'Came alone! Why didn't you write to me to come and fetch you?'

'I had no time. I took a sudden resolution. Poor, poor Eddy!'

'Ah, poor fellow, poor fellow!'

'His uncle has made love to me. I cannot bear it,' said Rosa, at once with a burst of tears, and a stamp of her little foot; 'I shudder with horror of him, and I have come to you to protect me and all of us from him. You will?'

'I will,' cried Mr Grewgious, with a sudden rush of amazing energy. 'Damn him!

> Confound his politics!
> Frustrate his knavish tricks!
> On Thee his hopes to fix?
> Damn him again!'[236]

After this most extraordinary outburst, Mr Grewgious, quite beside himself, plunged about the room, to all appearance undecided whether he was in a fit of loyal enthusiasm, or combative denunciation.

He stopped and said, wiping his face: 'I beg your pardon, my dear, but you will be glad to know I feel better. Tell me no more just now, or I might do it again. You must be refreshed and cheered. What did you take last? Was it breakfast, lunch, dinner, tea or supper? And what will you take next? Shall it be breakfast, lunch, dinner, tea or supper?'

The respectful tenderness with which, on one knee before her, he helped her to remove her hat, and disentangle her pretty hair from it, was quite a chivalrous sight. Yet who, knowing him only on the surface, would have expected chivalry – and of the true sort, too; not the spurious – from Mr Grewgious?

'Your rest too must be provided for,' he went on; 'and you shall have the prettiest chamber in Furnival's. Your toilet must be provided for, and you shall have everything that an unlimited head chambermaid – by which expression I mean a head chambermaid not limited as to outlay – can procure. Is that a bag?' he looked hard at it; sooth to say, it required hard looking at to be seen at all in a dimly lighted room: 'and is it your property, my dear?'

'Yes, sir. I brought it with me.'

'It is not an extensive bag,' said Mr Grewgious, candidly, 'though admirably calculated to contain a day's provision for a canary-bird. Perhaps you brought a canary-bird?'

Rosa smiled and shook her head.

'If you had, he should have been made welcome,' said Mr Grewgious, 'and I think he would have been pleased to be hung upon a nail outside and pit himself against our Staple sparrows; whose execution must be admitted to be not quite equal to their intention. Which is the case with so many of us! You didn't say what meal, my dear. Have a nice jumble of all meals.'

Rosa thanked him, but said she could only take a cup of tea. Mr Grewgious, after several times running out and in again to mention such supplementary items as marmalade, eggs, watercresses, salted fish and frizzled ham, ran across to Furnival's without his hat, to give his various directions. And soon afterwards they were realised in practice, and the board was spread.

'Lord bless my soul,' cried Mr Grewgious, putting the lamp upon it, and taking his seat opposite Rosa; 'what a new sensation for a poor old angular bachelor, to be sure!'

Rosa's expressive little eyebrows asked him what he meant?

'The sensation of having a sweet young presence in the place, that whitewashes it, paints it, papers it, decorates it with gilding, and makes it Glorious!' said Mr Grewgious. 'Ah me! Ah me!'

As there was something mournful in his sigh, Rosa, in touching him with her tea-cup, ventured to touch him with her small hand too.

'Thank you, my dear,' said Mr Grewgious. 'Ahem! Let's talk!'

'Do you always live here, sir?' asked Rosa.

'Yes, my dear.'

'And always alone?'

'Always alone; except that I have daily company in a gentleman by the name of Bazzard, my clerk.'

'*He* doesn't live here?'

'No, he goes his way, after office hours. In fact, he is off duty here, altogether, just at present; and a firm downstairs, with which I have business relations, lend me a substitute. But it would be extremely difficult to replace Mr Bazzard.'

'He must be very fond of you,' said Rosa.

'He bears up against it with commendable fortitude if he is,' returned Mr Grewgious, after considering the matter. 'But I doubt if he is. Not particularly so. You see, he is discontented, poor fellow.'

Mr Grewgious experiences a new sensation

'Why isn't he contented?' was the natural enquiry.

'Misplaced,' said Mr Grewgious, with great mystery.

Rosa's eyebrows resumed their inquisitive and perplexed expression.

'So misplaced,' Mr Grewgious went on, 'that I feel constantly apologetic towards him. And he feels (though he doesn't mention it) that I have reason to be.'

Mr Grewgious had by this time grown so very mysterious, that Rosa did not know how to go on. While she was thinking about it Mr Grewgious suddenly jerked out of himself for the second time: 'Let's talk. We were speaking of Mr Bazzard. It's a secret, and moreover it is Mr Bazzard's secret; but the sweet presence at my table makes me so unusually expansive that I feel I must impart it in inviolable confidence. What do you think Mr Bazzard has done?'

'Oh dear!' cried Rosa, drawing her chair a little nearer, and her mind reverting to Jasper, 'nothing dreadful, I hope?'

'He has written a play,' said Mr Grewgious, in a solemn whisper. 'A tragedy.'

Rosa seemed much relieved.

'And nobody,' pursued Mr Grewgious in the same tone, 'will hear, on any account whatever, of bringing it out.'

Rosa looked reflective, and nodded her head slowly; as who should say, 'Such things are, and why are they!'

'Now, you know,' said Mr Grewgious, '*I* couldn't write a play.'

'Not a bad one, sir?' said Rosa, innocently, with her eyebrows again in action.

'No. If I was under sentence of decapitation, and was about to be instantly decapitated, and an express arrived with a pardon for the condemned convict Grewgious if he wrote a play, I should be under the necessity of resuming the block, and begging the executioner to proceed to extremities – meaning,' said Mr Grewgious, passing his hand under his chin, 'the singular number, and this extremity.'

Rosa appeared to consider what she would do if the awkward supposititious case were hers.

'Consequently,' said Mr Grewgious, 'Mr Bazzard would have a sense of my inferiority to himself under any circumstances; but when I am his master, you know, the case is greatly aggravated.'

Mr Grewgious shook his head seriously, as if he felt the offence to be a little too much, though of his own committing.

'How came you to be his master, sir?' asked Rosa.

'A question that naturally follows,' said Mr Grewgious. 'Let's talk. Mr Bazzard's father, being a Norfolk farmer, would have furiously laid about him with a flail, a pitch-fork and every agricultural implement available for assaulting purposes on the slightest hint of his son's having written a play. So the son, bringing to me the father's rent (which I receive), imparted his secret, and pointed out that he was determined to pursue his genius, and that it would put him in peril of starvation, and that he was not formed for it.'

'For pursuing his genius, sir?'

'No, my dear,' said Mr Grewgious, 'for starvation. It was impossible to deny the position that Mr Bazzard was not formed to be starved, and Mr Bazzard then pointed out that it was desirable that I should stand between him and a fate so perfectly unsuited to his formation. In that way Mr Bazzard became my clerk, and he feels it very much.'

'I am glad he is grateful,' said Rosa.

'I didn't quite mean that, my dear. I mean, that he feels the degradation. There are some other geniuses that Mr Bazzard has become acquainted with, who have also written tragedies, which likewise nobody will on any account whatever hear of bringing out, and these choice spirits dedicate their plays to one another in a highly panegyrical manner. Mr Bazzard has been the subject of one of these dedications. Now, you know, *I* never had a play dedicated to *me*!'

Rosa looked at him as if she would have liked him to be the recipient of a thousand dedications.

'Which again, naturally, rubs against the grain of Mr Bazzard,' said Mr Grewgious. 'He is very short with me sometimes, and then I feel that he is meditating, "This blockhead my master! A fellow who couldn't write a tragedy on pain of death, and who will never have one dedicated to him with the most complimentary congratulations on the high position he has taken in the eyes of posterity!" Very trying, very trying. However, in giving him directions, I reflect beforehand: "Perhaps he may not like this," or, "He might take it ill if I asked that;" and so we get on very well. Indeed, better than I could have expected.'

'Is the tragedy named, sir?' asked Rosa.

'Strictly between ourselves,' answered Mr Grewgious, 'it has a dreadfully appropriate name. It is called *The Thorn of Anxiety*. But Mr Bazzard hopes – and I hope – that it will come out at last.'

It was not hard to divine that Mr Grewgious had related the Bazzard history thus fully, at least quite as much for the recreation of his ward's mind from the subject that had driven her there, as for the gratification of his own tendency to be social and communicative.

'And now, my dear,' he said at this point, 'if you are not too tired to tell me more of what passed today – but only if you feel quite able – I should be glad to hear it. I may digest it the better, if I sleep on it tonight.'

Rosa, composed now, gave him a faithful account of the interview. Mr Grewgious often smoothed his head while it was in progress, and begged to be told a second time those parts which bore on Helena and Neville. When Rosa had finished, he sat grave, silent and meditative for a while.

'Clearly narrated,' was his only remark at last, 'and, I hope, clearly put away here,' smoothing his head again. 'See, my dear,' taking her to the open window, 'where they live! The dark windows over yonder.'

'I may go to Helena tomorrow?' asked Rosa.

'I should like to sleep on that question tonight,' he answered doubtfully. 'But let me take you to your own rest, for you must need it.'

With that Mr Grewgious helped her to get her hat on again, and hung upon his arm the very little bag that was of no earthly use, and led her by the hand (with a certain stately awkwardness, as if he were going to walk a minuet) across Holborn, and into Furnival's Inn. At the hotel door, he confided her to the unlimited head chambermaid, and said that while she went up to see her room, he would remain below, in case she should wish it exchanged for another, or should find that there was anything she wanted.

Rosa's room was airy, clean, comfortable, almost gay. The unlimited had laid in everything omitted from the very little bag (that is to say, everything she could possibly need), and Rosa tripped down the great many stairs again, to thank her guardian for his thoughtful and affectionate care of her.

'Not at all, my dear,' said Mr Grewgious, infinitely gratified; 'it is I who thank you for your charming confidence and for your charming company. Your breakfast will be provided for you in a neat, compact and graceful little sitting-room (appropriate to your figure), and I will come to you at ten o'clock in the morning. I hope you don't feel very strange indeed, in this strange place.'

'Oh no, I feel so safe!'

'Yes, you may be sure that the stairs are fire-proof,' said Mr Grewgious, 'and that any outbreak of the devouring element would be perceived and suppressed by the watchmen.'

'I did not mean that,' Rosa replied. 'I mean, I feel so safe from him.'

'There is a stout gate of iron bars to keep him out,' said Mr Grewgious, smiling; 'and Furnival's is specially watched and lighted, and *I* live over the way!' In the stoutness of his knight-errantry, he seemed to think the last-named protection all sufficient. In the same spirit he said to the gate-porter as he went out, 'If someone staying in the hotel should wish to send across the road to me in the night, a crown will be ready for the messenger.' In the same spirit, he walked up and down outside the iron gate for the best part of an hour, with some solicitude; occasionally looking in between the bars, as if he had laid a dove in a high roost in a cage of lions, and had it on his mind that she might tumble out.

CHAPTER 21[237]

A Recognition

NOTHING OCCURRED in the night to flutter the tired dove; and the dove arose refreshed. With Mr Grewgious, when the clocks struck ten in the morning, came Mr Crisparkle, who had come at one plunge out of the river at Cloisterham.

'Miss Twinkleton was so uneasy, Miss Rosa,' he explained to her, 'and came round to ma and me with your note in such a state of wonder that, to quiet her, I volunteered on this service by the very first train to be caught in the morning. I wished at the time that you had come to me; but now I think it best that you did *as* you did, and came to your guardian.'

'I did think of you,' Rosa told him; 'but Minor Canon Corner was so near him – '

'I understand. It was quite natural.'

'I have told Mr Crisparkle,' said Mr Grewgious, 'all that you told me last night, my dear. Of course I should have written it to him immediately; but his coming was most opportune. And it was particularly kind of him to come, for he had but just gone.'

'Have you settled,' asked Rosa, appealing to them both, 'what is to be done for Helena and her brother?'

'Why really,' said Mr Crisparkle, 'I am in great perplexity. If even Mr Grewgious, whose head is much longer than mine, and who is a whole night's cogitation in advance of me, is undecided, what must I be!'

The unlimited here put her head in at the door – after having tapped, and been authorised to present herself – announcing that a gentleman wished for a word with another gentleman named Crisparkle, if any such gentleman were there. If no such gentleman were there, he begged pardon for being mistaken.

'Such a gentleman is here,' said Mr Crisparkle, 'but is engaged just now.'

'Oh, is it a dark gentleman?' interposed Rosa, retreating on her guardian.

'No, miss, more of a brown gentleman.'

'You are sure not with black hair?' asked Rosa, taking courage.

'Quite sure of that, miss. Brown hair and blue eyes.'

'Perhaps,' hinted Mr Grewgious, with habitual caution, 'it might be well to see him, reverend sir, if you don't object. When one is in a difficulty or at a loss, one never knows in what direction a way out may chance to open. It is a business principle of mine, in such a case, not to close up any direction, but to keep an eye on every direction that may present itself. I could relate an anecdote in point, but that it would be premature.'

'If Miss Rosa will allow me, then? Let the gentleman come in,' said Mr Crisparkle.

The gentleman came in; apologised, with a frank but modest grace, for not finding Mr Crisparkle alone; turned to Mr Crisparkle, and smilingly asked the unexpected question: 'Who am I?'

'You are the gentleman I saw smoking under the trees in Staple Inn, a few minutes ago.'

'True. There I saw you. Who else am I?'

Mr Crisparkle concentrated his attention on a handsome face, much sunburnt; and the ghost of some departed boy seemed to rise, gradually and dimly, in the room.

The gentleman saw a struggling recollection lighten up the minor canon's features and, smiling again, said: 'What will you have for breakfast this morning? You are out of jam.'

'Wait a moment!' cried Mr Crisparkle, raising his right hand. 'Give me another instant! Tartar!'

The two shook hands with the greatest heartiness, and then went the wonderful length – for Englishmen – of laying their hands each on the other's shoulders, and looking joyfully each into the other's face.

'My old fag!'[238] said Mr Crisparkle.

'My old master!' said Mr Tartar.

'You saved me from drowning!' said Mr Crisparkle.

'After which you took to swimming, you know!' said Mr Tartar.

'God bless my soul!' said Mr Crisparkle.

'Amen!' said Mr Tartar.

And then they fell to shaking hands most heartily again.

'Imagine,' exclaimed Mr Crisparkle, with glistening eyes: 'Miss Rosa Bud and Mr Grewgious, imagine Mr Tartar, when he was the smallest of juniors, diving for me, catching me, a big heavy senior, by the hair of my head, and striking out for the shore with me like a water-giant!'

'Imagine my not letting him sink, as I was his fag!' said Mr Tartar. 'But the truth being that he was my best protector and friend, and did me more good than all the masters put together, an irrational impulse seized me either to pick him up, or go down with him.'

'Hem! Permit me, sir, to have the honour,' said Mr Grewgious, advancing with extended hand, 'for an honour I truly esteem it. I am proud to make your acquaintance. I hope you didn't take cold. I hope you were not inconvenienced by swallowing too much water. How have you been since?'

It was by no means apparent that Mr Grewgious knew what he said, though it was very apparent that he meant to say something highly friendly and appreciative.

If heaven, Rosa thought, had but sent such courage and skill to her poor mother's aid! And he to have been so slight and young then!

'I don't wish to be complimented upon it, I thank you; but I think I have an idea,' Mr Grewgious announced, after taking a jog-trot or two across the room, so very unexpected and unaccountable that they all stared at him, doubtful whether he was choking or had the cramp – '*I think* I have an idea. I believe I have had the pleasure of seeing Mr Tartar's name as tenant of the top set in the house next the top set in the corner?'

'Yes, sir,' returned Mr Tartar. 'You are right so far.'

'I am right so far,' said Mr Grewgious. 'Tick that off;' which he did, with his right thumb on his left. 'Might you happen to know the name of your neighbour in the top set on the other side of the party-wall?' coming very close to Mr Tartar, to lose nothing of his face, in his shortness of sight.

'Landless.'

'Tick that off,' said Mr Grewgious, taking another trot, and then coming back. 'No personal knowledge, I suppose, sir?'

'Slight, but some.'

'Tick that off,' said Mr Grewgious, taking another trot, and again coming back. 'Nature of knowledge, Mr Tartar?'

'I thought he seemed to be a young fellow in a poor way, and I asked his leave – only within a day or so – to share my flowers up there with him; that is to say, to extend my flower-garden to his windows.'

'Would you have the kindness to take seats?' said Mr Grewgious. 'I *have* an idea!'

They complied; Mr Tartar none the less readily for being all abroad; and Mr Grewgious, seated in the centre, with his hands upon his knees, thus stated his idea, with his usual manner of having got the statement by heart.

'I cannot as yet make up my mind whether it is prudent to hold open communication under present circumstances, and on the part of the fair member of the present company, with Mr Neville or Miss Helena. I have reason to know that a local friend of ours (on whom I beg to bestow a passing but a hearty malediction, with the kind permission of my reverend friend) sneaks to and fro, and dodges up and down. When not doing so himself, he may have some informant skulking about, in the person of any watchman, porter, or suchlike hanger-on of Staple. On the other hand, Miss Rosa very naturally wishes to see her friend Miss Helena, and it would seem important that at least Miss Helena (if not her brother too, through her) should privately know from Miss Rosa's lips what has occurred, and what has been threatened. Am I agreed with generally in the views I take?'

'I entirely coincide with them,' said Mr Crisparkle, who had been very attentive.

'As I have no doubt I should,' added Mr Tartar, smiling, 'if I understood them.'

'Fair and softly, dear sir,' said Mr Grewgious; 'we shall fully confide in you directly, if you will favour us with your permission. Now, if our local friend should have any informant on the spot, it is tolerably clear that such informant can only be set to watch the chambers in the occupation of Mr Neville. He reporting to our local friend, who comes and goes there, our local friend would supply for himself, from his own previous knowledge, the identity of the parties. Nobody can be set to watch all Staple, or to concern himself with comers and goers to other sets of chambers: unless, indeed, mine.'

'I begin to understand to what you tend,' said Mr Crisparkle, 'and I highly approve of your caution.'

'I needn't repeat that I know nothing yet of the why and wherefore,' said Mr Tartar; 'but I also understand to what you tend, so let me say at once that my chambers are freely at your disposal.'

'There!' cried Mr Grewgious, smoothing his head triumphantly, 'now we have all got the idea. You have it, my dear?'

'I think I have,' said Rosa, blushing a little as Mr Tartar looked quickly towards her.

'You see, you go over to Staple with Mr Crisparkle and Mr Tartar,' said Mr Grewgious; 'I going in and out, and out and in, alone, in my usual way; you go up with those gentlemen to Mr Tartar's rooms; you look into Mr Tartar's flower-garden; you wait for Miss Helena's appearance there, or you signify to Miss Helena that you are close by; and you communicate with her freely, and no spy can be the wiser.'

'I am very much afraid I shall be – '

'Be what, my dear?' asked Mr Grewgious, as she hesitated. 'Not frightened?'

'No, not that,' said Rosa, shyly; 'in Mr Tartar's way. We seem to be appropriating Mr Tartar's residence so very coolly.'

'I protest to you,' returned that gentleman, 'that I shall think the better of it for evermore, if your voice sounds in it only once.'

Rosa, not quite knowing what to say about that, cast down her eyes, and turning to Mr Grewgious, dutifully asked if she should put her hat on? Mr Grewgious being of opinion that she could not do better, she withdrew for the purpose. Mr Crisparkle took the opportunity of giving Mr Tartar a summary of the distresses of Neville and his sister; the opportunity was quite long enough, as the hat happened to require a little extra fitting on.

Mr Tartar gave his arm to Rosa, and Mr Crisparkle walked, detached, in front.

'Poor, poor Eddy!' thought Rosa, as they went along.

Mr Tartar waved his right hand as he bent his head down over Rosa, talking in an animated way.

'It was not so powerful or so sun-browned when it saved Mr Crisparkle,' thought Rosa, glancing at it; 'but it must have been very steady and determined even then.'

Mr Tartar told her he had been a sailor, roving everywhere for years and years.

'When are you going to sea again?' asked Rosa.

'Never!'

Rosa wondered what the girls would say if they could see her crossing the wide street on the sailor's arm. And she feared that the passers-by must think her very little and very helpless, contrasted with the strong figure that could have caught her up and carried her out of any danger, miles and miles without resting.

She was thinking, further, that his far-seeing blue eyes looked as if they had been used to watch danger afar off, and to watch it without flinching, drawing nearer and nearer: when, happening to raise her own eyes, she found that he seemed to be thinking something about *them*.

This a little confused Rosebud, and may account for her never afterwards quite knowing how she ascended (with his help) to his garden in the air, and seemed to get into a marvellous country that came into sudden bloom like the country on the summit of the magic beanstalk.[239] May it flourish for ever!

CHAPTER 22

A Gritty State of Things Comes On

MR TARTAR'S CHAMBERS were the neatest, the cleanest and the best-ordered chambers ever seen under the sun, moon and stars.[240] The floors were scrubbed to that extent that you might have supposed the London blacks[241] emancipated for ever, and gone out of the land for good. Every inch of brasswork in Mr Tartar's possession was polished and burnished, till it shone like a brazen mirror. No speck, nor spot, nor spatter soiled the purity of any of Mr Tartar's household goods, large, small or middle-sized. His sitting-room was like the admiral's cabin, his bathroom was like a dairy, his sleeping-chamber, fitted all about with lockers and drawers, was like a seedsman's shop; and his nicely-balanced cot just stirred in the midst, as if it breathed. Everything belonging to Mr Tartar had quarters of its own assigned to it: his maps and charts had their quarters; his books had theirs; his brushes had theirs; his boots had theirs; his clothes had theirs; his case-bottles had theirs; his telescopes and other instruments had theirs. Everything was readily accessible. Shelf, bracket, locker, hook and drawer were equally within reach, and were equally contrived with a view to avoiding waste of room, and providing some snug inches of stowage for something that would have exactly fitted nowhere else. His gleaming little service of plate was so arranged upon his sideboard as that a slack salt-spoon would have instantly betrayed itself; his toilet implements were so arranged upon his dressing-table as that a toothpick of slovenly deportment could have been reported at a glance. So with the curiosities he had brought home from various voyages. Stuffed, dried, repolished or otherwise preserved, according to their kind; birds, fishes, reptiles, arms, articles of dress, shells, seaweeds, grasses, or memorials of coral reef; each was displayed in its especial place, and each could have been displayed in no better place. Paint and varnish seemed to be kept somewhere out of sight, in constant readiness to obliterate stray fingermarks wherever any might become perceptible in Mr Tartar's chambers. No man-of-war was ever kept more spick and span from careless touch. On this bright summer day, a neat awning was rigged over Mr Tartar's flower-garden as only a sailor can rig it, and there was a sea-going air upon the whole effect so delightfully complete that the flower-garden might have appertained to stern-windows afloat, and the whole concern might have bowled away gallantly with all on board if Mr Tartar had only clapped to his lips the speaking-trumpet that was slung in a corner and given hoarse orders to heave the anchor up, look alive there, men, and get all sail upon her!

Mr Tartar doing the honours of this gallant craft was of a piece with the rest. When a man rides an amiable hobby that shies at nothing and kicks nobody, it is always agreeable to find him riding it with a humorous sense of the droll side of the creature. When the man is a cordial and an earnest man by nature, and withal is perfectly fresh and genuine, it may be doubted whether he is ever seen to greater advantage than at such a time. So Rosa would have naturally thought (even if she *hadn't* been conducted over the ship with all the homage due to the First Lady of the Admiralty,[242] or First Fairy of the Sea) that it was charming to see and hear Mr Tartar half laughing at, and half rejoicing in, his various contrivances. So Rosa would have naturally thought, anyhow, that the sunburnt sailor showed to great advantage when, the inspection finished, he delicately withdrew out of his admiral's cabin, beseeching her to consider herself its queen, and waving her free of its flower-garden with the hand that had had Mr Crisparkle's life in it.

'Helena! Helena Landless! Are you there?'

'Who speaks to me? Not Rosa?' Then a second handsome face appearing.

'Yes, my darling!'

'Why, how did you come here, dearest?'

'I – I don't quite know,' said Rosa with a blush; 'unless I am dreaming!'

Why with a blush? For their two faces were alone with the other flowers. Are blushes among the fruits of the country of the magic beanstalk?

'I am not dreaming,' said Helena, smiling. 'I should take more for granted if I were. How do we come together – or so near together – so very unexpectedly?'

Unexpectedly indeed, among the dingy gables and chimney-pots of PJT's connection, and the flowers that had sprung from the salt sea. But Rosa, waking, told in a hurry how they came to be together, and all the why and wherefore of that matter.

'And Mr Crisparkle is here,' said Rosa, in rapid conclusion; 'and, could you believe it? long ago he saved his life!'

'I could believe any such thing of Mr Crisparkle,' returned Helena, with a mantling face.

(More blushes in the beanstalk country!)

'Yes, but it wasn't Crisparkle,' said Rosa, quickly putting in the correction.

'I don't understand, love.'

'It was very nice of Mr Crisparkle to be saved,' said Rosa, 'and he couldn't have shown his high opinion of Mr Tartar more expressively. But it was Mr Tartar who saved him.'

Helena's dark eyes looked very earnestly at the bright face among the leaves, and she asked, in a slower and more thoughtful tone: 'Is Mr Tartar with you now, dear?'

'No; because he has given up his rooms to me – to us, I mean. It is such a beautiful place!'

'Is it?'

'It is like the inside of the most exquisite ship that ever sailed. It is like – it is like – '

'Like a dream?' suggested Helena.

Rosa answered with a little nod, and smelled the flowers.

Helena resumed, after a short pause of silence, during which she seemed (or it was Rosa's fancy) to compassionate somebody: 'My poor Neville is reading in his own room, the sun being so very bright on this side just now. I think he had better not know that you are so near.'

'Oh, I think so too!' cried Rosa very readily.

'I suppose,' pursued Helena, doubtfully, 'that he must know by and by all you have told me; but I am not sure. Ask Mr Crisparkle's advice, my darling. Ask him whether I may tell Neville as much or as little of what you have told me as I think best.'

Rosa subsided into her state-cabin, and propounded the question. The minor canon was for the free exercise of Helena's judgement.

'I thank him very much,' said Helena, when Rosa emerged again with her report. 'Ask him whether it would be best to wait until any new maligning and pursuing of Neville on the part of this wretch shall disclose itself, or to try to anticipate it: I mean, so far as to find out whether any such goes on darkly about us?'

The minor canon found this point so difficult to give a confident opinion on that, after two or three attempts and failures, he suggested a reference to Mr Grewgious. Helena acquiescing, he betook himself (with a most unsuccessful assumption of lounging indifference) across the quadrangle to PJT's, and stated it. Mr Grewgious held decidedly to the general principle that if you could steal a march upon a brigand or a wild beast you had better do it; and he also held decidedly to the special case, that John Jasper was a brigand *and* a wild beast in combination.

Thus advised, Mr Crisparkle came back again and reported to Rosa, who in her turn reported to Helena. She now steadily pursuing her train of thought at her window, considered thereupon.

'We may count on Mr Tartar's readiness to help us, Rosa?' she enquired.

Oh yes! Rosa shyly thought so. Oh yes, Rosa shyly believed she could almost answer for that. But should she ask Mr Crisparkle? 'I think your authority on the point as good as his, my dear,' said Helena, sedately, 'and you needn't disappear again for that.' Odd of Helena!

'You see, Neville,' Helena pursued after more reflection, 'knows no one else here: he has not so much as exchanged a word with anyone else here. If Mr Tartar would call to see him openly and often; if he would spare a minute for the purpose frequently; if he would even do so almost daily; something might come of it.'

'Something might come of it, dear?' repeated Rosa, surveying her friend's beauty with a highly perplexed face. 'Something might?'

'If Neville's movements are really watched, and if the purpose really is to isolate him from all friends and acquaintance and wear his daily life out grain by grain (which would seem to be in the threat to you), does it not appear likely,' said Helena, 'that his enemy would in some way communicate with Mr Tartar to warn him off from Neville? In which case, we might not only know the fact, but might know from Mr Tartar what the terms of the communication were.'

'I see!' cried Rosa. And immediately darted into her state-cabin again.

Presently her pretty face reappeared, with a heightened colour, and she said that she had told Mr Crisparkle, and that Mr Crisparkle had fetched in Mr Tartar, and that Mr Tartar – 'who is waiting now, in case you want him,' added Rosa, with a half-look back, and in not a little confusion between the inside of the state-cabin and the out – had declared his readiness to act as she had suggested, and to enter on his task that very day.

'I thank him from my heart,' said Helena. 'Pray tell him so.'

Again not a little confused between the flower-garden and the cabin, Rosa dipped in with her message, and dipped out again with more assurances from Mr Tartar, and stood wavering in a divided state between Helena and him, which proved that confusion is not always necessarily awkward, but may sometimes present a very pleasant appearance.

'And now, darling,' said Helena, 'we will be mindful of the caution that has restricted us to this interview for the present, and will part. I hear Neville moving too. Are you going back?'

'To Miss Twinkleton's?' asked Rosa.

'Yes.'

'Oh, I could never go there any more. I couldn't indeed, after that dreadful interview!' said Rosa.

'Then where *are* you going, pretty one?'

'Now I come to think of it, I don't know,' said Rosa. 'I have settled nothing at all yet, but my guardian will take care of me. Don't be uneasy, dear. I shall be sure to be somewhere.'

(It did seem likely.)

'And I shall hear of my Rosebud from Mr Tartar?' enquired Helena.

'Yes, I suppose so; from – ' Rosa looked back again in a flutter, instead of supplying the name. 'But tell me one thing before we part, dearest Helena. Tell me – that you are sure, sure, sure, I couldn't help it.'

'Help it, love?'

'Help making him malicious and revengeful. I couldn't hold any terms with him, could I?'

'You know how I love you, darling,' answered Helena, with indignation; 'but I would sooner see you dead at his wicked feet.'[243]

'That's a great comfort to me! And you will tell your poor brother so, won't you? And you will give him my remembrance and my sympathy? And you will ask him not to hate me?'

With a mournful shake of the head, as if that would be quite a superfluous entreaty, Helena lovingly kissed her two hands to her friend, and her friend's two hands were kissed to her; and then she saw a third hand (a brown one) appear among the flowers and leaves, and help her friend out of sight.

The refection that Mr Tartar produced in the admiral's cabin by merely touching the spring knob of a locker and the handle of a drawer, was a dazzling enchanted repast. Wonderful macaroons, glittering liqueurs, magically-preserved tropical spices and jellies of celestial tropical fruits displayed themselves profusely at an instant's notice. But Mr Tartar could not make time stand still; and time, with his hard-hearted fleetness, strode on so fast, that Rosa was obliged to come down from the beanstalk country to earth and her guardian's chambers.

'And now, my dear,' said Mr Grewgious, 'what is to be done next? To put the same thought in another form; what is to be done with you?'

Rosa could only look apologetically sensible of being very much in her own way and in everybody else's. Some passing idea of living, fire-proof, up a good many stairs in Furnival's Inn for the rest of her life, was the only thing in the nature of a plan that occurred to her.

'It has come into my thoughts,' said Mr Grewgious, 'that as the respected lady, Miss Twinkleton, occasionally repairs to London in the recess, with the view of extending her connection, and being available for interviews with metropolitan parents, if any. Whether, until we have time in which to turn ourselves round, we might invite Miss Twinkleton to come and stay with you for a month?'

'Stay where, sir?'

'Whether,' explained Mr Grewgious, 'we might take a furnished lodging in town for a month, and invite Miss Twinkleton to assume the charge of you in it for that period?'

'And afterwards?' hinted Rosa.

'And afterwards,' said Mr Grewgious, 'we should be no worse off than we are now.'

'I think that might smooth the way,' assented Rosa.

'Then let us,' said Mr Grewgious, rising, 'go and look for a furnished lodging. Nothing could be more acceptable to me than the sweet presence of last evening, for all the remaining evenings of my existence; but these are not fit surroundings for a young lady. Let us set out in quest of adventures, and look for a furnished lodging. In the meantime, Mr Crisparkle here, about to return home immediately, will no doubt kindly see Miss Twinkleton, and invite that lady to co-operate in our plan.'

Mr Crisparkle, willingly accepting the commission, took his departure; Mr Grewgious and his ward set forth on their expedition.

As Mr Grewgious's idea of looking at a furnished lodging was to get on the opposite side of the street to a house with a suitable bill in the window, and stare at it; and then work his way tortuously to the back of the house, and stare at that; and then not go in, but make similar trials of another house, with the same result; their progress was but slow. At length he bethought himself of a widowed cousin, divers times removed, of Mr Bazzard's, who had once solicited his influence in the lodger world, and who lived in Southampton Street, Bloomsbury Square.[244] This lady's name, stated in uncompromising capitals of considerable size on a brass door-plate, and yet not lucidly stated as to sex or condition, was BILLICKIN.

Personal faintness and an overpowering personal candour were the distinguishing features of Mrs Billickin's organisation. She came languishing out from her own exclusive back parlour with the air of having been expressly brought-to for the purpose from an accumulation of several swoons.

'I hope I see you well, sir,' said Mrs Billickin, recognising her visitor with a bend.

'Thank you, quite well. And you, ma'am?' returned Mr Grewgious.

'I am as well,' said Mrs Billickin, becoming aspirational with excess of faintness, 'as I hever ham.'

'My ward and an elder lady,' said Mr Grewgious, 'wish to find a genteel lodging for a month or so. Have you any apartments available, ma'am?'

'Mr Grewgious,' returned Mrs Billickin, 'I will not deceive you; far from it. I *have* apartments available.' This with the air of adding: 'Convey me to the stake, if you will; but while I live, I will be candid.'

'And now, what apartments, ma'am?' asked Mr Grewgious, cosily. To tame a certain severity apparent on the part of Mrs Billickin.

'There is this sitting-room – which, call it what you will, it is the front parlour, miss,' said Mrs Billickin, impressing Rosa into the conversation: 'the back parlour being what I cling to and never part with; and there is two bedrooms at the top of the 'ouse with gas laid on.[245] I do not tell you that your bedroom floors is firm, for firm they are not. The gas-fitter himself allowed, that to make a firm job, he must go right under your jistes,[246] and it were not worth the outlay as a yearly tenant so to do. The piping is carried above your jistes, and it is best that it should be made known to you.'

Mr Grewgious and Rosa exchanged looks of some dismay, though they had not the least idea what latent horrors this carriage of the piping might involve. Mrs Billickin put her hand to her heart, as having eased it of a load.

'Well! The roof is all right, no doubt,' said Mr Grewgious, plucking up a little.

'Mr Grewgious,' returned Mrs Billickin, 'if I was to tell you, sir, that to have nothink above you is to have a floor above you, I should put a deception upon you which I will not do. No, sir. Your slates *will* rattle loose at that elewation[247] in windy weather, do your utmost, best or worst! I defy you, sir, be you who you may, to keep your slates tight, try how you can.' Here Mrs Billickin, having been warm with Mr Grewgious, cooled a little, not to abuse the moral power she held over him. 'Consequent,' proceeded Mrs Billickin, more mildly, but still firmly in her incorruptible candour: 'consequent it would be worse than of no use for me to traipse and travel up to the top of the 'ouse with you, and for you to say, "Mrs Billickin, what stain do I notice in the ceiling, for a stain I do consider it?" and for me to answer, "I do not understand you, sir." No, sir, I will not be so underhand. I *do* understand you before you pint it out. It is the wet, sir. It do come in, and it do not come in. You may lay dry there half your lifetime; but the time will come, and it is best that you should know it, when a dripping sop would be no name for you.'

Mr Grewgious looked much disgraced by being prefigured in this pickle.

'Have you any other apartments, ma'am?' he asked.

'Mr Grewgious,' returned Mrs Billickin, with much solemnity, 'I have. You ask me have I, and my open and my honest answer air, I have. The first and second floors is wacant, and sweet rooms.'

'Come, come! There's nothing against *them*,' said Mr Grewgious, comforting himself.

'Mr Grewgious,' replied Mrs Billickin, 'pardon me, there is the stairs. Unless your mind is prepared for the stairs, it will lead to inevitable disappointment. You cannot, miss,' said Mrs Billickin, addressing Rosa reproachfully, 'place a first floor, and far less a second, on the level footing of a parlour. No, you cannot do it, miss, it is beyond your power, and wherefore try?'

Mrs Billickin put it very feelingly, as if Rosa had shown a headstrong determination to hold the untenable position.

'Can we see these rooms, ma'am?' enquired her guardian.

'Mr Grewgious,' returned Mrs Billickin, 'you can. I will not disguise it from you, sir; you can.'

Mrs Billickin then sent into her back parlour for her shawl (it being a state fiction, dating from immemorial antiquity, that she could never go anywhere without being wrapped up), and having been enrobed by her attendant, led the way. She made various genteel pauses on the stairs for breath, and clutched at her heart in the drawing-room as if it had very nearly got loose, and she had caught it in the act of taking wing.

'And the second floor?' said Mr Grewgious, on finding the first satisfactory.

'Mr Grewgious,' replied Mrs Billickin, turning upon him with ceremony, as if the time had now come when a distinct understanding on a difficult point must be arrived at, and a solemn confidence established, 'the second floor is over this.'

'Can we see that too, ma'am?'

'Yes, sir,' returned Mrs Billickin, 'it is open as the day.'

That also proving satisfactory, Mr Grewgious retired into a window with Rosa for a few words of consultation, and then, asking for pen and ink, sketched out a line or two of agreement. In the meantime Mrs Billickin took a seat, and delivered a kind of index to, or abstract of, the general question.

'Five-and-forty shillings per week by the month certain at the time of year,' said Mrs Billickin, 'is only reasonable to both parties. It is not Bond Street nor yet St James's Palace;[248] but it is not pretended that it is. Neither is it attempted to be denied – for why should it? – that the archway leads to a mews.[249] Mewses must exist. Respecting attendance:[250] two is kep', at liberal wages. Words *has* arisen as to tradesmen, but dirty shoes on fresh hearth-stoning was attributable, and no wish for a commission on your orders. Coals is either *by* the fire, or *per* the scuttle.' She emphasised the prepositions as marking a subtle but immense difference. 'Dogs is not viewed with favour. Besides litter, they gets stole, and sharing suspicions is apt to creep in, and unpleasantness takes place.'

By this time Mr Grewgious had his agreement-lines, and his earnest-money,[251] ready. 'I have signed it for the ladies, ma'am,' he said, 'and you'll have the goodness to sign it for yourself, Christian and surname there, if you please.'

'Mr Grewgious,' said Mrs Billickin in a new burst of candour, 'no, sir! You must excuse the Christian name.'

Mr Grewgious stared at her.

'The door-plate is used as a protection,' said Mrs Billickin, 'and acts as such, and go from it I will not.'

Mr Grewgious stared at Rosa.

'No, Mr Grewgious, you must excuse me. So long as this 'ouse is known indefinite as Billickin's, and so long as it is a doubt with the riff-raff where Billickin may be hidin', near the street-door or down the airy,[252] and what his weight and size, so long I feel safe. But commit myself to a solitary female statement, no, miss! Nor would you for a moment wish,' said Mrs Billickin, with a strong sense of injury, 'to take that advantage of your sex, if you were not brought to it by inconsiderate example.'

Rosa reddening as if she had made some most disgraceful attempt to overreach the good lady, besought Mr Grewgious to rest content with any signature. And accordingly, in a baronial way,[253] the sign-manual *Billickin* got appended to the document.

Details were then settled for taking possession on the next day but one, when Miss Twinkleton might be reasonably expected; and Rosa went back to Furnival's Inn on her guardian's arm.

Behold Mr Tartar walking up and down Furnival's Inn, checking himself when he saw them coming, and advancing towards them!

'It occurred to me,' hinted Mr Tartar, 'that we might go up the river, the weather being so delicious and the tide serving. I have a boat of my own at the Temple Stairs.'[254]

'I have not been up the river for this many a day,' said Mr Grewgious, tempted.

'I was never up the river,' added Rosa.

Within half an hour they were setting this matter right by going up the river. The tide was running with them, the afternoon was charming. Mr Tartar's boat was perfect. Mr Tartar and Lobley (Mr Tartar's man) pulled a pair of oars. Mr Tartar had a yacht, it seemed, lying somewhere down by Greenhithe; and Mr Tartar's man had charge of this yacht, and was detached upon his present service. He was a jolly-favoured man, with tawny hair and whiskers, and a big red face. He was the dead image of the sun in old woodcuts,[255] his hair and whiskers answering for rays all around him. Resplendent in the bow of the boat, he was a shining sight, with a man-of-war's man's shirt on – or off, according to opinion – and his arms and breast tattooed all sorts of patterns. Lobley seemed to take it easily, and so did Mr Tartar; yet their oars bent as they pulled, and the boat bounded under them. Mr Tartar talked as if he were doing nothing, to Rosa who was really doing nothing, and to Mr Grewgious who was doing this much – that he steered all wrong; but what did that matter, when a turn of Mr Tartar's skilful wrist, or a mere grin of Mr Lobley's over the bow, put all to rights! The tide bore them on in the gayest and most sparkling manner, until they stopped to dine in some everlast-ingly-green garden, needing no matter-of-fact identification here; and then the tide obligingly turned – being devoted to that party alone for that day; and as they floated idly among some osier-beds, Rosa tried what she could do in the rowing way, and came off splendidly, being much assisted; and Mr Grewgious tried what he could do, and came off on his back, doubled up with an oar under his chin, being not assisted at all. Then there was an interval of rest under boughs (such rest!), what time Mr Lobley mopped and, arranging cushions, stretchers and the like, danced the tight-rope the whole length of the boat like a man to whom shoes were a superstition and stockings slavery;[256] and then came the sweet return among delicious odours of limes in bloom, and musical ripplings; and, all too soon, the great black city cast its shadow on the waters, and its dark bridges spanned them as death spans life, and the everlastingly-green garden seemed to be left for everlast-ing, unregainable and far away.

'Cannot people get through life without gritty stages, I wonder?' Rosa thought next day, when the town was very gritty again, and everything had a strange and an uncomfortable appearance on it of seeming to wait for something that wouldn't come. No. She began to think that, now the Cloisterham schooldays had glided past and gone, the gritty stages would begin to set in at intervals and make themselves wearily known!

Yet what did Rosa expect? Did she expect Miss Twinkleton? Miss Twinkleton duly came. Forth from her back parlour issued the Billickin to receive Miss Twinkleton, and war was in the Billickin's eye from that fell moment.

Miss Twinkleton brought a quantity of luggage with her, having all Rosa's as well as her own. The Billickin took it ill that Miss Twinkleton's mind, being sorely disturbed by this luggage, failed to take in her personal identity with that clearness of perception which was due to its demands. Stateliness mounted her gloomy throne upon the Billickin's brow in consequence. And when Miss Twinkleton, in agitation taking stock of her trunks and packages, of which she had seventeen, particularly counted in the Billickin herself as number eleven, the B found it necessary to repudiate.

'Things cannot too soon be put upon the footing,' said she, with a candour so demonstrative as to be almost obtrusive, 'that the person of the 'ouse is not a box, nor yet a bundle, nor a carpet-bag. No, I am 'ily obleeged to you, Miss Twinkleton, nor yet a beggar.'

This last disclaimer had reference to Miss Twinkleton's

Up the river

distractedly pressing two-and-sixpence on her, instead of the cabman.

Thus cast off, Miss Twinkleton wildly enquired, 'which gentle-man' was to be paid? There being two gentlemen in that position (Miss Twinkleton having arrived with two cabs), each gentleman on being paid held forth his two-and-sixpence on the flat of his open hand and, with a speechless stare and a dropped jaw, displayed his wrong to heaven and earth. Terrified by this alarming spectacle, Miss Twinkleton placed another shilling in each hand; at the same time appealing to the law in flurried accents, and re-counting her luggage this time with the two gentlemen in, who caused the total to come out complicated. Meanwhile the two gentlemen, each looking very hard at the last shilling, as if it might become eighteen-pence if he kept his eyes on it, grumblingly descended the door-steps, ascended their carriages, and drove away, leaving Miss Twinkleton bewildered on a bonnet-box in tears.

The Billickin beheld this manifestation of weakness without sympathy, and gave directions for 'a young man to be got in' to wrestle with the luggage. When that gladiator had disappeared from the arena, peace ensued, and the new lodgers dined.

But the Billickin had somehow come to the knowledge that Miss Twinkleton kept a school. The leap from that knowledge to the inference that Miss Twinkleton would set herself to teach *her* some-thing, was easy. 'But you don't do it,' soliloquised the Billickin; '*I* am not your pupil, whatever she,' meaning Rosa, 'may be, poor thing!'

Miss Twinkleton, on the other hand, having changed her dress and recovered her spirits, was animated by a bland desire to improve the occasion in all ways, and to be as serene a model as possible. In a happy compromise between her two states of exist-ence, she had already become, with her work-basket before her, the equably vivacious companion with a slight judicious flavouring of information, when the Billickin announced herself.

'I will not hide from you, ladies,' said the B, enveloped in the shawl of state, 'for it is not my character to hide neither my motives nor my actions, that I take the liberty to look in upon you to express a 'ope that your dinner was to your liking. Though not Professed but Plain,[257] still her wages should be a sufficient object to her to stimilate to soar above mere roast and biled.'

'We dined very well indeed,' said Rosa, 'thank you.'

'Accustomed,' said Miss Twinkleton with a gracious air, which to the jealous ears of the Billickin seemed to add 'my good woman' – 'accustomed to a liberal and nutritious, yet plain and salutary diet, we have found no reason to bemoan our absence from the ancient city and the methodical household in which the quiet routine of our lot has been hitherto cast.'

'I did think it well to mention to my cook,' observed the Billickin with a gush of candour, 'which I 'ope you will agree with me, Miss Twinkleton, was a right precaution, that the young lady being used to what we should consider here but poor diet, had better be brought forward by degrees. For, a rush from scanty feeding to generous feeding, and from what you may call messing to what you may call method, do require a power of constitution which is not often found in youth, particular when undermined by boarding-school!'

It will be seen that the Billickin now openly pitted herself against Miss Twinkleton, as one whom she had fully ascertained to be her natural enemy.

'Your remarks,' returned Miss Twinkleton, from a remote moral eminence, 'are well meant, I have no doubt; but you will permit me to observe that they develop a mistaken view of the subject, which can only be imputed to your extreme want of accurate information.'

'My informiation,' retorted the Billickin, throwing in an extra syllable for the sake of an emphasis at once polite and powerful – 'my informiation, Miss Twinkleton, were my own experience, which I believe is usually considered to be good guidance. But whether so or not, I was put in youth to a very genteel boarding-school, the mistress being no less a lady than yourself, of about your own age or it may be some years younger, and a poorness of blood flowed from the table which has run through my life.'

'Very likely,' said Miss Twinkleton, still from her distant eminence; 'and very much to be deplored. Rosa, my dear, how are you getting on with your work?'

'Miss Twinkleton,' resumed the Billickin, in a courtly manner, 'before retiring on the 'int, as a lady should, I wish to ask of yourself, as a lady, whether I am to consider that my words is doubted?'

'I am not aware on what ground you cherish such a supposition – ' began Miss Twinkleton again, when the Billickin again neatly stopped her.

'Do not, if you please, put suppositions betwixt my lips where none such have been imparted by myself. Your flow of words is great, Miss Twinkleton, and no doubt is expected from you by your pupils, and no doubt is considered worth the money. No doubt, I am sure. But not paying for flows of words, and not asking to be favoured with them here, I wish to repeat my question.'

'If you refer to the poverty of your circulation – ' began Miss

Twinkleton, when again the Billickin neatly stopped her.

'I have used no such expressions.'

'If you refer, then, to the poorness of your blood – '

'Brought upon me,' stipulated the Billickin, expressly, 'at a boarding-school – '

'Then,' resumed Miss Twinkleton, 'all I can say is, that I am bound to believe, on your asseveration, that it is very poor indeed. I cannot forbear adding, that if that unfortunate circumstance influences your conversation, it is much to be lamented, and it is eminently desirable that your blood were richer. Rosa, my dear, how are you getting on with your work?'

'Hem! Before retiring, miss,' proclaimed the Billickin to Rosa, loftily cancelling Miss Twinkleton, 'I should wish it to be understood between yourself and me that my transactions in future is with you alone. I know no elderly lady here, miss, none older than yourself.'

'A highly desirable arrangement, Rosa my dear,' observed Miss Twinkleton.

'It is not, miss,' said the Billickin, with a sarcastic smile, 'that I possess the mill I have heard of, in which old single ladies could be ground up young[258] (what a gift it would be to some of us!), but that I limit myself to you totally.'

'When I have any desire to communicate a request to the person of the house, Rosa my dear,' observed Miss Twinkleton with majestic cheerfulness, 'I will make it known to you, and you will kindly undertake, I am sure, that it is conveyed to the proper quarter.'

'Good-evening, miss,' said the Billickin, at once affectionately and distantly. 'Being alone in my eyes, I wish you good-evening with best wishes, and do not find myself drove, I am truly 'appy to say, into expressing my contempt for an indiwidual, unfortunately for yourself, belonging to you.'

The Billickin gracefully withdrew with this parting speech, and from that time Rosa occupied the restless position of shuttlecock between these two battledores. Nothing could be done without a smart match being played out. Thus, on the daily-arising question of dinner, Miss Twinkleton would say, the three being present together: 'Perhaps, my love, you will consult with the person of the house, whether she could procure us a lamb's fry;[259] or, failing that, a roast fowl.'

On which the Billickin would retort (Rosa not having spoken a word), 'If you was better accustomed to butcher's meat,[260] miss, you

would not entertain the idea of a lamb's fry. Firstly, because lambs
has long been sheep, and secondly, because there is such things as
killing-days, and there is not. As to roast fowls, miss, why you must
be quite surfeited with roast fowls, letting alone your buying, when
you market for yourself, the agedest of poultry with the scaliest of
legs, quite as if you was accustomed to picking 'em out for
cheapness. Try a little inwention, miss. Use yourself to 'ousekeeping
a bit. Come now, think of somethink else.'

To this encouragement, offered with the indulgent toleration of a
wise and liberal expert, Miss Twinkleton would rejoin, reddening:
'Or, my dear, you might propose to the person of the house a duck.'

'Well, Miss!' the Billickin would exclaim (still no word being
spoken by Rosa), 'you do surprise me when you speak of ducks! Not
to mention that they're getting out of season and very dear, it really
strikes to my heart to see you have a duck; for the breast, which is
the only delicate cuts in a duck, always goes in a direction which I
cannot imagine where, and your own plate comes down so miserable skin-and-bony! Try again, miss. Think more of yourself, and
less of others. A dish of sweetbreads[261] now, or a bit of mutton.
Something at which you can get your equal chance.'

Occasionally the game would wax very brisk indeed, and would be
kept up with a smartness rendering such an encounter as this quite
tame. But the Billickin almost invariably made by far the higher
score; and would come in with side hits of the most unexpected and
extraordinary description, when she seemed without a chance.

All this did not improve the gritty state of things in London, or
the air that London had acquired in Rosa's eyes of waiting for
something that never came. Tired of working and conversing with
Miss Twinkleton, she suggested working and reading: to which
Miss Twinkleton readily assented, as an admirable reader of tried
powers. But Rosa soon made the discovery that Miss Twinkleton
didn't read fairly. She cut the love-scenes, interpolated passages in
praise of female celibacy, and was guilty of other glaring pious
frauds. As an instance in point, take the glowing passage:

'Ever dearest and best adored,' said Edward, clasping the dear
head to his breast, and drawing the silken hair through his
caressing fingers, from which he suffered it to fall like golden
rain, 'ever dearest and best adored, let us fly from the unsympathetic world and the sterile coldness of the stony-hearted, to the
rich warm Paradise of Trust and Love.'

Miss Twinkleton's fraudulent version tamely ran thus:

'Ever engaged to me with the consent of our parents on both sides, and the approbation of the silver-haired rector of the district,' said Edward, respectfully raising to his lips the taper fingers so skilful in embroidery, tambour, crochet and other truly feminine arts, 'let me call on thy papa ere tomorrow's dawn has sunk into the west, and propose a suburban establishment, lowly it may be, but within our means, where he will be always welcome as an evening guest, and where every arrangement shall invest economy, and the constant interchange of scholastic acquirements, with the attributes of the ministering angel to domestic bliss.'

As the days crept on and nothing happened, the neighbours began to say that the pretty girl at Billickin's, who looked so wistfully and so much out of the gritty windows of the drawing-room, seemed to be losing her spirits. The pretty girl might have lost them but for the accident of lighting on some books of voyages and sea-adventure. As a compensation against their romance, Miss Twinkleton, reading aloud, made the most of all the latitudes and longitudes, bearings, winds, currents, offsets and other statistics (which she felt to be none the less improving because they expressed nothing whatever to her); while Rosa, listening intently, made the most of what was nearest to her heart. So they both did better than before.

CHAPTER 23

The Dawn Again

ALTHOUGH MR CRISPARKLE and John Jasper met daily under the cathedral roof, nothing at any time passed between them having reference to Edwin Drood, after the time, more than half a year gone by, when Jasper mutely showed the minor canon the conclusion and the resolution entered in his diary. It is not likely that they ever met, though so often, without the thoughts of each reverting to the subject. It is not likely that they ever met, though so often, without a sensation on the part of each that the other was a perplexing secret to him. Jasper as the denouncer and pursuer of Neville Landless, and Mr Crisparkle as his consistent advocate and protector, must at least have stood sufficiently in opposition to have speculated with keen interest each on the steadiness and next direction of the other's designs. But neither ever broached the theme.

False pretence not being in the minor canon's nature, he doubtless displayed openly that he would at any time have revived the subject, and even desired to discuss it. The determined reticence of Jasper, however, was not to be so approached. Impassive, moody, solitary, resolute, so concentrated on one idea, and on its attendant fixed purpose that he would share it with no fellow-creature, he lived apart from human life.[262] Constantly exercising an art which brought him into mechanical harmony with others, and which could not have been pursued unless he and they had been in the nicest mechanical relations and unison, it is curious to consider that the spirit of the man was in moral accordance or interchange with nothing around him. This indeed he had confided to his lost nephew, before the occasion for his present inflexibility arose.

That he must know of Rosa's abrupt departure, and that he must divine its cause, was not to be doubted. Did he suppose that he had terrified her into silence? or did he suppose that she had imparted to anyone – to Mr Crisparkle himself, for instance – the particulars of his last interview with her? Mr Crisparkle could not determine this in his mind. He could not but admit, however, as a just man, that it was not, of itself, a crime to fall in love with Rosa, any more than it was a crime to offer to set love above revenge.

The dreadful suspicion of Jasper, which Rosa was so shocked to have received into her imagination, appeared to have no harbour in Mr Crisparkle's. If it ever haunted Helena's thoughts or Neville's, neither gave it one spoken word of utterance. Mr Grewgious took no pains to conceal his implacable dislike of Jasper, yet he never referred it, however distantly, to such a source. But he was a reticent as well as an eccentric man; and he made no mention of a certain evening when he warmed his hands at the gatehouse fire, and looked steadily down upon a certain heap of torn and miry clothes upon the floor.

Drowsy Cloisterham, whenever it awoke to a passing reconsideration of a story above six months old and dismissed by the bench of magistrates, was pretty equally divided in opinion whether John Jasper's beloved nephew had been killed by his passionate rival, treacherously, or in an open struggle; or had, for his own purposes, spirited himself away. It then lifted up its head to notice that the bereaved Jasper was still ever devoted to discovery and revenge; and then dozed off again. This was the condition of matters, all round, at the period to which the present history has now attained.

The cathedral doors have closed for the night; and the choir-master, on a short leave of absence for two or three services, sets his face towards London. He travels thither by the means by which Rosa travelled, and arrives, as Rosa arrived, on a hot, dusty evening.

His travelling baggage is easily carried in his hand, and he repairs with it on foot to a hybrid hotel in a little square behind Aldersgate Street, near the General Post Office.[263] It is hotel, boarding-house or lodging-house[264] at its visitor's option. It announces itself, in the new *Railway Advertisers*,[265] as a novel enterprise, timidly beginning to spring up. It bashfully, almost apologetically, gives the traveller to understand that it does not expect him, on the good old constitutional hotel plan, to order a pint of sweet blacking[266] for his drinking, and throw it away; but insinuates that he may have his boots blacked instead of his stomach, and maybe also have bed, breakfast, attendance, and a porter up all night, for a certain fixed charge. From these and similar premises, many true Britons in the lowest spirits deduce that the times are levelling times, except in the article of high roads, of which there will shortly be not one in England.

He eats without appetite, and soon goes forth again. Eastward[267] and still eastward through the stale streets he takes his way, until he reaches his destination: a miserable court, specially miserable among many such.

He ascends a broken staircase, opens a door, looks into a dark stifling room, and says: 'Are you alone here?'

'Alone, deary; worse luck for me, and better for you,' replies a croaking voice. 'Come in, come in, whoever you be: I can't see you till I light a match, yet I seem to know the sound of your speaking. I'm acquainted with you, ain't I?'

'Light your match, and try.'

'So I will, deary, so I will; but my hand that shakes, as I can't lay it on a match all in a moment. And I cough so that, put my matches where I may, I never find 'em there. They jump and start, as I cough and cough, like live things. Are you off a voyage, deary?'

'No.'

'Not seafaring?'

'No.'

'Well, there's land customers, and there's water customers. I'm a mother to both. Different from Jack Chinaman t'other side the court. He ain't a father to neither. It ain't in him. And he ain't got the true secret of mixing, though he charges as much as me that has, and more if he can get it. Here's a match, and now where's the

Mr Greavgious has his suspicions

candle? If my cough takes me, I shall cough out twenty matches afore I gets a light.'

But she finds the candle, and lights it, before the cough comes on. It seizes her in the moment of success, and she sits down rocking herself to and fro, and gasping at intervals: 'Oh, my lungs is awful bad! my lungs is wore away to cabbage-nets!'[268] until the fit is over. During its continuance she has had no power of sight, or any other power not absorbed in the struggle; but as it leaves her, she begins to strain her eyes, and as soon as she is able to articulate, she cries, staring: 'Why, it's you!'

'Are you so surprised to see me?'

'I thought I never should have seen you again, deary. I thought you was dead, and gone to heaven.'

'Why?'

'I didn't suppose you could have kept away, alive, so long, from the poor old soul with the real receipt for mixing it. And you are in mourning too! Why didn't you come and have a pipe or two of comfort? Did they leave you money, perhaps, and so you didn't want comfort?'

'No.'

'Who was they as died, deary?'

'A relative.'

'Died of what, lovey?'

'Probably, Death.'

'We are short tonight!' cries the woman, with a propitiatory laugh. 'Short and snappish we are! But we're out of sorts for want of a smoke. We've got the all-overs, haven't us, deary? But this is the place to cure 'em in; this is the place where the all-overs is smoked off.'

'You may make ready, then,' replies the visitor, 'as soon as you like.'

He divests himself of his shoes, loosens his cravat, and lies across the foot of the squalid bed, with his head resting on his left hand.

'Now you begin to look like yourself,' says the woman approvingly. 'Now I begin to know my old customer indeed! Been trying to mix for yourself this long time, poppet?'

'I have been taking it now and then in my own way.'

'Never take it your own way. It ain't good for trade, and it ain't good for you. Where's my ink-bottle, and where's my thimble, and where's my little spoon? He's going to take it in a artful form now, my deary dear!'

Entering on her process, and beginning to bubble and blow[269] at the faint spark enclosed in the hollow of her hands, she speaks from time to time, in a tone of snuffling satisfaction, without breaking off. When he speaks, he does so without looking at her, and as if his thoughts were already roaming away by anticipation.

'I've got a pretty many smokes ready for you, first and last, haven't I, chuckey?'

'A good many.'

'When you first come, you was quite new to it; warn't ye?'

'Yes, I was easily disposed of, then.'

'But you got on in the world, and was able by and by to take your pipe with the best of 'em, warn't ye?'

'Ah; and the worst.'

'It's just ready for you. What a sweet singer you was when you first come! Used to drop your head, and sing yourself off like a bird! It's ready for you now, deary.'

He takes it from her with great care, and puts the mouthpiece to his lips. She seats herself beside him, ready to refill the pipe.

After inhaling a few whiffs in silence, he doubtingly accosts her with: 'Is it as potent as it used to be?'

'What do you speak of, deary?'

'What should I speak of, but what I have in my mouth?'

'It's just the same. Always the identical same.'

'It doesn't taste so. And it's slower.'

'You've got more used to it, you see.'

'That may be the cause, certainly. Look here – ' He stops, becomes dreamy, and seems to forget that he has invited her attention. She bends over him, and speaks in his ear.

'I'm attending to you. Says you just now, Look here. Says I now, I'm attending to ye. We was talking just before of your being used to it.'

'I know all that. I was only thinking. Look here. Suppose you had something in your mind; something you were going to do.'

'Yes, deary; something I was going to do?'

'But had not quite determined to do.'

'Yes, deary.'

'Might or might not do, you understand.'

'Yes.' With the point of a needle she stirs the contents of the bowl.

'Should you do it in your fancy, when you were lying here doing this?'

She nods her head. 'Over and over again.'

'Just like me! I did it over and over again. I have done it hundreds of thousands of times in this room.'

'It's to be hoped it was pleasant to do, deary.'

'It *was* pleasant to do!'

He says this with a savage air, and a spring or start at her. Quite unmoved she retouches or replenishes the contents of the bowl with her little spatula. Seeing her intent upon the occupation, he sinks into his former attitude.

'It was a journey, a difficult and dangerous journey. That was the subject in my mind. A hazardous and perilous journey, over abysses where a slip would be destruction. Look down, look down! You see what lies at the bottom there?'

He has darted forward to say it, and to point at the ground, as though at some imaginary object far beneath. The woman looks at him, as his spasmodic face approaches close to hers, and not at his pointing. She seems to know what the influence of her perfect quietude would be; if so, she has not miscalculated it, for he subsides again.

'Well; I have told you I did it here hundreds of thousands of times. What do I say? I did it millions and billions of times. I did it so often, and through such vast expanses of time, that when it was really done, it seemed not worth the doing, it was done so soon.'[270]

'That's the journey you have been away upon,' she quietly remarks.

He glares at her as he smokes; and then, his eyes becoming filmy, answers: 'That's the journey.'

Silence ensues. His eyes are sometimes closed and sometimes open. The woman sits beside him, very attentive to the pipe, which is all the while at his lips.

'I'll warrant,' she observes, when he has been looking fixedly at her for some consecutive moments, with a singular appearance in his eyes of seeming to see her a long way off, instead of so near him: 'I'll warrant you made the journey in many ways, when you made it so often?'

'No, always in one way.'

'Always in the same way?'

'Ay.'

'In the way in which it was really made at last?'

'Ay.'

'And always took the same pleasure in harping on it?'

'Ay.'

For the time he appears unequal to any other reply than this lazy monosyllabic assent. Probably to assure herself that it is not the assent of a mere automaton, she reverses the form of her next sentence.

'Did you never get tired of it, deary, and try to call up something else for a change?'

He struggles into a sitting posture, and retorts upon her: 'What do you mean? What did I want? What did I come for?'

She gently lays him back again, and before returning him the instrument he has dropped, revives the fire in it with her own breath; then says to him, coaxingly: 'Sure, sure, sure! Yes, yes, yes! Now I go along with you. You was too quick for me. I see now. You come o' purpose to take the journey. Why, I might have known it, through its standing by you so.'

He answers first with a laugh, and then with a passionate setting of his teeth: 'Yes, I came on purpose. When I could not bear my life, I came to get the relief, and I got it. It *was* one! It *was* one!' This repetition with extraordinary vehemence, and the snarl of a wolf.

She observes him very cautiously, as though mentally feeling her way to her next remark. It is: 'There was a fellow-traveller, deary.'

'Ha, ha, ha!' He breaks into a ringing laugh, or rather yell. 'To think,' he cries, 'how often fellow-traveller, and yet not know it! To think how many times he went the journey, and never saw the road!'

The woman kneels upon the floor, with her arms crossed on the coverlet of the bed, close by him, and her chin upon them. In this crouching attitude she watches him. The pipe is falling from his mouth. She puts it back, and laying her hand upon his chest, moves him slightly from side to side. Upon that he speaks, as if she had spoken.

'Yes! I always made the journey first, before the changes of colours and the great landscapes and glittering processions began. They couldn't begin till it was off my mind. I had no room till then for anything else.'

Once more he lapses into silence. Once more she lays her hand upon his chest, and moves him slightly to and fro, as a cat might stimulate a half-slain mouse. Once more he speaks, as if she had spoken.

'What? I told you so. When it comes to be real at last, it is so short that it seems unreal for the first time. Hark!'

'Yes, deary. I'm listening.'

'Time and place are both at hand.'[271]

He is on his feet, speaking in a whisper, and as if in the dark.

'Time, place and fellow-traveller,' she suggests, adopting his tone, and holding him softly by the arm.

'How could the time be at hand unless the fellow-traveller was? Hush! The journey's made. It's over.'

'So soon?'

'That's what I said to you. So soon. Wait a little. This is a vision.

I shall sleep it off. It has been too short and easy. I must have a better vision than this; this is the poorest of all. No struggle, no consciousness of peril, no entreaty – and yet I never saw *that* before.' With a start.

'Saw what, deary?'

'Look at it! Look what a poor, mean, miserable thing it is! *That* must be real. It's over.'

He has accompanied this incoherence with some wild unmeaning gestures; but they trail off into the progressive inaction of stupor, and he lies a log upon the bed.

The woman, however, is still inquisitive. With a repetition of her cat-like action she slightly stirs his body again, and listens; stirs it again, and listens; whispers to it, and listens. Finding it past all rousing for the time, she slowly gets upon her feet, with an air of disappointment, and flicks the face with the back of her hand in turning from it.

But she goes no further away from it than the chair upon the hearth. She sits in it, with an elbow on one of its arms, and her chin upon that hand, intent upon him. 'I heard ye say once,' she croaks under her breath, 'I heard ye say once, when I was lying where you're lying, and you were making your speculations upon me, "Unintelligible!" I heard you say so, of two more than me. But don't ye be too sure always; don't ye be too sure, beauty!'

Unwinking, cat-like and intent, she presently adds: 'Not so potent as it once was? Ah! Perhaps not at first. You may be more right there. Practice makes perfect. I may have learned the secret how to make ye talk, deary.'

He talks no more, whether or no. Twitching in an ugly way from time to time, both as to his face and limbs, he lies heavy and silent. The wretched candle burns down; the woman takes its expiring end between her fingers, lights another at it, crams the guttering frying morsel deep into the candlestick, and rams it home with the new candle, as if she were loading some ill-savoured and unseemly weapon of witchcraft; the new candle in its turn burns down; and still he lies insensible. At length what remains of the last candle is blown out, and daylight looks into the room.

It has not looked very long, when he sits up, chilled and shaking, slowly recovers consciousness of where he is, and makes himself ready to depart. The woman receives what he pays her with a grateful, 'Bless ye, bless ye, deary!' and seems, tired out, to begin making herself ready for sleep as he leaves the room.

But seeming may be false or true. It is false in this case; for, the

Sleeping it off

moment the stairs have ceased to creak under his tread, she glides after him, muttering emphatically: 'I'll not miss ye twice!'

There is no egress from the court but by its entrance. With a weird peep from the doorway, she watches for his looking back. He does not look back before disappearing, with a wavering step. She follows him, peeps from the court, sees him still faltering on without looking back, and holds him in view.

He repairs to the back of Aldersgate Street, where a door immediately opens to his knocking. She crouches in another doorway, watching that one, and easily comprehending that he puts up temporarily at that house. Her patience is unexhausted by hours. For sustenance she can, and does, buy bread within a hundred yards, and milk as it is carried past her.

He comes forth again at noon, having changed his dress, but carrying nothing in his hand, and having nothing carried for him. He is not going back into the country, therefore, just yet. She follows him a little way, hesitates instantaneously, turns confidently, and goes straight into the house he has quitted.

'Is the gentleman from Cloisterham indoors?'

'Just gone out.'

'Unlucky. When does the gentleman return to Cloisterham?'

'At six this evening.'

'Bless ye and thank ye. May the Lord prosper a business where a civil question, even from a poor soul, is so civilly answered!'

'I'll not miss ye twice!' repeats the poor soul in the street, and not so civilly. 'I lost ye last, where that omnibus you got into nigh your journey's end plied betwixt the station and the place. I wasn't so much as certain that you even went right on to the place. Now I know ye did. My gentleman from Cloisterham, I'll be there before ye, and bide your coming. I've swore my oath that I'll not miss ye twice!'

Accordingly, that same evening the poor soul stands in Cloisterham High Street, looking at the many quaint gables of the Nuns' House, and getting through the time as she best can until nine o'clock; at which hour she has reason to suppose that the arriving omnibus passengers may have some interest for her. The friendly darkness, at that hour, renders it easy for her to ascertain whether this be so or not; and it is so, for the passenger not to be missed twice arrives among the rest.

'Now let me see what becomes of you. Go on!'

An observation addressed to the air, and yet it might be addressed to the passenger, so compliantly does he go on along the High

Street until he comes to an arched gateway, at which he unexpectedly vanishes. The poor soul quickens her pace; is swift, and close
upon him in turning under the gateway; but only sees a postern
staircase on one side of it, and on the other side an ancient vaulted
room, in which a large-headed, grey-haired gentleman is writing,
under the odd circumstances of sitting open to the thoroughfare
and eyeing all who pass, as if he were toll-taker at the gateway,
though the way is free.

'Halloa!' he cries in a low voice, seeing her brought to a standstill: 'who are you looking for?'

'There was a gentleman passed in here this minute, sir. A
gentleman in mourning.'

'Of course there was. What do you want with him?'

'Where do he live, deary?'

'Live? Up that staircase.'

'Bless ye! Whisper. What's his name, deary?'

'Surname Jasper, Christian name John. Mr John Jasper.'

'Has he a calling, good gentleman?'

'Calling? Yes. Sings in the choir.'

'In the spire?'

'Choir.'

'What's that?'

Mr Datchery rises from his papers, and comes to his doorstep.
'Do you know what a cathedral is?' he asks, jocosely.

The woman nods.

'What is it?'

She looks puzzled, casting about in her mind to find a definition,
when it occurs to her that it is easier to point out the substantial
object itself, massive against the dark-blue sky and the early stars.

'That's the answer. Go in there at seven tomorrow morning, and
you may see Mr John Jasper, and hear him too.'

'Thank ye! Thank ye!'

The burst of triumph in which she thanks him does not escape the
notice of the single buffer of an easy temper living idly on his means.
He glances at her; clasps his hands behind him, as the wont of such
buffers is; and lounges along the echoing precincts at her side.

'Or,' he suggests, with a backward hitch of his head, 'you can go
up at once to Mr Jasper's rooms there.'

The woman eyes him with a cunning smile, and shakes her head.

'Oh! you don't want to speak to him?'

She repeats her dumb reply, and forms with her lips a soundless
'No.'

'You can admire him at a distance three times a day, whenever you like. It's a long way to come for that, though.'

The woman looks up quickly. If Mr Datchery thinks she is to be so induced to declare where she comes from, he is of a much easier temper than she is. But she acquits him of such an artful thought, as he lounges along, like the chartered bore of the city, with his uncovered grey hair blowing about, and his purposeless hands rattling the loose money in the pockets of his trousers.

The chink of the money has an attraction for her greedy ears. 'Wouldn't you help me to pay for my traveller's lodging, dear gentleman, and to pay my way along? I am a poor soul, I am indeed, and troubled with a grievous cough.'

'You know the travellers' lodging, I perceive, and are making direct for it,' is Mr Datchery's bland comment, still rattling his loose money. 'Been here often, my good woman?'

'Once in all my life.'

'Ay, ay?'

They have arrived at the entrance to the Monks' Vineyard. An appropriate remembrance, presenting an exemplary model for imitation, is revived in the woman's mind by the sight of the place. She stops at the gate, and says energetically: 'By this token, though you mayn't believe it, that a young gentleman gave me three-and-sixpence as I was coughing my breath away on this very grass. I asked him for three-and-sixpence, and he gave it me.'

'Wasn't it a little cool to name your sum?' hints Mr Datchery, still rattling. 'Isn't it customary to leave the amount open? Mightn't it have had the appearance, to the young gentleman – only the appearance – that he was rather dictated to?'

'Look'ee here, deary,' she replies, in a confidential and persuasive tone, 'I wanted the money to lay it out on a medicine as does me good, and as I deal in. I told the young gentleman so, and he gave it me, and I laid it out honest to the last brass farden. I want to lay out the same sum in the same way now; and if you'll give it me, I'll lay it out honest to the last brass farden again, upon my soul!'

'What's the medicine?'

'I'll be honest with you beforehand, as well as after. It's opium.'

Mr Datchery, with a sudden change of countenance, gives her a sudden look.

'It's opium, deary. Neither more nor less. And it's like a human creetur so far that you always hear what can be said against it, but seldom what can be said in its praise.'

Mr Datchery begins very slowly to count out the sum demanded of him. Greedily watching his hands, she continues to hold forth on the great example set him.

'It was last Christmas Eve, just arter dark, the once that I was here afore, when the young gentleman gave me the three-and-six.' Mr Datchery stops in his counting, finds he has counted wrong, shakes his money together, and begins again.

'And the young gentleman's name,' she adds, 'was Edwin.'

Mr Datchery drops some money, stoops to pick it up, and reddens with the exertion as he asks: 'How do you know the young gentleman's name?'

'I asked him for it, and he told it me. I only asked him the two questions, what was his Chris'en name, and whether he'd a sweetheart? And he answered, Edwin, and he hadn't.'

Mr Datchery pauses with the selected coins in his hand, rather as if he were falling into a brown study of their value, and couldn't bear to part with them. The woman looks at him distrustfully, and with her anger brewing for the event of his thinking better of the gift; but he bestows it on her as if he were abstracting his mind from the sacrifice, and with many servile thanks she goes her way.

John Jasper's lamp is kindled, and his lighthouse is shining when Mr Datchery returns alone towards it. As mariners on a dangerous voyage, approaching an iron-bound coast, may look along the beams of the warning light to the haven lying beyond it that may never be reached, so Mr Datchery's wistful gaze is directed to this beacon, and beyond.

His object in now revisiting his lodging is merely to put on the hat which seems so superfluous an article in his wardrobe. It is half-past ten by the cathedral clock when he walks out into the precincts again; he lingers and looks about him, as though, the enchanted hour when Mr Durdles may be stoned home having struck, he had some expectation of seeing the imp who is appointed to the mission of stoning him.

In effect, that power of evil is abroad. Having nothing living to stone at the moment, he is discovered by Mr Datchery in the unholy office of stoning the dead, through the railings of the churchyard. The imp finds this a relishing and piquing pursuit; firstly, because their resting-place is announced to be sacred; and secondly, because the tall headstones are sufficiently like themselves, on their beat in the dark, to justify the delicious fancy that they are hurt when hit.

Mr Datchery hails him with: 'Halloa, Winks!' He acknowledges the hail with: 'Halloa, Dick!' Their acquaintance seemingly having been established on a familiar footing.

'But, I say,' he remonstrates, 'don't yer go a-making my name public. I never means to plead to no name, mind yer. When they says to me in the lock-up, a-going to put me down in the book, "What's your name?" I says to them, "Find out." Likewise when they says, "What's your religion?" I says, "Find out." '

Which, it may be observed in passing, it would be immensely difficult for the State, however statistical, to do.[272]

'Asides which,' adds the boy, 'there ain't no family of Winkses.'

'I think there must be.'

'Yer lie, there ain't. The travellers[273] give me the name on account of my getting no settled sleep and being knocked up all night; whereby I gets one eye roused open afore I've shut the other. That's what Winks means. Deputy's the nighest name to indict me by: but yer wouldn't catch me pleading to that, neither.'

'Deputy be it always, then. We two are good friends; eh, Deputy?'

'Jolly good.'

'I forgave you the debt you owed me when we first became acquainted, and many of my sixpences have come your way since; eh, Deputy?'

'Ah! And what's more, yer ain't no friend o' Jarsper's. What did he go a-histing me off my legs for?'

'What indeed! But never mind him now. A shilling of mine is coming your way tonight, Deputy. You have just taken in a lodger I have been speaking to; an infirm woman with a cough.'

'Puffer,' assents Deputy, with a shrewd leer of recognition, and smoking an imaginary pipe, with his head very much on one side and his rolling eyes very much out of their places: 'Hopeum Puffer.'

'What is her name?'

''Er Royal Highness the Princess Puffer.'

'She has some other name than that; where does she live?'

'Up in London. Among the jacks.'

'The sailors?'

'I said so: jacks; and Chayner men;[274] and hother knifers.'

'I should like to know, through you, exactly where she lives.'

'All right. Give us 'old.'

A shilling passes; and, in that spirit of confidence which should pervade all business transactions between principals of honour, this piece of business is considered done.

'But here's a lark!' cries Deputy. 'Where do yer think 'er Royal Highness is a-goin' to tomorrow morning? Blest if she ain't a-goin' to the *kin–free–der–el*!' He greatly prolongs the word in his ecstasy, and smites his leg, and doubles himself up in a fit of shrill laughter.

'How do you know that, Deputy?'

''Cos she told me so just now. She said she must be hup and hout o' purpose. She ses, "Deputy, I must 'ave a early wash, and make myself as swell as I can, for I'm a-goin' to take a turn at the *kin–free–der–el*!" ' He separates the syllables with his former zest, and, not finding his sense of the ludicrous sufficiently relieved by stamping about on the pavement, breaks into a slow and stately dance, perhaps supposed to be performed by the dean.

Mr Datchery receives the communication with a well-satisfied though pondering face, and breaks up the conference. Returning to his quaint lodging, and sitting long over the supper of bread and cheese and salad and ale which Mrs Tope has left prepared for him, he still sits when his supper is finished. At length he rises, throws open the door of a corner cupboard, and refers to a few uncouth chalked strokes on its inner side.

'I like,' says Mr Datchery, 'the old tavern way of keeping scores.[275] Illegible except to the scorer. The scorer not committed, the scored debited with what is against him. Humph! A very small score this; a very poor score!'

He sighs over the contemplation of its poverty, takes a bit of chalk from one of the cupboard shelves, and pauses with it in his hand, uncertain what addition to make to the account.

'I think a moderate stroke,' he concludes, 'is all I am justified in scoring up;' so saying he suits the action to the word,[276] closes the cupboard, and goes to bed.

A brilliant morning shines on the old city. Its antiquities and ruins are surpassingly beautiful, with a lusty ivy gleaming in the sun, and the rich trees waving in the balmy air. Changes of glorious light from moving boughs, songs of birds, scents from gardens, woods, and fields – or, rather, from the one great garden of the whole cultivated island[277] in its yielding time – penetrate into the cathedral, subdue its earthy odour, and preach the Resurrection and the Life.[278] The cold stone tombs of centuries ago grow warm; and flecks of brightness dart into the sternest marble corners of the building, fluttering there like wings.

Comes Mr Tope with his large keys, and yawningly unlocks and sets open. Come Mrs Tope and attendant sweeping sprites. Come, in due time, organist and bellows-boy, peeping down from the red curtains in the loft, fearlessly flapping dust from books up at that remote elevation, and whisking it from stops and pedals. Come sundry rooks, from various quarters of the sky, back to the great tower; who may be presumed to enjoy vibration, and to know that bell and organ are going to give it them. Come a very small and straggling congregation indeed: chiefly from Minor Canon Corner and the precincts. Come Mr Crisparkle, fresh and bright; and his ministering brethren, not quite so fresh and bright. Come the choir in a hurry (always in a hurry, and struggling into their nightgowns at the last moment, like children shirking bed), and comes John Jasper leading their line. Last of all comes Mr Datchery into a stall, one of a choice empty collection very much at his service, and glancing about him for Her Royal Highness the Princess Puffer.

The service is pretty well advanced before Mr Datchery can discern Her Royal Highness. But by that time he has made her out, in the shade. She is behind a pillar, carefully withdrawn from the choirmaster's view, but regards him with the closest attention. All unconscious of her presence, he chants and sings. She grins when he is most musically fervid, and – yes, Mr Datchery sees her do it! – shakes her fist at him behind the pillar's friendly shelter.

Mr Datchery looks again, to convince himself. Yes, again! As ugly and withered as one of the fantastic carvings on the under brackets of the stall seats, as malignant as the Evil One, as hard as the big brass eagle holding the sacred books upon his wings (and, according to the sculptor's presentation of his ferocious attributes, not at all converted by them), she hugs herself in her lean arms, and then shakes both fists at the leader of the choir.

And at that moment, outside the grated door of the choir, having eluded the vigilance of Mr Tope by shifty resources in which he is an adept, Deputy peeps, sharp-eyed, through the bars, and stares astounded from the threatener to the threatened.

The service comes to an end, and the servitors disperse to breakfast. Mr Datchery accosts his last new acquaintance outside, when the choir (as much in a hurry to get their bedgowns off as they were but now to get them on) have scuffled away.

'Well, mistress. Good-morning. You have seen him?'

'*I've* seen him, deary; *I've* seen him!'

'And you know him?'

'Know him! Better far than all the reverend parsons put together know him.'

Mrs Tope's care has spread a very neat, clean breakfast ready for her lodger. Before sitting down to it, he opens his corner-cupboard door; takes his bit of chalk from its shelf; adds one thick line to the score, extending from the top of the cupboard door to the bottom; and then falls to with an appetite.

MASTER HUMPHREY'S CLOCK

Master Humphrey, from his Clockside in the Chimney-Corner

THE READER must not expect to know where I live. At present, it is true, my abode may be a question of little or no import to anybody; but if I should carry my readers with me, as I hope to do, and there should spring up between them and me feelings of homely affection and regard attaching something of interest to matters ever so slightly connected with my fortunes or my speculations, even my place of residence might one day have a kind of charm for them. Bearing this possible contingency in mind, I wish them to understand, in the outset, that they must never expect to know it.

I am not a churlish old man. Friendless I can never be, for all mankind are my kindred, and I am on ill terms with no one member of my great family. But for many years I have led a lonely, solitary life; what wound I sought to heal, what sorrow to forget, originally, matters not now; it is sufficient that retirement has become a habit with me, and that I am unwilling to break the spell which for so long a time has shed its quiet influence upon my home and heart.

I live in a venerable suburb of London, in an old house which in bygone days was a famous resort for merry roysterers and peerless ladies, long since departed. It is a silent, shady place, with a paved courtyard so full of echoes, that sometimes I am tempted to believe that faint responses to the noises of old times linger there yet, and that these ghosts of sound haunt my footsteps as I pace it up and down. I am the more confirmed in this belief, because, of late years, the echoes that attend my walks have been less loud and marked than they were wont to be; and it is pleasanter to imagine in them the rustling of silk brocade, and the light step of some lovely girl, than to recognise in their altered note the failing tread of an old man.

Those who like to read of brilliant rooms and gorgeous furniture would derive but little pleasure from a minute description of my simple dwelling. It is dear to me for the same reason that they would hold it in slight regard. Its worm-eaten doors, and low ceilings crossed by clumsy beams; its walls of wainscot, dark stairs, and gaping closets; its small chambers, communicating with each other by winding passages or narrow steps; its many nooks, scarce larger than its corner-cupboards; its very dust and dullness, are all dear to me. The moth and spider are my constant tenants; for in my house the one basks in his long sleep, and the other plies his busy loom secure and undisturbed. I have a pleasure in thinking on a summer's day how many butterflies have sprung for the first time into light and sunshine from some dark corner of these old walls.

When I first came to live here, which was many years ago, the neighbours were curious to know who I was, and whence I came, and why I lived so much alone. As time went on, and they still remained unsatisfied on these points, I became the centre of a popular ferment, extending for half a mile round, and in one direction for a full mile. Various rumours were circulated to my prejudice. I was a spy, an infidel, a conjurer, a kidnapper of children, a refugee, a priest, a monster. Mothers caught up their infants and ran into their houses as I passed; men eyed me spitefully, and muttered threats and curses. I was the object of suspicion and distrust – ay, of downright hatred too.

But when in course of time they found I did no harm, but, on the contrary, inclined towards them despite their unjust usage, they began to relent. I found my footsteps no longer dogged, as they had often been before, and observed that the women and children no longer retreated, but would stand and gaze at me as I passed their doors. I took this for a good omen, and waited patiently for better times. By degrees I began to make friends among these humble folks; and though they were yet shy of speaking, would give them 'good-day', and so pass on. In a little time, those whom I had thus accosted would make a point of coming to their doors and windows at the usual hour, and nod or curtsy to me; children, too, came timidly within my reach, and ran away quite scared when I patted their heads and bade them be good at school. These little people soon grew more familiar. From exchanging mere words of course with my older neighbours, I gradually became their friend and adviser, the depositary of their cares and sorrows, and sometimes, it may be, the reliever, in my small way, of their distresses. And now I never walk abroad but pleasant recognitions and smiling faces wait on Master Humphrey.

It was a whim of mine, perhaps as a whet to the curiosity of my neighbours, and a kind of retaliation upon them for their suspicions – it was, I say, a whim of mine, when I first took up my abode in this place, to acknowledge no other name than Humphrey. With my detractors, I was Ugly Humphrey. When I began to convert them into friends, I was Mr Humphrey and Old Mr Humphrey. At length I settled down into plain Master Humphrey, which was understood to be the title most pleasant to my ear; and so completely a matter of course has it become that sometimes, when I am taking my morning walk in my little courtyard, I overhear my barber – who has a profound respect for me, and would not, I am sure, abridge my honours for the world – holding forth on the other side of the wall, touching the state of 'Master Humphrey's' health, and communicating to some friend the substance of the conversation that he and Master Humphrey have had together in the course of the shaving which he has just concluded.

That I may not make acquaintance with my readers under false pretences, or give them cause to complain hereafter that I have withheld any matter which it was essential for them to have learnt at first, I wish them to know – and I smile sorrowfully to think that the time has been when the confession would have given me pain – that I am a misshapen, deformed old man.

I have never been made a misanthrope by this cause. I have never been stung by any insult, nor wounded by any jest upon my crooked figure. As a child I was melancholy and timid, but that was because the gentle consideration paid to my misfortune sank deep into my spirit and made me sad, even in those early days. I was but a very young creature when my poor mother died, and yet I remember that often when I hung around her neck, and oftener still when I played about the room before her, she would catch me to her bosom, and bursting into tears, would soothe me with every term of fondness and affection. God knows I was a happy child at those times – happy to nestle in her breast – happy to weep when she did – happy in not knowing why.

These occasions are so strongly impressed upon my memory, that they seem to have occupied whole years. I had numbered very, very few when they ceased for ever, but before then their meaning had been revealed to me.

I do not know whether all children are imbued with a quick perception of childish grace and beauty, and a strong love for it, but I was. I had no thought that I remember, either that I possessed it myself or that I lacked it, but I admired it with an intensity that I cannot describe. A little knot of playmates – they must have been beautiful, for I see them now – were clustered one day round my mother's knee in eager admiration of some picture representing a group of infant angels, which she held in her hand. Whose the picture was, whether it was familiar to me or otherwise, or how all the children came to be there, I forget; I have some dim thought it was my birthday, but the beginning of my recollection is that we were all together in a garden, and it was summer weather – I am sure of that, for one of the little girls had roses in her sash. There were many lovely angels in this picture, and I remember the fancy coming upon me to point out which of them represented each child there, and that when I had gone through my companions, I stopped and hesitated, wondering which was most like me. I remember the children looking at each other, and my turning red and hot, and their crowding round to kiss me, saying that they loved me all the same; and then, and when the old sorrow came into my dear mother's mild and tender look, the truth broke upon me for the first time, and I knew, while watching my awkward and ungainly sports, how keenly she had felt for her poor crippled boy.

I used frequently to dream of it afterwards, and now my heart aches for that child as if I had never been he, when I think how often he awoke from some fairy change to his own old form, and sobbed himself to sleep again.

Well, well – all these sorrows are past. My glancing at them may not be without its use, for it may help in some measure to explain why I have all my life been attached to the inanimate objects that people my chamber, and how I have come to look upon them rather in the light of old and constant friends than as mere chairs and tables which a little money could replace at will.

Chief and first among all these is my clock – my old, cheerful, companionable clock. How can I ever convey to others an idea of the comfort and consolation that this old clock has been for years to me!

It is associated with my earliest recollections. It stood upon the staircase at home (I call it home still mechanically), nigh sixty years ago. I like it for that; but it is not on that account, nor because it is a quaint old thing in a huge oaken case curiously and richly carved, that I prize it as I do. I incline to it as if it were alive, and could understand and give me back the love I bear it.

And what other thing that has not life could cheer me as it does? what other thing that has not life (I will not say how few things that have) could have proved the same patient, true, untiring friend?

How often have I sat in the long winter evenings feeling such society in its cricket-voice[1] that, raising my eyes from my book and looking gratefully towards it, the face reddened by the glow of the shining fire has seemed to relax from its staid expression and to regard me kindly! how often in the summer twilight, when my thoughts have wandered back to a melancholy past, have its regular whisperings recalled them to the calm and peaceful present! how often in the dead tranquillity of night has its bell broken the oppressive silence, and seemed to give me assurance that the old clock was still a faithful watcher at my chamber-door! My easy-chair, my desk, my ancient furniture, my very books, I can scarcely bring myself to love even these last like my old clock.

It stands in a snug corner, midway between the fireside and a low arched door leading to my bedroom. Its fame is diffused so extensively throughout the neighbourhood, that I have often the satisfaction of hearing the publican, or the baker, and sometimes even the parish-clerk,[2] petitioning my housekeeper (of whom I shall have much to say by and by) to inform him the exact time by Master Humphrey's clock. My barber, to whom I have referred, would sooner believe it than the sun. Nor are these its only distinctions. It has acquired, I am happy to say, another, inseparably connecting it not only with my enjoyments and reflections, but with those of other men; as I shall now relate.

I lived alone here for a long time without any friend or acquaintance. In the course of my wanderings by night and day, at all hours and seasons, in city streets and quiet country parts, I came to be familiar with certain faces, and to take it to heart as quite a heavy disappointment if they failed to present themselves each at its accustomed spot. But these were the only friends I knew, and beyond them I had none.

It happened, however, when I had gone on thus for a long time, that I formed an acquaintance with a deaf gentleman, which ripened into intimacy and close companionship. To this hour, I am ignorant of his name. It is his humour to conceal it, or he has a reason and purpose for so doing. In either case, I feel that he has a right to require a return of the trust he has reposed; and as he has never sought to discover my secret, I have never sought to penetrate his. There may have been something in this tacit confidence in each other flattering and pleasant to us both, and it may have imparted in the beginning an additional zest, perhaps, to our friendship. Be this as it may, we have grown to be like brothers, and still I only know him as the deaf gentleman.

I have said that retirement has become a habit with me. When I add that the deaf gentleman and I have two friends, I communicate nothing which is inconsistent with that declaration. I spend many hours of every day in solitude and study, have no friends or change of friends but these, only see them at stated periods, and am supposed to be of a retired spirit by the very nature and object of our association.

We are men of secluded habits, with something of a cloud upon our early fortunes, whose enthusiasm, nevertheless, has not cooled with age, whose spirit of romance is not yet quenched, who are content to ramble through the world in a pleasant dream, rather than ever waken again to its harsh realities. We are alchemists[3] who would extract the essence of perpetual youth from dust and ashes, tempt coy Truth in many light and airy forms from the bottom of her well, and discover one crumb of comfort or one grain of good in the commonest and least-regarded matter that passes through our crucible. Spirits of past times, creatures of imagination, and people of today are alike the objects of our seeking, and, unlike the objects of search with most philosophers, we can ensure their coming at our command.

The deaf gentleman and I first began to beguile our days with these fancies, and our nights in communicating them to each other. We are now four. But in my room there are six old chairs, and we have decided that the two empty seats shall always be placed at our table when we meet, to remind us that we may yet increase our company by that number, if we should find two men to our mind. When one among us dies, his chair will always be set in its usual place, but never occupied again; and I have caused my will to be so drawn out that when we are all dead the house shall be shut up, and the vacant chairs still left in their accustomed places. It is pleasant to think that even then our shades may, perhaps, assemble together as of yore we did, and join in ghostly converse.

One night in every week, as the clock strikes ten, we meet. At the second stroke of two, I am alone.

And now shall I tell how that my old servant, besides giving us note of time, and ticking cheerful encouragement of our proceedings, lends its name to our society, which for its punctuality and my love is christened 'Master Humphrey's Clock'? Now shall I tell how that in the bottom of the old dark closet, where the steady pendulum throbs and beats with healthy action, though the pulse of him who made it stood still long ago, and never moved again, there are piles of dusty papers constantly placed there by our hands, that we may link our enjoyments with my old friend, and draw means to beguile time from the heart of time itself? Shall I, or can I, tell with what a secret pride I open this repository when we meet at night, and still find new store of pleasure in my dear old clock?

Friend and companion of my solitude! mine is not a selfish love; I would not keep your merits to myself, but disperse something of pleasant association with your image through the whole wide world; I would have men couple with your name cheerful and healthy thoughts; I would have them believe that you keep true and honest time; and how it would gladden me to know that they recognised some hearty English work in Master Humphrey's clock!

THE CLOCK-CASE

It is my intention constantly to address my readers from the chimney-corner, and I would fain hope that such accounts as I shall give them of our histories and proceedings, our quiet speculations or more busy adventures, will never be unwelcome. Lest, however, I should grow prolix in the outset by lingering too long upon our little association, confounding the enthusiasm with which I regard this chief happiness of my life with that minor degree of interest which those to whom I address myself may be supposed to feel for it, I have deemed it expedient to break off as they have seen.

But, still clinging to my old friend, and naturally desirous that all its merits should be known, I am tempted to open (somewhat irregularly and against our laws, I must admit) the clock-case. The first roll of paper on which I lay my hand is in the writing of the deaf gentleman. I shall have to speak of him in my next paper; and how can I better approach that welcome task than by prefacing it with a production of his own pen, consigned to the safe keeping of my honest clock by his own hand?

The manuscript runs thus:

INTRODUCTION TO THE GIANT CHRONICLES

Once upon a time, that is to say, in this our time – the exact year, month and day are of no matter – there dwelt in the city of London a substantial citizen, who united in his single person the dignities of wholesale fruiterer, alderman, common-councilman and member of the worshipful Company of Patten-Makers; who had superadded to these extraordinary distinctions the important post and title of sheriff, and who at length, and to crown all, stood next in rotation for the high and honourable office of Lord Mayor.

He was a very substantial citizen indeed. His face was like the full moon in a fog, with two little holes punched out for his eyes, a very ripe pear stuck on for his nose, and a wide gash to serve for a mouth. The girth of his waistcoat was hung up and lettered in his tailor's shop as an extraordinary curiosity. He breathed like a heavy snorer, and his voice in speaking came thickly forth, as if it were oppressed and stifled by featherbeds. He trod the ground like an elephant, and eat and drank like – like nothing but an alderman, as he was.

This worthy citizen had risen to his great eminence from small beginnings. He had once been a very lean, weazen little boy, never dreaming of carrying such a weight of flesh upon his bones or of money in his pockets, and glad enough to take his dinner at a baker's door, and his tea at a pump. But he had long ago forgotten all this, as it was proper that a wholesale fruiterer, alderman, common-councilman, member of the worshipful Company of Patten-Makers, past sheriff and, above all, a Lord Mayor[4] that was to be, should; and he never forgot it more completely in all his life than on the eighth of November in the year of his election to the great golden civic chair, which was the day before his grand dinner at Guildhall.[5]

It happened that as he sat that evening all alone in his counting-house, looking over the bill of fare for next day, and checking off the fat capons in fifties, and the turtle-soup by the hundred quarts, for his private amusement – it happened that as he sat alone occupied in these pleasant calculations, a strange man came in and asked him how he did, adding, 'If I am half as much changed as you, sir, you have no recollection of me, I am sure.'

The strange man was not over and above well dressed, and was very far from being fat or rich-looking in any sense of the word, yet he spoke with a kind of modest confidence, and assumed an easy, gentlemanly sort of an air, to which nobody but a rich man can lawfully presume. Besides this, he interrupted the good citizen just as he had reckoned three hundred and seventy-two fat capons, and was carrying them over to the next column; and as if that were not aggravation enough, the learned recorder for the city of London[6] had only ten minutes previously gone out at that very same door, and had turned round and said, 'Good-night, my lord.' Yes, he had said, 'my lord'; – he, a man of birth and education, of the Honourable Society of the Middle Temple,[7] barrister-at-law – he who had an uncle in the House of Commons, and an aunt almost but not quite in the House of Lords (for she had married a feeble peer, and made him vote as she liked) – he, this man, this learned recorder, had said, 'my lord'. 'I'll not wait till tomorrow to give you your title, my Lord Mayor,' says he, with a bow and a smile; 'you are Lord Mayor de facto, if not de jure.[8] Good-night, my lord.'

The Lord Mayor elect thought of this, and turning to the stranger, and sternly bidding him 'go out of his private counting-house', brought forward the three hundred and seventy-two fat capons, and went on with his account.

'Do you remember,' said the other, stepping forward – '*do* you remember little Joe Toddyhigh?'

The port wine fled for a moment from the fruiterer's nose as he muttered, 'Joe Toddyhigh! What about Joe Toddyhigh?'

'*I* am Joe Toddyhigh,' cried the visitor. 'Look at me, look hard at me – harder, harder. You know me now? You know little Joe again? What a happiness to us both, to meet the very night before your grandeur! Oh! give me your hand, Jack – both hands – both, for the sake of old times.'

'You pinch me, sir. You're a-hurting of me,' said the Lord Mayor elect pettishly. 'Don't – suppose anybody should come – Mr Toddyhigh, sir.'

'Mr Toddyhigh!' repeated the other ruefully.

'Oh, don't bother,' said the Lord Mayor elect, scratching his head. 'Dear me! Why, I thought you was dead. What a fellow you are!'

Indeed, it was a pretty state of things, and worthy the tone of vexation and disappointment in which the Lord Mayor spoke. Joe Toddyhigh had been a poor boy with him at Hull,[9] and had oftentimes divided his last penny and parted his last crust to relieve his wants; for though Joe was a destitute child in those times, he was as faithful and affectionate in his friendship as ever man of might could be. They parted one day to seek their fortunes in different directions. Joe went to sea, and the now wealthy citizen begged his way to London. They separated with many tears, like foolish fellows as they were, and agreed to remain fast friends, and if they lived, soon to communicate again.

When he was an errand-boy, and even in the early days of his apprenticeship, the citizen had many a time trudged to the post office to ask if there were any letter from poor little Joe, and had gone home again with tears in his eyes when he found no news of his only friend. The world is a wide place, and it was a long time before the letter came; when it did, the writer was forgotten. It turned from white to yellow from lying in the post office with nobody to claim it, and in course of time was torn up with five hundred others and sold for wastepaper. And now at last, and when it might least have been expected, here was this Joe Toddyhigh turning up and claiming acquaintance with a great public character, who on the morrow would be cracking jokes with the Prime Minister of England, and who had only, at any time during the next twelve months, to say the word, and he could shut up Temple Bar, and make it no thoroughfare for the king himself!

'I am sure I don't know what to say, Mr Toddyhigh,' said the Lord Mayor elect; 'I really don't. It's very inconvenient. I'd sooner have given twenty pound – it's very inconvenient, really.'

A thought had come into his mind, that perhaps his old friend might say something passionate which would give him an excuse for being angry himself. No such thing. Joe looked at him steadily, but very mildly, and did not open his lips.

'Of course I shall pay you what I owe you,' said the Lord Mayor elect, fidgeting in his chair. 'You lent me – I think it was a shilling or some small coin – when we parted company, and that of course I shall pay with good interest. I can pay my way with any man, and always have done. If you look into the Mansion House[10] the day after tomorrow – some time after dusk – and ask for my private clerk, you'll find he has a draft for you. I haven't got time to say anything more just now, unless' – he hesitated, for coupled with a strong desire to glitter for once in all his glory in the eyes of his former companion was a distrust of his appearance, which might be more shabby than he could tell by that feeble light – 'unless you'd like to come to the dinner tomorrow. I don't mind your having this ticket, if you like to take it. A great many people would give their ears for it, I can tell you.'

His old friend took the card without speaking a word, and instantly departed. His sunburnt face and grey hair were present to the citizen's mind for a moment; but by the time he reached three hundred and eighty-one fat capons, he had quite forgotten him.

Joe Toddyhigh had never been in the capital of Europe before, and he wandered up and down the streets that night amazed at the number of churches and other public buildings, the splendour of the shops, the riches that were heaped up on every side, the glare of light in which they were displayed, and the concourse of people who hurried to and fro, indifferent, apparently, to all the wonders that surrounded them. But in all the long streets and broad squares, there were none but strangers; it was quite a relief to turn down a byway and hear his own footsteps on the pavement. He went home to his inn, thought that London was a dreary, desolate place, and felt disposed to doubt the existence of one true-hearted man in the whole worshipful Company of Patten-Makers. Finally, he went to bed, and dreamed that he and the Lord Mayor elect were boys again.

He went next day to the dinner; and when, in a burst of light and music, and in the midst of splendid decorations and surrounded by brilliant company, his former friend appeared at the head of the hall, and was hailed with shouts and cheering, he cheered and shouted with the best, and for the moment could have cried. The next moment he cursed his weakness in behalf of a man so changed and selfish, and quite hated a jolly-looking old gentleman opposite for declaring himself in the pride of his heart a Patten-Maker.

As the banquet proceeded, he took more and more to heart the rich citizen's unkindness; and that, not from any envy, but because he felt that a man of his state and fortune could all the better afford to recognise an old friend, even if he were poor and obscure. The more he thought of this, the more lonely and sad he felt. When the company dispersed and adjourned to the ballroom, he paced the hall and passages alone, ruminating in a very melancholy condition upon the disappointment he had experienced.

It chanced, while he was lounging about in this moody state, that he stumbled upon a flight of stairs, dark, steep and narrow, which he ascended without any thought about the matter, and so came into a little music-gallery, empty and deserted. From this elevated post, which commanded the whole hall, he amused himself in looking down upon the attendants who were clearing away the fragments of the feast very lazily, and drinking out of all the bottles and glasses with most commendable perseverance.

His attention gradually relaxed and he fell fast asleep.

When he awoke, he thought there must be something the matter with his eyes; but, rubbing them a little, he soon found that the moonlight was really streaming through the east window, that the lamps were all extinguished, and that he was alone. He listened, but no distant murmur in the echoing passages, not even the shutting of a door, broke the deep silence; he groped his way down the stairs, and found that the door at the bottom was locked on the other side. He began now to comprehend that he must have slept a long time, that he had been overlooked, and was shut up there for the night.

His first sensation, perhaps, was not altogether a comfortable one, for it was a dark, chilly, earthy-smelling place, and something too large, for a man so situated, to feel at home in. However, when the momentary consternation of his surprise was over, he made light of the accident, and resolved to feel his way up the stairs again, and make himself as comfortable as he could in the gallery until morning. As he turned to execute this purpose, he heard the clocks strike three.

Any such invasion of a dead stillness as the striking of distant clocks causes it to appear the more intense and insupportable when the sound has ceased. He listened with strained attention in the hope that some clock, lagging behind its fellows, had yet to strike – looking all the time into the profound darkness before him, until it seemed to weave itself into a black tissue, patterned with a hundred reflections of his own eyes. But the bells had all pealed out their warning for that once, and the gust of wind that moaned through the place seemed cold and heavy with their iron breath.

The time and circumstances were favourable to reflection. He tried to keep his thoughts to the current, unpleasant though it was, in which they had moved all day, and to think with what a romantic feeling he had looked forward to shaking his old friend by the hand before he died, and what a wide and cruel difference there was between the meeting they had had, and that which he had so often and so long anticipated. Still, he was disordered by waking to such sudden loneliness, and could not prevent his mind from running upon odd tales of people of undoubted courage, who, being shut up by night in vaults or churches, or other dismal places, had scaled great heights to get out, and fled from silence as they had never done from danger. This brought to his mind the moonlight through the window, and bethinking himself of it, he groped his way back up the crooked stairs – but very stealthily, as though he were fearful of being overheard.

He was very much astonished when he approached the gallery again, to see a light in the building: still more so, on advancing hastily and looking round, to observe no visible source from which it could proceed. But how much greater yet was his astonishment at the spectacle which this light revealed.

The statues of the two giants, Gog and Magog,[11] each above fourteen feet in height, those which had succeeded to still older and more barbarous figures after the Great Fire of London[12] and which stand in the Guildhall to this day, were endowed with life and motion. These guardian genii of the City had quitted their pedestals, and reclined in easy attitudes in the great stained-glass window. Between them was an ancient cask, which seemed to be full of wine; for the younger giant, clapping his huge hand upon it and throwing up his mighty leg, burst into an exulting laugh, which reverberated through the hall like thunder.

Joe Toddyhigh instinctively stooped down, and, more dead than alive, felt his hair stand on end, his knees knock together and a cold damp break out upon his forehead. But even at that minute curiosity prevailed over every other feeling and, somewhat reassured by the good-humour of the giants and their apparent unconsciousness of his presence, he crouched in a corner of the gallery, in as small a space as he could, and, peeping between the rails, observed them closely.

It was then that the elder Giant, who had a flowing grey beard, raised his thoughtful eyes to his companion's face, and in a grave and solemn voice addressed him thus:

FIRST NIGHT OF THE GIANT CHRONICLES

Turning towards his companion, the elder Giant uttered these words in a grave, majestic tone:

'Magog, does boisterous mirth beseem the giant warder of this ancient city? Is this becoming demeanour for a watchful spirit over whose bodiless head so many years have rolled, so many changes swept like empty air – in whose impalpable nostrils the scent of blood and crime, pestilence, cruelty and horror has been familiar as breath to mortals – in whose sight Time has gathered in the harvest of centuries, and garnered so many crops of human pride, affections, hopes and sorrows? Bethink you of our compact. The night wanes; feasting, revelry and music have encroached upon our usual hours of solitude, and morning will be here apace. Ere we are stricken mute again, bethink you of our compact.'

Pronouncing these latter words with more of impatience than quite accorded with his apparent age and gravity, the giant raised a long pole (which he still bears in his hand) and tapped his brother giant rather smartly on the head; indeed, the blow was so smartly administered, that the latter quickly withdrew his lips from the cask, to which they had been applied, and, catching up his shield and halberd, assumed an attitude of defence.

His irritation was but momentary, for he laid these weapons aside as hastily as he had assumed them, and said as he did so: 'You know, Gog, old friend, that when we animate these shapes which the Londoners of old assigned (and not unworthily) to the guardian genii of their city, we are susceptible of some of the sensations which belong to humankind. Thus when I taste wine, I feel blows; when I relish the one, I disrelish the other. Therefore, Gog, the more especially as your arm is none of the lightest, keep your good staff by your side, else we may chance to differ. Peace be between us!'

'Amen!' said the other, leaning his staff in the window-corner. 'Why did you laugh just now?'

'To think,' replied the giant Magog, laying his hand upon the cask, 'of him who owned this wine, and kept it in a cellar hoarded from the light of day for thirty years – "till it should be fit to drink," quoth he. He was two-score and ten years old when he buried it beneath his house, and yet never thought that he might be scarcely "fit to drink" when the wine became so. I wonder it never occurred to him to make himself unfit to be eaten. There is very little of him left by this time.'

'The night is waning,' said Gog mournfully.

'I know it,' replied his companion, 'and I see you are impatient. But look. Through the eastern window – placed opposite to us, that the first beams of the rising sun may every morning gild our giant faces – the moon-rays fall upon the pavement in a stream of light that to my fancy sinks through the cold stone and gushes into the old crypt below. The night is scarcely past its noon, and our great charge is sleeping heavily.'

They ceased to speak, and looked upward at the moon. The sight of their large, black, rolling eyes filled Joe Toddyhigh with such horror that he could scarcely draw his breath. Still they took no note of him, and appeared to believe themselves quite alone.

'Our compact,' said Magog after a pause, 'is, if I understand it, that instead of watching here in silence through the dreary nights, we entertain each other with stories of our past experience; with tales of the past, the present and the future; with legends of London and her sturdy citizens from the old simple times. That every night at midnight, when St Paul's[13] bell tolls out one, and we may move and speak, we thus discourse, nor leave such themes till the first grey gleam of day shall strike us dumb. Is that our bargain, brother?'

'Yes,' said the giant Gog, 'that is the league between us who guard this city, by day in spirit, and by night in body also; and never on ancient holidays have its conduits run wine more merrily than we will pour forth our legendary lore. We are old chroniclers from this time hence. The crumbled walls encircle us once more, the postern-gates are closed, the drawbridge is up and, pent in its narrow den beneath, the water foams and struggles with the sunken starlings. Jerkins and quarter-staves are in the streets again, the nightly watch is set, the rebel, sad and lonely in his Tower[14] dungeon, tries to sleep and weeps for home and children. Aloft upon the gates and walls are noble heads glaring fiercely down upon the dreaming city, and vexing the hungry dogs that scent them in the air, and tear the ground beneath with dismal howlings. The axe, the block, the rack, in their dark chambers, give signs of recent use. The Thames, floating past long lines of cheerful windows whence come a burst of music and a stream of light, bears suddenly to the palace wall the last red stain brought on the tide from Traitor's Gate.[15] But your pardon, brother. The night wears, and I am talking idly.'

The other giant appeared to be entirely of this opinion, for during the foregoing rhapsody of his fellow-sentinel he had been scratching his head with an air of comical uneasiness, or rather with an air that would have been very comical if he had been a dwarf or an ordinary-sized man. He winked too, and though it could not be doubted for a moment that he winked to himself, still he certainly cocked his enormous eye towards the gallery where the listener was concealed. Nor was this all, for he gaped; and when he gaped, Joe was horribly reminded of the popular prejudice on the subject of giants, and of their fabled power of smelling out Englishmen, however closely concealed.

His alarm was such that he nearly swooned, and it was some little time before his power of sight or hearing was restored. When he recovered he found that the elder giant was pressing the younger to commence the chronicles, and that the latter was endeavouring to excuse himself on the ground that the night was far spent, and it would be better to wait until the next. Well assured by this that he was certainly about to begin directly, the listener collected his faculties by a great effort, and distinctly heard Magog express himself to the following effect:

In the sixteenth century, and in the reign of Queen Elizabeth[16] of glorious memory (albeit her golden days are sadly rusted with blood), there lived in the city of London a bold young 'prentice who loved his master's daughter. There were no doubt within the walls a great many 'prentices in this condition, but I speak of only one, and his name was Hugh Graham.

This Hugh was apprenticed to an honest bowyer who dwelt in the ward of Cheype,[17] and was rumoured to possess great wealth. Rumour was quite as infallible in those days as at the present time, but it happened then as now to be sometimes right by accident. It stumbled upon the truth when it gave the old bowyer a mint of money. His trade had been a profitable one in the time of King Henry VIII,[18] who encouraged English archery to the utmost, and he had been prudent and discreet. Thus it came to pass that Mistress Alice, his only daughter, was the richest heiress in all his wealthy ward. Young Hugh had often maintained with staff and cudgel that she was the handsomest. To do him justice, I believe she was.

If he could have gained the heart of pretty Mistress Alice by knocking this conviction into stubborn people's heads, Hugh would have had no cause to fear. But though the bowyer's daughter smiled in secret to hear of his doughty deeds for her sake, and though her little waiting-woman reported all her smiles (and many more) to Hugh, and though he was at a vast expense in kisses and small coin to recompense her fidelity, he made no progress in his love. He durst not whisper it to Mistress Alice save on sure encouragement, and that she never gave him. A glance of her dark eye as she sat at the door on a summer's evening after prayer-time, while he and the neighbouring 'prentices exercised themselves in the street with blunted sword and buckler, would fire Hugh's blood so that none could stand before him; but then she glanced at others quite as kindly as on him, and where was the use of cracking crowns if Mistress Alice smiled upon the cracked as well as on the cracker?

Still Hugh went on, and loved her more and more. He thought of her all day, and dreamed of her all night long. He treasured up her every word and gesture, and had a palpitation of the heart whenever he heard her footstep on the stairs or her voice in an adjoining room. To him, the old bowyer's house was haunted by an angel; there was enchantment in the air and space in which she moved. It would have been no miracle to Hugh if flowers had sprung from the rush-strewn floors beneath the tread of lovely Mistress Alice.

Never did 'prentice long to distinguish himself in the eyes of his lady-love so ardently as Hugh. Sometimes he pictured to himself the house taking fire by night, and he, when all drew back in fear, rushing through flame and smoke and bearing her from the ruins in his arms. At other times he thought of a rising of fierce rebels, an attack upon the City, a strong assault upon the bowyer's house in particular, and he falling on the threshold pierced with numberless wounds in defence of Mistress Alice. If he could only enact some prodigy of valour, do some wonderful deed, and let her know that she had inspired it, he thought he could die contented.

Sometimes the bowyer and his daughter would go out to supper with a worthy citizen at the fashionable hour of six o'clock, and on such occasions Hugh, wearing his blue 'prentice cloak[19] as gallantly as 'prentice might, would attend with a lantern and his trusty club to escort them home. These were the brightest moments of his life. To hold the light while Mistress Alice picked her steps, to touch her hand as he helped her over broken ways, to have her leaning on his arm – it sometimes even came to that – this was happiness indeed!

When the nights were fair, Hugh followed in the rear, his eyes riveted on the graceful figure of the bowyer's daughter as she and the old man moved on before him. So they threaded the narrow winding streets of the city, now passing beneath the overhanging gables of old wooden houses whence creaking signs projected into the street, and now emerging from some dark and frowning gateway into the clear moonlight. At such times, or when the shouts of straggling brawlers met her ear, the bowyer's daughter would look timidly back at Hugh, beseeching him to draw nearer; and then how he grasped his club and longed to do battle with a dozen rufflers, for the love of Mistress Alice!

The old bowyer was in the habit of lending money on interest to the gallants of the Court, and thus it happened that many a richly dressed gentleman dismounted at his door. More waving plumes and gallant steeds, indeed, were seen at the bowyer's house and more embroidered silks and velvets sparkled in his dark shop and darker private closet than at any merchant's in the City. In those times no less than in the present it would seem that the richest-looking cavaliers often wanted money the most.

Of these glittering clients there was one who always came alone. He was nobly mounted, and, having no attendant, gave his horse in charge to Hugh while he and the bowyer were closeted within. Once as he sprang into the saddle Mistress Alice was seated at an upper window, and before she could withdraw he had doffed his jewelled cap and kissed his hand. Hugh watched him caracoling[20] down the street, and burnt with indignation. But how much deeper was the glow that reddened in his cheeks when, raising his eyes to the casement, he saw that Alice watched the stranger too!

He came again and often, each time arrayed more gaily than before, and still the little casement showed him Mistress Alice. At length one heavy day, she fled from home. It had cost her a hard struggle, for all her old father's gifts were strewn about her chamber as if she had parted from them one by one and knew that the time must come when these tokens of his love would wring her heart – yet she was gone.

She left a letter commanding her poor father to the care of Hugh, and wishing he might be happier than ever he could have been with her, for he deserved the love of a better and a purer heart than she had to bestow. The old man's forgiveness (she said) she had no power to ask, but she prayed God to bless him – and so ended with a blot upon the paper where her tears had fallen.

At first the old man's wrath was kindled, and he carried his wrong to the Queen's throne itself; but there was no redress, he learnt at Court, for his daughter had been conveyed abroad. This afterwards appeared to be the truth, as there came from France, after an interval of several years, a letter in her hand. It was written in trembling characters, and almost illegible. Little could be made out save that she often thought of home and her old dear pleasant room – and that she had dreamt her father was dead and had not blessed her – and that her heart was breaking.

The poor old bowyer lingered on, never suffering Hugh to quit his sight, for he knew now that he had loved his daughter, and that was the only link that bound him to earth. It broke at length and he died – bequeathing his old 'prentice his trade and all his wealth, and solemnly charging him with his last breath to revenge his child if ever he who had worked her misery crossed his path in life again.

From the time of Alice's flight, the tilting-ground, the fields, the fencing-school, the summer-evening sports, knew Hugh no more. His spirit was dead within him. He rose to great eminence and repute among the citizens, but was seldom seen to smile, and never mingled in their revelries or rejoicings. Brave, humane, and generous, he was beloved by all. He was pitied too by those who knew his story, and these were so many that when he walked along the streets alone at dusk, even the rude common people doffed their caps and mingled a rough air of sympathy with their respect.

One night in May – it was her birthnight, and twenty years since she had left her home – Hugh Graham sat in the room she had hallowed in his boyish days. He was now a grey-haired man, though still in the prime of life. Old thoughts had borne him company for many hours, and the chamber had gradually grown quite dark, when he was roused by a low knocking at the outer door.

He hastened down and, opening it, saw by the light of a lamp which he had seized upon the way, a female figure crouching in the portal. It hurried swiftly past him and glided up the stairs. He looked for pursuers. There were none in sight. No, not one.

He was inclined to think it a vision of his own brain, when suddenly a vague suspicion of the truth flashed upon his mind. He barred the door, and hastened wildly back. Yes, there she was – there, in the chamber she had quitted – there in her old innocent, happy home, so changed that none but he could trace one gleam of what she had been – there upon her knees – with her hands clasped in agony and shame before her burning face.

'My God, my God!' she cried, 'now strike me dead! Though I have brought death and shame and sorrow on this roof, oh, let me die at home in mercy!'

There was no tear upon her face then, but she trembled and glanced round the chamber. Everything was in its old place. Her bed looked as if she had risen from it but that morning. The sight of these familiar objects, marking the dear remembrance in which she had been held, and the blight she had brought upon herself, was more than the woman's better nature that had carried her there could bear. She wept and fell upon the ground.

A rumour was spread about, in a few days' time, that the bowyer's cruel daughter had come home, and that Master Graham had given her lodging in his house. It was rumoured too that he had resigned her fortune, in order that she might bestow it in acts of charity, and that he had vowed to guard her in her solitude, but that they were never to see each other more. These rumours greatly incensed all virtuous wives and daughters in the ward, especially when they appeared to receive some corroboration from the circumstance of Master Graham taking up his abode in another tenement hard by. The estimation in which he was held, however, forbade any questioning on the subject; and as the bowyer's house was close shut up, and nobody came forth when public shows and festivities were in progress, or to flaunt in the public walks, or to buy new fashions at the mercers' booths, all the well-conducted females agreed among themselves that there could be no woman there.

These reports had scarcely died away when the wonder of every good citizen, male and female, was utterly absorbed and swallowed up by a royal proclamation, in which her majesty, strongly censuring the practice of wearing long Spanish rapiers of preposterous length[21] (as being a bullying and swaggering custom, tending to bloodshed and public disorder), commanded that on a particular day therein named, certain grave citizens should repair to the City gates, and there, in public, break all rapiers worn or carried by persons claiming admission that exceeded, though it were only by a quarter of an inch, three standard feet in length.

Royal proclamations usually take their course, let the public wonder never so much. On the appointed day two citizens of high repute took up their stations at each of the gates, attended by a party of the City guard, the main body to enforce the Queen's will, and take custody of all such rebels (if any) as might have the temerity to dispute it, and a few to bear the standard measures and instruments for reducing all unlawful sword-blades to the prescribed dimensions. In pursuance of these arrangements, Master Graham and another were posted at Ludgate,[22] on the hill before St Paul's.

A pretty numerous company were gathered together at this spot, for, besides the officers in attendance to enforce the proclamation, there was a motley crowd of lookers-on of various degrees, who raised from time to time such shouts and cries as the circumstances called forth. A spruce young courtier was the first who approached: he unsheathed a weapon of burnished steel that shone and glistened in the sun, and handed it with the newest air to the officer, who, finding it exactly three feet long, returned it with a bow. Thereupon the gallant raised his hat, and crying, 'God save the Queen!' passed on amidst the plaudits of the mob. Then came another – a better courtier still – who wore a blade but two feet long, whereat the people laughed, much to the disparagement of his honour's dignity. Then came a third, a sturdy old officer of the army, girded with a rapier at least a foot and a half beyond her majesty's pleasure; at him they raised a great shout, and most of the spectators (but especially those who were armourers or cutlers) laughed very heartily at the breakage which would ensue. But they were disappointed; for the old campaigner, coolly unbuckling his sword and bidding his servant carry it home again, passed through unarmed, to the great indignation of all the beholders. They relieved themselves in some degree by hooting a tall blustering fellow, with a prodigious weapon, who stopped short on coming in sight of the preparations and after a little consideration turned back again. But all this time no rapier had been broken, although it was high noon, and all cavaliers of any quality or appearance were taking their way towards St Paul's Churchyard.[23]

During these proceedings, Master Graham had stood apart,

strictly confining himself to the duty imposed upon him, and taking little heed of anything beyond. He stepped forward now as a richly dressed gentleman on foot, followed by a single attendant, was seen advancing up the hill.

As this person drew nearer, the crowd stopped their clamour, and bent forward with eager looks. Master Graham standing alone in the gateway, and the stranger coming slowly towards him, they seemed, as it were, set face to face. The nobleman (for he looked one) had a haughty and disdainful air, which bespoke the slight estimation in which he held the citizen. The citizen, on the other hand, preserved the resolute bearing of one who was not to be frowned down or daunted, and who cared very little for any nobility but that of worth and manhood. It was perhaps some consciousness on the part of each of these feelings in the other that infused a more stern expression into their regards as they came closer together.

'Your rapier, worthy sir!' At the instant that he pronounced these words Graham started, and falling back some paces, laid his hand upon the dagger in his belt. 'You are the man whose horse I used to hold before the bowyer's door? You are that man? Speak!'

'Out, you 'prentice hound!' said the other.

'You are he! I know you well now!' cried Graham. 'Let no man step between us two, or I shall be his murderer.' With that he drew his dagger, and rushed in upon him.

The stranger had drawn his weapon from the scabbard, ready for the scrutiny, before a word was spoken. He made a thrust at his assailant, but the dagger which Graham clutched in his left hand being the dirk in use at that time for parrying such blows, promptly turned the point aside. They closed. The dagger fell rattling on the ground, and Graham, wresting his adversary's sword from his grasp, plunged it through his heart. As he drew it out it snapped in two, leaving a fragment in the dead man's body.

All this passed so swiftly that the bystanders looked on without an effort to interfere; but the man was no sooner down than an uproar broke forth which rent the air. The attendant rushing through the gate proclaimed that his master, a nobleman, had been set upon and slain by a citizen; the word quickly spread from mouth to mouth; St Paul's Cathedral and every bookshop, ordinary[24] and smoking-house in the churchyard poured out its stream of cavaliers and their followers, who, mingling together in a dense tumultuous body, struggled, sword in hand, towards the spot.

With equal impetuosity, and stimulating each other by loud cries and shouts, the citizens and common people took up the quarrel on their side, and encircling Master Graham a hundred deep, forced him from the gate. In vain he waved the broken sword above his head, crying that he would die on London's threshold for their sacred homes. They bore him on, and ever keeping him in the midst, so that no man could attack him, fought their way into the city.

The clash of swords and roar of voices, the dust and heat and pressure, the trampling under foot of men, the distracted looks and shrieks of women at the windows above as they recognised their relatives or lovers in the crowd, the rapid tolling of alarm-bells, the furious rage and passion of the scene, were fearful. Those who, being on the outskirts of each crowd, could use their weapons with effect, fought desperately, while those behind, maddened with baffled rage, struck at each other over the heads of those before them, and crushed their own fellows. Wherever the broken sword was seen above the people's heads, towards that spot the cavaliers made a new rush. Every one of these charges was marked by sudden gaps in the throng where men were trodden down, but as fast as they were made, the tide swept over them, and still the multitude pressed on again, a confused mass of swords, clubs, staves, broken plumes, fragments of rich cloaks and doublets, and angry, bleeding faces, all mixed up together in inextricable disorder.

The design of the people was to force Master Graham to take refuge in his dwelling, and to defend it until the authorities could interfere, or they could gain time for parley. But either from ignorance or in the confusion of the moment they stopped at his old house, which was closely shut. Some time was lost in beating the doors open and passing him to the front. About a score of the boldest of the other party threw themselves into the torrent while this was being done, and reaching the door at the same moment as himself cut him off from his defenders.

'I never will turn in such a righteous cause, so help me Heaven!' cried Graham, in a voice that at last made itself heard, and confronting them as he spoke. 'Least of all will I turn upon this threshold which owes its desolation to such men as ye. I give no quarter, and I will have none! Strike!'

For a moment they stood at bay. At that moment a shot from an unseen hand, apparently fired by some person who had gained access to one of the opposite houses, struck Graham in the brain, and he fell dead. A low wail was heard in the air – many people in the concourse cried that they had seen a spirit glide across the little casement window of the bowyer's house. . .

A dead silence succeeded. After a short time some of the flushed and heated throng laid down their arms and softly carried the body within doors. Others fell off or slunk away in knots of two or three, others whispered together in groups, and before a numerous guard which then rode up could muster in the street, it was nearly empty.

Those who carried Master Graham to the bed upstairs were shocked to see a woman lying beneath the window with her hands clasped together. After trying to recover her in vain, they laid her near the citizen, who still retained, tightly grasped in his right hand, the first and last sword that was broken that day at Ludgate.

The giant uttered these concluding words with sudden precipitation; and on the instant the strange light which had filled the hall faded away. Joe Toddyhigh glanced involuntarily at the eastern window, and saw the first pale gleam of morning. He turned his head again towards the other window in which the giants had been seated. It was empty. The cask of wine was gone, and he could dimly make out that the two great figures stood mute and motionless upon their pedestals.

After rubbing his eyes and wondering for full half an hour, during which time he observed morning come creeping on apace, he yielded to the drowsiness which overpowered him and fell into a refreshing slumber. When he awoke it was broad day; the building was open, and workmen were busily engaged in removing the vestiges of last night's feast.

Stealing gently down the little stairs, and assuming the air of some early lounger who had dropped in from the street, he walked up to the foot of each pedestal in turn, and attentively examined the figure it supported. There could be no doubt about the features of either; he recollected the exact expression they had worn at different passages of their conversation, and recognised in every line and lineament the giants of the night. Assured that it was no vision, but that he had heard and seen with his own proper senses, he walked forth, determining at all hazards to conceal himself in the Guildhall again that evening. He further resolved to sleep all day, so that he might be very wakeful and vigilant, and above all that he might take notice of the figures at the precise moment of their becoming animated and subsiding into their old state, which he greatly reproached himself for not having done already.

CORRESPONDENCE TO MASTER HUMPHREY

Sir – Before you proceed any further in your account of your friends and what you say and do when you meet together, excuse me if I proffer my claim to be elected to one of the vacant chairs in that old room of yours. Don't reject me without full consideration; for if you do, you will be sorry for it afterwards – you will, upon my life.

I enclose my card, sir, in this letter. I never was ashamed of my name, and I never shall be. I am considered a devilish gentlemanly fellow, and I act up to the character. If you want a reference, ask any of the men at our club. Ask any fellow who goes there to write his letters, what sort of conversation mine is. Ask him if he thinks I have the sort of voice that will suit your deaf friend and make him hear, if he can hear anything at all. Ask the servants what they think of me. There's not a rascal among 'em, sir, but will tremble to hear my name. That reminds me – don't you say too much about that housekeeper of yours; it's a low subject, damned low.

I tell you what, sir. If you vote me into one of those empty chairs, you'll have among you a man with a fund of gentlemanly information that'll rather astonish you. I can let you into a few anecdotes about some fine women of title, that are quite high life, sir – the tiptop sort of thing. I know the name of every man who has been out on an affair of honour within the last five-and-twenty years; I know the private particulars of every cross and squabble that has taken place upon the turf, at the gaming-table or elsewhere during the whole of that time. I have been called the gentlemanly chronicle. You may consider yourself a lucky dog; upon my soul, you may congratulate yourself, though I say so.

It's an uncommon good notion that of yours, not letting anybody know where you live. I have tried it, but there has always been an anxiety respecting me which has found me out. Your deaf friend is a cunning fellow to keep his name so close. I have tried that too, but have always failed. I shall be proud to make his acquaintance – tell him so, with my compliments.

You must have been a queer fellow when you were a child, confounded queer. It's odd, all that about the picture in your first paper – prosy, but told in a devilish gentlemanly sort of way. In places like that I could come in with great effect with a touch of life – don't you feel that?

I am anxiously waiting for your next paper to know whether your friends live upon the premises, and at your expense, which I take it for granted is the case. If I am right in this impression, I know a charming fellow (an excellent companion and most delightful company) who will be proud to join you. Some years ago he seconded a great many prizefighters, and once fought an amateur match himself; since then he has driven several mails, broken at different periods all the lamps on the right-hand side of Oxford Street,[25] and six times carried away every bell-handle in Bloomsbury Square,[26] besides turning off the gas in various thoroughfares. In point of gentlemanliness he is unrivalled, and I should say that next to myself he is of all men the best suited to your purpose.

Expecting your reply,

I am,

&c. &c.

* * *

Master Humphrey informs this gentleman that his application, both as it concerns himself and his friend, is rejected.

CHAPTER 2

Master Humphrey, from his Clockside in the Chimney-Corner

MY OLD COMPANION tells me it is midnight. The fire glows brightly, crackling with a sharp and cheerful sound, as if it loved to burn. The merry cricket on the hearth (my constant visitor), this ruddy blaze, my clock, and I, seem to share the world among us, and to be the only things awake. The wind, high and boisterous but now, has died away and hoarsely mutters in its sleep. I love all times and seasons each in its turn, and am apt, perhaps, to think the present one the best; but past or coming I always love this peaceful time of night, when long-buried thoughts, favoured by the gloom and silence, steal from their graves, and haunt the scenes of faded happiness and hope.

The popular faith in ghosts has a remarkable affinity with the whole current of our thoughts at such an hour as this, and seems to be their necessary and natural consequence. For who can wonder that man should feel a vague belief in tales of disembodied spirits wandering through those places which they once dearly affected, when he himself, scarcely less separated from his old world than they, is for ever lingering upon past emotions and bygone times, and hovering, the ghost of his former self, about the places and people that warmed his heart of old? It is thus that at this quiet hour I haunt the house where I was born, the rooms I used to tread, the scenes of my infancy, my boyhood and my youth; it is thus that I prowl around my buried treasure (though not of gold or silver), and mourn my loss; it is thus that I revisit the ashes of extinguished fires, and take my silent stand at old bedsides. If my spirit should ever glide back to this chamber when my body is mingled with the dust, it will but follow the course it often took in the old man's lifetime, and add but one more change to the subjects of its contemplation.

In all my idle speculations I am greatly assisted by various legends connected with my venerable house, which are current in the neighbourhood, and are so numerous that there is scarce a cupboard or corner that has not some dismal story of its own. When I first entertained thoughts of becoming its tenant, I was assured that it was haunted from roof to cellar, and I believe that the bad opinion in which my neighbours once held me had its rise in my not being torn to pieces, or at least distracted with terror, on the night I took possession; in either of which cases I should doubtless have arrived by a short cut at the very summit of popularity.

But traditions and rumours all taken into account, who so abets me in every fancy, and chimes with my every thought, as my dear deaf friend? and how often have I cause to bless the day that brought us two together! Of all days in the year I rejoice to think that it should have been Christmas Day, with which from childhood we associate something friendly, hearty and sincere.

I had walked out to cheer myself with the happiness of others, and, in the little tokens of festivity and rejoicing, of which the streets and houses present so many upon that day, had lost some hours. Now I stopped to look at a merry party hurrying through the snow on foot to their place of meeting, and now turned back to see a whole coachful of children safely deposited at the welcome house. At one time, I admired how carefully the working man carried the baby in its gaudy hat and feathers, and how his wife, trudging patiently on behind, forgot even her care of her gay clothes, in exchanging greeting with the child as it crowed and laughed over the father's shoulder; at another, I pleased myself with some passing scene of gallantry or courtship, and was glad to believe that for a season half the world of poverty was gay.

As the day closed in, I still rambled through the streets, feeling a companionship in the bright fires that cast their warm reflection on the windows as I passed, and losing all sense of my own loneliness in imagining the sociality and kind-fellowship that everywhere prevailed. At length I happened to stop before a tavern, and, encountering a bill of fare in the window, it all at once brought it into my head to wonder what kind of people dined alone in taverns upon Christmas Day.

Solitary men are accustomed, I suppose, unconsciously to look upon solitude as their own peculiar property. I had sat alone in my room on many, many anniversaries of this great holiday, and had never regarded it but as one of universal assemblage and rejoicing. I had excepted, and with an aching heart, a crowd of prisoners and beggars; but *these* were not the men for whom the Tavern doors were open. Had they any customers, or was it a mere form? – a form, no doubt.

Trying to feel quite sure of this, I walked away; but before I had gone many paces, I stopped and looked back. There was a provoking air of business in the lamp above the door which I could not overcome. I began to be afraid there might be many customers – young men, perhaps, struggling with the world, utter strangers in this great place, whose friends lived at a long distance off, and whose means were too slender to enable them to make the journey. The supposition gave rise to so many distressing little pictures that, in preference to carrying them home with me, I determined to encounter the realities. So I turned and walked in.

I was at once glad and sorry to find that there was only one person in the dining-room; glad to know that there were not more, and sorry that he should be there by himself. He did not look so old as I, but like me he was advanced in life, and his hair was nearly white. Though I made more noise in entering and seating myself than was quite necessary, with the view of attracting his attention and saluting him in the good old form of that time of year, he did not raise his head, but sat with it resting on his hand, musing over his half-finished meal.

I called for something which would give me an excuse for remaining in the room (I had dined early, as my housekeeper was engaged at night to partake of some friend's good cheer), and sat where I could observe without intruding on him. After a time he looked up. He was aware that somebody had entered, but could see very little of me, as I sat in the shade and he in the light. He was sad and thoughtful, and I forbore to trouble him by speaking.

Let me believe it was something better than curiosity which riveted my attention and impelled me strongly towards this gentleman. I never saw so patient and kind a face. He should have been surrounded by friends, and yet here he sat dejected and alone when all men had their friends about them. As often as he roused himself from his reverie he would fall into it again, and it was plain that, whatever were the subject of his thoughts, they were of a melancholy kind, and would not be controlled.

He was not used to solitude. I was sure of that; for I know by myself that if he had been, his manner would have been different, and he would have taken some slight interest in the arrival of another. I could not fail to mark that he had no appetite; that he tried to eat in vain; that time after time the plate was pushed away, and he relapsed into his former posture.

His mind was wandering among old Christmas days, I thought. Many of them sprung up together, not with a long gap between each, but in unbroken succession like days of the week. It was a great change to find himself for the first time (I quite settled that it *was* the first) in an empty silent room with no soul to care for. I could not help following him in imagination through crowds of pleasant faces, and then coming back to that dull place with its bough of mistletoe sickening in the gas, and sprigs of holly parched up already by a simoom of roast and boiled. The very waiter had gone home; and his representative, a poor, lean, hungry man, was keeping Christmas in his jacket.

I grew still more interested in my friend. His dinner done, a decanter of wine was placed before him. It remained untouched for a long time, but at length with a quivering hand he filled a glass and raised it to his lips. Some tender wish to which he had been accustomed to give utterance on that day, or some beloved name that he had been used to pledge, trembled upon them at the moment. He put it down very hastily – took it up once more – again put it down – pressed his hand upon his face – yes – and tears stole down his cheeks, I am certain.

Without pausing to consider whether I did right or wrong, I stepped across the room, and sitting down beside him laid my hand gently on his arm.

'My friend,' I said, 'forgive me if I beseech you to take comfort and consolation from the lips of an old man. I will not preach to you what I have not practised, indeed. Whatever be your grief, be of a good heart – be of a good heart, pray!'

'I see that you speak earnestly,' he replied, 'and kindly I am very sure, but – '

I nodded my head to show that I understood what he would say; for I had already gathered, from a certain fixed expression in his face, and from the attention with which he watched me while I spoke, that his sense of hearing was destroyed. 'There should be a freemasonry between us,' said I, pointing from himself to me to explain my meaning; 'if not in our grey hairs, at least in our misfortunes. You see that I am but a poor cripple.'

I never felt so happy under my affliction, since the trying moment of my first becoming conscious of it, as when he took my hand in his with a smile that has lighted my path in life from that day, and we sat down side by side.

This was the beginning of my friendship with the deaf gentleman; and when was ever the slight and easy service of a kind word in season repaid by such attachment and devotion as he has shown to me!

He produced a little set of tablets and a pencil to facilitate our conversation, on that our first acquaintance; and I well remember how awkward and constrained I was in writing down my share of the dialogue, and how easily he guessed my meaning before I had written half of what I had to say. He told me in a faltering voice that he had not been accustomed to be alone on that day – that it had always been a little festival with him; and seeing that I glanced at his dress in the expectation that he wore mourning, he added hastily that it was not that; if it had been he thought he could have borne it better. From that time to the present we have never touched upon this theme. Upon every return of the same day we have been together; and although we make it our annual custom to drink to each other hand in hand after dinner, and to recall with affectionate garrulity every circumstance of our first meeting, we always avoid this one as if by mutual consent.

Meantime we have gone on strengthening in our friendship and regard and forming an attachment which, I trust and believe, will only be interrupted by death, to be renewed in another existence. I scarcely know how we communicate as we do; but he has long since ceased to be deaf to me. He is frequently my companion in my walks, and even in crowded streets replies to my slightest look or gesture, as though he could read my thoughts. From the vast number of objects which pass in rapid succession before our eyes, we frequently select the same for some particular notice or remark; and when one of these little coincidences occurs, I cannot describe the pleasure which animates my friend, or the beaming countenance he will preserve for half an hour afterwards at least.

He is a great thinker from living so much within himself, and, having a lively imagination, has a facility of conceiving and enlarging upon odd ideas which renders him invaluable to our little body, and greatly astonishes our two friends. His powers in this respect are much assisted by a large pipe, which he assures us once belonged to a German student. Be this as it may, it has undoubtedly a very ancient and mysterious appearance, and is of such capacity that it takes three hours and a half to smoke it out. I have reason to believe that my barber, who is the chief authority of a knot of gossips who congregate every evening at a small tobacconist's hard by, has related anecdotes of this pipe and the grim figures that are carved upon its bowl at which all the smokers in the neighbourhood have stood aghast; and I know that my housekeeper, while she holds it in high veneration, has a superstitious feeling connected with it which would render her exceedingly unwilling to be left alone in its company after dark.

Whatever sorrow my dear friend has known, and whatever grief may linger in some secret corner of his heart, he is now a cheerful, placid, happy creature. Misfortune can never have fallen upon such a man but for some good purpose; and when I see its traces in his gentle nature and his earnest feeling, I am the less disposed to murmur at such trials as I may have undergone myself. With regard to the pipe, I have a theory of my own; I cannot help thinking that it is in some manner connected with the event that brought us together; for I remember that it was a long time before he even talked about it; that when he did, he grew reserved and melancholy; and that it was a long time yet before he brought it forth. I have no curiosity, however, upon this subject; for I know that it promotes his tranquillity and comfort, and I need no other inducement to regard it with my utmost favour.

Such is the deaf gentleman. I can call up his figure now, clad in sober grey, and seated in the chimney-corner. As he puffs out the smoke from his favourite pipe, he casts a look on me brimful of cordiality and friendship, and says all manner of kind and genial things in a cheerful smile; then he raises his eyes to my clock, which is just about to strike, and, glancing from it to me and back again, seems to divide his heart between us. For myself, it is not too much to say that I would gladly part with one of my poor limbs, could he but hear the old clock's voice.

Of our two friends, the first has been all his life one of that easy, wayward, truant class whom the world is accustomed to designate as nobody's enemies but their own. Bred to a profession for which he never qualified himself, and reared in the expectation of a fortune he has never inherited, he has undergone every vicissitude of which such an existence is capable. He and his younger brother, both orphans from their childhood, were educated by a wealthy relative, who taught them to expect an equal division of his property; but too indolent to court, and too honest to flatter, the elder gradually lost ground in the affections of a capricious old man, and the younger, who did not fail to improve his opportunity, now triumphs in the possession of enormous wealth. His triumph is to hoard it in solitary wretchedness, and probably to feel with the expenditure of every shilling a greater pang than the loss of his whole inheritance ever cost his brother.

Jack Redburn – he was Jack Redburn at the first little school he went to, where every other child was mastered and surnamed, and he has been Jack Redburn all his life, or he would perhaps have been a richer man by this time – has been an inmate of my house these eight years past. He is my librarian, secretary, steward and first minister; director of all my affairs and inspector-general of my household. He is something of a musician, something of an author, something of an actor, something of a painter, very much of a carpenter, and an extraordinary gardener, having had all his life a wonderful aptitude for learning everything that was of no use to him. He is remarkably fond of children, and is the best and kindest nurse in sickness that ever drew the breath of life. He has mixed with every grade of society, and known the utmost distress; but there never was a less selfish, a more tender-hearted, a more enthusiastic or a more guileless man; and I dare say, if few have done less good, fewer still have done less harm in the world than he. By what chance Nature forms such whimsical jumbles I don't know; but I do know that she sends them among us very often, and that the king of the whole race is Jack Redburn.

I should be puzzled to say how old he is. His health is none of the best, and he wears a quantity of iron-grey hair, which shades his face and gives it rather a worn appearance; but we consider him quite a young fellow notwithstanding; and if a youthful spirit, surviving the roughest contact with the world, confers upon its possessor any title to be considered young, then he is a mere child.

The only interruptions to his careless cheerfulness are on a wet Sunday, when he is apt to be unusually religious and solemn, and sometimes of an evening, when he has been blowing a very slow tune on the flute. On these last-named occasions he is apt to incline towards the mysterious, or the terrible. As a specimen of his powers in this mood, I refer my readers to the extract from the clock-case which follows this paper: he brought it to me not long ago at midnight, and informed me that the main incident had been suggested by a dream of the night before.

His apartments are two cheerful rooms looking towards the garden, and one of his great delights is to arrange and rearrange the furniture in these chambers, and put it in every possible variety of position. During the whole time he has been here, I do not think he has slept for two nights running with the head of his bed in the same place; and every time he moves it is to be the last. My housekeeper was at first well-nigh distracted by these frequent changes; but she has become quite reconciled to them by degrees, and has so fallen in with his humour, that they often consult together with great gravity upon the next final alteration. Whatever his arrangements are, however, they are always a pattern of neatness; and every one of the manifold articles connected with his manifold occupations is to be found in its own particular place. Until within the last two or three years he was subject to an occasional fit (which usually came upon him in very fine weather), under the influence of which he would dress himself with peculiar care, and, going out under pretence of taking a walk, disappear for several days together. At length, after the interval between each outbreak of this disorder had gradually grown longer and longer, it wholly disappeared; and now he seldom stirs abroad, except to stroll out a little way on a summer's evening. Whether he yet mistrusts his own constancy in this respect, and is therefore afraid to wear a coat, I know not; but we seldom see him in any other upper garment than an old spectral-looking dressing-gown, with very disproportionate pockets, full of a miscellaneous collection of odd matters, which he picks up wherever he can lay his hands upon them.

Everything that is a favourite with our friend is a favourite with us; and thus it happens that the fourth among us is Mr Owen Miles, a most worthy gentleman, who had treated Jack with great kindness before my deaf friend and I encountered him by an accident, to which I may refer on some future occasion. Mr Miles was once a very rich merchant; but receiving a severe shock in the death of his wife, he retired from business, and devoted himself to a quiet, unostentatious life. He is an excellent man, of thoroughly sterling character: not of quick apprehension, and not without some amusing prejudices, which I shall leave to their own development. He holds us all in profound veneration; but Jack Redburn he esteems as a kind of pleasant wonder that he may venture to approach familiarly. He believes, not only that no man ever lived who could do so many things as Jack, but that no man ever lived who could do anything so well; and he never calls my attention to any of his ingenious proceedings, but he whispers in my ear, nudging me at the same time with his elbow: 'If he had only made it his trade, sir – if he had only made it his trade!'

They are inseparable companions; one would almost suppose that, although Mr Miles never by any chance does anything in the way of assistance, Jack could do nothing without him. Whether he is reading, writing, painting, carpentering, gardening, flute-playing, or what not, there is Mr Miles beside him, buttoned up to the chin in his blue coat, and looking on with a face of incredulous delight, as though he could not credit the testimony of his own senses, and had a misgiving that no man could be so clever but in a dream.

These are my friends; I have now introduced myself and them.

THE CLOCK-CASE

A CONFESSION FOUND IN A PRISON
IN THE TIME OF CHARLES II

I held a lieutenant's commission in his majesty's army, and served abroad in the campaigns of 1677 and 1678. The treaty of Nijmegen[27] being concluded, I returned home, and retiring from the service, withdrew to a small estate lying a few miles east of London, which I had recently acquired in right of my wife.

This is the last night I have to live, and I will set down the naked truth without disguise. I was never a brave man, and had always been from my childhood of a secret, sullen, distrustful nature. I speak of myself as if I had passed from the world; for while I write this, my grave is digging, and my name is written in the black-book of death.

Soon after my return to England, my only brother was seized with mortal illness. This circumstance gave me slight or no pain; for since we had been men, we had associated but very little together. He was open-hearted and generous, handsomer than I, more accomplished, and generally beloved. Those who sought my acquaintance abroad or at home, because they were friends of his, seldom attached themselves to me long, and would usually say, in our first conversation, that they were surprised to find two brothers so unlike in their manners and appearance. It was my habit to lead them on to this avowal; for I knew what comparisons they must draw between us; and having a rankling envy in my heart, I sought to justify it to myself.

We had married two sisters. This additional tie between us, as it may appear to some, only estranged us the more. His wife knew me well. I never struggled with any secret jealousy or gall when she was present but that woman knew it as well as I did. I never raised my eyes at such times but I found hers fixed upon me; I never bent them on the ground or looked another way but I felt that she overlooked me always. It was an inexpressible relief to me when we quarrelled, and a greater relief still when I heard abroad that she was dead. It seems to me now as if some strange and terrible foreshadowing of what has happened since must have hung over us then. I was afraid of her; she haunted me; her fixed and steady look comes back upon me now, like the memory of a dark dream, and makes my blood run cold.

She died shortly after giving birth to a child – a boy. When my brother knew that all hope of his own recovery was past, he called my wife to his bedside, and confided this orphan, a child of four years old, to her protection. He bequeathed to him all the property he had, and willed that, in case of his child's death, it should pass to my wife, as the only acknowledgment he could make her for her care and love. He exchanged a few brotherly words with me, deploring our long separation; and being exhausted, fell into a slumber, from which he never awoke.

We had no children; and as there had been a strong affection between the sisters, and my wife had almost supplied the place of a mother to this boy, she loved him as if he had been her own. The child was ardently attached to her; but he was his mother's image in face and spirit, and always mistrusted me.

I can scarcely fix the date when the feeling first came upon me; but I soon began to be uneasy when this child was by. I never roused myself from some moody train of thought but I marked him looking at me; not with mere childish wonder, but with something of the purpose and meaning that I had so often noted in his mother. It was no effort of my fancy, founded on close resemblance of feature and expression. I never could look the boy down. He feared me, but seemed by some instinct to despise me while he did so; and even when he drew back beneath my gaze – as he would when we were alone, to get nearer to the door – he would keep his bright eyes upon me still.

Perhaps I hide the truth from myself, but I do not think that, when this began, I meditated to do him any wrong. I may have thought how serviceable his inheritance would be to us, and may have wished him dead; but I believe I had no thought of compassing his death. Neither did the idea come upon me at once, but by very slow degrees, presenting itself at first in dim shapes at a very great distance, as men may think of an earthquake or the last day; then drawing nearer and nearer, and losing something of its horror and improbability; then coming to be part and parcel – nay nearly the whole sum and substance – of my daily thoughts, and resolving itself into a question of means and safety; not of doing or abstaining from the deed.

While this was going on within me, I never could bear that the child should see me looking at him, and yet I was under a fascination which made it a kind of business with me to contemplate his slight and fragile figure and think how easily it might be done. Sometimes I would steal upstairs and watch him as he slept; but usually I hovered in the garden near the window of the room in which he learnt his little tasks; and there, as he sat upon a low seat beside my wife, I would peer at him for hours together from behind a tree; starting, like the guilty wretch I was, at every rustling of a leaf, and still gliding back to look and start again.

Hard by our cottage, but quite out of sight and (if there were any wind astir) of hearing too, was a deep sheet of water. I spent days in shaping with my pocketknife a rough model of a boat, which I finished at last and dropped in the child's way. Then I withdrew to a secret place, which he must pass if he stole away alone to swim this bauble, and lurked there for his coming. He came neither that day nor the next, though I waited from noon till nightfall. I was sure that I had him in my net, for I had heard him prattling of the toy, and knew that in his infant pleasure he kept it by his side in bed. I felt no weariness or fatigue, but waited patiently, and on the third day he passed me, running joyously along, with his silken hair streaming in the wind, and he singing – God have mercy upon me! – singing a merry ballad – who could hardly lisp the words.

I stole down after him, creeping under certain shrubs which grow in that place, and none but devils know with what terror I, a strong full-grown man, tracked the footsteps of that baby as he approached the water's brink. I was close upon him, had sunk upon my knee and raised my hand to thrust him in, when he saw my shadow in the stream and turned round.

His mother's ghost was looking from his eyes. The sun burst forth from behind a cloud; it shone in the bright sky, the glistening earth, the clear water, the sparkling drops of rain upon the leaves. There were eyes in everything. The whole great universe of light was there to see the murder done. I know not what he said; he came of bold and manly blood, and, child as he was, he did not crouch or fawn upon me. I heard him cry that he would try to love me – not that he did – and then I saw him running back towards the house. The next I saw was my own sword naked in my hand, and he lying at my feet stark dead – dabbled here and there with blood, but otherwise no different from what I had seen him in his sleep – in the same attitude too, with his cheek resting upon his little hand.

I took him in my arms and laid him – very gently now that he was dead – in a thicket. My wife was from home that day, and would not return until the next. The window of our bedroom, the only sleeping-room on that side of the house, was but a few feet from the ground, and I resolved to descend from it at night and bury him in the garden. I had no thought that I had failed in my design, no thought that the water would be dragged and nothing found, that the money must now lie waste, since I must encourage the idea that the child was lost or stolen. All my thoughts were bound up and knotted together in the one absorbing necessity of hiding what I had done.

How I felt when they came to tell me that the child was missing, when I ordered scouts in all directions, when I gasped and trembled at everyone's approach, no tongue can tell or mind of man conceive. I buried him that night. When I parted the boughs and looked into the dark thicket, there was a glowworm shining like the visible spirit of God upon the murdered child. I glanced down into his grave when I had placed him there, and still it gleamed upon his breast; an eye of fire looking up to heaven in supplication to the stars that watched me at my work.

I had to meet my wife, and break the news, and give her hope that the child would soon be found. All this I did – with some appearance, I suppose, of being sincere, for I was the object of no suspicion. This done, I sat at the bedroom window all day long, and watched the spot where the dreadful secret lay.

It was in a piece of ground which had been dug up to be newly turfed, and which I had chosen on that account, as the traces of my spade were less likely to attract attention. The men who laid down the grass must have thought me mad. I called to them continually to expedite their work, ran out and worked beside them, trod down the earth with my feet, and hurried them with frantic eagerness. They had finished their task before night, and then I thought myself comparatively safe.

I slept – not as men do who awake refreshed and cheerful, but I did sleep, passing from vague and shadowy dreams of being hunted down, to visions of the plot of grass, through which now a hand, and now a foot, and now the head itself was starting out. At this point I always woke and stole to the window, to make sure that it was not really so. That done, I crept to bed again; and thus I spent the night in fits and starts, getting up and lying down full twenty times, and dreaming the same dream over and over again – which was far worse than lying awake, for every dream had a whole night's suffering of its own. Once I thought the child was alive, and that I had never tried to kill him. To wake from that dream was the most dreadful agony of all.

The next day I sat at the window again, never once taking my eyes from the place, which, although it was covered by the grass, was as plain to me – its shape, its size, its depth, its jagged sides, and all – as if it had been open to the light of day. When a servant walked across it, I felt as if he must sink in; when he had passed, I looked to see that his feet had not worn the edges. If a bird lighted there, I was in terror lest by some tremendous interposition it should be instrumental in the discovery; if a breath of air sighed across it, to me it whispered murder. There was not a sight or a sound – how ordinary, mean or unimportant soever – but was fraught with fear. And in this state of ceaseless watching I spent three days.

On the fourth there came to the gate one who had served with me abroad, accompanied by a brother officer of his whom I had never seen. I felt that I could not bear to be out of sight of the place. It was a summer evening, and I bade my people take a table and a flask of wine into the garden. Then I sat down *with my chair upon the grave*, and being assured that nobody could disturb it now without my knowledge, tried to drink and talk.

They hoped that my wife was well – that she was not obliged to keep her chamber – that they had not frightened her away. What could I do but tell them with a faltering tongue about the child? The officer whom I did not know was a down-looking man, and kept his eyes upon the ground while I was speaking. Even that terrified me. I could not divest myself of the idea that he saw something there which caused him to suspect the truth. I asked him hurriedly if he supposed that – and stopped. 'That the child has been murdered?' said he, looking mildly at me: 'Oh no! what could a man gain by murdering a poor child?' I could have told him what a man gained by such a deed, no one better: but I held my peace and shivered as with an ague.

Mistaking my emotion, they were endeavouring to cheer me with the hope that the boy would certainly be found – great cheer that was for me! – when we heard a low deep howl, and presently there sprang over the wall two great dogs, who, bounding into the garden, repeated the baying sound we had heard before.

'Bloodhounds!' cried my visitors.

What need to tell me that! I had never seen one of that kind in all my life, but I knew what they were and for what purpose they had come. I grasped the elbows of my chair, and neither spoke nor moved.

'They are of the genuine breed,' said the man whom I had known abroad, 'and being out for exercise have no doubt escaped from their keeper.'

Both he and his friend turned to look at the dogs, who with their noses to the ground moved restlessly about, running to and fro, and up and down and across, and round in circles, careering about like wild things, and all this time taking no notice of us, but ever and again repeating the yell we had heard already, then dropping their noses to the ground again and tracking earnestly here and there. They now began to snuff the earth more eagerly than they had done yet, and although they were still very restless, no longer beat about in such wide circuits, but kept near to one spot, and constantly diminished the distance between themselves and me.

At last they came up close to the great chair on which I sat and, raising their frightful howl once more, tried to tear away the wooden rails that kept them from the ground beneath. I saw how I looked, in the faces of the two who were with me.

'They scent some prey,' said they, both together.

'They scent no prey!' cried I.

'In heaven's name, move!' said the one I knew, very earnestly, 'or you will be torn to pieces.'

'Let them tear me from limb to limb, I'll never leave this place!' cried I. 'Are dogs to hurry men to shameful deaths? Hew them down, cut them in pieces.'

'There is some foul mystery here!' said the officer whom I did not know, drawing his sword. 'In King Charles's name, assist me to secure this man.'

They both set upon me and forced me away, though I fought and bit and caught at them like a madman. After a struggle, they got me quietly between them; and then, my God! I saw the angry dogs tearing at the earth and throwing it up into the air like water.

What more have I to tell? That I fell upon my knees, and with chattering teeth confessed the truth, and prayed to be forgiven. That I have since denied, and now confess to it again. That I have been tried for the crime, found guilty, and sentenced. That I have not the courage to anticipate my doom, or to bear up manfully against it. That I have no compassion, no consolation, no hope, no friend. That my wife has happily lost for the time those faculties which would enable her to know my misery or hers. That I am alone in this stone dungeon with my evil spirit, and that I die tomorrow.

*   *   *

[*The Old Curiosity Shop* begins here.]28

CORRESPONDENCE

Master Humphrey has been favoured with the following letter written on strongly scented paper, and sealed in light-blue wax with the representation of two very plump doves interchanging beaks. It does not commence with any of the usual forms of address, but begins as is here set forth.

Bath,[29] *Wednesday night*

Heavens! into what an indiscretion do I suffer myself to be betrayed! To address these faltering lines to a total stranger, and that stranger one of a conflicting sex! – and yet I am precipitated into the abyss, and have no power of self-snatchation (forgive me if I coin that phrase) from the yawning gulf before me.

Yes, I am writing to a man; but let me not think of that, for madness is in the thought. You will understand my feelings? Oh yes, I am sure you will; and you will respect them too, and not despise them – will you?

Let me be calm. That portrait – smiling as once he smiled on me; that cane – dangling as I have seen it dangle from his hand I know not how oft; those legs that have glided through my nightly dreams and never stopped to speak; the perfectly gentlemanly though false original – can I be mistaken? Oh no, no.

Let me be calmer yet; I would be calm as coffins. You have published a letter from one whose likeness is engraved, but whose name (and wherefore?) is suppressed. Shall *I* breathe that name! Is it – but why ask when my heart tells me too truly that it is!

I would not upbraid him with his treachery; I would not remind him of those times when he plighted the most eloquent of vows, and procured from me a small pecuniary accommodation; and yet I would see him – see him did I say – *him* – alas! such is woman's nature. For as the poet beautifully says – but you will already have anticipated the sentiment. Is it not sweet? Oh yes!

It was in this city (hallowed by the recollection) that I met him first; and assuredly if mortal happiness be recorded anywhere, then those rubbers with their three-and-sixpenny points are scored on tablets of celestial brass. He always held an honour – generally two. On that eventful night we stood at eight.[30] He raised his eyes (luminous in their seductive sweetness) to my agitated face. '*Can* you?' said he, with peculiar meaning. I felt the gentle pressure of his foot on mine; our corns throbbed in unison. '*Can* you?' he said again; and every lineament of his expressive countenance added the words 'resist me?' I murmured, 'No,' and fainted.

They said, when I recovered, it was the weather. *I* said it was the nutmeg in the negus.[31] How little did they suspect the truth! How little did they guess the deep mysterious meaning of that enquiry! He called next morning on his knees; I do not mean to say that he actually came in that position to the house-door, but that he went down upon those joints directly the servant had retired. He brought some verses in his hat, which he said were original, but which I have since found were Milton's;[32] likewise a little bottle labelled laudanum;[33] also a pistol and a sword-stick. He drew the latter, uncorked the former, and clicked the trigger of the pocket firearm. He had come, he said, to conquer or to die. He did not die. He wrested from me an avowal of my love, and let off the pistol out of a back window previous to partaking of a slight repast.

Faithless, inconstant man! How many ages seem to have elapsed since his unaccountable and perfidious disappearance! Could I still forgive him both that and the borrowed lucre that he promised to pay next week! Could I spurn him from my feet if he approached in penitence, and with a matrimonial object! Would the blandishing enchanter still weave his spells around me, or should I burst them all and turn away in coldness! I dare not trust my weakness with the thought.

My brain is in a whirl again. You know his address, his occupations, his mode of life – are acquainted, perhaps, with his inmost thoughts. You are a humane and philanthropic character; reveal all you know – all; but especially the street and number of his lodgings. The post is departing, the bellman rings – pray heaven it be not the knell of love and hope to

BELINDA.[34]

PS – Pardon the wanderings of a bad pen and a distracted mind. Address to the post office. The bellman, rendered impatient by delay, is ringing dreadfully in the passage.

PPS – I open this to say that the bellman is gone, and that you must not expect it till the next post; so don't be surprised when you don't get it.

* * *

Master Humphrey does not feel himself at liberty to furnish his fair correspondent with the address of the gentleman in question, but he publishes her letter as a public appeal to his faith and gallantry.

CHAPTER 3

Master Humphrey's Visitor

WHEN I AM in a thoughtful mood, I often succeed in diverting the current of some mournful reflections by conjuring up a number of fanciful associations with the objects that surround me, and dwelling upon the scenes and characters they suggest.

I have been led by this habit to assign to every room in my house and every old staring portrait on its walls a separate interest of its own. Thus, I am persuaded that a stately dame, terrible to behold in her rigid modesty, who hangs above the chimneypiece of my bedroom, is the former lady of the mansion. In the courtyard below is a stone face of surpassing ugliness, which I have somehow – in a kind of jealousy, I am afraid – associated with her husband. Above my study is a little room with ivy peeping through the lattice, from which I bring their daughter, a lovely girl of eighteen or nineteen years of age, and dutiful in all respects save one, that one being her devoted attachment to a young gentleman on the stairs, whose grandmother (degraded to a disused laundry in the garden) piques herself upon an old family quarrel, and is the implacable enemy of their love. With such materials as these I work out many a little drama, whose chief merit is that I can bring it to a happy end at will. I have so many of them on hand that if on my return home one of these evenings I were to find some bluff old wight of two centuries ago comfortably seated in my easy chair, and a lovelorn damsel vainly appealing to his heart, and leaning her white arm upon my clock itself, I verily believe I should only express my surprise that they had kept me waiting so long, and never honoured me with a call before.

I was in such a mood as this, sitting in my garden yesterday morning under the shade of a favourite tree, revelling in all the bloom and brightness about me, and feeling every sense of hope and enjoyment quickened by this most beautiful season of spring, when my meditations were interrupted by the unexpected appearance of my barber at the end of the walk, who I immediately saw was coming towards me with a hasty step that betokened something remarkable.

My barber is at all times a very brisk, bustling, active little man – for he is, as it were, chubby all over, without being stout or unwieldy – but yesterday his alacrity was so very uncommon that it quite took me by surprise. For could I fail to observe when he came up to me that his grey eyes were twinkling in a most extraordinary manner, that his little red nose was in an unusual glow, that every line in his round bright face was twisted and curved into an expression of pleased surprise, and that his whole countenance was radiant with glee? I was still more surprised to see my housekeeper, who usually preserves a very staid air, and stands somewhat upon her dignity, peeping round the hedge at the bottom of the walk, and exchanging nods and smiles with the barber, who twice or thrice looked over his shoulder for that purpose. I could conceive no announcement to which these appearances could be the prelude, unless it were that they had married each other that morning.

I was, consequently, a little disappointed when it only came out that there was a gentleman in the house who wished to speak with me.

'And who is it?' said I.

The barber, with his face screwed up still tighter than before, replied that the gentleman would not send his name, but wished to see me. I pondered for a moment, wondering who this visitor might be, and I remarked that he embraced the opportunity of exchanging another nod with the housekeeper, who still lingered in the distance.

'Well!' said I, 'bid the gentleman come here.'

This seemed to be the consummation of the barber's hopes, for he turned sharp round, and actually ran away.

Now, my sight is not very good at a distance, and therefore when the gentleman first appeared in the walk, I was not quite clear whether he was a stranger to me or otherwise. He was an elderly gentleman, but came tripping along in the pleasantest manner conceivable, avoiding the garden-roller and the borders of the beds with inimitable dexterity, picking his way among the flower-pots, and smiling with unspeakable good humour. Before he was half-way up the walk he began to salute me; then I thought I knew him; but when he came towards me with his hat in his hand, the sun shining on his bald head, his bland face, his bright spectacles, his fawn-coloured tights, and his black gaiters – then my heart warmed towards him, and I felt quite certain that it was Mr Pickwick.[35]

'My dear sir,' said that gentleman as I rose to receive him, 'pray be seated. Pray sit down. Now, do not stand on my account. I must insist upon it, really.' With these words Mr Pickwick gently pressed me down into my seat, and taking my hand in his, shook it again and again with a warmth of manner perfectly irresistible. I endeavoured to express in my welcome something of that heartiness and pleasure which the sight of him awakened, and made him sit down beside me. All this time he kept alternately releasing my hand and grasping it again, and surveying me through his spectacles with such a beaming countenance as I never till then beheld.

'You knew me directly!' said Mr Pickwick. 'What a pleasure it is to think that you knew me directly!'

I remarked that I had read his adventures very often, and his features were quite familiar to me from the published portraits. As I thought it a good opportunity of adverting to the circumstance, I condoled with him upon the various libels on his character which had found their way into print. Mr Pickwick shook his head, and for a moment looked very indignant, but, smiling again directly, added that no doubt I was acquainted with Cervantes' introduction to the second part of *Don Quixote*, and that it fully expressed his sentiments on the subject.[36]

'But now,' said Mr Pickwick, 'don't you wonder how I found you out?'

'I shall never wonder, and, with your good leave, never know,' said I, smiling in my turn. 'It is enough for me that you give me this gratification. I have not the least desire that you should tell me by what means I have obtained it.'

'You are very kind,' returned Mr Pickwick, shaking me by the hand again; 'you are so exactly what I expected! But for what particular purpose do you think I have sought you, my dear sir? Now what *do* you think I have come for?'

Mr Pickwick put this question as though he were persuaded that it was morally impossible that I could by any means divine the deep purpose of his visit, and that it must be hidden from all human ken. Therefore, although I was rejoiced to think that I had anticipated his drift, I feigned to be quite ignorant of it, and after a brief consideration shook my head despairingly.

'What should you say,' said Mr Pickwick, laying the forefinger of his left hand upon my coat-sleeve, and looking at me with his head thrown back, and a little on one side – 'what should you say if I confessed that after reading your account of yourself and your little society, I had come here, a humble candidate for one of those empty chairs?'

'I should say,' I returned, 'that I know of only one circumstance which could still further endear that little society to me, and that would be the associating with it my old friend – for you must let me call you so – my old friend, Mr Pickwick.'

As I made him this answer every feature of Mr Pickwick's face fused itself into one all-pervading expression of delight. After shaking me heartily by both hands at once, he patted me gently on the back, and then – I well understood why – coloured up to the eyes, and hoped with great earnestness of manner that he had not hurt me.

If he had, I would have been content that he should have repeated the offence a hundred times rather than suppose so; but as he had not, I had no difficulty in changing the subject by making an enquiry which had been upon my lips twenty times already.

'You have not told me,' said I, 'anything about Sam Weller.'

'Oh! Sam,' replied Mr Pickwick, 'is the same as ever. The same true, faithful fellow that he ever was. What should I tell you about Sam, my dear sir, except that he is more indispensable to my happiness and comfort every day of my life?'

'And Mr Weller senior?'[37] said I.

'Old Mr Weller,' returned Mr Pickwick, 'is in no respect more altered than Sam, unless it be that he is a little more opinionated than he was formerly, and perhaps at times more talkative. He spends a good deal of his time now in our neighbourhood, and has so constituted himself a part of my bodyguard, that when I ask permission for Sam to have a seat in your kitchen on clock nights (supposing your three friends think me worthy to fill one of the chairs), I am afraid I must often include Mr Weller too.'

I very readily pledged myself to give both Sam and his father a free admission to my house at all hours and seasons, and this point settled, we fell into a lengthy conversation which was carried on with as little reserve on both sides as if we had been intimate friends from our youth, and which conveyed to me the comfortable assurance that Mr Pickwick's buoyancy of spirit, and indeed all his old cheerful characteristics, were wholly unimpaired. As he had spoken of the consent of my friends as being yet in abeyance, I repeatedly assured him that his proposal was certain to receive their most joyful sanction, and several times entreated that he would give me leave to introduce him to Jack Redburn and Mr Miles (who were near at hand) without further ceremony.

To this proposal, however, Mr Pickwick's delicacy would by no means allow him to accede, for he urged that his eligibility must be formally discussed, and that, until this had been done, he could not think of obtruding himself further. The utmost I could obtain from him was a promise that he would attend upon our next night of meeting, that I might have the pleasure of presenting him immediately on his election.

Mr Pickwick, having with many blushes placed in my hands a small roll of paper, which he termed his 'qualification', put a great many questions to me touching my friends, and particularly Jack Redburn, whom he repeatedly termed 'a fine fellow', and in whose favour I could see he was strongly predisposed. When I had satisfied him on these points, I took him up into my room, that he might make acquaintance with the old chamber which is our place of meeting.

'And this,' said Mr Pickwick, stopping short, 'is the clock! Dear me! And this is really the old clock!'

I thought he would never have come away from it. After advancing towards it softly, and laying his hand upon it with as much respect and as many smiling looks as if it were alive, he set himself to consider it in every possible direction, now mounting on a chair to look at the top, now going down upon his knees to examine the bottom, now surveying the sides with his spectacles almost touching the case, and now trying to peep between it and the wall to get a slight view of the back. Then he would retire a pace or two and look up at the dial to see it go, and then draw near again and stand with his head on one side to hear it tick, never failing to glance towards me at intervals of a few seconds each, and nod his head with such complacent gratification as I am quite unable to describe. His admiration was not confined to the clock either, but extended itself to every article in the room; and really, when he had gone through them every one, and at last sat himself down in all the six chairs, one after another, to try how they felt, I never saw such a picture of good-humour and happiness as he presented, from the top of his shining head down to the very last button of his gaiters.

I should have been well pleased, and should have had the utmost enjoyment of his company, if he had remained with me all day, but my favourite, striking the hour, reminded him that he must take his leave. I could not forbear telling him once more how glad he had made me, and we shook hands all the way downstairs.

We had no sooner arrived in the hall than my housekeeper, gliding out of her little room (she had changed her gown and cap, I observed), greeted Mr Pickwick with her best smile and curtsy; and the barber, feigning to be accidentally passing on his way out, made him a vast number of bows. When the housekeeper curtsied, Mr Pickwick bowed with the utmost politeness, and when he bowed, the housekeeper curtsied again; between the housekeeper and the barber, I should say that Mr Pickwick faced about and bowed with undiminished affability fifty times at least.

I saw him to the door; an omnibus was at the moment passing the corner of the lane, which Mr Pickwick hailed and ran after with extraordinary nimbleness. When he had got about half-way, he turned his head, and seeing that I was still looking after him and that I waved my hand, stopped, evidently irresolute whether to come back and shake hands again, or to go on. The man behind the omnibus shouted, and Mr Pickwick ran a little way towards him: then he looked round at me, and ran a little way back again. Then there was another shout, and he turned round once more and ran the other way. After several of these vibrations, the man settled the question by taking Mr Pickwick by the arm and putting him into the carriage; but his last action was to let down the window and wave his hat to me as it drove off.

I lost no time in opening the parcel he had left with me. The following were its contents –

MR PICKWICK'S TALE

A good many years have passed away since old John Podgers lived in the town of Windsor,[38] where he was born, and where, in course of time, he came to be comfortably and snugly buried. You may be sure that in the time of King James I,[39] Windsor was a very quaint queer old town, and you may take it upon my authority that John Podgers was a very quaint queer old fellow; consequently he and Windsor fitted each other to a nicety, and seldom parted company even for half a day.

John Podgers was broad, sturdy, Dutch-built, short, and a very hard eater, as men of his figure often are. Being a hard sleeper likewise, he divided his time pretty equally between these two recreations, always falling asleep when he had done eating, and always taking another turn at the trencher when he had done sleeping, by which means he grew more corpulent and more drowsy every day of his life. Indeed it used to be currently reported that when he sauntered up and down the sunny side of the street before dinner (as he never failed to do in fair weather), he enjoyed his soundest nap; but many people held this to be a fiction, as he had several times been seen to look after fat oxen on market-days, and had even been heard, by persons of good credit and reputation, to chuckle at the sight, and say to himself with great glee, 'Live beef, live beef!' It was upon this evidence that the wisest people in Windsor (beginning with the local authorities, of course) held that John Podgers was a man of strong, sound sense, not what is called smart, perhaps, and it might be of a rather lazy and apoplectic turn, but still a man of solid parts, and one who meant much more than he cared to show. This impression was confirmed by a very dignified way he had of shaking his head and imparting, at the same time, a pendulous motion to his double chin; in short, he passed for one of those people who, being plunged into the Thames, would make no vain efforts to set it afire, but would straightway flop down to the bottom with a deal of gravity, and be highly respected in consequence by all good men.

Being well to do in the world, and a peaceful widower – having a great appetite, which, as he could afford to gratify it, was a luxury and no inconvenience, and a power of going to sleep, which, as he had no occasion to keep awake, was a most enviable faculty – you will readily suppose that John Podgers was a happy man. But appearances are often deceptive when they least seem so, and the truth is that, notwithstanding his extreme sleekness, he was rendered uneasy in his mind and exceedingly uncomfortable by a constant apprehension that beset him night and day.

You know very well that in those times there flourished divers evil old women who, under the name of witches, spread great disorder through the land, and inflicted various dismal tortures upon Christian men; sticking pins and needles into them when they least expected it, and causing them to walk in the air with their feet upwards, to the great terror of their wives and families, who were naturally very much disconcerted when the master of the house unexpectedly came home, knocking at the door with his heels and combing his hair on the scraper. These were their commonest pranks, but they every day played a hundred others, of which none were less objectionable, and many were much more so, being improper besides; the result was that vengeance was denounced against all old women, with whom even the king himself had no sympathy (as he certainly ought to have had), for with his own most gracious hand he penned a most gracious consignment of them to everlasting wrath, and devised most gracious means for their confusion and slaughter,[40] in virtue whereof scarcely a day passed but one witch at the least was most graciously hanged, drowned or roasted in some part of his dominions. Still the press teemed with strange and terrible news from the north or the south, or the east or the west, relative to witches and their unhappy victims in some corner of the country, and the public's hair stood on end to that degree that it lifted its hat off its head, and made its face pale with terror.

You may believe that the little town of Windsor did not escape the general contagion. The inhabitants boiled a witch on the king's birthday and sent a bottle of the broth to court, with a dutiful address expressive of their loyalty. The king, being rather frightened by the present, piously bestowed it upon the Archbishop of Canterbury, and returned an answer to the address, wherein he gave them golden rules for discovering witches, and laid great stress upon certain protecting charms, and especially horseshoes. Immediately the townspeople went to work nailing up horseshoes over every door, and so many anxious parents apprenticed their children to farriers to keep them out of harm's way, that it became quite a genteel trade, and flourished exceedingly.

In the midst of all this bustle John Podgers ate and slept as usual, but shook his head a great deal oftener than was his custom, and was observed to look at the oxen less, and at the old women more. He had a little shelf put up in his sitting-room, whereon was displayed, in a row which grew longer every week, all the witchcraft literature of the time; he grew learned in charms and exorcisms, hinted at certain questionable females on broomsticks whom he had seen from his chamber window, riding in the air at night, and was in constant terror of being bewitched. At length, from perpetually dwelling upon this one idea, which, being alone in his head, had all its own way, the fear of witches became the single passion of his life. He, who up to that time had never known what it was to dream, began to have visions of witches whenever he fell asleep; waking, they were incessantly present to his imagination likewise; and, sleeping or waking, he had not a moment's peace. He began to set witch-traps in the highway, and was often seen lying in wait round the corner for hours together, to watch their effect. These engines were of simple construction, usually consisting of two straws disposed in the form of a cross, or a piece of a Bible cover with a pinch of salt upon it; but they were infallible, and if an old woman chanced to stumble over them (as not unfrequently happened, the chosen spot being a broken and stony place), John started from a doze, pounced out upon her, and hung round her neck till assistance arrived, when she was immediately carried away and drowned. By dint of constantly inveigling old ladies and disposing of them in this summary manner, he acquired the reputation of a great public character; and as he received no harm in these pursuits beyond a scratched face or so, he came, in the course of time, to be considered witch-proof.

There was but one person who entertained the least doubt of John Podgers's gifts, and that person was his own nephew, a wild, roving young fellow of twenty who had been brought up in his uncle's house and lived there still – that is to say, when he was at home, which was not as often as it might have been. As he was an apt scholar, it was he who read aloud every fresh piece of strange and terrible intelligence that John Podgers bought; and this he always did of an evening in the little porch in front of the house, round which the neighbours would flock in crowds to hear the direful news – for people like to be frightened, and when they can be frightened for nothing and at another man's expense, they like it all the better.

One fine midsummer evening, a group of persons were gathered in this place, listening intently to Will Marks (that was the nephew's name), as with his cap very much on one side, his arm coiled slyly round the waist of a pretty girl who sat beside him, and his face screwed into a comical expression intended to represent extreme gravity, he read – with heaven knows how many embellishments of his own – a dismal account of a gentleman down in Northamptonshire under the influence of witchcraft and taken forcible possession of by the Devil, who was playing his very self with him. John Podgers, in a high sugar-loaf hat[41] and short cloak, filled the opposite seat, and surveyed the auditory with a look of mingled pride and horror very edifying to see; while the hearers, with their heads thrust forward and their mouths open, listened and trembled, and hoped there was a great deal more to come. Sometimes Will stopped for an instant to look round upon his eager audience, and then, with a more comical expression of face than before and a settling of himself comfortably, which included a squeeze of the young lady before mentioned, he launched into some new wonder surpassing all the others.

The setting sun shed his last golden rays upon this little party, who, absorbed in their present occupation, took no heed of the approach of night, or the glory in which the day went down, when the sound of a horse, approaching at a good round trot, invading the silence of the hour, caused the reader to make a sudden stop, and the listeners to raise their heads in wonder. Nor was their wonder diminished when a horseman dashed up to the porch, and abruptly checking his steed, enquired where one John Podgers dwelt.

'Here!' cried a dozen voices, while a dozen hands pointed out sturdy John, still basking in the terrors of the pamphlet.

The rider, giving his bridle to one of those who surrounded him, dismounted and approached John, hat in hand, but with great haste.

'Whence come ye?' said John.

'From Kingston, master.'

'And wherefore?'

'On most pressing business.'

'Of what nature?'

'Witchcraft.'

Witchcraft! Everybody looked aghast at the breathless messenger, and the breathless messenger looked equally aghast at everybody – except Will Marks, who, finding himself unobserved, not only squeezed the young lady again, but kissed her twice. Surely he must have been bewitched himself, or he never could have done it – and the young lady too, or she never would have let him.

'Witchcraft!' cried Will, drowning the sound of his last kiss, which was rather a loud one.

The messenger turned towards him, and with a frown repeated the word more solemnly than before; then told his errand, which was, in brief, that the people of Kingston[42] had been greatly terrified for some nights past by hideous revels, held by witches beneath the gibbet within a mile of the town, and related and deposed to by chance wayfarers who had passed within ear-shot of the spot; that the sound of their voices in their wild orgies had been plainly heard by many persons; that three old women laboured under strong suspicion, and that precedents had been consulted and solemn council had, and it was found that to identify the hags some single person must watch upon the spot alone; that no single person had the courage to perform the task; and that he had been despatched express to solicit John Podgers to undertake it that very night, as being a man of great renown who bore a charmed life and was proof against unholy spells.

John received this communication with much composure, and said in a few words, that it would have afforded him inexpressible pleasure to do the Kingston people so slight a service, if it were not for his unfortunate propensity to fall asleep, which no man regretted more than himself upon the present occasion, but which quite settled the question. Nevertheless, he said, there *was* a gentleman present (and here he looked very hard at a tall farrier), who, having been engaged all his life in the manufacture of horseshoes, must be quite invulnerable to the power of witches, and who, he had no doubt, from his own reputation for bravery and good-nature, would readily accept the commission. The farrier politely thanked him for his good opinion, which it would always be his study to deserve, but added that, with regard to the present little matter, he couldn't think of it on any account, as his departing on such an errand would certainly occasion the instant death of his wife, to whom, as they all knew, he was tenderly attached. Now, so far from this circumstance being notorious, everybody had suspected the reverse, as the farrier was in the habit of beating his lady rather more than tender husbands usually do; all the married men present, however, applauded his resolution with great vehemence, and one and all declared that they would stop at home and die if needful (which happily it was not) in defence of their lawful partners.

This burst of enthusiasm over, they began to look, as by one consent, toward Will Marks, who, with his cap more on one side than ever, sat watching the proceedings with extraordinary unconcern. He had never been heard openly to express his disbelief in witches, but had often cut such jokes at their expense as left it to be inferred; publicly stating on several occasions that he considered a broomstick an inconvenient charger, and one especially unsuited to the dignity of the female character, and indulging in other free remarks of the same tendency, to the great amusement of his wild companions.

As they looked at Will they began to whisper and murmur among themselves, and at length one man cried, 'Why don't you ask Will Marks?'

As this was what everybody had been thinking of, they all took up the word, and cried in concert, 'Ah! why don't you ask Will?'

'*He* don't care,' said the farrier.

'Not he,' added another voice in the crowd.

'He don't believe in it, you know,' sneered a little man with a yellow face and a taunting nose and chin, which he thrust out from under the arm of a long man before him.

'Besides,' said a red-faced gentleman with a gruff voice, 'he's a single man.'

'That's the point!' said the farrier; and all the married men murmured, ah! that was it, and they only wished they were single themselves; they would show him what spirit was, very soon.

The messenger looked towards Will Marks beseechingly.

'It will be a wet night, friend, and my grey nag is tired after yesterday's work – '

Here there was a general titter.

'But,' resumed Will, looking about him with a smile, 'if nobody else puts in a better claim to go, for the credit of the town I am your man, and I would be if I had to go afoot. In five minutes I shall be in the saddle, unless I am depriving any worthy gentleman here of the honour of the adventure, which I wouldn't do for the world.'

But here arose a double difficulty, for not only did John Podgers combat the resolution with all the words he had, which were not many, but the young lady combated it too with all the tears she had, which were very many indeed. Will, however, being inflexible, parried his uncle's objections with a joke, and coaxed the young lady into a smile in three short whispers. As it was plain that he had set his mind upon it, and would go, John Podgers offered him a few first-rate charms out of his own pocket, which he dutifully declined to accept; and the young lady gave him a kiss, which he also returned.

'You see what a rare thing it is to be married,' said Will, 'and how careful and considerate all these husbands are. There's not a man among them but his heart is leaping to forestall me in this adventure, and yet a strong sense of duty keeps him back. The husbands in this one little town are a pattern to the world, and so must the wives be too, for that matter, or they could never boast half the influence they have!'

Waiting for no reply to this sarcasm, he snapped his fingers and withdrew into the house, and thence into the stable, while some busied themselves in refreshing the messenger, and others in baiting his steed. In less than the specified time he returned by another way, with a good cloak hanging over his arm, a good sword girded by his side, and leading his good horse caparisoned for the journey.

'Now,' said Will, leaping into the saddle at a bound, 'up and away. Upon your mettle, friend, and push on. Good-night!'

He kissed his hand to the girl, nodded to his drowsy uncle, waved his cap to the rest – and off they flew pell-mell, as if all the witches in England were in their horses' legs. They were out of sight in a minute.

The men who were left behind shook their heads doubtfully, stroked their chins, and shook their heads again. The farrier said that certainly Will Marks was a good horseman, nobody should ever say he denied that: but he was rash, very rash, and there was no telling what the end of it might be; what did he go for, that was what he wanted to know? He wished the young fellow no harm, but why did he go? Everybody echoed these words, and shook their heads again, having done which they wished John Podgers good-night and straggled home to bed.

The Kingston people were in their first sleep when Will Marks and his conductor rode through the town and up to the door of a house where sundry grave functionaries were assembled, anxiously expecting the arrival of the renowned Podgers. They were a little disappointed to find a gay young man in his place; but they put the best face upon the matter, and gave him full instructions how he was to conceal himself behind the gibbet, and watch and listen to the witches, and how at a certain time he was to burst forth and cut and slash among them vigorously, so that the suspected parties might be found bleeding in their beds next day, and thoroughly confounded. They gave him a great quantity of wholesome advice besides, and – which was more to the purpose with Will – a good supper. All these things being done, and midnight nearly come, they sallied forth to show him the spot where he was to keep his dreary vigil.

The night was by this time dark and threatening. There was a rumbling of distant thunder, and a low sighing of wind among the trees, which was very dismal. The potentates of the town kept so uncommonly close to Will that they trod upon his toes, or stumbled against his ankles, or nearly tripped up his heels at every step he took, and, besides these annoyances, their teeth chattered so with fear that he seemed to be accompanied by a dirge of castanets.

At last they made a halt at the opening of a lonely, desolate space, and, pointing to a black object at some distance, asked Will if he saw that, yonder.

'Yes,' he replied. 'What then?'

Informing him abruptly that it was the gibbet where he was to watch, they wished him good-night in an extremely friendly manner, and ran back as fast as their feet would carry them.

Will walked boldly to the gibbet, and, glancing upwards when he came under it, saw – certainly with satisfaction – that it was empty, and that nothing dangled from the top but some iron chains, which swung mournfully to and fro as they were moved by the breeze. After a careful survey of every quarter he determined to take his station with his face towards the town; both because that would place him with his back to the wind, and because, if any trick or surprise were attempted, it would probably come from that direction in the first instance. Having taken these precautions, he wrapped his cloak about him so that it left the handle of his sword free and ready to his hand and, leaning against the gallows-tree with his cap not quite so much on one side as it had been before, took up his position for the night.

SECOND CHAPTER OF MR PICKWICK'S TALE

We left Will Marks leaning under the gibbet with his face towards the town, scanning the distance with a keen eye which sought to pierce the darkness and catch the earliest glimpse of any person or persons that might approach towards him. But all was quiet, and, save the howling of the wind as it swept across the heath in gusts, and the creaking of the chains that dangled above his head, there was no sound to break the sullen stillness of the night. After half an hour or so this monotony became more disconcerting to Will than the most furious uproar would have been, and he heartily wished for some one antagonist with whom he might have a fair stand-up fight, if it were only to warm himself.

Truth to tell, it was a bitter wind, and seemed to blow to the very heart of a man whose blood, heated but now with rapid riding, was the more sensitive to the chilling blast. Will was a daring fellow, and cared not a jot for hard knocks or sharp blades; but he could not persuade himself to move or walk about, having just that vague expectation of a sudden assault which made it a comfortable thing to have something at his back, even though that something were a gallows-tree. He had no great faith in the superstitions of the age, still such of them as occurred to him did not serve to lighten the time, or to render his situation the more endurable. He remembered how witches were said to repair at that ghostly hour to churchyards and gibbets, and suchlike dismal spots, to pluck the bleeding mandrake[43] or scrape the flesh from dead men's bones, as choice ingredients for their spells; how, stealing by night to lonely places, they dug graves with their finger-nails, or anointed themselves, before riding in the air, with a delicate pomatum made of the fat of infants newly boiled. These, and many other fabled practices of a no less agreeable nature, and all having some reference to the circumstances in which he was placed, passed and repassed in quick succession through the mind of Will Marks, and adding a shadowy dread to that distrust and watchfulness which his situation inspired, rendered it, upon the whole, sufficiently uncomfortable. As he had foreseen, too, the rain began to descend heavily, and driving before the wind in a thick mist, obscured even those few objects which the darkness of the night had before imperfectly revealed.

'Look!' shrieked a voice. 'Great heaven, it has fallen down, and stands erect as if it lived!'

The speaker was close behind him; the voice was almost at his ear.

Will threw off his cloak, drew his sword, and darting swiftly round, seized a woman by the wrist, who, recoiling from him with a dreadful shriek, fell struggling upon her knees. Another woman, clad, like her whom he had grasped, in mourning garments, stood rooted to the spot on which they were, gazing upon his face with wild and glaring eyes that quite appalled him.

'Say,' cried Will, when they had confronted each other thus for some time, 'what are ye?'

'Say what are *you*,' returned the woman, 'who trouble even this obscene resting-place of the dead, and strip the gibbet of its honoured burden? Where is the body?'

He looked in wonder and affright from the woman who questioned him to the other whose arm he clutched.

'Where is the body?' repeated the questioner more firmly than before. 'You wear no livery which marks you for the hireling of the government. You are no friend to us, or I should recognise you, for the friends of such as we are few in number. What are you then, and wherefore are you here?'

'I am no foe to the distressed and helpless,' said Will. 'Are ye among that number? ye should be by your looks.'

'We are!' was the answer.

'Is it ye who have been wailing and weeping here under cover of the night?' said Will.

'It is,' replied the woman sternly; and pointing, as she spoke, towards her companion, 'she mourns a husband, and I a brother. Even the bloody law that wreaks its vengeance on the dead does not make that a crime, and if it did 'twould be alike to us who are past its fear or favour.'

Will glanced at the two females, and could barely discern that the one whom he addressed was much the elder, and that the other was young and of a slight figure. Both were deadly pale, their garments wet and worn, their hair dishevelled and streaming in the wind, themselves bowed down with grief and misery; their whole appearance most dejected, wretched and forlorn. A sight so different from any he had expected to encounter touched him to the quick, and all idea of anything but their pitiable condition vanished before it.

'I am a rough, blunt yeoman,'[44] said Will. 'Why I came here is told in a word; you have been overheard at a distance in the silence of the night, and I have undertaken a watch for hags or spirits. I came here expecting an adventure, and prepared to go through with any. If there be aught that I can do to help or aid you, name it, and on the faith of a man who can be secret and trusty, I will stand by you to the death.'

'How comes this gibbet to be empty?' asked the elder female.

'I swear to you,' replied Will, 'that I know as little as yourself. But this I know, that when I came here an hour ago or so, it was as it is now; and if, as I gather from your question, it was not so last night, sure I am that it has been secretly disturbed without the knowledge of the folks in yonder town. Bethink you, therefore, whether you have no friends in league with you or with him on whom the law has done its worst, by whom these sad remains have been removed for burial.'

The women spoke together, and Will retired a pace or two while they conversed apart. He could hear them sob and moan, and saw that they wrung their hands in fruitless agony. He could make out little that they said, but between whiles he gathered enough to assure him that his suggestion was not very wide of the mark, and that they not only suspected by whom the body had been removed, but also whither it had been conveyed. When they had been in conversation a long time, they turned towards him once more. This time the younger female spoke.

'You have offered us your help?'

'I have.'

'And given a pledge that you are still willing to redeem?'

'Yes. So far as I may, keeping all plots and conspiracies at arm's length.'

'Follow us, friend.'

Will, whose self-possession was now quite restored, needed no second bidding, but with his drawn sword in his hand, and his cloak so muffled over his left arm as to serve for a kind of shield without offering any impediment to its free action, suffered them to lead the way. Through mud and mire, and wind and rain, they walked in silence a full mile. At length they turned into a dark lane, where, suddenly starting out from beneath some trees where he had taken shelter, a man appeared, having in his charge three saddled horses. One of these (his own apparently), in obedience to a whisper from the women, he consigned to Will, who, seeing that they mounted, mounted also. Then, without a word spoken, they rode on together, leaving the attendant behind.

They made no halt nor slackened their pace until they arrived near Putney.[45] At a large wooden house which stood apart from any other they alighted, and giving their horses to one who was already waiting, passed in by a side door, and so up some narrow creaking stairs into a small panelled chamber, where Will was left alone. He had not been here very long when the door was softly opened and there entered to him a cavalier[46] whose face was concealed beneath a black mask.

Will stood upon his guard, and scrutinised this figure from head to foot. The form was that of a man pretty far advanced in life, but of a firm and stately carriage. His dress was of a rich and costly kind, but so soiled and disordered that it was scarcely to be recognised for one of those gorgeous suits which the expensive taste and fashion of the time prescribed for men of any rank or station.

He was booted and spurred, and bore about him even as many tokens of the state of the roads as Will himself. All this he noted, while the eyes behind the mask regarded him with equal attention. This survey over, the cavalier broke silence.

'Thou'rt young and bold, and wouldst be richer than thou art?'

'The two first I am,' returned Will. 'The last I have scarcely thought of. But be it so. Say that I would be richer than I am; what then?'

'The way lies before thee now,' replied the Mask.

'Show it me.'

'First let me inform thee, that thou wert brought here tonight lest thou shouldst too soon have told thy tale to those who placed thee on the watch.'

'I thought as much when I followed,' said Will. 'But I am no blab, not I.'

'Good,' returned the Mask. 'Now listen. He who was to have executed the enterprise of burying that body, which, as thou hast suspected, was taken down tonight, has left us in our need.'

Will nodded, and thought within himself that if the Mask were to attempt to play any tricks, the first eyelet-hole on the left-hand side of his doublet, counting from the buttons up the front, would be a very good place in which to pink him neatly.

'Thou art here, and the emergency is desperate. I propose this task to thee. Convey the body (now coffined in this house), by means that I shall show, to the Church of St Dunstan[47] in London tomorrow night, and thy service shall be richly paid. Thou'rt about to ask whose corpse it is. Seek not to know. I warn thee, seek not to know. Felons hang in chains on every moor and heath. Believe, as others do, that this was one, and ask no further. The murders of state policy, its victims or avengers, had best remain unknown to such as thee.'

'The mystery of this service,' said Will, 'bespeaks its danger. What is the reward?'

'One hundred golden unities,'[48] replied the cavalier. 'The danger to one who cannot be recognised as the friend of a fallen cause is not great, but there is some hazard to be run. Decide between that and the reward.'

'What if I refuse?' said Will.

'Depart in peace, in God's name,' returned the Mask in a melancholy tone, 'and keep our secret, remembering that those who brought thee here were crushed and stricken women, and that those who bade thee go free could have had thy life with one word, and no man the wiser.'

Men were readier to undertake desperate adventures in those times than they are now. In this case the temptation was great, and the punishment, even in case of detection, was not likely to be very severe, as Will came of a loyal stock, and his uncle was in good repute, and a passable tale to account for his possession of the body and his ignorance of the identity might be easily devised.

The cavalier explained that a covered cart had been prepared for the purpose; that the time of departure could be arranged so that he should reach London Bridge at dusk, and proceed through the City after the day had closed in; that people would be ready at his journey's end to place the coffin in a vault without a minute's delay; that officious enquirers in the streets would be easily repelled by the tale that he was carrying for interment the corpse of one who had died of the plague; and in short showed him every reason why he should succeed, and none why he should fail. After a time they were joined by another gentleman, masked like the first, who added new arguments to those which had been already urged; the wretched wife, too, added her tears and prayers to their calmer representations; and in the end, Will, moved by compassion and good-nature, by a love of the marvellous, by a mischievous anticipation of the terrors of the Kingston people when he should be missing next day, and finally, by the prospect of gain, took upon himself the task, and devoted all his energies to its successful execution.

The following night, when it was quite dark, the hollow echoes of old London Bridge[49] responded to the rumbling of the cart which contained the ghastly load, the object of Will Marks' care. Sufficiently disguised to attract no attention by his garb, Will walked at the horse's head, as unconcerned as a man could be who was sensible that he had now arrived at the most dangerous part of his undertaking, but full of boldness and confidence.

It was now eight o'clock. After nine, none could walk the streets without danger of their lives, and even at this hour, robberies and murder were of no uncommon occurrence. The shops upon the bridge were all closed; the low wooden arches thrown across the way were like so many black pits, in every one of which ill-favoured fellows lurked in knots of three or four; some standing upright against the wall, lying in wait; others skulking in gateways, and thrusting out their uncombed heads and scowling eyes; others crossing and recrossing, and constantly jostling both horse and man to provoke a quarrel; others stealing away and summoning their companions in a low whistle. Once, even in that short passage, there was the noise of scuffling and the clash of swords behind him, but Will, who knew the City and its ways, kept straight on and scarcely turned his head.

The streets being unpaved, the rain of the night before had converted them into a perfect quagmire, which the splashing waterspouts from the gables, and the filth and offal cast from the different houses, swelled in no small degree. These odious matters being left to putrefy in the close and heavy air, emitted an insupportable stench, to which every court and passage poured forth a contribution of its own. Many parts, even of the main streets, with their projecting stories tottering overhead and nearly shutting out the sky, were more like huge chimneys than open ways. At the corners of some of these, great bonfires were burning to prevent infection from the plague,[50] of which it was rumoured that some citizens had lately died; and few, who availing themselves of the light thus afforded paused for a moment to look around them, would have been disposed to doubt the existence of the disease, or wonder at its dreadful visitations.

But it was not in such scenes as these, or even in the deep and miry road, that Will Marks found the chief obstacles to his progress. There were kites and ravens feeding in the streets (the only scavengers the City kept), who, scenting what he carried, followed the cart or fluttered on its top, and croaked their knowledge of its burden and their ravenous appetite for prey. There were distant fires, where the poor wood-and-plaster tenements wasted fiercely, and whither crowds made their way, clamouring eagerly for plunder, beating down all who came within their reach, and yelling like devils let loose. There were single-handed men flying from bands of ruffians, who pursued them with naked weapons, and hunted them savagely; there were drunken, desperate robbers issuing from their dens and staggering through the open streets where no man dared molest them; there were vagabond servitors returning from the Bear Garden,[51] where had been good sport that day, dragging after them their torn and bleeding dogs, or leaving them to die and rot upon the road. Nothing was abroad but cruelty, violence and disorder.

Many were the interruptions which Will Marks encountered from these stragglers, and many the narrow escapes he made. Now some stout bully would take his seat upon the cart, insisting to be driven to his own home, and now two or three men would come down upon him together, and demand that on peril of his life he showed them what he had inside. Then a party of the City watch, upon their rounds, would draw across the road, and not satisfied with his tale, question him closely, and revenge themselves by a little cuffing and hustling for maltreatment sustained at other hands that night. All these assailants had to be rebutted, some by fair words, some by foul, and some by blows. But Will Marks was not the man to be stopped or turned back now he had penetrated so far, and though he got on slowly, still he made his way down Fleet Street and reached the church at last.

As he had been forewarned, all was in readiness. Directly he stopped, the coffin was removed by four men, who appeared so suddenly that they seemed to have started from the earth. A fifth mounted the cart, and scarcely allowing Will time to snatch from it a little bundle containing such of his own clothes as he had thrown off on assuming his disguise, drove briskly away. Will never saw cart or man again.

He followed the body into the church, and it was well he lost no time in doing so, for the door was immediately closed. There was no light in the building save that which came from a couple of torches borne by two men in cloaks, who stood upon the brink of a vault. Each supported a female figure, and all observed a profound silence.

By this dim and solemn glare, which made Will feel as though light itself were dead, and its tomb the dreary arches that frowned above, they placed the coffin in the vault, with uncovered heads, and closed it up. One of the torchbearers then turned to Will, and stretched forth his hand, in which was a purse of gold. Something told him directly that those were the same eyes which he had seen beneath the mask.

'Take it,' said the cavalier in a low voice, 'and be happy. Though these have been hasty obsequies, and no priest has blessed the work, there will not be the less peace with thee thereafter for having laid his bones beside those of his little children. Keep thy own counsel, for thy sake no less than ours, and God be with thee!'

'The blessing of a widowed mother on thy head, good friend!' cried the younger lady through her tears; 'the blessing of one who has now no hope or rest but in this grave!'

Will stood with the purse in his hand, and involuntarily made a gesture as though he would return it, for though a thoughtless fellow, he was of a frank and generous nature. But the two gentlemen, extinguishing their torches, cautioned him to be gone, as their common safety would be endangered by a longer delay; and at the same time their retreating footsteps sounded through the church. He turned, therefore, towards the point at which he had entered, and seeing by a faint gleam in the distance that the door was again partially open, groped his way towards it and so passed into the street.

Meantime the local authorities of Kingston had kept watch and ward all the previous night, fancying every now and then that dismal shrieks were borne towards them on the wind, and frequently winking to each other, and drawing closer to the fire as they drank the health of the lonely sentinel, upon whom a clerical gentleman present was especially severe by reason of his levity and youthful folly. Two or three of the gravest in the company, who were of a theological turn, propounded to him the question whether such a character was not but poorly armed for single combat with the

Devil, and whether he himself would not have been a stronger opponent; but the clerical gentleman, sharply reproving them for their presumption in discussing such questions, clearly showed that a fitter champion than Will could scarcely have been selected, not only for that, being a child of Satan, he was the less likely to be alarmed by the appearance of his own father, but because Satan himself would be at his ease in such company, and would not scruple to kick up his heels to an extent which it was quite certain he would never venture before clerical eyes, under whose influence (as was notorious) he became quite a tame and milk-and-water character.

But when next morning arrived, and with it no Will Marks, and when a strong party repairing to the spot, as a strong party ventured to do in broad day, found Will gone and the gibbet empty, matters grew serious indeed. The day passing away and no news arriving, and the night going on also without any intelligence, the thing grew more tremendous still; in short, the neighbourhood worked itself up to such a comfortable pitch of mystery and horror, that it is a great question whether the general feeling was not one of excessive disappointment, when, on the second morning, Will Marks returned.

However this may be, back Will came in a very cool and collected state, and appearing not to trouble himself much about anybody except old John Podgers, who, having been sent for, was sitting in the town hall crying slowly, and dozing between whiles. Having embraced his uncle and assured him of his safety, Will mounted on a table and told his story to the crowd.

And surely they would have been the most unreasonable crowd that ever assembled together if they had been in the least respect disappointed with the tale he told them; for besides describing the witches' dance to the minutest motion of their legs, and performing it in character on the table, with the assistance of a broomstick, he related how they had carried off the body in a copper cauldron, and so bewitched him that he lost his senses until he found himself lying under a hedge at least ten miles off, whence he had straightway returned as they then beheld. The story gained such universal applause that it soon afterwards brought down express from London the great witch-finder of the age, the heaven-born Hopkins,[52] who having examined Will closely on several points, pronounced it the most extraordinary and the best accredited witch-story ever known, under which title it was published at the Three Bibles on London Bridge,[53] in small quarto, with a view of the cauldron from an original drawing, and a portrait of the clerical gentleman as he sat by the fire.

On one point Will was particularly careful: and that was to describe, for the witches he had seen, three impossible old females, whose likenesses never were or will be. Thus he saved the lives of the suspected parties, and of all other old women who were dragged before him to be identified.

This circumstance occasioned John Podgers much grief and sorrow, until happening one day to cast his eyes upon his house-keeper, and observing her to be plainly afflicted with rheumatism, he procured her to be burnt as an undoubted witch. For this service to the state he was immediately knighted, and became from that time Sir John Podgers.

Will Marks never gained any clue to the mystery in which he had been an actor, nor did any inscription in the church, which he often visited afterwards, nor any of the limited enquiries that he dared to make, yield him the least assistance. As he kept his own secret, he was compelled to spend the gold discreetly and sparingly. In the course of time he married the young lady of whom I have already told you, whose maiden name is not recorded, with whom he led a prosperous and happy life. Years and years after this adventure, it was his wont to tell her upon a stormy night that it was a great comfort to him to think those bones, to whomsoever they might have once belonged, were not bleaching in the troubled air, but were mouldering away with the dust of their own kith and kindred in a quiet grave.

FURTHER PARTICULARS OF MASTER HUMPHREY'S VISITOR

Being very full of Mr Pickwick's application, and highly pleased with the compliment he had paid me, it will be readily supposed that long before our next night of meeting I communicated it to my three friends, who unanimously voted his admission into our body. We all looked forward with some impatience to the occasion which would enroll him among us, but I am greatly mistaken if Jack Redburn and myself were not by many degrees the most impatient of the party.

At length the night came, and a few minutes after ten Mr Pickwick's knock was heard at the street-door. He was shown into a lower room, and I directly took my crooked stick and went to accompany him upstairs, in order that he might be presented with all honour and formality.

'Mr Pickwick,' said I, on entering the room, 'I am rejoiced to see you – rejoiced to believe that this is but the opening of a long series of visits to this house, and but the beginning of a close and lasting friendship.'

That gentleman made a suitable reply with a cordiality and frankness peculiarly his own, and glanced with a smile towards two persons behind the door, whom I had not at first observed, and whom I immediately recognised as Mr Samuel Weller and his father.

It was a warm evening, but the elder Mr Weller was attired, notwithstanding, in a most capacious greatcoat, and his chin enveloped in a large speckled shawl, such as is usually worn by stage coachmen on active service. He looked very rosy and very stout, especially about the legs, which appeared to have been compressed into his top-boots with some difficulty. His broad-brimmed hat he held under his left arm, and with the forefinger of his right hand he touched his forehead a great many times in acknowledgment of my presence.

'I am very glad to see you in such good health, Mr Weller,' said I.

'Why, thankee, sir,' returned Mr Weller, 'the axle an't broke yet. We keeps up a steady pace – not too sewere, but vith[54] a moderate degree o' friction – and the consekens is that ve're still a runnin' and comes in to the time reg'lar. – My son Samivel, sir, as you may have read on in history,' added Mr Weller, introducing his first-born.

I received Sam very graciously, but before he could say a word his father struck in again.

'Samivel Veller, sir,' said the old gentleman, 'has conferred upon me the ancient title o' grandfather vich had long laid dormouse,[55] and wos s'posed to be nearly hex–tinct in our family. Sammy, relate a anecdote o' vun o' them boys – that 'ere little anecdote about young Tony sayin' as he *would* smoke a pipe unbeknown to his mother.'

'Be quiet, can't you?' said Sam; 'I never see such a old magpie – never!'

'That 'ere Tony is the blessedest boy,' said Mr Weller, heedless of this rebuff, 'the blessedest boy as ever *I* see in *my* days! of all the charmin'est infants as ever I heerd tell on, includin' them as was kivered over by the robin-redbreasts arter they'd committed sooicide with blackberries,[56] there never wos any like that 'ere little Tony. He's alvays a playin' with a quart pot, that boy is! To see him a settin' down on the doorstep pretending to drink out of it, and fetching a long breath artervards, and smoking a bit of firevood, and sayin', "Now I'm grandfather" – to see him a doin' that at two year old is better than any play as wos ever wrote. "Now I'm grandfather!" He wouldn't take a pint pot if you wos to make him a present on it, but he gets his quart, and then he says, "Now I'm grandfather!" '

Mr Weller was so overpowered by this picture that he straightway fell into a most alarming fit of coughing, which must certainly have been attended with some fatal result but for the dexterity and promptitude of Sam, who, taking a firm grasp of the shawl just under his father's chin, shook him to and fro with great violence, at the same time administering some smart blows between his shoulders. By this curious mode of treatment Mr Weller was finally recovered, but with a very crimson face, and in a state of great exhaustion.

'He'll do now, Sam,' said Mr Pickwick, who had been in some alarm himself.

'He'll do, sir!' cried Sam, looking reproachfully at his parent. 'Yes, he *will* do one o' these days – he'll do for hisself and then he'll wish he hadn't. Did anybody ever see sich a inconsiderate old file – laughing into conwulsions afore company, and stamping on the floor as if he'd brought his own carpet vith him and wos under a wager to punch the pattern out in a given time? He'll begin again in a minute. There – he's a goin' off – I said he would!'

In fact, Mr Weller, whose mind was still running upon his precocious grandson, was seen to shake his head from side to side, while a laugh, working like an earthquake, below the surface, produced various extraordinary appearances in his face, chest and shoulders – the more alarming because unaccompanied by any noise whatever. These emotions, however, gradually subsided, and after three or four short relapses he wiped his eyes with the cuff of his coat, and looked about him with tolerable composure.

'Afore the governor vith-draws,' said Mr Weller, 'there is a pint respecting vich Sammy has a qvestion to ask. Vile that qvestion is a perwadin' this here conwersation, p'raps the gen'l'men vill permit me to re–tire.'

'Wot are you goin' away for?' demanded Sam, seizing his father by the coat-tail.

'I never see such a undootiful boy as you, Samivel,' returned Mr Weller. 'Didn't you make a solemn promise, amountin' almost to a speeches o' wow, that you'd put that 'ere qvestion on my account?'

'Well, I'm agreeable to do it,' said Sam, 'but not if you go cuttin' away like that, as the bull turned round and mildly observed to the drover ven they wos a goadin' him into the butcher's door. The fact is, sir,' said Sam, addressing me, 'that he wants to know somethin' respectin' that 'ere lady as is housekeeper here.'

'Ay. What is that?'

'Vy, sir,' said Sam, grinning still more, 'he wishes to know vether she – '

'In short,' interposed old Mr Weller decisively, a perspiration breaking out upon his forehead, 'vether that 'ere old creetur is or is not a widder.'

Mr Pickwick laughed heartily, and so did I, as I replied decisively that my housekeeper was a spinster.

'There!' cried Sam, 'now you're satisfied. You hear she's a spinster.'

'A wot?' said his father, with deep scorn.

'A spinster,' replied Sam.

Mr Weller looked very hard at his son for a minute or two, and then said, 'Never mind vether she makes jokes or not, that's no matter. Wot I say is, is that 'ere female a widder, or is she not?'

'Wot do you mean by her making jokes?' demanded Sam, quite aghast at the obscurity of his parent's speech.

'Never you mind, Samivel,' returned Mr Weller gravely; 'puns may be wery good things or they may be wery bad 'uns, and a female may be none the better or she may be none the vurse for making of 'em; that's got nothing to do vith widders.'

'Vy now,' said Sam, looking round, 'would anybody believe as a man at his time o' life could be running his head agin spinsters and punsters being the same thing?'

'There an't a straw's difference between 'em,' said Mr Weller. 'Your father didn't drive a coach for so many years, not to be ekal to his own langvidge as far as *that* goes, Sammy.'

Avoiding the question of etymology, upon which the old gentleman's mind was quite made up, he was several times assured that the housekeeper had never been married. He expressed great satisfaction on hearing this, and apologised for the question, remarking that he had been greatly terrified by a widow not long before, and that his natural timidity was increased in consequence.

'It wos on the rail,' said Mr Weller, with strong emphasis; 'I wos a goin' down to Birmingham by the rail,[57] and I wos locked up in a close carriage vith a living widder. Alone we wos; the widder and me wos alone; and I believe it wos only because we *wos* alone, and there wos no clergyman in the conwayance, that that 'ere widder didn't marry me afore ve reached the half-way station. Ven I think how she began a screaming as we wos a goin' under them tunnels in the dark – how she kept on a faintin' and ketchin' hold o' me – and how I tried to bust open the door as was tight-locked and perwented all escape – Ah! It was a awful thing, most awful!'

Mr Weller was so very much overcome by this retrospect that he was unable, until he had wiped his brow several times, to return any reply to the question whether he approved of railway communication, notwithstanding that it would appear from the answer which he ultimately gave that he entertained strong opinions on the subject.

'I con–sider,' said Mr Weller, 'that the rail is unconstitootional and an inwaser o' priwileges, and I should wery much like to know what that 'ere old Carter as once stood up for our liberties[58] and wun 'em too – I should like to know wot he vould say, if he wos alive now, to Englishmen being locked up vith widders, or with anybody again their wills. Wot a old Carter would have said, a old Coachman may say, and I as–sert that in that pint o' view alone, the rail is an inwaser. As to the comfort, vere's the comfort o' sittin' in a harm-cheer lookin' at brick walls or heaps o' mud, never comin' to a public-house, never seein' a glass o' ale, never goin' through a pike, never meetin' a change o' no kind (horses or othervise), but alvays comin' to a place, ven you come to one at all, the wery picter o' the last, vith the same p'leesemen standing about, the same blessed old bell a-ringin', the same unfort'nate people standing behind the bars, a-waitin' to be let in; and everythin' the same except the name, vich is wrote up in the same sized letters as the last name, and vith the same colours. As to the *h*onour and dignity o' travellin', vere can that be vithout a coachman; and wot's the rail to sich coachmen and guards as is sometimes forced to go by it, but a outrage and a insult? As to the pace, wot sort o' pace do you think I, Tony Veller, could have kept a coach goin' at, for five hundred thousand pound a mile, paid in adwance afore the coach was on the road? And as to the ingein – a nasty, wheezin', creakin', gaspin', puffin', bustin' monster, alvays out o' breath, with a shiny green-and-gold back, like a unpleasant beetle in that 'ere gas magnifier – as to the ingein as is alvays a pourin' out red-hot coals at night, and black smoke in the day, the sensiblest thing it does, in my opinion, is, ven there's somethin' in the vay, and it sets up that 'ere frightful scream vich seems to say, "Now here's two hundred and forty passengers in the very greatest extremity o' danger, and here's their two hundred and forty screams in vun!" '

By this time I began to fear that my friends would be rendered impatient by my protracted absence. I therefore begged Mr Pickwick to accompany me upstairs, and left the two Mr Wellers in the care of the housekeeper, laying strict injunctions upon her to treat them with all possible hospitality.

CHAPTER 4

The Clock

As we were going upstairs, Mr Pickwick put on his spectacles, which he had held in his hand hitherto; arranged his neckerchief, smoothed down his waistcoat, and made many other little preparations of that kind which men are accustomed to be mindful of when they are going among strangers for the first time and are anxious to impress them pleasantly. Seeing that I smiled, he smiled too, and said that if it had occurred to him before he left home, he would certainly have presented himself in pumps and silk stockings.

'I would, indeed, my dear sir,' he said very seriously; 'I would have shown my respect for the society, by laying aside my gaiters.'

'You may rest assured,' said I, 'that they would have regretted your doing so very much, for they are quite attached to them.'

'No, really!' cried Mr Pickwick, with manifest pleasure. 'Do you think they care about my gaiters? Do you seriously think that they identify me at all with my gaiters?'

'I am sure they do,' I replied.

'Well, now,' said Mr Pickwick, 'that is one of the most charming and agreeable circumstances that could possibly have occurred to me!'

I should not have written down this short conversation, but that it developed a slight point in Mr Pickwick's character, with which I was not previously acquainted. He has a secret pride in his legs. The manner in which he spoke, and the accompanying glance he bestowed upon his tights, convince me that Mr Pickwick regards his legs with much innocent vanity.

'But here are our friends,' said I, opening the door and taking his arm in mine; 'let them speak for themselves – Gentlemen, I present to you Mr Pickwick.'

Mr Pickwick and I must have been a good contrast just then. I, leaning quietly on my crutch-stick, with something of a careworn, patient air; he, having hold of my arm, and bowing in every direction with the most elastic politeness, and an expression of face whose sprightly cheerfulness and good-humour knew no bounds. The difference between us must have been more striking yet, as we advanced towards the table, and the amiable gentleman, adapting his jocund step to my poor tread, had his attention divided between treating my infirmities with the utmost consideration, and affecting to be wholly unconscious that I required any.

I made him personally known to each of my friends in turn. First, to the deaf gentleman, whom he regarded with much interest, and accosted with great frankness and cordiality. He had evidently some vague idea, at the moment, that my friend being deaf must be dumb also; for when the latter opened his lips to express the pleasure it afforded him to know a gentleman of whom he had heard so much, Mr Pickwick was so extremely disconcerted, that I was obliged to step in to his relief.

His meeting with Jack Redburn was quite a treat to see. Mr Pickwick smiled, and shook hands, and looked at him through his spectacles, and under them, and over them, and nodded his head approvingly, and then nodded to me, as much as to say, 'This is just the man; you were quite right;' and then turned to Jack and said a few hearty words, and then did and said everything over again with unimpaired vivacity. As to Jack himself, he was quite as much delighted with Mr Pickwick as Mr Pickwick could possibly be with him. Two people never can have met together since the world began, who exchanged a warmer or more enthusiastic greeting.

It was amusing to observe the difference between this encounter and that which succeeded, between Mr Pickwick and Mr Miles. It was clear that the latter gentleman viewed our new member as a kind of rival in the affections of Jack Redburn, and besides this, he had more than once hinted to me, in secret, that although he had no doubt Mr Pickwick was a very worthy man, still he did consider that some of his exploits were unbecoming a gentleman of his years and gravity. Over and above these grounds of distrust, it is one of his fixed opinions that the law never can by possibility do anything wrong; he therefore looks upon Mr Pickwick as one who has justly suffered in purse and peace for a breach of his plighted faith to an unprotected female, and holds that he is called upon to regard him with some suspicion on that account. These causes led to a rather cold and formal reception; which Mr Pickwick acknowledged with the same stateliness and intense politeness as was displayed on the other side. Indeed, he assumed an air of such majestic defiance, that I was fearful he might break out into some solemn protest or declaration, and therefore inducted him into his chair without a moment's delay.

This piece of generalship was perfectly successful. The instant he took his seat, Mr Pickwick surveyed us all with a most benevolent aspect, and was taken with a fit of smiling full five minutes long. His interest in our ceremonies was immense. They are not very numerous or complicated, and a description of them may be comprised in very few words. As our transactions have already been, and must necessarily continue to be, more or less anticipated by being presented in these pages at different times, and under various forms, they do not require a detailed account.

Our first proceeding when we are assembled is to shake hands all round, and greet each other with cheerful and pleasant looks. Remembering that we assemble not only for the promotion of our happiness, but with the view of adding something to the common stock, an air of languor or indifference in any member of our body would be regarded by the others as a kind of treason. We have never had an offender in this respect; but if we had, there is no doubt that he would be taken to task pretty severely.

Our salutation over, the venerable piece of antiquity from which we take our name is wound up in silence. The ceremony is always performed by Master Humphrey himself (in treating of the club, I may be permitted to assume the historical style, and speak of myself in the third person), who mounts upon a chair for the purpose, armed with a large key. While it is in progress, Jack Redburn is required to keep at the farther end of the room under the guardianship of Mr Miles, for he is known to entertain certain aspiring and unhallowed thoughts connected with the clock, and has even gone so far as to state that if he might take the works out for a day or two, he thinks he could improve them. We pardon him his presumption in consideration of his good intentions, and his keeping this respectful distance, which last penalty is insisted on, lest by secretly wounding the object of our regard in some tender part, in the ardour of his zeal for its improvement, he should fill us with dismay and consternation.

This regulation afforded Mr Pickwick the highest delight, and seemed, if possible, to exalt Jack in his good opinion.

The next ceremony is the opening of the clock-case (of which Master Humphrey has likewise the key), the taking from it as many papers as will furnish forth our evening's entertainment, and arranging in the recess such new contributions as have been provided since our last meeting. This is always done with peculiar solemnity. The deaf gentleman then fills and lights his pipe, and we once more take our seats round the table before mentioned, Master Humphrey acting as president – if we can be said to have any president, where all are on the same social footing – and our friend Jack as secretary. Our preliminaries being now concluded, we fall into any train of conversation that happens to suggest itself, or proceed immediately to one of our readings. In the latter case, the paper selected is consigned to Master Humphrey, who flattens it carefully on the table and makes dog's ears in the corner of every page, ready for turning over easily; Jack Redburn trims the lamp with a small machine of his own invention which usually puts it out; Mr Miles looks on with great approval notwithstanding; the deaf gentleman draws in his chair, so that he can follow the words on the paper or on Master Humphrey's lips as he pleases; and Master Humphrey himself, looking round with mighty gratification, and glancing up at his old clock, begins to read aloud.

Mr Pickwick's face, while his tale was being read, would have attracted the attention of the dullest man alive. The complacent motion of his head and forefinger as he gently beat time, and corrected the air with imaginary punctuation, the smile that mantled on his features at every jocose passage, and the sly look he stole around to observe its effect, the calm manner in which he shut his eyes and listened when there was some little piece of description, the changing expression with which he acted the dialogue to himself, his agony that the deaf gentleman should know what it was all about, and his extraordinary anxiety to correct the reader when he hesitated at a word in the manuscript, or substituted a wrong one, were alike worthy of remark. And when at last, endeavouring to communicate with the deaf gentleman by means of the finger alphabet, with which he constructed such words as are unknown in any civilised or savage language, he took up a slate and wrote in large text, one word in a line, the question, 'How – do – you – like – it?' – when he did this, and handing it over the table awaited the reply, with a countenance only brightened and improved by his great excitement, even Mr Miles relaxed, and could not forbear looking at him for the moment with interest and favour.

'It has occurred to me,' said the deaf gentleman, who had watched Mr Pickwick and everybody else with silent satisfaction – 'it has occurred to me,' said the deaf gentleman, taking his pipe from his lips, 'that now is our time for filling our only empty chair.'

As our conversation had naturally turned upon the vacant seat, we lent a willing ear to this remark, and looked at our friend enquiringly.

'I feel sure,' said he, 'that Mr Pickwick must be acquainted with somebody who would be an acquisition to us; that he must know the man we want. Pray let us not lose any time, but set this question at rest. Is it so, Mr Pickwick?'

The gentleman addressed was about to return a verbal reply, but remembering our friend's infirmity, he substituted for this kind of answer some fifty nods. Then taking up the slate and printing on it a gigantic 'Yes', he handed it across the table and, rubbing his hands as he looked round upon our faces, protested that he and the deaf gentleman quite understood each other, already.

'The person I have in my mind,' said Mr Pickwick, 'and whom I should not have presumed to mention to you until some time hence, but for the opportunity you have given me, is a very strange old man. His name is Bamber.'

'Bamber!' said Jack. 'I have certainly heard the name before.'

'I have no doubt, then,' returned Mr Pickwick, 'that you remember him in those adventures of mine (the Posthumous Papers of our old club, I mean), although he is only incidentally mentioned; and, if I remember right, appears but once.'[59]

'That's it,' said Jack. 'Let me see. He is the person who has a grave interest in old mouldy chambers and the Inns of Court, and who relates some anecdotes having reference to his favourite theme – and an odd ghost story – is that the man?'

'The very same. Now,' said Mr Pickwick, lowering his voice to a mysterious and confidential tone, 'he is a very extraordinary and remarkable person; living, and talking, and looking, like some strange spirit, whose delight is to haunt old buildings; and absorbed in that one subject which you have just mentioned, to an extent which is quite wonderful. When I retired into private life, I sought him out, and I do assure you that the more I see of him, the more strongly I am impressed with the strange and dreamy character of his mind.'

'Where does he live?' I enquired.

'He lives,' said Mr Pickwick, 'in one of those dull, lonely old places with which his thoughts and stories are all connected; quite alone, and often shut up close for several weeks together. In this dusty solitude he broods upon the fancies he has so long indulged, and when he goes into the world, or anybody from the world without goes to see him, they are still present to his mind and still his favourite topic. I may say, I believe, that he has brought himself to entertain a regard for me, and an interest in my visits; feelings which I am certain he would extend to Master Humphrey's Clock if he were once tempted to join us. All I wish you to understand is that he is a strange, secluded visionary, in the world but not of it; and as unlike anybody here as he is unlike anybody elsewhere that I have ever met or known.'

Mr Miles received this account of our proposed companion with rather a wry face, and after murmuring that perhaps he was a little mad, enquired if he were rich.

'I never asked him,' said Mr Pickwick.

'You might know, sir, for all that,' retorted Mr Miles, sharply.

'Perhaps so, sir,' said Mr Pickwick, no less sharply than the other, 'but I do not. Indeed,' he added, relapsing into his usual mildness, 'I have no means of judging. He lives poorly, but that would seem to be in keeping with his character. I never heard him allude to his circumstances, and never fell into the society of any man who had the slightest acquaintance with them. I have really told you all I know about him, and it rests with you to say whether you wish to know more, or know quite enough already.'

We were unanimously of opinion that we would seek to know more; and as a sort of compromise with Mr Miles (who, although he said, 'Yes – oh! certainly – he should like to know more about the gentleman – he had no right to put himself in opposition to the general wish,' and so forth, shook his head doubtfully and hemmed several times with peculiar gravity), it was arranged that Mr

Pickwick should carry me with him on an evening visit to the subject of our discussion, for which purpose an early appointment between that gentleman and myself was immediately agreed upon; it being understood that I was to act upon my own responsibility, and to invite him to join us or not, as I might think proper. This solemn question determined, we returned to the clock-case (where we have been forestalled by the reader), and between its contents, and the conversation they occasioned, the remainder of our time passed very quickly.

When we broke up, Mr Pickwick took me aside to tell me that he had spent a most charming and delightful evening. Having made this communication with an air of the strictest secrecy, he took Jack Redburn into another corner to tell him the same, and then retired into another corner with the deaf gentleman and the slate, to repeat the assurance. It was amusing to observe the contest in his mind whether he should extend his confidence to Mr Miles, or treat him with dignified reserve. Half a dozen times he stepped up behind him with a friendly air, and as often stepped back again without saying a word; at last, when he was close at that gentleman's ear and upon the very point of whispering something conciliating and agreeable, Mr Miles happened suddenly to turn his head, upon which Mr Pickwick skipped away, and said with some fierceness, 'Good-night, sir – I was about to say good-night, sir – nothing more;' and so made a bow and left him.

'Now, Sam,' said Mr Pickwick, when he had got downstairs.

'All right, sir,' replied Mr Weller. 'Hold hard, sir. Right arm fust – now the left – now one strong conwulsion, and the greatcoat's on, sir.'

Mr Pickwick acted upon these directions, and being further assisted by Sam, who pulled at one side of the collar, and Mr Weller, who pulled hard at the other, was speedily enrobed. Mr Weller senior then produced a full-sized stable lantern, which he had carefully deposited in a remote corner on his arrival, and enquired whether Mr Pickwick would have 'the lamps alight'.

'I think not tonight,' said Mr Pickwick.

'Then if this here lady vill per–mit,' rejoined Mr Weller, 'we'll leave it here, ready for next journey. This here lantern, mum,' said Mr Weller, handing it to the housekeeper, 'vunce belonged to the celebrated Bill Blinder as is now at grass, as all on us vill be in our turns. Bill, mum, wos the hostler as had charge o' them two vell-known piebald leaders that run in the Bristol fast coach, and vould never go to no other tune but a sutherly vind and a cloudy sky, which wos consekvently played incessant, by the guard, wenever they wos on duty. He wos took wery bad one arternoon, arter having been off his feed, and wery shaky on his legs for some veeks; and he says to his mate, "Matey," he says, "I think I'm a-goin' the wrong side o' the post, and that my foot's wery near the bucket. Don't say I an't," he says, "for I know I am, and don't let me be interrupted," he says, "for I've saved a little money, and I'm a-goin' into the stable to make my last vill and testymint." "I'll take care as nobody interrupts," says his mate, "but you on'y hold up your head, and shake your ears a bit, and you're good for twenty years to come." Bill Blinder makes him no answer, but he goes avay into the stable, and there he soon artervards lays himself down a'tween the two piebalds, and dies – previously a writin' outside the corn-chest, "This is the last vill and testymint of Villiam Blinder." They wos nat'rally wery much amazed at this, and arter looking among the litter, and up in the loft, and vere not, they opens the corn-chest, and finds that he'd been and chalked his vill inside the lid; so the lid was obligated to be took off the hinges, and sent up to Doctor Commons to be proved, and under that 'ere wery instrument this here lantern was passed to Tony Veller; vich circumstarnce, mum, gives it a wally in my eyes, and makes me rekvest, if you vill be so kind, as to take partickler care on it.'

The housekeeper graciously promised to keep the object of Mr Weller's regard in the safest possible custody, and Mr Pickwick, with a laughing face, took his leave. The bodyguard followed, side by side;

old Mr Weller buttoned and wrapped up from his boots to his chin; and Sam, with his hands in his pockets and his hat half off his head, remonstrating with his father as he went on his extreme loquacity.

I was not a little surprised, on turning to go upstairs, to encounter the barber in the passage at that late hour; for his attendance is usually confined to some half-hour in the morning. But Jack Redburn, who finds out (by instinct, I think) everything that happens in the house, informed me, with great glee, that a society in imitation of our own had been that night formed in the kitchen, under the title of 'Mr Weller's Watch', of which the barber was a member; and that he could pledge himself to find means of making me acquainted with the whole of its future proceedings, which I begged him, both on my own account and that of my readers, by no means to neglect doing.

*   *   *

[*The Old Curiosity Shop* is contnued here, completing Chapter IV.]

CHAPTER 5

Mr Weller's Watch

IT SEEMS THAT the housekeeper and the two Mr Wellers were no sooner left together on the occasion of their first becoming acquainted, than the housekeeper called to her assistance Mr Slithers, the barber, who had been lurking in the kitchen in expectation of her summons; and with many smiles and much sweetness introduced him as one who would assist her in the responsible office of entertaining her distinguished visitors.

'Indeed,' said she, 'without Mr Slithers I should have been placed in quite an awkward situation.'

'There is no call for any hock'erdness, mum,' said Mr Weller with the utmost politeness; 'no call wotsumever. A lady,' added the old gentleman, looking about him with the air of one who establishes an incontrovertible position – 'a lady can't be hock'erd. Natur' has otherwise purwided.'

The housekeeper inclined her head and smiled yet more sweetly. The barber, who had been fluttering about Mr Weller and Sam in a state of great anxiety to improve their acquaintance, rubbed his hands and cried, 'Hear, hear! Very true, sir;' whereupon Sam turned about and steadily regarded him for some seconds in silence.

'I never knew,' said Sam, fixing his eyes in a ruminative manner upon the blushing barber – 'I never knew but vun o' your trade, but *he* wos worth a dozen, and wos indeed dewoted to his callin'!'

'Was he in the easy shaving way, sir,' enquired Mr Slithers; 'or in the cutting and curling line?'

'Both,' replied Sam; 'easy shavin' was his natur', and cuttin' and curlin' was his pride and glory. His whole delight wos in his trade. He spent all his money in bears, and run in debt for 'em besides, and there they wos a growling avay down in the front cellar all day long, and ineffectooally gnashing their teeth, vile the grease o' their relations[60] and friends wos being re–tailed in gallipots in the shop above, and the first-floor winder wos ornamented vith their heads; not to speak o' the dreadful aggrawation it must have been to 'em to see a man alvays a walkin' up and down the pavement outside, vith the portrait of a bear in his last agonies, and underneath in large letters, "Another fine animal wos slaughtered yesterday at Jinkinson's!" Hows'ever, there they wos, and there Jinkinson wos, till he wos took wery ill with some inn'ard disorder, lost the use of his legs, and wos confined to his bed, vere he laid a wery long time, but sich wos his pride in his profession, even then, that wenever he wos worse than usual the doctor used to go downstairs and say, "Jinkinson's wery low this mornin'; we must give the bears a stir;" and as sure as ever they stirred 'em up a bit and made 'em roar, Jinkinson opens his eyes if he wos ever so bad, calls out, "There's the bears!" and rewives agin.'

'Astonishing!' cried the barber.

'Not a bit,' said Sam, 'human natur' neat as imported. Vun day the doctor happenin' to say, "I shall look in as usual tomorrow mornin'," Jinkinson catches hold of his hand and says, "Doctor," he says, "will you grant me one favour?" "I will, Jinkinson," says the doctor. "Then, doctor," says Jinkinson, "vill you come unshaved, and let me shave you?" "I will," says the doctor. "God bless you," says Jinkinson. Next day the doctor came, and arter he'd been shaved all skilful and reg'lar, he says, "Jinkinson," he says, "it's wery plain this does you good. Now," he says, "I've got a coachman as has got a beard that it 'ud warm your heart to work on, and though the footman," he says, "hasn't got much of a beard, still he's a-trying it on vith a pair o' viskers to that extent that razors is Christian charity. If they take it in turns to mind the carriage when it's a waitin' below," he says, "wot's to hinder you from operatin' on both of 'em ev'ry day as well as upon me? You've got six children," he says, "wot's to hinder you from shavin' all their heads and keepin' 'em shaved? You've got two assistants in the shop downstairs, wot's to hinder you from cuttin' and curlin' them as often as you like? Do this," he says, "and you're a man agin." Jinkinson squeedged the doctor's hand and begun that wery day; he kept his tools upon the bed, and wenever he felt hisself gettin' worse, he turned to at vun o' the children who wos a runnin' about the house vith heads like clean Dutch cheeses,[61] and shaved him agin. Vun day the lawyer come to make his vill; all the time he wos a takin' it down, Jinkinson was secretly a clippin' avay at his hair vith a large pair of scissors. "Wot's that 'ere snippin' noise?" says the lawyer every now and then; "it's like a man havin' his hair cut." "It *is* wery like a man havin' his hair cut," says poor Jinkinson, hidin' the scissors, and lookin' quite innocent. By the time the lawyer found it out, he was wery nearly bald. Jinkinson wos kept alive in this vay for a long time, but at last vun day he has in all the children vun arter another, shaves each on 'em wery clean, and gives him vun kiss on the crown o' his head; then he has in the two assistants, and arter cuttin' and curlin' of 'em in the first style of elegance, says he should like to hear the woice o' the greasiest bear, vich rekvest is immediately complied with; then he says that he feels wery happy in his mind and vishes to be left alone; and then he dies, previously cuttin' his own hair and makin' one flat curl in the wery middle of his forehead.'

This anecdote produced an extraordinary effect, not only upon Mr Slithers, but upon the housekeeper also, who evinced so much anxiety to please and be pleased, that Mr Weller, with a manner betokening some alarm, conveyed a whispered enquiry to his son whether he had gone 'too fur'.

'Wot do you mean by too fur?' demanded Sam.

'In that 'ere little compliment respectin' the want of hock'erdness in ladies, Sammy,' replied his father.

'You don't think she's fallen in love with you in consekens o' that, do you?' said Sam.

'More unlikelier things have come to pass, my boy,' replied Mr Weller in a hoarse whisper; 'I'm always afeerd of inadwertent captivation, Sammy. If I know'd how to make myself ugly or unpleasant, I'd do it, Samivel, rayther than live in this here state of perpetival terror!'

Mr Weller had, at that time, no further opportunity of dwelling upon the apprehensions which beset his mind, for the immediate occasion of his fears proceeded to lead the way downstairs, apologising as they went for conducting him into the kitchen, which apartment, however, she was induced to proffer for his accommodation in preference to her own little room, the rather as it afforded greater facilities for smoking, and was immediately adjoining the ale-cellar. The preparations which were already made sufficiently proved that these were not mere words of course, for on the deal table were a sturdy ale-jug and glasses, flanked with clean pipes and a plentiful supply of tobacco for the old gentleman and his son, while on a dresser hard by was goodly store of cold meat and other eatables. At sight of these arrangements Mr Weller was at first distracted between his love of joviality and his doubts whether they were not to be considered as so many evidences of captivation having already taken place; but he soon yielded to his natural impulse, and took his seat at the table with a very jolly countenance.

'As to imbibin' any o' this here flagrant veed, mum, in the presence of a lady,' said Mr Weller, taking up a pipe and laying it down again, 'it couldn't be. Samivel, total abstinence, if *you* please.'

'But I like it of all things,' said the housekeeper.

'No,' rejoined Mr Weller, shaking his head – 'no.'

'Upon my word I do,' said the housekeeper. 'Mr Slithers knows I do.'

Mr Weller coughed, and notwithstanding the barber's confirmation of the statement, said 'no' again, but more feebly than before. The housekeeper lighted a piece of paper, and insisted on applying it to the bowl of the pipe with her own fair hands; Mr Weller resisted; the housekeeper cried that her fingers would be burnt; Mr Weller gave way. The pipe was ignited, Mr Weller drew a long puff of smoke, and detecting himself in the very act of smiling on the housekeeper, put a sudden constraint upon his countenance and looked sternly at the candle, with a determination not to captivate himself, or encourage thoughts of captivation in others. From this iron frame of mind he was roused by the voice of his son.

'I don't think,' said Sam, who was smoking with great composure and enjoyment, 'that if the lady wos agreeable it 'ud be wery far out o' the vay for us four to make up a club of our own like the governors does upstairs, and let him,' Sam pointed with the stem of his pipe towards his parent, 'be the president.'

The housekeeper affably declared that it was the very thing she had been thinking of. The barber said the same. Mr Weller said nothing, but he laid down his pipe as if in a fit of inspiration, and performed the following manoeuvres.

Unbuttoning the three lower buttons of his waistcoat and pausing for a moment to enjoy the easy flow of breath consequent upon this process, he laid violent hands upon his watchchain, and slowly and with extreme difficulty drew from his fob an immense double-cased silver watch, which brought the lining of the pocket with it, and was not to be disentangled but by great exertions and an amazing redness of face. Having fairly got it out at last, he detached the outer case and wound it up with a key of corresponding magnitude; then put the case on again, and having applied the watch to his ear to ascertain that it was still going, gave it some half-dozen hard knocks on the table to improve its performance.

'That,' said Mr Weller, laying it on the table with its face upwards, 'is the title and emblem o' this here society. Sammy, reach them two stools this vay for the wacant cheers. Ladies and gen'l'men, Mr Weller's Watch is vound up and now a-goin'. Order!'

By way of enforcing this proclamation, Mr Weller, using the watch after the manner of a president's hammer, and remarking with great pride that nothing hurt it, and that falls and concussions of all kinds materially enhanced the excellence of the works and assisted the regulator, knocked the table a great many times, and declared the association formally constituted.

'And don't let's have no grinnin' at the cheer, Samivel,' said Mr Weller to his son, 'or I shall be committin' you to the cellar, and then p'r'aps we may get into what the 'Merrikins[62] call a fix and the English a qvestion o' privileges.'

Having uttered this friendly caution, the president settled himself in his chair with great dignity, and requested that Mr Samuel would relate an anecdote.

'I've told one,' said Sam.

'Wery good, sir; tell another,' returned the chair.

'We wos a talking jist now, sir,' said Sam, turning to Slithers, 'about barbers. Pursuing that 'ere fruitful theme, sir, I'll tell you in a wery few words a romantic little story about another barber as p'r'aps you may never have heerd.'

'Samivel!' said Mr Weller, again bringing his watch and the table into smart collision, 'address your obserwations to the cheer, sir, and not to priwate indiwiduals!'

'And if I might rise to order,' said the barber in a soft voice, and looking round him with a conciliatory smile as he leant over the table, with the knuckles of his left hand resting upon it – 'if I *might* rise to order, I would suggest that "barbers" is not exactly the kind of language which is agreeable and soothing to our feelings. You, sir, will correct me if I'm wrong, but I believe there *is* such a word in the dictionary as hairdressers.'

'Well, but suppose he wasn't a hairdresser,' suggested Sam.

'Wy then, sir, be parliamentary[63] and call him vun all the more,' returned his father. 'In the same vay as ev'ry gen'l'man in another place is a honourable, ev'ry barber in this place is a hairdresser. Ven you read the speeches in the papers, and see as vun gen'lman says of another, "the honourable member, if he vill allow me to call him so", you vill understand, sir, that that means, "if he vill allow me to keep up that 'ere pleasant and uniwersal fiction". '

It is a common remark, confirmed by history and experience, that great men rise with the circumstances in which they are placed. Mr Weller came out so strong in his capacity of chairman, that Sam was for some time prevented from speaking by a grin of surprise, which held his faculties enchained, and at last subsided in a long whistle of a single note. Nay, the old gentleman appeared even to have astonished himself, and that to no small extent, as was demonstrated by the vast amount of chuckling in which he indulged after the utterance of these lucid remarks.

'Here's the story,' said Sam. 'Vunce upon a time there wos a young hairdresser as opened a wery smart little shop vith four wax dummies in the winder, two gen'l'men and two ladies – the gen'lmen vith blue dots for their beards, wery large viskers, oudacious heads of hair, uncommon clear eyes, and nostrils of amazin' pinkness; the ladies vith their heads o' one side, their right forefingers on their lips, and their forms deweloped beautiful, in vich last respect they had the adwantage over the gen'l'men, as wasn't allowed but wery little shoulder, and terminated rayther abrupt in fancy drapery. He had also a great many hairbrushes and toothbrushes bottled up in the winder, neat glass-cases on the counter, a floor-clothed cuttin'-room upstairs, and a weighin'-macheen in the shop, right opposite the door. But the great attraction and ornament wos the dummies, which this here young hairdresser wos constantly a-runnin' out in the road to look at, and constantly a-runnin' in again to touch up and polish; in short, he wos so proud on 'em, that ven Sunday come, he wos always wretched and mis'rable to think they wos behind the shutters, and looked anxiously for Monday on that account. Vun o' these dummies wos a favrite vith him beyond the others; and ven any of his acquaintance asked him wy he didn't get married – as the young ladies he know'd, in partickler, often did – he used to say, "Never! I never vill enter into the bonds of vedlock," he says, "until I meet vith a young 'ooman as realises my idea o' that 'ere fairest dummy vith the light hair. Then, and not till then," he says, "I vill approach the altar." All the young ladies he know'd as had got dark hair told him this wos wery sinful, and that he wos wurshippin' a idle; but them as wos at all near the same shade as the dummy coloured up wery much, and wos observed to think him a wery nice young man.'

'Samivel,' said Mr Weller, gravely, 'a member o' this associashun bein' one o' that 'ere tender sex which is now immedetly referred to, I have to rekvest that you vill make no reflections.'

'I ain't a-makin' any, am I?' enquired Sam.

'Order, sir!' rejoined Mr Weller, with severe dignity. Then, sinking the chairman in the father, he added, in his usual tone of voice: 'Samivel, drive on!'

Sam interchanged a smile with the housekeeper, and proceeded:

'The young hairdresser hadn't been in the habit o' makin' this avowal above six months, ven he en–countered a young lady as wos the wery picter o' the fairest dummy. "Now," he says, "it's all up. I am a slave!" The young lady wos not only the picter o' the fairest dummy, but she wos wery romantic, as the young hairdresser was, too, and he says, "Oh!" he says, "here's a community o' feelin', here's a flow o' soul!" he says, "here's a interchange o' sentiment!"[64] The young lady didn't say much, o' course, but she expressed herself agreeable, and shortly artervards vent to see him vith a mutual friend. The hairdresser rushes out to meet her, but d'rectly she sees the dummies she changes colour and falls a tremblin' wiolently. "Look up, my love," says the hairdresser, "behold your imige in my winder, but not correcter than in my art!" "My imige!" she says. "Yourn!" replies the hairdresser. "But whose imige is *that*?" she says, a-pinting at vun o' the gen'l'men. "No vun's, my love," he says, "it is but a idea." "A idea!" she cries: "it is a portrait, I feel it is a portrait, and that 'ere noble face must be in the millingtary!" "Wot do I hear!" says he, a crumplin' his curls. "Villiam Gibbs," she says, quite firm, "never renoo the subject. I respect you as a friend," she says, "but my affections is set upon that manly brow." "This," says the hairdresser, "is a reg'lar blight, and in it I perceive the hand of Fate. Farevell!" Vith these vords he rushes into the shop, breaks the dummy's nose vith a blow of his curlin'-irons, melts him down at the parlour fire, and never smiles artervards.'

'The young lady, Mr Weller?' said the housekeeper.

'Why, ma'am,' said Sam, 'finding that Fate had a spite agin her, and everybody she come into contact vith, she never smiled neither, but read a deal o' poetry and pined avay – by rayther slow degrees, for she ain't dead yet. It took a deal o' poetry to kill the hairdresser, and some people say arter all that it was more the gin and water as caused him to be run over; p'r'aps it was a little o' both, and came o' mixing the two.'

The barber declared that Mr Weller had related one of the most interesting stories that had ever come within his knowledge, in which opinion the housekeeper entirely concurred.

'Are you a married man, sir?' enquired Sam.

The barber replied that he had not that honour.

'I s'pose you mean to be?' said Sam.

'Well,' replied the barber, rubbing his hands smirkingly, 'I don't know, I don't think it's very likely.'

'That's a bad sign,' said Sam; 'if you'd said you meant to be vun o' these days, I should ha' looked upon you as bein' safe. You're in a wery precarious state.'

'I am not conscious of any danger, at all events,' returned the barber.

'No more wos I, sir,' said the elder Mr Weller, interposing; 'those vere my symptoms, exactly. I've been took that vay twice. Keep your vether eye open, my friend, or you're gone.'

There was something so very solemn about this admonition, both in its matter and manner, and also in the way in which Mr Weller still kept his eye fixed upon the unsuspecting victim, that nobody cared to speak for some little time, and might not have cared to do so for some time longer if the housekeeper had not happened to sigh, which called off the old gentleman's attention and gave rise to a gallant enquiry whether 'there wos anythin' wery piercin' in that 'ere little heart?'

'Dear me, Mr Weller!' said the housekeeper, laughing.

'No, but is there anythin' as agitates it?' pursued the old gentleman. 'Has it always been obderrate, always opposed to the happiness o' human creeturs? Eh? Has it?'

At this critical juncture for her blushes and confusion, the housekeeper discovered that more ale was wanted, and hastily withdrew into the cellar to draw the same, followed by the barber, who insisted on carrying the candle. Having looked after her with a very complacent expression of face, and after him with some disdain, Mr Weller caused his glance to travel slowly round the kitchen, until at length it rested on his son.

'Sammy,' said Mr Weller, 'I mistrust that barber.'

'Wot for?' returned Sam; 'wot's he got to do with you? You're a nice man, you are, arter pretendin' all kinds o' terror, to go a payin' compliments and talkin' about hearts and piercers.'

The imputation of gallantry appeared to afford Mr Weller the utmost delight, for he replied in a voice choked by suppressed laughter, and with the tears in his eyes.

'Wos I a-talkin' about hearts and piercers – wos I though, Sammy, eh?'

'Wos you? of course you wos.'

'She don't know no better, Sammy, there ain't no harm in it – no danger, Sammy; she's only a punster. She seemed pleased, though, didn't she? O' course, she wos pleased, it's nat'ral she should be, wery nat'ral.'

'He's wain of it!' exclaimed Sam, joining in his father's mirth. 'He's actually wain!'

'Hush!' replied Mr Weller, composing his features, 'they're a-comin' back – the little heart's a-comin' back. But mark these wurds o' mine once more, and remember 'em ven your father says he said 'em. Samivel, I mistrust that 'ere deceitful barber.'

CHAPTER 6

Master Humphrey, from his Clockside in the Chimney-Corner

TWO OR THREE EVENINGS after the institution of Mr Weller's Watch, I thought I heard, as I walked in the garden, the voice of Mr Weller himself at no great distance; and stopping once or twice to listen more attentively, I found that the sounds proceeded from my housekeeper's little sitting-room, which is at the back of the house. I took no further notice of the circumstance at that time, but it formed the subject of a conversation between me and my friend Jack Redburn next morning, when I found that I had not been deceived in my impression. Jack furnished me with the following particulars; and as he appeared to take extraordinary pleasure in relating them, I have begged him in future to jot down any such domestic scenes or occurrences that may please his humour, in order that they may be told in his own way. I must confess that, as Mr Pickwick and he are constantly together, I have been influenced, in making this request, by a secret desire to know something of their proceedings.

On the evening in question, the housekeeper's room was arranged with particular care, and the housekeeper herself was very smartly dressed. The preparations, however, were not confined to mere showy demonstrations, as tea was prepared for three persons, with a small display of preserves and jams and sweet cakes, which heralded some uncommon occasion. Miss Benton (my housekeeper bears that name) was in a state of great expectation, too, frequently going to the front door and looking anxiously down the lane, and more than once observing to the servant-girl that she expected company, and hoped no accident had happened to delay them.

A modest ring at the bell at length allayed her fears, and Miss Benton, hurrying into her own room and shutting herself up, in order that she might preserve that appearance of being taken by surprise which is so essential to the polite reception of visitors, awaited their coming with a smiling countenance.

'Good ev'nin', mum,' said the older Mr Weller, looking in at the door after a prefatory tap. 'I'm afeerd we've come in rayther arter the time, mum, but the young colt being full o' wice, has been' a boltin' and shyin' and gettin' his leg over the traces to sich a extent that if he an't wery soon broke in, he'll wex me into a broken heart, and then he'll never be brought out no more except to learn his letters from the writin' on his grandfather's tombstone.'

With these pathetic words, which were addressed to something outside the door about two feet six from the ground, Mr Weller introduced a very small boy firmly set upon a couple of very sturdy legs, who looked as if nothing could ever knock him down. Besides having a very round face strongly resembling Mr Weller's, and a stout little body of exactly his build, this young gentleman, standing with his little legs very wide apart, as if the top-boots were familiar to them, actually winked upon the housekeeper with his infant eye, in imitation of his grandfather.

'There's a naughty boy, mum,' said Mr Weller, bursting with delight, 'there's a immoral Tony. Wos there ever a little chap o' four year and eight months old as vinked his eye at a strange lady afore?'

As little affected by this observation as by the former appeal to his feelings, Master Weller elevated in the air a small model of a coach whip which he carried in his hand, and addressing the housekeeper with a shrill 'Ya – hip!' enquired if she was 'going down the road'; at which happy adaptation of a lesson he had been taught from infancy, Mr Weller could restrain his feelings no longer, but gave him twopence on the spot.

'It's in wain to deny it, mum,' said Mr Weller, 'this here is a boy arter his grandfather's own heart, and beats out all the boys as ever wos or will be. Though at the same time, mum,' added Mr Weller, trying to look gravely down upon his favourite, 'it was wery wrong on him to want to be put over all the posts as we come along, and wery cruel on him to force poor grandfather to lift him cross-legged over every vun of 'em. He wouldn't pass vun single blessed post, mum, and at the top o' the lane there's seven-and-forty on 'em all in a row, and wery close together.'

Here Mr Weller, whose feelings were in a perpetual conflict between pride in his grandson's achievements and a sense of his own responsibility, and the importance of impressing him with moral truths, burst into a fit of laughter, and, suddenly checking himself, remarked in a severe tone that little boys as made their grandfathers put 'em over posts never went to heaven at any price.

By this time the housekeeper had made tea, and little Tony, placed on a chair beside her, with his eyes nearly on a level with the top of the table, was provided with various delicacies which yielded him extreme contentment. The housekeeper (who seemed rather afraid of the child, notwithstanding her caresses) then patted him on the head, and declared that he was the finest boy she had ever seen.

'Wy, mum,' said Mr Weller, 'I don't think you'll see a many sich, and that's the truth. But if my son Samivel vould give me my vay, mum, and only dis–pense vith his . . . *might* I wenter to say the vurd?'

'What word, Mr Weller?' said the housekeeper, blushing slightly.

'Petticuts, mum,' returned that gentleman, laying his hand upon the garments of his grandson. 'If my son Samivel, mum, vould only dis–pense vith these here, you'd see such a alteration in his appearance, as the imagination can't depicter.'

'But what would you have the child wear instead, Mr Weller?' said the housekeeper.

'I've offered my son Samivel, mum, agen and agen,' returned the old gentleman, 'to purwide him at my own cost vith a suit o' clothes as 'ud be the makin' on him, and form his mind in infancy for those pursuits as I hope the family o' the Vellers vill alvays dewote themselves to. Tony, my boy, tell the lady wot them clothes are as grandfather says father ought to let you vear.'

'A little white hat and a little sprig weskut and little knee cords and little top-boots and a little green coat with little bright buttons and a little welwet collar,' replied Tony, with great readiness and no stops.

'That's the cos–toom, mum,' said Mr Weller, looking proudly at the housekeeper. 'Once make sich a model on him as that, and you'd say he *wos* a angel!'

Perhaps the housekeeper thought that in such a guise young Tony would look more like the angel at Islington[65] than anything else of that name, or perhaps she was disconcerted to find her previously conceived ideas disturbed, as angels are not commonly represented in top-boots and sprig waistcoats. She coughed doubtfully, but said nothing.

'How many brothers and sisters have you, my dear?' she asked, after a short silence.

'One brother and no sister at all,' replied Tony. 'Sam his name is, and so's my father's. Do you know my father?'

'Oh yes, I know him,' said the housekeeper, graciously.

'Is my father fond of you?' pursued Tony.

'I hope so,' rejoined the smiling housekeeper.

Tony considered a moment, and then said, 'Is my grandfather fond of you?'

This would seem a very easy question to answer, but instead of replying to it, the housekeeper smiled in great confusion, and said that really children did ask such extraordinary questions that it was the most difficult thing in the world to talk to them. Mr Weller took upon himself to reply that he was very fond of the lady; but the housekeeper entreating that he would not put such things into the child's head, Mr Weller shook his own while she looked another way, and seemed to be troubled with a misgiving that captivation was in progress. It was, perhaps, on this account that he changed the subject precipitately.

'It's wery wrong in little boys to make game o' their grandfathers, an't it, mum?' said Mr Weller, shaking his head waggishly, until Tony looked at him, when he counterfeited the deepest dejection and sorrow.

'Oh, very sad!' assented the housekeeper. 'But I hope no little boys do that?'

'There is vun young Turk,[66] mum,' said Mr Weller, 'as havin' seen his grandfather a little overcome vith drink on the occasion of a friend's birthday, goes a reelin' and staggerin' about the house, and makin' believe that he's the old gen'l'm'n.'

'Oh, quite shocking!' cried the housekeeper,

'Yes, mum,' said Mr Weller; 'and previously to so doin', this here young traitor that I'm a speakin' of, pinches his little nose to make it red, and then he gives a hiccup and says, "I'm all right," he says; "give us another song!" Ha, ha! "Give us another song," he says. Ha, ha, ha!'

In his excessive delight, Mr Weller was quite unmindful of his moral responsibility, until little Tony kicked up his legs, and, laughing immoderately, cried, 'That was me, that was;' whereupon the grandfather, by a great effort, became extremely solemn.

'No, Tony, not you,' said Mr Weller. 'I hope it warn't you, Tony. It must ha' been that 'ere naughty little chap as comes sometimes out o' the empty watch-box[67] round the corner – that same little chap as wos found standing on the table afore the looking-glass pretending to shave himself vith a oyster-knife.'

'He didn't hurt himself, I hope?' observed the housekeeper.

'Not he, mum,' said Mr Weller proudly; 'bless your heart, you might trust that 'ere boy vith a steam-engine a'most, he's such a knowin' young – ' But suddenly recollecting himself and observing that Tony perfectly understood and appreciated the compliment, the old gentleman groaned and observed that 'it wos all wery shockin' – wery'.

'Oh, he's a bad 'un,' said Mr Weller, 'is that 'ere watch-box boy, makin' such a noise and litter in the backyard, he does, waterin' wooden horses and feedin' of 'em vith grass, and perpetivally spillin' his little brother out of a veelbarrow and frightenin' his mother out of her vits, at the wery moment wen she's expectin' to increase his stock of happiness vith another play-feller – Oh, he's a bad one! He's even gone so far as to put on a pair of paper spectacles as he got his father to make for him, and walk up and down the garden vith his hands behind him in imitation of Mr Pickwick – but Tony don't do sich things, oh no!'

'Oh no!' echoed Tony.

'He knows better, he does,' said Mr Weller. 'He knows that if he wos to come sich games as these nobody wouldn't love him, and that his grandfather in partickler couldn't abear the sight on him; for vich reasons Tony's always good.'

'Always good,' echoed Tony; and his grandfather immediately took him on his knee and kissed him, at the same time, with many nods and winks, slyly pointing at the child's head with his thumb, in order that the housekeeper, otherwise deceived by the admirable manner in which he, Mr Weller, had sustained his character, might not suppose that any other young gentleman was referred to, and might clearly understand that the boy of the watch-box was but an imaginary creation, and a fetch of Tony himself, invented for his improvement and reformation.

Not confining himself to a mere verbal description of his grandson's abilities, Mr Weller, when tea was finished, invited him by various gifts of pence and halfpence to smoke imaginary pipes, drink visionary beer from real pots, imitate his grandfather without reserve, and in particular to go through the drunken scene, which threw the old gentleman into ecstasies and filled the housekeeper with wonder. Nor was Mr Weller's pride satisfied with even this display, for when he took his leave he carried the child, like some rare and astonishing curiosity, first to the barber's house and afterwards to the tobacconist's, at each of which places he repeated his performances with the utmost effect to applauding and delighted audiences. It was half-past nine o'clock when Mr Weller was last seen carrying him home upon his shoulder, and it has been whispered abroad that at that time the infant Tony was rather intoxicated.

[*The Old Curiosity Shop* is continued from here to the end without farther break. Master Humphrey is revived, thus, at the close of *The Old Curiosity Shop*, merely to introduce *Barnaby Rudge*.]

I was musing the other evening upon the characters and incidents with which I had been so long engaged; wondering how I could ever have looked forward with pleasure to the completion of my tale, and reproaching myself for having done so, as if it were a kind of cruelty to those companions of my solitude whom I had now dismissed, and could never again recall; when my clock struck ten. Punctual to the hour, my friends appeared.

On our last night of meeting we had finished the story which the reader has just concluded. Our conversation took the same current as the meditations which the entrance of my friends had interrupted, and *The Old Curiosity Shop* was the staple of our discourse.

I may confide to the reader now, that in connection with this little history I had something upon my mind; something to communicate which I had all along with difficulty repressed; something I had deemed it, during the progress of the story, necessary to its interest to disguise, and which, now that it was over, I wished, and was yet reluctant, to disclose.

To conceal anything from those to whom I am attached is not in my nature. I can never close my lips where I have opened my heart. This temper, and the consciousness of having done some violence to it in my narrative, laid me under a restraint which I should have had great difficulty in overcoming but for a timely remark from Mr Miles, who, as I hinted in a former paper, is a gentleman of business habits, and of great exactness and propriety in all his transactions.

'I could have wished,' my friend objected, 'that we had been made acquainted with the single gentleman's name.[68] I don't like his withholding his name. It made me look upon him at first with suspicion, and caused me to doubt his moral character, I assure you. I am fully satisfied by this time of his being a worthy creature; but in this respect he certainly would not appear to have acted at all like a man of business.'

'My friends,' said I, drawing to the table, at which they were by this time seated in their usual chairs, 'do you remember that this story bore another title besides that one we have so often heard of late?'

Mr Miles had his pocket-book out in an instant, and, referring to an entry therein, rejoined, 'Certainly. *Personal Adventures of Master Humphrey*. Here it is. I made a note of it at the time.'

I was about to resume what I had to tell them, when the same Mr Miles again interrupted me, observing that the narrative originated in a personal adventure of my own, and that was no doubt the reason for its being thus designated.

This led me to the point at once.

'You will one and all forgive me,' I returned, 'if for the greater convenience of the story, and for its better introduction, that adventure was fictitious. I had my share, indeed – no light or trivial one – in the pages we have read, but it was not the share I feigned to have at first. The younger brother, the single gentleman, the nameless actor in this little drama, stands before you now.'

It was easy to see they had not expected this disclosure.

'Yes,' I pursued. 'I can look back upon my part in it with a calm, half-smiling pity for myself as for some other man. But I am he, indeed; and now the chief sorrows of my life are yours.'

I need not say what true gratification I derived from the sympathy and kindness with which this acknowledgment was received; nor how often it had risen to my lips before; nor how difficult I had found it – how impossible, when I came to those passages which touched me most, and most nearly concerned me – to sustain the character I had assumed. It is enough to say that I replaced in the clock-case the record of so many trials – sorrowfully, it is true, but with a softened sorrow which was almost pleasure; and felt that in living through the past again, and communicating to others the lesson it had helped to teach me, I had been a happier man.

We lingered so long over the leaves from which I had read, that as I consigned them to their former resting-place, the hand of my trusty clock pointed to twelve, and there came towards us upon the wind the voice of the deep and distant bell of St Paul's as it struck the hour of midnight.

'This,' said I, returning with a manuscript I had taken at the moment, from the same repository, 'to be opened to such music, should be a tale where London's face by night is darkly seen, and where some deed of such a time as this is dimly shadowed out. Which of us here has seen the working of that great machine whose voice has just now ceased?'

Mr Pickwick had, of course, and so had Mr Miles. Jack and my deaf friend were in the minority.

I had seen it but a few days before, and could not help telling them of the fancy I had about it.

I paid my fee of twopence, upon entering, to one of the money-changers who sit within the temple;[69] and falling, after a few turns up and down, into the quiet train of thought which such a place awakens, paced the echoing stones like some old monk whose present world lay all within its walls. As I looked afar up into the lofty dome, I could not help wondering what were his reflections whose genius reared that mighty pile,[70] when, the last small wedge of timber fixed, the last nail driven into its home for many centuries, the clang of hammers, and the hum of busy voices gone, and the Great Silence whole years of noise had helped to make, reigning undisturbed around, he mused, as I did now, upon his work, and lost himself amid its vast extent. I could not quite determine whether the contemplation of it would impress him with a sense of greatness or of insignificance; but when I remembered how long a time it had taken to erect, in how short a space it might be traversed even to its remotest parts, for how brief a term he, or any of those who cared to bear his name, would live to see it, or know of its existence, I imagined him far more melancholy than proud, and looking with regret upon his labour done. With these thoughts in my mind, I began to ascend, almost unconsciously, the flight of steps leading to the several wonders of the building, and found myself before a barrier where another money-taker sat, who demanded which among them I would choose to see. There were the stone gallery, he said, and the whispering gallery, the geometrical staircase, the room of models, the clock – the clock being quite in my way, I stopped him there, and chose that sight from all the rest.

I groped my way into the turret which it occupies, and saw before me, in a kind of loft, what seemed to be a great, old oaken press with folding doors. These being thrown back by the attendant (who was sleeping when I came upon him, and looked a drowsy fellow, as though his close companionship with Time had made him quite indifferent to it), disclosed a complicated crowd of wheels and chains in iron and brass – great, sturdy, rattling engines – suggestive of breaking a finger put in here or there, and grinding the bone to powder – and these were the clock! Its very pulse, if I may use the word, was like no other clock. It did not mark the flight of every moment with a gentle second stroke, as though it would check old Time, and have him stay his pace in pity, but measured it with one sledgehammer beat, as if its business were to crush the seconds as they came trooping on, and remorselessly to clear a path before the Day of Judgement.

I sat down opposite to it, and hearing its regular and never-changing voice, that one deep constant note, uppermost amongst all the noise and clatter in the streets below – marking that, let that tumult rise or fall, go on or stop – let it be night or noon, tomorrow or today, this year or next – it still performed its functions with the same dull constancy, and regulated the progress of the life around, the fancy came upon me that this was London's heart, and that when it should cease to beat, the city would be no more.

It is night. Calm and unmoved amidst the scenes that darkness favours, the great heart of London throbs in its giant breast. Wealth and beggary, vice and virtue, guilt and innocence, repletion and the direst hunger, all treading on each other and crowding together, are gathered round it. Draw but a little circle above the clustering housetops, and you shall have within its space everything with its opposite extreme and contradiction close beside. Where yonder feeble light is shining, a man is but this moment dead. The taper at a few yards' distance is seen by eyes that have this instant opened on the world. There are two houses separated by but an inch or two of wall. In one, there are quiet minds at rest; in the other, a waking conscience that one might think would trouble the very air. In that close corner where the roofs shrink down and cower together as if to hide their secrets from the handsome street hard by, there are such dark crimes, such miseries and horrors, as could be hardly told in whispers. In the handsome street, there are folks asleep who have dwelt there all their lives, and have no more knowledge of these things than if they had never been, or were transacted at the remotest limits of the world – who, if they were hinted at, would shake their heads, look wise and frown and say they were impossible and out of nature – as if all great towns were not. Does not this heart of London, that nothing moves, nor stops, nor quickens – that goes on the same let what will be done – does it not express the city's character well?

The day begins to break, and soon there is the hum and noise of life. Those who have spent the night on doorsteps and cold stones crawl off to beg; they who have slept in beds come forth to their occupation, too, and business is astir. The fog of sleep rolls slowly off, and London shines awake. The streets are filled with carriages and people gaily clad. The jails are full, too, to the throat, nor have the workhouses or hospitals much room to spare. The courts of law are crowded. Taverns have their regular frequenters by this time, and every mart of traffic has its throng. Each of these places is a world, and has its own inhabitants; each is distinct from, and almost unconscious of, the existence of any other. There are some few people well to do, who remember to have heard it said that numbers of men and women – thousands, they think it was – get up in London every day, unknowing where to lay their heads at night; and that there are quarters of the town where misery and famine always are. They don't believe it quite – there may be some truth in it, but it is exaggerated, of course. So, each of these thousand worlds goes on, intent upon itself, until night comes again – first with its lights and pleasures, and its cheerful streets; then with its guilt and darkness.

Heart of London, there is a moral in thy every stroke! as I look on at thy indomitable working, which neither death, nor press of life, nor grief, nor gladness out of doors will influence one jot, I seem to hear a voice within thee which sinks into my heart, bidding me, as I elbow my way among the crowd, have some thought for the meanest wretch that passes, and, being a man, to turn away with scorn and pride from none that bear the human shape.

I am by no means sure that I might not have been tempted to enlarge upon the subject had not the papers that lay before me on the table been a silent reproach for even this digression. I took them up again when I had got thus far, and seriously prepared to read.

The handwriting was strange to me, for the manuscript had been fairly copied. As it is against our rules, in such a case, to enquire into the authorship until the reading is concluded, I could only glance at the different faces round me, in search of some expression which should betray the writer. Whoever he might be, he was prepared for this, and gave no sign for my enlightenment.

I had the papers in my hand, when my deaf friend interposed with a suggestion.

'It has occurred to me,' he said, 'bearing in mind your sequel to the tale we have finished, that if such of us as have anything to relate of our own lives could interweave it with our contribution to the Clock, it would be well to do so. This need be no restraint upon us, either as to time, or place, or incident, since any real passage of this kind may be surrounded by fictitious circumstances, and represented by fictitious characters. What if we make this an article of agreement among ourselves?'

The proposition was cordially received, but the difficulty appeared to be that here was a long story written before we had thought of it.

'Unless,' said I, 'it should have happened that the writer of this tale – which is not impossible, for men are apt to do so when they write – has actually mingled with it something of his own endurance and experience.'

Nobody spoke, but I thought I detected in one quarter that this was really the case.

'If I have no assurance to the contrary,' I added, therefore, 'I shall take it for granted that he has done so, and that even these papers come within our new agreement. Everybody being mute, we hold that understanding if you please.'

And here I was about to begin again, when Jack informed us softly, that during the progress of our last narrative, Mr Weller's Watch had adjourned its sittings from the kitchen, and regularly met outside our door, where he had no doubt that august body would be found at the present moment. As this was for the convenience of listening to our stories, he submitted that they might be suffered to come in, and hear them more pleasantly.

To this we one and all yielded a ready assent, and the party being discovered, as Jack had supposed, and invited to walk in, entered (though not without great confusion at having been detected), and were accommodated with chairs at a little distance.

Then, the lamp being trimmed, the fire well stirred and burning brightly, the hearth clean swept, the curtains closely drawn, the clock wound up, we entered on our new story – *Barnaby Rudge*.

[The following is the final appearance of Master Humphrey's Clock. It forms the conclusion of *Barnaby Rudge*.][71]

It is again midnight. My fire burns cheerfully; the room is filled with my old friend's sober voice; and I am left to muse upon the story we have just now finished.

It makes me smile, at such a time as this, to think if there were anyone to see me sitting in my easy-chair, my grey head hanging down, my eyes bent thoughtfully upon the glowing embers, and my crutch – emblem of my helplessness – lying upon the hearth at my feet, how solitary I should seem. Yet though I am the sole tenant of this chimney-corner, though I am childless and old, I have no sense of loneliness at this hour but am the centre of a silent group whose company I love.

Thus, even age and weakness have their consolations. If I were a younger man, if I were more active, more strongly bound and tied to life, these visionary friends would shun me, or I should desire to fly from them. Being what I am, I can court their society, and delight in it; and pass whole hours in picturing to myself the shadows that perchance flock every night into this chamber, and in imagining with pleasure what kind of interest they have in the frail, feeble mortal who is its sole inhabitant.

All the friends I have ever lost I find again among these visitors. I love to fancy their spirits hovering about me, feeling still some earthly kindness for their old companion, and watching his decay. 'He is weaker, he declines apace, he draws nearer and nearer to us, and will soon be conscious of our existence.' What is there to alarm me in this? It is encouragement and hope.

These thoughts have never crowded on me half so fast as they have done tonight. Faces I had long forgotten have become familiar to me once again; traits I had endeavoured to recall for years have come before me in an instant; nothing is changed but me; and even I can be my former self at will.

Raising my eyes but now to the face of my old clock, I remember, quite involuntarily, the veneration, not unmixed with a sort of childish awe, with which I used to sit and watch it as it ticked, unheeded in a dark staircase corner. I recollect looking more grave and steady when I met its dusty face, as if, having that strange kind of life within it, and being free from all excess of vulgar appetite, and warning all the house by night and day, it were a sage. How often have I listened to it as it told the beads of time, and wondered at its constancy! How often watched it slowly pointing round the dial, and, while I panted for the eagerly expected hour to come, admired, despite myself, its steadiness of purpose and lofty freedom from all human strife, impatience and desire!

I thought it cruel once. It was very hard of heart, to my mind, I remember. It was an old servant even then; and I felt as though it ought to show some sorrow; as though it wanted sympathy with us in our distress, and were a dull, heartless, mercenary creature. Ah!

how soon I learnt to know that in its ceaseless going on, and in its being checked or stayed by nothing, lay its greatest kindness, and the only balm for grief and wounded peace of mind.

Tonight, tonight, when this tranquillity and calm are on my spirits, and memory presents so many shifting scenes before me, I take my quiet stand at will by many a fire that has been long extinguished, and mingle with the cheerful group that cluster round it. If I could be sorrowful in such a mood, I should grow sad to think what a poor blot I was upon their youth and beauty once, and now how few remain to put me to the blush; I should grow sad to think that such among them as I sometimes meet with in my daily walks are scarcely less infirm than I; that time has brought us to a level; and that all distinctions fade and vanish as we take our trembling steps towards the grave.

But memory was given us for better purposes than this, and mine is not a torment but a source of pleasure. To muse upon the gaiety and youth I have known suggests to me glad scenes of harmless mirth that may be passing now. From contemplating them apart, I soon become an actor in these little dramas and, humouring my fancy, lose myself among the beings it invokes.

When my fire is bright and high, and a warm blush mantles in the walls and ceiling of this ancient room; when my clock makes cheerful music, like one of those chirping insects who delight in the warm hearth, and are sometimes, by a good superstition, looked upon as the harbingers of fortune and plenty to that household in whose mercies they put their humble trust; when everything is in a ruddy genial glow, and there are voices in the crackling flame, and smiles in its flashing light, other smiles and other voices congregate around me, invading, with their pleasant harmony, the silence of the time.

For then a knot of youthful creatures gather round my fireside, and the room re-echoes to their merry voices. My solitary chair no longer holds its ample place before the fire, but is wheeled into a smaller corner, to leave more room for the broad circle formed about the cheerful hearth. I have sons, and daughters, and grand-children, and we are assembled on some occasion of rejoicing common to us all. It is a birthday, perhaps, or perhaps it may be Christmastime; but, be it what it may, there is rare holiday among us; we are full of glee.

In the chimney-corner, opposite myself, sits one who has grown old beside me. She is changed, of course; much changed; and yet I recognise the girl even in that grey hair and wrinkled brow. Glancing from the laughing child who half hides in her ample skirts, and half peeps out – and from her to the little matron of twelve years old, who sits so womanly and so demure at no great distance from me – and from her again, to a fair girl in the full bloom of early womanhood, the centre of the group, who has glanced more than once towards the opening door, and by whom the children, whispering and tittering among themselves, *will* leave a vacant chair, although she bids them not – I see her image thrice repeated, and feel how long it is before one form and set of features wholly pass away, if ever, from among the living. While I am dwelling upon this, and tracing out the gradual change from infancy to youth, from youth to perfect growth, from that to age, and thinking, with an old man's pride, that she is comely yet, I feel a slight thin hand upon my arm, and, looking down, see seated at my feet a crippled boy – a gentle, patient child – whose aspect I know well. He rests upon a little crutch – I know it too – and leaning on it as he climbs my footstool, whispers in my ear, 'I am hardly one of these, dear grandfather, although I love them dearly. They are very kind to me, but you will be kinder still, I know.'

I have my hand upon his neck and stoop to kiss him – when my clock strikes, my chair is in its old spot, and I am alone.

What if I be? What if this fireside be tenantless, save for the presence of one weak old man? From my house-top I can look upon a hundred homes, in every one of which these social companions are matters of reality. In my daily walks I pass a thousand men whose cares are all forgotten, whose labours are made light, whose dull routine of work from day to day is cheered and brightened by their glimpses of domestic joy at home. Amid the struggles of this struggling town what cheerful sacrifices are made; what toil endured with readiness; what patience shown and fortitude displayed for the mere sake of home and its affections! Let me thank heaven that I can people my fireside with shadows such as these; with shadows of bright objects that exist in crowds about me; and let me say, 'I am alone no more.'

I never was less so – I write it with a grateful heart – than I am tonight. Recollections of the past and visions of the present come to bear me company; the meanest man to whom I have ever given alms appears, to add his mite of peace and comfort to my stock; and whenever the fire within me shall grow cold, to light my path upon this earth no more, I pray that it may be at such an hour as this, and when I love the world as well as I do now.

THE DEAF GENTLEMAN FROM HIS OWN APARTMENT

Our dear friend laid down his pen at the end of the foregoing paragraph, to take it up no more. I little thought ever to employ mine upon so sorrowful a task as that which he has left me, and to which I now devote it.

As he did not appear among us at his usual hour next morning, we knocked gently at his door. No answer being given, it was softly opened; and then, to our surprise, we saw him seated before the ashes of his fire, with a little table I was accustomed to set at his elbow when I left him for the night at a short distance from him, as though he had pushed it away with the idea of rising and retiring to his bed. His crutch and footstool lay at his feet as usual, and he was dressed in his chamber-gown, which he had put on before I left him. He was reclining in his chair, in his accustomed posture, with his face towards the fire, and seemed absorbed in meditation – indeed, at first, we almost hoped he was.

Going up to him, we found him dead. I have often, very often, seen him sleeping, and always peacefully, but I never saw him look so calm and tranquil. His face wore a serene, benign expression, which had impressed me very strongly when we last shook hands; not that he had ever had any other look, God knows; but there was something in this so very spiritual, so strangely and indefinably allied to youth, although his head was grey and venerable, that it was new even in him. It came upon me all at once when on some slight pretence he called me back upon the previous night to take me by the hand again, and once more say, 'God bless you.'

A bell-rope hung within his reach, but he had not moved towards it; nor had he stirred, we all agreed, except, as I have said, to push away his table, which he could have done, and no doubt did, with a very slight motion of his hand. He had relapsed for a moment into his late train of meditation, and, with a thoughtful smile upon his face, had died.

I had long known it to be his wish that whenever this event should come to pass we might be all assembled in the house. I therefore lost no time in sending for Mr Pickwick and for Mr Miles, both of whom arrived before the messenger's return.

It is not my purpose to dilate upon the sorrow and affectionate emotions of which I was at once the witness and the sharer. But I may say, of the humbler mourners, that his faithful housekeeper was fairly heartbroken; that the poor barber would not be comforted; and that I shall respect the homely truth and warmth of heart of Mr Weller and his son to the last moment of my life.

'And the sweet old creetur, sir,' said the elder Mr Weller to me in the afternoon, 'has bolted. Him as had no wice, and was so free from temper that a infant might ha' drove him, has been took at last with that 'ere unawoidable fit o' staggers as we all must come to, and gone off his feed for ever! I see him,' said the old gentleman, with a moisture in his eye, which could not be mistaken – 'I see him gettin', every journey, more and more groggy; I says to Samivel, "My boy! the grey's a-goin' at the knees;" and now my predilictions is fatally werified, and him as I could never do enough to serve, or show my likin' for, is up the great uniwersal spout o' natur'.'[72]

I was not the less sensible of the old man's attachment because he expressed it in his peculiar manner. Indeed, I can truly assert of both him and his son, that notwithstanding the extraordinary dialogues they held together, and the strange commentaries and corrections with which each of them illustrated the other's speech, I do not think it possible to exceed the sincerity of their regret; and that I am sure their thoughtfulness and anxiety in anticipating the discharge of many little offices of sympathy would have done honour to the most delicate-minded persons.

Our friend had frequently told us that his will would be found in a box in the clock-case, the key of which was in his writing-desk. As he had told us also that he desired it to be opened immediately after his death, whenever that should happen, we met together that night for the fulfilment of his request.

We found it where he had told us, wrapped in a sealed paper, and with it a codicil of recent date, in which he named Mr Miles and Mr Pickwick his executors – as having no need of any greater benefit from his estate than a generous token (which he bequeathed to them) of his friendship and remembrance.

After pointing out the spot in which he wished his ashes to repose, he gave to 'his dear old friends', Jack Redburn and myself, his house, his books, his furniture – in short, all that his house contained; and with this legacy more ample means of maintaining it in its present state than we, with our habits and at our terms of life, can ever exhaust. Besides these gifts, he left to us, in trust, an annual sum of no insignificant amount, to be distributed in charity among his accustomed pensioners – they are a long list – and such other claimants on his bounty as might, from time to time, present themselves. And as true charity not only covers a multitude of sins, but includes a multitude of virtues, such as forgiveness, liberal construction, gentleness and mercy to the faults of others, and the remembrance of our own imperfections and advantages, he bade us not enquire too closely into the venial errors of the poor, but finding that they *were* poor, first to relieve and then endeavour – at an advantage – to reclaim them.

To the housekeeper he left an annuity, sufficient for her comfortable maintenance and support through life. For the barber, who had attended him many years, he made a similar provision. And I may make two remarks in this place: first, that I think this pair are very likely to club their means together and make a match of it; and secondly, that I think my friend had this result in his mind, for I have heard him say, more than once, that he could not concur with the generality of mankind in censuring equal marriages made in later life, since there were many cases in which such unions could not fail to be a wise and rational source of happiness to both parties.

The elder Mr Weller is so far from viewing this prospect with any feelings of jealousy, that he appears to be very much relieved by its contemplation; and his son, if I am not mistaken, participates in this feeling. We are all of opinion, however, that the old gentleman's danger, even at its crisis, was very slight, and that he merely laboured under one of those transitory weaknesses to which persons of his temperament are now and then liable, and which become less and less alarming at every return, until they wholly subside. I have no doubt he will remain a jolly old widower for the rest of his life, as he has already enquired of me, with much gravity, whether a writ of habeas corpus would enable him to settle his property upon Tony beyond the possibility of recall; and has, in my presence, conjured his son, with tears in his eyes, that in the event of his ever becoming amorous again, he will put him in a strait-waistcoat until the fit is past, and distinctly inform the lady that his property is 'made over'.

Although I have very little doubt that Sam would dutifully comply with these injunctions in a case of extreme necessity, and that he would do so with perfect composure and coolness, I do not apprehend things will ever come to that pass, as the old gentleman seems perfectly happy in the society of his son, his pretty daughter-in-law, and his grandchildren, and has solemnly announced his determination to 'take arter the old 'un in all respects'; from which I infer that it is his intention to regulate his conduct by the model of Mr Pickwick, who will certainly set him the example of a single life.

I have diverged for a moment from the subject with which I set out, for I know that my friend was interested in these little matters, and I have a natural tendency to linger upon any topic that occupied his thoughts or gave him pleasure and amusement. His remaining wishes are very briefly told. He desired that we would make him the frequent subject of our conversation; at the same time, that we would never speak of him with an air of gloom or restraint, but frankly, and as one whom we still loved and hoped to meet again. He trusted that the old house would wear no aspect of mourning, but that it would be lively and cheerful; and that we would not remove or cover up his picture, which hangs in our dining-room, but make it our companion as he had been. His own room, our place of meeting, remains, at his desire, in its accustomed state; our seats are placed about the table as of old; his easy-chair, his desk, his crutch, his footstool, hold their accustomed places, and the clock stands in its familiar corner. We go into the chamber at stated times to see that all is as it should be, and to take care that the light and air are not shut out, for on that point he expressed a strong solicitude. But it was his fancy that the apartment should not be inhabited; that it should be religiously preserved in this condition, and that the voice of his old companion should be heard no more.

My own history may be summed up in very few words; and even those I should have spared the reader but for my friend's allusion to me some time since. I have no deeper sorrow than the loss of a child – an only daughter, who is living, and who fled from her father's house but a few weeks before our friend and I first met. I had never spoken of this even to him, because I have always loved her, and I could not bear to tell him of her error until I could tell him also of her sorrow and regret. Happily I was enabled to do so some time ago. And it will not be long, with heaven's leave, before she is restored to me; before I find in her and her husband the support of my declining years.

For my pipe, it is an old relic of home, a thing of no great worth, a poor trifle, but sacred to me for her sake.

Thus, since the death of our venerable friend, Jack Redburn and I have been the sole tenants of the old house; and, day by day, have lounged together in his favourite walks. Mindful of his injunctions, we have long been able to speak of him with ease and cheerfulness, and to remember him as he would be remembered. From certain allusions which Jack has dropped, to his having been deserted and cast off in early life, I am inclined to believe that some passages of his youth may possibly be shadowed out in the history of Mr Chester and his son,[73] but seeing that he avoids the subject, I have not pursued it.

My task is done. The chamber in which we have whiled away so many hours – not, I hope, without some pleasure and some profit – is deserted; our happy hour of meeting strikes no more; the chimney-corner has grown cold; and Master Humphrey's clock has stopped for ever.

HUNTED DOWN

MOST OF US see some romances in life. In my capacity as chief manager of a Life Assurance office, I think I have within the last thirty years seen more romances than the generality of men, however unpromising the opportunity may, at first sight, seem.

As I have retired and live at my ease, I possess the means, that I used to want, of considering what I have seen at leisure. My experiences have a more remarkable aspect, so reviewed, than they had when they were in progress. I have come home from the play now, and can recall the scenes of the drama upon which the curtain has fallen, free from the glare, bewilderment and bustle of the theatre.

Let me recall one of these romances of the real world.

There is nothing truer than physiognomy,[1] taken in connection with manner. The art of reading that book of which eternal wisdom obliges every human creature to present his or her own page, with the individual character written on it, is a difficult one, perhaps, and is little studied. It may require some natural aptitude, and it must require (for everything does) some patience and some pains. That these are not usually given to it – that numbers of people accept a few stock commonplace expressions of the face as the whole list of characteristics, and neither seek nor know the refinements that are truest – that you, for instance, give a great deal of time and attention to the reading of music, Greek, Latin, French, Italian, Hebrew, if you please, and do not qualify yourself to read the face of the master or mistress looking over your shoulder teaching it to you – I assume to be five hundred times more probable than improbable. Perhaps a little self-sufficiency may be at the bottom of this; facial expression requires no study from you, you think; it comes by nature to you to know enough about it, and you are not to be taken in.

I confess, for my part, that I *have* been taken in, over and over again. I have been taken in by acquaintances, and I have been taken in (of course) by friends; far oftener by friends than by any other class of persons. How came I to be so deceived? Had I quite misread their faces?

No. Believe me, my first impression of those people, founded on face and manner alone, was invariably true. My mistake was in suffering them to come nearer to me and explain themselves away.

2

The partition which separated my own office from our general outer office in the City was of thick plate-glass. I could see through it what passed in the outer office, without hearing a word. I had it put up in place of a wall that had been there for years – ever since the house was built. It is no matter whether I did or did not make the change in order that I might derive my first impression of strangers, who came to us on business, from their faces alone, without being influenced by anything they said. Enough to mention that I turned my glass partition to that account, and that a Life Assurance office is at all times exposed to be practised upon by the most crafty and cruel of the human race.

It was through my glass partition that I first saw the gentleman whose story I am going to tell.

He had come in without my observing it, and had put his hat and umbrella on the broad counter, and was bending over it to take some papers from one of the clerks. He was about forty or so, dark, exceedingly well dressed in black – being in mourning – and the hand he extended with a polite air, had a particularly well-fitting black-kid glove upon it. His hair, which was elaborately brushed and oiled, was parted straight up the middle; and he presented this parting to the clerk, exactly (to my thinking) as if he had said, in so many words: 'You must take me, if you please, my friend, just as I show myself. Come straight up here, follow the gravel path, keep off the grass, I allow no trespassing.'

I conceived a very great aversion to that man the moment I thus saw him.

He had asked for some of our printed forms, and the clerk was giving them to him and explaining them. An obliged and agreeable smile was on his face, and his eyes met those of the clerk with a sprightly look. (I have known a vast quantity of nonsense talked about bad men not looking you in the face. Don't trust that conventional idea. Dishonesty will stare honesty out of countenance any day in the week if there is anything to be got by it.)

I saw, in the corner of his eyelash, that he became aware of my looking at him. Immediately he turned the parting in his hair toward the glass partition, as if he said to me with a sweet smile, 'Straight up here, if you please. Off the grass!'

In a few moments he had put on his hat and taken up his umbrella, and was gone.

I beckoned the clerk into my room, and asked, 'Who was that?'

He had the gentleman's card in his hand. 'Mr Julius Slinkton, Middle Temple.'[2]

'A barrister, Mr Adams?'

'I think not, sir.'

'I should have thought him a clergyman, but for his having no Reverend here,' said I.

'Probably, from his appearance,' Mr Adams replied, 'he is reading for orders.'

I should mention that he wore a dainty white cravat, and dainty linen altogether.

'What did he want, Mr Adams?'

'Merely a form of proposal, sir, and form of reference.'

'Recommended here? Did he say?'

'Yes, he said he was recommended here by a friend of yours. He noticed you, but said that as he had not the pleasure of your personal acquaintance he would not trouble you.'

'Did he know my name?'

'Oh yes, sir! He said, "There *is* Mr Sampson, I see!" '

'A well-spoken gentleman, apparently?'

'Remarkably so, sir.'

'Insinuating manners, apparently?'

'Very much so, indeed, sir.'

'Hah!' said I. 'I want nothing at present, Mr Adams.'

Within a fortnight of that day I went to dine with a friend of mine, a merchant, a man of taste, who buys pictures and books, and the first man I saw among the company was Mr Julius Slinkton. There he was, standing before the fire, with good large eyes and an open expression of face; but still (I thought) requiring everybody to come at him by the prepared way he offered, and by no other.

I noticed him ask my friend to introduce him to Mr Sampson, and my friend did so. Mr Slinkton was very happy to see me. Not too happy; there was no overdoing of the matter; happy in a thoroughly well-bred, perfectly unmeaning way.

'I thought you had met,' our host observed.

'No,' said Mr Slinkton. 'I did look in at Mr Sampson's office, on your recommendation; but I really did not feel justified in troubling Mr Sampson himself, on a point in the everyday routine of an ordinary clerk.'

I said I should have been glad to show him any attention on our friend's introduction.

'I am sure of that,' said he, 'and am much obliged. At another time, perhaps, I may be less delicate. Only, however, if I have real business; for I know, Mr Sampson, how precious business time is, and what a vast number of impertinent people there are in the world.'

I acknowledged his consideration with a slight bow. 'You were thinking,' said I, 'of effecting a policy on your life.'

'Oh dear no! I am afraid I am not so prudent as you pay me the compliment of supposing me to be, Mr Sampson. I merely enquired for a friend. But you know what friends are in such matters. Nothing may ever come of it. I have the greatest reluctance to trouble men of business with enquiries for friends, knowing the probabilities to be a thousand to one that the friends will never follow them up. People are so fickle, so selfish, so inconsiderate. Don't you, in your business, find them so every day, Mr Sampson?'

I was going to give a qualified answer; but he turned his smooth, white parting on me with its 'Straight up here, if you please!' and I answered, 'Yes.'

'I hear, Mr Sampson,' he resumed presently, for our friend had a new cook, and dinner was not so punctual as usual, 'that your profession has recently suffered a great loss.'

'In money?' said I.

He laughed at my ready association of loss with money, and replied, 'No, in talent and vigour.'

Not at once following out his allusion, I considered for a moment. '*Has* it sustained a loss of that kind?' said I. 'I was not aware of it.'

'Understand me, Mr Sampson. I don't imagine that you have retired. It is not so bad as that. But Mr Meltham – '

'Oh, to be sure!' said I. 'Yes! Mr Meltham, the young actuary[3] of the "Inestimable".'[4]

'Just so,' he returned in a consoling way.

'He is a great loss. He was at once the most profound, the most original, and the most energetic man I have ever known connected with Life Assurance.'

I spoke strongly; for I had a high esteem and admiration for Meltham; and my gentleman had indefinitely conveyed to me some suspicion that he wanted to sneer at him. He recalled me to my guard by presenting that trim pathway up his head, with its infernal 'Not on the grass, if you please – the gravel.'

'You knew him, Mr Slinkton?'

'Only by reputation. To have known him as an acquaintance, or as a friend, is an honour I should have sought if he had remained in society, though I might never have had the good fortune to attain it, being a man of far inferior mark. He was scarcely above thirty, I suppose?'

'About thirty.'

'Ah!' he sighed in his former consoling way. 'What creatures we are! To break up, Mr Sampson, and become incapable of business at that time of life! – Any reason assigned for the melancholy fact?'

('Humph!' thought I, as I looked at him. 'But I *won't* go up the track, and I *will* go on the grass.')

'What reason have you heard assigned, Mr Slinkton?' I asked, point-blank.

'Most likely a false one. You know what rumour is, Mr Sampson. I never repeat what I hear; it is the only way of paring the nails and shaving the head of rumour. But when *you* ask me what reason I have heard assigned for Mr Meltham's passing away from among men, it is another thing. I am not gratifying idle gossip then. I was told, Mr Sampson, that Mr Meltham had relinquished all his avocations and all his prospects, because he was, in fact, broken-hearted. A disappointed attachment I heard – though it hardly seems probable, in the case of a man so distinguished and so attractive.'

'Attractions and distinctions are no armour against death,' said I.

'Oh, she died? Pray pardon me. I did not hear that. That, indeed, makes it very, very sad. Poor Mr Meltham! She died? Ah, dear me! Lamentable, lamentable!'

I still thought his pity was not quite genuine, and I still suspected an unaccountable sneer under all this, until he said, as we were parted, like the other knots of talkers, by the announcement of dinner: 'Mr Sampson, you are surprised to see me so moved on behalf of a man whom I have never known. I am not so disinterested as you may suppose. I have suffered, and recently too, from death myself. I have lost one of two charming nieces, who were my constant companions. She died young – barely three-and-twenty; and even her remaining sister is far from strong. The world is a grave!'

He said this with deep feeling, and I felt reproached for the coldness of my manner. Coldness and distrust had been engendered in me, I knew, by my bad experiences; they were not natural to me; and I often thought how much I had lost in life, losing trustfulness, and how little I had gained, gaining hard caution. This state of mind being habitual to me, I troubled myself more about this conversation than I might have troubled myself about a greater matter. I listened to his talk at dinner, and observed how readily other men responded to it, and with what a graceful instinct he adapted his subjects to the knowledge and habits of those he talked with. As, in talking with me, he had easily started the subject I might be supposed to understand best, and to be the most interested in, so, in talking with others, he guided himself by the same rule. The company was of a varied character; but he was not at fault, that I could discover, with any member of it. He knew just as much of each man's pursuit as made him agreeable to that man in reference to it, and just as little as made it natural in him to seek modestly for information when the theme was broached.

As he talked and talked – but really not too much, for the rest of us seemed to force it upon him – I became quite angry with myself. I took his face to pieces in my mind, like a watch, and examined it in detail. I could not say much against any of his features separately; I could say even less against them when they were put together. 'Then is it not monstrous,' I asked myself, 'that because a man happens to part his hair straight up the middle of his head, I should permit myself to suspect, and even to detest, him?'

(I may stop to remark that this was no proof of my sense. An observer of men who finds himself steadily repelled by some apparently trifling thing in a stranger is right to give it great weight. It may be the clue to the whole mystery. A hair or two will show where a lion is hidden. A very little key will open a very heavy door.)

I took my part in the conversation with him after a time, and we got on remarkably well. In the drawing-room, I asked the host how long he had known Mr Slinkton. He answered, not many months; he had met him at the house of a celebrated painter then present, who had known him well when he was travelling with his nieces in Italy for their health. His plans in life being broken by the death of one of them, he was reading with the intention of going back to college as a matter of form, taking his degree, and going into orders. I could not but argue with myself that here was the true explanation of his interest in poor Meltham, and that I had been almost brutal in my distrust on that simple head.

3

On the very next day but one I was sitting behind my glass partition, as before, when he came into the outer office, as before. The moment I saw him again without hearing him, I hated him worse than ever.

It was only for a moment that I had this opportunity; for he waved his tightfitting black glove the instant I looked at him, and came straight in.

'Mr Sampson, good-day! I presume, you see, upon your kind permission to intrude upon you. I don't keep my word in being justified by business, for my business here – if I may so abuse the word – is of the slightest nature.'

I asked, was it anything I could assist him in?

'I thank you, no. I merely called to enquire outside whether my dilatory friend had been so false to himself as to be practical and sensible. But, of course, he has done nothing. I gave him your papers with my own hand, and he was hot upon the intention, but of course he has done nothing. Apart from the general human disinclination to do anything that ought to be done, I dare say there is a specialty about assuring one's life. You find it like will-making. People are so superstitious, and take it for granted they will die soon afterwards.'

'Up here, if you please; straight up here, Mr Sampson. Neither to the right nor to the left.' I almost fancied I could hear him breathe the words as he sat smiling at me, with that intolerable parting exactly opposite the bridge of my nose.

'There is such a feeling sometimes, no doubt,' I replied; 'but I don't think it obtains to any great extent.'

'Well,' said he, with a shrug and a smile, 'I wish some good angel would influence my friend in the right direction. I rashly promised his mother and sister in Norfolk[5] to see it done, and he promised them that he would do it. But I suppose he never will.'

He spoke for a minute or two on indifferent topics, and went away.

I had scarcely unlocked the drawers of my writing-table next morning, when he reappeared. I noticed that he came straight to the door in the glass partition, and did not pause a single moment outside.

'Can you spare me two minutes, my dear Mr Sampson?'

'By all means.'

'Much obliged,' laying his hat and umbrella on the table; 'I came early, not to interrupt you. The fact is, I am taken by surprise in reference to this proposal my friend has made.'

'Has he made one?' said I.

'Ye–es,' he answered, deliberately looking at me; and then a bright idea seemed to strike him – 'or he only tells me he has. Perhaps that may be a new way of evading the matter. By Jupiter, I never thought of that!'

Mr Adams was opening the morning's letters in the outer office. 'What is the name, Mr Slinkton?' I asked.

'Beckwith.'

I looked out at the door and requested Mr Adams, if there were a proposal in that name, to bring it in. He had already laid it out of his hand on the counter. It was easily selected from the rest, and he gave it me. Alfred Beckwith. Proposal to effect a policy with us for two thousand pounds. Dated yesterday.

'From the Middle Temple, I see, Mr Slinkton.'

'Yes. He lives on the same staircase with me; his door is opposite. I never thought he would make me his reference though.'

'It seems natural enough that he should.'

'Quite so, Mr Sampson; but I never thought of it. Let me see.' He took the printed paper from his pocket. 'How am I to answer all these questions?'

'According to the truth, of course,' said I.

'Oh, of course!' he answered, looking up from the paper with a smile; 'I meant they were so many. But you do right to be particular. It stands to reason that you must be particular. Will you allow me to use your pen and ink?'

'Certainly.'

'And your desk?'

'Certainly.'

He had been hovering about between his hat and his umbrella for a place to write on. He now sat down in my chair, at my blotting-paper and inkstand, with the long walk up his head in accurate perspective before me, as I stood with my back to the fire.

Before answering each question he ran over it aloud, and discussed it. How long had he known Mr Alfred Beckwith? That he had to calculate by years upon his fingers. What were his habits? No difficulty about them; temperate in the last degree, and took a little too much exercise, if anything. All the answers were satisfactory. When he had written them all, he looked them over, and finally signed them in a very pretty hand. He supposed he had now done with the business. I told him he was not likely to be troubled any further. Should he leave the papers there? If he pleased. Much obliged. Good-morning.

I had had one other visitor before him; not at the office, but at my own house. That visitor had come to my bedside when it was not yet daylight, and had been seen by no one else but by my faithful confidential servant.

A second reference paper (for we required always two) was sent down into Norfolk, and was duly received back by post. This, likewise, was satisfactorily answered in every respect. Our forms were all complied with; we accepted the proposal, and the premium for one year was paid.

4

For six or seven months I saw no more of Mr Slinkton. He called once at my house, but I was not at home; and he once asked me to dine with him in the Temple, but I was engaged. His friend's assurance was effected in March. Late in September or early in October I was down at Scarborough for a breath of sea-air, where I met him on the beach. It was a hot evening; he came toward me with his hat in his hand; and there was the walk I had felt so strongly disinclined to take in perfect order again, exactly in front of the bridge of my nose.

He was not alone, but had a young lady on his arm.

She was dressed in mourning, and I looked at her with great interest. She had the appearance of being extremely delicate, and her face was remarkably pale and melancholy; but she was very pretty. He introduced her as his niece, Miss Niner.

'Are you strolling, Mr Sampson? Is it possible you can be idle?'

It *was* possible, and I *was* strolling.

'Shall we stroll together?'

'With pleasure.'

The young lady walked between us, and we walked on the cool sea sand, in the direction of Filey.[6]

'There have been wheels here,' said Mr Slinkton. 'And now I look again, the wheels of a hand-carriage! Margaret, my love, your shadow without doubt!'

'Miss Niner's shadow?' I repeated, looking down at it on the sand.

'Not that one,' Mr Slinkton returned, laughing. 'Margaret, my dear, tell Mr Sampson.'

'Indeed,' said the young lady, turning to me, 'there is nothing to tell – except that I constantly see the same invalid old gentleman at all times, wherever I go. I have mentioned it to my uncle, and he calls the gentleman my shadow.'

'Does he live in Scarborough?' I asked.

'He is staying here.'

'Do you live in Scarborough?'

'No, I am staying here. My uncle has placed me with a family here, for my health.'

'And your shadow?' said I, smiling.

'My shadow,' she answered, smiling too, 'is – like myself – not very robust, I fear; for I lose my shadow sometimes, as my shadow loses me at other times. We both seem liable to confinement to the house. I have not seen my shadow for days and days; but it does oddly happen, occasionally, that wherever I go, for many days together, this gentleman goes. We have come together in the most unfrequented nooks on this shore.'

'Is this he?' said I, pointing before us.

The wheels had swept down to the water's edge, and described a great loop on the sand in turning. Bringing the loop back towards us, and spinning it out as it came, was a hand-carriage, drawn by a man.

'Yes,' said Miss Niner, 'this really is my shadow, uncle.'

As the carriage approached us and we approached the carriage, I saw within it an old man, whose head was sunk on his breast, and who was enveloped in a variety of wrappers. He was drawn by a very quiet but very keen-looking man, with iron-grey hair, who was slightly lame. They had passed us, when the carriage stopped, and the old gentleman within, putting out his arm, called to me by my name. I went back, and was absent from Mr Slinkton and his niece for about five minutes.

When I rejoined them, Mr Slinkton was the first to speak. Indeed, he said to me in a raised voice before I came up with him: 'It is well you have not been longer, or my niece might have died of curiosity to know who her shadow is, Mr Sampson.'

'An old East India director,'[7] said I. 'An intimate friend of our friend's, at whose house I first had the pleasure of meeting you. A certain Major Banks. You have heard of him?'

'Never.'

'Very rich, Miss Niner; but very old, and very crippled. An

amiable man, sensible – much interested in you. He has just been expatiating on the affection that he has observed to exist between you and your uncle.'

Mr Slinkton was holding his hat again, and he passed his hand up the straight walk, as if he himself went up it serenely, after me.

'Mr Sampson,' he said, tenderly pressing his niece's arm in his, 'our affection was always a strong one, for we have had but few near ties. We have still fewer now. We have associations to bring us together that are not of this world, Margaret.'

'Dear uncle!' murmured the young lady, and turned her face aside to hide her tears.

'My niece and I have such remembrances and regrets in common, Mr Sampson,' he feelingly pursued, 'that it would be strange indeed if the relations between us were cold or indifferent. If I remember a conversation we once had together, you will understand the reference I make. Cheer up, dear Margaret. Don't droop, don't droop. My Margaret! I cannot bear to see you droop!'

The poor young lady was very much affected, but controlled herself. His feelings, too, were very acute. In a word, he found himself under such great need of a restorative that he presently went away to take a bath of sea-water, leaving the young lady and me sitting by a point of rock, and probably presuming – but that, you will say, was a pardonable indulgence in a luxury – that she would praise him with all her heart.

She did, poor thing! With all her confiding heart, she praised him to me, for his care of her dead sister and for his untiring devotion in her last illness. The sister had wasted away very slowly, and wild and terrible fantasies had come over her toward the end, but he had never been impatient with her, or at a loss; had always been gentle, watchful and self-possessed. The sister had known him, as she had known him, to be the best of men, the kindest of men, and yet a man of such admirable strength of character as to be a very tower for the support of their weak natures while their poor lives endured.

'I shall leave him, Mr Sampson, very soon,' said the young lady; 'I know my life is drawing to an end; and when I am gone, I hope he will marry and be happy. I am sure he has lived single so long only for my sake, and for my poor, poor sister's.'

The little hand-carriage had made another great loop on the damp sand, and was coming back again, gradually spinning out a slim figure of eight, half a mile long.

'Young lady,' said I, looking around, laying my hand upon her

arm and speaking in a low voice, 'time presses. You hear the gentle
murmur of that sea?'

She looked at me with the utmost wonder and alarm, saying,
'Yes!'

'And you know what a voice is in it when the storm comes?'

'Yes!'

'You see how quiet and peaceful it lies before us, and you know
what an awful sight of power without pity it might be, this very
night!'

'Yes!'

'But if you had never heard or seen it, or heard of it in its cruelty,
could you believe that it beats every inanimate thing in its way to
pieces, without mercy, and destroys life without remorse?'

'You terrify me, sir, by these questions!'

'To save you, young lady, to save you! For God's sake, collect
your strength and collect your firmness! If you were here alone, and
hemmed in by the rising tide on the flow to fifty feet above your
head, you could not be in greater danger than the danger you are
now to be saved from.'

The figure on the sand was spun out, and straggled off into a
crooked little jerk that ended at the cliff very near us.

'As I am, before heaven and the judge of all mankind, your friend,
and your dead sister's friend, I solemnly entreat you, Miss Niner,
without one moment's loss of time, to come to this gentleman with
me!'

If the little carriage had been less near to us, I doubt if I could
have got her away; but it was so near that we were there before she
had recovered the hurry of being urged from the rock. I did not
remain there with her two minutes. Certainly within five, I had the
inexpressible satisfaction of seeing her – from the point we had sat
on, and to which I had returned – half supported and half carried up
some rude steps notched in the cliff by the figure of an active man.
With that figure beside her, I knew she was safe anywhere.

I sat alone on the rock, awaiting Mr Slinkton's return. The
twilight was deepening and the shadows were heavy, when he came
round the point, with his hat hanging at his buttonhole, smoothing
his wet hair with one of his hands, and picking out the old path with
the other and a pocket-comb.

'My niece not here, Mr Sampson?' he said, looking about.

'Miss Niner seemed to feel a chill in the air after the sun was
down, and has gone home.'

He looked surprised, as though she were not accustomed to do anything without him; even to originate so slight a proceeding.

'I persuaded Miss Niner,' I explained.

'Ah!' said he. 'She is easily persuaded – for her good. Thank you, Mr Sampson; she is better within doors. The bathing-place was farther than I thought, to say the truth.'

'Miss Niner is very delicate,' I observed.

He shook his head and drew a deep sigh. 'Very, very, very. You may recollect my saying so. The time that has since intervened has not strengthened her. The gloomy shadow that fell upon her sister so early in life seems, in my anxious eyes, to gather over her, ever darker, ever darker. Dear Margaret, dear Margaret! But we must hope.'

The hand-carriage was spinning away before us at a most indecorous pace for an invalid vehicle, and was making most irregular curves upon the sand. Mr Slinkton, noticing it after he had put his handkerchief to his eyes, said: 'If I may judge from appearances, your friend will be upset, Mr Sampson.'

'It looks probable, certainly,' said I.

'The servant must be drunk.'

'The servants of old gentlemen will get drunk sometimes,' said I.

'The major draws very light, Mr Sampson.'

'The major does draw light,' said I.

By this time the carriage, much to my relief, was lost in the darkness. We walked on for a little, side by side over the sand, in silence. After a short while he said, in a voice still affected by the emotion that his niece's state of health had awakened in him, 'Do you stay here long, Mr Sampson?'

'Why, no. I am going away tonight.'

'So soon? But business always holds you in request. Men like Mr Sampson are too important to others to be spared to their own need of relaxation and enjoyment.'

'I don't know about that,' said I. 'However, I am going back.'

'To London?'

'To London.'

'I shall be there, too, soon after you.'

I knew that as well as he did. But I did not tell him so. Any more than I told him what defensive weapon my right hand rested on in my pocket, as I walked by his side. Any more than I told him why I did not walk on the sea side of him with the night closing in.

We left the beach, and our ways diverged. We exchanged good-night, and had parted indeed, when he said, returning, 'Mr Sampson, *may* I ask? Poor Meltham, whom we spoke of – dead yet?'

'Not when I last heard of him; but too broken a man to live long, and hopelessly lost to his old calling.'

'Dear, dear, dear!' said he, with great feeling. 'Sad, sad, sad! The world is a grave!' And so went his way.

It was not his fault if the world were not a grave; but I did not call that observation after him, any more than I had mentioned those other things just now enumerated. He went his way, and I went mine with all expedition. This happened, as I have said, either at the end of September or beginning of October. The next time I saw him, and the last time, was late in November.

5

I had a very particular engagement to breakfast in the Temple. It was a bitter north-easterly morning, and the sleet and slush lay inches deep in the streets. I could get no conveyance, and was soon wet to the knees; but I should have been true to that appointment though I had to wade to it up to my neck in the same impediments.

The appointment took me to some chambers in the Temple. They were at the top of a lonely corner house overlooking the river. The name MR ALFRED BECKWITH was painted on the outer door. On the door opposite, on the same landing, the name MR JULIUS SLINKTON. The doors of both sets of chambers stood open, so that anything said aloud in one set could be heard in the other.

I had never been in those chambers before. They were dismal, close, unwholesome and oppressive; the furniture, originally good, and not yet old, was faded and dirty – the rooms were in great disorder; there was a strong prevailing smell of opium, brandy and tobacco; the grate and fire-irons were splashed all over with unsightly blotches of rust; and on a sofa by the fire, in the room where breakfast had been prepared, lay the host, Mr Beckwith, a man with all the appearances of the worst kind of drunkard, very far advanced upon his shameful way to death.

'Slinkton is not come yet,' said this creature, staggering up when I went in; 'I'll call him – Halloa! Julius Caesar![8] Come and drink!' As he hoarsely roared this out, he beat the poker and tongs together in a mad way, as if that were his usual manner of summoning his associate.

The voice of Mr Slinkton was heard through the clatter from the opposite side of the staircase, and he came in. He had not expected the pleasure of meeting me. I have seen several artful men brought to a stand, but I never saw a man so aghast as he was when his eyes rested on mine.

'Julius Caesar,' cried Beckwith, staggering between us, 'Mist' Sampson! Mist' Sampson, Julius Caesar! Julius, Mist' Sampson, is the friend of my soul. Julius keeps me plied with liquor, morning, noon and night. Julius is a real benefactor. Julius threw the tea and coffee out of the window when I used to have any. Julius empties all the water-jugs of their contents, and fills 'em with spirits. Julius winds me up and keeps me going. Boil the brandy, Julius!'

There was a rusty and furred saucepan in the ashes – the ashes looked like the accumulation of weeks – and Beckwith, rolling and staggering between us as if he were going to plunge headlong into the fire, got the saucepan out, and tried to force it into Slinkton's hand.

'Boil the brandy, Julius Caesar! Come! Do your usual office. Boil the brandy!'

He became so fierce in his gesticulations with the saucepan that I expected to see him lay open Slinkton's head with it. I therefore put out my hand to check him. He reeled back to the sofa, and sat there panting, shaking and red-eyed, in his rags of dressing-gown, looking at us both. I noticed then that there was nothing to drink on the table but brandy, and nothing to eat but salted herrings, and a hot, sickly, highly peppered stew.

'At all events, Mr Sampson,' said Slinkton, offering me the smooth gravel path for the last time, 'I thank you for interfering between me and this unfortunate man's violence. However you came here, Mr Sampson, or with whatever motive you came here, at least I thank you for that.'

'Boil the brandy,' muttered Beckwith.

Without gratifying his desire to know how I came there, I said, quietly, 'How is your niece, Mr Slinkton?'

He looked hard at me, and I looked hard at him.

'I am sorry to say, Mr Sampson, that my niece has proved treacherous and ungrateful to her best friend. She left me without a word of notice or explanation. She was misled, no doubt, by some designing rascal. Perhaps you may have heard of it.'

'I did hear that she was misled by a designing rascal. In fact, I have proof of it.'

'Are you sure of that?' said he.

'Quite.'

'Boil the brandy,' muttered Beckwith. 'Company to breakfast, Julius Caesar. Do your usual office – provide the usual breakfast, dinner, tea and supper. Boil the brandy!'

The eyes of Slinkton looked from him to me, and he said, after a moment's consideration, 'Mr Sampson, you are a man of the world, and so am I. I will be plain with you.'

'Oh no, you won't,' said I, shaking my head.

'I tell you, sir, I will be plain with you.'

'And I tell you you will not,' said I. 'I know all about you. *You* plain with anyone? Nonsense, nonsense!'

'I plainly tell you, Mr Sampson,' he went on, with a manner almost composed, 'that I understand your object. You want to save your funds, and escape from your liabilities; these are old tricks of trade with you office-gentlemen. But you will not do it, sir; you will not succeed. You have not an easy adversary to play against, when you play against me. We shall have to enquire, in due time, when and how Mr Beckwith fell into his present habits. With that remark, sir, I put this poor creature, and his incoherent wanderings of speech, aside, and wish you a good-morning and a better case next time.'

While he was saying this, Beckwith had filled a half-pint glass with brandy. At this moment, he threw the brandy at his face, and threw the glass after it. Slinkton put his hands up, half blinded with the spirit, and cut with the glass across the forehead. At the sound of the breakage, a fourth person came into the room, closed the door, and stood at it; he was a very quiet but very keen-looking man, with iron-grey hair, and slightly lame.

Slinkton pulled out his handkerchief, assuaged the pain in his smarting eyes, and dabbled the blood on his forehead. He was a long time about it, and I saw that in the doing of it, a tremendous change came over him, occasioned by the change in Beckwith – who ceased to pant and tremble, sat upright, and never took his eyes off him. I never in my life saw a face in which abhorrence and determination were so forcibly painted as in Beckwith's then.

'Look at me, you villain,' said Beckwith, 'and see me as I really am. I took these rooms, to make them a trap for you. I came into them as a drunkard, to bait the trap for you. You fell into the trap, and you will never leave it alive. On the morning when you last went to Mr Sampson's office, I had seen him first. Your plot has been known to both of us, all along, and you have been counterplotted all along. What? Having been cajoled into putting that prize of two thousand pounds in your power, I was to be done to death with brandy, and, brandy not proving quick enough, with something quicker? Have I never seen you, when you thought my senses gone, pouring from your little bottle into my glass? Why, you murderer and forger, alone here with you in the dead of night, as I have so often been, I have had my hand upon the trigger of a pistol, twenty times, to blow your brains out!'

This sudden starting up of the thing that he had supposed to be his imbecile victim into a determined man, with a settled resolution to hunt him down and be the death of him, mercilessly expressed from head to foot, was, in the first shock, too much for him. Without any figure of speech, he staggered under it. But there is no greater mistake than to suppose that a man who is a calculating criminal is, in any phase of his guilt, otherwise than true to himself, and perfectly consistent with his whole character. Such a man commits murder, and murder is the natural culmination of his course; such a man has to outface murder, and will do it with hardihood and effrontery. It is a sort of fashion to express surprise that any notorious criminal, having such crime upon his conscience, can so brave it out. Do you think that if he had it on his conscience at all, or had a conscience to have it upon, he would ever have committed the crime?

Perfectly consistent with himself, as I believe all such monsters to be, this Slinkton recovered himself, and showed a defiance that was sufficiently cold and quiet. He was white, he was haggard, he was changed; but only as a sharper who had played for a great stake and had been outwitted and had lost the game.

'Listen to me, you villain,' said Beckwith, 'and let every word you hear me say be a stab in your wicked heart. When I took these rooms, to throw myself in your way and lead you on to the scheme that I knew my appearance and supposed character and habits would suggest to such a devil, how did I know that? Because you were no stranger to me. I knew you well. And I knew you to be the cruel wretch who, for so much money, had killed one innocent girl while she trusted him implicitly, and who was by inches killing another.'

Slinkton took out a snuffbox, took a pinch of snuff, and laughed.

'But see here,' said Beckwith, never looking away, never raising his voice, never relaxing his face, never unclenching his hand. 'See what a dull wolf you have been, after all! The infatuated drunkard who never drank a fiftieth part of the liquor you plied him with, but poured it away, here, there, everywhere – almost before your eyes; who bought over the fellow you set to watch him and to ply him, by outbidding you in his bribe, before he had been at his work three days; with whom you have observed no caution, yet who was so bent on ridding the earth of you as a wild beast, that he would have defeated you if you had been ever so prudent; that drunkard whom you have, many a time, left on the floor of this room, and who has even let you go out of it, alive and undeceived, when you have turned him over with your foot – has, almost as often, on the same night, within an hour, within a few minutes, watched you awake, had his hand at your pillow when you were asleep, turned over your papers, taken samples from your bottles and packets of powder, changed their contents, rifled every secret of your life!'

He had had another pinch of snuff in his hand, but had gradually let it drop from between his fingers to the floor; where he now smoothed it out with his foot, looking down at it the while.

'That drunkard,' said Beckwith, 'who had free access to your rooms at all times, that he might drink the strong drinks that you left in his way and be the sooner ended, holding no more terms with you than he would hold with a tiger, has had his master-key for all your locks, his test for all your poisons, his clue to your cipher-writing. He can tell you, as well as you can tell him, how long it took to complete that deed, what doses there were, what intervals, what signs of gradual decay upon mind and body; what distempered fancies were produced, what observable changes, what physical pain. He can tell you, as well as you can tell him, that all this was recorded day by day, as a lesson of experience for future service. He can tell you, better than you can tell him, where that journal is at this moment.'

Slinkton stopped the action of his foot, and looked at Beckwith.

'No,' said the latter, as if answering a question from him. 'Not in the drawer of the writing-desk that opens with a spring; it is not there, and it never will be there again.'

'Then you are a thief!' said Slinkton.

Without any change whatever in the inflexible purpose, which it was quite terrific even to me to contemplate, and from the power of which I had always felt convinced it was impossible for this wretch to escape, Beckwith returned, 'And I am your niece's shadow, too.'

With an imprecation Slinkton put his hand to his head, tore out some hair, and flung it to the ground. It was the end of the smooth walk; he destroyed it in the action, and it will soon be seen that his use for it was past.

Beckwith went on: 'Whenever you left here, I left here. Although I understood that you found it necessary to pause in the completion of that purpose, to avert suspicion, still I watched you close, with the poor confiding girl. When I had the diary, and could read it word by word – it was only about the night before your last visit to Scarborough – you remember the night? you slept with a small flat vial tied to your wrist – I sent to Mr Sampson, who was kept out of view. This is Mr Sampson's trusty servant standing by the door. We three saved your niece among us.'

Slinkton looked at us all, took an uncertain step or two from the place where he had stood, returned to it, and glanced about him in a very curious way – as one of the meaner reptiles might, looking for a hole to hide in. I noticed at the same time, that a singular change took place in the figure of the man – as if it collapsed within his clothes, and they consequently became ill-shapen and ill-fitting.

'You shall know,' said Beckwith, 'for I hope the knowledge will be bitter and terrible to you, why you have been pursued by one man, and why, when the whole interest that Mr Sampson represents would have expended any money in hunting you down, you have been tracked to death at a single individual's charge. I hear you have had the name of Meltham on your lips sometimes?'

I saw, in addition to those other changes, a sudden stoppage come upon his breathing.

'When you sent the sweet girl whom you murdered (you know with what artfully made-out surroundings and probabilities you sent her) to Meltham's office, before taking her abroad to originate the transaction that doomed her to the grave, it fell to Meltham's lot to see her and to speak with her. It did not fall to his lot to save her, though I know he would freely give his own life to have done it. He admired her – I would say he loved her deeply, if I thought it possible that you could understand the word. When she was sacrificed, he was thoroughly assured of your guilt. Having lost her, he had but one object left in life, and that was to avenge her and destroy you.'

I saw the villain's nostrils rise and fall convulsively; but I saw no moving at his mouth.

'That man Meltham,' Beckwith steadily pursued, 'was as absolutely certain that you could never elude him in this world, if he devoted himself to your destruction with his utmost fidelity and earnestness, and if he divided the sacred duty with no other duty in life, as he was certain that in achieving it he would be a poor instrument in the hands of Providence, and would do well before heaven in striking you out from among living men. I am that man, and I thank God that I have done my work!'

If Slinkton had been running for his life from swift-footed

savages, a dozen miles, he could not have shown more emphatic signs of being oppressed at heart and labouring for breath than he showed now, when he looked at the pursuer who had so relentlessly hunted him down.

'You never saw me under my right name before; you see me under my right name now. You shall see me once again in the body, when you are tried for your life. You shall see me once again in the spirit, when the cord is round your neck, and the crowd are crying against you!'

When Meltham had spoken these last words, the miscreant suddenly turned away his face, and seemed to strike his mouth with his open hand. At the same instant, the room was filled with a new and powerful odour[9] and, almost at the same instant, he broke into a crooked run, leap, start – I have no name for the spasm – and fell, with a dull weight that shook the heavy old doors and windows in their frames.

That was the fitting end of him.

When we saw that he was dead, we drew away from the room, and Meltham, giving me his hand, said, with a weary air, 'I have no more work on earth, my friend. But I shall see her again elsewhere.'

It was in vain that I tried to rally him. He might have saved her, he said; he had not saved her, and he reproached himself; he had lost her, and he was broken-hearted.

'The purpose that sustained me is over, Sampson, and there is nothing now to hold me to life. I am not fit for life; I am weak and spiritless; I have no hope and no object; my day is done.'

In truth, I could hardly have believed that the broken man who then spoke to me was the man who had so strongly and so differently impressed me when his purpose was before him. I used such entreaties with him, as I could; but he still said, and always said, in a patient, undemonstrative way – nothing could avail him – he was broken-hearted.

He died early in the next spring. He was buried by the side of the poor young lady for whom he had cherished those tender and unhappy regrets; and he left all he had to her sister. She lived to be a happy wife and mother; she married my sister's son, who succeeded poor Meltham; she is living now, and her children ride about the garden on my walking-stick when I go to see her.

HOLIDAY ROMANCE
in four parts

PART ONE

Introductory Romance from the Pen of William Tinkling, Esq. – Aged Eight

THIS BEGINNING-PART is not made out of anybody's head, you know. It's real. You must believe this beginning-part more than what comes after, else you won't understand how what comes after came to be written. You must believe it all; but you must believe this most, please. I am the editor of it. Bob Redforth (he's my cousin, and shaking the table on purpose) wanted to be the editor of it; but I said he shouldn't because he couldn't. *He* has no idea of being an editor.

Nettie Ashford is my bride. We were married in the right-hand closet in the corner of the dancing-school, where first we met, with a ring (a green one) from Wilkingwater's toy-shop. *I* owed for it out of my pocket-money. When the rapturous ceremony was over, we all four went up the lane and let off a cannon (brought loaded in Bob Redforth's waistcoat-pocket) to announce our nuptials. It flew right up when it went off, and turned over. Next day, Lieutenant-Colonel Robin Redforth was united, with similar ceremonies, to Alice Rainbird. This time the cannon burst with a most terrific explosion, and made a puppy bark.

My peerless bride was, at the period of which we now treat, in captivity at Miss Grimmer's. Drowvey and Grimmer is the partnership, and opinion is divided which is the greatest beast. The lovely bride of the colonel was also immured in the dungeons of the same establishment. A vow was entered into, between the colonel and myself, that we would cut them out on the following Wednesday when walking two and two.

Under the desperate circumstances of the case, the active brain of the colonel, combining with his lawless pursuit (he is a pirate), suggested an attack with fireworks. This, however, from motives of humanity, was abandoned as too expensive.

Lightly armed with a paperknife buttoned up under his jacket, and waving the dreaded black flag at the end of a cane, the colonel took command of me at 2 p.m. on the eventful and appointed day. He had drawn out the plan of attack on a piece of paper, which was rolled up round a hoop-stick. He showed it to me. My position and my full-length portrait (but my real ears don't stick out horizontal) was behind a corner lamp-post, with written orders to remain there till I should see Miss Drowvey fall. The Drowvey who was to fall was the one in spectacles, not the one with the large lavender bonnet. At that signal I was to rush forth, seize my bride, and fight my way to the lane. There a junction would be effected between myself and the colonel; and putting our brides behind us, between ourselves and the palings, we were to conquer or die.

The enemy appeared – approached. Waving his black flag, the colonel attacked. Confusion ensued. Anxiously I awaited my signal; but my signal came not. So far from falling, the hated Drowvey in spectacles appeared to me to have muffled the colonel's head in his outlawed banner, and to be pitching into him with a parasol. The one in the lavender bonnet also performed prodigies of valour with her fists on his back. Seeing that all was for the moment lost, I fought my desperate way hand to hand to the lane. Through taking the back road, I was so fortunate as to meet nobody, and arrived there uninterrupted.

It seemed an age ere the colonel joined me. He had been to the jobbing tailor's to be sewn up in several places, and attributed our defeat to the refusal of the detested Drowvey to fall. Finding her so obstinate, he had said to her, '*Die, recreant!*' but had found her no more open to reason on that point than the other.

My blooming bride appeared, accompanied by the colonel's bride, at the dancing-school next day. What? Was her face averted from me? Hah? Even so. With a look of scorn, she put into my hand a bit of paper, and took another partner. On the paper was pencilled, 'Heavens! Can I write the word? Is my husband a cow?'

In the first bewilderment of my heated brain, I tried to think what slanderer could have traced my family to the ignoble animal mentioned above. Vain were my endeavours. At the end of that dance I whispered the colonel to come into the cloakroom, and I showed him the note.

'There is a syllable wanting,' said he, with a gloomy brow.

'Hah! What syllable?' was my enquiry.

'She asks, can she write the word? And no; you see she couldn't,' said the colonel, pointing out the passage.

'And the word was?' said I.

'Cow–cow–coward,' hissed the pirate-colonel in my ear, and gave me back the note.

Feeling that I must for ever tread the earth a branded boy – person I mean – or that I must clear up my honour, I demanded to be tried by a court-martial. The colonel admitted my right to be tried. Some difficulty was found in composing the court, on account of the Emperor of France's aunt refusing to let him come out. He was to be the president. Ere yet we had appointed a substitute, he made his escape over the back-wall, and stood among us, a free monarch.

The court was held on the grass by the pond. I recognised, in a certain admiral among my judges, my deadliest foe. A coconut had given rise to language that I could not brook; but confiding in my innocence, and also in the knowledge that the President of the United States (who sat next him) owed me a knife, I braced myself for the ordeal.

It was a solemn spectacle, that court. Two executioners with pinafores reversed led me in. Under the shade of an umbrella I perceived my bride, supported by the bride of the pirate-colonel. The president, having reproved a little female ensign for tittering on a matter of life or death, called upon me to plead, 'Coward or no coward, guilty or not guilty?' I pleaded in a firm tone, 'No coward and not guilty.' (The little female ensign being again reproved by the president for misconduct, mutinied, left the court, and threw stones.)

My implacable enemy, the admiral, conducted the case against me. The colonel's bride was called to prove that I had remained behind the corner lamp-post during the engagement. I might have been spared the anguish of my own bride's being also made a witness to the same point, but the admiral knew where to wound me. Be still, my soul, no matter. The colonel was then brought forward with his evidence.

It was for this point that I had saved myself up, as the turning-point of my case. Shaking myself free of my guards – who had no business to hold me, the stupids, unless I was found guilty – I asked the colonel what he considered the first duty of a soldier? Ere he could reply, the President of the United States rose and informed the court, that my foe, the admiral, had suggested 'Bravery', and that prompting a witness wasn't fair. The president of the court immediately ordered the admiral's mouth to be filled with leaves, and tied up with string. I had the satisfaction of seeing the sentence carried into effect before the proceedings went further.

I then took a paper from my trousers-pocket, and asked, 'What do you consider, Colonel Redford, the first duty of a soldier? Is it obedience?'

'It is,' said the colonel.

'Is that paper – please to look at it – in your hand?'

'It is,' said the colonel.

'Is it a military sketch?'

'It is,' said the colonel.

'Of an engagement?'

'Quite so,' said the colonel.

'Of the late engagement?'

'Of the late engagement.'

'Please to describe it, and then hand it to the president of the court.'

From that triumphant moment my sufferings and my dangers were at an end. The court rose up and jumped, on discovering that I had strictly obeyed orders. My foe, the admiral, who though muzzled was malignant yet, contrived to suggest that I was dishonoured by having quitted the field. But the colonel himself had done as much, and gave his opinion, upon his word and honour as a pirate, that when all was lost the field might be quitted without disgrace. I was going to be found 'No coward and not guilty', and my blooming bride was going to be publicly restored to my arms in a procession, when an unlooked-for event disturbed the general rejoicing. This was no other than the Emperor of France's aunt catching hold of his hair. The proceedings abruptly terminated, and the court tumultuously dissolved.

It was when the shades of the next evening but one were beginning to fall, ere yet the silver beams of Luna touched the earth, that four forms might have been descried slowly advancing towards the weeping willow on the borders of the pond, the now deserted scene of the day before yesterday's agonies and triumphs. On a nearer approach, and by a practised eye, these might have been identified as the forms of the pirate-colonel with his bride, and of the day before yesterday's gallant prisoner with his bride.

On the beauteous faces of the nymphs dejection sat enthroned. All four reclined under the willow for some minutes without speaking, till at length the bride of the colonel poutingly observed, 'It's of no use pretending any more, and we had better give it up.'

'Hah!' exclaimed the pirate. 'Pretending?'

'Don't go on like that; you worry me,' returned his bride.

The lovely bride of Tinkling echoed the incredible declaration.

The two warriors exchanged stony glances.

'If,' said the bride of the pirate-colonel, 'grown-up people *won't* do what they ought to do, and *will* put us out, what comes of our pretending?'

'We only get into scrapes,' said the bride of Tinkling.

'You know very well,' pursued the colonel's bride, 'that Miss Drowvey wouldn't fall. You complained of it yourself. And you know how disgracefully the court-martial ended. As to our marriage; would my people acknowledge it at home?'

'Or would my people acknowledge ours?' said the bride of Tinkling.

Again the two warriors exchanged stony glances.

'If you knocked at the door and claimed me, after you were told to go away,' said the colonel's bride, 'you would only have your hair pulled, or your ears, or your nose.'

'If you persisted in ringing at the bell and claiming me,' said the bride of Tinkling to that gentleman, 'you would have things dropped on your head from the window over the handle, or you would be played upon by the garden-engine.'

'And at your own homes,' resumed the bride of the colonel, 'it would be just as bad. You would be sent to bed, or something equally undignified. Again, how would you support us?'

The pirate-colonel replied in a courageous voice, 'By rapine!' But his bride retorted, 'Suppose the grown-up people wouldn't be rapined?' 'Then,' said the colonel, 'they should pay the penalty in blood.' – 'But suppose they should object,' retorted his bride, 'and wouldn't pay the penalty in blood or anything else?'

A mournful silence ensued.

'Then do you no longer love me, Alice?' asked the colonel.

'Redforth! I am ever thine,' returned his bride.

'Then do you no longer love me, Nettie?' asked the present writer.

'Tinkling! I am ever thine,' returned my bride.

We all four embraced. Let me not be misunderstood by the giddy. The colonel embraced his own bride, and I embraced mine. But two times two make four.

'Nettie and I,' said Alice mournfully, 'have been considering our position. The grown-up people are too strong for us. They make us ridiculous. Besides, they have changed the times. William Tinkling's baby brother was christened yesterday. What took place? Was any king present? Answer, William.'

I said no, unless disguised as Great-Uncle Chopper.

'Any queen?'

There had been no queen that I knew of at our house. There might have been one in the kitchen, but I didn't think so, or the servants would have mentioned it.

'Any fairies?'

None that were visible.

'We had an idea among us, I think,' said Alice, with a melancholy smile, 'we four, that Miss Grimmer would prove to be the wicked fairy, and would come in at the christening with her crutch-stick, and give the child a bad gift. Was there anything of that sort? Answer, William.'

I said that ma had said afterwards (and so she had), that Great-Uncle Chopper's gift was a shabby one; but she hadn't said a bad one. She had called it shabby, electrotyped, second-hand, and below his income.

'It must be the grown-up people who have changed all this,' said Alice. '*We* couldn't have changed it, if we had been so inclined, and we never should have been. Or perhaps Miss Grimmer *is* a wicked fairy after all, and won't act up to it because the grown-up people have persuaded her not to. Either way, they would make us ridiculous if we told them what we expected.'

'Tyrants!' muttered the pirate-colonel.

'Nay, my Redforth,' said Alice, 'say not so. Call not names, my Redforth, or they will apply to pa.'

'Let 'em,' said the colonel. 'I do not care. Who's he?'

Tinkling here undertook the perilous task of remonstrating with his lawless friend, who consented to withdraw the moody expressions above quoted.

'What remains for us to do?' Alice went on in her mild, wise way. 'We must educate, we must pretend in a new manner, we must wait.'

The colonel clenched his teeth – four out in front, and a piece of another, and he had been twice dragged to the door of a dentist-despot, but had escaped from his guards. 'How educate? How pretend in a new manner? How wait?'

'Educate the grown-up people,' replied Alice. 'We part tonight. Yes, Redforth' – for the colonel tucked up his cuffs – 'part to night! Let us in these next holidays, now going to begin, throw our thoughts into something educational for the grown-up people, hinting to them how things ought to be. Let us veil our meaning under a mask of romance; you, I and Nettie. William Tinkling being the plainest and quickest writer, shall copy out. Is it agreed?'

The colonel answered sulkily, 'I don't mind.' He then asked, 'How about pretending?'

'We will pretend,' said Alice, 'that we are children; not that we are those grown-up people who won't help us out as they ought, and who understand us so badly.'

The colonel, still much dissatisfied, growled, 'How about waiting?'

'We will wait,' answered little Alice, taking Nettie's hand in hers, and looking up to the sky, 'we will wait – ever constant and true – till the times have got so changed as that everything helps us out, and nothing makes us ridiculous, and the fairies have come back. We will wait – ever constant and true – till we are eighty, ninety or one hundred. And then the fairies will send *us* children, and we will help them out, poor pretty little creatures, if they pretend ever so much.'

'So we will, dear,' said Nettie Ashford, taking her round the waist with both arms and kissing her. 'And now if my husband will go and buy some cherries for us, I have got some money.'

In the friendliest manner I invited the colonel to go with me; but he so far forgot himself as to acknowledge the invitation by kicking out behind, and then lying down on his stomach on the grass, pulling it up and chewing it. When I came back, however, Alice had nearly brought him out of his vexation, and was soothing him by telling him how soon we should all be ninety.

As we sat under the willow-tree and ate the cherries (fair, for Alice shared them out), we played at being ninety. Nettie complained that she had a bone in her old back, and it made her hobble; and Alice sang a song in an old woman's way, but it was very pretty, and we were all merry. At least, I don't know about merry exactly, but all comfortable.

There was a most tremendous lot of cherries; and Alice always had with her some neat little bag or box or case to hold things. In it that night was a tiny wine glass. So Alice and Nettie said they would make some cherry-wine to drink our love at parting.

Each of us had a glassful, and it was delicious; and each of us drank the toast, 'Our love at parting.' The colonel drank his wine last; and it got into my head directly that it got into his directly. Anyhow, his eyes rolled immediately after he had turned the glass upside down; and he took me on one side and proposed in a hoarse whisper, that we should, 'Cut 'em out still.'

'How did he mean?' I asked my lawless friend.

'Cut our brides out,' said the colonel, 'and then cut our way, without going down a single turning, bang to the Spanish main!'

We might have tried it, though I didn't think it would answer; only we looked round and saw that there was nothing but moonlight under the willow-tree, and that our pretty, pretty wives were gone. We burst out crying. The colonel gave in second, and came to first; but he gave in strong.

We were ashamed of our red eyes, and hung about for half an hour to whiten them. Likewise a piece of chalk round the rims, I doing the colonel's, and he mine, but afterwards found in the bedroom looking-glass not natural, besides inflammation. Our conversation turned on being ninety. The colonel told me he had a pair of boots that wanted soling and heeling; but he thought it hardly worth while to mention it to his father, as he himself should so soon be ninety, when he thought shoes would be more convenient. The colonel also told me, with his hand upon his hip, that he felt himself already getting on in life and turning rheumatic. And I told him the same. And when they said at our house at supper (they are always bothering about something) that I stooped, I felt so glad!

This is the end of the beginning-part that you were to believe most.

PART TWO

Romance from the Pen of
Miss Alice Rainbird – Aged Seven

THERE WAS ONCE a king, and he had a queen; and he was the manliest of his sex, and she was the loveliest of hers. The king was, in his private profession, under government. The queen's father had been a medical man out of town.

They had nineteen children, and were always having more. Seventeen of these children took care of the baby; and Alicia, the eldest, took care of them all. Their ages varied from seven years to seven months.

Let us now resume our story.

One day the king was going to the office, when he stopped at the fishmonger's to buy a pound and a half of salmon, not too near the tail, which the queen (who was a careful housekeeper) had requested him to send home. Mr Pickles, the fishmonger, said, 'Certainly, sir; is there any other article? Good-morning.'

The king went on towards the office in a melancholy mood; for quarter-day was such a long way off, and several of the dear children were growing out of their clothes. He had not proceeded far, when Mr Pickles's errand-boy came running after him, and said, 'Sir, you didn't notice the old lady in our shop.'

'What old lady?' enquired the king. 'I saw none.'

Now the king had not seen any old lady, because this old lady had been invisible to him, though visible to Mr Pickles's boy. Probably because he messed and splashed the water about to that degree, and flopped the pairs of soles down in that violent manner, that, if she had not been visible to him, he would have spoilt her clothes.

Just then the old lady came trotting up. She was dressed in shot-silk of the richest quality, smelling of dried lavender.

'King Watkins I, I believe?' said the old lady.

'Watkins,' replied the king, 'is my name.'

'Papa, if I am not mistaken, of the beautiful Princess Alicia?' said the old lady.

'And of eighteen other darlings,' replied the king.

'Listen. You are going to the office,' said the old lady.

It instantly flashed upon the king that she must be a fairy, or how could she know that?

'You are right,' said the old lady, answering his thoughts. 'I am the good Fairy Grandmarina. Attend! When you return home to dinner, politely invite the Princess Alicia to have some of the salmon you bought just now.'

'It may disagree with her,' said the king.

The old lady became so very angry at this absurd idea, that the king was quite alarmed, and humbly begged her pardon.

'We hear a great deal too much about this thing disagreeing, and that thing disagreeing,' said the old lady, with the greatest contempt it was possible to express. 'Don't be greedy. I think you want it all yourself.'

The king hung his head under this reproof, and said he wouldn't talk about things disagreeing any more.

'Be good, then,' said the Fairy Grandmarina, 'and don't. When the beautiful Princess Alicia consents to partake of the salmon – as I think she will – you will find she will leave a fish-bone on her plate. Tell her to dry it, and to rub it, and to polish it till it shines like mother-of-pearl, and to take care of it as a present from me.'

'Is that all?' asked the king.

'Don't be impatient, sir,' returned the Fairy Grandmarina, scolding him severely. 'Don't catch people short, before they have done speaking. Just the way with you grown-up persons. You are always doing it.'

The king again hung his head, and said he wouldn't do so any more.

'Be good, then,' said the Fairy Grandmarina, 'and don't! Tell the Princess Alicia, with my love, that the fish-bone is a magic present which can only be used once; but that it will bring her, that once, whatever she wishes for, *provided she wishes for it at the right time*. That is the message. Take care of it.'

The king was beginning, 'Might I ask the reason?' when the fairy became absolutely furious.

'*Will* you be good, sir?' she exclaimed, stamping her foot on the ground. 'The reason for this, and the reason for that, indeed! You are always wanting the reason. No reason. There! Hoity toity me! I am sick of your grown-up reasons.'

The king was extremely frightened by the old lady's flying into such a passion, and said he was very sorry to have offended her, and he wouldn't ask for reasons any more.

'Be good, then,' said the old lady, 'and don't!'

With those words, Grandmarina vanished, and the king went on and on and on, till he came to the office. There he wrote and wrote and wrote, till it was time to go home again. Then he politely invited the Princess Alicia, as the fairy had directed him, to partake of the salmon. And when she had enjoyed it very much, he saw the fish-bone on her plate, as the fairy had told him he would, and he delivered the fairy's message, and the Princess Alicia took care to dry the bone, and to rub it, and to polish it, till it shone like mother-of-pearl.

And so, when the queen was going to get up in the morning, she said, 'Oh, dear me, dear me; my head, my head!' and then she fainted away.

The Princess Alicia, who happened to be looking in at the chamber-door, asking about breakfast, was very much alarmed when she saw her royal mamma in this state, and she rang the bell for Peggy, which was the name of the lord chamberlain. But remembering where the smelling-bottle was, she climbed on a chair and got it; and after that she climbed on another chair by the bedside, and held the smelling-bottle to the queen's nose; and after that she jumped down and got some water; and after that she jumped up again and wetted the queen's forehead; and, in short, when the lord chamberlain came in, that dear old woman said to the little princess, 'What a trot you are! I couldn't have done it better myself!'

But that was not the worst of the good queen's illness. Oh, no! She was very ill indeed, for a long time. The Princess Alicia kept the seventeen young princes and princesses quiet, and dressed and undressed and danced the baby, and made the kettle boil, and heated the soup, and swept the hearth, and poured out the medicine, and nursed the queen, and did all that ever she could, and was as busy, busy, busy as busy could be; for there were not many servants at that palace for three reasons: because the king was short of money, because a rise in his office never seemed to come, and because quarter-day was so far off that it looked almost as far off and as little as one of the stars.

But on the morning when the queen fainted away, where was the magic fish-bone? Why, there it was in the Princess Alicia's pocket! She had almost taken it out to bring the queen to life again, when she put it back, and looked for the smelling-bottle.

After the queen had come out of her swoon that morning, and was dozing, the Princess Alicia hurried upstairs to tell a most particular secret to a most particularly confidential friend of hers, who was a duchess. People did suppose her to be a doll; but she was really a duchess, though nobody knew it except the princess.

This most particular secret was the secret about the magic fish-bone, the history of which was well known to the duchess, because the princess told her everything. The princess kneeled down by the bed on which the duchess was lying, full-dressed and wide awake, and whispered the secret to her. The duchess smiled and nodded. People might have supposed that she never smiled and nodded; but she often did, though nobody knew it except the princess.

Then the Princess Alicia hurried downstairs again, to keep watch in the queen's room. She often kept watch by herself in the queen's room; but every evening, while the illness lasted, she sat there watching with the king. And every evening the king sat looking at her with a cross look, wondering why she never brought out the magic fish-bone. As often as she noticed this, she ran upstairs, whispered the secret to the duchess over again, and said to the duchess besides, 'They think we children never have a reason or a meaning!' And the duchess, though the most fashionable duchess that ever was heard of, winked her eye.

'Alicia,' said the king, one evening, when she wished him good-night.

'Yes, papa.'

'What is become of the magic fish-bone?'

'In my pocket, papa!'

'I thought you had lost it?'

'Oh, no, papa!'

'Or forgotten it?'

'No, indeed, papa.'

And so another time the dreadful little snapping pug-dog, next door, made a rush at one of the young princes as he stood on the steps coming home from school, and terrified him out of his wits; and he put his hand through a pane of glass, and bled, bled, bled. When the seventeen other young princes and princesses saw him bleed, bleed, bleed, they were terrified out of their wits too, and screamed themselves black in their seventeen faces all at once. But the Princess Alicia put her hands over all their seventeen mouths, one after another, and persuaded them to be quiet because of the sick queen. And then she put the wounded prince's hand in a basin of fresh cold water, while they stared with their twice seventeen are thirty-four, put down four and carry three,[1] eyes, and then she looked in the hand for bits of glass, and there were fortunately no bits of glass there. And then she said to two chubby-legged princes, who were sturdy though small, 'Bring me in the royal rag-bag: I must snip and stitch and cut and contrive.' So these two young princes tugged at the royal rag-bag, and lugged it in; and the Princess Alicia sat down on the floor, with a large pair of scissors and a needle and thread, and snipped and stitched and cut and contrived, and made a bandage, and put it on, and it fitted beautifully; and so when it was all done, she saw the king her papa looking on by the door.

'Alicia.'

'Yes, papa.'

'What have you been doing?'

'Snipping, stitching, cutting and contriving, papa.'

'Where is the magic fish-bone?'

'In my pocket, papa.'

'I thought you had lost it?'

'Oh, no, papa.'

'Or forgotten it?'

'No, indeed, papa.'

After that, she ran upstairs to the duchess, and told her what had passed, and told her the secret over again; and the duchess shook her flaxen curls, and laughed with her rosy lips.

Well! and so another time the baby fell under the grate. The seventeen young princes and princesses were used to it; for they were almost always falling under the grate or down the stairs; but the baby was not used to it yet, and it gave him a swelled face and a black eye. The way the poor little darling came to tumble was that he was out of the Princess Alicia's lap just as she was sitting, in a great coarse apron that quite smothered her, in front of the kitchen-fire, beginning to peel the turnips for the broth for dinner; and the way she came to be doing that was that the king's cook had run away that morning with her own true love, who was a very tall but very tipsy soldier. Then the seventeen young princes and princesses, who cried at everything that happened, cried and roared. But the Princess Alicia (who couldn't help crying a little herself) quietly called to them to be still, on account of not throwing back the queen upstairs, who was fast getting well, and said, 'Hold your tongues, you wicked little monkeys, every one of you, while I examine baby!' Then she examined baby, and found that he hadn't broken anything; and she held cold iron to his poor dear eye, and smoothed his poor dear face, and he presently fell asleep in her arms. Then she said to the seventeen princes and princesses, 'I am afraid to let him down yet, lest he should wake and feel pain; be good, and you shall all be cooks.' They jumped for joy when they heard that, and began making themselves cooks' caps out of old newspapers. So to one she gave the salt-box, and to one she gave the barley, and to one she gave the herbs, and to one she gave the turnips, and to one she gave the carrots, and to one she gave the onions, and to one she gave the spice-box, till they were all cooks, and all running about at work, she sitting in the middle, smothered in the great coarse apron, nursing baby. By and by the broth was done; and the baby woke up, smiling, like an angel, and was trusted to the sedatest princess to hold, while the other princes and princesses were squeezed into a far-off corner to look at the Princess Alicia turning out the saucepanful of broth, for fear (as they were always getting into trouble) they should get splashed and scalded. When the broth came tumbling out, steaming beautifully, and smelling like a nosegay good to eat, they clapped their hands. That made the baby clap his hands; and that, and his looking as if he had a comic toothache, made all the princes and princesses laugh. So the Princess Alicia said, 'Laugh and be good; and after dinner we will make him a nest on the floor in a corner, and he shall sit in his nest and see a dance of eighteen cooks.' That delighted the young princes and princesses, and they ate up all the broth, and washed up all the plates and dishes, and cleared away, and pushed the table into a corner; and then they in their cooks' caps, and the Princess Alicia in the smothering coarse apron that belonged to the cook that had run away with her own true love that was the very tall but very tipsy soldier, danced a dance of eighteen cooks before the angelic baby, who forgot his swelled face and his black eye, and crowed with joy.

And so then, once more the Princess Alicia saw King Watkins I, her father, standing in the doorway looking on, and he said, 'What have you been doing, Alicia?'

'Cooking and contriving, papa.'

'What else have you been doing, Alicia?'

'Keeping the children light-hearted, papa.'

'Where is the magic fish-bone, Alicia?

'In my pocket, papa.'

'I thought you had lost it?'

'Oh, no, papa!'

'Or forgotten it?'

'No, indeed, papa.'

The king then sighed so heavily, and seemed so low-spirited, and sat down so miserably, leaning his head upon his hand, and his elbow upon the kitchen-table pushed away in the corner, that the seventeen princes and princesses crept softly out of the kitchen, and left him alone with the Princess Alicia and the angelic baby.

'What is the matter, papa?'

'I am dreadfully poor, my child.'

'Have you no money at all, papa?'

'None, my child.'

'Is there no way of getting any, papa?'

'No way,' said the king. 'I have tried very hard, and I have tried all ways.'

When she heard those last words, the Princess Alicia began to put her hand into the pocket where she kept the magic fish-bone.

'Papa,' said she, 'when we have tried very hard, and tried all ways, we must have done our very, very best?'

'No doubt, Alicia.'

'When we have done our very, very best, papa, and that is not enough, then I think the right time must have come for asking help of others.' This was the very secret connected with the magic fish-bone, which she had found out for herself from the good Fairy Grandmarina's words, and which she had so often whispered to her beautiful and fashionable friend, the duchess.

So she took out of her pocket the magic fish-bone, that had been dried and rubbed and polished till it shone like mother-of-pearl; and she gave it one little kiss, and wished it was quarter-day. And immediately it *was* quarter-day; and the king's quarter's salary came rattling down the chimney, and bounced into the middle of the floor.

But this was not half of what happened – no, not a quarter; for immediately afterwards the good Fairy Grandmarina came riding in, in a carriage and four (peacocks), with Mr Pickles's boy up behind, dressed in silver and gold, with a cocked-hat, powdered-hair, pink silk stockings, a jewelled cane and a nosegay. Down jumped Mr Pickles's boy, with his cocked-hat in his hand, and wonderfully polite (being entirely changed by enchantment), and handed Grandmarina out; and there she stood, in her rich shot-silk smelling of dried lavender, fanning herself with a sparkling fan.

'Alicia, my dear,' said this charming old fairy, 'how do you do? I hope I see you pretty well? Give me a kiss.'

The Princess Alicia embraced her; and then Grandmarina turned to the king, and said rather sharply, 'Are you good?' The king said he hoped so.

'I suppose you know the reason *now*, why my god-daughter here,' kissing the princess again, 'did not apply to the fish-bone sooner?' said the fairy.

The king made a shy bow.

'Ah! but you didn't *then*?' said the fairy.

The king made a shyer bow.

'Any more reasons to ask for?' said the fairy.

The king said no, and he was very sorry.

'Be good, then,' said the fairy, 'and live happy ever afterwards.'

Then Grandmarina waved her fan, and the queen came in most splendidly dressed; and the seventeen young princes and princesses, no longer grown out of their clothes, came in, newly fitted out from top to toe, with tucks in everything to admit of its being let out. After that, the fairy tapped the Princess Alicia with her fan, and the smothering coarse apron flew away, and she appeared exquisitely dressed, like a little bride, with a wreath of orange-flowers and a silver veil. After that, the kitchen dresser changed of itself into a wardrobe, made of beautiful woods and gold and looking glass, which was full of dresses of all sorts, all for her and all exactly fitting her. After that, the angelic baby came in, running alone, with his face and eye not a bit the worse, but much the better. Then Grandmarina begged to be introduced to the duchess; and, when the duchess was brought down, many compliments passed between them.

A little whispering took place between the fairy and the duchess; and then the fairy said out loud, 'Yes, I thought she would have told you.' Grandmarina then turned to the king and queen, and said, 'We are going in search of Prince Certainpersonio. The pleasure of your company is requested at church in half an hour precisely.' So she and the Princess Alicia got into the carriage; and Mr Pickles's boy handed in the duchess, who sat by herself on the opposite seat; and then Mr Pickles's boy put up the steps and got up behind, and the peacocks flew away with their tails behind.

Prince Certainpersonio was sitting by himself, eating barley-sugar, and waiting to be ninety. When he saw the peacocks, followed by the carriage, coming in at the window it immediately occurred to him that something uncommon was going to happen.

'Prince,' said Grandmarina, 'I bring you your bride.' The moment the fairy said those words, Prince Certainpersonio's face left off being sticky, and his jacket and corduroys changed to peach-bloom velvet, and his hair curled, and a cap and feather flew in like a bird and settled on his head. He got into the carriage by the fairy's invitation; and there he renewed his acquaintance with the duchess, whom he had seen before.

In the church were the prince's relations and friends, and the Princess Alicia's relations and friends, and the seventeen princes and princesses, and the baby, and a crowd of the neighbours. The marriage was beautiful beyond expression. The duchess was brides-maid, and beheld the ceremony from the pulpit, where she was supported by the cushion of the desk.

Grandmarina gave a magnificent wedding-feast afterwards, in which there was everything and more to eat, and everything and more to drink. The wedding-cake was delicately ornamented with white satin ribbons, frosted silver and white lilies, and was forty-two yards round.

When Grandmarina had drunk her love to the young couple, and Prince Certainpersonio had made a speech, and everybody had cried, Hip, hip, hip, hurrah! Grandmarina announced to the king and queen that in future there would be eight quarter-days in every year, except in leap-year, when there would be ten. She then turned to Certainpersonio and Alicia, and said, 'My dears, you will have thirty-five children, and they will all be good and beautiful. Seventeen of your children will be boys, and eighteen will be girls. The hair of the whole of your children will curl naturally. They will never have the measles, and will have recovered from the whooping-cough[2] before being born.'

On hearing such good news, everybody cried out, 'Hip, hip, hip, hurrah!' again.

'It only remains,' said Grandmarina in conclusion, 'to make an end of the fish-bone.'

So she took it from the hand of the Princess Alicia, and it instantly flew down the throat of the dreadful little snapping pug-dog, next door, and choked him, and he expired in convulsions.

PART THREE

Romance from the Pen of Lieutenant-Colonel Robin Redforth – Aged Nine

THE SUBJECT of our present narrative would appear to have devoted himself to the pirate profession at a comparatively early age. We find him in command of a splendid schooner of one hundred guns loaded to the muzzle, ere yet he had had a party in honour of his tenth birthday.

It seems that our hero, considering himself spited by a Latin-grammar master, demanded the satisfaction due from one man of honour to another. Not getting it, he privately withdrew his haughty spirit from such low company, bought a second-hand pocket-pistol, folded up some sandwiches in a paper bag, made a bottle of Spanish liquorice-water[3] and entered on a career of valour.

It were tedious to follow Boldheart (for such was his name) through the commencing stages of his story. Suffice it, that we find him bearing the rank of Captain Boldheart, reclining in full uniform on a crimson hearth-rug spread out upon the quarterdeck of his schooner the *Beauty*, in the China Seas. It was a lovely evening; and, as his crew lay grouped about him, he favoured them with the following melody:

> 'Oh landsmen are folly!
> Oh pirates are jolly!
> Oh diddleum Dolly,
>   Di!
> [*Chorus*] Heave yo.'

The soothing effect of these animated sounds floating over the waters, as the common sailors united their rough voices to take up the rich tones of Boldheart, may be more easily conceived than described.

It was under these circumstances that the lookout at the masthead gave the word, 'Whales!'

All was now activity.

'Where away?' cried Captain Boldheart, starting up.

'On the larboard bow, sir,' replied the fellow at the masthead, touching his hat. For such was the height of discipline on board of the *Beauty*, that, even at that height, he was obliged to mind it, or be shot through the head.

'This adventure belongs to me,' said Boldheart. 'Boy, my harpoon. Let no man follow;' and leaping alone into his boat, the captain rowed with admirable dexterity in the direction of the monster.

All was now excitement.

'He nears him!' said an elderly seaman, following the captain through his spyglass.

'He strikes him!' said another seaman, a mere stripling, but also with a spyglass.

'He tows him towards us!' said another seaman, a man in the full vigour of life, but also with a spyglass.

In fact, the captain was seen approaching, with the huge bulk following. We will not dwell on the deafening cries of 'Boldheart! Boldheart!' with which he was received, when, carelessly leaping on the quarterdeck, he presented his prize to his men. They afterwards made two thousand four hundred and seventeen pound ten and sixpence by it.

Ordering the sail to be braced up, the captain now stood west-north-west. The *Beauty* flew rather than floated over the dark blue waters. Nothing particular occurred for a fortnight, except taking, with considerable slaughter, four Spanish galleons, and a snow[4] from South America, all richly laden. Inaction began to tell upon the spirits of the men. Captain Boldheart called all hands aft, and said, 'My lads, I hear there are discontented ones among ye. Let any such stand forth.'

After some murmuring, in which the expressions, 'Ay, ay, sir!' 'Union Jack,' 'Avast,' 'Starboard,' 'Port,' 'Bowsprit,' and similar indications of a mutinous undercurrent, though subdued, were audible, Bill Boozey, captain of the foretop, came out from the rest. His form was that of a giant, but he quailed under the captain's eye.

'What are your wrongs?' said the captain.

'Why, d'ye see, Captain Boldheart,' replied the towering mariner, 'I've sailed, man and boy, for many a year, but I never yet know'd the milk served out for the ship's company's teas to be so sour as 'tis aboard this craft.'

At this moment the thrilling cry, 'Man overboard!' announced to the astonished crew that Boozey, in stepping back, as the captain (in mere thoughtfulness) laid his hand upon the faithful pocket-pistol which he wore in his belt, had lost his balance and was struggling with the foaming tide.

All was now stupefaction.

But with Captain Boldheart, to throw off his uniform coat, regardless of the various rich orders with which it was decorated, and to plunge into the sea after the drowning giant, was the work of a moment. Maddening was the excitement when boats were lowered; intense the joy when the captain was seen holding up the drowning man with his teeth; deafening the cheering when both were restored to the main deck of the *Beauty*. And, from the instant of his changing his wet clothes for dry ones, Captain Boldheart had no such devoted though humble friend as William Boozey.

Boldheart now pointed to the horizon, and called the attention of his crew to the taper spars of a ship lying snug in harbour under the guns of a fort.

'She shall be ours at sunrise,' said he. 'Serve out a double allowance of grog, and prepare for action.'

All was now preparation.

When morning dawned, after a sleepless night, it was seen that the stranger was crowding on all sail to come out of the harbour and offer battle. As the two ships came nearer to each other, the stranger fired a gun and hoisted Roman colours. Boldheart then perceived her to be the Latin-grammar master's bark. Such indeed she was, and had been tacking about the world in unavailing pursuit, from the time of his first taking to a roving life.

Boldheart now addressed his men, promising to blow them up if he should feel convinced that their reputation required it, and giving orders that the Latin-grammar master should be taken alive. He then dismissed them to their quarters, and the fight began with a broadside from the *Beauty*. She then veered around, and poured in another. The *Scorpion* (so was the bark of the Latin-grammar master appropriately called) was not slow to return her fire; and a terrific cannonading ensued, in which the guns of the *Beauty* did tremendous execution.

The Latin-grammar master was seen upon the poop, in the midst of the smoke and fire, encouraging his men. To do him justice, he was no craven, though his white hat, his short grey trousers, and his long snuff-coloured surtout reaching to his heels (the self-same coat in which he had spited Boldheart), contrasted most unfavourably with the brilliant uniform of the latter. At this moment, Boldheart, seizing a pike and putting himself at the head of his men, gave the word to board.

A desperate conflict ensued in the hammock-nettings – or some-where in about that direction – until the Latin-grammar master, having all his masts gone, his hull and rigging shot through, and seeing Boldheart slashing a path towards him, hauled down his flag himself, gave up his sword to Boldheart, and asked for quarter. Scarce had he been put into the captain's boat, ere the *Scorpion* went down with all on board.

On Captain Boldheart's now assembling his men, a circumstance occurred. He found it necessary with one blow of his cutlass to kill the cook, who, having lost his brother in the late action, was making at the Latin-grammar master in an infuriated state, intent on his destruction with a carving-knife.

Captain Boldheart then turned to the Latin-grammar master, severely reproaching him with his perfidy, and put it to his crew what they considered that a master who spited a boy deserved.

They answered with one voice, 'Death.'

'It may be so,' said the captain; 'but it shall never be said that Boldheart stained his hour of triumph with the blood of his enemy. Prepare the cutter.'

The cutter was immediately prepared.

'Without taking your life,' said the captain, 'I must yet for ever deprive you of the power of spiting other boys. I shall turn you adrift in this boat. You will find in her two oars, a compass, a bottle of rum, a small cask of water, a piece of pork, a bag of biscuit, and my Latin grammar. Go! and spite the natives, if you can find any.'

Deeply conscious of this bitter sarcasm, the unhappy wretch was put into the cutter, and was soon left far behind. He made no effort to row, but was seen lying on his back with his legs up, when last made out by the ship's telescopes.

A stiff breeze now beginning to blow, Captain Boldheart gave orders to keep her sou'-sou'-west,[5] easing her a little during the night by falling off a point or two west by west, or even by south-west, if she complained much. He then retired for the night, having in truth much need of repose. In addition to the fatigues he had undergone, this brave officer had received sixteen wounds in the engagement, but had not mentioned it.

In the morning a white squall came on, and was succeeded by other squalls of various colours. It thundered and lightened heavily for six weeks. Hurricanes then set in for two months. Waterspouts and tornadoes followed. The oldest sailor on board – and he was a very old one – had never seen such weather. The *Beauty* lost all idea where she was, and the carpenter reported six feet two of water in the hold. Everybody fell senseless at the pumps every day.

Provisions now ran very low. Our hero put the crew on short allowance, and put himself on shorter allowance than any man in the ship. But his spirit kept him fat. In this extremity, the gratitude of Boozey, the captain of the foretop, whom our readers may remember, was truly affecting. The loving though lowly William repeatedly requested to be killed and preserved for the captain's table.

We now approach a change of affairs.

One day during a gleam of sunshine, and when the weather had moderated, the man at the masthead – too weak now to touch his hat, besides its having been blown away – called out, 'Savages!'

All was now expectation.

Presently fifteen hundred canoes, each paddled by twenty savages, were seen advancing in excellent order. They were of a light green colour (the savages were), and sang, with great energy, the following strain:

> Choo a choo a choo tooth.
>   Muntch, muntch. Nycey!
> Choo a choo a choo tooth.
>   Muntch, muntch. Nycey!

As the shades of night were by this time closing in, these expressions were supposed to embody this simple people's views of the evening hymn. But it too soon appeared that the song was a translation of 'For what we are going to receive',[6] &c.

The chief, imposingly decorated with feathers of lively colours, and having the majestic appearance of a fighting parrot, no sooner understood (he understood English perfectly) that the ship was the *Beauty*, Captain Boldheart, than he fell upon his face on the deck, and could not be persuaded to rise until the captain had lifted him up, and told him he wouldn't hurt him. All the rest of the savages also fell on their faces with marks of terror, and had also to be lifted up one by one. Thus the fame of the great Boldheart had gone before him, even among these children of nature.

Turtles and oysters were now produced in astonishing numbers; and on these and yams the people made a hearty meal. After dinner the chief told Captain Boldheart that there was better feeding up at the village, and that he would be glad to take him and his officers there. Apprehensive of treachery, Boldheart ordered his boat's crew to attend him completely armed. And well were it for other commanders if their precautions – But let us not anticipate.

When the canoes arrived at the beach, the darkness of the night was illumined by the light of an immense fire. Ordering his boat's crew (with the intrepid though illiterate William at their head) to keep close and be upon their guard, Boldheart bravely went on, arm in arm with the chief.

But how to depict the captain's surprise when he found a ring of savages singing in chorus that barbarous translation of 'For what we are going to receive', &c., which has been given above, and dancing hand in hand round the Latin-grammar master, in a hamper with his head shaved, while two savages floured him, before putting him to the fire to be cooked!

Boldheart now took counsel with his officers on the course to be adopted. In the meantime, the miserable captive never ceased begging pardon and imploring to be delivered. On the generous Boldheart's proposal, it was at length resolved that he should not be cooked, but should be allowed to remain raw, on two conditions, namely:

1. That he should never, under any circumstances, presume to teach any boy anything any more.
2. That, if taken back to England, he should pass his life in travelling to find out boys who wanted their exercises done, and should do their exercises for those boys for nothing, and never say a word about it.

Drawing the sword from its sheath, Boldheart swore him to these conditions on its shining blade. The prisoner wept bitterly, and appeared acutely to feel the errors of his past career.

The captain then ordered his boat's crew to make ready for a volley, and, after firing, to reload quickly. 'And expect a score or two on ye to go head over heels,' murmured William Boozey; 'for I'm a-looking at ye.' With those words, the derisive though deadly William took a good aim.

'Fire!'

The ringing voice of Boldheart was lost in the report of the guns and the screeching of the savages. Volley after volley awakened the numerous echoes. Hundreds of savages were killed, hundreds wounded, and thousands ran howling into the woods. The Latin-grammar master had a spare nightcap lent him, and a long-tail coat, which he wore hind side before. He presented a ludicrous though pitiable appearance, and serve him right.

We now find Captain Boldheart, with this rescued wretch on board, standing off for other islands. At one of these, not a cannibal island, but a pork and vegetable one, he married (only in fun on his part) the king's daughter. Here he rested some time, receiving from the natives great quantities of precious stones, gold dust, elephants' teeth, and sandalwood, and getting very rich. This, too, though he almost every day made presents of enormous value to his men.

The ship being at length as full as she could hold of all sorts of valuable things, Boldheart gave orders to weigh the anchor, and turn the *Beauty*'s head towards England. These orders were obeyed with three cheers; and ere the sun went down full many a hornpipe had been danced on deck by the uncouth though agile William.

We next find Captain Boldheart about three leagues off Madeira,[7] surveying through his spyglass a stranger of suspicious appearance making sail towards him. On his firing a gun ahead of her to bring her to, she ran up a flag, which he instantly recognised as the flag from the mast in the back-garden at home.

Inferring from this that his father had put to sea to seek his long-lost son, the captain sent his own boat on board the stranger to enquire if this was so, and, if so, whether his father's intentions were strictly honourable. The boat came back with a present of greens and fresh meat, and reported that the stranger was the *Family*, of twelve hundred tons, and had not only the captain's father on board, but also his mother, with the majority of his aunts and uncles, and all his cousins. It was further reported to Boldheart that the whole of these relations had expressed themselves in a becoming manner, and were anxious to embrace him and thank him for the glorious credit he had done them. Boldheart at once invited them to breakfast next morning on board the *Beauty*, and gave orders for a brilliant ball that should last all day.

It was in the course of the night that the captain discovered the hopelessness of reclaiming the Latin-grammar master. That thankless traitor was found out, as the two ships lay near each other, communicating with the *Family* by signals, and offering to give up Boldheart. He was hanged at the yardarm the first thing in the morning, after having it impressively pointed out to him by Boldheart that this was what spiters came to.

The meeting between the captain and his parents was attended with tears. His uncles and aunts would have attended their meeting with tears too, but he wasn't going to stand that. His cousins were very much astonished by the size of his ship and the discipline of his men, and were greatly overcome by the splendour of his uniform. He kindly conducted them round the vessel, and pointed out everything worthy of notice. He also fired his hundred guns, and found it amusing to witness their alarm.

The entertainment surpassed everything ever seen on board ship and lasted from ten in the morning until seven the next morning. Only one disagreeable incident occurred. Captain Boldheart found himself obliged to put his cousin Tom in irons, for being disrespectful. On the boy's promising amendment, however, he was humanely released after a few hours' close confinement.

Boldheart now took his mother down into the great cabin, and asked after the young lady with whom, it was well known to the world, he was in love. His mother replied that the object of his affections was then at school at Margate,[8] for the benefit of sea-bathing (it was the month of September), but that she feared the young lady's friends were still opposed to the union. Boldheart at once resolved, if necessary, to bombard the town.

Taking the command of his ship with this intention, and putting all but fighting men on board the *Family*, with orders to that vessel to keep in company, Boldheart soon anchored in Margate Roads.[9] Here he went ashore well armed, and attended by his boat's crew (at their head the faithful though ferocious William), and demanded to see the mayor, who came out of his office.

'Dost know the name of yon ship, mayor?' asked Boldheart fiercely.

'No,' said the mayor, rubbing his eyes, which he could scarce believe, when he saw the goodly vessel riding at anchor.

'She is named the *Beauty*,' said the captain.

'Hah!' exclaimed the mayor, with a start. 'And you, then, are Captain Boldheart?'

'The same.'

A pause ensued. The mayor trembled.

'Now, mayor,' said the captain, 'choose! Help me to my bride, or be bombarded.'

The mayor begged for two hours' grace, in which to make enquiries respecting the young lady. Boldheart accorded him but one; and during that one placed William Boozey sentry over him, with a drawn sword, and instructions to accompany him wherever he went, and to run him through the body if he showed a sign of playing false.

At the end of the hour the mayor reappeared more dead than alive, closely waited on by Boozey more alive than dead.

'Captain,' said the mayor, 'I have ascertained that the young lady is going to bathe. Even now she waits her turn for a machine.[10] The tide is low, though rising. I, in one of our town-boats,[11] shall not be suspected. When she comes forth in her bathing-dress into the shallow water from behind the hood of the machine, my boat shall intercept her and prevent her return. Do you the rest.'

'Mayor,' returned Captain Boldheart, 'thou hast saved thy town.'

The captain then signalled his boat to take him off, and, steering her himself, ordered her crew to row towards the bathing-ground, and there to rest upon their oars. All happened as had been arranged. His lovely bride came forth, the mayor glided in behind her, she became confused, and had floated out of her depth, when, with one skilful touch of the rudder and one quivering stroke from the boat's crew, her adoring Boldheart held her in his strong arms. There her shrieks of terror were changed to cries of joy.

Before the *Beauty* could get underway, the hoisting of all the flags in the town and harbour, and the ringing of all the bells, announced to the brave Boldheart that he had nothing to fear. He therefore determined to be married on the spot, and signalled for a clergyman and clerk, who came off promptly in a sailing-boat named the *Skylark*.[12] Another great entertainment was then given on board the *Beauty*, in the midst of which the mayor was called out by a messenger. He returned with the news that government had sent down to know whether Captain Boldheart, in acknowledgment of the great services he had done his country by being a pirate, would consent to be made a lieutenant-colonel. For himself he would have spurned the worthless boon; but his bride wished it, and he consented.

Only one thing further happened before the good ship *Family* was dismissed, with rich presents to all on board. It is painful to record (but such is human nature in some cousins) that Captain Boldheart's unmannerly cousin Tom was actually tied up to receive three dozen with a rope's end 'for cheekiness and making game', when Captain Boldheart's lady begged for him, and he was spared. The *Beauty* then refitted, and the captain and his bride departed for the Indian Ocean to enjoy themselves for evermore.

PART FOUR

Romance from the Pen of
Miss Nettie Ashford – Aged Half-Past Six

THERE IS A COUNTRY, which I will show you when I get into maps,[13] where the children have everything their own way. It is a most delightful country to live in. The grown-up people are obliged to obey the children, and are never allowed to sit up to supper, except on their birthdays. The children order them to make jam and jelly and marmalade, and tarts and pies and puddings, and all manner of pastry. If they say they won't, they are put in the corner[14] till they do. They are sometimes allowed to have some; but when they have some, they generally have powders given them afterwards.

One of the inhabitants of this country, a truly sweet young creature of the name of Mrs Orange, had the misfortune to be sadly plagued by her numerous family. Her parents required a great deal of looking after, and they had connections and companions who were scarcely ever out of mischief. So Mrs Orange said to herself, 'I really cannot be troubled with these torments any longer: I must put them all to school.'

Mrs Orange took off her pinafore, and dressed herself very nicely, and took up her baby, and went out to call upon another lady of the name of Mrs Lemon, who kept a preparatory establishment.[15] Mrs Orange stood upon the scraper to pull at the bell, and give a ring-ting-ting.

Mrs Lemon's neat little housemaid, pulling up her socks as she came along the passage, answered the ring-ting-ting.

'Good-morning,' said Mrs Orange. 'Fine day. How do you do? Mrs Lemon at home?'

'Yes, ma'am.'

'Will you say Mrs Orange and baby?'

'Yes, ma'am. Walk in.'

Mrs Orange's baby was a very fine one, and real wax all over. Mrs Lemon's baby was leather and bran. However, when Mrs Lemon came into the drawing-room with her baby in her arms, Mrs

Orange said politely, 'Good-morning. Fine day. How do you do? And how is little Tootleumboots?'

'Well, she is but poorly. Cutting her teeth, ma'am,' said Mrs Lemon.

'Oh, indeed, ma'am!' said Mrs Orange. 'No fits, I hope?'

'No, ma'am.'

'How many teeth has she, ma'am?'

'Five, ma'am.'

'My Emilia, ma'am, has eight,' said Mrs Orange. 'Shall we lay them on the mantelpiece side by side, while we converse?'

'By all means, ma'am,' said Mrs Lemon. 'Hem!'

'The first question is, ma'am,' said Mrs Orange, 'I don't bore you?'

'Not in the least, ma'am,' said Mrs Lemon. 'Far from it, I assure you.'

'Then pray *have* you,' said Mrs Orange – '*have* you any vacancies?'

'Yes, ma'am. How many might you require?'

'Why, the truth is, ma'am,' said Mrs Orange, 'I have come to the conclusion that my children' – oh, I forgot to say that they call the grown-up people children in that country! – 'that my children are getting positively too much for me. Let me see. Two parents, two intimate friends of theirs, one godfather, two godmothers, and an aunt. *Have* you as many as eight vacancies?'

'I have just eight, ma'am,' said Mrs Lemon.

'Most fortunate! Terms moderate, I think?'

'Very moderate, ma'am.'

'Diet good, I believe?'

'Excellent, ma'am.'

'Unlimited?'

'Unlimited.'

'Most satisfactory! Corporal punishment dispensed with?'

'Why, we do occasionally shake,' said Mrs Lemon, 'and we have slapped. But only in extreme cases.'

'*Could* I, ma'am,' said Mrs Orange – '*could* I see the establishment?'

'With the greatest of pleasure, ma'am,' said Mrs Lemon.

Mrs Lemon took Mrs Orange into the schoolroom, where there were a number of pupils. 'Stand up, children,' said Mrs Lemon; and they all stood up.

Mrs Orange whispered to Mrs Lemon, 'There is a pale, bald child, with red whiskers, in disgrace. Might I ask what he has done?'

'Come here, White,' said Mrs Lemon, 'and tell this lady what you have been doing.'

'Betting on horses,' said White sulkily.

'Are you sorry for it, you naughty child?' said Mrs Lemon.

'No,' said White. 'Sorry to lose, but shouldn't be sorry to win.'

'There's a vicious boy for you, ma'am,' said Mrs Lemon. 'Go along with you, sir. This is Brown, Mrs Orange. Oh, a sad case, Brown's! Never knows when he has had enough. Greedy. How is your gout, sir?'

'Bad,' said Brown.

'What else can you expect?' said Mrs Lemon. 'Your stomach is the size of two. Go and take exercise directly. Mrs Black, come here to me. Now, here is a child, Mrs Orange, ma'am, who is always at play. She can't be kept at home a single day together; always gadding about and spoiling her clothes. Play, play, play, play, from morning to night, and to morning again. How can she expect to improve?'

'Don't expect to improve,' sulked Mrs Black. 'Don't want to.'

'There is a specimen of her temper, ma'am,' said Mrs Lemon. 'To see her when she is tearing about, neglecting everything else, you would suppose her to be at least good-humoured. But bless you! ma'am, she is as pert and flouncing a minx as ever you met with in all your days!'

'You must have a great deal of trouble with them, ma'am,' said Mrs Orange.

'Ah, I have, indeed, ma'am!' said Mrs Lemon. 'What with their tempers, what with their quarrels, what with their never knowing what's good for them, and what with their always wanting to domineer, deliver me from these unreasonable children!'

'Well, I wish you good-morning, ma'am,' said Mrs Orange.

'Well, I wish you good-morning, ma'am,' said Mrs Lemon.

So Mrs Orange took up her baby and went home, and told the family that plagued her so that they were all going to be sent to school. They said they didn't want to go to school; but she packed up their boxes, and packed them off.

'Oh dear me, dear me! Rest and be thankful!' said Mrs Orange, throwing herself back in her little armchair. 'Those troublesome troubles are got rid of, please the pigs!'

Just then another lady, named Mrs Alicumpaine, came calling at the street-door with a ring-ting-ting.

'My dear Mrs Alicumpaine,' said Mrs Orange, 'how do you do? Pray stay to dinner. We have but a simple joint of sweet-stuff, followed by a plain dish of bread and treacle; but, if you will take us as you find us, it will be *so* kind!'

'Don't mention it,' said Mrs Alicumpaine. 'I shall be too glad. But what do you think I have come for, ma'am? Guess, ma'am.'

'I really cannot guess, ma'am,' said Mrs Orange.

'Why, I am going to have a small juvenile party tonight,' said Mrs Alicumpaine; 'and if you and Mr Orange and baby would but join us, we should be complete.'

'More than charmed, I am sure!' said Mrs Orange.

'So kind of you!' said Mrs Alicumpaine. 'But I hope the children won't bore you?'

'Dear things! Not at all,' said Mrs Orange. 'I dote upon them.'

Mr Orange here came home from the city; and he came, too, with a ring-ting-ting.

'James, love,' said Mrs Orange, 'you look tired. What has been doing in the city today?'

'Trap, bat and ball, my dear,' said Mr Orange, 'and it knocks a man up.'

'That dreadfully anxious City, ma'am,' said Mrs Orange to Mrs Alicumpaine; 'so wearing, is it not?'

'Oh, so trying!' said Mrs Alicumpaine. 'John has lately been speculating in the peg-top ring; and I often say to him at night, "John, *is* the result worth the wear and tear?" '

Dinner was ready by this time: so they sat down to dinner; and while Mr Orange carved the joint of sweet-stuff, he said, 'It's a poor heart that never rejoices. Jane, go down to the cellar, and fetch a bottle of the Upest ginger-beer.'

At teatime, Mr and Mrs Orange and baby and Mrs Alicumpaine went off to Mrs Alicumpaine's house. The children had not come yet; but the ballroom was ready for them, decorated with paper flowers.

'How very sweet!' said Mrs Orange. 'The dear things! How pleased they will be!'

'I don't care for children myself,' said Mr Orange, gaping.

'Not for girls?' said Mrs Alicumpaine. 'Come! you care for girls?'

Mr Orange shook his head, and gaped again. 'Frivolous and vain, ma'am.'

'My dear James,' cried Mrs Orange, who had been peeping about, 'do look here. Here's the supper for the darlings, ready laid in the room behind the folding-doors. Here's their little pickled salmon, I do declare! And here's their little salad, and their little roast beef and fowls, and their little pastry, and their wee, wee, wee champagne!'

'Yes, I thought it best, ma'am,' said Mrs Alicumpaine, 'that they should have their supper by themselves. Our table is in the corner here, where the gentlemen can have their wine glass of negus, and their egg sandwich, and their quiet game at beggar-my-neighbour, and look on. As for us, ma'am, we shall have quite enough to do to manage the company.'

'Oh, indeed, you may say so! Quite enough, ma'am,' said Mrs Orange.

The company began to come. The first of them was a stout boy, with a white topknot and spectacles. The housemaid brought him in and said, 'Compliments, and at what time was he to be fetched!' Mrs Alicumpaine said, 'Not a moment later than ten. How do you do, sir? Go and sit down.' Then a number of other children came; boys by themselves, and girls by themselves, and boys and girls together. They didn't behave at all well. Some of them looked through quizzing-glasses at others, and said, 'Who are those? Don't know them.' Some of them looked through quizzing-glasses[16] at others, and said, 'How do?' Some of them had cups of tea or coffee handed to them by others, and said, 'Thanks; much!' A good many boys stood about, and felt their shirt-collars. Four tiresome fat boys *would* stand in the doorway, and talk about the newspapers, till Mrs Alicumpaine went to them and said, 'My dears, I really cannot allow you to prevent people from coming in. I shall be truly sorry to do it; but, if you put yourself in everybody's way, I must positively send you home.' One boy, with a beard and a large white waistcoat, who stood straddling on the hearth-rug warming his coat-tails, *was* sent home. 'Highly incorrect, my dear,' said Mrs Alicumpaine, handing him out of the room, 'and I cannot permit it.'

There was a children's band – harp, cornet and piano – and Mrs Alicumpaine and Mrs Orange bustled among the children to persuade them to take partners and dance. But they were so obstinate! For quite a long time they would not be persuaded to take partners and dance. Most of the boys said, 'Thanks; much! But not at present.' And most of the rest of the boys said, 'Thanks; much! But never do.'

'Oh, these children are very wearing!' said Mrs Alicumpaine to Mrs Orange.

'Dear things! I dote upon them; but they *are* wearing,' said Mrs Orange to Mrs Alicumpaine.

At last they did begin in a slow and melancholy way to slide about to the music; though even then they wouldn't mind what they were told, but would have this partner, and wouldn't have that partner, and showed temper about it. And they wouldn't smile – no, not on any account they wouldn't; but, when the music stopped, went round and round the room in dismal twos, as if everybody else was dead.

'Oh, it's very hard indeed to get these vexing children to be entertained!' said Mrs Alicumpaine to Mrs Orange.

'I dote upon the darlings; but it is hard,' said Mrs Orange to Mrs Alicumpaine.

They were trying children, that's the truth. First, they wouldn't sing when they were asked; and then, when everybody fully believed they wouldn't, they would. 'If you serve us so any more, my love,' said Mrs Alicumpaine to a tall child, with a good deal of white back, in mauve silk trimmed with lace, 'it will be my painful privilege to offer you a bed, and to send you to it immediately.'

The girls were so ridiculously dressed, too, that they were in rags before supper. How could the boys help treading on their trains? And yet when their trains were trodden on, they often showed temper again, and looked as black, they did! However, they all seemed to be pleased when Mrs Alicumpaine said, 'Supper is ready, children!' And they went crowding and pushing in, as if they had had dry bread for dinner.

'How are the children getting on?' said Mr Orange to Mrs Orange, when Mrs Orange came to look after baby. Mrs Orange had left baby on a shelf near Mr Orange while he played at beggar-my-neighbour, and had asked him to keep his eye upon her now and then.

'Most charmingly, my dear!' said Mrs Orange. 'So droll to see their little flirtations and jealousies! Do come and look!'

'Much obliged to you, my dear,' said Mr Orange; 'but I don't care about children myself.'

So Mrs Orange, having seen that baby was safe, went back without Mr Orange to the room where the children were having supper.

'What are they doing now?' said Mrs Orange to Mrs Alicumpaine.

'They are making speeches, and playing at parliament,' said Mrs Alicumpaine to Mrs Orange.

On hearing this, Mrs Orange set off once more back again to Mr Orange, and said, 'James dear, do come. The children are playing at parliament.'

'Thank you, my dear,' said Mr Orange, 'but I don't care about parliament myself.'

So Mrs Orange went once again without Mr Orange to the room where the children were having supper, to see them playing at parliament. And she found some of the boys crying, 'Hear, hear, hear!' while other boys cried, 'No, no!' and others, 'Question!' 'Spoke!' and all sorts of nonsense that ever you heard. Then one of those tiresome fat boys who had stopped the doorway told them he was on his legs (as if they couldn't see that he wasn't on his head, or on his anything else) to explain, and that, with the permission of his honourable friend, if he would allow him to call him so (another tiresome boy bowed), he would proceed to explain. Then he went on for a long time in a sing-song (whatever he meant), did this troublesome fat boy, about that he held in his hand a glass; and about that he had come down to that house that night to discharge what he would call a public duty; and about that, on the present occasion, he would lay his hand (his other hand) upon his heart, and would tell honourable gentlemen that he was about to open the door to general approval. Then he opened the door by saying, 'To our hostess!' and everybody else said, 'To our hostess!' and then there were cheers. Then another tiresome boy started up in sing-song, and then half a dozen noisy and nonsensical boys at once. But at last Mrs Alicumpaine said, 'I cannot have this din. Now, children, you have played at parliament very nicely; but parliament gets tiresome after a little while, and it's time you left off, for you will soon be fetched.'

After another dance (with more tearing to rags than before supper), they began to be fetched; and you will be very glad to be told that the tiresome fat boy who had been on his legs was walked off first without any ceremony. When they were all gone, poor Mrs Alicumpaine dropped upon a sofa, and said to Mrs Orange, 'These children will be the death of me at last, ma'am – they will indeed!'

'I quite adore them, ma'am,' said Mrs Orange; 'but they *do* want variety.'

Mr Orange got his hat, and Mrs Orange got her bonnet and her baby, and they set out to walk home. They had to pass Mrs Lemon's preparatory establishment on their way.

'I wonder, James dear,' said Mrs Orange, looking up at the window, 'whether the precious children are asleep!'

'I don't care much whether they are or not, myself,' said Mr Orange.

'James dear!'

'You dote upon them, you know,' said Mr Orange. 'That's another thing.'

'I do,' said Mrs Orange rapturously. 'Oh, I *do*!'

'I don't,' said Mr Orange.

'But I was thinking, James love,' said Mrs Orange, pressing his arm, 'whether our dear, good, kind Mrs Lemon would like them to stay the holidays with her.'

'If she was paid for it, I daresay she would,' said Mr Orange.

'I adore them, James,' said Mrs Orange, 'but *suppose* we pay her, then!'

This was what brought that country to such perfection, and made it such a delightful place to live in. The grown-up people (that would be in other countries) soon left off being allowed any holidays after Mr and Mrs Orange tried the experiment; and the children (that would be in other countries) kept them at school as long as ever they lived, and made them do whatever they were told.

GEORGE SILVERMAN'S EXPLANATION

First Chapter

IT HAPPENED in this wise –

But, sitting with my pen in my hand looking at those words again, without descrying any hint in them of the words that should follow, it comes into my mind that they have an abrupt appearance. They may serve, however, if I let them remain, to suggest how very difficult I find it to begin to explain my explanation. An uncouth phrase: and yet I do not see my way to a better.

Second Chapter

IT HAPPENED in *this* wise –

But, looking at those words, and comparing them with my former opening, I find they are the self-same words repeated. This is the more surprising to me, because I employ them in quite a new connection. For indeed I declare that my intention was to discard the commencement I first had in my thoughts, and to give the preference to another of an entirely different nature, dating my explanation from an anterior period of my life. I will make a third trial, without erasing this second failure, protesting that it is not my design to conceal any of my infirmities, whether they be of head or heart.

Third Chapter

NOT AS YET directly aiming at how it came to pass, I will come upon it by degrees. The natural manner, after all, for God knows that is how it came upon me.

My parents were in a miserable condition of life, and my infant home was a cellar in Preston.[1] I recollect the sound of father's

Lancashire clogs[2] on the street pavement above, as being different in my young hearing from the sound of all other clogs; and I recollect that, when mother came down the cellar-steps, I used tremblingly to speculate on her feet having a good or an ill-tempered look – on her knees – on her waist – until finally her face came into view, and settled the question. From this it will be seen that I was timid, and that the cellar-steps were steep, and that the doorway was very low.

Mother had the gripe and clutch of poverty upon her face, upon her figure, and not least of all upon her voice. Her sharp and high-pitched words were squeezed out of her, as by the compression of bony fingers on a leathern bag; and she had a way of rolling her eyes about and about the cellar, as she scolded, that was gaunt and hungry. Father, with his shoulders rounded, would sit quiet on a three-legged stool, looking at the empty grate, until she would pluck the stool from under him, and bid him go bring some money home. Then he would dismally ascend the steps; and I, holding my ragged shirt and trousers together with a hand (my only braces), would feint and dodge from mother's pursuing grasp at my hair.

A worldly little devil was mother's usual name for me. Whether I cried for that I was in the dark, or for that it was cold, or for that I was hungry, or whether I squeezed myself into a warm corner when there was a fire, or ate voraciously when there was food, she would still say, 'Oh, you worldly little devil!' And the sting of it was that I quite well knew myself to be a worldly little devil. Worldly as to wanting to be housed and warmed, worldly as to wanting to be fed, worldly as to the greed with which I inwardly compared how much I got of those good things with how much father and mother got, when, rarely, those good things were going.

Sometimes they both went away seeking work; and then I would be locked up in the cellar for a day or two at a time. I was at my worldliest then. Left alone, I yielded myself up to a worldly yearning for enough of anything (except misery), and for the death of mother's father, who was a machine-maker at Birmingham,[3] and on whose decease, I had heard mother say, she would come into a whole courtful of houses 'if she had her rights'. Worldly little devil, I would stand about, musingly fitting my cold bare feet into cracked bricks and crevices of the damp cellar-floor – walking over my grandfather's body, so to speak, into the courtful of houses, and selling them for meat and drink, and clothes to wear.

At last a change came down into our cellar. The universal change came down even as low as that – so will it mount to any height on which a human creature can perch – and brought other changes with it.

We had a heap of I don't know what foul litter in the darkest corner, which we called 'the bed'. For three days mother lay upon it without getting up, and then began at times to laugh. If I had ever heard her laugh before, it had been so seldom that the strange sound frightened me. It frightened father too; and we took it by turns to give her water. Then she began to move her head from side to side, and sing. After that, she getting no better, father fell a-laughing and a-singing; and then there was only I to give them both water, and they both died.

Fourth Chapter

WHEN I WAS lifted out of the cellar by two men, of whom one came peeping down alone first, and ran away and brought the other, I could hardly bear the light of the street. I was sitting in the roadway, blinking at it, and at a ring of people collected around me, but not close to me, when, true to my character of worldly little devil, I broke silence by saying, 'I am hungry and thirsty!'

'Does he know they are dead?' asked one of another.

'Do you know your father and mother are both dead of fever?' asked a third of me severely.

'I don't know what it is to be dead. I supposed it meant that, when the cup rattled against their teeth and the water spilt over them. I am hungry and thirsty.' That was all I had to say about it.

The ring of people widened outward from the inner side as I looked around me; and I smelt vinegar, and what I know to be camphor,[4] thrown in towards where I sat. Presently someone put a great vessel of smoking vinegar on the ground near me; and then they all looked at me in silent horror as I ate and drank of what was brought for me. I knew at the time they had a horror of me, but I couldn't help it.

I was still eating and drinking, and a murmur of discussion had begun to arise respecting what was to be done with me next, when I heard a cracked voice somewhere in the ring say, 'My name is Hawkyard, Mr Verity Hawkyard, of West Bromwich.'[5] Then the ring split in one place; and a yellow-faced, peak-nosed gentleman, clad all in iron-grey to his gaiters, pressed forward with a policeman and another official of some sort. He came forward close to the vessel of smoking vinegar; from which he sprinkled himself carefully, and me copiously.

'He had a grandfather at Birmingham, this young boy, who is just dead too,' said Mr Hawkyard.

I turned my eyes upon the speaker, and said in a ravening manner, 'Where's his houses?'

'Hah! Horrible worldliness on the edge of the grave,' said Mr Hawkyard, casting more of the vinegar over me, as if to get my devil out of me. 'I have undertaken a slight – a very slight – trust in behalf of this boy; quite a voluntary trust: a matter of mere honour, if not of mere sentiment: still I have taken it upon myself, and it shall be (oh, yes, it shall be!) discharged.'

The bystanders seemed to form an opinion of this gentleman much more favourable than their opinion of me.

'He shall be taught,' said Mr Hawkyard, '(Oh, yes, he shall be taught!); but what is to be done with him for the present? He may be infected. He may disseminate infection.' The ring widened considerably. 'What is to be done with him?'

He held some talk with the two officials. I could distinguish no word save 'farmhouse'. There was another sound several times repeated, which was wholly meaningless in my ears then, but which I knew afterwards to be 'Hoghton Towers'.

'Yes,' said Mr Hawkyard. 'I think that sounds promising; I think that sounds hopeful. And he can be put by himself in a ward, for a night or two, you say?'

It seemed to be the police-officer who had said so; for it was he who replied, Yes! It was he, too, who finally took me by the arm, and walked me before him through the streets, into a whitewashed room in a bare building, where I had a chair to sit in, a table to sit at, an iron bedstead and good mattress to lie upon, and a rug and blanket to cover me. Where I had enough to eat, too, and was shown how to clean the tin porringer, in which it was conveyed to me, until it was as good as a looking-glass. Here, likewise, I was put in a bath, and had new clothes brought to me; and my old rags were burnt, and I was camphored and vinegared and disinfected in a variety of ways.

When all this was done – I don't know in how many days or how few, but it matters not – Mr Hawkyard stepped in at the door, remaining close to it, and said, 'Go and stand against the opposite wall, George Silverman. As far off as you can. That'll do. How do you feel?'

I told him that I didn't feel cold, and didn't feel hungry, and didn't feel thirsty. That was the whole round of human feelings, as far as I knew, except the pain of being beaten.

'Well,' said he, 'you are going, George, to a healthy farmhouse to be purified. Keep in the air there as much as you can. Live an out-of-door life there, until you are fetched away. You had better not say much – in fact, you had better be very careful not to say anything – about what your parents died of, or they might not like to take you in. Behave well, and I'll put you to school. Oh, yes! I'll put you to school, though I'm not obligated to do it. I am a servant of the Lord, George; and I have been a good servant to him, I have, these five-and-thirty years. The Lord has had a good servant in me, and he knows it.'

What I then supposed him to mean by this, I cannot imagine. As little do I know when I began to comprehend that he was a prominent member of some obscure denomination or congregation, every member of which held forth to the rest when so inclined, and among whom he was called Brother Hawkyard. It was enough for me to know, on that day in the ward, that the farmer's cart was waiting for me at the street corner. I was not slow to get into it; for it was the first ride I ever had in my life.

It made me sleepy, and I slept. First, I stared at Preston streets as long as they lasted; and, meanwhile, I may have had some small dumb wondering within me whereabouts our cellar was; but I doubt it. Such a worldly little devil was I, that I took no thought who would bury father and mother, or where they would be buried, or when. The question whether the eating and drinking by day, and the covering by night, would be as good at the farmhouse as at the ward superseded those questions.

The jolting of the cart on a loose stony road awoke me; and I found that we were mounting a steep hill, where the road was a rutty by-road through a field. And so, by fragments of an ancient terrace, and by some rugged outbuildings that had once been fortified, and passing under a ruined gateway we came to the old farmhouse in the thick stone wall outside the old quadrangle of Hoghton Towers:[6] which I looked at like a stupid savage, seeing no specialty in, seeing no antiquity in; assuming all farmhouses to resemble it; assigning the decay I noticed to the one potent cause of all ruin that I knew – poverty; eyeing the pigeons in their flights, the cattle in their stalls, the ducks on the pond, and the fowls pecking about the yard, with a hungry hope that plenty of them might be killed for dinner while I stayed there; wondering whether the scrubbed dairy vessels, drying in the sunlight, could be goodly porringers out of which the master ate his belly-filling food, and which he polished when he had done, according to my ward experience; shrinkingly doubtful whether the shadows, passing over that airy height on the bright spring day, were not something in the nature of frowns – sordid, afraid, unadmiring – a small brute to shudder at.

To that time I had never had the faintest impression of duty. I had had no knowledge whatever that there was anything lovely in this life. When I had occasionally slunk up the cellar-steps into the street, and glared in at shop-windows, I had done so with no higher feelings than we may suppose to animate a mangy young dog or wolf-cub. It is equally the fact that I had never been alone, in the sense of holding unselfish converse with myself. I had been solitary often enough, but nothing better.

Such was my condition when I sat down to my dinner that day, in the kitchen of the old farmhouse. Such was my condition when I lay on my bed in the old farmhouse that night, stretched out opposite the narrow mullioned window, in the cold light of the moon, like a young vampire.

Fifth Chapter

WHAT DO I KNOW of Hoghton Towers? Very little; for I have been gratefully unwilling to disturb my first impressions. A house, centuries old, on high ground a mile or so removed from the road between Preston and Blackburn, where the first James of England, in his hurry to make money by making baronets, perhaps made some of those remunerative dignities. A house, centuries old, deserted and falling to pieces, its woods and gardens long since grassland or ploughed up, the Rivers Ribble and Darwen[7] glancing below it, and a vague haze of smoke, against which not even the supernatural prescience of the first Stuart could foresee a counter-blast, hinting at steam-power, powerful in two distances.

What did I know then of Hoghton Towers? When I first peeped in at the gate of the lifeless quadrangle, and started from the mouldering statue becoming visible to me like its guardian ghost; when I stole round by the back of the farmhouse, and got in among the ancient rooms, many of them with their floors and ceilings falling, the beams and rafters hanging dangerously down, the plaster dropping as I trod, the oaken panels stripped away, the windows half walled up, half broken; when I discovered a gallery commanding the old kitchen, and looked down between balustrades upon a massive old table and benches, fearing to see I know not what dead-alive creatures come in and seat themselves, and look up with I know not what dreadful eyes, or lack of eyes, at me; when all over the house I was awed by gaps and chinks where the sky stared sorrowfully at me, where the birds passed, and the ivy rustled, and the stains of winter weather blotched the rotten floors; when down at the bottom of dark pits of staircase, into which the stairs had sunk, green leaves trembled, butterflies fluttered and bees hummed in and out through the broken doorways; when encircling the whole ruin were sweet scents, and sights of fresh green growth and ever-renewing life that I had never dreamed of – I say, when I passed into such clouded perception of these things as my dark soul could compass, what did I know then of Hoghton Towers?

I have written that the sky stared sorrowfully at me. Therein have I anticipated the answer. I knew that all these things looked sorrowfully at me; that they seemed to sigh or whisper, not without pity for me, 'Alas! poor worldly little devil!'

There were two or three rats at the bottom of one of the smaller pits of broken staircase when I craned over and looked in. They were scuffling for some prey that was there; and, when they started and hid themselves close together in the dark, I thought of the old life (it had grown old already) in the cellar.

How not to be this worldly little devil? how not to have a repugnance towards myself as I had towards the rats? I hid in a corner of one of the smaller chambers, frightened at myself, and crying (it was the first time I had ever cried for any cause not purely physical), and I tried to think about it. One of the farm-ploughs came into my range of view just then; and it seemed to help me as it went on with its two horses up and down the field so peacefully and quietly.

There was a girl of about my own age in the farmhouse family, and she sat opposite to me at the narrow table at mealtimes. It had come into my mind, at our first dinner, that she might take the fever from me. The thought had not disquieted me then. I had only speculated how she would look under the altered circumstances, and whether she would die. But it came into my mind now that I might try to prevent her taking the fever by keeping away from her. I knew I should have but scrambling board if I did; so much the less worldly and less devilish the deed would be, I thought.

From that hour, I withdrew myself at early morning into secret corners of the ruined house, and remained hidden there until she went to bed. At first, when meals were ready, I used to hear them calling me; and then my resolution weakened. But I strengthened it again by going farther off into the ruin, and getting out of hearing. I often watched for her at the dim windows; and, when I saw that she was fresh and rosy, felt much happier.

Out of this holding her in my thoughts, to the humanising of myself, I suppose some childish love arose within me. I felt, in some sort, dignified by the pride of protecting her – by the pride of making the sacrifice for her. As my heart swelled with that new feeling, it insensibly softened about mother and father. It seemed to have been frozen before, and now to be thawed. The old ruin and all the lovely things that haunted it were not sorrowful for me only, but sorrowful for mother and father as well. Therefore did I cry again, and often too.

The farmhouse family conceived me to be of a morose temper, and were very short with me; though they never stinted me in such broken fare as was to be got out of regular hours. One night when I lifted the kitchen latch at my usual time, Sylvia (that was her pretty name) had but just gone out of the room. Seeing her ascending the opposite stairs, I stood still at the door. She had heard the clink of the latch, and looked round.

'George,' she called to me in a pleased voice, 'tomorrow is my birthday; and we are to have a fiddler, and there's a party of boys and girls coming in a cart, and we shall dance. I invite you. Be sociable for once, George.'

'I am very sorry, miss,' I answered; 'but I – but, no; I can't come.'

'You are a disagreeable, ill-humoured lad,' she returned disdainfully; 'and I ought not to have asked you. I shall never speak to you again.'

As I stood with my eyes fixed on the fire, after she was gone, I felt that the farmer bent his brows upon me.

'Eh, lad!' said he; 'Sylvy's right. You're as moody and broody a lad as never I set eyes on yet.'

I tried to assure him that I meant no harm; but he only said coldly, 'Maybe not, maybe not! There, get thy supper, get thy supper; and then thou canst sulk to thy heart's content again.'

Ah! if they could have seen me next day, in the ruin, watching for the arrival of the cart full of merry young guests; if they could have seen me at night, gliding out from behind the ghostly statue, listening to the music and the fall of dancing feet, and watching the lighted farmhouse windows from the quadrangle when all the ruin was dark; if they could have read my heart, as I crept up to bed by the back way, comforting myself with the reflection, 'They will take no hurt from me' – they would not have thought mine a morose or an unsocial nature.

It was in these ways that I began to form a shy disposition; to be of a timidly silent character under misconstruction; to have an inexpressible, perhaps a morbid, dread of ever being sordid or worldly. It was in these ways that my nature came to shape itself to such a mould, even before it was affected by the influences of the studious and retired life of a poor scholar.

Sixth Chapter

BROTHER HAWKYARD (as he insisted on my calling him) put me to school, and told me to work my way. 'You are all right, George,' he said. 'I have been the best servant the Lord has had in his service for this five-and-thirty year (oh, I have!); and he knows the value of such a servant as I have been to him (oh, yes, he does!); and he'll prosper your schooling as a part of my reward. That's what *he*'ll do, George. He'll do it for me.'

From the first I could not like this familiar knowledge of the ways of the sublime, inscrutable Almighty, on Brother Hawkyard's part. As I grew a little wiser, and still a little wiser, I liked it less and less. His manner, too, of confirming himself in a parenthesis – as if, knowing himself, he doubted his own word – I found distasteful. I cannot tell how much these dislikes cost me; for I had a dread that they were worldly.

As time went on, I became a foundation-boy on a good Found–ation,[8] and I cost Brother Hawkyard nothing. When I had worked my way so far, I worked yet harder, in the hope of ultimately getting a presentation to college and a fellowship. My health has never been strong (some vapour from the Preston cellar cleaves to me, I think); and what with much work and some weakness, I came again to be regarded – that is, by my fellow-students – as unsocial.

All through my time as a foundation-boy, I was within a few miles of Brother Hawkyard's congregation; and whenever I was what we called a leave-boy on a Sunday,[9] I went over there at his desire. Before the knowledge became forced upon me that outside their place of meeting these brothers and sisters were no better than the rest of the human family, but on the whole were, to put the case mildly, as bad as most, in respect of giving short weight in their shops, and not speaking the truth – I say, before this knowledge became forced upon me, their prolix addresses, their inordinate conceit, their daring ignorance, their investment of the Supreme Ruler of heaven and earth with their own miserable meannesses and littlenesses, greatly shocked me. Still, as their term for the frame of mind that could not perceive them to be in an exalted state of grace was the 'worldly' state, I did for a time suffer tortures under my enquiries of myself whether that young worldly-devilish spirit of mine could secretly be lingering at the bottom of my non-appreciation.

Brother Hawkyard was the popular expounder in this assembly, and generally occupied the platform (there was a little platform with a table on it, in lieu of a pulpit) first, on a Sunday afternoon. He was by trade a dry-salter. Brother Gimblet, an elderly man with a crabbed face, a large dog's-eared shirt-collar and a spotted blue neckerchief reaching up behind to the crown of his head, was also a dry-salter and an expounder. Brother Gimblet professed the greatest admiration for Brother Hawkyard, but (I had thought more than once) bore him a jealous grudge.

Let whosoever may peruse these lines kindly take the pains here to read twice my solemn pledge that what I write of the language and customs of the congregation in question I write scrupulously, literally, exactly, from the life and the truth.

On the first Sunday after I had won what I had so long tried for, and when it was certain that I was going up to college, Brother Hawkyard concluded a long exhortation thus: 'Well, my friends and fellow-sinners, now I told you when I began that I didn't know a word of what I was going to say to you (and no, I did not!), but that it was all one to me because I knew the Lord would put into my mouth the words I wanted.'

('That's it!' from Brother Gimblet.)

'And he did put into my mouth the words I wanted.'

('So he did!' from Brother Gimblet.)

'And why?'

('Ah, let's have that!' from Brother Gimblet.)

'Because I have been his faithful servant for five-and-thirty years, and because he knows it. For five-and-thirty years! And he knows it, mind you! I got those words that I wanted on account of my wages. I got 'em from the Lord, my fellow-sinners. "Down!" I said.

"Here's a heap of wages due; let us have something down, on account." And I got it down, and I paid it over to you; and you won't wrap it up in a napkin, nor yet in a towel, nor yet pocketankercher,[10] but you'll put it out at good interest. Very well. Now, my brothers and sisters and fellow-sinners, I am going to conclude with a question, and I'll make it so plain (with the help of the Lord, after five-and-thirty years, I should rather hope!) as that the Devil shall not be able to confuse it in your heads – which he would be overjoyed to do.'

('Just his way. Crafty old blackguard!' from Brother Gimblet.)

'And the question is this, Are the angels learned?'

('Not they. Not a bit on it!' from Brother Gimblet, with the greatest confidence.)

'Not they. And where's the proof? Sent ready-made by the hand of the Lord. Why, there's one among us here now, that has got all the learning that can be crammed into him. I got him all the learning that could be crammed into him. His grandfather' (this I had never heard before) 'was a brother of ours. He was Brother Parksop. That's what he was. Parksop; Brother Parksop. His worldly name was Parksop, and he was a brother of this brotherhood. Then wasn't he Brother Parksop?'

('Must be. Couldn't help hisself!' from Brother Gimblet.)

'Well, he left that one now here present among us to the care of a brother-sinner of his (and that brother-sinner, mind you, was a sinner of a bigger size in his time than any of you; praise the Lord!), Brother Hawkyard. Me. *I* got him without fee or reward – without a morsel of myrrh, or frankincense,[11] nor yet amber, letting alone the honeycomb – all the learning that could be crammed into him. Has it brought him into our temple, in the spirit? No. Have we had any ignorant brothers and sisters, that didn't know round O from crooked S, come in among us meanwhile? Many. Then the angels are *not* learned; then they don't so much as know their alphabet. And now, my friends and fellow-sinners, having brought it to that, perhaps some brother present – perhaps you, Brother Gimblet – will pray a bit for us?'

Brother Gimblet undertook the sacred function, after having drawn his sleeve across his mouth and muttered, 'Well! I don't know as I see my way to hitting any of you quite in the right place neither.' He said this with a dark smile, and then began to bellow. What we were specially to be preserved from, according to his solicitations, was despoilment of the orphan, suppression of testamentary intentions on the part of a father or (say) grandfather, appropriation of the orphan's house-property, feigning to give in charity to the wronged one from whom we withheld his due; and that class of sins. He ended with the petition, 'Give us peace!' which, speaking for myself, was very much needed after twenty minutes of his bellowing.

Even though I had not seen him, when he rose from his knees, steaming with perspiration, glance at Brother Hawkyard, and even though I had not heard Brother Hawkyard's tone of congratulating him on the vigour with which he had roared, I should have detected a malicious application in this prayer. Unformed suspicions to a similar effect had sometimes passed through my mind in my earlier schooldays, and had always caused me great distress; for they were worldly in their nature, and wide, very wide, of the spirit that had drawn me from Sylvia. They were sordid suspicions, without a shadow of proof. They were worthy to have originated in the unwholesome cellar. They were not only without proof, but against proof; for was I not myself a living proof of what Brother Hawkyard had done? and without him, how should I ever have seen the sky look sorrowfully down upon that wretched boy at Hoghton Towers?

Although the dread of a relapse into a stage of savage selfishness was less strong upon me as I approached manhood and could act in an increased degree for myself, yet I was always on my guard against any tendency to such relapse. After getting these suspicions under my feet, I had been troubled by not being able to like Brother Hawkyard's manner or his professed religion. So it came about that, as I walked back that Sunday evening, I thought it would be an act of reparation for any such injury my struggling thoughts had unwillingly done him, if I wrote, and placed in his hands, before going to college, a full acknowledgment of his goodness to me, and an ample tribute of thanks. It might serve as an implied vindication of him against any dark scandal from a rival brother and expounder, or from any other quarter.

Accordingly, I wrote the document with much care. I may add with much feeling too; for it affected me as I went on. Having no set studies to pursue in the brief interval between leaving the Foundation and going to Cambridge, I determined to walk out to his place of business and give it into his own hands.

It was a winter afternoon, when I tapped at the door of his little counting-house, which was at the farther end of his long, low shop. As I did so (having entered by the backyard, where casks and boxes were taken in, and where there was the inscription, 'Private way to the counting-house'), a shopman called to me from the counter that he was engaged.

'Brother Gimblet' (said the shopman, who was one of the brotherhood) 'is with him.'

I thought this all the better for my purpose, and made bold to tap again. They were talking in a low tone, and money was passing; for I heard it being counted out.

'Who is it?' asked Brother Hawkyard, sharply.

'George Silverman,' I answered, holding the door open. 'May I come in?'

Both brothers seemed so astounded to see me that I felt shyer than usual. But they looked quite cadaverous in the early gaslight, and perhaps that accidental circumstance exaggerated the expression of their faces.

'What is the matter?' asked Brother Hawkyard.

'Ay! what is the matter?' asked Brother Gimblet.

'Nothing at all,' I said, diffidently producing my document: 'I am only the bearer of a letter from myself.'

'From yourself, George?' cried Brother Hawkyard.

'And to you,' said I.

'And to me, George?'

He turned paler, and opened it hurriedly; but looking over it, and seeing generally what it was, became less hurried, recovered his colour, and said, 'Praise the Lord!'

'That's it!' cried Brother Gimblet. 'Well put! Amen.'

Brother Hawkyard then said, in a livelier strain, 'You must know, George, that Brother Gimblet and I are going to make our two businesses one. We are going into partnership. We are settling it now. Brother Gimblet is to take one clear half of the profits (oh, yes! he shall have it; he shall have it to the last farthing).'

'DV!' said Brother Gimblet, with his right fist firmly clenched on his right leg.

'There is no objection,' pursued Brother Hawkyard, 'to my reading this aloud, George?'

As it was what I expressly desired should be done, after yesterday's prayer, I more than readily begged him to read it aloud. He did so; and Brother Gimblet listened with a crabbed smile.

'It was in a good hour that I came here,' he said, wrinkling up his eyes. 'It was in a good hour, likewise, that I was moved yesterday to depict for the terror of evildoers a character the direct opposite of Brother Hawkyard's. But it was the Lord that done it: I felt him at it while I was perspiring.'

After that it was proposed by both of them that I should attend the congregation once more before my final departure. What my shy reserve would undergo, from being expressly preached at and prayed at, I knew beforehand. But I reflected that it would be for the last time, and that it might add to the weight of my letter. It was well known to the brothers and sisters that there was no place taken for me in *their* paradise; and if I showed this last token of deference to Brother Hawkyard, notoriously in despite of my own sinful inclinations, it might go some little way in aid of my statement that he had been good to me, and that I was grateful to him. Merely stipulating, therefore, that no express endeavour should be made for my conversion – which would involve the rolling of several brothers and sisters on the floor, declaring that they felt all their sins in a heap on their left side, weighing so many pounds avoirdupois, as I knew from what I had seen of those repulsive mysteries – I promised.

Since the reading of my letter, Brother Gimblet had been at intervals wiping one eye with an end of his spotted blue neckerchief, and grinning to himself. It was, however, a habit that brother had, to grin in an ugly manner even when expounding. I call to mind a delighted snarl with which he used to detail from the platform the torments reserved for the wicked (meaning all human creation except the brotherhood), as being remarkably hideous.

I left the two to settle their articles of partnership, and count money; and I never saw them again but on the following Sunday. Brother Hawkyard died within two or three years, leaving all he possessed to Brother Gimblet, in virtue of a will dated (as I have been told) that very day.

Now I was so far at rest with myself, when Sunday came, knowing that I had conquered my own mistrust, and righted Brother Hawkyard in the jaundiced vision of a rival, that I went, even to that coarse chapel, in a less sensitive state than usual. How could I foresee that the delicate, perhaps the diseased, corner of my mind, where I winced and shrank when it was touched, or was even approached, would be handled as the theme of the whole proceedings?

On this occasion it was assigned to Brother Hawkyard to pray, and to Brother Gimblet to preach. The prayer was to open the ceremonies; the discourse was to come next. Brothers Hawkyard and Gimblet were both on the platform; Brother Hawkyard on his knees at the table, unmusically ready to pray; Brother Gimblet sitting against the wall, grinningly ready to preach.

'Let us offer up the sacrifice of prayer, my brothers and sisters and fellow-sinners.' Yes; but it was I who was the sacrifice. It was our poor, sinful, worldly-minded brother here present who was wrestled for. The now-opening career of this our unawakened brother might lead to his becoming a minister of what was called 'the church'. That was what *he* looked to. The church. Not the chapel, Lord. The church. No rectors, no vicars, no archdeacons, no bishops, no archbishops, in the chapel, but, oh Lord! many such in the church. Protect our sinful brother from his love of lucre. Cleanse from our unawakened brother's breast his sin of worldly-mindedness. The prayer said infinitely more in words, but nothing more to any intelligible effect.

Then Brother Gimblet came forward, and took (as I knew he would) the text, 'My kingdom is not of this world.' Ah! but whose was, my fellow-sinners? Whose? Why, our brother's here present was. The only kingdom he had an idea of was of this world. ('That's it!' from several of the congregation.) What did the woman do when she lost the piece of money? Went and looked for it. What should our brother do when he lost his way? ('Go and look for it,' from a sister.) Go and look for it, true. But must he look for it in the right direction, or in the wrong? ('In the right,' from a brother.) There spake the prophets! He must look for it in the right direction, or he couldn't find it. But he had turned his back upon the right direction, and he wouldn't find it. Now, my fellow-sinners, to show you the difference betwixt worldly-mindedness and unworldly-mindedness, betwixt kingdoms not of this world and kingdoms *of* this world, here was a letter wrote by even our worldly-minded brother unto Brother Hawkyard. Judge, from hearing of it read, whether Brother Hawkyard was the faithful steward that the Lord had in his mind only t'other day, when, in this very place, he drew you the picter of the unfaithful one; for it was him that done it, not me. Don't doubt that!

Brother Gimblet then groaned and bellowed his way through my composition, and subsequently through an hour. The service closed with a hymn, in which the brothers unanimously roared, and the sisters unanimously shrieked at me – that I by wiles of worldly gain was mocked, and they on waters of sweet love were rocked; that I with mammon struggled in the dark, while they were floating in a second ark.[12]

I went out from all this with an aching heart and a weary spirit: not because I was quite so weak as to consider these narrow creatures interpreters of the Divine Majesty and Wisdom, but because I was weak enough to feel as though it were my hard fortune to be misrepresented and misunderstood when I most tried to subdue any risings of mere worldliness within me, and when I most hoped that, by dint of trying earnestly, I had succeeded.

Seventh Chapter

MY TIMIDITY and my obscurity occasioned me to live a secluded life at college, and to be little known. No relative ever came to visit me, for I had no relative. No intimate friends broke in upon my studies, for I made no intimate friends. I supported myself on my scholarship, and read much. My college time was otherwise not so very different from my time at Hoghton Towers.

Knowing myself to be unfit for the noisier stir of social existence, but believing myself qualified to do my duty in a moderate, though earnest way, if I could obtain some small preferment in the church, I applied my mind to the clerical profession. In due sequence I took orders, was ordained, and began to look about me for employment. I must observe that I had taken a good degree, that I had succeeded in winning a good fellowship, and that my means were ample for my retired way of life. By this time I had read with several young men; and the occupation increased my income, while it was highly interesting to me. I once accidentally overheard our greatest don say, to my boundless joy, that he heard it reported of Silverman that his gift of quiet explanation, his patience, his amiable temper, and his conscientiousness made him the best of coaches. May my 'gift of quiet explanation' come more seasonably and powerfully to my aid in this present explanation than I think it will!

It may be in a certain degree owing to the situation of my college-rooms (in a corner where the daylight was sobered), but it is in a much larger degree referable to the state of my own mind, that I seem to myself, on looking back to this time of my life, to have been always in the peaceful shade. I can see others in the sunlight; I can see our boats' crews and our athletic young men on the glistening water, or speckled with the moving lights of sunlit leaves; but I myself am always in the shadow looking on. Not unsympathetically – God forbid! – but looking on alone, much as I looked at Sylvia from the shadows of the ruined house, or looked at the red gleam shining through the farmer's windows, and listened to the fall of dancing feet, when all the ruin was dark that night in the quadrangle.

I now come to the reason for my quoting that laudation of myself above given. Without such reason, to repeat it would have been mere boastfulness.

Among those who had read with me was Mr Fareway, second son of Lady Fareway, widow of Sir Gaston Fareway, baronet. This young gentleman's abilities were much above the average; but he came of a rich family and was idle and luxurious. He presented himself to me too late, and afterwards came to me too irregularly, to admit of my being of much service to him. In the end, I considered it my duty to dissuade him from going up for an examination which he could never pass; and he left college without a degree. After his departure, Lady Fareway wrote to me, representing the justice of my returning half my fee, as I had been of so little use to her son. Within my knowledge a similar demand had not been made in any other case; and I most freely admit that the justice of it had not occurred to me until it was pointed out. But I at once perceived it, yielded to it, and returned the money –

Mr Fareway had been gone two years or more, and I had forgotten him, when he one day walked into my rooms as I was sitting at my books.

Said he, after the usual salutations had passed, 'Mr Silverman, my mother is in town here, at the hotel, and wishes me to present you to her.'

I was not comfortable with strangers, and I dare say I betrayed that I was a little nervous or unwilling. 'For,' said he, without my having spoken, 'I think the interview may tend to the advancement of your prospects.'

It put me to the blush to think that I should be tempted by a worldly reason, but I rose immediately.

Said Mr Fareway, as we went along, 'Are you a good hand at business?'

'I think not,' said I.

Said Mr Fareway then, 'My mother is.'

'Truly?' said I.

'Yes: my mother is what is usually called a managing woman. Doesn't make a bad thing, for instance, even out of the spendthrift habits of my eldest brother abroad. In short, a managing woman. This is in confidence.'

He had never spoken to me in confidence, and I was surprised by his doing so. I said I should respect his confidence, of course, and said no more on the delicate subject. We had but a little way to walk, and I was soon in his mother's company. He presented me, shook hands with me, and left us two (as he said) to business.

I saw in my Lady Fareway a handsome, well-preserved lady of somewhat large stature, with a steady glare in her great round dark eyes that embarrassed me.

Said my lady, 'I have heard from my son, Mr Silverman, that you would be glad of some preferment in the church.' I gave my lady to understand that was so.

'I don't know whether you are aware,' my lady proceeded, 'that we have a presentation to a living? I say *we* have; but, in point of fact, *I* have.'

I gave my lady to understand that I had not been aware of this.

Said my lady, 'So it is: indeed I have two presentations – one to two hundred a year, one to six. Both livings are in our county – North Devonshire – as you probably know. The first is vacant. Would you like it?'

What with my lady's eyes, and what with the suddenness of this proposed gift, I was much confused.

'I am sorry it is not the larger presentation,' said my lady, rather coldly; 'though I will not, Mr Silverman, pay you the bad compliment of supposing that *you* are, because that would be mercenary – and mercenary I am persuaded you are not.'

Said I, with my utmost earnestness, 'Thank you, Lady Fareway, thank you, thank you! I should be deeply hurt if I thought I bore the character.'

'Naturally,' said my lady. 'Always detestable, but particularly in a clergyman. You have not said whether you will like the living?'

With apologies for my remissness or indistinctness, I assured my lady that I accepted it most readily and gratefully. I added that I hoped she would not estimate my appreciation of the generosity of her choice by my flow of words; for I was not a ready man in that respect when taken by surprise or touched at heart.

'The affair is concluded,' said my lady; 'concluded. You will find the duties very light, Mr Silverman. Charming house; charming little garden, orchard, and all that. You will be able to take pupils. By the by! No: I will return to the word afterwards. What was I going to mention, when it put me out?'

My lady stared at me, as if I knew. And I didn't know. And that perplexed me afresh.

Said my lady, after some consideration, 'Oh, of course, how very dull of me! The last incumbent – least mercenary man I ever saw –

in consideration of the duties being so light and the house so delicious, couldn't rest, he said, unless I permitted him to help me with my correspondence, accounts and various little things of that kind; nothing in themselves, but which it worries a lady to cope with. Would Mr Silverman also like to – ? Or shall I – ?'

I hastened to say that my poor help would be always at her ladyship's service.

'I am absolutely blessed,' said my lady, casting up her eyes (and so taking them off me for one moment), 'in having to do with gentlemen who cannot endure an approach to the idea of being mercenary!' She shivered at the word. 'And now as to the pupil.'

'The – ?' I was quite at a loss.

'Mr Silverman, you have no idea what she is. She is,' said my lady, laying her touch upon my coat-sleeve, 'I do verily believe, the most extraordinary girl in this world. Already knows more Greek and Latin than Lady Jane Grey.[13] And taught herself! Has not yet, remember, derived a moment's advantage from Mr Silverman's classical acquirements. To say nothing of mathematics, which she is bent upon becoming versed in, and in which (as I hear from my son and others) Mr Silverman's reputation is so deservedly high!'

Under my lady's eyes I must have lost the clue, I felt persuaded; and yet I did not know where I could have dropped it.

'Adelina,' said my lady, 'is my only daughter. If I did not feel quite convinced that I am not blinded by a mother's partiality; unless I was absolutely sure that when you know her, Mr Silverman, you will esteem it a high and unusual privilege to direct her studies – I should introduce a mercenary element into this conversation, and ask you on what terms – '

I entreated my lady to go no further. My lady saw that I was troubled, and did me the honour to comply with my request.

Eight Chapter

EVERYTHING IN MENTAL acquisition that her brother might have been, if he would, and everything in all gracious charms and admirable qualities that no one but herself could be – this was Adelina.

I will not expatiate upon her beauty; I will not expatiate upon her intelligence, her quickness of perception, her powers of memory, her sweet consideration, from the first moment, for the slow-paced tutor who ministered to her wonderful gifts. I was thirty then; I am over sixty now: she is ever present to me in these hours as she was in those, bright and beautiful and young, wise and fanciful and good.

When I discovered that I loved her, how can I say? In the first day? in the first week? in the first month? Impossible to trace. If I be (as I am) unable to represent to myself any previous period of my life as quite separable from her attracting power, how can I answer for this one detail?

Whensoever I made the discovery, it laid a heavy burden on me. And yet, comparing it with the far heavier burden that I afterwards took up, it does not seem to me now to have been very hard to bear. In the knowledge that I did love her, and that I should love her while my life lasted, and that I was ever to hide my secret deep in my own breast, and she was never to find it, there was a kind of sustaining joy or pride, or comfort, mingled with my pain.

But later on – say, a year later on – when I made another discovery, then indeed my suffering and my struggle were strong. That other discovery was –

These words will never see the light, if ever, until my heart is dust; until her bright spirit has returned to the regions of which, when imprisoned here, it surely retained some unusual glimpse of remembrance; until all the pulses that ever beat around us shall have long been quiet; until all the fruits of all the tiny victories and defeats achieved in our little breasts shall have withered away. That discovery was that she loved me.

She may have enhanced my knowledge, and loved me for that; she may have overvalued my discharge of duty to her, and loved me for that; she may have refined upon a playful compassion which she would sometimes show for what she called my want of wisdom, according to the light of the world's dark lanterns, and loved me for that; she may – she must – have confused the borrowed light of what I had only learned, with its brightness in its pure, original rays; but she loved me at that time, and she made me know it.

Pride of family and pride of wealth put me as far off from her in my lady's eyes as if I had been some domesticated creature of another kind. But they could not put me farther from her than I put myself when I set my merits against hers. More than that. They could not put me, by millions of fathoms, half so low beneath her as I put myself when in imagination I took advantage of her noble trustfulness, took the fortune that I knew she must possess in her own right, and left her to find herself, in the zenith of her beauty and genius, bound to poor rusty, plodding me.

No! Worldliness should not enter here at any cost. If I had tried to keep it out of other ground, how much harder was I bound to try to keep it out from this sacred place!

But there was something daring in her broad, generous character, that demanded at so delicate a crisis to be delicately and patiently addressed. And many and many a bitter night (oh, I found I could cry, for reasons not purely physical, at this pass of my life!) I took my course.

My lady had, in our first interview, unconsciously overstated the accommodation of my pretty house. There was room in it for only one pupil. He was a young gentleman near coming of age, very well connected, but what is called a poor relation. His parents were dead. The charges of his living and reading with me were defrayed by an uncle; and he and I were to do our utmost together for three years towards qualifying him to make his way. At this time he had entered into his second year with me. He was well-looking, clever, energetic, enthusiastic, bold; in the best sense of the term, a thorough young Anglo-Saxon.

I resolved to bring these two together.

Ninth Chapter

SAID I, ONE NIGHT, when I had conquered myself, 'Mr Granville' – Mr Granville Wharton his name was – 'I doubt if you have ever yet so much as seen Miss Fareway.'

'Well, sir,' returned he, laughing, 'you see her so much yourself that you hardly leave another fellow a chance of seeing her.'

'I am her tutor, you know,' said I.

And there the subject dropped for that time. But I so contrived as that they should come together shortly afterwards. I had previously so contrived as to keep them asunder; for while I loved her – I mean before I had determined on my sacrifice – a lurking jealousy of Mr Granville lay within my unworthy breast.

It was quite an ordinary interview in the Fareway Park but they talked easily together for some time: like takes to like, and they had many points of resemblance. Said Mr Granville to me, when he and I sat at our supper that night, 'Miss Fareway is remarkably beautiful, sir, remarkably engaging. Don't you think so?' 'I think so,' said I. And I stole a glance at him, and saw that he had reddened and was thoughtful. I remember it most vividly, because the mixed feeling of grave pleasure and acute pain that the slight circumstance caused me was the first of a long, long series of such mixed impressions under which my hair turned slowly grey.

I had not much need to feign to be subdued; but I counterfeited to be older than I was in all respects (heaven knows! my heart being all too young the while), and feigned to be more of a recluse and bookworm than I had really become, and gradually set up more and more of a fatherly manner towards Adelina. Likewise I made my tuition less imaginative than before; separated myself from my poets and philosophers; was careful to present them in their own light, and me, their lowly servant, in my own shade. Moreover, in the matter of apparel I was equally mindful; not that I had ever been dapper that way; but that I was slovenly now.

As I depressed myself with one hand, so did I labour to raise Mr Granville with the other; directing his attention to such subjects as I too well knew interested her, and fashioning him (do not deride or misconstrue the expression, unknown reader of this writing; for I have suffered!) into a greater resemblance to myself in my solitary one strong aspect. And gradually, gradually, as I saw him take more and more to these thrown-out lures of mine, then did I come to know better and better that love was drawing him on, and was drawing her from me.

So passed more than another year; every day a year in its number of my mixed impressions of grave pleasure and acute pain; and then these two, being of age and free to act legally for themselves, came before me hand in hand (my hair being now quite white) and entreated me that I would unite them together. 'And indeed, dear tutor,' said Adelina, 'it is but consistent in you that you should do this thing for us, seeing that we should never have spoken together that first time but for you, and that but for you we could never have met so often afterwards.' The whole of which was literally true; for I had availed myself of my many business attendances on, and conferences with, my lady, to take Mr Granville to the house and leave him in the outer room with Adelina.

I knew that my lady would object to such a marriage for her daughter, or to any marriage that was other than an exchange of her for stipulated lands, goods and moneys. But looking on the two, and seeing with full eyes that they were both young and beautiful; and knowing that they were alike in the tastes and acquirements that will outlive youth and beauty; and considering that Adelina had a fortune now, in her own keeping; and considering further that Mr Granville, though for the present poor, was of a good family that had never lived in a cellar in Preston; and believing that their love would endure, neither having any great discrepancy to find out in the other – I told them of my readiness to do this thing which Adelina asked of her dear tutor, and to send them forth, husband and wife, into the shining world with golden gates that awaited them.

It was on a summer morning that I rose before the sun to compose myself for the crowning of my work with this end; and my dwelling being near to the sea, I walked down to the rocks on the shore, in order that I might behold the sun in his majesty.

The tranquillity upon the deep, and on the firmament, the orderly withdrawal of the stars, the calm promise of coming day, the rosy suffusion of the sky and waters, the ineffable splendour that then burst forth, attuned my mind afresh after the discords of the night. Methought that all I looked on said to me, and that all I heard in the sea and in the air said to me, 'Be comforted, mortal, that thy life is so short. Our preparation for what is to follow has endured, and shall endure, for unimaginable ages.'

I married them. I knew that my hand was cold when I placed it on their hands clasped together; but the words with which I had to accompany the action I could say without faltering, and I was at peace.

They being well away from my house and from the place after our simple breakfast, the time was come when I must do what I had pledged myself to them that I would do – break the intelligence to my lady.

I went up to the house, and found my lady in her ordinary business-room. She happened to have an unusual amount of commissions to entrust to me that day; and she had filled my hands with papers before I could originate a word.

'My lady,' I then began, as I stood beside her table.

'Why, what's the matter?' she said quickly, looking up.

'Not much, I would fain hope, after you shall have prepared yourself, and considered a little.'

'Prepared myself; and considered a little! You appear to have prepared *yourself* but indifferently, anyhow, Mr Silverman.' This mighty scornfully, as I experienced my usual embarrassment under her stare.

Said I, in self-extenuation once for all, 'Lady Fareway, I have but to say for myself that I have tried to do my duty.'

'For yourself?' repeated my lady. 'Then there are others con-cerned, I see. Who are they?'

I was about to answer, when she made towards the bell with a dart that stopped me, and said, 'Why, where is Adelina?'

'Forbear! be calm, my lady. I married her this morning to Mr Granville Wharton.'

She set her lips, looked more intently at me than ever, raised her right hand, and smote me hard upon the cheek.

'Give me back those papers! give me back those papers!' She tore them out of my hands, and tossed them on her table. Then seating herself defiantly in her great chair, and folding her arms, she stabbed me to the heart with the unlooked-for reproach, 'You worldly wretch!'

'Worldly?' I cried. 'Worldly?'

'This, if you please' – she went on with supreme scorn, pointing me out as if there were someone there to see – 'this, if you please, is the disinterested scholar, with not a design beyond his books! This, if you please, is the simple creature whom anyone could overreach in a bargain! This, if you please, is Mr Silverman! Not of this world; not he! He has too much simplicity for this world's cunning. He has too much singleness of purpose to be a match for this world's double-dealing. What did he give you for it?'

'For what? And who?'

'How much,' she asked, bending forward in her great chair, and insultingly tapping the fingers of her right hand on the palm of her left – 'how much does Mr Granville Wharton pay you for getting him Adelina's money? What is the amount of your percentage upon Adelina's fortune? What were the terms of the agreement that you proposed to this boy when you, the Reverend George Silverman, licensed to marry, engaged to put him in possession of this girl? You made good terms for yourself, whatever they were. He would stand a poor chance against your keenness.'

Bewildered, horrified, stunned by this cruel perversion, I could not speak. But I trust that I looked innocent, being so.

'Listen to me, shrewd hypocrite,' said my lady, whose anger increased as she gave it utterance; 'attend to my words, you cunning schemer, who have carried this plot through with such a practised double face that I have never suspected you. I had my projects for my daughter; projects for family connection; projects for fortune. You have thwarted them and overreached me; but I am not one to be thwarted and overreached without retaliation. Do you mean to hold this living another month?'

'Do you deem it possible, Lady Fareway, that I can hold it another hour, under your injurious words?'

'Is it resigned, then?'

'It was mentally resigned, my lady, some minutes ago.'

'Don't equivocate, sir. *Is* it resigned?'

'Unconditionally and entirely; and I would that I had never, never come near it!'

'A cordial response from me to *that* wish, Mr Silverman! But take this with you, sir. If you had not resigned it, I would have had you deprived of it. And though you have resigned it, you will not get quit of me as easily as you think for. I will pursue you with this story. I will make this nefarious conspiracy of yours, for money, known. You have made money by it, but you have at the same time made an enemy by it. *You* will take good care that the money sticks to you; *I* will take good care that the enemy sticks to you.'

Then said I finally, 'Lady Fareway, I think my heart is broken. Until I came into this room just now, the possibility of such mean wickedness as you have imputed to me never dawned upon my thoughts. Your suspicions – '

'Suspicions! Pah!' said she indignantly. 'Certainties.'

'Your certainties, my lady, as you call them, your suspicions as I call them, are cruel, unjust, wholly devoid of foundation in fact. I can declare no more; except that I have not acted for my own profit or my own pleasure. I have not in this proceeding considered myself. Once again, I think my heart is broken. If I have unwittingly done any wrong with a righteous motive, that is some penalty to pay.'

She received this with another and more indignant 'Pah!' and I made my way out of her room (I think I felt my way out with my hands, although my eyes were open), almost suspecting that my voice had a repulsive sound, and that I was a repulsive object.

There was a great stir made, the bishop was appealed to, I received a severe reprimand and narrowly escaped suspension. For years a cloud hung over me and my name was tarnished.

But my heart did not break, if a broken heart involves death; for I lived through it.

They stood by me, Adelina and her husband, through it all. Those who had known me at college, and even most of those who had only known me there by reputation, stood by me too. Little by little, the belief widened that I was not capable of what was laid to my charge. At length, I was presented to a college-living[14] in a sequestered place, and there I now pen my explanation. I pen it at my open window, in the summertime, and before me lies the churchyard, equal resting-place for sound hearts, wounded hearts and broken hearts. I pen it for the relief of my own mind, not foreseeing whether or no it will ever have a reader.

NOTES

Any word or phrase used in one of its primary meanings as given in a comprehensive and readily accessible dictionary is not annotated. The following abbreviations are used: *BCP* (*The Book of Common Prayer*); CD (Charles Dickens); *MED* (*The Mystery of Edwin Drood*); *OED* (*The Oxford English Dictionary*, 2nd edition, 1989). Shakespeare references are to The Riverside Shakespeare, ed. G. Blakemore Evans and J. J. M. Tobin, Houghton Mifflin Company, New York and Boston, 2nd edition 1997. Wendy S. Jacobson's *Companion* to *MED* has been an invaluable source of information, as have previous editions of the novel, edited by Margaret Cardwell, A. J. Cox, Steven Connor and David Paroissien. These, together with other books and articles cited in the notes, are listed in the Bibliography, pp. xxvii–xxx. All dates are CE (Common Era, formerly AD) unless indicated by BCE (before Common Era, formerly BC).

In the nineteenth century British currency was based on a system of 12 pence (12*d.*) to the shilling (1*s.* or 1/-) and 20 shillings (20*s.*) to the pound (£). Copper coins were the penny (1*d.*), half-penny (½*d.*) and farthing (¼*d.*). Silver coins included the crown (5*s.* or 5/-), half-crown (2*s. 6d.* or 2/6), shilling, sixpence (6*d.*) and threepenny (3*d.*) pieces. Gold sovereigns (£1), half sovereigns (10*s.* or 10/-) and bank-notes for higher denominations were also in circulation. Professional fees (e.g., for doctors or lawyers), were usually charged in guineas, a guinea being 21*s.*

The Mystery of Edwin Drood

1 (p. 3) *The Dawn*   'The Prologue' in the manuscript
2 (p. 3) *Maybe . . . attendants*   This Eastern vision is influenced by *The Arabian Nights*, one of CD's favourite books, known since childhood, of which he owned a six-volume edition.
3 (p. 3) *Lascar*   an East Indian sailor from the region of Bombay (now Mumbai)
4 (p. 3) *this woman*   In May 1869 CD and friends visited criminal areas in London and saw an old woman smoking opium, on whom this character is based (see Forster, Book XII, Chap. I).

5 (p. 4) *Chinamen*   Opium smoking was particularly associated with China, where the British were active in trading the substance.

6 (p. 4) *no ships coming in*   Steven Connor points out that a shortage of opium could explain the high market price in spite of a fall in demand.

7 (p. 4) *dreffle*   represents the speaker's pronunciation of 'dreadful'

8 (p. 4) *the true secret of mixing it . . . horn spoon*   The woman prepares the drug first by heating the raw opium to separate its narcotic element, and then by re-heating (in a non-conductive horn spoon) the resulting viscous substance until it is solid and can be smoked in a pipe.

9 (p. 6) *this unclean spirit of imitation*   Mark 1: 25–6: 'And Jesus rebuked him, saying, Hold thy peace, and come out of him. And when the unclean spirit had torn him, and cried with a loud voice, he came out of him.'

10 (p. 6) *an old Cathedral*   Cloisterham is based on Rochester, close to CD's home in Kent (see 'Cloisterham and Rochester: a Note', where the locations of the novel are discussed.)

11 (p. 6) *vesper service*   the evening service

12 (p. 6) *sacristan . . . sanctuary . . . chancel*   a church functionary, responsible for tolling the bell and assisting the clergy in various ways . . . the holiest part of a church . . . the east end of the church, usually housing the choir, the altar and the sanctuary

13 (p. 6) *When the wicked man*   Ezekiel 18:27: ' . . . when the wicked man turneth away from his wickedness that he hath committed, and doeth that which is lawful and right, he shall save his soul alive', a text used in both Morning and Evening Prayers in *BCP*. The next words are 'I acknowledge my transgressions: and my sin is ever before me' (Psalms 51:3). CD's notes for the first number of *MED* read 'Touch the key note / "When the Wicked Man" – .'

14 (p. 7) *A Dean and a Chapter Also*   A dean is the senior administrator of a cathedral and is responsible for its fabric as well as being in control of its services; next in rank to a bishop, but independent of him, the dean manages the cathedral with the help of the chapter, composed of the canons, the clergy attached to the cathedral.

15 (p. 7) *clerical bird*   A rook's plumage – black with a whitish face – resembles clerical dress. See the nursery rhyme, 'Who killed Cock Robin?': 'Who'll be the parson? / I, said the Rook, / With my little book, / I'll be the parson.'

16 (p. 7) *wings his way homeward*   William Shakespeare (1563–1616), *Macbeth* (c.1606), 3,2, 50–1: 'Light thickens, and the crow / Makes wing to th' rooky wood'. The lines occur in the scene before Banquo's murder. This is the first of many allusions to *Macbeth* throughout *MED*.

17 (p. 7) *Close* the precinct of a cathedral, usually containing houses for the clergy

18 (p. 7) *Not only is the day waning, but the year* an indication of the novel's close adherence to the succession of the seasons

19 (p. 7) *Virginia creeper* an American climbing plant, common in England, related to the vine, with deep red leaves in autumn

20 (p. 7) *Their fallen leaves lie strewn thickly about* compare John Milton (1608–74), *Paradise Lost* (1667), 1, 300–3 (adapted from Virgil's *Aeneid*, 6): 'he stood and called / His legions, angel forms, who lay entranced / Thick as autumnal leaves that strow the brooks / In Vallombrosa'

21 (p. 7) *cast them forth* a phrase used several times in the Bible; see Psalms 147: 17: 'He casteth forth his ice like morsels: who can stand before his cold?'

22 (p. 7) *Chief Verger* bearer of the staff of office for bishops and other dignitaries; usually also a church caretaker

23 (p. 9) *Mr Jasper's heart may not be too much set upon his nephew* Job 7:17: 'What is man, that thou shouldest magnify him? and that thou shouldest set thine heart upon him?'

24 (p. 9) *Our affections . . . in this transitory world* Communion Service, *BCP*: 'And we most humbly beseech thee of thy goodness, O Lord, to comfort and succour all them, who in this transitory life are in trouble, sorrow, need, sickness, or any other adversity.'

25 (p. 9) *at present 'in residence'* Under the terms of the Ecclesiastical Commissioners Act (1841) the dean had to live on cathedral premises for at least eight months each year.

26 (p. 9) *minor canon* a diocesan clergyman who took part in cathedral services but was not a member of the Chapter, and was usually chosen for his ability to sing the services because he often had to stand in for absent canons

27 (p. 10) *Alternate Musical Wednesdays* a choir or glee club meeting fortnightly

28 (p. 10) *'Tell me, shep–herds . . .'* from 'The Wreath', a glee by Joseph Mazzinghi (1765–1844): 'Ye shepherds, tell me, have you seen? /My Flora pass this way?''

29 (p. 10) *Septimus* indicating that Crisparkle is the seventh born in his family: see the opening of Chapter 6

30 (p. 10) *moddley-coddley* to pamper or take excessive care of; more commonly 'molly-coddle'; the earliest use of the phrase cited in *OED*

31 (p. 11) *Marseillaise-wise* the usual manner of singing the French national anthem

32 (p. 12) *'Begone . . . clay'* conflation of the opening lines of a popular song by John Playford (1613–93), from *The Musical Companion* (1667), set as a glee by John Sale: 'Begone, dull Care, I prithee

begone from me, / Begone, dull Care, you and I shall never agree' and 'Too much care will make a young man grey, / And too much care will turn an old man to clay.'

33 (p. 13) *opium for a pain*   a common use for the drug, then readily available as pills, as laudanum or in many proprietary medicines

34 (p. 14) *lay precentor, or lay clerk*   non-clerical leader of a church or cathedral choir

35 (p. 14) *No wretched monk . . . stalls and seats and desks*   Monks stood throughout long services, but were able to lean against tip-up seats called misericords, the undersides of which were often carved with scenes from the Bible, mythology and everyday life.

36 (p. 16) *engineering into the East*   In the nineteenth century British engineers designed and supervised many major projects in the Middle East and Asia; see also notes 51 and 101.

37 (p. 16) *my wife . . . the day*   from the second verse of 'Begone, dull care' (see note 32)

38 (p. 16) *'Nothing half so sweet in life'*   Thomas Moore (1779–1852), 'Love's Young Dream', *Irish Melodies* (1807–35): 'there's nothing half so sweet in life / As love's young dream.'

39 (p. 17) *small salad*   mustard and cress

40 (p. 17) *the ogre . . . his bread*   In the stories of 'Jack and the Beanstalk' and 'Jack the Giant-Killer' the giant cries 'Fee, fau, fum, / I smell the blood of an Englishman, / Be he alive, or be he dead, / I'll grind his bones to make my bread'. See Charles Faulkner's article for a discussion of how CD uses these stories in *MED*

41 (p. 18) *receiving the foul fiend*   Compare Shakespeare, *King Lear* (1604–5), 3, 4, 127, where Edgar refers to the devil as the 'foul fiend'; in theatrical performances the Devil often entered and exited through a trapdoor in the stage.

42 (p. 18) *scarlet beans*   another reference to Jack the Giant-Killer

43 (p. 18) *a stiff-necked generation*   Exodus 33:5: 'Ye are a stiff-necked people.'

44 (p. 18) *walled up alive . . . world alive ever since*   a punishment for nuns who broke their vows of chastity and became pregnant.

45 (pp. 18–19) *animal magnetism*   a term often applied to mesmerism

46 (p. 19) *Tunbridge Wells*   a fashionable spa resort, about 26 miles west of Rochester

47 (p. 20) *transported*   Criminals were transported to the American colonies from the early seventeenth century until Independence in 1776. Various locations in Australia were developed as penal colonies from 1790, but the last transportation to Botany Bay was in 1840, and by the mid 1860s the practice has been abolished altogether.

48 (p. 20) *the mark goes round*   'In schools, a badge worn by the pupil

who has last committed some particular fault. *to pass the mark*: to get rid of the badge in detecting a schoolfellow in the same fault' (*OED*).

49 (p. 20) *Wandering Jewess* derived from the wandering Jew, a legendary figure said to have taunted Christ on the cross and to have been condemned to wander until the Second Coming

50 (p. 21) *an acidulated drop* a boiled sweet flavoured with tartaric acid

51 (p. 24) *Egypt . . . country* The Suez Canal opened in November 1869, but interest in Egypt had been steadily increasing since the early years of the nineteenth century when, following Napoleon's defeat in the Revolutionary Wars, the country became more accessible to British travellers and antiquarians, who began to excavate archaeological sites and to ship home their finds. Egyptian exhibitions, such as Belzoni's (see note 53) were extremely popular, and the history of Egypt, now better known and understood, offered a new subject for the curriculum of schools like Miss Twinkleton's.

52 (p. 25) *Isises . . . Ibises . . . Cheopses . . . Pharaohses* Isis was wife of the God Osiris . . . the ibis was a sacred bird in ancient Egypt . . . Cheops was the Pharaoh who built the Great Pyramid

53 (p. 25) *Belzoni* Giovanni Batista Belzoni (1778–1823), Italian Egypt-ologist, whose exhibitions at the Egyptian Hall in London's Piccadilly in 1821–2 were extremely popular

54 (p. 28) *you Egyptian boys . . . phantoms* Divination from a pool of ink was common in Egypt and other Asian countries. Indians practise it in Wilkie Collins's, *The Moonstone* (1868), First Period, Chapter III; see also the opening sentence of *Adam Bede* (1859) by George Eliot (1819–80): 'With a single drop of ink for a mirror, the Egyptian sorcerer undertakes to reveal to any chance comer far-reaching visions of the past.' Gypsies, thought at the time to be Egyptians, were also said to use this method of divination. See also 'The Magic Crystal', *Household Words*, 2, 14 December 1850, 284–8.

55 (p. 28) *'dresses at'* '*dress at*. to dress and adorn in order to enamour or gain the affection of a person' (*OED*)

56 (p. 28) *My Lord* usual mode of address to a bishop of the Church of England

57 (p. 29) *eight-day clock* running for eight days before being wound

58 (p. 30) *'When the French' . . . infancy* Sapsea is nearly sixty and is recalling a popular toast of 1804, when Napoleon was camped at Boulogne with an army of invasion.

59 (p. 31) *it is not good . . . alone* Genesis 2: 18: 'And the Lord God said, it is not good that man should be alone; I will make him an help meet for him.'

60 (p. 31) *the finger of scorn* Shakespeare, *Othello* (1603), 4, 2, 53–5: 'but alas, to make me / The fixed figure for the time of scorn / To point his slow unmoving finger at!'.

61 (p. 32) *wasting . . . air*   compare Thomas Gray (1716–71), *Elegy Written in a Country Church-Yard* (1751): 'Full many a flower is born to blush unseen, / And waste its sweetness on the desert air.'

62 (p. 32) *Man . . . disposes*   see Thomas à Kempis (1380–1471) *De Imitatione Christi* [*The Imitation of Christ*]: 'Man proposes, heaven disposes'; see also Proverbs 16: 9: 'A man's heart deviseth his way: but the Lord directeth his steps'; more commonly 'Man proposes, God disposes'

63 (p. 33) *the chartered libertine*   Shakespeare, *Henry V* (1599), I, 1, 44–8: 'When he speaks, / The air, a charter'd libertine, is still'

64 (p. 34) *the bench of justices*   the local magistrates

65 (p. 34) *dipping . . . Death*   figures sometimes found on public clocks, moving as described whenever the clock strikes; also to be found in waxwork and other exhibitions

66 (p. 34) *Catechism . . . life*   see the Catechism in *BCP*: 'that I should keep God's holy will and commandments, and walk in the same all the days of my life'

67 (p. 35) *wards*   the configurations on a key, matching those in the lock

68 (p. 36) *as though . . . iron*   Ostriches swallow hard objects to aid digestion; hence the popular belief about their diet.

69 (p. 37) *Mulled*   missed (from 'mull', a miss or muddle)

70 (p. 37) *cock-shy*   a throw at a target, as at a fair

71 (p. 37) *Widdy . . . warning*   a variation on a song accompanying a children's chasing-game. The catcher sings 'Whiddy, whiddy way, / If you don't come, I won't play', and the targets reply 'Warning once, warning twice, warning three times over; / When the cock crows out come I / Whiddy whiddy wake-cock. Warning', and the chase begins.

72 (p. 37) *note of preparation*   Shakespeare, *Henry V*, Chorus, 4, 12–14: 'The armorers . . . . / With busy hammer closing rivets up, / Give dreadful note of preparation.'

73 (p. 37) *Travellers' Twopenny . . . Deputy*   a cheap lodging-house . . . an ironical use of the name given to workhouse officials

74 (p. 38) *the common folk . . . turf and brambles*   The cemetery contains unconsecrated ground, reserved for suicides, paupers and unbaptised infants, who would be wrapped as described rather than being placed in coffins

75 (p. 38) *Peter the Wild Boy*   a feral child discovered in a wood near Hanover in 1724 and brought to England in 1725, where he died in 1785

76 (p. 39) *National Education*   Demands for a national system of education grew during the 1860s, CD supporting the campaign. The Education Act of 1870 was the first important step towards free and compulsory education for all children.

77 (p. 40) *hanged by the neck . . . until they are dead*   The wording of the death sentence was: 'The sentence of this Court upon you is, that you be taken from this place to a lawful prison and thence to a place of execution and that you be hanged by the neck until you are dead.' Capital punishment was abolished in Great Britain in 1965.

78 (p. 41) *lights of rush or cotton dip*   made by dipping a reed or a cotton wick in grease and producing only a dim light

79 (p. 41) *according to a custom . . . Saint Stephen*   CD was concerned that the police did not offer the public enough protection against hooligans: see 'The Ruffian' in *The Uncommercial Traveller* (1860) . . . Stephen, the first Christian martyr, was stoned to death

80 (p. 42) *Chanticleer*   the cock in the medieval French fable *Reynard the Fox* and 'The Nun's Priest's Tale', in *The Canterbury Tales* (begun *c.*1387) by Geoffrey Chaucer (*c.*1343–1400)

81 (p. 42) *six weak little . . . lighted*   Compare Pip in *Great Expectations* (1860–1), five of whose brothers have died; the (thirteen) originals of those graves are in Cooling churchyard near Rochester

82 (p. 43) *pier-glass*   a tall mirror, usually hung between windows

83 (p. 43) *Chancery . . . Noble Art*   the action in boxing of locking an opponent's head under your arm; see also CD's attack on the Court of Chancery, whose victims could be locked for years in legal actions, in *Bleak House* (1852–3)

84 (p. 43) *the dress of a china shepherdess . . . colours*   Porcelain figures in brightly coloured pastoral costumes had been manufactured since the early eighteenth century in the Meissen factory at Dresden and were popular as table decorations.

85 (p. 44) *Haven of Philanthropy*   CD has in mind Exeter Hall in the Strand, a non-sectarian building opened in 1831 and used for meetings by religious, scientific, educational and charitable organisations. As the portrait of Luke Honeythunder (see note 88) suggests, CD was sceptical of much philanthropic activity, which he saw as self-important, bullying and. patronising. Further comments on the attitude Exeter Hall represented for CD may be found in 'The Niger Expedition', *Examiner*, 19 August 1848 and 'A Handful of Humbugs', *All the Year Round*, 12 September 1863. The building was demolished in 1907.

86 (p. 45) *the paths of peace*   Proverbs 3:17: 'Her ways are the ways of pleasantness, and all her paths are peace.'

87 (p. 45) *an inmate to be read with*   Neville will be a resident student of Crisparkle's

88 (p. 43) *Luke Honeythunder*   This character appears to be based on John Bright (1811–89), radical politician and philanthropist, known for his abrasive and hectoring manner.

89 (p. 46) *Superior Family Souchong*   a fine black China tea

90 (p. 46) *corporation preferment in London City*   a clerical living in the gift of the Lord Mayor and Aldermen of the City of London

91 (p. 46) *the fairy bride that is to be*   alluding to the song 'The Mistletoe Bough', with words by T. H. Bayley about a young bride who hides in a chest during a Christmas game, and whose skeleton is found many years later, and perhaps suggesting something about the development of the plot of *MED*

92 (p. 47) *In those days . . . railway*   From 1844 it was possible to travel from London Bridge to Maidstone, and then continue to Rochester, twenty miles away, by omnibus. Strood station, near Rochester, on the line from Victoria, was opened in 1853.

93 (p. 47) *to ruin the money market . . . church and state if it succeeded*   Railways were the object of heavy investment in the nineteenth century and a failed company could seriously affect the stock market. Many, like Sapsea, saw in the coming of the railways, especially if trains were allowed to run on Sundays, a threat to religious and civil stability.

94 (p. 47) *Elephant . . . Castle*   The ancient Elephant and Castle inn stood at the meeting point, south of the Thames, of roads into London from Kent and Surrey.

95 (p. 48) *The worm will , when –*   See Shakespeare, *3 Henry VI* (1590–1) 2, 2, 17: 'The smallest worm will turn, being trodden on.'

96 (p. 49) *you were to abolish . . . shoot them*   In 1865 Governor John Eyre of Jamaica was threatened with prosecution (a course of action supported by John Bright: see note 88) after he dealt with an insurrection by declaring a period of martial law during which three hundred people were killed and many imprisoned. CD supported the Eyre Defence Fund which helped the Governor to be exonerated.

97 (p. 49) *the apple of the eye . . . to sweep off the face of the earth . . . love your brother as yourself*   biblical references used ironically to indicate the aggressive nature of Honeythunder's philanthropy: see Psalms 17:8 and Proverbs 7:2 . . . Genesis 6:7 . . . Leviticus 19:18 and Matthew 19:19

98 (p. 51) *Ceylon*   now Sri Lanka, occupied by the British since 1796, and a British colony since 1802

99 (p. 54) *dressed as a boy*   an important hint for those readers who believe that Datchery is a disguised Helena Landless

100 (p. 56) *the future wives and mothers of England*   an allusion to Mrs Sarah Ellis, author of *The Women of England* (1839), *The Daughters of England* (1842), *The Mothers of England* and *The Wives of England* (both 1843), which advocate a subordinate role for women

101 (p. 60) *'Going to wake up Egypt a little . . . Doing, working, engineering*   see notes 37 and 51

102 (p. 62) *stirrup-cup*   a drink taken by fox-hunters before setting out

103 (p. 63) *Juno . . . Venus*   Roman goddesses of power, wisdom, chastity and love

104 (p. 64) *The world . . . choose*   John Milton (1608–74), *Paradise Lost* (1667), 12:646–7: 'The World was all before them, where to choose / Their place of rest, and Providence their guide'

105 (p. 64) *pluck the golden fruit that hangs ripe on the tree for him*   a reference to the golden apples of the Hesperides, Juno's gift to Jupiter on their wedding day

106 (p. 67) *The south . . . lists*   John 3:8: 'The wind bloweth where it listeth'

107 (p. 70) *birds of the air*   Ecclesiastes 10:20: ' . . . a bird of the air shall carry the voice, and that which hath wings shall tell the matter.'

108 (p. 71) *the Graces*   in Greek mythology personifying beauty (Euphrosyne), grace (Aglaia) and charm (Thalia)

109 (p. 71) *Peter Piper . . . picked*   a popular tongue-twister: 'If Peter Piper picked a peck of pickled pepper / Where's the peck of pickled pepper Peter Piper picked?'

110 (p. 72) *Queen Elizabeth's . . . Tilbury fort*   Queen Elizabeth reviewed and spoke to her troops at Tilbury on 8 August 1588 after the Spanish Armada had been dispersed but while there was still a threat of invasion. She is usually represented as being alone on this occasion, so Mrs Tisher takes on an imaginary role. See the brief account of this event in CD's *A Child's History of England* (1851–4), Chapter 31.

111 (p. 72) *the bard of Avon . . . the immortal Shakespeare . . . the Swan of his native river*   frequently used epithets for Shakespeare; see Ben Jonson (*c.*1573–1637), 'To the Memory of . . . Shakespeare' (1623): 'Sweet Swan of Avon'

112 (p. 72) *Rumour . . . tongues . . . elsewhere*   Shakespeare, *Henry IV, Part 2* (1598), Induction (stage direction): 'Enter RUMOUR, painted full of tongues' . . . rumour is often personified in Shakespeare: see 2 *Henry VI* (1590–1) 3, 1, 197–8, *Julius Caesar* (1599) 2, 4, 18–19 and *Macbeth* 4, 2, 19–21

113 (p. 72) *Who drew . . . Jew*   Miss Twinkleton misremembers the couplet, 'This is the Jew / That Shakespeare drew', a tribute to Charles Macklin's celebrated performance as Shylock in February 1741, lines sometimes attributed to Alexander Pope (1688–1744).

114 (p. 72) *Monsieur la Fontaine*   Jean de la Fontaine (1621–95), whose poetic versions of Aesop's *Fables* appeared in 1668, 1678 and 1694

115 (p. 72) *'airy nothings'*   Shakespeare, *A Midsummer Night's Dream* (1595–6), 5, 1, 15–17: 'And as imagination bodies forth / The form of things unknown, the poet's pen / Turns them to shapes, and gives to aery nothing / A local habitation and a name.'

116 (p. 74) *My visits . . . between*   See Robert Blair (1699–1746), 'The Grave' (1743), 586–9: 'its visits, / Like those of angels, short, and far

between'; but CD could also have derived the phrase from Thomas Campbell (1777–1844), *The Pleasures of Hope* (1799), ii, 378: ' ... oh! leave the light of HOPE behind! / What though my wingèd hours of bliss have been, / Like angel-visits, few and far between.'

117 (p. 75) *the Celestial Nine*   the Muses of Greek mythology

118 (p. 76) *a bear ... cotillion*   dancing bears were still exhibited in the nineteenth century ... a French quadrille or square dance

119 (p. 77) *personality*   in the sense of 'distinctive, personal or individual charcater' (*OED*) such as might be inferred from the name Bud

120 (p. 77) *pen-and-ink-ubus*   apparently a well-worn pun even in the nineteenth century

121 (p. 80) *the throat of Old Time*   Time is usually personified as an old man with a scythe.

122 (p. 80) *grill-gate of the chancel*   The east end of a cathedral is often divided off by such gates, of iron or, more rarely, wood.

123 (p. 85) *Constantia*   red wine, valued as a tonic, from a vineyard near Cape Town, South Africa

124 (p. 85) *Handel in a flowing wig*   Georg Friedrich Handel (1685–1759), composer, resident in England from 1712; probably alluding to the much-reproduced portrait by Thomas Hudson (1701–79) in the National Portrait Gallery

125 (p. 86) *japanned*   laquered and decorated in an Oriental style

126 (p. 86) *ladies' fingers*   long thin sponge cakes

127 (p. 86) *like the highly popular lamb ... led to the slaughter*   Isaiah 53:7: ' ... he is brought as a lamb to the slaughter, and as a sheep before her shearers is dumb, so he openeth not his mouth'. Just before he died CD replied to a correspondent who had written to complain about the tastelessness of this apparent reference to Christ: 'I have always striven in my writings to express veneration for the life and lessons of Our Saviour; because I feel it ... But I have never made proclamation of this from the house tops' (to John Makeham, 8 June 1870, *Letters*, XII, p. 548).

128 (p. 87) *Lady Macbeth ... seas that roll*   see *Macbeth*, 2, 2, 57–60; 5, 1, 50–2 : 'Will all great Neptune's oceans wash this blood / Clean from my hand? No: this my hand will rather / The multitudinous seas incarnadine, / Making the green one red'; 'All the perfumes of Arabia will not sweeten this little hand'

129 (p. 90) *the Searcher of all hearts*   Romans 8:27: 'And he that searcheth the hearts knoweth what is the mind of the Spirit, because he maketh intercession for the saints according to the will of God'; see also the Collect for Holy Communion, *BCP*: 'Almighty God, unto whom all hearts be open, all desires known, and from whom no secrets are hid'

130 (p. 92) *'What is the matter? Who did it?'* see *Macbeth*, 3, 4, 47: 'Which of you have done this?', Macbeth's words when he sees Banquo's ghost

131 (p. 96) *Old Bourne* a tributary of the Fleet, which once flowed down Holborn, a main thoroughfare in central London, north of the Strand.

132 (p. 96) *Staple Inn* formerly one of the Inns of Chancery, medieval establishments with the power to validate barristers, built round a quadrangle at the west of Holborn

133 (p. 96) *a little hall with a little lantern in its roof* Built in 1581, the hall of Staple Inn has a wooden roof with a windowed lantern in the centre.

134 (p. 97) *PJT 1747* the initials of Principal John Thompson, President of Staple Inn in 1747

135 (p. 97) *convey . . . Pistol says* Shakespeare, *The Merry Wives of Windsor* (1597), 1, 3, 30: '"Convey," the wise it call it. "Steal"? foh! a *fico* for the phrase!'; a euphemism for stealing, conveyancing being the legal act of transferring property (usually houses) from one owner to another

136 (p. 97) *a pretty fat receivership* 'A receiver is appointed by the court to receive money on behalf of others, frequently in regard to a deceased state or bankruptcy' (Jacobson, p. 111).

137 (p. 97) *under the dry vine and fig tree* 1 Kings 4: 25: 'And Judah and Israel dwelt safely, every man under his vine and under his fig tree.'

138 (p. 98) *the hotel in Furnival's Inn* Wood's Hotel, in the archway of this former Inn of Chancery, where CD lived, 1834–7

139 (p. 98) *a fabulous familiar* a spirit who performs magical acts for a sorcerer, like the genie in the story of Aladdin from the *Arabian Nights*

140 (p. 98) *that baleful tree of Java* the upas tree (*Antiaris toxicari*) whose vapour was believed to kill everything in its vicinity

141 (p. 99) *made-dish* a dish containing a variety of ingredients, usually re-cooked

142 (p. 101) *Circumlocution Department* an imaginary government office, devoted to 'How not to do it'; compare the Circumlocution Office in CD's *Little Dorrit* (1855–7), Chap. 10

143 (p. 101) *National Gallery* in Trafalgar Square, London, designed by William Wilkins and built 1832–8 to contain the national collection of paintings

144 (p. 101) *Dr Kitchener's . . . Harvey* William Kitchiner [sic] (c. 1775–1835), author of *The Cook's Oracle* (1817), the subject of two odes by Thomas Hood (1799–1845) . . . a sauce invented by Peter Harvey for use in his inn, later marketed by his sister

145 (p. 101) *like Macbeth's leg . . . Duncan* When playing Macbeth CD's friend, the actor William Charles Macready (1793–1873), would

leave his leg and foot in sight on the stage for some time to signify reluctance before departing to murder Duncan (see *Macbeth*, 2, 1).

146 (p. 103) *charity boy . . . catechism*   a pupil at a charitable school . . . a set of questions and answers about Christian doctrine, to be found in *BCP*

147 (p. 104) *trench upon*   'to encroach or infringe on . . . a region which is the domain of another' (*OED*)

148 (p. 105) *Joss*   pidgin English for an Eastern idol (rather than, as implied here, a devotee)

149 (p. 106) *ashes among ashes, and dust among dust*   ' . . . we therefore commit his body to the ground; earth to earth, ashes to ashes, dust to dust; in sure and certain hope of the Resurrection to eternal life' (Burial Service, *BCP*)

150 (p. 108) *Mayor of Cloisterham*   the chief magistrate or head of the council of a town or city

151 (p. 108) *'going up' with addresses*   delivering addresses to the monarch on behalf of a town or city, often resulting in a knighthood for the mayor

152 (p. 108) *Of such is the salt of the earth*   Matthew 5: 13 and Mark 10: 14: 'Ye art the salt of the earth' and ' . . . of such is the kingdom of God'

153 (p. 109) *kickshaw ditties*   cheap or worthless (and in this case foreign – the name derives from the French *quelque chose*) songs

154 (p. 109) *the genuine George III . . . hearts of oak*   George III (reigned 1760–1820) was the first Hanoverian monarch to be born and brought up in England . . . See David Garrick (1717–79), 'Heart of Oak' in *Harlequin's Invasion* (1759): 'Heart of oak are our ships / Heart of oak are our men'; a common image in popular nationalistic songs, many dating from George III's reign, including some in Charles Dibdin's *Songs, Naval and National* (1841), owned by CD

155 (p. 109) *Archbishop of York or Canterbury*   the two archbishops of the Church of England, Canterbury being the senior

156 (p. 109) *fetch*   a ghost or double of a living person

157 (p. 110) *a lover of the picturesque*   The 'tombs, vaults, towers, and ruins' mentioned by Jasper are among the stage properties of the 'Graveyard School' of eighteenth-century poets, including Thomas Gray (whose *Elegy Written in a Country Churchyard* is the best-known example of the genre) and Thomas Warton (1728–90). This melancholy poetry was one of the forerunners of English Romanticism, but also, and perhaps more relevant to this novel, of the Gothic Revival, predominant in European culture in the late eighteenth and early nineteenth centuries, and an influence on CD's work.

158 (p. 112) *the lamplighter . . . aghast at the idea of abolishing*   Lamplighters with their ladders and oil-lamps were familiar figures

in English towns and cities, and although gas lamps also needed to be lighted by hand, local authorities often resisted their introduction. Nonetheless gas lighting, first introduced in London in 1820, spread steadily throughout the country during the nineteenth century.

159 (p. 112) *pea-jacket*   a short woollen overcoat, as worn by sailors

160 (p. 113) *Dance of Death*   a series of drawings by Hans Holbein (?1497–1543), of which CD owned an 1833 edition

161 (p. 113) *'animal spirits, or ardent?'*   The phrase 'animal spirits' had been used since the sixteenth century to describe the means by which the brain, usually described as the soul or the will, is able to operate in the physical body. 'Ardent' spirits, which Durdles has been imbibing from his bottle, jug and tumbler, are alcoholic, with a fiery taste.

162 (p. 113) *quicklime*   calcium oxide (CaO), highly corrosive unless slaked with water; wrongly believed to hasten the decomposition of corpses; perhaps a hint of how Jasper plans to dispose of Edwin's body

163 (p. 116) *Chairs to mend*   the street-cry of itinerant bodgers or chair menders

164 (p. 118) *aeronauts*   a reference to ballooning, a popular pastime in the nineteenth century

165 (p. 118) *calenture*   a fever affecting people in hot climates, occasionally leading to delusions causing the sufferers to leap from high places

166 (p. 120) *wouldn't go home till morning*   parody of John Buckstone (1802–79), 'Billy Taylor', to the tune 'We Won't Go Home Till Morning', from the air 'Malborough' [sic] or 'Malbrook', dating from campaigns led by the Duke of Marlborough (1650–1722) against France in the years 1702–11: 'On such an occasion as this, / All time and nonsense scorning, / Nothing shall come amiss, / And we won't go home till morning.'

167 (p. 120) *'bellows me!'*   Bellows was a slang term for the lungs and at boxing matches the spectators would cry 'bellows him well!', encouraging one of the fighters not to spare his opponent but to knock the breath out of him.

168 (p. 121) *'the half'* . . . *'the term'*   The school year was divided into two halves, with the break at Christmas. Following the recommendations of the Taunton Commission of 1867–8, however, and in accordance with the practice of universities and the law, the school year was divided into four terms.

169 (p. 122) *little Rickitts . . . steel drops daily*   These iron chloride drops are for anaemia, but note the pun on rickets, a bone-softening condition caused by vitamin deficiency, common among the poor.

170 (p. 122) *pomatum*   scented hair ointment

171 (p. 122) '*at home*'   an informal social gathering

172 (p. 122) *a drawing room*   an ironical use of a phrase used to describe a royal reception

173 (p. 122) *brown Holland*   coarse linen

174 (p. 122) *pound-cake*   a rich, sweet cake, so-called because it contains a pound of each ingredient

175 (pp. 122–3) *Mr Addison's impressive tragedy*   Joseph Addison (1672–1719), *Cato* (1713)

176 (p. 123) *Spartan general . . . specify*   Before the battle of Thermopylae (480BCE), where three hundred Spartans resisted the Persian army, Leonidas told his men 'let us dine cheerfully here, for tonight we shall sup with Pluto'. In Greek mythology, Pluto is the king of the underworld.

177 (p. 123) *next friend at law*   a legal term for next of kin or a close friend

178 (p. 124) *Rosebud in her bower*   Rosamund Clifford (d. 1176?) was known as 'Fair Rosamond'. Her beauty attracted Henry II (reigned 1154–1189), who built a bower for her in the centre of a labyrinth at Woodstock near Oxford, where she died, possibly poisoned by Henry's wife, Queen Eleanor. In *A Child's History of England* (Chapter 12) CD casts doubt on the authenticity of this 'pretty story', and tells a different version which has Rosamond dying in a nunnery.

179 (p. 129) *what do you see from the turret?*   In the story of Bluebeard, his last wife, afraid that she is about to be murdered like her predecessors, begs for time to say her prayers and meanwhile asks her sister to keep watch for their brothers who are coming to their rescue: 'Sister Anne, Sister Anne, what do you see from the tower?' See the discussion of this allusion in Faulkner, pp. 85–6.

180 (p. 132) *When Shall These Three Meet Again?*   *Macbeth*, 1, 1, 1: 'When shall we three meet again?'

181 (p. 132) *currants . . . sugar*   ingredients for Christmas pudding or Christmas cake

182 (p. 132) *Twelfth . . . Harlequin*   an ornamental cake eaten on Twelfth-night (5 January), at the end of the Christmas season . . . a mischievous figure in a multi-coloured costume, adopted into English pantomime from the Italian *commedia dell-arte*; an appropriate figure for Twelfth-night celebrations, when many established social hierarchies were subverted

183 (p. 132) *waxwork . . . China*   CD may have had in mind Letter 45 of *Letters from a Citizen of the World to His Friends in the* East (1760) by Oliver Goldsmith (?1730–1774) which describes the reactions of a Chinese philosopher to various exhibitions he has seen in London.

Also, compare Mrs Jarley's waxworks in *The Old Curiosity Shop* (1840–1).

184 (p. 132) *Jacksonini*   Clowns often adopted Italian-sounding names, Italy being the home of pantomime. In 1838 CD edited *Memoirs of Joseph Grimaldi* (1779–1837), a clown born in England to an Italian father; see also 'Private Theatres' in *Sketches by Boz* (1836–7).

185 (p. 135) *his own . . . body*   Juvenal (1st century), *Satires*, x, 356: '*mens sana in corpore sano*' ['a healthy mind in a healthy body'], the tacit philosophy of many English public (i.e. private, fee-paying) schools

186 (p. 140) *bottomless pit*   Hell; see Revelations 20:1: 'And I saw an angel come down from heaven, having the key of the bottomless pit and a great chain in his hand.'

187 (p. 140) *to have . . . this law*   'Lord have mercy upon us, and incline our hearts to keep this law', the congregation's response to the Ten Commandments in the Communion service in *BCP*

188 (p. 140) *a large . . . silk*   Luke Fildes, illustrator of *MED*, said that CD told him that Edwin was to be strangled with the scarf (see Jacobson, pp. 131–2). It has also been suggested that Jasper is a member of the Indian religious sect the Phanigars or Thuggees, devotees of the death-goddess Kali, who committed ritual murder in her name.

189 (p. 143) *chimneys topple*   see *Macbeth* 2, 3, 54–6, on the night of Duncan's murder: 'The night has been unruly. Where we lay, / Our chimneys were blown down, (and, as they say) / Lamentings heard i' th' air; strange screams of death.'

190 (p. 144) *Tilted Wagon*   with a tilt, a canvas cover

191 (p. 145) *to set his mark upon some of them*   Genesis 4:15: 'And the Lord set a mark upon Cain, lest any finding him should kill him.'

192 (p. 146) *Where is your nephew? . . . Why do you ask me?*   compare God's question to Cain after he has murdered Abel, Genesis 4:9: 'And the Lord said unto Cain, Where is Abel thy brother? And he said, I know not: Am I my brother's keeper?'

193 (p. 148) *Mr Sapsea's parlour*   the Mayor's office or private room

194 (p. 148) *He washed his hands as clean as he could*   Matthew 27:24: 'When Pilate saw that he could prevail nothing . . . he took water, and washed his hands before the multitude, saying, I am innocent of the blood of this just person'

195 (p. 152) *the castles . . . for him*   'castles in the air': daydreams of plans for the future

196 (p. 153) *a seven day's wonder*   something that is 'news' for a short time; usually nine days, but compare the seven wonders of the world

197 (p. 156) *airy tongues that syllable men's names*   Milton, *Comus* (*A Maske presented at Ludlow-castle, 1634*), 205–9: 'What might this be? A thousand fantasies / Begin to throng into my memory / Of calling

shapes, and beck'ning shadows dire, / And airy tongues, that syllable men's names / On Sands, and Shoars, and desert Wildernesses.'

198 (p. 157) *grey hairs with sorrow to the grave*   an allusion to the story of Joseph, Genesis 42:38: 'if mischief befall him by the way in the which ye go, then shall ye bring down my grey hair with sorrow to the grave'

199 (p. 157) *the last man*   Thomas Browne (1605–82), *Religio Medici* (1642, 1643), 1.58: 'my desires onely are (and I shall be happy therein,) to be but the last man, and bring up the Rere in Heaven'; Thomas Campbell and Thomas Hood both wrote poems with this title.

200 (p. 157) *in the words of Bentham . . . number*   The utilitarian philosopher Jeremy Bentham (1748–1832) argued that society should be organised according to 'the greatest happiness of the greatest number'. CD attacked this philosophy in *Hard Times* (1854).

201 (p. 158) *Jasper laboured night and day*   1 Thessalonians 2:9: 'For ye remember, brethren, our labour and travail: for labouring night and day, because we would not be chargeable to any of you, we preached unto you the gospel of God'; see also 2 Thessalonians 3:8

202 (p. 159) *'The days of taking sanctuary are past'*   In former times criminals and other fugitives could take refuge in churches, which were regarded as consecrated spaces, outside the jurisdiction of the secular authorities. The practice was legislatively abolished in 1723.

203 (p. 160) *'we clergy need do nothing emphatically'*   a topical reference; Cardwell draws attention to 'The Duty of Keeping the Church Insignificant' (*Spectator*, 9 October 1869), criticising the Church of England's appointment of clergy with no extreme views, to avoid criticism

204 (p. 160) *and he went . . . name and fame*   Genesis 4:13–14: 'And Cain said unto the Lord, My punishment is greater than I can bear. Thou hast driven me out this day from the face of the earth; and from thy face shall I be hid; and I shall be fugitive and a vagabond in the earth; and it shall come to pass; that every one that findeth me shall slay me.'

205 (pp. 160–1) *phrenological formation . . . those organs*   Phrenology was a pseudo-scientific practice developed and popularised by the Viennese Franz Joseph Gall (1757–1828), who argued that mental functions could be associated with particular areas ('organs') in the brain, the size of the organ being a guide to an individual's propensity towards a particular trait of mind, personality or behaviour. With the aid of phrenological heads marking the position of these organs a person's head could be 'read'. The theory was applied to education, criminology and penology and

used by many (including novelists) for psychological purposes. The organ of combativeness, relevant here, was said to lie behind the ear.

206 (p. 161) *Fancy . . . mill*   boxing . . . fight

207 (p. 161) *Frosty-Faced Fogo*   Nicknamed for his pock-marked skin, Jack Fogo was a boxing promoter and sports writer in the early nineteenth century

208 (p. 163) *swept off the face of the earth by a deed of violence*   Genesis 6:7: 'And the Lord said, I will destroy man whom I have created from the face of the earth'

209 (p. 163) *Abel! Cain!*   see Genesis 4:1–17

210 (p. 163) *The Commandments say, no murder*   Exodus 20:13 and Deuteronomy 5:17: 'Thou shalt not kill', but see also Communion in *BCP*: 'Thou shalt do no murder'

211 (p. 163) *you shall bear no false witness*   Exodus 20:16: 'Thou shalt not bear false witness against thy neighbour'; see also Deuteronomy 5:20

212 (p. 164) *necessity . . . oppressed*   see The Litany in *BCP*: 'We beseech thee to hear us, good Lord. That it may please thee to succour, help, and comfort, all that are in danger, necessity, and tribulation.'

213 (p. 164) *playing-fields keeping a wicket*   In cricket the wicket-keeper stands behind the stumps and gathers the ball when it goes past the batsman; alertness, fearlessness, rapid reactions and a safe pair of hands are required of the player occupying this position.

214 (p. 164) *caps . . . if they like*   the proverbial expression is 'if the cap fits, wear it'

215 (p. 165) *I will not bow down to a false God of your making*   Exodus 20:3–5: 'Thou shalt have no other gods before me. Thou shalt not make unto thee any graven image . . . Thou shalt not bow down thyself to them, nor serve them'; see also Deuteronomy 5:7–9

216 (p. 165) *turn heaven's creatures into swine and wild beasts*   perhaps a submerged allusion to Book 10 of the *Odyssey* by Homer (eighth to ninth centuries BCE), where the sorceress Circe turns Odysseus's crew into swine

217 (p. 165) *run amuck like so many mad Malays*   There was a popular belief that Malays behave in this manner when under the influence of opium, as described by Thomas de Quincey (1785–1859) in *Confessions of an English Opium Eater* (1822).

218 (p. 167) *'I feel marked and tainted'*   another allusion to the story of Cain: see note 192

219 (p. 167) *to be so tied to a stake*   see *Macbeth* 5, 7, 1–2: : 'They have tied me to a stake; I cannot fly'

220 (p. 168) *while the grass grows, the steed starves*   proverbial expression first recorded in English in the mid-fourteenth century

221 (p. 171) *the yet unfinished and undeveloped railway station*   London Bridge station opened in modest buildings in 1836; a proper station was built, 1840–44 and rebuilt in 1849.

222 (p. 171) *my name is Tartar*   'Tar' (as in 'Jolly Jack Tar') is a slang name for a sailor.

223 (p. 174) *buffer*   colloquialism for a fellow or a chap, usually middle-aged to elderly

224 (p. 175) *game . . . butter*   a hiding and finding game in which seekers are told whether they are 'hot' or 'cold' according to how close they are to the hidden object. A nineteenth century version of the game begins, 'Hot boil'd beans and very good butter / If you please to come to supper!'

225 (p. 177) *making a leg*   bowing with one leg in front of him

226 (p. 179) *the end crowns the work*   Shakespeare, *Trolius and Cressida* (*c.*1603), 4, 5, 224: 'The end crowns all'

227 (p. 179) *the secrets of the prison-house*   Shakespeare, *Hamlet* 1, 5, 13–4: 'I am forbid / To tell the secrets of my prison-house'; the speaker is the ghost of Hamlet's murdered father.

228 (p. 180) *Apollo . . . his lyre*   the god of music and poetry, often represented with a lyre

229 (p. 180) *Mister Sapsea . . . occupation*   CD varies a rhyme often written by schoolchildren in their books. The formula usually runs: '— is my name / England is my nation / — is my dwelling-place / And Heaven's my expectation'.

230 (p. 182) *made of the dust of the earth*   Genesis 2:7: 'And the Lord formed man of the dust of the ground.'

231 (p. 182) *kennels*   central or side gutters to carry sewage down a street

232 (p. 182) *Bedouins*   pilgrims to Cloisterham are ironically likened to these tent-dwelling nomadic Arabs

233 (p. 182) *askant*   sideways, sceptically (a variation on 'askance')

234 (p. 188) *as certainly as night follows day*   Shakespeare, *Hamlet* 1, 3, 78–80: 'This above all: to thine own self be true, / And it must follow, as the night the day, / That thou canst not then be false to any man'

235 (p. 192) *over the housetops*   Railway viaducts, often passing through densely populated areas, carried trains to the centre of London, so the phrase describes a literal reality and yet has associations with the flights undertaken by characters in fairy tales.

236 (p. 193) *Confound . . . him again!*   variation on the second verse of the British national anthem by Henry Carey (1693?–1743): 'Confound their Politicks, / Frustrate their Knavish Tricks, / On him our Hopes we fix, / God save us all.'

237 (p. 199) *Chapter 21*   After CD's death Forster restored the cuts the author had made in the proofs of the fifth number. This made the

number too long so Forster carried the extra matter forward to the sixth number as this new separate chapter.

238 (p. 200) *fag*   in English public schools a junior boy who acted as a servant to one of his seniors

239 (p. 204) *a marvellous country . . . beanstalk*   another reference to Jack and the Beanstalk

240 (p. 204) *under the sun, moon, and stars*   Deuteronomy 4:19 'And lest thou lift up thine eyes unto heaven, and when thou seest the sun, and the moon, and the stars, even all the host of heaven'

241 (p. 204) *the London blacks*   specks of soot

242 (p. 205) *First Lady of the Admiralty*   The First Lord is the government official (not necessarily a sailor) in charge of the Royal Navy.

243 (p. 208) *I would sooner see you dead at his wicked feet*   Shakespeare, *The Merchant of Venice* (1596–7), 3, 1, 87–90: 'I would my daughter were dead at my foot, and the jewels in her ear! Would she were hears'd at my foot, and the ducats in her coffin!'

244 (p. 210) *Southampton Street, Bloomsbury Square*   a quiet respectable area of central London

245 (p. 210) *gas laid on*   Gas was being installed in London's private houses from the 1840s.

246 (p. 210) *jistes*   Mrs Billickins's pronunciation of joists: Forster says that CD recorded in his notebook this pronunciation (by a servant at his home at Tavistock House): see Forster, Book IX, Chap. VII.

247 (p. 211) *elewation*   The pronunciation of 'v' as 'w' was common in the nineteenth century among working-class people in London and south-east England.

248 (p. 212) *Bond Street . . . St James's Palace*   a highly fashionable street . . . a royal palace

249 (p. 212) *mews*   A street with stabling for horses, often running between two back-to-back terraces of houses. The smell sometimes made apparently smart addresses less than desirable.

250 (p. 212) *attendance*   servants

251 (p. 212) *agreement lines . . . earnest money*   preliminary contract . . . deposit

252 (p. 213) *down the airy*   An area is a small paved court, reached by steps from the street, giving access to the basement of a house.

253 (p. 213) *in a baronial way*   English barons sign with their surnames only

254 (p. 213) *Temple Stairs . . . Greenhithe*   on the Thames near the Inns of Court . . . south-east of London, near the Thames, roughly midway between London and Rochester

255 (p. 213) *The dead image of the sun in old woodcuts*   The sun was often represented as a broadly smiling face surrounded by beams of light.

256 (p. 214) *like a man . . . stockings slavery*   Sailors usually went bare-foot while at sea and found shoes and stockings uncomfortable.

257 (p. 216) *not Professed but Plain*   a cook, who could be relied upon to produce English dishes, as opposed to a professional chef, familiar with foreign cusines

258 (p. 218) *the mill I have heard of, in which young ladies could be ground up young*   The early nineteenth century industrial ballad 'Man-chester's Improving Daily' includes the verse 'The spinning-jennies whirl along, /Performing strange things, I've been told, sir, / For twisting fresh and making young / All maids who own they're grown too old, sir.' Many young women were literally 'ground' in accidents involving industrial machinery.

259 (p. 218) *lamb's fry*   the testicles of castrated lambs; a delicacy

260 (p. 218) *butcher's meat*   from animals slaughtered by butchers, as opposed to fowl and game

261 (p. 219) *sweetbreads*   the pancreas cooked as food

262 (p. 221) *he lived apart from human life*   Jacobson (p. 174) quotes Macbeth's words 'troops of friends, / I must not look to have' (5, 3, 25–6) and points out that Macready's interpretation of the role, with which CD was very familiar, emphasised Macbeth's increasing isolation.

263 (p. 222) *a hybrid hotel . . . behind Aldersgate Street, near the General Post Office*   The profusion of hotels in this area, opened to accommodate the ever-increasing number of rail passengers, makes this one impossible to identify.

264 (p. 222) *hotel, boarding-house or lodging-house*   a descending order of status, the choice as to description suggesting the democratising tendency of the railways

265 (p. 222) *the new Railway Advertisers*   Early publications with details of routes and train times such as the *Railway Times* (from 1837) and *Bradshaw's Railway Timetable* (first published in 1839 and issued monthly from 1841) included advertisements for accommodation in the vicinity of the major London stations.

266 (p. 222) *a pint of sweet blacking*   poor, treacly wine, reminiscent of boot polish

267 (p. 222) *Eastward*   from Aldersgate Street towards the docks

268 (p. 224) *cabbage-nets*   used to cook cabbages by suspending them over a pot of boiling water; a vivid and rather unpleasant metaphor for the state of Princess Puffer's lungs

269 (p. 224) *bubble and blow*   see *Macbeth*, 4, 1, 10–11: 'Double, double, toil and trouble; / Fire burn and cauldron bubble'

270 (p. 226) *'when it was really done, it seemed not worth the doing, it was done so soon'*   compare *Macbeth* 1, 7, 1–2: 'If it were done, when 'tis done, then 'twere well / It were done quickly .'

271 (p. 227) *time and place are both at hand*   see *Macbeth* 1, 7, 51–4 'Nor time, nor place, / Did then adhere, and yet you would make both: / They have made themselves, and that their fitness now / Does unmake you'

272 (p. 234) *Which . . . it would be immensely difficult for the State, however statistical, to do*   Governments in the nineteenth century relied increasingly on the collection of statistical data about the state of the nation. This ironical comment reveals CD's deep scepticism of the statistical approach in either the understanding or the solution of social problems.

273 (p. 234) *The travellers*   the lodging house

274 (p. 234) *jacks . . . Chayner men*   sailors . . . Chinamen

275 (p. 235) *the old tavern way of keeping scores*   Publicans kept a record of customers' debts by chalking them on a board.

276 (p. 235) *suits the action to the word*   Shakespeare, *Hamlet* 3, 2, 17–22: 'Suit the action to the word, the word to the action, with this special observance, that you o'erstep not the modesty of nature: for any thing so o'erdone is from the purpose of playing, whose end, both at the first and now, was and is, to hold the mirror up to nature'

277 (p. 235) *the one great garden of the whole cultivated island*   The county of Kent, famous for its orchards, hop fields and market gardens, is often referred to as 'the garden of England'. There may also be a submerged reference to the Garden of Eden.

278 (p. 235) *the Resurrection and the Life*   John 11: 25: 'I am the resurrection, and the life: he that believeth in me, though he were dead, yet shall he live'; the opening sentence of the Burial Service in *BCP*

Master Humphrey's Clock

1 (p. 243) *cricket-voice*   suggesting that the ticking of the clock resembles the sound made by this insect

2 (p. 243) *parish-clerk*   a lay member of the congregation in a Church of England parish who acts as recording officer and leads the responses during services

3 (p. 244) *alchemists*   Alchemy was an early stage of modern chemistry, and alchemists were particularly concerned to find a means of transforming base metal into gold.

4 (p. 247) *alderman, common-councilman . . . sheriff . . . Lord Mayor*   representatives elected in wards of the Corporation of London . . . the city's chief officer of justice . . . the prestigious and influential head of the Corporation, elected annually

5 (p. 247) *Guildhall*   Elections to the offices mentioned in the previous note were held in the Guildhall, the oldest parts of which

date from the fifteenth century, although a building used for ceremonial purposes had probably existed on the site since the eleventh century.

6 (p. 248) *recorder for the city of London*   a judge in a city or borough court

7 (p. 248) *Honourable Society of the Middle Temple*   The name derives from the Knights Templar, an order founded in the eleventh century to protect pilgrims to Jerusalem. The Knights occupied several sites in London and from the mid-sixteenth century the Middle Temple was used for the training and accommodation of lawyers.

8 (p. 248) *de facto . . . de jure*   actual, but not legally recognised . . . rightful or legal

9 (p. 248) *Hull*   a fishing port and manufacturing city on the north-east coast

10 (p. 249) *the Mansion House*   the official residence of the Lord Mayor of London, built between 1739 and 1752 on the site of the Stocks Market near the Bank of England

11 (p. 252) *Gog and Magog*   a pair of legendary giants, seen as protectors of the City of London, whose effigies were carried in City processions, including the annual Lord Mayor's Show

12 (p. 252) *the Great Fire of London*   The fire of 2–4 September 1666 destroyed over 450 acres of London, mostly within the city walls.

13 (p. 254) *St. Paul's*   The first cathedral on the site, formerly occupied by a Roman temple, was founded in 604. The fourth cathedral, begun in the late eleventh century, was demolished after considerable damage in the Great Fire, and Christopher Wren's building was erected between 1675 and 1710.

14 (p. 254) *Tower*   the Tower of London, begun by William I (reigned 1066–87) and completed by Edward I (1272–1307), London's principal fortress, used as a court, a prison, especially for those accused of treason and heresy, and as a place of execution.

15 (p. 254) *Traitor's Gate*   a gate giving direct access from the Thames to the Tower

16 (p. 255) *the reign of Queen Elizabeth*   Elizabeth I (b. 1533), reigned 1558–1603

17 (p. 255) *the ward of Cheype*   the electoral division of the City that includes Cheapside, centre of the market area of medieval London

18 (p. 255) *Henry VIII*   Henry VIII (b. 1491), reigned 1509–47

19 (p. 256) *blue 'prentice cloak*   worn by those apprenticed to trades and crafts in the City

20 (p. 257) *caracoling*   describing a half-turn or wheel in equestrian dressage

21 (p. 260) *a royal proclamation . . . Spanish rapiers of preposterous length*   The exaggerated dress fashions of the Elizabethan period were often

attributed to foreign influences, and in 1580 a royal proclamation limited the length of swords to three feet and daggers to twelve inches, in both cases including the handle.

22 (p. 260) *Ludgate* named after a gate supposedly built by King Lud in 66 BCE; Ludgate Hill runs eastward from Ludgate Circus (at the junction with Fleet Street) to St Paul's

23 (p. 260) *St Paul's Churchyard* the continuation of Ludgate Hill on the south side of the Cathedral, and until the Great Fire the centre of the London book trade; previously used as a place of execution for religious martyrs and those convicted of treason, such as the Gunpowder Plot conspirators of 1605

24 (p. 261) *ordinary* an eating place serving meals at a fixed charge.

25 (p. 266) *Oxford Street* at that time largely composed of houses and places of entertainment

26 (p. 266) *Bloomsbury Square* a fashionable residential area since the seventeenth century

27 (p. 275) *the campaigns of 1677 and 1678. The treaty of Nijmegen* The Treaty brought to an end the Franco-Dutch War of 1672–78. England at first reluctantly participated as an ally of France, under the terms of a previous agreement with Louis XIV of France, but made a separate peace by the Treaty of Westminster in 1674. It is possible that the narrator, as a Protestant, joined the war on the Dutch side, since a strong element in England's reluctance to continue fighting the Dutch was a sense that there was little point in Protestants warring with each other. It was only a decade later that William of Orange, who emerged from the war with France with increased power, was invited to take the throne of England. The campaigns of 1677 and 1678 resulted in French victories at Cassel and Ghent.

28 (p. 281) *The Old Curiosity Shop* Serialisation of CD's novel in the context of *Master Humphrey's Clock* began in April 1840 (in number 4); after number 8 the device of Master Humphrey as the novel's narrator was discontinued, and the novel occupied the whole of numbers 12–45 (see p. 314) until its completion in February 1841.

29 (p. 282) *Bath* the best-known and most fashionable English spa town

30 (p. 282) *those rubbers . . . stood at eight* referring to scores at whist, a popular card game at watering places

31 (p. 282) *negus* a drink of sherry or port with hot water, sugar and spices

32 (p. 283) *Milton* John Milton (1608–74), English poet

33 (p. 283) *laudanum* a tincture of opium, popular (and readily available) in the nineteenth century, both as a treatment for medical disorders and as a narcotic

34 (p. 283) *Belinda* a popular eighteenth-century name, often given to

young women in fiction and drama, as in *Belinda* (1801) by Maria Edgeworth (1768–1849), and appropriate to the old-fashioned note struck by this letter

35 (p. 286) *Mr Pickwick*   the hero of CD's first novel, *Pickwick Papers* (1836–7)

36 (p. 286) *Cervantes' . . . Don Quixote*   the popular and influential picaresque novel by Miguel de Cervantes (1547–1616), published in two parts in 1605 and 1615, and first read by CD as a child

37 (p. 287) *Sam Weller . . . Mr Weller Senior*   Pickwick's servant and his father, two of the most popular characters in *Pickwick Papers*

38 (p. 289) *Windsor*   A town on the Thames west of London whose castle, begun in the twelfth century, has been a royal residence ever since; it was particularly favoured by Queen Victoria (reigned 1837–1901).

39 (p. 289) *King James I*   James I of England and VI of Scotland (b. 1566), reigned 1603–25

40 (p. 291) *he penned a most gracious . . . confusion and slaughter*   James was known to take a deep interest in witchcraft and in 1597, when he was still King of Scotland only, he published in Edinburgh a work called *Daemonologie* in which he discussed an alternative or parallel dark kingdom. In 1604, soon after he acceded to the English throne, a statute was passed reinforcing the 1563 act against witchcraft. While it is unlikely that James had any direct influence on this statute, his accession will undoubtedly have revived interest in the issue. During his reign James intervened in a number of cases to rebuke over-zealous judges when women had been falsely accused and convicted of witchcraft. As a result there were no further major witchcraft panics in England until the early 1630s.

41 (p. 292) *a high sugar-loaf hat*   conical in shape, as worn in the seventeenth century

42 (p. 294) *Kingston*   a riverside market town to the west of London and until 1750 the location of the only bridge above the Thames after London Bridge

43 (p. 298) *to pluck the bleeding mandrake*   Mandrake roots, often forked in shape, can resemble a human figure and were believed to scream when uprooted.

44 (p. 299) *yeoman*   a small farmer, often idealised as a symbol of English honesty, courage and industry

45 (p. 300) *Putney*   A popular and peaceful riverside suburb, west of the City, since the sixteenth century, Putney underwent considerable expansion in the seventeenth and eighteenth centuries. The Putney Debates among Cromwell's army in 1647 took place in its parish church.

46 (p. 301) *a cavalier*   a knight or gallant; perhaps, given the early

seventeenth century setting of this tale, an anticipation of the English
Civil War (1642–49) when the Royalists were known as Cavaliers

47 (p. 301) *the Church of St Dunstan*   in Fleet Street, one of the best-
known London churches

48 (p. 302) *golden unities*   A unite [sic] was a coin of the reign of James
I, worth at first twenty shillings and later twenty-two shillings. CD's
(incorrect) form of the plural is not in *OED*.

49 (p. 302) *old London Bridge*   Old London Bridge, a much repaired and
adapted medieval structure, was crowded with houses and a chapel.
The heads of executed traitors were displayed on its gates. The
present bridge was opened in 1831.

50 (p. 303) *the plague*   The Great Plague of London in 1664–65
postdates the setting of this story, but smaller outbreaks had
occurred since the time of the Black Death in the 1340s.

51 (p. 306) *the Bear Garden*   on Bankside, used until the late seventeenth century for a variety of purposes, including dog-fighting.

52 (p. 306) *the heaven-born Hopkins*   Matthew Hopkins (d. 1647) was
responsible for the discovery and execution of many 'witches'
between 1644 and 1647, before he was himself exposed and hanged
as a sorcerer.

53 (p. 306) *the Three Bibles on London Bridge*   untraced; presumably the
sign of a fictional bookseller /publisher.

54 (p. 308) *'vith'*   see *MED* note 248

55 (p. 308) *'dormouse'*   Mr Weller's mistake for 'dormant'; apposite in
its own way

56 (p. 308) *'them as was . . . with blackberries'*   a reference to the story of
the Babes in the Wood who perished while fleeing from a murderous
uncle and were 'buried' in leaves by robins; often seen as symbols of
innocent childhood

57 (p. 311) *'I wos a goin' down to Birmingham by the rail'*   The railway
line between Birmingham (Curzon Street) and London (Euston) was
completed in September 1838

58 (p. 311) *'old Carter as stood up for our liberties'*   Mr Weller is
presumably referring to Magna Carta, signed in 1215, by which the
English barons extracted certain liberties from King John (b. ?1167,
reigned 1199–1216)

59 (p. 317) *'Bamber . . . appears but once'*   see *Pickwick Papers*, Chap. XXI

60 (p. 323) *'the grease o' their relations'*   Bear grease was used in the
making of hair cream.

61 (p. 324) *'like clean Dutch cheeses'*   round and smooth, like a whole
Gouda or Edam cheese

62 (p. 326) *''Merrikins'*   Americans

63 (p. 327) *'parliamentary'*   exaggeratedly polite and flattering

64 (p. 328) *'here's a community . . . o' sentiment'*   an echo of Alexander

Pope (1688–1744): 'There St John mingles with my flowing bowl / The feast of reason and the flow of soul' (*Satires and Epistles of Horace Imitated: To Mr Fortescue*, 1733)

65 (p. 334) *'the angel at Islington'*   A coaching inn of this name had stood at Islington, the staging post closest to London on the Great North Road, since at least the sixteenth century.

66 (p. 334) *'young Turk'*   a lively (and perhaps rebellious or icono-clastic) member of an organisation or generation

67 (p. 335) *'watch-box'*   a watchman's hut

68 (p. 337) *the single gentleman's name*   This character, who appears in Chap. XXXIV of *The Old Curiosity Shop*, is later revealed as the estranged younger brother of Old Trent and so Nell's great-uncle.

69 (p. 338) *the money-changers who sit within the temple*   Christ's ex-pulsion of the money-changers from the temple in Jerusalem is described in Matthew 21: 12 and Mark 11: 15. Here, CD's narrator comments ironically on the commercialisation of St Paul's as a tourist destination, even in the nineteenth century. The end of the paragraph makes it clear that access to particular parts of the Cathedral attracted further charges.

70 (p. 338) *whose genius reared that mighty pile*   Christopher Wren (1632–1723); see note 33

71 (p. 341) *Barnaby Rudge*   serialised in *Master Humphrey's Clock* February–November 1841

72 (p. 346) *'And the sweet old creetur . . . the great universal spout o' nature''*   Mr Weller's elegy for Master Humphrey is a virtuoso recital of epithets and euphemisms for death, drawn from his experience as a coachman.

73 (p. 349) *Mr Chester and his son*   Sir John and Edward Chester: characters in *Barnaby Rudge*

'Hunted Down'

1 (p. 353) *physiognomy*   the practice of reading character from the face

2 (p. 355) *Middle Temple*   see *Master Humphrey's Clock*, note 7

3 (p. 356) *actuary*   in the insurance business, one who calculates risks

4 (p. 356) *the "Inestimable"*   a fictitious insurance company

5 (p. 359) *Norfolk*   a county on the east coast of England

6 (p. 361) *Scarborough . . . Filey*   resorts on the east coast of Yorkshire

7 (p. 362) *An old East India director*   The East India Company traded profitably on the sub-continent from the late seventeenth century until it lost its privileges after the Indian Mutiny of 1857

8 (p. 366) *Julius Caesar*   a joke deriving from Slinkton's given name

9 (p. 372) *a new and powerful odour*   Slinkton has perhaps taken cyanide which acts quickly and has a strong smell.

'Holiday Romance'

1 (p. 386) *twice seventeen . . . carry three* an echo of how Alice has learned to add up; an example of CD's efforts to give the narrative a child-like tone

2 (p. 390) *measles . . . whooping-cough* a useful fairy gift, since in the nineteenth century these complaints could have serious, even fatal, consequences for children

3 (p. 391) *Spanish liquorice-water* water flavoured with liquorice, often used by children as a kind of play-alcohol

4 (p. 392) *a snow* a vessel similar to a a brigantine

5 (p. 394) *sou'-so'-west . . . west* Robin delights in using nautical language

6 (p. 395) *For what we are going to receive* A grace before meals which continues 'may we be truly thankful'. The implication is that the natives are cannibals.

7 (p. 397) *Madeira* an island off the north-west coast of Africa, under the control of Spain, famous for a fortified white wine

8 (p. 398) *Margate* a resort on the coast of Kent, convenient for London

9 (p. 398) *Roads* navigable waters offering access and anchorage

10 (p. 399) *machine* a wooden hut on wheels, used both for changing into bathing costumes and for pushing modest bathers out to a depth for swimming

11 (p. 399) *town-boats* local boats, registered in Margate

12 (p. 399) *a sailing-boat named the* Skylark a common name for pleasure boats, hence the catch-phrase 'All aboard the *Skylark*!'

13 (p. 400) *when I get into maps* Nettie's education has not yet reached map-reading

14 (p. 400) *put in the corner* a punishment for naughty children

15 (p. 400) *a preparatory establishment* a school (usually residential) that prepared boys for entry into public schools; at this time, also a general term for a first school

16 (p. 404) *quizzing-glasses* monocles

'George Silverman's Explanation'

1 (p. 411) *Preston* an industrial city in north Lancashire whose population grew from 12,000 in 1801 to 69,000 in 1851 and in 1869 had 69 factories, overwhelmingly for the cotton trade

2 (p. 412) *Lancashire clogs* wooden shoes, worn by workers because they are hard-wearing

3 (p. 412) *Birmingham* one of the first English cities to be industrialised, its population growing from 71,000 in 1801 to

144,000 in 1831; famous for engineering, the production of iron and brass and the mass manufacture of cheap goods

4 (p. 413) *vinegar . . . camphor*   used as stimulants to revive someone who has fainted

5 (p. 413) *West Bromwich*   part of the Birmingham conurbation

6 (p. 415) *Hoghton Towers . . . Preston and Blackburn*   a late sixteenth and early seventeenth century house south-east of Preston and south-west of Blackburn, visited by CD in April 1867 (see Introduction, pp. xx)

7 (p. 416) *Rivers Ribble and Darwen*   rivers running to the north of Hoghton Towers, the Ribble through Preston and the Darwen just north of Blackburn.

8 (p. 419) *a foundation-boy on a good Foundation*   a pupil at a charitable school offering free education

9 (p. 419) *a leave-boy on a Sunday*   George would be allowed leave from the school on a number of Sundays each term

10 (p. 421) *pocketankercher*   a colloquial pronunciation of pocket-hand-kerchief

11 (p. 421) *myrrh, or frankincense*   two of the three gifts (the other was gold) brought to the infant Jesus by the wise men or Magi: see Matthew 2:11

12 (p. 425) *that I by wiles . . . second ark*   untraced, but presumably the words of a hymn

13 (p. 429) *more Greek and Latin than Lady Jane Grey*   Lady Jane (1537–54) was a pretender to the throne of England and was noted for her scholarship. Proclaimed queen in 1553, she was executed after Sir Thomas Wyatt's rebellion in 1554.

14 (p. 435) *a college-living*   a clerical living in the gift of one of the colleges at Oxford or Cambridge